SEP. -- 1997

Jackson-Opoku, Sandra.
The river where blood is born.

FRANKLIN TOWNSHIP PUBLIC LIBRARY

3 6613 00116 8040

D0561059

THE
River Where
Blood Is Born

THE
River Where
Blood Is Born

Sandra Jackson-Opoku

ONE WORLD
Ballantine Books
New York

A One World Book
Published by Ballantine Books

Copyright © 1997 by Sandra Jackson-Opoku

Artwork for "The Spider's Web" and
"Beadwork" copyright © 1997
by Don Davis

All rights reserved under International
and Pan-American Copyright Conventions. Published
in the United States by Ballantine Books, a division of Random
House, Inc., New York, and simultaneously in Canada
by Random House of Canada Limited, Toronto.

http://www.randomhouse.com

LIBRARY OF CONGRESS CATALOGING-IN-PUBLICATION DATA
Jackson-Opoku, Sandra.
The river where blood is born / Sandra Jackson-Opoku — 1st ed.
p.   cm.
ISBN 0-345-39514-X (hc)
I. Title.
PS3560.A2473R58   1997
813'.54—dc21   97-16504
                                                         CIP

Text design by Holly Johnson

Manufactured in the United States of America

First Edition: September 1997

10 9 8 7 6 5 4 3 2 1

To The Bridges I Crossed Over On . . .
Mary Ella, Oceal, Golina

To Those Who Come Behind Me . . .
Kimathi, Adjoa, Starlotta, Menelik

And For Ancestor Sister . . .
Amoke

FRANKLIN TOWNSHIP PUBLIC LIBRARY
485 DEMOTT LANE
SOMERSET, NJ 08873

Contents

I've known rivers
older than the flow
of human blood in human veins. . . .

my soul has grown deep
like the rivers

—LANGSTON HUGHES
THE NEGRO SPEAKS OF RIVERS

"A Nine-Veined River That Begins in Blood"

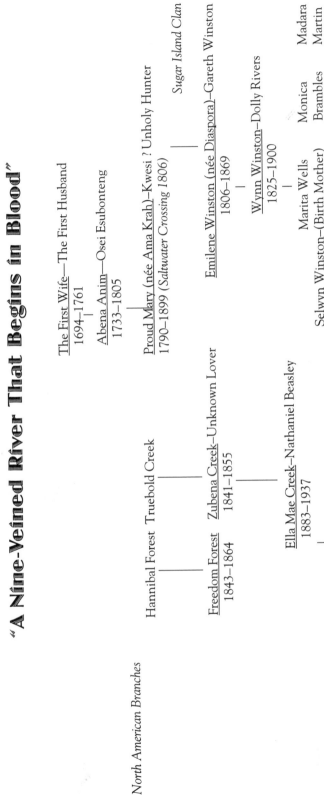

North American Branches

The First Wife—The First Husband
1694–1761

Abena Anim—Osei Esubonteng
1733–1805

Proud Mary (née Ama Krah)–Kwesi ? Unholy Hunter
1790–1899 (*Saltwater Crossing 1806*)

Sugar Island Clan

Emilene Winston (née Diaspora)–Gareth Winston
1806–1869

Wynn Winston–Dolly Rivers
1825–1900

Marita Wells

Selwyn Winston–(Birth Mother)
1872–1982

–Darlene Josephs
(Adopted Mother)

Monica
Brambles

Madara
Martin

Hannibal Forest   Truebold Creek

Zubena Creek–Unknown Lover
1841–1855

Freedom Forest
1843–1864

Ella Mae Creek–Nathaniel Beasley
1883–1937

Two Rivers Clan

Bohema "Big Momma"
Simon Winfield–Beasley–Hosea Ennols   Joe Lee Bullocks
1883–1979

Rita Winston
1949–

Beverly Winston
1940– Trevor Barrett

Sara Winston
1947–
(*Saltwater Crossing 1959*)

Joe Lee   Berta Mae
Bullocks Jr.– Robbins
1905–1949
"King"

Truly   Angus
Ennols–Jaspars
1903–1976

Callie Mae   Benjamin
Bullocks – Peeples
1932–

Lola   Clyde
Jaspers–Brown
1927–

Alma   – Kwesi Omobowale –? Trevor Barrett
(née Allie Mae) Peeples
1954–

Cinnamon
(née Pat) Brown
1951–

(*Saltwater Crossing 1983*)

The Ninth-Born Child?
1984–

Lost River Clan

Earlene   Ivory
Winfield–Josephs
1896–1979

Darlene Kwesi
Josephs–Amagashie
1929–

(*Saltwater Crossing 1970*)

Zenzeli   The Ninth-
Amagashie   Born Child?
1973–   1984–

PROLOGUE

Love at Waterfall

Even now in the hereafter, I still savor the taste of something sweet. I offer no excuse for myself. In mortal life the elders warned that if I habitually raided hives, I would come to know bee sting. That if I wallowed so much in sweetness, I would find it difficult to endure in times of want.

But you know the proverb. *Too much advice is no advice.* My discipline was lax and I overindulged, mouth relaxing open to the nectar of wildflowers, the sap of sun-ripened fruits. I enjoyed the tang of my husband's honey long after I had become an elder myself.

It is said that only when a woman passes childbearing, does she come into her full power. Her menses, no longer spent monthly, returns to nourish its host. Her womb closes onto itself like a cowrie shell, a shrine no man is meant to enter. But I was my husband's only wife. How could I deny him conjugal bliss in his old age? How could I deny myself?

And here I stand, Gatekeeper of the Great Beyond. There are no men in this village, there have never been. It is a thing we never thought to question. We are spirit workers, women who have transcended life's earthly pleasures.

But at times I find myself seized by longings I thought lost in the body I left behind. The memory of hard hands at the curve of my back. The surrender of self to the sweetness of flesh. There is a very thin line between wish and prayer; taboos may be broken in spirit, as well as the flesh. It is on account of such indiscretion that we may all be punished.

The moment which would disrupt our way of life and forever trouble the surface of our tranquil waters happens as I take my sunset constitutional. Those times when work has ended and a woman wants a moment to be alone with her own needs. And love always tastes sweetest at twilight.

May I draw you a map? My path to perdition leads downhill toward the first cataract which feeds the River Where Blood Is Born. It twists like a snake through the forest, descending to meet the water at its own level. We come upon a spot just beyond the warm-water inlet where cocoons await their blossoming into birth, near the bridge these unborn daughters eventually cross over into life.

It is as in the inexorable course of lovemaking. Where river rushes toward land's end, it has no recourse. It must rebecome, must leave the earth and meet the air. Must hang suspended, fracturing the waning light. And float, rather than fall.

The cascade murmurs like the musical moan from deep within a man's chest. Each drop drifts earthward to collect itself into a shimmering pool of joy, before gathering momentum to float onward.

Our meeting at the bottom of the waterfall has happened so often, it has become ritual. I call him, and he becomes. His body, flint black and shiny, emerges from the rock face beneath the tumbling waters. He moves toward me and I am ready.

His breath is the wind that lifts my wrapper and I pirouette, shameless as a young girl in mating dance. My skirts billow above my waist like sails. With no *amoasi* to stay my comfort, I settle my seminakedness into a curve of stone worn smooth by water, warmed by sun. I open my legs and wait, prepared for the familiar rush of sensation; the kiss of setting sun upon my face; the surge, the wet murmur of falling waters.

"Come to me, my love," I whisper in anticipation.

But the answer I receive is harsh and unexpected, a dash of frigid water down the back. My lover's coos vanish, his image retreats into the stone cliff. I hear instead the voice of my ancient enemy, rising behind me from the protected inlet of our nursery. There is a man in our midst, someone other than the phantom lover I conjure in my moments of weakness. Uncertain whether I have been seen, I yank down my skirts and rise to search him out, following the sound of his voice.

"Eh-heh. When spider webs unite, can they not bind a lion? Such a net I will weave from this sacred silk, nothing I capture can escape."

I open the door to admit a man, and this one slips in? I leave the gateway unguarded and this is what enters? Do you see him? Can you hear him? Will you imagine the gall of this spider of a man? Singing his own praises. Misquoting proverbs in his mischief making. He thinks his misdeeds go unnoticed.

It is not his own web that Ananse works. He poaches from our sacred river, playing fast and loose with our very futures. See him there, crouched beneath the joists of the bridge, hidden like the unwelcome visitor he is. Testing the weave of each bobbing cocoon, the unformed bud of each delicate daughter. Reaching into waters and fishing out unlived lives, wet as raw silk. Laughing his lisping laugh and unwinding. Waving his spindly limbs and reeling. Tossing about the silken mass like a malevolent cat. And spinning a cobweb of confusion from the river of our generations.

He has already unraveled silken threads from nine cocoons, when I reach into the crevice where he has secreted himself. I watch him squirm and wonder aloud why I shouldn't simply crush him between the balls of my fingers.

"I beg-o, Mistress Gatekeeper," Kwaku Ananse wails. "You would never do me such a badness. No luck can come to a woman who kills a spider. Nana would never forgive."

"We will see what the Queen Mother herself has to say about that. I suggest, however, that you ready your soul to meet your ancestors."

And that, my people, is how Kwaku Ananse, the spider who is a man, the man who is a spider, came into possession of this story. There are those of you who may say he came to it by trickery. I prefer to call it the fine art of negotiation. Even I can't help but admire a man who can think on his feet.

Yes, Ananse is hauled before the stool of the Queen Mother of the River Where Blood Is Born, cowering but crafty. For he, the undisputed master of all stories, had had just enough time to concoct one of his own.

You must watch carefully or you will miss the precise moment when the mist gathers itself from water and rises. Do you know how many aspects can exist in one blueness? Aqua, azure, indigo. Cobalt, turquoise, sapphire, sky.

I will call your attention to how subtly the blues cascade, shimmering in her garments as she walks. And the sound of living waters; is its music like anything you've ever heard? Of course not. But then you are not within your earthly domain. You are in the realm of a goddess. What else should be expected?

But do not be deceived by the Queen Mother of the River Where Blood Is Born. Yes, her songs are sweet, but often mournful. Because her waters are placid does not mean they are shallow. Do not be fooled by the softness of her smile, the humor that murmurs in the melody of her words. For she is one who can be as temperamental as she is tender.

She has been known to rage, you know. Her blue waters have been seen frothing white, tumbling toward ocean. Bubbling over banks. Do not mistake kindness for weakness. Even Ananse knows better. He quickly unfurls a cobweb of confusion, a dragnet of flattery.

"Eh, but you are beautiful, Queen Mother," he exclaims, shielding his bulging eyes from her glory. "Do you want a poor man to go blind?"

"Well," she murmurs, music in her laughter. "I had in mind a rather more severe punishment."

"Yes, yes," he hurries to agree. "Pluck me limb from limb, throw the pieces to the dogs. Roast me on your open fire, drown me in your deepest waters. I can die happy today, for I have visited your palace. I have seen with my own eyes the magnificence of your village. Eh, I cannot wait . . ."

And here he begins to contradict himself . . .

". . . to run home to my village, to tell my people what I've seen."

"Foolish little man," the goddess trills. "You think it is that easy to back away from death? You think you can bathe in blood waters and ever again be dry?"

"And don't forget," I remind her. "This man is more than just a trespasser. He has behaved badly. Look at his handiwork."

I produce the tangled mass of mischief Ananse has made.

"But what is this?" she asks in alarm.

"Bits and pieces of unlived lives, unspoken voices from the daughters of your descent. Like this Ama Krah, a daughter of Africa destined to wander . . ."

I tug one line from the tangle of silk. The fragment of untold story is revealed, reflected in full upon the face of the waters . . .

They had reached the confluence, the place where the Black met the Blood. A mother's voice seemed to call to them upriver, a voice that only Ama heard. A wind seemed to tug them downriver, a force which only Ama felt. They stood confused in the crotch of land where rivers meet. Looking first one way, then the other.

What name does one give to the not knowing, the wondering? Which road to take? Which river to follow? Which voice to answer? They waited for a sign, and finding none, abandoned the way of water . . .

"A traveler," Ananse interjects. "There must be one in every family. Imagine the possibilities, Queen Mother. Word of your name, news of your fame will wander the world alongside her. And tales like this, of a daughter named Diaspora; can we let such a journey go unchronicled?"

You may not remember my face. You may never hear my story. So I have left it here for the time after I am gone. A sweetwater song in saltwater blues. It whispers in the waves of this wide, wide river. It has sifted through leagues of sea and settled into sand. It is in the current that begins in a surge at one shore and ends in a wave at another. And my voice is just one among many. I am not the only one here who sings or moans . . .

"I beg to differ," I interrupt. "I know pain when I see it. And these women's wanderings have little in them of the pleasure trip."

Our Queen Mother's eyes cloud, a mixture of pride and regret. It is true that our daughters' destiny rests on the knees of the gods. But even in heaven we respect the power of mystery. Just how far into tomorrow does one have the right to prospect? How much of the future can we handle before the fact?

Of course we are curious to know the people our children will become. But to preview your daughters' growing pains before they have even had a chance to live them out? To see such delicate rites tossed about like toys? To witness the unfolding of your futures at the hands of a man like Kwaku Ananse? It is a predicament, indeed.

"Ah," she sighs sadly. And even the sound of her sigh is like gently running water. "It is a bad guest who takes leave of his host by spitting into the well. Pray tell me now, before you meet your punishment, friend Ananse. Whatever possessed you to dip into my sacred waters, to dabble into the lives of my unborn daughters? Have I ever tampered with, or attempted to reel the weave of your wives' egg sacs?"

"Queen Mother of the River Where Blood Is Born, my name is Kwaku Ananse."

"I am well aware of your name, unfortunate one. It is your story that causes one to wonder."

This was just the opening he needed. Ananse begins to embellish the very lie he had been spinning.

"I am a weaver, as was my father and his father before him. I was trained at the village of master weavers, you must know of it? The place where royal *kente* cloth is made from pure silk, the finest in the land. Yes, I do not like to boast . . ."

It is not true, of course. Ananse lives to sing his own praises.

". . . but in no time, I was the greatest of all weavers. Mine were the most brilliant colors, the finest threads, the most intricate designs. I soon became bored working ordinary fibers, unraveling and reinventing the weave of imported silks.

And I began to experiment with story. Have you ever seen story cloth, Queen Mother?"

Like a wave that ripples the surface of water, her ageless brow creases in wonder.

"A story cloth? No, I must say that I haven't. It sounds intriguing."

Ananse probes the tangle of silk and teases out yet another story line.

"First listen to the voice of a motherless child a long way from home; songs from the life of one Earlene."

I even had a brief fling with stardom in the forties and off I went to Europe singing Swing Low, Sweet Chariot *to folks who couldn't understand the words. But it's not about words when that coming for to carry me home echoes from way deep down. It's about memory on top of memory, layered like the strata of earth, like the levels of underground water.*

As if this was not enough, he extracted yet another thread from his ball of mischief.

"And you may be happy to know that a certain descendant called Darlene will lead a more settled life." Another tug, another bit of story unfolds.

. . . The big, comfortable woman with the kind face and ready ear. A woman forever in the kitchen cooking while the party's going on. Or at home baby-sitting while others are out tasting the world's flavors . . .

Well, honey, I'm here to tell you. I was ready to take my life out of moth-balls and put it on. Wadn't no sense of me playing momma to no more grown folks. Putting everybody's needs ahead of my own. I was tired of sitting in the kitchen nibbling the chicken backs of life . . .

"And so," Ananse continues. "I collect threads and fragments from the most fascinating, the most colorful of stories, and work them into a fabric that is the envy of all weavers. And the garments made from such *kente?* Why, they are worn by only the most beautiful of women."

In spite of herself, the Queen Mother becomes entangled in Ananse's web of deceit, his tissue of lies.

"Indeed, the most beautiful?"

"But, yes. The highest of royalty, the most magnificent of ancestors, the most eminent of goddesses . . ."

And here he pauses to let his point settle.

"The most eminent of goddesses?" Predictably, the Queen's fury stirs, like wind upon the water. I love her well enough to know her flaws, one of which is vanity. And why not? She has earned the right to be prideful. "And why have I not been included among them? Why have I not been given my own story-cloth robe to wear?"

"But that is why I am here, oh beautiful Queen Mother! I was planning a sur-prise gift, fashioned of silk from cocoons found here in your very own river. This,

Queen Mother, is the material true art is made from; patterns and textures from the rich imagination of a certain one of your children who will be called Sara . . ."

The river was slim as a blue ribbon and slow moving, more of a country branch some joker decided to call Broad. It gurgled like a baby as it meandered along, and Sara heard voices; invisible mermaids who whispered secrets to her.
. . . One day the mermaids would help her build a boat, and she would sail away upon this river. She consulted a tattered atlas and plotted her escape route. She would go up to the Shenandoah, down the Potomac, across the Chesapeake Bay, out to the Atlantic Ocean, down to the Caribbean, and back to her island home . . .

"No, I say, and no again," the Queen insists. "These are no mere silkmoth larvae you've dared to handle with your unclean hands; these are the souls of my unborn daughters. It is not proper to disrupt the fabric of their lives before they've had a chance to live them. It is their story to make, not yours."

"But this is not my power, Queen Mother," the wily one protests. "I do not craft their stories. I only collect them, assembling the raw materials into a garment that befits the beauty of its wearer. To forecast your daughters' destiny is one thing; but to drape its vestments about your shoulders! Your future need not loom in the distance, when there is a loom master anxious to serve you. Let us reach boldly into tomorrow, grasp its shining threads, and weave them into a work of wonder. Witness the tale of a woman who will be known as Big Momma . . ."

. . . I knew that the Klan was riding the night. Colored folks losing their land and their lives. Simon Winfield just wanted better for his daughter. And I watched them boarding that barge. I waved them off. He said he was taking Early to see some of his people up in Cape Girardeau. She wasn't even two years old yet. Wasn't even talking good. But she talked that morning. Said Bye-bye, Mama just as clear. And they took off, upriver. Ain't never seen them again, neither one of them.

I can see now that the goddess is caught, trapped in Kwaku Ananse's web of trickery.

"If anyone should have the right to tell this story, it should be me," I protest, knowing now he has gained the upper hand. "After all, I am the Gatekeeper. The intermediary between unborn souls, the world of the living, and the ancestors who watch over them all. It is I who send our children out across the bridge, onto their life's journey. And when it ends, I alone greet them here at the gate, and guide them to their final rest in this selfsame village. Why not create story cloth from the life of your own descendants, Ananse? What of Ntikuma, your misbegotten son? You are not of the Queen Mother's clan. You are not even a woman."

"Ah, but who creates a child?" Ananse dances around the point. "Is it the mother alone? The world of the living will not be like this village here, an abode of women. Fathers, brothers, lovers will enter their stories time and again."

He extracts another thread. An image emerges from the anguished life of one who will become Cinnamon . . .

I don't set out meaning to break men's hearts. It's like I'm hungry all the time, but I can't seem to find the right food. So I taste a little bit of everything. It's like something's out there calling me, and I can't figure out who it is. So I go looking for the voice in every man I meet . . .

And if that foretaste of sadness leaves a bitter taste in your mouth, it hasn't affected Kwaku Ananse in the slightest. He turns to the Queen, stretching as wide a grin as his shrunken little face can muster.

"I have heard of your beauty, your kindness. I know that in all the universe there is not more loving a mother to be found. Ah, this is the ultimate challenge of the master storyteller: to create, from the most delicate materials, a story cloth of such finery, of such magnificence . . ."

"Of such lies," I interject, sorry that I didn't crush this interloper when first I had the chance.

"I know that I am small and weak," he counters with affected humility. "Certainly, there have been men more handsome . . ."

"Behold," I breathe. "He stumbles upon the path of lies, and accidentally blurts out the truth."

". . . but there is no greater griot than I. And you are without poet to sing your praises here in this palace."

"Queen Mother has her priestess in the world of the living," I point out, "and her linguist in the hereafter. We all serve her well."

"Allow me to join ranks with them. Even though I am not of your clan. Although I may not be a woman. After all, the great storytellers have been weavers, and all the best weavers are men. It is not I who have made it so. It is the way it has always been.

"It has never been among our people, a woman's work to weave, save perhaps a basket with which to carry the load of her life. Women are bearers, deliverers. The salt which makes food taste sweet, the water without which life cannot exist. I am a mere man, a spider at that. But it is only proper that I, owner of all the stories on earth, be allowed access to this one. It shall be my finest work."

The Queen Mother regards him carefully, shaking her blue-turbaned head. She turns to me and sighs.

"I may come to regret this. Admittedly, he is a rascal. But as for me, I would like to see the creation of such a story cloth. I would like to drape this garment about my shoulders. If he has these skills indeed, let the spider reveal them."

Now, Ananse begins to be cocky with new-found confidence.

"But you realize that I am more than a spider, much more than just a man. I am the one who spins the rainbow, who rides the winds, who can even negotiate the skies on a line of my own making. I am he who is called upon to knit the birth caul worn by the seventh son of the seventh son. I am the world's greatest storyteller because I am the world's greatest watcher, the one overlooked in corners. You see?" he continues, pleased to have proven his point at the expense of these unborn souls. "It is not the fly on the wall who knows the story. Winged but witless, he has no more desire than to find the nearest lump of sugar to rest upon, the most fragrant pile of excrement upon which to feast.

He is slow, blundering. Destined to end up a smear on a swat, a morsel in the tangle of my web.

"I am not mighty like the elephant, nor splendidly maned like the lion. Few are the poets who sing my praises. But though small, I have never been defeated, even by larger enemies. History flows from my spinnerets. I was here at the beginning, and will yet be at the end. Carrying my loom, my calabash of silks and threads. I alone can reel and work your tangled skein of story, of songs and daughters."

"It seems, Queen Mother," I point out, "that Kwaku Ananse is overly adept at weaving the web of self-congratulation. He may be too preoccupied singing his own praises to do justice to yours."

"I see so. You must not forget, Ananse, that you are merely a teller of this tale, not a player in it. And you cannot be the sole griot voice of my clan. Tell the story, Kwaku Ananse, but also teach the art. Animate my daughters with your magic. In each of my generations, there must be at least one who masters her own voice, who learns to work the warp and the weft of her own life."

Ananse reaches again into his bag of tricks.

"But who among them is worthy? Perhaps a daughter like this one, who will be called Alma . . ."

> For years the story beads rested in the corner of my underwear drawer. I'd take them out now and then, but only because they reminded me of her. But there must be more to their secrets than memory. Alone in the long hours of Caribbean night I laid them across my bare, hungry body. They seemed to glisten like they had a light of their own. Endless, like a river that returns to itself.
>
> And now I desperately seek the way back to myself, to my source . . .

The Queen Mother slowly inclines her head in assent.

"In each generation," she reminds him. "At least one."

"And what will be my reward," asks the crafty spider, rubbing together all eight of his hairy legs, "for passing on so valuable a skill?"

"Only if you are successful, my friend. Only if the story you render is so flawless, is of such exquisite quality that it is surpassed by none, will I leave you with your own life."

"Eh! Payment enough, oh Great One," Ananse murmurs smoothly, scrabbling toward the bridge with a tangled skein of silk balanced atop his head. "I must prepare for the work ahead of me. I must find the first thread before I start the story, for all stories must begin at the beginning. There is only one favor I ask. In this story I shall weave and you shall one day wear, take the lion's share for yourself. But then if you please, let just the tiniest scrap float back to me."

And that is how one Kwaku Ananse came into possession of the materials to weave the story that is about to unfold. Whether he does justice to the Queen Mother's name remains to be seen. But let me tell you something, my people.

That spider may have eight eyes in his head, but he does not see all. Even though I inhabit this quiet village of women, I have something to say. I have a story to tell too.

Day after day as I watch the bridge stretching from this village of death to the world of the living, as I welcome new ancestors into eternity, as I tend the unborn souls sheltered in the inlet of these sacred waters, and occasionally slip away . . . I also work. I watch and I work.

Notice this sweetgrass basket that rests beside me, the plain utilitarian object Ananse says it is woman's work to weave, a woman's fate to carry? Come closer, have a look inside. Its subtle simplicity could be easily overlooked.

You see, this basket holds beads of many sorts and sizes, as delicate as drops of water. Some more complex and intricate than any spider's design. I collect them as our daughters enter this village and deposit their waist beads at death's gate.

If you look closely you can discern within each bead the hues of blues; this woman's birth, that one's budding of breasts; the first blood, the sacrament of sex, childbearing, old age, death. Feel their surfaces, the ridges of happiness and hollows of heartbreak. Hear in them as they meet each other, the sound of living waters.

It is true we were captured in Ananse's web of deceit. Yet we must shoulder our share of blame, for we know full well this happenstance is rooted in weakness. We are blessed with divine graces and cursed with human frailties, ours being the twin sins of vanity and lust.

The Queen Mother fancies gossamer garments to adorn her beauty. And even a goddess can be swayed by flattery. I cannot fault her. But for my weakness for love's sweet honey, I would never know the bite of this one's venom. In order to celebrate one's triumphs, one must also admit her failings. I trust this lesson will not be lost on our daughters to be.

Still, the thing that Ananse has started is now water under the bridge. The spider's web cannot be unwound, nor the past undone. It is now our future that he weaves, a commission which carries the Queen Mother's blessing. But which of us knows the story best?

Perhaps you've heard the fable about the struggle between the lioness and the hunter. The cat does her damage with tooth and claw, ripping away the hunter's left hand. He fights with spear and machete, hacking off the lion's tail. The fight rages on, yet neither foe can manage to best the other.

In the end the lioness slinks away to the bush to lick her wounds, the hunter limps back to his village. He is bloody but triumphant, holding aloft the severed tail with his one good hand. Word of his exploits resound far and wide, even to the place where the lioness reclines with her pride, nursing her tailless stump.

"How dare he boast of victory," she complains, "when neither of us won the battle?"

"No one will challenge the hunter," returns a wizened old headwoman, flicking her tail to fan the flies, "until the lioness learns to tell her own story."

He thinks he has bested the Gatekeeper, this insect of a man called Kwaku Ananse. Yes, the spider has his nine sets of yarns to spin. But remember that cats have nine lives, too. As Ananse dazzles you with his fanciful designs and shimmering threads, please allow yourself to appreciate the simplicity of my craft. As you see, I am stringing these beads on a length of lion's tail. If it is a woman's art, then this is a woman's story.

PART I

HEADWATERS

The Spider's Web

I have no problem with a little healthy competition. If the Gatekeeper wishes to try her hand at storytelling, let her match wits with me and see which one emerges with his tail intact. But in fairness she must be forewarned; there is a reason I am known as the greatest storyteller on earth. It is not for nothing I am called the master trickster. When I lose a hand, another one grows in its place. And when spider webs unite, they can tie up a lion.

You have seen a she-cat paw at yarn, play with it, become entangled in the threads. But have you ever seen her work it? She perches at her post with a basket of blue beads, claiming to string nine lives. Well, I weave nine threads, nine daughters, nine destinies in my magic loom. And don't forget, the rights to work this story have been granted me by the Queen Mother herself.

If Madam Gatekeeper knows not the difference between a dilettante's craft and a master's art, I shall be delighted to teach her and all who doubt.

Ah, these women. It is true they are your children. But do they really know you, Queen River Mother, as they claim they do? I doubt it.

You have not been given half your proper honor. Poets have sung your praises on one or two occasions. They herald your past, stand witness to your present. But your mysteries cannot be mastered unless one is willing to part the veil, to pass through the mist that shrouds your queendom. And those who make the journey rarely return to tell the tale. Thus it is a rare griot who knows the ways of your waters, who can stitch your story from the three strands of time—past, present, and future.

As I have often said, each cloth begins with the first thread. Each story begins at the beginning. But who knows the source of your waters? Who can claim to have charted your waters? Better men than I have tried and failed. One could venture a guess. Ground flow? Mountain spring? Reservoir? It matters not.

What we know is that it flows deep and shallow over black earth and red; over mountain, through forest, across savanna. In the wet times it may surge over its banks, in drought it has been known to run dry. It has coursed through the land, like blood, or trickled down the face of it, like tears.

It has been a lost river, running underground for a time to reappear at some point in the distance. It hungers to join the sea, but it has been known to turn back to the place where it is born. And it always emerges from adversity, reinvented. In rain and drought, fat times and famine, it ever endures.

We hear tell of its secrets. "As woman gives birth to children, so water gives birth to gods." We have heard that there are voices that murmur in its meander and thunder in its wake, voices that all can hear but few can understand.

We cannot be sure where your river begins, but we do know that the beginnings of things are sacred. I believe there are infinite beginnings. A multitude of sources. Geneses upon geneses. Herstory is woven as tightly as a multihued length of kente cloth. Who but the weaver knows where the first thread begins? Who but the earth knows where the first waters stirred?

And consider this act of ingratitude! They worship the earth as Mother, though your people have always flowed like the rivers. Fleeing flood and famine, following fortune. Ambling forth with babies on backs, cattle plodding behind them, forests opening before them. Moving easy across fields, tumbling fiercely over falls. Carving out new courses, forging new languages, absorbing new blood. Ever flowing into the future.

There are infinite beginnings. Such as one not so long ago. I say it as I see it, from my customary hiding place in the farthest corner.

Nine Daughters

The night is rich with spirits. Asase Yaa, the Earth Mother, rests in her temple of consecrated fields. The air is thick with the smoky incense of tamped-down cooking fires. And voices gurgle in the flow of nearby waters.

Into this spirit-heavy night, the First Wife creeps from her bed of straw and earth. In the fertile moonlight the infertile First Wife makes a night journey. Takes a well-trodden path to a place away from the village. Connected by a slim trail snaking uphill through tall grasses, like an artery flowing into the heart.

The artery ends at a clearing. Above it, an outcropping of fieldstone as flat as a tabletop. Atop the table lies the scattered remains of a feast. Below the table, water bubbles forth from the red clay like blood. It tumbles downhill, gathering force and volume as it flows off toward the forest. The waters gurgle like the gut of one well fed.

Beneath the river shrine is a simple shelter with thatched roof and earthen walls. The First Wife pauses outside the doorway, calls out a woman's name. Her clear cry pierces the night, rustles the grasses. A voice within bids her enter.

Inside, the Old Woman. Herbalist. Healer. Priestess of many powers. Worker of roots and seer of dreams. Wakeful as those who live close to the ancestors must be. The First Wife bends to enter and beholds the Old Woman, bathed in blue moonlight. A brass basin balanced upon her head. Her face, arms, and legs whitened with clay.

Gnarled and strong as cane, she sits on her sacred stool, amidst her bones and jars, her animal-skin bags full of secrets, her powders, her amulets.

"Daughter," the Priestess greets her.

"Mother," the First Wife answers. Though her water did not break in this one's womb. "Mother, I have come for your help. My pain is so much that the life that was once honey now tastes of bitter leaf. I am the laughingstock of all my age mates."

"Daughter, I know this. I felt your suffering before you knew it yourself. It is only through suffering that we learn to love life. One who has not known suffering will hear weeping and think it is song. Come and sit."

The old hands finger a clutch of cowrie shells, joined together by strips of antelope hide. Each cowrie, curled and closed as a vulva. These hands know the swells and surfaces of each, as a mother knows the faces of her many children.

"Mother, I have done everything I know." Her voice throbs with seasons of sadness. "I make sacrifice to my ancestors. I nurse, and bathe, and care for the fertility doll called *Akwaaba* as I would my own child. But she ever mocks me, she whose name means *welcome*. I remain an empty shell. Can you beg the River Mother to help me?"

The Priestess chants in a language that is known to few. She sings praises of a goddess who is mother to many. She begins to quiver like one possessed; she *is* one possessed as the spirit settles upon her.

She tosses the cowries, then bends to study the oracle, the miracle. The basin balanced upon her head tilts, but never falls. The configuration of the cluster pleases her. And she smiles.

"Daughter, do not despair," she tells her. "You will bear."

The First Wife is afraid of this hope the Priestess has handed her. She has held on to hope all these years like the loyal First Wife that she is. But hope has proven unfaithful. It has betrayed her again and again.

"Mother, are you sure?"

"Are the ancestors blind? Does the River Mother lie?" She points to the cluster of white against dark ground. A plump cowrie, a smaller one balanced against it. "You see it? That is you with a baby on your back. You will bear."

Joy washes over the First Wife, clear as blue moonlight. She slumps, weak with the happiness of the moment. The ancestors did not lie. The River Mother was not blind.

The Priestess gathers her cowrie children into the palm of one hand.

"Wait." The First Wife holds up a hand, unwilling to challenge the spirits with more questions, yet unable to stem their insistent flow. "Mother, will the first child be a daughter?"

The old woman sighs, grows still. The brass basin still balanced atop her head, she bends low and tosses the shells again. She studies the pattern of their fall.

"Yes, my dear. A daughter."

"We thank God." The First Wife smiles. "And the second? Will I be blessed enough to bear again?"

She tosses.

"A daughter." And again. "Again a daughter."

Nine times the cowrie shells brush the beaten earth. Their smooth sides kiss crumbs of soil. Nine tosses of cowries as curved and secret as wombs before the pattern breaks. The brass basin tips, but never topples.

"Nine daughters? Not a son among them?" Fat with her fortune, she is nonetheless disappointed. "Will I give my husband no son at all to work his farm and harvest his yam? No son to inherit my elder brother?"

The Priestess touches her children, lightly. Marveling at the arrangement, the fall of fate.

"Each one may not issue from your womb. But you carry nine generations of daughters in you. Nine daughters, nine destinies." Of this she is certain. "Don't you see them, curved like a river? Each one separate, yet connected?"

She reads the geometry of the pattern. She begins to speak in tongues, chanting a chorus of words that click like waist beads when a woman walks. Neither can make meaning of the refrain.

ama emilene
big momma earlene
sara darlene
cinnamon alma

"When a mother waits a lifetime to bring a child amongst us, she ages from her place on the other side. Your first child will be born an old soul."

ama emilene
big momma earlene
sara darlene
cinnamon alma

"Fruit never falls far from the tree. But when the wind blows, its seeds can be carried. The second child will be a bit lazy, but independent and clever."

ama emilene
big momma earlene
sara darlene
cinnamon alma

"When a tree is bent from the beginning, it grows twisted. But if through fortune or fortitude its origins are upright, the tree grows straight. Your third-born child will be firm minded, though pampered and petted."

ama emilene
big momma earlene
sara darlene
cinnamon alma

"She who sings at dawn captures the sun. The fourth-born child will be calm and bright."

ama emilene
big momma earlene
sara darlene
cinnamon alma

"And then there are those warrior souls, sent forth fighting to carve their path in the world. The fifth child will be born aggressive."

ama emilene
big momma earlene

sara darlene
cinnamon alma

"Each flower comes to seed in its own time. Your sixth child will be a late-season bloomer; slow to blossom, but eager to learn."

ama emilene
big momma earlene
sara darlene
cinnamon alma

"One who breaks ranks may one day lead the herd. The seventh child will be born a leader."

ama emilene
big momma earlene
sara darlene
cinnamon alma

"It is one thing to lead, and another to be a guide. The eighth-born child will be helpful."

ama emilene
big momma earlene
sara darlene
cinnamon alma

"And the ninth daughter? Well, the ninth child always brings fortune and luck to the mother who bears her."

"Nine daughters," the First Wife repeats, stunned with blessings. "And will they too be fruitful?"

"They will be as the okro fruit; blessed with many seeds. They will bear children and their children will bear children. You carry generations in your womb. You will not suffer hunger when you join the ancestors, Daughter. Many shall be the ones who come behind to honor your name."

The First Wife sighs, accepting her fate.

"And will they be good daughters? Will they work the fields and cook the yam and bring honor on their ancestors' names?"

The Old One squints at her shell children and shakes her head, the basin still balanced there. The answer is not to be found there. She takes the basin from her head and gazes into the sacred river waters it contains. She dips a small, curved calabash shell into it. She asks the River Mother to steady her hand. She closes her eyes and slowly pours.

Nine drops of water fall on the floor of beaten earth. Glowing as if they had a light of their own. And then they find their path, flowing together in rivulets to form one way of water.

"Some will stay close to home. Others will stray. Some will cross waters to other lands. Others will work the land of their mothers. Some will be dancers, others stumblers. And one, my daughter, will be a child of this river."

"A blood sacrifice?" The First Wife is alarmed. "The River Mother would want my child?"

"One of your daughters will be called by the one who is the soul of our people, who is mother to us all. This one must guard the shrine of the River Where Blood Is Born. One day she will be called, and she must come."

The Priestess takes up a hand broom of dry grasses. She brushes the floor. What was once holy water is now damp earth. She scoops up the cowries into the warm hollow of her hand, holds them for a moment. She returns them to the darkness of their resting place.

"It is enough."

She is a woman straddling a river. One foot planted in the land of the living, the other in the place of the ancestors. It is not easy to keep balance. It is not prudent to lean so far and listen so long to the spirit world that one grows weak and topples into it before her time.

"It is enough. Have you brought your gift?"

The First Wife brings out her offering. A pure black cock, trussed like a package. Three speckled guinea eggs. A length of cloth. A jar of red palm oil.

The Old One nods.

"It is good. The ancestors will eat well. But it grows late now. Go to your husband, Daughter. Tonight is ripe for creation. Go to him with your fortune."

And the Priestess returns to her own. Tender of the shrine. Guardian of the Place Where Blood Is Born. The full moon shimmers like a swollen ovum as the First Wife returns along the artery. Returns to the growling of sleeping goats and the snores of other women's children. Home to her husband's love, the seed and spirit of her waiting daughters.

And that is just one genesis. A seed of many seeds. A nine-veined river that begins in blood. A river that will beget rivers.

Many are the women who will emerge from the Queen Mother's blood, who will flow forth from your waters into the waiting world. Unless they look back as they move forward, how will they remember the Place Where Blood Is Born? How can they really know you are the mother of all journeys?

Beadwork

Kwaku Ananse can only see the story from the outside looking in. He promises a tapestry woven from three strands of time. But spider webs are spun in air, not on earth.

How can this man be expected to master any but the time in which he lives? Our history is a cowrie with both an outer shell and a hidden heart. Unless you know both sides, you stumble in the present and blunder in the future.

Ananse is so proprietary of our Nine Daughters, you would think he was the rightful father. Little does he credit the faith and action of women that set these events into motion. He may work the raw materials of our daughters' futures, but I still guard their souls.

Though I am trapped here in the afterworld, I can see quite clearly that the most important work of life takes place before birth. I tend the tightly curled cocoons of the unborn, and know each one's beginnings. I sort these story beads, and see in them the lives of the departed. I see the story, my people, from the inside out.

Before Birth

The Priestess approached the bridge cautiously, a bowlful of offerings in her outstretched hands. She hesitated before crossing the river. As is customary when anyone approaches the entrance to this village, the Gatekeeper greeted her at the gate.

"Welcome, Sister. You must be dry after so long a journey. Will you take water?"

"Thank you." The Priestess paused at the portal, shaking her head. "But I am not thirsty."

"Then why not rest your *amoasi* and waist beads here with me? The weight of them must weary you."

"No, Sister," she answered warily, one foot remaining on the bridge. "I am not here to stay. I respectfully beg audience with the Queen Mother of the River Where Blood Is Born. Can you bring her to me?"

Before her question could be answered, Queen Mother of the River rose from the mist, clad gorgeously in gold and *kente* cloth, encircled in beads the color of running water.

"Who calls my name? And what does she ask of me?"

"It is only your servant, most beneficent Queen Mother of the River," the Priestess answered. "I come on behalf of a woman with a wish, a daughter of mine."

"Of yours?"

"And yours," the Priestess hastened to say. "Of course she is your daughter first. You, after all, are the mother of all our people, Queen Mother of the River Where Blood Is Born. It is your sacred blood that sings sweetly in our veins. Indeed we are all your sons and daughters."

"Your praises are sweet," the Queen Mother interrupted. "But what brings you here?"

"Must I have another mission, save to praise your name? Does a good child visit her mother for any other reason but to look upon her loving face?"

"Your tongue flows sweet with honey, Daughter. But it is a bad mother who will see her child wanting, and not ask what she needs. I say again, what brings you here?"

"As always, Mother, you are wise beyond understanding. Patient beyond indulgence. A child of yours begs favor. I felt her pain before she even knew the name to call it. She laments the emptiness of her body, as hollow as a dried calabash. She wants to feel life bouncing in her belly, to stretch open and give another one passage into the world of the living."

The Queen Mother contemplated the request.

"Does she not know the pain she calls down upon herself?"

"She says, Queen Mother, that the pain of childlessness is so much greater than childbirth could possibly be."

"She doesn't know the half of it. Pain does not end with birth, but only begins. Raising a crop is work harder and longer than any plowing, any planting. Hardship is a mother's constant harvest."

"She believes, Queen Mother, that hardship makes one strong."

"True." The Queen Mother nodded. "But a spoiled child's eyes are bigger than her belly. She begs for food that she cannot possibly eat. How do I know that what she beseeches now as a blessing won't blossom into bitterness when her breasts fall and her hair grays? When the sweet taste of sleep is constantly snatched from her mouth? How do I know she will not live to curse my name instead of praise it? Every woman is not made to mother."

"You are right, as always," the Priestess agreed. "It is not enough to sow a seed. Unattended, it may be eaten by birds before it germinates. It may sprout only to wither and die. It may bloom to be ravaged by rats. A crop must be tended well. And our daughter, she prays to you not only for children. She also begs a bit of the wisdom required to bring her crop to a bountiful harvest."

The laughter of the Queen Mother was a wonder to behold, a symphony of birdsong and rain. It rolled from her body as resonant as a waterfall.

"Your daughter is lucky to have you to plead her case, a honey-tongued charmer such as you are. How can I say no? The next time our daughter sleeps with her husband, I will beseech the Great God to bless their union."

"Praises to you, Queen Mother. Goddess of goodness and grace. We will never stop celebrating your blessings."

"But," the Queen Mother warned, "there is something she must know. That one of the children she begets, the daughter of deepest memory. That one will be mine."

"But what else? Every child is yours. Are you not Queen Mother of the River Where Blood Is Born, mother to all our people?"

"This one," the goddess insisted, "I have special plans for. When it is time, she must come to me."

"A small enough sacrifice. A woman with a bowlful of rice will not begrudge the one grain fallen. When must the child be sent to serve you?"

"She must come to me of her own accord. When it is her time, when she hears me calling out to her, she must make her way here to my side."

"Mother, you are beyond generosity. You will excuse my departure now. Our daughter will be happy to hear this news."

"Dear servant of mine," the Queen Mother teased. "Our constant visitor. Why must you hurry away? Why not stay here and share in the delicious meal you have brought us?"

The Priestess backed away, warily.

"Eh. No, Queen Mother. I am not worthy to eat with the ancestors."

"What kind of guest is it who only stands in the doorway and will not come inside? Who brings offerings of food, but never tastes of it? One day you must sit down and sup with us."

"But death is no sleeping room for frequent visitors," the Priestess pleaded. "If I should remain behind, who will serve you in the land of the living? Who will tend your shrine, encourage your people to celebrate your festival, and see that you are fed? Even now the ungrateful among them are forgetting your name. My work calls, Queen Mother of the River. I must return."

The Queen Mother and Gatekeeper stood beside the bridge of time, watching the Priestess beat a hasty retreat back into the land of the living.

"Ah, she is crafty, that one. How many seasons has she seen?"

"She is old," the Gatekeeper answered. "But agile. And she loves life too much to leave it. However much she comes to beg, she always keeps one foot planted firmly on the bridge. She never comes completely over to this side."

"She will," Queen Mother predicted. "She has been a faithful servant to me. But even though the old woman is strong and hearty, she will not live forever. And one of these days she will join us, as do they all."

"But she does serve you well, Queen Mother. We would not want your name to fall among those of the forgotten gods, those who wither from neglect and die. After she is gone . . . ?"

The Queen Mother smiled her certainty.

"An unborn daughter has been dedicated to me. A new priestess will arise among my people. And my name will always be praised."

Beadwork

As the Gatekeeper I saw it as Ananse never could, so many lifetimes ago. In his infinite wisdom, he has predicted that the first child will be born an old soul. Yet there is more to the story than meets the eye, you will soon come to know. A struggle with more fury, even greater odds than that which takes place now between Gatekeeper and Spider.

And when such forces are unleashed, even an old soul may be lured, lost, or stolen beyond the guidance of her ancestors. When a child is separated from her source, as a tail severed from the lion's body, blood still spurts from the unhealed wound. Phantom pain haunts the amputated limb. And though she no longer holds her in her arms, a mother's voice may call out to her, even in the silence of her exile.

To Follow the Black or the Blood

T wo women lived in the bush miles outside a certain village in Ashanti. They were banished women, forced to flee the same village home some years before.

Yaa Aidoo was a small round woman with three small round daughters. And one son. It was because of the son that Yaa had been driven away; a son born after too many weeks in the womb.

People said that even before birth he knew himself to be a son of sin and was therefore loath to leave his sanctuary in the village of the unborn. He came into the world colorless, as most newborn creatures do. But sunlight brought no blush to his skin. He remained a pale shade of yellow. He would have been thought albino, were it not for the tuft of slick black hair which sprang from the center of his head.

Kwesi was born with black eyes wide open. The midwife stared at the oddly colored child. Kwesi stared solemnly back. Surely this was no ordinary infant looking her in the eye like a man. He continued to regard her with unblinking almond eyes.

Before nightfall the rumor had already circulated through the village. The Elder Acheampong's third wife had given birth to a half-caste child. They had heard of such things happening on the coast, where the whites were known to mix freely among the women. But never here, in the heart of the forest region. And surely he is the son of some sinister magic, this little one looking at his elders with the eyes of a man.

Kwesi's afterbirth was not buried under a fig tree in his family compound, as was the custom of his people. It was wrapped in the banana leaf upon which it had been delivered and thrown into the river.

There was not the usual concern that witches might learn his name before he did, call it, and claim him. There was not the customary wait of one week before the child's secret name was whispered into his ear at daybreak, before witches were up and about, before being announced in public.

Kwesi was his name day. Everyone, including the witches, knew that he had been born on a Sunday morning. He was never given another name, one that might bless him with the bravery of his father's brother, Boahene the hunter, or the sweet tongue of his grandfather Ansere, the storyteller. Kwesi

27

would have to go into the world like that single tuft of hair; nearly bald, nearly nameless.

Nor was there the customary wait of three weeks before the new child was outdoored. Kwesi would never be presented to the community of his kin. By Tuesday nightfall, Yaa Aidoo and her son were driven from the village. In a household where wickedness reigns, the shame belongs to all who reside therein.

The crime was adultery, an abomination itself. To make matters worse, the adulteress must have fraternized with some pale-blooded stranger. Women whispered, men wagered as to who might have sired the child. Some said that it was a wandering white sailor from one of the slaving ships that plied the coastal waters. Others swore it must have been one of the Muslim medicine men at the Asantehene's royal court in Kumasi.

Yaa Aidoo pleaded witchcraft. Muttering weak pleas and protestations, she crept away the next morning clasping the newborn close to her chest. She was accompanied by a hail of insults and one or two stones. She trudged off toward the bush, bemoaning her fate. She, Yaa Aidoo, had never been unfaithful to her husband. She had even made sacrifice that the river deity might finally bless them with the birth of a boy. How could she explain the unusual appearance of her son, except that some evil apparition had assaulted her in her sleep? That white witches had come in the cover of the night to suck her son's color?

All the way into the bush that sprang up as sudden as a shout beyond the village farms, Yaa Aidoo protested her innocence. No one heard except the creatures of the forest. She stumbled downriver into what is now known as *Deep Bush*. Here the water that fed the thirst and washed the bodies of the villagers, water nearly the same color as the rich black land over which it flowed, became something else. Within Deep Bush, it made an uneasy alliance with a river that flowed down from the red mountains, its waters tinged the bloody color of its soil.

They converged, these rivers. Crashing together with the soundless fury of enemies in the act of copulation, they met but did not mix. Flowing side by side, the Black and the Blood were known as *Two Rivers That Hate Each Other*.

The villagers knew of this phenomenon. It was one they spoke of in whispers. Legend had it that once a woman's curiosity, or quest for magic, had carried her downriver to where the Black met the Blood. And her curiosity, or quest for magic, had caused her to wade out to the center current, and to mix within a small calabash she carried, water from both sides of the rivers. Her lifeless body was found later by her family, floating motionless in the same spot.

It was in this unholy place of Deep Bush and bad blood that Yaa Aidoo found she could go no further. She stopped, drank river water from the black side, wiped away with leaves the blood of childbirth which still flowed between her legs, and fed the uncrying child at her breast. They rested on a cushion of decaying leaves.

Some hours later, the sun almost setting, Yaa Aidoo awakened to the sound of women crying. She wondered at first at the health of her own mind. She knew that no one lived in Deep Bush. Could those cries she heard be the magnified sound of her own weeping?

Half rising from her bed of leaves, Yaa Aidoo looked upriver and saw her three round-faced daughters marching in single file with bundles upon their heads. Singing a chorus of tears with intermittent solo ululations.

It seemed that the good wives of Elder Acheampong did not cherish the idea that daughters of evil might remain in their midst. Was it not said that no matter how hard he tries, *the dog can never be cured of his desire to steal meat?* And was it not also said that *what the mother has not learned, she can never teach the child?*

If the bitch would steal meat, then so too the pups. What worse than having daughters of adultery living in your compound? They could be expected to do no better than the mother, so they too must be driven out. One cannot fell a trunk and leave its branches.

Thus, Yaa Aidoo, her alleged half-caste son, and three round-faced daughters came to find sanctuary on the banks of the black side of Two Rivers That Hate Each Other, within Deep Bush, some miles outside a certain village in Ashanti.

Not two years after, the animals of the forest came to witness another woman's banishment. Her loud cries of protestation raised birds from trees and sent bush rats scurrying to find their holes.

Abena Anim, mistress of the *adowa* singers, was not a young woman. But her voice was strong, as loud as any man's. She too had been driven away by the good citizens of the village. Her crime was even more shocking than Yaa Aidoo's had been. It was the abomination of witchcraft.

This whispering had started when Abena, barren for every one of her fifty-odd years, had suddenly given birth to an extraordinarily beautiful girlchild. People knew well the ability of evil spirits to take on the shape of something pleasing, as a child with eyes shining like twin moons in a midnight sky. She was born on Saturday; Ama was her name day. At her naming ceremony she was given the name Krah, meaning *soul*.

A length of *kente* cloth appeared as a gift for the child, and no one could account for the benefactor. Abena told everyone it was an anonymous blessing from Kwaku Ananse.

But at the child's outdooring, the midwife would whisper to all who listened that this could never be a normal infant. And this time the whispering was done discreetly. Abena Anim was not a small woman in this village. Despite her childlessness, Abena had long been the senior and favored wife of Osei Esubonteng, the chief. It was often said that Abena was the true power behind the royal stool, the chief's seat of authority.

"Ah, well," the villagers reasoned. "It is the wife who knows her husband. And when the chief has good counsel, his reign is peaceful."

It was widely known that Abena had her husband's ear on matters of village affairs. Oftentimes those who had requests to make would not approach the chief directly, but rather through the good offices of his senior wife, Abena Anim. Of course, this put her in perpetual conflict with the queen mother of their particular village, who felt her role as the rightful *whispering voice* behind the stool was being continually usurped. But the queen mother wisely held her tongue until such time as she could unseat the pretender.

Abena was also known to be a woman of deep medicine. She practiced the healing arts with herbs and magic. She was often able to cure everything from fever to madness in one treatment. But it was also known that those with the power to heal also had the power to harm.

It was quietly whispered that Abena Anim had bewitched her husband long ago, had cooked spells into the food she fed him. Why else would Chief Esubonteng continue to sleep with a woman whose breasts had fallen, a woman who had given him no child? Especially when he had young, fertile wives with whom to share his bed. How else would a mere wife have so much influence that people often called her *the chief's head*?

It was murmured that Abena Anim turned herself into an owl and flew about at night, long after decent people were in their beds. This is what was whispered about the chief's wife, though none of it was uttered in her presence.

"No one," the villagers reasoned, "tests the depths of a river with both feet."

And so she was admired by many, disliked by some, envied by others, and feared by all, this Abena Anim, mistress of the *adowa* singers.

But when Abena Anim gave birth the whisperings grew louder. At her advanced age, such a feat was unheard of. Those who had disputed the rumors of witchcraft grew conspicuously silent. Those who supported it looked over their shoulders and whispered in louder voices.

"After all, is it not Abena who comes from a mountain village where everyone is a witch?"

"And what barren woman would suddenly give birth after fifty-seven seasons? Mistress of the *adowa* must sing sweetly when the witches gather to eat."

"I hear that she flies out to Deep Bush each night to sleep with Sasabonsam, demon of the forest."

"Eh? So that is who fathered the child then? Not only a witch, but an adulteress."

"And one who sleeps with monsters. The fruit of such unholiness must indeed be tainted."

A young pregnant woman, wife in fact to Elder Acheampong, husband of the banished Yaa Aidoo, was washing her clothing at the bend of the Black River one day. She heard (she said) a rustling in the bush behind her and turned to witness Abena Anim's stooped figure, crouching in the grasses. Abena Anim (the woman said) squatted there, chewing on something and fastening upon her a look so evil it would cause a grown woman to urinate upon herself. And did.

Abandoning her washing, the young wife fled screaming into the village and collapsed in the room of her husband's senior wife. Where she immediately miscarried.

This was all the proof the good villagers needed. Who was such a woman, such a witch who would suck the blood of the unborn as one would suck the juice from an orange? Who caused infants to shrivel in the womb before they had seen sunlight? Would they allow such an evil woman to remain among them? The answer was a resounding *No!* And what was to happen, happened swiftly.

That evening, a group of women led by the chief's own sister (mother of his maternal nephews, his legitimate heirs) approached the queen mother's palace. They were women with a common problem: recurrent miscarriages. This collection of women came forth to swear that their losses had been caused by Abena Anim, the chief's own wife.

How else had this gray-haired woman been able to bear, they claimed, but through stealing life from the wombs of others? This witch Abena was a devourer of unborn infants and they, the good women of the village, could not stand by and allow her to wreak her evil magic. The queen mother held the chief's counsel the very next morning.

He was loath to drive his woman away. In truth, he not only loved Abena Anim, he also depended upon her. The chief had good counsel in her, and his reign indeed was peaceful.

But one man, chief though he be, could not go against an entire village. Could not go against the voice of the queen mother, could not go against his own sister, mother to his heirs. Could not go against women grieving their lost children. And for once in many years, Osei Esubonteng made a decision without consulting his elder wife. The village was united in one sentiment: Abena must go! The chief had no choice but to comply.

And so, in the very early hours of the day, singing (mingled with the lusty cries of an infant) was heard above the morning sounds of the village. Abena's strong voice carried over the crow of roosters, the thud of cooking pots, the voices of mothers scolding their children. The good villagers heard strains of song that once moved them to dance, that could call up the dead from their rest, and wondered about the wisdom of testing a witch's powers. If Sasabonsam was a fearsome wizard when living a normal life, what does he become now that he cackles from the top of an odum tree, his beard touching the ground—that same odum tree that sprouts a crop of gnomes like fruit.

Ama Krah tied to her back, her talking drum tucked firmly beneath her armpit, Abena made a tour of the village. Going first to the room of Acheampong's young wife who had been washing by the river that day, Abena performed a drum and song serenade.

A mere woman has shut herself up,
    ashamed to come out . . .

A quarrelsome woman lies in the
    sand . . .

Barren woman.
    Behold, behold,
    The childless woman!

Abena Anim stood by, singing and drumming loudly until the wives of the household appeared in concert to drive her away. She repeated this performance at the compounds of each of her enemies.

With her task complete, Abena Anim marched downriver into Deep Bush.

Followed the river as it twisted crookedly into the thickness of forest. Until it met the river of blood and became something else.

Now, shortly past the confluence Abena came upon a palm tree that had been felled by lightning. A jagged scorched scar marked the separation of tree from trunk. The tree had fallen in such a way that it bridged the Two Rivers That Hate Each Other from bank to bank. To Abena it seemed a sign. With Ama gurgling on her back, she crossed over.

Abena stood a long while on the bank on the side of blood. Shielding her eyes against the sun, she gazed upriver as if she could see clear to the source. But after a time she shook her head. An irresistible force seemed to turn her away from the source, and in the direction of the river's flow.

She trudged downriver, following a threadbare path that hugged the bank. Far into Deep Bush she walked, until the path ended at a giant mangrove. The tree stood like a sentry, its hollow roots straddling the riverbank.

Abena knew of this place. She had not seen it before, but had heard of it. It was used as a forest shelter by the occasional hunter spending a night in the bush on the track of prey. But even hunters, who were known to be among the bravest of men, did not often venture so far into this area of Deep Bush where wild things ruled the night; wild things that could not always be felled by spear or trap.

It was here that Abena decided to make her home. Using the mangrove roots as the framework, she constructed a small hut of river clay and palm fronds. She unwrapped and ate the last of the food she had brought from the village. She fed Ama at her fallen breast. Then crawled inside her hut to rest. She had no way of knowing that Yaa Aidoo and her family had carved out a home of sorts, across the stream, downriver.

And so it happened that two women and their daughters came to reside in the far flung bush, two hours outside a certain village in Ashanti, on the banks of the Black and the Blood, Two Rivers That Hate Each Other. Two women, their daughters, and the man. Who was first a boy.

He grew to manhood in a world bounded on all sides by a blue-green monster that grew two limbs for every one that was cut. A beast that crept into the farms they hacked out of thin forest soil. A world of wild animals that must be tracked and killed and eaten, lest you be tracked and killed and eaten by them. He grew up with a taste for bush meat that was considered taboo in the world just two hours upriver on the Black: man-ape, crocodile, python. He grew up not knowing the feel of sandals on his feet. He grew and his head sprouted the untamed locks that marked him as a fetish child. He grew up nearly naked, but with an animal-skin loincloth to stay the swing of his private parts. And from that loincloth, curiously enough, swung a European pocketwatch on a gold chain.

One day he'd heard a faint, persistent clicking and followed it to its source. The disc glinted, half buried beneath dead leaves on the forest floor. He picked up the object and gingerly examined it. He touched a piece that protruded slightly. It sprang open to reveal a hidden face etched with strange symbols, with black lines that moved by some unknown magic.

"White man medicine," he murmured, convinced he'd uncovered the talisman of some powerful *obruni* wizard.

The place beyond forest he thought of as simply *outside*. And the shiny bauble of *white man medicine* was one of few things from outside that made its way into his world.

His was a world where the sky was seldom seen, filtered as always by the blue-green foliage overhead. It was a world full of noises: the constant gurgle of the river, the *kura kura gook gook* cry of the giant crested plantain eater, the cawing of river eagles, the call of herons, the occasional bark of hyenas, the screaming of monkeys, the grunting of giant forest hogs.

It was a world of woods and women, a world bisected by the enmity of the Black and the Blood.

Kwesi was loved by every woman in Deep Bush, all six of them. His mother and his three round-faced sisters. Ama, the daughter of Abena Anim. Even the stern face of the aging Abena was known to grudgingly crease into smile at the sight of Kwesi's mane, his gold-brown body breaking through brush with the shiny disc of white man medicine dangling from his waist, a gift of freshly killed antelope slung across his back. He was the common denominator between these two families of the forest, the one thing that all the women shared. And one of the many things they fought over.

Yaa Aidoo hated Abena Anim with an all-consuming passion. Abena gladly returned the favor. There was no solace in their similar sufferings. In that closed-in world of dank and overgrown green, the spirits of suspicion had been planted in Yaa's mind. Had taken root and grown twisted branches. The pleasant face of Kwesi's mother was transformed into a grotesque mask when she spoke of *that witch on the other side of the river*.

On most mornings the two women would go to the river to bathe, collect the day's ration of black or red-tinged water, and enact their daily ritual. They never addressed one another directly, but their enmity was as thick as smoke in the air. Yaa's round face contorted as she cried out across the waters. Her voice, high and shrill, echoed up and down that stretch of Two Rivers. Waking bad spirits from their day's rest. Spirits that slipped from their beds on the banks and noiselessly slid into the water, darting about the women's legs in the shape of fish, feasting on the ire.

Yaa would always begin. She would turn to her daughters. If they did not happen to be about, she addressed the sky.

"Why has this witch come to trouble me today?" Aggressively flinging aside the skin wrapper tied just above her breasts, she would squat to dip up a calabash of water from her side of the river. "Is she not happy enough to go flying about each night? Yes, flying. Last night I left my mat to relieve myself in the bush and there she was. The shameless witch, sitting in the shape of an owl on the limb of her rotten mangrove tree. Why has this woman come to plague me? Do witches never sleep?"

Downriver and cross-stream, Abena would turn her back and scoop up water to wash her wrinkled body.

"Who is she to speak to me, Abena Anim, wife of a chief?" her heavy voice would growl. She furiously slapped the cloth she washed back and forth against water-smoothed rocks. "Who is her mother? A nobody, a slave. Who is her father? A drunkard and a thief. How dare their wretched daughter raise her wretched voice in oath against her betters?"

"Great God in the Sky," Yaa might cry into the blue-green-filtered heavens. "May no witch dirty my name on her tongue this morning! How can she say someone is a slave without knowing her origin? Is she not content to have driven me from my village with her witchcraft?"

"My witchcraft? So now I am the hairy *obruni* sailor? So now I am the white man Yaa Aidoo opened her legs to and got her half-caste son?"

"Let no witch speak my name this morning-o!" Yaa Aidoo would call back across the river.

"Daughter of a slave," Abena Anim sang back.

And so each morning the duet rang, a curious call and response. Yaa was always there to open song with her shrilling soprano, Abena to sing chorus in her booming baritone. And when the opera of abuse was over both women would come away feeling cleansed.

Ignoring his mother's caution to never cross over to where *that witch and her daughter* lived in the roots of the mangrove, Kwesi began wading across as soon as he was old enough to follow his curiosity. Before Ama had reached sufficient size to help Abena cultivate her small patch of yams and garden eggs, Kwesi would lend his labor. When one season, Abena's farm failed altogether and mother and daughter might have starved, Kwesi helped feed them with provisions pilfered from his family's own store of food, as well as meat from his traps.

And one season when the spirits of swamp fever rode Kwesi for weeks, Abena would cross the river and sneak into the boy's hut at night. She bathed his face and fed him a tea of fever grass. Eventually Yaa Aidoo had heard a sound in the night and went to investigate. She found Abena bent over her sick son and sent one of her round-faced daughters scurrying for the cutlass with which she would remove the head of the witch who was trying to eat the life out of her only male child.

Abena vanished into the night and there were no more visits. By then, however, Kwesi's fever had broken and the spirits left him. He soon resumed his wild life of hunting and wandering.

Yaa Aidoo kept the wilderness of forest life as far from her three round-faced daughters as she could. She kept the forest at bay and her daughters at her side as she weeded the garden, chopped at the brush, boiled the cocoyam on an open fire. But to hold at home the son with the locks of a lion, born with the eyes of a man, this was a losing battle.

Kwesi wandered at will, staying away for hours, sometimes days at a time. He would hunt and trap, a skill he learned by surreptitiously following village hunters out in Deep Bush. He harvested wild fruits, raided village farms, and continued his forays to the mangrove hut across Two Rivers. He was drawn like a magnet to the other side. He knew that when the time was ripe, stories might fall as plump as palm fruits from Abena Anim's lips.

She told them of Ananse, a wily trickster who through guile had gained possession of all the tales on earth; a man who liked nothing better than avoiding work and dabbling in other peoples' affairs. Legends of *mmoetia*, a magical race of gnomes less than two feet high. Stories of a time before the *obruni*, men without color, came to their lands. Of bow and arrow, then gunpowder battles, where elder women fought bravely alongside their men. Of families and festivals in the nearby village where she had been the chief's senior wife. Of ancestors and a great river goddess in a mountain village where she had been born. Stories of a time beyond memory, when their people first came to these lands. Before the reign of women waned. When women ruled the world, as the Great Mother Goddess ruled the sky.

Sometimes they would sit on the riverbank, woman, girl, and boy. Abena would stare upriver for long moments, as if she could see to its source.

"If you were to follow one of these rivers to the place it begins," she would say, "you would come to a village that is shrouded in magic. Ancestors sit in the surrounding trees. It is the sacred sanctuary of the River Mother. The unholy hunters would never find prey there. Spirits would pluck off their genitals and eat their eyes. And how brave can a hunter be without his testicles? How many antelope can he spear blind?"

Kwesi had never seen the unholy hunters, but he lived in mortal fear of them. These men, according to Abena Anim, were hunters of human flesh. They could be distinguished from other hunters only by the talismans of human teeth they wore around their necks. They killed those of their kind, salted the meat, and sent it on giant boats to be sold across the waters.

During Kwesi's frequent forays into the forest he kept a vigilant watch. But signs of hidden hunters were not all he looked for. With the years he witnessed Ama's transformation from infant riding her mother's bent back to a girl no less wild or adventurous than himself.

It was not long before she began to join him on his wanderings through the forest. They would stalk animals with poison-tipped spears, set and check traps, and make occasional forays into their banned village where they raided farms and went back to the forest with all the yams they could carry. And they always kept watch for the possible approach of things unholy.

But once they were careless. They were caught, but not by hunters. They had gone to a clearing downriver to check Kwesi's fishing nets and to share in their bounty of fruits from the village farms. They heard a sudden rustling in the bush behind them, and turned to find Akua, the youngest of Kwesi's round-faced sisters.

She backed away, a gourd of water on her head and a plump hand clasped to her mouth. From the horror in her eyes, she might just have witnessed her brother cozied up to a deadly green mamba.

"Eh! What have I seen?" she cried. "Our mother will know of this, Kwesi."

"She will not." Kwesi sprang to his feet in alarm, the mangoes in his lap falling and rolling onto the forest floor. Ama merely reclined, sucked sweet pulp, and watched the scene between siblings.

"I will tell our mother," Akua promised, turning to run. "She will know that you have befriended this daughter of a witch."

Kwesi's wild forest life had shaped his body as lithe and taut as some of the young animals he hunted. So when he sprang, his sister at first thought she had been attacked by one of the baboons that lived near the forest's edge.

"Oh, my mother," she screamed. "Help me. I am killed."

"You be quiet," Kwesi warned, giving her two sharp knocks to the head. Though she was older, Kwesi was larger and stronger. The dangerous glitter of black eyes in his gold-brown face drove away any thoughts of fighting back. She threw her arms over her head and wept noisily.

"You are not to tell our mother or *anyone* what you have seen here," her brother threatened, gripping her head by the two plaits which were conveniently placed on either side of it. "If you do, I will kill you. And I will leave your body for the hyenas."

"No, no. I will say nothing, Kwesi. Please let me go. Our mother is waiting for the water."

Kwesi fetched the fallen calabash and refilled it from the river. He helped Akua replace it on the coil of twisted leaves she wore to cushion her head against the weight. With a frightened glance over her shoulder, Akua crept off toward home.

As soon as she had darted rabbitlike into the bush, Kwesi began to cry. He had never struck any of his sisters before. Though he had killed more times than he could remember, had cut off the head of striking vipers, he had never touched another human being in anger. He was a child who had known wildness in the woods, but kindness in the hearts of women. And what he had just done frightened him. He could not comprehend this desire to protect Ama, a desire so strong he had threatened to kill his own sister.

"Stop crying!" Ama shook him harshly. "You were right to beat that girl. If you hadn't done so, she would have told your mother. And she would surely stop us from being together. Would you like such a thing?"

Kwesi's tears evaporated under her burning stare. He looked back at the girl standing above him. Ama, after almost fourteen seasons, was becoming a very pretty girl. She looked nothing at all like her mother, Abena Anim of wrinkled skin and flattened breasts. Ama's skin was as smooth as the skin of the papaya, her eyes as black and gleaming as papaya seeds. She was almost as agile and strong as Kwesi himself, but lately she was looking less and less like a boy.

From the smooth plane of a chest once flat like his, breasts were beginning to bud. Her full, dark lips were now slower to smile. But when they did, the smile lingered a bit at the corners. She had taken to looking not at him when he spoke, but at some unseen spot on the ground.

Kwesi, now somewhere around sixteen, looked at his age mate as if he had never seen her before. Whenever he looked at her, something trembled in him, as if he were being tracked by leopards. Never having known the feelings men feel, he was unable to recognize what the trembling was. He only knew that it both frightened and fascinated him.

He wondered if his mother was right, that Abena Anim had opened her legs to a spirit and gotten this child called Ama Krah. Otherwise, how could she be so unbearably beautiful?

"Kwesi," Ama murmured conspiratorially. She gave him one of her new smiles that lingered. "You will let no one stop our being together. If they try, you will kill them."

Kwesi could only nod his head in mute agreement. And wonder if Ama, daughter of a witch, had indeed bewitched him.

Whatever will he had evaporated. He only wanted to touch Ama, to feel the brown silk of her skin. He found his hand reaching beneath her loincloth, resting it against the gentle thrust of her buttocks. He found his fingers straying to the cups of her breasts, and squeezing the berries which bloomed there. He wondered if they would be sweet like berries, and lowered his mouth to taste each one.

Ama sighed, grasped him by his locks and held his head firmly against her, surrendering herself to the explorations of Kwesi's tongue and fingertips.

Now that her daughter was erupting into womanhood, Kwesi's continual presence made Abena Anim nervous. He would wade across Two Rivers as always with a hand of bananas, a bundle of smoked fish, or ripe mangoes stolen from the village. But more and more often, Abena would step onto the bank and wave him away.

When Ama broke her first blood, Abena bathed her in Blood River waters. She closed her away in a shelter high in the trees, shaved her head, rubbed her body with shea butter, and draped her in the once-vivid *kente* she claimed had been an anonymous outdooring present from Kwaku Ananse. She fashioned an *amoasi* of clean white cloth and placed it between her daughter's legs. She anchored it in place with a doubled length *beads of water*; a string of heirloom trade beads wrapped around her waist. She fed her mashed yam and eggs from her own hands, as if she were a baby again. She sang her songs, told her stories, and gave her warnings.

"A girl must not bear fruit until her body is ready to bloom. A woman must not take seed until she has been blessed for birth. The ancestors would be offended, and calamitous events could take place. You may not be able to mother the child you bear. This river here, our very sustenance, could overflow its banks. Unholy hunters could come."

She brought her food, more than enough. She made her to understand that she must not leave the shelter for six days. And Abena went out to tend her garden.

But Ama Krah was not a child who could sit silent in the trees. Was not a new woman made for stillness. When she became bored, she would climb down and sneak away to meet her Kwesi. And with him she would do as they always did: fish, hunt, talk, and play.

On the fifth day Abena made a surprise visit and found her daughter missing. Having tracked her by the trail of sounds, the boy's and girl's laughter echoing across the water, she found them on the other side of the river. They had just roasted and eaten a bush fowl, but their hunger remained unsatisfied. They reclined in each other's arms, lazily testing the tastes of various places.

Ama's mouth wandered his face, finding his lips.

"This one is like mango."

Kwesi allowed her mouth to tease his, then suddenly captured her darting tongue between his teeth.

"And this one," he proclaimed, "is like melon."

Abena's looming shadow fell across the couple. She yanked her daughter up and beat her as she had never done.

"Oh, you cry?" Abena was unmoved by Ama's tears. "Then cry blood, disobedient daughter."

Kwesi's three sisters scurried to the riverbank to watch.

"What is she doing on our side of the river?" demanded Akosua, the eldest.

"Do you see how she is beating the girl?" chortled Akua gleefully. "She will kill her. She will surely kill her."

Said Aduama, the middle sister, "It takes a witch to murder her own child."

When the beating was finished Abena grabbed her sobbing daughter roughly by the hand and without a backward glance, dragged her back across Two Rivers.

From that day, Kwesi was no longer welcome on the other side. Abena tried her best to keep Ama under her eye. But something wild seemed to be growing in her. She refused to complete her *beragoro*, the nubility rites. When she saw Abena coming toward her carrying shea butter and *kente* cloth, she bolted and hid.

Now and again when the moon was full, she would slip away to Kwesi's hut, or wander to a spot in the forest where a hunter's shelter had been hastily erected. As silent as a forest creature, she would creep in, crouch over the man inside, and watch the rise and fall of his chest as he slept. She would count how many times she could lightly touch it before his eyes fluttered open. Sometimes she would flee into the darkness. Often she would stay. She would not return until long after nightfall, her body wet with sweat. And Abena would sniff the air, despairing at the unfamiliar odors clinging to her daughter's body.

Abena offered up fervent prayers and sacrifices, hoping to stave off the devastation she knew could follow the breaking of such a deep taboo. She faulted herself, and the desperation of raising a daughter with no village to call home.

The troubled mother rarely slept, and when she did her rest was visited by turbulent dreams. One night she dreamed that a young boy came to her hut, offering to share the contents of his cooking pot. He dished out a heaping serving into her calabash. But when she reached in to grasp a piece of meat, she discovered the soup was filled with human body parts. Fingers and eyeballs, teeth and toes floated to the surface and bobbed, like driftwood on troubled seas.

Curiously enough, another person in their forest shared that same nightmare. Later that same night Kwesi was awakened by breath on his face. He had sleepily reached for his cutlass and was about to strike, when he saw that it was Ama. Eyes glittering in the dark, she leaned over him.

"Ama," he whispered in alarm. "What are you doing here? Where is your mother?"

"She is gone."

A full moon shone through the cracks of Kwesi's thatch roof. In moonlight, a strange lingering smile lit Ama's lips.

"My mother is gone and I have come to you, Kwesi."

He did not know what to say, or what to do. He was drawn to the light in

Ama's eyes, the smile at the corners of her lips, her wet body glowing in the moonlight. A soft, worn *kente* cloth was tied above her breasts. Her skin smelled of shea butter. He could only imagine that this was what a mammy water would look like, that spirit of deep waters whose songs seduced unwary men to their deaths.

"Kwesi," Ama spoke. She removed her cloth. *Beads of water* coiled like a blue river around her waist.

"No!" The shout was neither hers, nor his. It was his mother's. Ama was suddenly pulled backward through the small entrance of the hut. Kwesi tried to hold on to her arms, but she was dragged away by a more determined force.

Kwesi squeezed out behind her and saw his mother's hands fastened around the throat of the naked girl. Something wild in him made him leap. Made him pry his mother's hands away. While Ama, stunned and coughing, stumbled away into the night, Yaa Aidoo struggled from Kwesi's restraining hands and lunged after her.

"Daughter of a witch!" she screamed as Ama plunged into the river. "You will not eat my son tonight."

Her round-faced daughters appeared, eyes languid with sleep. They picked up stones and lazily threw them across the river at the fleeing figure.

"Daughter of a witch," they called in trio.

Kwesi dashed to the bank. The moon lit the scene: four women, shouting and throwing stones and branches across Two Rivers. But he could see no one on the other side. Hungry spirits swirled in the shallows.

Kwesi would have waded across after her, but was held back by eight strong arms. They wrapped his own, his neck and legs and body. Screams echoed into the night.

"You will not go! You will not follow that witch across the water. I will kill you first."

Akua, the youngest, who had been hurling stones and insults the hardest, turned to her brother and pointed.

"He was with her," she cried. "I saw them that day, together. Kwesi said he would kill me if I ever told. She has bewitched him."

"So the witches would turn my son against his own blood?" Yaa Aidoo muttered. "This will never be."

With the help of her daughters, round faces crumpled in rage, Kwesi was beaten. Beaten so that the devils within him would take flight. Beaten with fallen branches and bare hands. Again and again. He fell into semiconsciousness. Night spirits cackled in the wind, swished through the brush, and whirled in to lap up the edges of anger and spilled blood.

Sunlight filtering through holes in the thatch pried Kwesi's eyes open many hours later. He had apparently been dragged into his mud hut and dumped upon his mat. Every part of his body was swollen.

He struggled up and squeezed out into daylight. Neither his mother nor his sisters were about. He stumbled into the river and stooped to bring water to his ravaged face. He found Ama's *kente* cloth abandoned at the bank, and retrieved it.

He crossed the river and inhaled, his nostrils catching the faint, sweet odor of her musk. Following the scent, he tracked her.

He found her, naked but for the blue beads about her waist. She sat on a fallen log upriver from the mangrove hut, silent and staring into the bush.

"Where is the hunter?" she asked when Kwesi greeted her, draping the *kente* cloth about her.

"What kind of question is that? You know that I am the hunter."

She shook her head impatiently, looking back toward the bush.

"Ama, what is it? Has my family hurt you?"

She shook her head again.

"Where is your mother?"

Ama pointed toward the mangrove hut.

"She is inside. She has gone."

Inside, Abena Anim lay facedown on the dirt floor. Her fingers were dug in, her back arched. Frozen in motion. Half her head lay flattened beneath a huge stone.

"She is gone," Ama called dully from the doorway.

"Who did this?" Kwesi tried to fan away the flies which hung thickly about the bludgeoned head. "Tell me, who has killed your mother?"

"The hunter."

"What hunter? Tell me, Ama. Did you do this thing?"

"She drove you away when she found us together. She drove my hunter away, too. She said he was unholy. You promised to kill anyone who kept us apart. But you did not. So the hunter has."

"Ama, who is this hunter?"

Ama's gaze returned to the bush.

"He came in the night to take me away. But I did not go. I hid in the trees." She beckoned him, still naked, from the doorway.

"Come away from there, Kwesi. She stinks."

Inexplicably, he followed her. She led him away, downriver to a part of the forest they seldom frequented. There stood a crudely built shelter he had never seen before.

"Who has built this place?" Kwesi wanted to know. He was suddenly seized by a nameless fear.

"The hunter," she answered, taking his hand and pulling him inside.

Later, the setting sun drove shadows into Ama's black eyes. She shivered in Kwesi's arms.

"Night is coming." Her voice seemed far away. "I do not like the night. Bad things come to trouble me in the night."

Kwesi held her, stroking the papaya smoothness of her dark skin. He had never known the company of men, though he had seen many wild things mating in the woods. How ever had Ama known what to do?

To rub the dangling disc of *white man medicine* against his thigh. To thrust his loincloth aside and grasp the column of rock that rose up to meet her. To guide his hands to such warm, moist places. To place himself within herself and move him. To milk him with her hips until everything he was surged out of him and into her. How had she learned these things?

He wanted to ask her as they lay in the grass afterwards. But before he could find the words, Ama had pushed him roughly from her, her eyes wild with sudden fear.

"I couldn't sleep last night. She," Ama pointed in the direction of the hut, "she kept calling my name. She came out here and tried to pull me back to the mangrove with her. Listen. She is coming again."

Women's voices, high and shrill, broke through the silence. But Kwesi knew those voices. They cried out his name.

"She is coming." Ama sat bolt upright. "You must kill her."

"No, Ama. There is something we must do."

Under the cover of trees, they made their way back to the mangrove hut. Kwesi dragged out the corpse of Abena Anim. Ama squatted nearby, throwing stones at the scavenger birds that came to gather. It was a hasty burial, made hastier by the cries of his mother and sisters across the river.

The four women stood at the riverbank. They called the name of brother and son. Ama shouted back.

"No! Go away. He will kill you-o!"

The women looked at each other. There was a hesitation. A hesitation sixteen years ancient, deeper than the river that ran black and blood. Deeper than the blue-green of forest. None of them had ever crossed to the other side. None of them ever thought that they would.

"He will kill you," Ama screeched again.

They plunged.

Kwesi pulled Ama by the hand.

"Come quickly. We must leave this place."

The boy and girl knew ways through the forest, even in moonlight. So often had they raided the village farms and hunted the forest animals, they'd torn tiny paths through the brush. These they now used. Though Yaa Aidoo and her daughters called and followed, they were soon left behind.

Tiredness and pain pulled at Kwesi's body, preyed on Ama's mind. She thought she heard someone calling. A mother's voice, calling her by name. But they kept walking, knowing they must not stop until they had left all they knew behind them.

Many more times than one, they had watched Abena Anim, a woman old enough to be her own daughter's great-grandmother. They had listened to her tales as she toiled in her garden or gathered herbs by Two Rivers. Had grown to near man- and near womanhood seeing Abena Anim gaze upriver with eyes that saw more than they could ever know.

"There is a place, children. A village at the headwaters of one of these rivers. It is the place where I was born. Now, to find that place, which river would you follow? The Black or the Blood?"

Kwesi had never known what to answer. Abena Anim would smile at his confusion.

"If it is your home, why don't you return there?" Kwesi would always wonder. "Why have you lived so long in this bush if you have another place to go?"

And Abena's eyes would become troubled.

"Even as I hear my mother's voice calling, something equally powerful pulls me away. It is as though I were a doll two sisters struggle for, without the will to move on my own. But one day children, I will."

And one of the children would ask her, "Then which river will *you* follow?"

Abena would answer with a riddle.

"What is first seen when a woman gives birth? The black of the child's head, or the blood of birth?"

Neither of them had seen a child born in their forest home. How could they know the answer?

They had reached the confluence, the place where the Black met the Blood. A mother's voice seemed to call to them upriver, a voice that only Ama heard. A wind seemed to tug them downriver, a force which only Ama felt. They stood confused in the crotch of land where rivers met. Looking first one way, then the other.

What name does one give to the not knowing, the wondering? Which road to take? Which river to follow? Which voice to answer? They waited for a sign, and finding none, abandoned the way of water.

They went back into Deep Bush, the blue-green beast that had always been their home. There was no longer a path to follow, so they made one. Night became day, then night again. They stalked wild things, and without knowing were being stalked. They hunted, and were hunted.

So the way that was would find them. Wearing their talismans of human teeth and other body parts, unholy hunters would come. And tear them from each other. Lead them beyond forest to coasts of gold. Imprison them in stacked stone mountains. Load them onto wooden coffins. Carry them across the waves of a water wider than reason. Saltier than tears. And more brilliant a blue-green than the deepest bush.

The Spider's Web

Q ueen Mother of the River Where Blood Is Born, a humble weaver such as myself can only applaud the Gatekeeper for her fine storytelling. She may prove to be a more worthy adversary than first I imagined.

But within this downpour of details, there is a small puddle that your Gatekeeper has artfully sidestepped. How can she tell the whole story and omit a chapter such as the one to come? It is not an easy truth to swallow, but we all must take the bitter with the sweet.

Though some have accused me of being unfeeling, I do indeed bemoan the trials of your first daughter. I do taste your tears in the rain, hear your voice in the wind as you moan her name; Ama, Ama Krah.

But may I remind you that she has been something of a headstrong daughter? Should it come as a surprise that her fate has fallen into the hands of a very wicked man? Do not blame your humble storyteller; I am but the man who carries the message.

I have seen it with my own eyes, heard the man boasting with my own ears. The trials of your first daughter, Ama Krah, begin at a place near the coast, where a tongue of bitter tide reaches in to plunder the mouth of Sweet River.

Bitter Tíde

It couldn't have been more painful if he had struck me down with his own fists. I had had but one taste, one tantalizing bite and that tasty dish was snatched from my open mouth. If only he had waited until I ate my fill, perhaps I might have allowed him my leavings. Everyone knows you do not take from a man that which he has prepared for his own palate.

It is like the scent of offal that remains behind, even when the act has been buried. Memory seizes the mind like a monkey which mistakes a hunter's head for its mother's back.

I was the eldest child of my mother, the laughingstock of all my age mates. *Don't mind that one,* they would often joke. *Though the calf is born with balls, he gives them up to become a bullock.*

My mother had no daughter to assist in her woman's work. So she tried to make a woman of me. I went about with younger siblings tied to my back, worked the farm with the women, cooked groundnut stew on the coal pot. The other boys jeered, called me a woman's boy when they saw me bent over the cooking fire. But that did not prevent them from coming to taste my meat at mealtimes.

One day I had pounded fufu, crushed fresh palm kernels in the mortar, and made a meal for myself. Steam rose from my calabash, hot and spicy. I tore off a ball of fufu, dipped it into the stew, and tasted. Ah! Could the second taste ever match the first? I would never know.

My mother stepped from her room and sent me to the river for water, a task everyone knows is reserved for girls. When I returned, a boy from a neighboring village was sitting before my calabash, wiping up the last bit of stew with the last ball of fufu. Why did my mother need water at the precise moment when I sat down to eat my food?

Ah! But these women will betray you. And other men, they will take what is yours. I learned my lesson early. You must become a predator, or forever scurry in the bush as prey. That is why I have grown to love the solitude of forests, the passion of the hunt.

But at times it is not enough to snare an antelope, to fell a buffalo. There are times when a hunter hungers for greater prey. There are moments when the release of the arrow, when the spurt of blood, or the thrill of the kill does not satisfy.

When a man lays down his traps and spears for other weapons. When he yearns to plunge into the valley of fresh, charmed flesh.

But these women will betray you. The girl would come to weep and curse and yes, even strike me, when she saw what I had done for her. For us. She, who did nothing but complain about the old woman. *My mother hoards me like salt. She refuses to let me climb down from her back.* You would think she'd be grateful to me for removing that witch from our path.

After I killed her mother, the girl would no longer have me. Though I called, she would not come. She hid from me. She went to lie with another in the shelter I built to spare Mother Earth the insult of our mating.

And now she dares call me unholy. See her and that half-caste boy, rutting like beasts on the bare ground, desecrating Asase Yaa, our Mother Earth. Even hunters like myself know that one does not sleep with a woman in his mother's bed.

And other men will take what is yours. Who does he think he is, this forest dweller who has never seen the inside of any city? This one to whom she habitually opens her legs? After all, it was I who first crushed her palm kernel, who cracked this coconut, who opened up the passage he now plunders.

Is she dazzled by the trinket this bush boy wears at his waist? I would wager he's never known the red rawness of the European's skin. The feeble click of his *white man medicine* is nothing compared to the might of a white man's musket, spitting fire from the hands.

I am no longer a woman's boy, you know. In my manhood I am the husband of three wives. I drink European liquor. I have tasted the meat, cured the hides, and worn the skin of many animals. I have seen human prey trembling in death throes. My mates and I have captured whole villages. Grown men prostrate themselves before me, begging me to spare their lives. This one dares to trifle with the likes of me?

Hah! He believes himself to be a hunter because he may trap a bird or fell an antelope. He is but a bush rat, a small rabbit waiting to wander into my snares. For the greatest of all hunters is the warrior; he who tracks the human animal.

Any hunter will tell you this is true. To kill a beast, you must first become that beast. You must come to know the ways of antelope, know the heart of elephant. You must live as the lion, think as the lion, be as the lion. Only then can you capture the lion.

I have tracked them for many days now. They bathe in the waters of the Sweet River, singing to each other and washing away the soil of their latest mating. Ah! If these forest dwellers only knew what lies at the mouth of this river.

No man devours a dish I prepare for my own palate. This small boy hunter will soon know what it is to become the game. Perhaps I will watch him beg for his life, and then let him meet the metal of my musket. Perhaps I will sell him downriver to the *obruni* traders at Elmina. As for her, she must also pay. She will answer to me, or by the Great God in the Sky, I will know the reason why.

I would sooner have the white men ride her, see her sold across ocean waves, than let a bush boy feast on a meal prepared for my own palate.

Beadwork

The spider thinks I cannot follow the feeble machinations of this flesh peddler, a man so foul he cannot smell his own stench? I, Gatekeeper of the Great Beyond. Does he not realize I can reach across this river and crush the two of them like the insects they are?

Yet I cannot openly oppose Ananse without offending the Queen Mother. So I am content to bide my time. It is not unknown for a spider to become trapped in his own web of vanity.

But Kwaku Ananse cannot possibly know that the moment Ama Krah set out on her uncertain journey, her mother Abena Anim would cross the bridge to the Village of the Ancestors, deposit her waist beads and amoasi with me, and enter our gates.

I read anguish in those beads of water, like sediment stirred up from the river's bottom. We are heading for a stretch of troubled waters—Watch out for your daughters is their plaintive message.

And I am reminded of what came before. Ananse places our daughters' fate squarely in the hands of this unholy hunter, not knowing he is but an agent of a greater greed.

Then again, perhaps the spider had more of a part in this than any of us may ever know. For once Ananse makes mischief in a place, things are never again the same. It may not be deliberate malice. Perhaps he is like a child playing with a large ant's nest. Perhaps he upsets the order of things at whim, just to see what surprises may erupt.

Could he be the one behind the banishment, when my people were disgorged from their first river-delta home? Was he there when they went trekking across deserts while graverobbers plundered the tombs of the ones left behind? Could he have joined them on their journey to new lands, plotting his machinations along the way? Peppering men's eyes with discontent? Pitting them against their women in a struggle that continues to this day?

Do you think he may have fanned a certain family quarrel to the point where two sisters, Queen Mothers of the River and the Ocean, waged war upon each other? And in the ensuing confusion, welcomed certain strangers into the people's new homes?

Was he onshore to greet the first slave ship? Might he have perched atop their war weapons, thrilling to the rumble of musket fire and cannon roar? Sipped whiskey with the coastal kings, counting the first shackled captives brought onboard?

I cannot prove that Ananse's hand was behind this particular matter. But I've been told that a giant spider's web had been seen in the area.

Troubled Waters

Nothing happens without a reason. The pattern of the rainfall, the force and rhythm of the winds, the slant of the sun's rays. None of it is accidental. We cannot always know the cause, only that one exists.

In this particular case, those who read the signs made it their business to be nowhere in the area. For isn't it said that *those who habitually play between the sea goddess and the river goddess are crushed by the grinding stone?*

Wet sheets of wind whipped the sky. Waters boiled over banks and seeped through fields. Waves crashed against shores and lightning cleaved stormclouds like a flashing cutlass. Thunder rumbled, great trees were uprooted, villages destroyed.

Two discontented goddesses warred. *When two elephants fight, it is the grass which suffers.* And the Great God wept at the savagery of the struggle.

"How can you say that she is yours, worthless woman?" Queen Mother of the River challenged. "Bloodthirsty witch whose waters hold my peoples' bones. You have swallowed too many of my children whole. You will not claim this one."

Queen Mother of the Sea waved her billowing blue gown.

"Ah! Are you the one who is calling me worthless? Does a puny river cow have a word to say in the presence of the mighty whale? How dare such an insignificant creature as you even raise her voice to address the Queen Mother of the Sea?"

"And do you know who I am? Have you visited my palace? It is only when you have crossed the river, you can say that the crocodile has a lump on his snout."

"I do not reach into your forests and pluck your children, you know. What kind of mother is it whose son sells brother, whose daughter ransoms sister? Your children have not been raised well, I fear. The ruin of a nation begins in the homes of its people."

"Prostitute," Queen Mother of the River spat back at her. "If I and my sisters did not feed you, would you ever have grown as fat and foolish as you are? We know full well that you lie on your back and let the strangers crawl your body at will. Why do you wet-nurse the white men? Why not take as sacrifice those whose wooden coffins have become shrines to your terrible hungers? Why do you suck my blood, devour my children? You are no better than a mammy water spitting tears."

"Feed me?" roared the angry ocean. "You should count yourself lucky that I accept this murky urine you call river water. Without me, the sea, you would be a road that leads to nowhere."

"Be careful what you say," came the warning. "That the sea is saltwater is well known. But the rain still pours into it."

"I have already told you that I do not steal your brats. They are brought to me by the white men, and also by many of their own kind. And if I like meat, should I refuse a meal that is offered me?"

"You will not eat this one," the Queen Mother of the River promised. "You cannot claim her. She has been dedicated to me."

"Some women are born to drink saltwater. She will find her way home to my arms."

"I will shelter her in my forests."

"I will be the water that flows from her eyes. And one day those tears will become a road that she will follow to me. Home to the billowing blue of my saltwater bosom."

The river wearied, overpowered against the onslaught of the ocean's rambunctious will. Her waters stilled. She ebbed with the tide, leaving her enemy in a froth of fury, and with a promise on her lips.

"The destiny God assigns us cannot be avoided. She is not your daughter. You will not claim her."

You will know who is the child's true mother when her journey takes her far from home. One woman is loath to let her go: *If I can't have her here with me, then no one shall.* The true mother weeps at her departure but says, *Go, my daughter. Go with my blessings.*

The River Mother has never yet lied. In the end it was as she predicted. Yes, our daughter was turned away from the river of blood, lured downriver beyond her forest home.

Yes, a terrible hurricane did rage, it ravaged the shores and the ships that rode the waters with claws of wind and terrible sheets of water. But it was as the River Mother foretold. And Queen Mother of the Ocean could be heard lamenting from her shrine fathoms beneath the seas.

She has come to me, my saltwater daughter. Chains upon her body, new life uncurling inside her. Brought to me as a sacrifice by the unholy hunters and white priests of power with whom I have entered into a death pact.

But my sister, Queen Mother of the River, was right. I have made her to come to me, but I cannot claim her. Your destiny is beyond me, Ama Krah, daughter of Abena Anim, granddaughter to the First Wife. You will take the secrets of your blood to other shores.

PART II

ESTUARY

The Spider's Web

Do I build ships and sail them? Do I possess guns and gold mines, Queen Mother? I am a weaver, not a warrior. A storyteller, not a sailor. So how can responsibility for Ama Krah's tragic voyage be laid at my feet?

Yet the circumstances do appeal to the adventurer in me. I have always wanted to wander, not just from one market town to another, but away across waters.

I do not need the meddlesome Gatekeeper to remind me that I am but a chronicler of this tale, not a player in it. But I ask you, Queen Mother, how does a spider follow your daughters' journey unless he makes one of his own?

There is a voyage to stow away upon, languages to be learned, histories to witness. And as I pick up a new daughter's thread and weave it into the story, do keep in mind the Priestess' earlier prophesy: Fruit never falls far from the tree, but when the wind blows, its seeds can be carried. *The second child will be a bit lazy, but independent and clever.*

A Daughter Named Díaspora

I f I could tell my story I would. If I had a voice in my mouth that I could command, others would know my name.

Mine would be a short story. I have only just come into being. But this is what I know of the world.

From inside my vessel I knew such a rocking. A heavy sway in my way of water. But now I am without her, the vessel which held me in a stormy peace for my time.

My mother did not want to give me to this world. Though I am new, this I know. She did not want to deliver me from the place which had become too small to contain me. She did not want to surrender me, though I demanded to be free. She wanted to keep me inside her, as a ship trapped in the belly of a bottle. Even though I had broken the cork and spilled the water. Even though I twisted and struggled to make my way out.

She pressed her knees together and did not howl against the pain that came as regular as a heartbeat. Though I made my way to the neck and beat at the opening. She dug nails into rotting wood and would not push. Would not move. I called, but she would not release me from the place that had become a prison.

So I pushed my own way out. Slithered through the neck of the vessel and out of the opening. I gave birth to myself.

And though I have escaped from my vessel I find myself still within a vessel. It is a huge cradle of splintered wood that rocks and sways. It is a cradle rocked by wind and water. And I am not the only one in it who cries for food to fill me and for dark arms to hold me. I am not the only one here who moans. Perhaps I have been delivered from one prison to another.

But now that I am here I am beginning to know the world. I know neither my father's name nor my own. But I do know her. Dark as night sky. Rivers flowing from her breasts and eyes.

I have come to know other things too. The taste of sweetwater that comes before the milk. The thick black sky of night that is so like the dark place where I have come from. But it is not a close darkness. It is a far darkness that is studded with lights I can see but not touch.

I am in the world now and she holds me to herself, cuddling me in a cloth of many colors. I know she would return me to eternity, would offer us both to the spirit in wide blue waters that surge around us. But I know that she will not.

For though I am new I know that we have some destiny to play out at the end of our passage. I fear that I will not have long to know her. I think that she knows this too. For she stares hungrily at me; my hands, my body, my eyes. She plucks me from her breast to closely examine my face. As if to memorize it now so that she will know me again.

And perhaps this knowledge is why she has not named me. To give a name to that which is not yours to keep is to hasten the moment and sharpen the pain of separation.

So I am wise in the wisdom of newness, the ancient wisdom I must lose only to seek again. But I am nameless. And since she will not name me I name myself. *Diaspora.*

You may not remember my face. You may never hear my story. So I have left it here for the time after I am gone. A sweetwater song in saltwater blues. It whispers in the waves of this wide, wide river. It has sifted through leagues of sea and settled into sand. It is in the current that begins in a surge at one shore and ends in a wave at another. And my voice is just one among many. I am not the only one here who sings or moans.

We are not lost. We are not nameless. We are not silent. Listen if you pass this way, traveler. Hear us.

Beadwork

*W*hat New World awaits them? How many worlds can there be under the same sun? This is something we have not seen.

We have seen people captured, but never yoked and shackled. We have seen people taken against their will, but never transplanted in such numbers. We have seen blood sacrifice, but not mass suicide. And perhaps those who lie in underwater graves are the lucky ones. What greater horror awaits our first-born daughter, and her own first-born daughter on the other side? What hope can there be with life mate gone, father unknown?

Still they are not beyond our aid. It is not the nature of fresh water to cross salt water, for a river to transverse an ocean. But our daughters are headed for a world they call New. And we, their ancestor mothers, are alive in their blood.

They are not alone, the ones who cross over. They take us along.

Last Voyage of the Sable Venus

DAY 1

Having ably disposed of our trading goods a fortnight in port, the good ship *Sable Venus* set sail from the Gold Coast on this eighth day of March in the year of our Lord 1806.

I expect we shall fetch a fair price in Barbadoes for our cargo of ivory, gold, spices, and some 437 healthy Coromantee Negroes. An even larger return might have been realized with judicious tight packing, as the factor at Elmina Castle holds stock of some 200 additional Negroes, prepared for loading. But one's hands are tied by Parliament's strictures on the numbers our vessels carry, such strictures being a thorn in the side of any Guineaman captain these past ten years or more.

What untold losses such capricious laws have caused cannot be measured; increasing the outlay of capital for a slaving voyage, while at the same time diminishing our profits. The result being that our enemies will soon reach their ultimate aim: the eventual prohibition of the slave trade. This may well be my last voyage.

DAY 7

These campaigns of war among the Guinea natives are for the express purpose of plundering and carrying off prisoners of war, which they then sell to the traders on the coast. Other slaves we receive from the local kings, who sell them into bondage for their crimes. Some natives have been known to sell off the excess of wives and children they can no longer feed. Indeed, the Negroes have such large families it is an act of Christian kindness to take some off their hands.

Yet I have good reason to believe that of the Negroes purchased, a great part are kidnapped. Panic is such in these last days of the trade, that any desperate adventurer seeks to fatten his fortune by panyaring. Kidnapping has become so common I have noticed Negro children make a game of it while playing on deck.

One of my sailors reported that while in port, he ventured out to explore the surrounding country. Why he wished to wander those pestilential forests, abounding with wild beasts and dangerous natives, I am sure I cannot say. In any case, during such wanderings he chanced upon two natives, bathing themselves in a local river.

As he watched he saw men steal out of the bushes and seize them. While the girl was immediately captured, the boy somehow contrived to escape and was given chase. The seaman chose not to linger in the vicinity, as it is not unknown for even white men to be captured and sold by unscrupulous panyarers. I do not doubt however that the girl, and the boy if recaptured, found their way into custody at Elmina Castle.

These Guinea factors take great care in the purchase of their Negroes. Groups of them are brought in great coffles, marched to the coast from areas as far as 500 miles distant. Their mouths are examined for tooth decay, in order to know an old one from a young one. When a tooth is found missing, it is noted down as a deduction in the price. The eyesight of each is observed, the voice is called into request. Every joint is made to crack. The surgeon is even forced to examine the privities of both men and women with the nicest scrutiny, as the yaws and *lues venerea*, or clap, are very common here.

A few days before they are loaded on, their heads are shaven. They are marked with a hot pip or silver brand, sufficiently heated to blister the skin. This is indispensable, in order that upon arrival the consignees may know which of the slaves belong to them.

Among any regrets at seeing this trade come to its end, I have no comfort or affection for the inhabitants of the slave coast, otherwise than it helps my fortune.

The great wealth of the Fanti people makes them so proud and haughty that a white man trading there must stand bare before them. Almost every king along the Gold Coast holds note on land where the European forts are built, and duly receives rent for use of such land. The English factors dare not in the least contradict them, and are often in such fear for their safety that they are confined to the castle without stirring abroad.

I have found the traders to be a most crafty and treacherous lot, who would sell their mother for the price of a tot of rum. The factors themselves are sad excuses for men, few if any among them having the benefit of education or moral principles. Many are addicted to strong liquors, and overfond of native women, whose hot and lewd tempers soon waste their bodies and consume what little substance they have. Yet they express not the slightest Christian shame over such debauchery.

Heaven is high and Europe is far away; so goes the Guinea factor's motto.

DAY 12

We have lost 59 Negroes thus far, due to an epidemic of the bloody flux. Among the men in the hold, the women between decks, those that are with child in the great cabin, and the children in the steerage, I fear that the most valued have suffered the greater losses.

The men-Negroes are of necessity shackled in irons two by two, which makes it difficult for them to turn or move. Although it is washed daily with seawater, the hold in which they lie resembles nothing so much as a killing-house floor, running with filth and blood. We have encountered a series of fitful storms and tarpaulin cloth is dropped to cover openings in the hold, lest the creatures below drown with the incoming waves.

The air has become hot and thick, the pestilential odours reaching even up to my cabin. The Negroes within have commenced a mournful howling. The linguist tells me that they sing, *White man, white man, we are dying.*

Every morning more instances are found of the living and the dead shackled together. Each day some three or four more are brought up on deck and tossed overboard. I have likewise lost 11 more members of my crew.

The storms show no sign of abatement. Some action must be taken soon, lest we continue to lose large numbers of valuable cargo.

DAY 19

I regret to report that it has been necessary to put down an attempted mutiny. We have lost some seven Coromantees to suicide by jumping overboard, and we were forced to hang three of their leaders as an example to the others.

I know full well that Gold Coast slaves are highly prized by the English, and generally fetch a better price than those from other regions. I have seen the Ibo boys cry and wail piteously when they are marked, while the Coromantine boys accept the procedure without a whimper.

The Ibos are of such weakness that large numbers of otherwise healthy Negroes will pine away and die from no cause other than fixed melancholia. The Coromantees are without exception strong willed and hardy, and there was never a rascal or coward born among them. Yet they also are haughty, ferocious, and stubborn; a nation of Negroes uncommonly prone to rebellion.

They are so willful and loath to leave their own country, that they often leap into the sea. We must take careful watch ere they join the sharks, of which a prodigious number keep about the ships, and will follow her hence to Barbadoes to feed on those gone overboard.

The next cruelty to buying human flesh, one would naturally think, should be to eat it. Some Negroes are prepossessed with the notion that they are being carried across to be sold to a race of white cannibals, and it is better to be eaten by sharks than by Europeans. They have a more dreadful apprehension of Barbadoes than we do of hell, though in truth they live better there than in their own country.

As a Christian kindness, I allowed the men-Negroes to come upon deck during the storm in order that they may escape the stifling heat and pestilence of the hold. Such action would prove a grievous error on my part.

The mutiny began at midnight. The Negroes fell upon the sentries and endeavoured to get their cutlasses from them, but the lanyards were so twisted in the scuffle, that they could not get them off. Several of the Negroes, perceiving white men coming toward them with arms in their hands, quitted the sentries and jumped over the ship's side into the sea.

We secured those remaining and had them removed below. They would not be subdued, but kept up a great noise. I called the linguists and ordered them to bid the men-Negroes between decks be quiet.

I asked what had induced them to mutiny. They answered I was a great rogue to buy them in order to carry them away from their own country and that they were resolved to regain their liberty if possible. I told them if they should gain their point and escape to the shore, it would be of little use to them, because their countrymen would capture them and sell them to other ships. This served my purpose, and there has been no trouble at all since that incident.

I regret that several of the finest of the lot had to be hanged, but there was no helping it. These abolitionists would undoubtedly weep crocodile tears and issue forth cries about *Ethiopia stretching out her hands unto God*. But the many acts of violence Negroes have committed by murdering whole crews and destroying ships calls for the use of the same confinement as if they were wolves or wild boars.

Of course, the seamen on deck that night were stripped bare and given twenty lashes each. I trust we shall not suffer a repeat of the incident.

DAY 25

Why not the visage of Her Majesty, our Queen? Why not any of innumerable gentlewomen of noble birth? Indeed, why not our Virgin Mary, the most immaculate of all white womanhood? The *Sable Venus*, her masthead the bust of a naked she-savage carved from ebony; who could possibly have thought to affix such an effigy to a Christian sailing vessel? It is small wonder the crew aboard conducts itself accordingly.

We have entered the doldrums and drift about, waiting for the trade winds. The heat is overpowering and I have taken to my cabin, though rest is hard to find what with the continuous shrieks of the women-Negroes on deck. It gives me no joy to know the poor creatures are so used, but the voyage has been hard and the seamen must have their ease.

Provisions have become quite unpalatable. When soup was brought to me this midday, one huge hairy spider swam about in it like a sea bather at Brighton. I dashed the bowl away in disgust, but the insect scurried off before I was able to crush it with my boot.

I must also contend with the noise of a crying babe born in the great cabin just three days ago. One scarcely closes one's eyes before the creature's bleating assaults the ear. The price of the child's ailing mother will no doubt be lowered, and one can realize little, if anything at all, from the sale of such a tiny pickaninny. It is only the greatest forbearance that stays me from seizing the noisesome child and throwing it to the sharks.

DAY 30

We have lost another 20 slaves and 6 sailors. The *Sable Venus* is most terribly undermanned. And we are so straitened for provisions that if we are another ten days at sea, we must either eat the slaves that die or make the living walk the plank.

It is times like these that I wonder who here are the slaves; they that howl in the hold below, the half-starved seamen, the naked women and children on deck, or indeed myself, Lloyd Merriweather, captain of this accursed vessel.

No other man upon earth is called upon to endure so much misery as they do who carry Negroes. By their willful rebellion, by their sickness and mortality, our voyages are ruined and our pockets emptied. We pine and fret ourselves to death, and to so much pain for so little purpose.

Perhaps the abolitionists are right; that this trade injures the trader as much as it does the traded. That the life of the Guineaman captain brings a numbness upon the heart and renders it indifferent to the sufferings of our fellow creatures. Perhaps I should count it lucky that I am sailing my last voyage on an African slaver.

DAY 32

I heard the call of *Land, ho!* And yesterday the sight of Bridgetown Harbour welcomed my weary eyes.

This morning the West Indian factor looked over the cargo and picked out the slaves who were diseased. These were quickly auctioned off, one mulatto woman I am told purchasing a Negro dying of the flux for one dollar. Those still alive among the Negroes marked for consignment were claimed. Then prices were set for the remaining healthy slaves, who were sold by scramble.

The scramble is a sight which I, in all my voyages of these past three and thirty years, still find shocking. The purchasers, all well-dressed white men, wait onshore for the sound of a gunshot which informs all that the sale has opened.

Then a great mob rushes onboard with tallies and cards in their hands, charging through the barricado door with the ferocity of brutes. They swarm upon the unsuspecting Negroes, wrapping their choices with several handkerchiefs joined.

I am sure the poor creatures believed themselves herded like sheep to slaughter. Some 20 to 30 of them jumped overboard in panic, but I believe they were taken up again. A woman-Negro clutching her babe in a soiled cloth somehow endeavoured to escape, and ran screaming like a madwoman through the streets of Bridgetown before she was apprehended.

No, it is not an amiable trade, this slaving business. But then, neither is the trade of a butcher. Yet wouldn't all say that a mutton chop is a good thing? Who would say that the sale should be abolished for the suffering caused the sheep?

We expect to take on a good cargo of molasses and rum here. The seamen will take their leisure, and the *Sable Venus* will be outfitted for its return to Liverpool.

And such, I expect, will end my last voyage to the New World. I am weary with the trade and all it has spawned—the factors, the traders, the sickness, the slaves, the sugar. I will return to Britain and pray that I never see a black man's face again in life. So signed;

CAPTAIN LLOYD ELIJAH MERRIWEATHER

Cropover

17 February, 1827
The Rivers of St. Philips
Barbadoes, West India

My Sister:

Alas, dear Eleanor. I fear that the news of the thing may reach you even on the heels of this missive. If you do not recognize this as my hand, know that it is being recorded by my faithful Emilene as I lie dying in this accursed wilderness.

How I do wish for the fresh green hills and fair climes of our native land. How I envy you to be there now, perhaps walking the flagstone path winding through the gardens and up the hillside. Perhaps gathering flowers at day's end. Perhaps sipping tea and conversing with gentlewomen of your class about such matters as fashion and frolic and the chance of coming rain. Or reading aloud by the warmth of your parlour fire, your children gathered about you.

Those few that remain of my days are destined to be spent in this manor house perched atop a rocky green hill. I look out my window and see the cane fields of The Rivers estate spread below me. The view is at once a pleasing and menacing one. For if one stretches one's sights just so, one might discern flashes of white amongst the green of cane. It is They.

They cover their black heads with white against the sun. They chop the cane with their wickedly sharp blades, with which they might easily sever a human head. They are as ants, dark and darting wherever a foot is planted or stone unturned. They are everywhere in this land that is mockingly called *Little England*.

We deceive ourselves with the illusion that we are masters here. No man is master. It is Cane which rules. Perchance a coincidence that such a name brings to mind the first man in creation to kill his own brother? Cane. You would know it as the staff the old man leans upon, the rod which punishes the wayward child.

We know it as the stalk that grows straight up from the ground. It runs riot throughout the land, cultivated with the care that Mama gave her roses. It grows nearly up to our doorsteps. It is an unbending great god which forces us all to bow down before it. It is as vile, and violent, as the slaves who tend it. Have you ever known a plant, my sister, which when cut can snap back and disembowel a man?

And it is our own weakness which has made this so. Our yearning for the gold it buys. Our craving for a lump to sweeten our tea. Our lust for rum to warm our toddy. We are as much slaves to this thing as the Godless Blacks. When I first landed here I could not get enough to chew of the sticky sweet heart of cane. I took succor in sugar all day long. The house slaves always kept me in fresh supply. It became a way for me, as quoth the Bard, *of making the hard way sweet.*

You will never know how moved I was at your good-hearted invitation. In truth, nothing would have given me more pleasure than to have ended my days in my own country, tucked within the comforting embrace of you and your loved ones. Nor will you know how keenly I wished to return even when Gareth died last year. I felt that my reason for stopping in this wicked place was at last no more. I felt that the gates to hell had somehow swung open and I was finally and forever free. But in the end, I could not go. I could not enjoy my freedom knowing that They had won over me.

Would that I knew then what I know now, lying pale and wasted upon my deathbed. That in the end, They must win, just as Satan will claim his souls. I know that it will be soon when they are eating from our Delft china and cutting their meat with the Sheffield silver that was your wedding gift to me. It will not be long before they are drinking Gareth's last cask of rum from our Waterford crystal.

For such is the misery of white lives in this black wilderness. They outnumber us ten to one and they wait, as vultures do, to feast on our carrion. If these words of mine ring contrary to your memories of the sunny girl I once was, know that this island has made me so. There is here a sense of closing in. This is not the open freedom of our island home. Here, the land holds one in limitation. For the black brutes are everywhere and wherever you roam you will be pursued by them to land's end. There is no escape.

What lunatic could have thought to call this estate *The Rivers?* For there is not a single one to be found, unless one were to count the sickly stream that flows in the far field. Indeed, one could comb the island itself and not find a body of water, save those that seethe underground.

There are those who say we are lucky to live in a land without rivers. That water bubbles up clean from underground caverns. That there are no sluggish stands of water to breed disease and the bothersome mosquitoes which infect Europeans in this part of the world with deadly swamp fever. But Eleanor, there are other fevers than that of the blood. There are other diseases which kill softly, yet just as surely.

If this place has changed me, it changed him more. Gareth, the one whose name means "gentle." What a cruel irony that would become. Oh, you remember the excitement in the very air of him. The dashing gentleman planter from the West Indies, the handsome and rakish suitor who would court me, claim my hand, and marry me all in a fortnight. And then whisk me off on the good ship *Liberty,* my heart and hope chest full. Away to the New World, where I would be the lady of my prince's manor. It was a fairy-tale dream that evaporated the moment I stepped foot on these accursed shores.

In this hell, my prince became a troll, a stranger I chanced to brush past in the full rooms of this empty manor house. He was a man forever counting; counting the fruit of his harvests, counting his silver, counting his slaves. 'Twas a pity I could give him no child to count among them.

But he found his comfort elsewhere. The manor became littered with gold coin enough for him to count on all hands—the yellow bastards gotten him by the black wenches he owns. It is only in death's arms that I may reveal to you the utter shame and despair my life here has been.

My only solace has been the faithful love of my dear Emilene. No doubt you have tired of hearing of her in my letters over the years. But my pride in her is boundless. Though she is black, she is not like the others here. Have I told you how she came to The Rivers?

I found her some one and twenty years before, when I myself was new to this island. At the market in Bridgetown Harbour, I spied a newborn babe suckling at the breast of a she-heathen, fresh from the shores of Guinea. The savage crouched in the dirt completely naked, but for a length of blue beads about her waist. She swaddled her little one in a threadbare, striated cloth. Perhaps this gaudy replica of tartan plaid might once have been clean. The rag was now most certainly foul and verminous. I took Christian pity on the babe bundled inside, no more than a fortnight's age. When I stopped to pet the child, the factor offered her as a gift.

Oh, how the Guinea heathen cried and cursed me in her savage tongue when they prized Emilene from her arms. So fervent and fiendish were her curses that the factor himself threatened to slit her tongue for her insolence. So tightly did she clasp the swaddling rag, that it rent in the struggle.

If only she had known what that daughter would become under my mercy, she would have fallen on her dark knees and begged my thanks. But for me, she most surely would have died.

As you well know, I have reared this girl as I would my own blood. She is very quick of mind, Eleanor. She speaks not in the broken patois of her kind, but in perfect up-country English. Her manners are ever so dainty and graceful. She sews a fine hand, she pours a perfect cup. Her reading of poetry is most exquisite. Oh, it is surely a sight to behold. This African maiden, dark as midnight, her woolly locks pulled back in a bun, wearing the snow-white frocks she favors, reciting Keats in a manner that would rival the most refined Englishwoman.

But sometimes I do wonder if 'twould have been kinder to have left her to suffer in the seasoning camp, or perish in the passage to New Orleans. For she wears this life as she does her fine garments of linen and lace: with difficult grace. She is like me, lonely in spirit, and being unlike those of her kind, so despised.

When Emilene reached her womanhood, this manor swarmed with the men who would make her theirs, both the black and the white. From the lowliest field slave with nothing to offer but a space beside him on his pallet, to the loftiest gentleman planter who offered me a fine price for her hand. But I shooed them away as I would these tropic vultures which descend upon you should you sit still too long in the sunlight. For in a man's touch can be nought but misery. That has been my lesson to her. I thought this knowledge, and my love, could save her.

But how could I reckon the depravity to which Gareth had descended? The one man with whom I held her safe, the one who had been almost as a father to her, would be the one to despoil her innocence. But even the thickest, darkest cloak may reveal a farthing tucked into the deepest pocket. Even in evil there are blessings to be found.

Although the notion may strike you as perverse, the child of Emilene and Gareth is like a grandson to me. He is called Wynn. And he is as fair of grace as he is dark of face, a fine golden fellow.

It will soon be Cropover. Here it surpasses even the Yuletide celebration. For of course They do not properly worship our Lord, but the Green God Cane. The bringing in of the sugar harvest gives the black ones cause for unholy revelry in savage dance and rummy song. The whites hold themselves scarcely better. Indeed, white becomes blacker as each day goes by.

One often sees a low caste of European, those whom even house slaves look down upon as *poor backra*. Irishmen for the most (though I daresay one might find those of our own English among the lot), go about with loads on their heads and babes tied to their backs. The most degraded among them toil in fields and sleep in beds beside the blacks, speaking the same patois, eating from the same pots, birthing free-born mulatto bastards who will grow up believing they are our equals. Nay, our betters.

The white man's day here will soon be no more. They are as doomed as the festering souls of the heathen Africans. Those who stay will be infected or destroyed. This I know in my blood as well as I know there will be yet another harvest. Each time fields are lit ablaze like the fires of Hades, I am reminded of the hell I have lived the past twenty-five of my years. When they burn the cane to prepare for the gathering, the fire blackens the earth as if a pestilence had come upon the land. Soon the blackness will spread until it has driven out the white. I count it a blessing that I will not be here to witness yet another season.

This is why you must understand why I do what I must do. When this letter to you is complete I will send Emilene for the solicitor. You will find this all after I am gone, but I wish to tell you now in my own words.

My spirit would not let me pass on to you any acre of this tainted soil, my sister. It holds a curse for every white hand which touches it. It is with this knowledge that I have decided that all I have shall pass on to Emilene and the child. I feel in my heart that they will do all they can to uphold the approbation of our good name, a name they both share. Even when the black plague descends upon this green island, there will be at least one here to honor the name of Winston.

I trust that I have made you to understand, and that in doing so you will respect my deeds and wishes. And I have yet one more request to make of you. Is the lone elm tree still standing upon that hill overlooking the moors? For that is where I wish to be buried. Should the tiniest voice live on after me, I shall finally exalt in the apogee of Sir Walter—*My foot is on my native heath*.

And so I end my last earthly words to you. I am finished now. I will be gone when this letter reaches you, but do not mourn my passing. Know that I will have traveled on to a better place, for I have already lived my hell. And always remember, dear sister, that my love for you, the best of my blood, will burn ever brighter when we meet again in glory.

Everlastingly,
Mercy McDunn Winston

Voices in the Rain

peak your voice, wench!

Can those words have been addressed to me? For it has never been, and will likely never be that I shall have a voice to call my own. I am like a slave whose vocal chords have been swollen closed with *dumb cane*. From such time as I can remember, Mother Mercy has always spoken for me. She would hurry to answer a question before I could even contemplate my own response.

"No, Nanny Griggs, Emilene has never liked mangoes."

"Yes, Gareth. I believe Emilene would enjoy a ride out to Bridgetown."

Is it little wonder that I barely speak? That my voice has no more power than tears falling into the ocean? That no matter how I try to magnify the sound, my speech is so faltering I am always being asked to repeat myself. Mother Mercy would usually do it for me.

During those unspeakable nights of last year's rains, I would close my ears to the panting, and my mind to the rutting. As raindrops beat my dormered roof, I imagined them to be voices; the patter of unnamed women, bidding me to sing with them, to run with them like rivers. But I did not know the words to their song and had nowhere to run. I have never known rivers on this, my island home.

Sometimes the voices I hear come not from the rains without, but the memories within my own head. And even these do not belong to me. They are something owned, like all else I have.

Should I sit quiet in the garden, smiling at the memory of some small enjoyment, Mother Mercy might examine my face.

"Pray tell, my girl, what reason have you to wear such a self-pleased smirk?"

Mother Mercy never failed to probe any sentiment I might evince, whether voiced or silent.

"You haven't touched a morsel, dear child. Indeed, you must be feeling unwell tonight."

It has been such all my life. That I must first and always turn to Mother Mercy to know what to want, how to think, what to feel. The gown to wear, the proper Bible verse to quote, the needlepoint design to stitch. And while I may no longer be owned in body, I have yet to regain a voice enslaved from birth.

Mother Mercy was fond of me in her own way. I do not doubt that I had her love. What I have suffered from, and hungered for all these years, is a mother's touch. Perhaps she feared to handle me, ere the blackness of my skin soil her dainty white hands. Or even become a permanent stain upon her person.

But oh, how I've longed for the caress of a cool hand against my forehead on a fevered night, a kiss upon my cheek, a fond embrace, a comforting hand clasped in mine. At times I have wondered if I were even there. As if silent, black, and untouched, I had simply begun to fade away.

When a small child, my hunger for touch was satisfied by the attention of my nanny. Having run to my mother fallen and bruised, I would be sent unhandled to the black hands of Nanny Griggs. And those hands would tenderly apply the poultices of oil of palm and crushed aloe. Those hands would patiently plait the knotted hair Mother Mercy proclaimed *most difficult*.

Nanny's hands were small and quick, alighting upon my body like healing brown birds. Did Mother Mercy know that I was bathed in herbs like leaf of life, my skin rubbed with salves made from coconut oil and madar flowers? She could not have known the blessings in those balms that bonded us, the practices she would undoubtedly dismiss as *ungodly and heathen*.

As a child I was frightened of thunderstorms, and Nanny Griggs would come to sleep at the foot of my bed. I could not see her face except in the flashes of lightning, yet her voice was like music in the room. Rain against the roof underscored her words, like drumbeat. She told fanciful and primitive tales like *Brother Nancy's Feeding Tree.*

In old Guinea Land, they call him Kwaku Ananse. Here now we name him Brother Nancy. And this is how Brother Nancy come to live 'pon this island.

One time Obeah Woman of the River and Obeah Woman of the Sea, them quarrel so a hurricane come upon the land. Next come a long time dry. No food a grow. Brother Hunger, him visit all God creatures. Brother Death come, too. But him no find Brother Nancy, man. He fish upon the sea.

"Is selfish obeah women." He cast his line upon the water, but no fish a bite. "How is man to eat?"

"Ca-aa-aw! Caw, caw!"

Blackbird come a flying fat and sassy so, Brother Nancy think she don't miss much meals. Is blackbird getting food, may can be a bite in it for him.

"Sister Blackbird," he call. "Where you might be flying this fine day?"

"I coming from my feeding tree. Is so much food I eat this morning, I near too heavy to fly."

Is "food" Brother Nancy hear blackbird say?

"Why you don't share? Just look at me, nuh. Is only skin and bones."

"But, Brother Spider," she a tell him back. "I don't carry a crumble at-all, at-all. Even small load make me too heavy to fly."

"Eh. And you never offer to take me there?"

"The feeding tree on an island in the ocean, man. Is far, far, far."

"Sister Blackbird," he tell her. "May I borrow a small few of your feathers."

Spider self, him cannot fly at all. May be the wind might take him, come carry him away. But Brother Nancy lose so much fat, wind lift him like dry leaf. He pick up two tail feather and fly along so. They soon come upon a feeding tree with nice, fat fruit.

Brother Nancy, he eat and he eat and he eat. Sun going down in the sky, and Brother Nancy still eating.

"Nighttime a coming," Sister Blackbird say. "Is time to go."

Brother Nancy still eating. Time pass again, Sister Blackbird say: "Is bird I be, not bat. I no like to fly in the night."

But still Brother Nancy still eating. Time pass again and Sister Blackbird say: "Nighttime a coming and I won't tarry. Come if you will, stay if you must."

And off home she fly. Brother Nancy eating never stop until his belly ready to burst. He see the sun slip down the sky like gravy down a greedy man chin.

"Is time. I flew this way. I must go back same."

Brap! Brother Nancy heavy, so! Each time he jump upon the air, he fall back upon the beach. Brother Nancy say, he must to swim for it. He jump in the water and blup! Down he go like a stone, right down to the bottom, where was Obeah Woman of the Sea, picking she teeth with a whalebone. And she vex so.

"Brother Nancy, I go beat you, man."

"Ah, Auntie Obeah Woman. You go beat your own nephew?"

She don't believe she get spider for nephew. But Obeah Woman tell him, say: "Is true? Make you stay and have a sup with me."

She take Brother Nancy back to the island, make a fire, and give him calabash of boiling sea water.

"If you are my nephew, make you drink this one time."

"Brrr." He put the calabash to his mouth. "Is cold, cold. Make I rest it in the setting sun, it come even hotter."

And so she did, and so Brother Nancy drink the water. Obeah Woman see he a family member. She must help him find the way back home.

She call her son Tarpon, make him bring a boat. Brother Nancy get in, bid Tarpon take him ashore.

But as they go, Obeah Woman think again about hot water in the sun. And slow-slow-slow, she know is trick Brother Nancy trick her. She send a storm.

"Tarpon," she call cross the wave. "Come back home."

Brother Nancy, he cover Tarpon ear.

"Is my mother a call?" Tarpon say.

"Me, I no hear nothing. Storm a coming, Brother Tarpon. Make I cover your ear so no water come in."

"Tarpon, I say. Come back home."

Obeah Woman of the Sea, she call and she call. But he no hear.

"Row on," Brother Nancy cry in the wind and the waves. "Row on."

But Tarpon, him bearings gone, row in wrong direction. Is shark he pass in water, is big-big ship. When land a come, Brother Nancy get down and look around. People here is same like home, but not the same again.

"I no think," Brother Nancy say, "that I am in my own country again."

My story, child; 'tis true or no be true, 'tis sweet or no be sweet, take a little now, and let some come back to me.

Her Nancy tales never failed to excite a small child's imagination. But nothing can replace a mother's love. Despite Nanny's stories and healing hands, I still yearned to know my Mother Mercy's touch. Especially after Nanny was gone.

I somehow knew without being told that Nanny's secrets were black and awful and must never be brought to light. I never feared the candles burning, the animal bones, the upturned pots about her quarters. These and the tales she told all hinted of African ignorance and obeah.

But there was something else, something singularly menacing in the person Nanny became in moonlight. With fire shining in the sweat of her brown face, she presided like some primitive queen over the slave meetings, the songs and wild dances, the drums softly beating. There was something sinister about the shady places in her balm garden.

Nanny knew well enough to keep such activities quiet. Why she deemed it prudent to be so open about this particular matter, I could never say; perhaps Mother Mercy might:

We had gone to meet a ship in Bridgetown Harbour said to be bringing in a cargo of rice. A group of slaves were gathered about a Negro sailor whose strange accent suggested he was a freeman from the mainland. It was nothing untoward to come upon free black seamen, some even masters of their own vessels. They were the talking drums of the ocean waves, bringing the outside world to our news-starved ears. The man, an impossibly black sailor whose ragged garb belied his regal bearing, ruffled the pages of a foreign journal.

"Our friend Wilberforce has turned the King's hand. It is all written here," he proclaimed to the black crowd, most of them unable, if they tried, to ascertain the veracity of his statement. "*Parliament entertains talks of abolishing slavery throughout the Commonwealth.*"

"Parliament does talk," bellowed a naysayer among the group. Indeed, the idea had been mooted among the slaves for months. "He talk and he talk. And to this day we still slaves in Barbados."

The Yankee Jack-tar shouted him down.

"The decree comes from King George himself! Britain is afraid, my friends. Afraid the West Indies will burn like Santo Domingo did in '91."

Nanny, one of the few slaves I knew who could read and write, snatched the paper unceremoniously from his hands to see the news herself.

"Is true, true," she announced finally. "No matter what planter man say, big boy, Barbados Parliament them a say. God come a tell it to King George, just like me a tell it so. Is true we free in Barbados this year."

No sooner had we returned to The Rivers, did Nanny make haste to pass the news in a most public way. She wielded her pages like a cane cutter's machete. The word *emancipation* was chanted at midnight meetings, found its way into Cropover celebration songs, was uttered boldly in the slave quarters, and whispered in the very kitchen of the great house. Nanny took the message and sent it echoing like drumbeats throughout the parish.

"The damn fool slave have no need to work for the *backra* again. I read it with my own eyes. Come New Year's Day of God's next year, all who has toiled must go free."

And when New Year's Day had come and gone with the slaves yet unfree,

Nanny remained stubborn and defiant. She chastised grown men for their fear and faithlessness.

"Is free we free in Barbados, you no see it? The *backra* must give what King George him a promise. Even if Barbados burn the way they do in Saint Domingo. Before this year end we all must go free."

I felt painfully full within earshot of this dangerous notion. But being a child without voice, there was no way to speak the unspeakable. I continued to take food at my parents' table, to sleep at night in my spindle bed, to let Mother Mercy speak my voice, and to wait.

But I was unprepared for the abrupt departure of my touchstone. She left the first night of Cropover, while Mother Mercy and Father Winston gathered the slaves in the yard to hand out the holiday allotment of rum, molasses, and salt fish. Nanny called me to the kitchen and said she was going to bachannal, the Crop-over festivities the slaves celebrated surreptitiously in the woods and gullies away from the estate.

I begged, as always, to be taken along. Nanny shook her head, pressing a faded cloth into my hands. It was sewn together from woven strips, though one edge was ragged as if an end were torn away. The faded orange and red patterns were faintly familiar, though I was sure I had never seen it before. It was stained and worn, smelling of dust and old sweat.

"Have it, Emilene girlchild. Is the only thing left from your mother. Not Mother Mercy, mind you. The black one that bore you. You come off the ship swaddled up in it."

I had heard snatches of story in and about the slave quarters. That I was born aboard an African slaver and adopted by Mother Mercy upon landing in Barbados. That my mother had soon been seasoned and sold, never to be seen again on this island. But I had no memory of this black mother. I had no need of this rag. I was the child of Mother Mercy and Father Winston. I made to return the cloth to Nanny.

"Is the only thing on earth you own. Take and remember the mother who bore you."

And she had disappeared into the night. Leaving me to wonder how I could remember one I had never known.

The whites knew of these bachannals, of course. Such activities were frowned upon; Christian women like Mother Mercy complained of the drums and the rum and the licentious behavior they unleashed. Land-owning men like Father Winston grumbled that these all-night parties made his slaves late to the fields in the morning. And late they were indeed. Many of the slaves would never report for work the next, or any other morning.

It was almost a relief when I heard the shouts. When I looked down from the hilltop and saw the fires burning. For the secret had left the cover of night, and now lived in the open daylight. It was no longer trapped inside me.

I had grown accustomed to being spoken for, spoken of, spoken around as if I weren't there. No notice was taken of me when Father Winston discussed the news at the table. There were visitors that night, officials from the governor's mansion.

"Aye, we cornered the bloody gang at Simmons' plantation, Bussa and all his boys." Gareth always spoke much too loudly. Mother Mercy said the voice gave away his coarse, working-class origins.

"But of course," Mother primly pointed out, "they could not have been *all his boys*, if Nanny were among them."

"Fighting as hard and cursing as loud as any man. If you could have seen the hag; barely did I recognize her me ownself. Bare of chest, long tits hanging like a goat's udder. She wore a wide girdle round her waist, with nine or ten different knives hanging in sheaths to it. Many of which I doubt not had been bathed in human blood. A bloody she-devil, if ever there was."

"Which only goes to show," Mother turned her head to me, "the world of difference between a woman, and a lady."

Governor Cobbemere nodded solemnly.

"And they stoutly maintained until the end, that this island belonged to them and not to the white men."

The news spread and the blood flowed. Slaves were rounded up from every corner of the island. I heard the outcome one night as I lay sleepless; the screams of pain and shouts of defiance. The next morning was as quiet as the night had been raucous. Mother Mercy insisted I keep indoors, but I watched it from the alcove window in the upper story.

Silent slaves scurried about the property, cutting down the ones who'd been hanged the night before, arranging the bodies aboard donkey carts for hasty burial in the far field. I had not heard Nanny's voice among the cries that night, nor seen her small body dangling from a mahogany tree like fruit on Brother Nancy's feeding tree.

Those who had not been slain in battle or executed were said to have been sentenced to deportation to Sierra Leone. I prayed that Nanny was among them.

I had expected Bussa's rebellion to yield no deliverance, so was not surprised when none came. After Nanny was gone I accepted my fate. I was no daughter of Mercy. I was a pampered pet of the Winston household, owned body, soul, and voice. And so likely would live out my days, silent and untouched.

Faint hope of healing through human hands would flare briefly like a candle flame, then just as quickly be snuffed out.

Robert was a near-white boy from Simmons' estate, a mustee carpenter who hired out his time. When Father Winston bought a set of matched Arabians, Robert came on as workman for the new stables. I would cut hibiscus in the flower garden, or perch in the verandah swing with my needlework. And watch him from the corner of my eyes, admiring the brown wonder of his body.

Robert was not a large man. He was quite slender, barely taller than myself. But his wiry strength was evident in his work. Shirtless, the sun glinting off his slight brown shoulders, he sawed and hammered, hoisted impossibly large loads of lumber.

One day I sat over an unread volume of Byron, calculating when I might safely chance to steal a glance at Robert. And I was suddenly aware of a working man's scent, the strong smell of sweat and sawdust. I looked up and Robert stood before me. Hat in one hand, fist closed over something small in the other. He opened his hand to me.

An angel rested in it, tiny and perfect. A slave with the strength to hew planks of lumber from mighty logs was also a man with a touch so light it could wrest angels from mahogany boughs. I looked at it closely, wordlessly.

It recalled an earlier moment, when as a child I had persisted in the belief that, like my parents, I too must certainly be white. And Nanny Griggs had thrust the looking glass into my hands. I experienced the same shock of seeing that small black face framed in the oval mirror. For the face of the angel, perfectly carved in mahogany, was my own.

Confused and frightened, I thrust it back at him. But Robert smiled and held his empty hand open to the sky. He backed toward the stair, almost falling off the landing. He had said not a word. Robert, I was to learn, was a man almost as silent as myself. Yet he knew what it was to touch. And I would learn to savor the feel of it.

Robert hired his time for five full summers, working day and night, paying out the lion's share to his master and saving what remained of his wages. Nanny's bundles of dried herbs were long gone, but memories of where they grew lived on in my mind. I would pick the carpenter grass and cowfoot leaf, steep them in water and coconut oil. And in the evenings extract splinters from his joints and bathe his beaten, callused hands.

In the time between Nanny's disappearance and Robert's love, I had felt myself turning gray as the cold stone statues in the flower garden. The untouched silence of my soul spreading over me, threatening to consume me with sure and steady death.

In Robert's hands I was becoming warm, alive, supple. His mouth on mine, tender and worshipful, his hard hands at the curve of my back. He gave me back my life, and in turn I gave him everything he asked. I would have given more. But my hand in marriage was not mine to give.

Robert was said to be son of the union of a house slave and the plantation bookkeeper at Simmons' estate. Everyone assumed he was working to impress his father, or to purchase his emancipation. But he did not attempt to buy his own freedom. He took his earnings to Father Winston and begged for mine. I had never seen Mother Mercy so angry. She called me to her rooms, her face set and grim.

"How can he imagine, black slave that he is, that I would consent to give him my child, the only thing that matters in the world to me? That you would soil your purity to lie beside him; what a curious notion. You cannot possibly want such a man."

I was all too accustomed to Mother Mercy speaking my mind. It surprised me to hear the hesitant sound of my own voice.

"But he is a good man, Mother Mercy. And a kind one. I do believe he cares for me."

"Never." My mother's voice rose, shrill and insistent. "All that I have done for you, all that I have made of you. You will never be wasted on the empty promises of such a foul, faithless creature. I will hear nothing more on the subject."

I did not tell Mother Mercy that the purity she protected had long since been sacrificed; time and again, since first I lifted my skirts beneath the midnight moon, underneath the mango tree.

I did not mention other trees that sheltered us in the coppice of woods beyond the great house; the texture of mahogany bark against my back, the secrets the night winds whispered through ceiba cotton leaves. I did not confess the tender aspects of his carpenter's tool; the slenderness at the root, the bent trunk, the flaring at the head. The manner in which he moved inside me, like a royal palm waving in the trade winds.

I uttered not a word. My voice retreated to its customary hiding place. Mother Mercy's vigilance ensured there'd be no more nighttime visits to the coppice. Undiscouraged, Robert sent word to me through my serving girl, Sarah. Our escape was planned, both our passages paid. But I could not find a voice to reply. His message went unanswered and Robert traveled on, to where I cannot say.

Sarah had always been a sweet soul, a grandchild of Nanny Griggs'. We had played together in the yard as children. If she touched me not with hand, it was with laughter and deed.

She would hurry through her scullery duties to keep my company, strolling with me through the garden, sitting with me to needlepoint on the verandah. I would tax her memory for the stories Nanny once told, of Brother Nancy and his animal world, of a land called Guinea that would call us home after death. Sarah never tired of looking at the pictures in my old books of stories and nursery rhymes, hungering to decipher the symbols on the printed page.

"And this one." She pointed to a word. "Is what?"

"C-A-T. Cat. *Pussy cat, pussy cat where have you been? I've been to London to look at the queen.*"

She burst into delighted laughter.

"Caroline? She ugly like monkey, man. Poor puss, him couldna find no better to look at in London?"

We shared old stories and made up laughable new ones, odd mixtures of the jumbies and spirits of the slave quarters, and the witches and trolls of European fairy tales. Sarah had already begun learning to read when I noticed the bloated condition of her belly.

"Sarah, could it possibly be that you are with child?" Silent soul that I was, it was difficult even finding voice to ask this delicate question.

"Oh no, Miss Emilene," Sarah insisted to the day she delivered Moses. "Is not true. I never yet lay down with any man."

Moses was such a beautiful child. As good as gold, his dusty blond curls and golden brown face. What a wonderful thing it was to touch his warm, soft skin. When awake, he would grasp my finger with amazing strength, and attempt to direct it into his mouth. And he smiled when sleeping, a peaceful, contented smile. Nanny Griggs once said that when a sleeping babe smiles, angels are whispering in its ear.

Sarah's milk soon dried up. The dear boy could not take the boiled, sweetened goat's milk. He'd hungrily suck it from the teat cloth, then quickly bring it back up again. He began to cry piteously, to lose weight.

One day I took him to my room, trying to rock him into forgetfulness of his empty stomach. He rooted around for my breast like a precious baby chick. In desperation, I opened my bodice.

It was most frustrating for him, I am sure. He would suckle hard at the dry teat, then his little face would crumple in rage. He would weep, then suckle again. Suckle, then weep. I told myself this intermittent crying was better than the constant wailing. The nipple seemed to soothe him for short moments. And oh, his dear little mouth at my breast.

I would nurse him so for hours each day. In time I noticed that he sucked more contentedly, his crying ceased. I looked down one day, surprised to notice a wet spot on the bodice of my covered breast. I tentatively looked inside. As Moses lustily suckled one breast, a thin, white substance dribbled from the other. By some miracle, my body was bringing forth the milk Moses needed to keep him alive. My dear God, how I came to love that child.

I continued to wet nurse, for Sarah was quite poorly for a time. She lay in bed, listless and weeping, insisting that the child could not be hers. Anyone with eyes could see both the maternity in the babe's broad features, and the paternity in its blond curls and blue eyes. He was not the first such child born on the Winston estate. Nor would he be the last.

As with the others, Mother Mercy lost little time. The child was sold away at ten months of age, as soon as he had begun to walk. Before he had even been properly weaned. Sarah, who had slowly learned to love little Moses, slipped into a pining so deep that she never recovered from it. And I, I thought my very heart would break. My breasts rebelled at his absence, engorged like stones with unspent milk. My eyes were dry with unshed tears.

Nanny Griggs' healing hands. Robert's gentle kisses. The balm of Sarah's smile. The suckling of Moses' tender mouth. Though I had never been a child to snuggle against a mother's bosom or perch upon a father's knee, I had those precious moments of touching that warmed my soul. I soon came to know the cold terror of a wounding, punishing touch.

He never called out, nor did I. I would close my eyes tightly, pretending not to know the one who pushed roughly into my bed chamber. Not to recognize the roaming hands, the rum breath, the harsh, raspy panting. And when it was over the hard-boned body collapsing upon mine. I would lie awake, fearful in my spindle bed. Praying that this night would not be one I would be visited by this stranger's touch. But he would always come, night upon night.

I could imagine how easy it had been for Sarah to make herself disbelieve. In the brightness of day, the nightly intrusions could be forgotten. The others were not so easy. The monthly flow dry as an empty fountain. The breasts, swelling shamefully. The meals, disgorged moments after dining. The body, bursting the seams of white cotton gowns.

And throughout it all, memories of Moses. Brown dimples flashing, blond curls bouncing. His warm hand grasping my finger. His tender mouth, suckling my breast. The bright, satisfied gleam in his dark blue eyes as he took his first step. And the empty reality of his absence.

I sat alone on the verandah one evening, reading until the light finally failed. There seemed to be a message for me in Burns' melancholy admonition.

Say, sages, what's the charm on earth
can turn death's dart aside?

I visited Nanny Griggs' balm garden, remembering the dark secrets whispered into my ear. The secrets I once longed to forget.

"The manweed kill hard, the lady kill easy. Devil's nightshade, cook up in the food, he kill in weeks. Madam Fate; a little pinch over time, she kill in months, sometimes years."

I picked the herbs and measured them carefully, putting larger amounts into Father Winston's meals. Smaller portions into Mother Mercy's tea. Father died six weeks before little Wynn was born. Mother Mercy, right before Cropover this year.

Bayley sent around his big boy, offering to purchase The Rivers for some paltry sum. I am most uncomfortable sitting alone with a man so infamous his cruelties have become legend throughout the parish.

"The man so wicked, kill become a part of his name. First time he kill William, then he kill Quashie. Now he kill Patrick."

Kilpatrick's face becomes more bloated by the year, from rum and whoring and whipping slaves. After Robert's marriage offer was declined, he had soon come around offering to buy me for himself. Mercifully, Mother had given him no less flat a rejection. I shudder at the possibility of it. Rather I should leap from the heights of Mount Pleasant, than belong to such a creature. Never again, I resolved from that moment, would I be touched but by a man of my own choosing.

Wynn nurses fitfully with the unaccustomed weight of wool about his head. His little fist flails, dislodging the nursing shawl. Kilpatrick squints through reddened eyes, staring greedily at my uncovered breast. I reach to tuck the nursing shawl securely around my shoulder.

" 'Tis a kindness to you," he slurs in his drunken brogue, "is Master Bayley's offer. What can such a naygur as yourself know of running a sugar estate? So what say you now, eh? Speak your voice, wench!"

I look around, almost expecting Mother Mercy to answer for me. But she is gone, both my white parents are. Sleeping their eternal nightshade rest on an island miles across the ocean. My infant son stirs in my arms, rooting to find nourishment at my breast. The rain begins to fall, spattering gently against the roof, speaking to me in voices. *We are not lost, we are not nameless, we are not silent.*

" 'Tis neither wench nor nigger you see before you, sir."

Kilpatrick flinches, as if recoiling from a blow. I stand suddenly, shifting Wynn's weight to my shoulder. Deprived of the nipple and startled by my voice, he begins to cry. Even I am stunned at the force of my words, the voice which whips from my lips like hurricane winds.

"I am called Emilene. Emilene Winston. A daughter of the Diaspora and mistress of this estate. I expect that I and my son will be staying on. The Rivers is not for sale, by your leave, Mr. Kilpatrick. Take that message to your master."

The Spider's Web

Your second-born daughter did not do badly for herself in the end.

And if she would end her days on a land without rivers? She would inherit a property called The Rivers and all that it contained. And if she continued to hold some of her own kind in semislavery well past the point of Emancipation? And if the term black backra would be hissed at her retreating back? Could she be expected to come down from her hill and share their poverty, their meager pots, their chattel houses?

The one who claimed her own voice would leave no diaries behind. But after she is gone, one will be able to read her story in dainty needlestitched designs, disquieting though they may be: women dancing in flames, brown angels flanked by white corpses, human hands hanging from ceiba cotton trees.

Having claimed her voice and sworn to never again be touched, but by a man of my own choosing, she would seek and find none worthy. Emilene, born Diaspora, would choose to live a life without. Happily? Well, what is happiness? She would find her happiness in motherhood.

Alas, no children would be born from the union of her male child Wynn and the highborn, highbrown maiden Emilene would choose for him. Perhaps it was not meant to be for a boy born in bastardy. But one serving girl in the household he shared with Emilene and his unhappy wife would prove fruitful enough. His children and their children would bear children. The Rivers would never be empty.

And what would become of her birth mother, your first-born daughter? What can I say, but that Ama Krah journeyed on? She journeyed on with nothing to remind her of home but her waist beads, a scrap of kente cloth, and her pride.

This nomad daughter would come to inhabit Amerindian villages and wander through battlefields. She moved through impossible places; I could not always follow the bloody footprints she left behind. She moved so fast that she discarded names like outgrown snakeskin, and continually grew them anew.

Ama Krah, Africa's daughter, would only settle when age had slowed her steps, when blood rooted her to this uneasy earth. She would find her way to a sodden point of land between two rivers, and find that she could go no further. And when Ama Krah was ready to join her ancestors, she would come from a new land and with a different name.

And that is how I happen to overhear that final conversation. I listen from the crack between the pages of Jeremiah 9:5. Have you noticed that as annoying as they are, elephants are barely bothered by the buzzing of mosquitoes? After all, it takes more than a mosquito to drink an elephant's blood.

Words at the Wake

Lordy mercy, look at all these peoples. Hand me some of that pecan pie 'fore it gets all gone. Wish Sister Mary coulda been here to see her ownself off. Woulda done her right proud.

Yes, indeed. This is the first wake in thirty-something years old Mary done missed. Was a good church mother if ever there was one. You know Proud Mary sitting at the right hand of the Lord. Justa mumbling her way through glory, honey.

Girl, hush your mouth. You know it ain't right to speak ill of the dead. Course, Mary was a tie-tongued somebody, wasn't she? Wonder how come.

Honey, they tell me it was some old mumbling Africa talk. You know she was a salt-water woman, don't you? Come all the way from Africa. Never did learn her no English.

Everybody knowed that. But if she didn't know English, how come Mary had so mucha understanding? She could listen at you, figure everything you was saying and then some. She may not could talk, but old Proud Mary had a plenty sense. Oh, the Lord works in mysterious ways, his wonders to perform.

Yes, and so do the devil.

The devil? What the devil got to do with it?

Well, the way I hear tell . . . oh, hey there, Sister Olean.

Olean Foley, how you keeping, child? I ain't seen you in a month of Sundays.

Don't Sister Mary look just as natural? Seem like she just laying up there sleeping . . . Yes, the good Lord done laid her down to rest. Well, run on along, Olean. I see you at Sunday service.

Olean look right foolish in all that yellow. I don't know what she got on her mind.

Yes, I do. See how she swishing up to Reverend Halliday over there? Some womens ain't got no shame.

Sho you right. More to be pitied than scorned. All gussied up like she at a wedding 'stead of a wake. Girl, do you see that? I don't believe it.

See what?

Big old spider, riding that Bible laying 'cross Proud Mary's breast. If it's anything I hate worser than sin, it's a nasty spider. There it go across the floor. Step on it quick, 'fore it gets away.

Naw, honey. They say it's bad luck to kill a spider. It ain't bothering you none, let it go on about its business.

Hmmph. How you know that spider ain't no heathenish hoodoo sent straight from hell? It's a lot y'all don't know about Proud Mary.

Like what?

See that scrap of rag and them old blue beads that girl Bohema carryin' round like it was religion? Somebody need to whup her narrow behind, take that mess to the boneyard. It ain't nothing but some African hoodoo they need to be burying right along with Mary.

I like to see somebody try to get that rag and beads away from that baby. They have a fight on they hands. That's Ella Mae's youngest child, Proud Mary's natural shadow. She just wanted a little something to remember her great grandmama by.

Well, you tell me if you catch her carryin' round that tongue. You recollect how when Proud Mary went to mumbling, she always kept her mouth covered? Ain't nobody never seed the inside of it. I hear tell, now don't you breathe a word of it. They tell me Proud Mary cut her own tongue out at the root. Umm-hmm.

Child, peoples will say anything. First she can't speak no English, now she ain't got no tongue. Why in God's name would a person cut out they own tongue?

It wasn't till her old age that Mary got religion, you know. When she was a young woman she was supposed to had trucked in all kinds of devilish conjure and carrying on. That's how I hear it. They tell me she used that tongue in some kinda spell that was suppose to make her live long as Methusalum. But you know how colored folk talk. I wouldn't put too much truck in that.

I don't know, Sister. She was way up in years, that's for sure. Had to be a hundred if she was a day. Mary lived so long she buried all two of her childrens. You recollect Proud Mary had two natural-born children of her own.

How you know they was natural born? Was you the midwife?

Far as I know, she whelped both of them her ownself. They say that no sooner did Proud Mary come across the water, she run off from Louisiana and commence to living in the woods. Mary was way too old to be breeding, if you ask me. That was the year that old Mississippi flooded so bad, sipe water rose up the porch. You had to get in a rowboat just to cross the road. Mary was already gray-headed when she come up here that spring, had Zubena on her back and Freedom in her belly. Don't ask me who they papa was.

Freedom was 'bout a pure-blooded nigger as you could get, but seems to me like that Zubena had some Injin or some Gypsy in her. You remember Zubena, don't you? Kind of copper-skinned and slick-headed. And just as wild and headstrong as a wolf pup. Come from being raised in the woods, I reckon. She couldn't speak a mumbling word when Mary first brung her up here.

Only stands to reason, don't it? What the mama don't know, how she going to teach? Ain't right to have no baby up in the woods by yourself. It takes a whole family to raise up a child, can't no one woman in the woods do it all by herself. Ain't had no home-training, that's how Zubena come to a bad end like she did.

A unchurched heathen if ever there was one.

You know Zubena wasn't but a little bitty thang when she crossed over. Po' child. She passed while she was birthing Ella Mae. Shoot, Mary 'bout the only mother little Ella knowed. And Mary's Freedom. Child, I don't even like to think on it. White folk can be so mean.

Lord knows we was proud of that boy. They say Freedom had on his blue army jacket when they cut him down from that tree. Two years fighting those rebels down South, and had the scars to prove it. Had to come back here and get hisself lynched by the Cairo crackers. Yet wearing that Union jacket when Mary took him up to Mound City and buried him.

I don't care how old you get, you ain't suppose to bury your childrens. You bury your only childrens, who going to bury you?

Now, you know Proud Mary had plenty of peoples to put her away. She ain't had but the one grandbaby. But child, Ella Mae Beasley got close to twenty childrens and grand-childrens together. Cairo just full of Proud Mary peoples.

I hear she even got some other peoples off somewhere. A family she had 'fore she come up here to Cairo.

Sho nuff? Where they at?

I don't know, child. They 'bout down South somewhere; Mary mighta had to leave them behind. So many peoples lost touch of they kin when they run off from slavery. First you got peoples, then you don't, just drylongso like it wasn't nothing wrong with it. It's a hurting thing.

Honey, do you know how long it been since slavery times? Forty years if a day. Them other folks might be in they grave by now.

Well, you sho' know that's where Old Mary going tomorrow morning. I ain't heard of no hoodoo that strong it can wake up the dead. Lessen Mary raise up from that cooling board bound to be another Lazarus, and Jesus Christ come down from heaven.

Now, honey. Proud Mary lived to a good old age and when she left here she was ready. Seen her down to the Point last week, had them old hoodoo beads hanging round her waist, that rag in her hand, and her Bible on her breast, just like she got it now. Holding on to that rag and that Bible, steady watching the water. Proud Mary was ready to cross that river, child. She way over on the other side.

Beadwork

From our village in eternity, one hundred years would be but a raindrop in the river. But these have not been normal times. It has been one hard century for our daughters. But we can't hold the unborn here, protecting them from pain. We must send them out into life.

They may be dying like flies in the world out there, but they're fighting like lions before they come home. It is true that ancestors are no longer as strong as we once were, but we are not powerless. We reach in and help where we can.

About this name-changing business. Correct me if I'm wrong, but hasn't that tale-tell spider been sporting new names? Kwaku Ananse in the Old World, Brother Nancy in the New? Yes, our daughters have changed their names. Many more will do the same. They are becoming new women in their trials, reinventing themselves in this peculiar place.

But I must admit, some of these new ways, we don't quite know what to make of. Sometimes a mother and daughter meet in the hereafter, with unexpected results. Sometimes a soul is allowed to cross over long before her time. See that child over there, more girl than woman? Gold in her ears and fire in her eyes? Watch out for that one.

Yet each soul has a purpose, if only to fertilize ground for the generation to come. Even calamities and catastrophe are not without meaning. That, unfortunately, is a fact with which we now contend.

The Queen Mother of the River Where Blood Is Born has not been herself lately. A goddess must be remembered in order to thrive. With no priestess among the living to celebrate her name, the Queen Mother keeps to her bed, waiting for the daughter of deep memory to return. I sit here at the gate, stringing my beads, worrying, and watching a wild child among us pick a fight with anybody who will give her the time of day.

As the argument rages, I see movement in the distance. It seems we have a newcomer. Yes, a woman is crossing the bridge, arms full of baskets and bundles. A white cloth wrapped around her head, a chewstick in her mouth, a kente-wrapped Bible in her hands, and battered, beaten shackles around her legs.

I prepare for a homecoming.

A Remembered One

"Welcome, sister. Welcome to eternity."

She drinks deeply of the water the Gatekeeper offers. When she passes over, her *amoasi*, a doubled rope of blue beads, drops down from around her waist. She steps out of them, wipes her mouth, and looks around to get her bearings.

Nothing's for certain, they say on the other side, *except death and taxes.*

It just goes to show what little the living know. The changes lived out in life carry over into this village of eternity. Some women are clad in rags, others wrapped in the finest raiment. Some wear goat-leather sandals, others buckskin moccasins. They do things ancestors never used to do in death before; play cards, smoke pipes, read Bibles. It is impossible to get *akpeteshie* and palm wine these days, so the ones that drink have to content themselves with white lightning and bathtub gin.

New breeds of ancestor have entered the blood. One woman wears long black braids about her smooth brown face, her elongated eyes turned toward the east. She hasn't said much since she entered the village and announced her credentials.

"Changing Woman. Ancestor goddess of the Apache People, a child of the water."

She sits there smoking her pipe, occasionally changing from a baby to an old woman, to a child, and back again. At this moment she is quietly watching the antics of that wild child. If the girl is one of her Apache daughters, perhaps she will take her in hand.

"I don't hold with all this mixing of religions." The Troublemaker jangles her gold earrings aggressively. She has taken it upon herself to drive someone from the village today. "Either you belong here or you don't."

"But, Sister," responds the one confronted, "what does it matter which name we call our Great God by? Whether we be black or brown, whether we call ourselves *ancestor* or *saint*?"

You have to strain your ear to hear a voice of reason these days. The old ones are fading from forgetfulness. They squat near the table, waiting for a crumb to fall.

"These saints come marching in, trying to turn hoodoo into Sunday school. Look at this one," she points out the woman wrapped in blue, "with her holy self. Who you the mother of?"

"Of God," she replies gently, matter of fact.

"Well, your God ain't none of mine. What business you got being in this gathering when all you all's head folk is mens? The father and the son. What happened to the mother and the daughter?"

The woman wrapped in blue is unperturbed.

"But there is the Holy Ghost, who has no gender. It is merely the spirit of God, inhabiting a body of flesh."

"And that God is a man," the Troublemaker retorts. "What's the difference between letting the Holy Ghost in, and any other old man that wants to get inside?"

"May God forgive you, sister," the other murmurs. "For the sacrilege you utter."

"I don't need you to ask no man's forgiveness of me, Miss Mary. Neither Jesus nor his Daddy got a thing to say to me. If I was you, I'd fight for my propers. Wouldn't be no Jesus if he didn't have a mama. And another thing. How can you give birth to that big-headed boychild of yours, and still have the nerve to call yourself a virgin?"

There is another strange one in the village, almost as silent and withdrawn as the Troublemaker is loud and coarse. She showed up at the gate one morning, stiff as a board in her British accent and linen gown, carrying not a single bead or any reference to recommend herself. She produced a frayed scrap of *kente* she said had been left behind by her birth mother.

And since that day, the Needleworker has been a disquieting presence among the ancestors. She says little, keeps her own counsel, busies herself stitching needlework designs. A frown of concern creases her brow when she notices the new ancestor entering the village. As usual she says nothing, but bends her head to bite a loose thread.

"You're home now," the Gatekeeper welcomes. "Don't be a stranger. Get to know people."

The woman steps through the mist, stops and stares hard at the young troublemaker, still itching to pitch a fight. Before she can be warned, she has walked up to her with open arms. She is getting to know the wrong kind.

"Zubena," she whispers, "is that you?"

The young one is taken aback. She looks the woman up and down, then turns away.

"Who invited this haint here? This ain't no séance. You better go find you a house to haunt, baby."

The woman draws back puzzled, shaking her head.

"I am no ghost, Zubena, my child. I am an ancestor like you, recently departed."

"So, what you doing here? Family reunion going on in the campgrounds. If you hurry over there, you may be able to find some of your kinfolk."

"I am more interested," the newcomer explains, "in the world of the living. I am studying songs and daughters. I want to learn what you know."

"Now, wait a minute, honey. We got work to do. Some of us here been watching these women cut up for near 'bout a hundred years, waiting to see which one of them is coming back to the river like she supposed to."

"I was one of the women you watched," the new one confesses. "My soul was at war with my blood and I couldn't find my way back to the Place Where Blood Is Born."

"Hmmph. That's your problem, not ours. Maybe if you act right, you might get to be born again, go back over there and tend to your mistakes. One thing's for sure. You can't come straight up here to the top. You got to start at the bottom and work your way up."

"I am concerned," she insists, "about my daughters."

"Who ain't? Question is, how many mothers we going to have taking care of business? It's getting crowded. Too many cooks spoil the broth. I think you going to have to leave, honey."

Zubena is gently shushed by one of the older ones.

"Silence, sister. You're little more than a newcomer yourself. Who are you to judge? In the old days one such as you would never have sat among the ancestors. Only when a child's hands are clean, can she eat with her elders."

"And what's wrong with me?"

The woman can only shake her head.

"You . . . one who has died so young. Who has died in childbirth, a birth her body had not been blessed for giving. The only reason you count yourself an ancestor at all is that someone wrenched that child from your stilled body and breathed life into her. And the child who has grown to become Ella Mae Beasley has no memory of you. When she calls for her mother, she calls out for another woman. Not you."

"Don't think I don't know," Zubena tosses her head, earrings jangling, "that y'all hate me just because I'm beautiful."

"Is that what the man told you?" The Needleworker, rarely heard from, cuts in icily. "The one who got you into this predicament? Who laid you down, planted the seed, then left you alone when your belly began to rise? When you gave birth to a child you had not been blessed to receive? When you died in the effort? And what good does all your beauty do you now, foolish girl? There is no man here to admire it."

"Who says somebody got to ask your leave-taking before they lay down with a man and make a baby from it? I got just as much right to sit here as any one of you. And I dare the first one of you to put me out."

She glares around her at all in the gathering. There are no takers. But then a voice, like a young girl crying, can be heard. It is faint, but distinct.

"Nana! Help me, Nana."

"Listen. Somebody out there is calling on one of us." All ears prick up, faces turned toward the bridge. "But that could be anyone. Nana means grandmother, old woman. Who is she asking for?"

"It is me," the newcomer answers. "She is a daughter of mine, and she needs my help. What can we do for her?"

All those assembled gather around the river. Clearly reflected in the waters is this scene: a child of no more than thirteen, tossing and writhing in a narrow wooden bed beside a window. An early morning sun rises pink behind patched curtains. The girl's face is contorted with the agony of a birth her young body is unprepared for giving.

There is silence for a heartbeat. Then a debate arises.

Some believe the girl's sin should be met with silence. That the time to ask for ancestors' blessings is before, not after, the child has been made. She made her bed hard, she must be left to writhe in it. Others call for compassion, mercy, understanding. Some wonder if the one struggling to come into the world might indeed be the one we've been waiting for so long. And what if a choice must be made; should we sacrifice the mother to save the child?

"What gives us the right to interfere with our children's lives? It is not our business," the Needleworker opines, "to meddle in the affairs of our descendants. Let God decide."

"Let God decide?" Zubena snorts derisively. "Ain't you the one that made her only son marry up with a woman he didn't love? If your boy Wynn had the chance to pick his own wife, maybe you wouldn't have wound up with a Big House full of bastards."

While the debate rages on, the new ancestor takes action. She opens up her mothering arms, just as she had earlier to the troubled one in their midst. She plunges bony, twisted hands into the water.

In the world of the living her hands find flesh. They touch first the young one's face, and the pain leaves it. They soothe the pulsing belly, bulging too large for the frail body. One hand reaches in between the legs and gently, expertly widens a way which had been too narrow. One hand holding the portal open, the other reaches up with the next squeeze of labor, and firmly presses down on the belly.

It happens so quickly that later on the woman-girl would say she did not remember how her first child was actually born. She would say she did not recall the last labor pains, the overwhelming urge to bear down, the interminable instant of stretching open, nor the delivery itself. She would say that in the last moments she felt her great-grandmother's hands on her, saw blue mist swirling, and heard the sound of running water. And she was gone from her body until the moment Earlene, her newborn daughter, was placed in her arms.

The water runs red. Our midwife, the new ancestor, draws hands from the river, dripping blood.

"It is like seeing myself again. Like *being* myself so many long years ago, struggling to bring harvest before the fruit is ripe. And such has been my punishment; I would give birth three times, and live to lose all three. I took a man's love as my due, and lost it long before I ever learned the joy of giving in return. If only I could have seen Kwesi once again, and shown him the woman I have become. If only I could see my mother, and tell her the things I now know. Blood is seen before birth."

"I am here," a voice answers. Abena Anim, a woman squatting with the ragged ones, rises. Her image is faded, like a rag that has been washed too many times. But this mistress of the *adowa*, her voice is still strong. "I know you, my child. I too have learned things, even in death. I have watched you from my place as an ancestor. You, who never had a family, have lived to mother three generations. You, who never had a village, have built your own. I have seen you grow

from a headstrong daughter to a wise mother. Do good and it lives in your descendants. Do evil and it lives in them likewise."

At this she turns and pointedly regards Zubena, the Troublemaker. But the
subtle scolding falls to the wayside, ignored in an orgy of greed.

"Well, what you brung to eat? We hungry and you can't eat with us unless you
bring something to the table."

Drying her hands against her Sunday go to meeting dress, the new one
quickly unwraps the bundles she's brought along. She uncovers fragrant-smelling
pots and dishes. Even the protester is impressed.

"Well, look at all this. Didn't your people put you away in fine style? You must
have a lot of children coming behind you. What do they call you, anyway?"

"They call me Proud Mary . . ." she begins.

The Troublemaker rolls her eyes.

"Lord, not another saint. Don't tell me you're coming up in here preaching
Jesus."

". . . but that is not the name I was born with. Mine were no virgin births. My
soul was at war with my blood, and I made life before my body was blessed
for giving. I came across water, seed in me. Lost my firstborn on the sugar isle.
My body was bought, my tongue was slit. I wandered the world without voice,
never able to speak to my children, or sing to my grandchildren, or tell a man I
loved him."

"You got an eternity to tell your life story, honey." The girl with gold earrings
begins to pick through the food. "It's dinnertime."

The voice of a silent one is suddenly heard. The blue mist clears and she can
be seen, sitting upon her royal stool. Her vigor has faded, but she is beautiful still.

"What a terrible thing it is to die without wisdom," whispers the Queen
Mother of the River. "I fear that one here is not ready to sit among us."

"That's what I was trying to tell this hardheaded haint," Zubena responds,
mouth crammed with food. "But y'all wouldn't listen."

"Headstrong child, wild as a wolf pup," the Queen Mother says gently.
"Daughter of the forest. Had not this woman's memories kept you alive, you would
have died a second time; the death of a disremembered ancestor. Do you not recognize the face of your own mother?"

"My mother? This ain't none of my mother. My mother ain't never called a
clear word in her life."

"I was not always the dumb mumbler you knew me as," the newcomer
explains. "When my tongue was taken, I could not say my true name to those in
the place I found myself. The worst thing about being voiceless, of being enslaved,
was losing my name. Some called me Saltwater Woman. River Walker. Proud
Mary. There is no one left behind who knows Ama Krah, *soul born on Saturday*.
My life is gone, but I have reclaimed my voice. All I wish now is to be able to
speak to my daughters."

She reaches toward the girl. "Come and embrace me, my second-born child."

Zubena shies away, regarding her with a mixture of fear and contempt. So
busy she is glaring that she doesn't notice the fingers of mist rising up from the

river until they have taken hold of her. She wails like a newborn baby as she is carried from the gathering, pulled backward through the gate, and out across the bridge into the land of the living. All in attendance heave a collective sigh of relief; all, that is, except one.

"I fear for the lost ones," breathes Saltwater Ama, the new ancestor.

"That one wasn't ready yet. Do not worry yourself, Daughter," the Queen Mother reassures. "She will be reborn, given a chance to rebecome."

"I had another daughter," Ama remembers. "A child I never had the chance to know."

The Queen Mother of the River Where Blood Is Born smiles tenderly, takes the woman's face between her hands.

"Look around you, my dear. She is among us."

And when she does, Saltwater Ama Krah encounters a familiar image. The woman is recognized not by her face, but the carefully folded square of *kente* cloth pinned against the linen bodice of the Needleworker's white dress.

"A daughter named Diaspora," Saltwater Ama murmurs. "My first-born child."

"The name is Emilene." The Needleworker critically regards the woman with outstretched arms. As prim and proper as Zubena was fiery and fierce, she unpins the worn scrap of *kente* and places it in her hand. "I believe this belongs to you. I have been waiting several lifetimes to relieve myself of this rag."

Anger wars with grief, and finally wins out.

"Where is your respect? Is this how that child-stealing Englishwoman has taught you to speak to your mother?"

"I do not know you, madam," the Needleworker returns. "You are simply the slave woman whose body I passed through. You are not my mother."

"I was never a slave," Ama explains sadly. "I was enslaved. And no bearded white man ever emancipated me. I fought my way free. But these tears I shed are not for myself. They are for the life I gave aboard a slave ship, when the elements around me, the Queen Mother of the Ocean herself, demanded her death. I weep for the bitter woman she has become."

"I gave birth to myself," the Needleworker reminded. "And I have always been my own mother. Kindly leave me to my needlework."

Ama Krah, Proud Mary, can only turn away in pain. The Queen Mother washes her face with cool water, soothes the mothering ache in her empty arms.

"Your daughter lived her life as a motherless child. Give her time to know you."

"It seems that even in death," Ama Krah sighs, "I am destined to lose my daughters. Will I ever hold one of them in my arms again? And what will become of the others, the motherless ones beyond us in the world of the living? The new blood among us will soon be wrenched from her source. When I reached into the present and touched the newborn child, I sensed seasons of separation within her and succeeding generations. Who will watch over them, protect them, remind them whose children they are?"

"You will. Proud Mary, Saltwater Woman, Ama Krah, daughter of Abena Anim, mother of Diaspora, of Freedom, and of Zubena. You are among us now, in your rightful place. They will never be motherless as long as we are with them.

The lost cannot be forgotten, for they are our wealth. Though a ghost is poor in possessions, at least she has the pride of her descendants."

"And what if our names should be unknown to those of our blood in the living world, as my name was to my daughters?" Ama wonders. "What names shall they call upon in their moment of need?"

"Our names are unimportant. Though we are known by many names, we have but one purpose. The head itself has two ears, but it does not hear in twos. We watch over our blood in the land of the living, helping where we can. Waiting to find the daughter of deepest memory and bring her home to us one day. We can reach through from the spirit world as you just have, my dear. Touching the souls of those descendants who seem lost."

"Will they know who we are?" the new ancestor worries. "Will they even realize that we are there?"

"Though your true name may be unknown to them, your spirit has not been forgotten, as has befallen so many of us here." The Queen Mother gestures toward the most poorly among us. "We are honored to share this meal prepared by those who loved you so well. You are a remembered one in the land of the living, and your presence here gives us new strength. Welcome, Daughter. Let us eat."

Proud Mary, Saltwater Woman, Ama Krah, smiles and calls out clearly in her reclaimed voice.

"So. Does anybody here like pecan pie?"

PART III

BACKWATER

Beadwork

What becomes of the lost ones?

How could we know that this question would come to haunt us? How could we know it would come to pass that several of our daughters would wander in the wilderness, disconnected from the river of their lifeline, where they "couldn't hear nobody pray"?

What have they to follow when the river goes underground?

Can we say that we were there in the breeze, in the trees that bent like brown women whispering secrets? Did they know that those whisperings were the secrets of their birthright? Were we there in the hurricane that blew one island-born daughter out into the world, carried beyond Caribbean? When another one stayed, planted by the rivers of water? Were we there in the mountain that moved her?

Did they hear our voices, feel our presence? If we were indeed unheard, unseen, unfelt, were we truly ever there? And if the daughter of deepest memory should appear in this quale, how would she know which way will take her home?

Sometimes I feel I want to tremble.

And the Priestess' earlier prediction is recalled:

She who sings at dawn captures the sun. The fourth-born child will be calm and bright.

And then there are those warrior souls, sent forth fighting to carve their path in the world. The fifth child will be born aggressive.

Each flower comes to seed in its own time. Your sixth child will be a late-season bloomer; slow to blossom, but eager to learn.

There have been no reports from the web of history. Kwaku Ananse, in predictable trickster fashion, is nowhere to be found. There is an empty space in this stretch of story beads. So we watch the waters, and await a word from the world of the living.

Can we get a witness?

My Little River

Mine is the soul of a wild child living in a city woman. I guess you could call me a country slicker. Spent most of my six decades living with steel and concrete, streets that stay lit after dark, water running hot and cold from kitchen taps.

But every now and then I feel something welling up in me, like the memory of a wilderness I have never known. Like water bubbling up from the bottom of a spring. Where this backwoods nostalgia comes from I will never know. Even the faint memories I have of a life outside the city are of a country more cultivated. Acres of rolling farmland, fields of green corn, cows in pasture.

I have never been much of an outdoors person. I don't like to camp or hunt like some colored folks I know. Yet I find myself longing for the mystery of deep forest, craving to chew on sweet blades of clover. I am fascinated with the sound of birds and the color of wildflowers. And the urge that will strike me now and again to explore unknown bodies of water. To see where they lead and how deep they run.

From time to time I'll go outside the city, some place where green dominates gray. I'll stand on a bridge overlooking a winding river, or sit on the shores of a lake and watch wild waterbirds. Feel at home among them, like one long-legged crane myself, a crest of white flaming up from its black head.

And I'll wonder what I've always wondered. Just what do they hear that makes them all rise as one out of the water, as sudden and sure as souls standing in service when the reverend calls them to *amen*? What is the magnet that moves them, that makes the V unwavering, that keeps them on the invisible route south come winter?

Is it land that calls them or water? Or something in the blood that knows where home should be? Yes. That must be it. I recognized it suddenly that morning crossing a bridge over the Illinois. I glanced out and saw a ribbon of river winding off into who knows where. Next thing I knew I was getting off at the next exit: *Simon's Acres, Illinois*.

Simon. That's funny; I had me a father named Simon. I remember him in the same way I do the birds and wildflowers that were a part of a life I lived before this patch of hair on my temple became white. And I've had it for a long time. People always tell me how striking the white crest of hair looks against the black. They never see the scalp underneath, the quarter-sized patch of skin with the pigment burned out.

Pappa's hair was neither white nor black. It was gone. I remember him big and black and strong. I remember him dark, his bald head shiny with sweat. I remember him throwing me up so high that the green ground would rush away and the blue sky would fly down to meet me. I remember him singing spirituals in his crackly baritone: *didn't it rain, children . . . steal away to Jesus . . . my soul looks back and wonders how I got over*. I remember him telling stories by a potbelly stove in a smoky one-room shack.

Now what did I want to say that for? Shack. I've always hated that word. They only call it a shack when it's Black folks' houses; otherwise it's a cabin. I once toured this replica of Lincoln's log cabin at a county fair, and if I had lived there instead of Abraham you better believe they'd be calling it *Earlene's Log Shack*. I guess when you're one of the darker folk you cast a shadow over all the logs and chinks and soot and creaky floors and field mice and windows caulked with rags, and what would have been a cabin becomes a shotgun shack.

Can somebody tell me just what makes a cabin a shack? Is it just the color of the occupants? Or a flimsiness of construction? A poverty of spirit? Not the house my father built.

So I drove that country road toward Simon's Acres, the town. And thought about Simon, the man. I drove past cornfields and remembered him the way I always do. A shadowy, far-off memory like when you watch one of those late-night movies half awake and the next morning you wonder if you didn't just dream the whole thing up.

You know, I did dream of Pappa just last night. I had been up late packing, getting ready for this trip. I guess I should have expected it. Anytime something big gets ready to happen—first day of school, getting married, approaching my due date, getting divorced, going back to school after forty-something years—I dream of Pappa. Or I dream the house is on fire. Sometimes both in the same dream.

It seemed like the farmland would go on forever when at last I saw the sign: SIMON'S ACRES, FOUNDED 1905, POPULATION 500. There were probably more than five hundred folks living in my high-rise apartment building in Detroit, which I was now about five hundred miles away from.

I had a family back home rooting for me. My tribe, as I like to call them, are a son and daughter in their forties, grandchildren in their teens and twenties, and a two-year-old angel who calls me *gray-ma* because she can't pronounce *great-grandma*. They were so proud when I showed them the poster those college kids had made up.

> *In commemoration of the 90th anniversary*
> *of the Emancipation Proclamation, 1863–1953*
> *Earlene Josephs sings "Songs of Freedom"*

But when I talked about driving out to the Quad Cities for the engagement, their reaction was just what I expected.

"Momma, don't drive that long way all by yourself. It takes all day. Why don't you just fly? You can be there in an hour."

I yessed them to death. Said a lot of *uh-huhs* and *you're rights*. Then when it was time to leave I got up and left. I had been living my life too long to let some children tell me how to get where I'm going.

Can you imagine what they'd have to say if they knew I had taken the scenic route and was out wandering the back roads of some rural Illinois town, memories jangling around in my mind like change in some old pocketbook? They'd probably be reserving my space in the old folks' home. And what could I say in my own defense? *You can take Old Girl out of the country, but you can't take the country out of Old Girl?* Or would I have said that the river called and I answered?

Well, I don't know if either argument would hold water. As citified as I'd become in my old age, I probably would run if someone as much as mentioned the word *outhouse*. And there was no sign of the river that I could have sworn had called my name and made me leave the highway.

By now the endless stretch of cornfields was beginning to be broken by farmhouses and barns set back from the road. I turned right at the next intersection and found myself in town, what there was of it. A gas station, a run-down motel, a general store. I pulled into the gas station, even though I was on *Full*.

A young white girl sat behind the counter looking like she wouldn't pump a tank of gas if her life depended on it. Sure enough, when I pushed through the flimsy screen door, she looked me up and down and said:

"It's self-service, here, miss."

She went back to watching soap operas on a little postage stamp–sized TV perched atop her cash register. Even though I had given up smoking some ten years ago at the urging of my grandson, I asked for a pack of Pall Malls and made a big deal about fishing around in my pocketbook for change. Cleared my throat and tried to make conversation.

"It's been a long time since I've been around here."

Her acne-pitted face registered mild disbelief, then she shrugged and turned back to the screen. She might as well have answered: *Of course you're lying, but do I give a damn?*

"Did a Simon Winfield ever live in these parts?" I persisted. Don't ask me why. Just humor me, an old lady, either making small talk or pulling at straws.

"I don't know." Her gray eyes were as blank as the flickering screen. "Where'd he live at?"

"Not sure I recall." I kept digging through my pocketbook while my mind went digging through the recesses of memory, trying to dredge up any shred of information to show this teenager and myself I was neither lying nor crazy. "About forty acres, somewhere near the river. A pond out back in a stand of woods."

"Glass Pond? Oh, you must mean old lady Bryn Mawr's place. That's hardly any forty acres though. Hey, ain't you got nothing smaller than that?" She frowned at the twenty I handed her. So I got it back and gave her back the cigarettes I never wanted in the first place.

"Sorry I disturbed you. You get back to work now," I called sweetly on my way out the door. My sarcasm was lost, drowned in the quicksand of the TV love story. She went back to *Search for Tomorrow* while I continued to hunt for yesterday.

Reason would have had me turn right around and get back on the highway to the Quad Cities. But there was that magnet again. What odd fancy of mine that Simon's forty and the acres that named this town might be one and the same? I don't know. Call me senile. I couldn't even begin to explain it. So I just told myself I'd look at the river and then go on about my business.

Singing hasn't really been my business for a long time, no more so than directing the church choir and maybe a Sunday solo every now and then. I'm a happy has-been now. But once I was a Singer. They called it gospel, but I was strictly into the old stuff. Spirituals spoke to something deep within me, to a time beyond even my advanced memory, before people were able to praise the Lord with any instrument but the human voice.

I even had a brief fling with stardom in the forties and off I went to Europe singing *Swing Low, Sweet Chariot* to folks who couldn't understand the words. But it's not about words when that *coming for to carry me home* echoes from way deep down. It's about memory on top of memory, layered like the strata of earth, like the levels of underground water. And you don't have to hear the words to know the feeling of *a motherless child a long way from home.*

People always say that's such a mournful song. But not to me. I've never had a mother to my memory, but I somehow feel myself surrounded by the presence of many mothers, bending to embrace me. I know I am somebody's child; I take that song and make it my own.

Sometimes I feel like I'm Jesus' child
and he tells me you are not alone.
He says, true believer, you are not alone.

So I let the folks pay me for what I had been doing in the Missionary Baptist Church most of my life. I took the little piece of change I made and put myself through school, became a grade school music teacher, and didn't think too much more about it. But every now and then some college students go rifling through the oldies bin and tell themselves they're rediscovering me.

And I find myself singing spirituals at somebody's gospel festival, singing a cappella or accompanying myself on piano while the rest of them bring down the house with their drums and electric guitars. Explaining to the young folks about these songs everybody sings nowadays on TV commercials, long car rides, and around campfires. *Kum Ba Ya* means *come by here.* And it was just as likely to be a call for a ride on the Underground Railroad as a request for a visit from Jesus.

My daughter Darlene is always telling me, Momma, *you've got to update your repertoire; don't nobody want to hear those old-timey slave songs.* But somebody has to sing the old songs. Otherwise no one will remember that *We Shall Overcome* and *Ain't Gonna Let Nobody Turn Me Around* is the same freedom folks been singing about for four hundred years. I sing those songs and hear my father's voice, singing to me. Singing through me.

It was these songs, in fact, that I should have been rehearsing. I was due to check into the hotel that night for a concert the next afternoon and here I was still east of the Mississippi looking for my lost father in the white folks' land.

I drove past the town limits sign and right into the next town, Lovitt. I was beginning to think it was one long cornfield, when I finally caught sight of a Black woman hanging laundry out back of a white clapboard house. By the time I had parked and gotten out she had disappeared. So I went up to the door.

But the woman who opened it was little, white, and rosy cheeked; about five feet tall. She stood there leaning on two canes and peering expectantly over the tops of wire-rimmed glasses. Her snow-white hair and red cheeks kind of put me in mind of Mrs. Santa Claus.

"Yes," said Mrs. Claus. "Can I help you, hon?"

Her voice was nasal and slightly Southern, yet somehow I knew she'd been living around this little midwestern river town all her life.

"Am I still in Simon's Acres?"

"Right outside of it," she answered. "What are you looking for?"

"Do you know if Simon's place is around here anywhere? A little one-roomed wooden cabin."

"Not that old shack that used to be here? That burned down when I was a girl. My daddy built this house on that spot nearly sixty years ago."

Was it the suddenness of sunlight spiking off the woman's steel-rimmed glasses? Was it the five-hundred-mile drive from Detroit on nothing but coffee and toast? Or was it the memory of a sixty-year-old fire that flashed in my mind? That made my knees go weak and my head dizzy and my ears hear a voice that hadn't been heard since 1903.

Early! Get on out of here. Run to the water, child!

Water. Either I was in it, or it was in me. I opened my eyes on somebody's flowered sofa, a middle-aged Black woman with a glass in her hand forcing water down my windpipe. I came to, coughing and sputtering.

"Girl, get that water away from me."

The woman drew back, hand on hip.

"Well, you were begging for it a minute ago. Miss Bryn Mawr said you were so thirsty you fainted on her doorstep."

"I'm sorry, sugar. I guess I was." I took the water and drank it. It tasted like well water. "Weren't you the one hanging laundry out back? I saw you from the road."

"You can get on back to work now, Flossie," a sharp voice called out. The jolly-looking old woman who had met me at the door now sat in a corner chair across the room.

"Yes, ma'am." Flossie tossed her a look that even in my dazed eyes looked like thinly veiled contempt. And sashayed into another room.

"Where you from, dear? Peoria?" The woman's eyes twinkled with eager curiosity. "I don't believe I've seen you around here."

"No, I drove in from Detroit."

"All the way out here in Lovitt. What brings you to these parts?" My, she was nosy. But I guess fainting on her doorstep gave her the right to inquire.

"I'm on my way to Davenport, Iowa. Thought I'd stop here and see this town. I believe I might have some family here."

She shook her head and chuckled softly.

"Oh, no. Ain't no coloreds in this town. Ain't never been, as far as I know and I've been living here near on seventy-five years."

I was sitting sideways on the sofa, semireclined. My back was propped up with throw pillows. I don't know how I got there; I guess Flossie must have been recruited to drag me in.

It was a tiny living room, connected to a tiny dining room by sliding wooden doors. As small as the rooms were, their ceilings were at least ten feet high. It gave the feeling of being in a cell, especially as crammed and crowded as the rooms were with oversized furniture and bric-a-brac. Through the dim lighting I could see a huge colonial dining table, buffet, and chifforobe in the next room. The living room held the large sofa I was sitting on, several overstuffed easy chairs, various end tables, and an old upright piano set against one wall.

The top of the piano seemed to have been designated the family photo gallery. The top of it and the wall behind it were crammed with photos of kids in Sunday clothes, gradually aging into graduation poses and wedding pictures.

"What a pretty girl." I pointed to an old-fashioned portrait in sepia tones of a light-haired, smiling young woman with flowers in her hair.

"That's me. Taken about 1904, I imagine. Must have been fifteen years old. My daddy had just finished building the house and we all got our pictures taken. You know, I was married the very next year, right here in this room."

"Well, you were quite a beauty, Mrs. . . ."

"Bryn Mawr," she beamed at me. "Elmira Bryn Mawr."

She was the type of woman who would tell her life story at the drop of a hat, then expect you to tell yours. Here I was, a stranger who had fainted at her doorstep and she was merrily chatting away about how the children had left one by one and gone off to the city, and she being all alone had to sell off the farmland acre by acre, but she was still holding on to the house and surrounding property because her old daddy and her late husband, Michael, God bless their souls, would have wanted it that way, though it did get lonely living out here in the middle of nowhere and the children were always pestering her about coming to live with them, but how could she leave a place where she had spent so many happy years, especially at her age? I tell you, that's just the way the woman talked. Nonstop.

"Bryn Mawr," I repeated, sipping on water. Her rambling was unwinding a spool deep down somewhere, its end buried in the fluff of her chitchat. Names and faces whirled just below the surface of recognition. I struggled to sort them out.

"Oh, yes. That's my married name, of course. I was born Elmira Brady."

I looked at her closely, all white and red. Though she'd looked like a blonde in the old portrait, I decided she must have been a redhead. There was a certain sharpness of feature, the faded freckles and thin lips. It was not quite a familiar face, but then again it was.

I suddenly had to get away. If I escaped the chatter and got somewhere quiet I knew I could start piecing things together. I arose abruptly and thanked her for her kindness.

Flossie was out on the front porch with a broom, beating the daylights out of an old rug that hung across the railing. She muttered softly under her breath as I passed her.

"Beg pardon?" I paused on the first step, thinking she'd spoken to me. I had wanted to have a word with her anyway.

"Wasn't talking to nobody but myself, miss." She was of the complexion called *brownskin*. Her tan cheeks glowed with exertion as she brought broom down on rug. Out in the daylight she looked younger, about in her mid-forties. "It's just that old woman and her penny-pinching ways. I don't see how on earth a body can be so damn cheap."

"What a shame."

"Shame? It's a crime! That old hag got a drying machine and vacuum cleaner too, and she still wants me to line dry all her washing and clean these rugs by hand. Just to save a nickel on the lights. I swear, that woman gone work me to death."

"You don't say." I descended another step. "I guess some folks don't know slavery ended ninety years ago."

"Somebody need to tell that to Miss Bryn Mawr. I got to come all the way out here from Peoria to do all her nasty work and she don't pay me but seventy-five cents an hour."

"Girl, you are kidding me." I was genuinely shocked. My thirteen-year-old granddaughter got more for baby-sitting. "And she seemed like such a nice old woman."

"She's sometimey." Flossie paused to wipe sweat from brow and rest hands on hips. "Ain't nothing worse than being sometimey. If you going to be nice, go ahead and be nice. If you going to be evil, then be evil. But goddamn it, don't be sometimey! I tell you, one of these days I'm going to give that old woman a good piece of my mind."

"Flossie? That's your name, isn't it?" I hurried to get a word in, because she was beginning to resemble the despised Miss Bryn Mawr in that once she got started talking she didn't seem to know how to stop. "Do you know of any Black people who once lived in this town? Maybe a Winfield family?"

"Black folks? In Lovitt?" she hooted humorlessly. "That'll be the day."

"Well, how about Simon's Acres?"

"Look, miss." She went back to beating Miss Bryn Mawr's butt in effigy. "This is pure-dee Klan country. Only Black faces you find around here is going to be the maids and the farmhands. You must be in the wrong town."

She was so dead certain of it that I thought for a moment of letting the sun set on me headed toward Davenport, where I belonged. But I still hadn't seen the river yet.

So again good sense deserted me. The setting sun found me facedown on the too-soft bed of a room at The Bluffs, the same motel I'd passed earlier in town. I called the college folks and told them I'd be there for sound check in the morning. Then I called my group at home and lied. Said I had reached Davenport safe and sound. And I slept.

It came on me again that night, but stronger. Stronger than ever before. A dream, but not so much a dream as a certainty that the room was burning. I lay paralyzed in the oversoft single bed, but in my mind I was crawling through smoke. Fingers of flames snatched at my hair, my clothes. Ropes of smoke waved like witch's hair from the ceiling. Reached out like human hands to fasten around my neck. Fists of hot air pounded at my chest. I kicked and fought and coughed, trying to escape it.

And that is how I awoke. Clawing and fighting for the still, empty air. Gasping and coughing for breath. My eyes opened to the darkened room with unfamiliar shapes crouching in the shadows. Through the curtained window I saw the motel's vacancy sign blinking on and off. There was no smoke, no fire. But still my lungs were burning, hungry to breathe clean air.

I made my way along the wall to the door. I opened it. The night air rushed toward me, black and fresh. I gulped it down like well water. Then took a look around me.

It could have been a picture. The night transformed the mundane little town. There in a shallow valley it sat, surrounded by slopes of low hills, like the open palm of a hand. Nothing moved in the moonlight. Even the stars were unblinking.

I could hear a river. I could feel it rushing somewhere nearby. And in the darkness I moved toward the water like a magnet. I might have still been dreaming, I guess. Sleepwalking. I moved barefoot across the road, through a path in the trees. Sure-footed and drawn to a water I could not see.

Perhaps against the possibilities of old ladies wandering in the night, someone had put up a barrier at the end of the path. I looked down the bluff and the water was not blue as I expected. Do you know how a silver ribbon might glint against a backdrop of black velvet? Like it had a light of its own? The river did so in this moonlight, twisting into dark hills and disappearing. But I knew that beyond those hills it still glowed, just as surely as I knew the sun did somewhere, despite this darkness.

The next morning I made a beeline for old lady Bryn Mawr's. Instead of going to the house, I parked up the road a piece and walked out across the fields.

Some distance from the house was a rotting old barn. I pried at the door and peered into the darkness, smelling rather than seeing the bales of fresh hay.

Beyond the barn some distance was a stand of trees. They leaned in toward one another in a semicircle, like women whispering secrets to each other. I moved toward the trees, feeling rather than knowing that something was waiting inside for me. As I walked in the quiet morning light, a crow cawed overhead, dived into the trees and out of sight.

I walked into those woods with the same serene confidence as when I walked into church come a Sunday. As when I walked onstage knowing that the Lord had blessed me with a good song to sing. And though I had done more walking here lately than I had in a while, like the song said: *I Don't Feel Noways Tired.*

It was cool inside that shelter of trees. The branches overhead had grown together and light barely filtered through. The trees stood like sentinels, like brown women with leafy green Sunday hats. Like a host of mothers, bending to embrace me. The ground within sloped in like a saucer, toward the source of water I knew I would find.

It was a small, rounded pool still as glass. But it stirred just a bit at the center, fed by a spring beneath the rocky soil. From one end of the pond, where the semicircle of trees opened up, a narrow stream emerged and flowed away. Like the stem of a flower, or the winding string on a child's balloon.

You already know about this fascination I have with bodies of water. I can't explain it. Sometimes I drive over to Lake St. Clair and just stand there, staring at the waves. When I travel to other cities I try to visit local rivers. I cross bridges and find myself wondering about the waters below, where they come from and where they're going.

Once at a picnic I got a sudden urge to wade across the narrows of what I thought was a shallow river. Halfway across, the bottom dropped from under my feet and I went under. You think that somebody who liked water so much would have learned how to swim.

"Now that would have been a real stupid death," Jonas, my man at the time, had told me while rubbing me down with a big, rough picnic blanket. "We would have read about you in tomorrow's paper: *Middle-aged woman drowns in the Belle River. Friends said she'd been despondent.*"

But even as I'd coughed up rank water, I had been filled with a curious calm. Like on the banks of the Jordan that year when the choir went to the Holy Land. And I had known that someday I was coming back to be baptized where John washed Jesus. Or as I was now, sitting still with my shoes off. Dangling my feet in the water. And waiting for whatever would happen to happen.

Didn't it rain, children?
Rain, oh, my Lord.
Oh, my Lord, didn't it
Oh, didn't it rain?

It did rain that night. It rained down water and fire.

Have you ever seen a fire burning in the rain? Have you ever smelled it? That's probably what saved the barn. Because I last remember it burning too, just as lightning came down showing me the way to run to my little river.

My Lord he calls me,
He calls me by the thunder.
The trumpet sounds within-a my soul,
I ain't got long to stay here.

But before thunder it was twilight. I was sitting on the porch with some cornbread my pappa had made. I was eating it mixed up with buttermilk, eating it right from a mason jar with my fingers, while I waited for the lightning bugs to come out and my pappa to come home from the fields. Sitting there with an old lop-eared dog we called Shadrach.

By the time I caught sight of him, the lightning bugs had been out for a while and the mosquitoes, too. A row of lightning bugs lay neatly on the gray porch floorboards, their wings torn off but their fires still blinking. Mosquitoes weren't as easy to catch. By the time I saw my pappa's beat-up straw hat coming over the rise my legs were a bumpy mass of welts, red from scratching.

But Pappa wasn't alone. The two white men who walked on either side of him were bare headed. Shadrach ran barking to meet them, just like he always did when Pappa came home. One of the white men gave him a kick that sent him yelping into the weeds.

"Early, gone on in the house," Pappa called out. "Get to bed."

"But, Pappa . . ."

"Do as I say, child. Get on."

I went to bed but not to sleep. I listened at the voices and tried to think who they belonged to.

"Nigger, you're going to sign this thing."

That sounded like a white man I knew as Will Brady. A man with a mass of white curls and rosy red cheeks.

"No. I don't believe I will."

That was Pappa's voice, low and tired.

"Looks to me like this nigger needs some persuading."

That voice I didn't recognize. I heard a crack like something breaking. Then a low grunt, like my pappa made when he went to lift up something heavy. The noises and the voices kept on until I got too tired to listen and fell into an uneasy sleep.

I don't remember whether I dreamed that night or not. But I do know that when I woke up the room was burning. The curtains at the window. The table in the corner. And my pappa, facedown on the floor. A falling spark lit a small blaze in the center of his back. He rocked from side to side, trying to put it out.

I ran and got the water bucket. It was too heavy to carry so I dragged it. Wisps of smoke wrapped like rope around my throat. New fires sprang up around me. The water put out the fire on Pappa, but he did not move. Did not get up and pick me up and carry me out of there. The voice that came out of him was not the same one that told stories, that sang *This Little Light of Mine*.

"Early! Get on out of here."

Part of the ceiling fell, on fire. The bucket that had carried the water caught ablaze. A flaming cinder landed on my temple and I smelled the burning hair before I felt the burning flesh. I screamed and clasped my head, putting out the fire with my bare hand. Still I hesitated, turned back toward my father's figure, facedown on the floor. His legs were straight, arms spread-eagled like Jesus on the cross.

"I'm right behind you, child. Run to the water, now."

I ran.

Out of the flaming frame of doorway, to the outside where it was raining. Did you know that rainwater on a wooden fire hits the burning pieces and makes a sizzling sound? Do you know the smell of it?

I ran around back to find shelter in the barn. The wet wind had carried the flames there, too. There was lightning in the sky, lighting up the fields and the hills beyond. Lighting up the stand of woods my father had planted, trees standing like little girls whispering secrets to each other.

And I ran to the shelter of my little river.

Green trees are bending
Poor sinners stand trembling.
The trumpet sounds within-a my soul
I ain't got long to stay here.

Elmira was waiting in the open doorway of the kitchen. As I approached the house I could see Flossie scowling, standing in the shadows behind her. But Elmira was not frowning. Her rosy cheeks were dimpled in a smile of welcome. She lifted one of her canes and waved me inside.

"Come on in, hon. I forget your name."

"Earlene."

"Well, come on in and take a load off. Flossie, pour Earlene some Coca-Cola."

The kitchen was much more spacious, almost cheerful compared to the crowded stiffness in the front parts of the house. There were brown and white gingham curtains at the windows, a worn wooden table and mismatched chairs. An ancient black potbelly stove stood in the far corner. A pot of something good-smelling simmered on a much newer, white kitchen stove in the other.

Flossie, still frowning, opened the refrigerator door, removed a bottle of Coke, and handed it to me unopened. Elmira eased herself down into a kitchen chair and waved me to another one.

"Flossie said she seen you wandering out back. What on earth were you looking for?"

"My little river."

"What little river? Ain't nothing back there but that old irrigation ditch. I been meaning to have that thing drained, too. We had a rainstorm back in '49 and the thing swole up so, it carved a path clear out to the Illinois. My husband, Michael, drowned in it, God rest his soul. Where you come from, anyway? Chicago?"

"Right here." I patted the kitchen table. "Right here. This was once my home."

Elmira set down her bottle of pop and peered at me over wire-rimmed glasses.

"You must be mistaken, hon. My daddy built this house."

"Yes, he did." I nodded. "Built it on land he stole after he left my father for dead and burned his house down around him."

A strangled sound came from Flossie, stirring a pot at the stove. She wheeled around and glared at me, the spoon still in her hand.

"Girl, you're trailing grease all over my kitchen floor," Elmira called sharply. "You get a rag and get that up, hear me?"

She turned back to me smiling, shaking her white curls with a confidential air. As if to say, *good help is so hard to find.*

"You must still have a touch of that sunstroke or whatever it was. Like I told you yesterday, ain't no colored ever lived around here. Nor ever will. This is strictly white man's country. We don't hold with all that race mixing you all do up in Chicago."

I looked out the window at the barn, weathered and sagging. I could see the stand of trees beyond it in the distance.

"You know, my pappa planted those trees before I was born, Elmira. I remember him telling me, *Early, these trees is older than you are.* They must be close to seventy-five years old by now. Just about your age."

Elmira was not smiling now. She blinked at me over the top of her glasses. Each hand grasped a cane so tightly I thought she was about to rise to standing. But she didn't. I continued.

"I imagine the trees that had been here before must have been cleared somewhere between the time the Indians were run off this land, and when my pappa got his forty acres. Or maybe he cleared them himself. I don't think so, though. Even though he was a farmer, Pappa liked trees. He said that your crops take away from the land. Trees give back to it."

"Hmmph," snorted Flossie, running water through a rag at the sink.

"Pappa worked that farm all by himself. Not another man as far as I can remember. Not even a mule. I remember him saying, just as plain as day: *I got my forty acres, don't need no mule.* He got out there and hitched that plough to his own back. He said it wasn't even work. Said that river land was so rich, you just touch it and things spring up growing. I don't remember what all he planted: corn, okra, tomatoes, beans. We always had plenty to eat. Not always meat, but always food."

Flossie, on hands and knees wiping up the floor, looked up at me. The frown still hadn't left her face. "And what about your momma? Where was she at in all this?"

"Flossie, tend to your business. You hear me?" Elmira turned on her with swift fury. "You've got too much work to sit around here yapping. Go on up there and make my bed."

Flossie struggled to get to her feet and I leaned over and offered her a hand up. She stared at it distrustingly for a moment before she took it and pulled herself to standing. Though Elmira had told her to go upstairs I could see her beyond the doorway to the dining room, waiting and listening.

"My mother," I continued, loud enough for Flossie to hear. "I don't remember her. Never knew what became of her. Whether she died when I was a baby, or whether she just up and left us, I never found out. And Pappa never spoke about her, either. I guess he might have told me someday, if he had lived. What you got cooking there? It smells good."

Elmira obligingly sniffed the air.

"Cabbage and catfish, I believe. And Flossie means to make some cornbread too, if she gets around to it. She's a good cook you know, but so lazy."

"Catfish," I repeated. "Me and Pappa fished a lot. There wasn't much to catch in the pond out there, but we'd go down to the river with our poles and string."

"We used to do quite a bit of fishing ourselves." Elmira tilted her head in remembrance. "Of course, the river was a lot cleaner back then. We'd even swim out there in the summer, and go skating in the winter. Can't hardly get in it now, much less eat out of it. Every since they turned that Chicago River around, the Illinois hasn't been the same."

"No, I guess it hasn't. But it was good fishing back then, wasn't it? Catfish and mullets and bluegills. Don't care how small a fish I caught, Pappa would take it on back home. Clean it and cook it for us. How far is the river?"

Elmira screwed her eyes tight, considering.

"Oh, I'd say about half a mile. What would you say, Flossie? Half a mile?"

"Damned if I know." Flossie, irritated at having been caught eavesdropping, could now be heard stomping up the stairs.

"It seemed further than that back then."

"Well, it always does when you're young," Elmira agreed.

"That's true. And I was pretty young, just five or six years old. Pappa had to leave me here, not in your house now. I'm talking about the one that used to be here. Because of course, he had to tend the fields and I couldn't keep up with him. So I was left to fend for myself. And no sooner did Pappa leave than I'd make a beeline for the river. I'd play up and down the bluffs, chuck rocks, go down to the bank and wade. I'd try to fish, but I never could catch anything without Pappa being there. Or I'd just sit there, looking off in either direction and wonder what kind of places the river ran through. One day Pappa caught me at it and he whipped me good."

"Did he?" Elmira shook her head, clucking. "Well, I guess you had it coming."

"Oh, yes. But I didn't understand. I just boo-hooed for the rest of the day. Not from the whipping. But for the loss of the river that I thought was mine. Pappa was so mad. *You ain't old enough to handle all that water, little old girl. You can't even swim yet. Supposing you were to fall in? Don't let me catch you around there no more.*

"But later Pappa took me up on his lap and he said: *Early, I tell you what. We're going to make you your own little river. Now what you think about that?* And he did. With a shovel and a pickax and his own hands. My pappa dug me my own little river right off that pond in the woods he planted. To wade in and fish out of and dream of one day traveling on."

Flossie appeared abruptly in the doorway.

"You're going to have to leave now. Miss Bryn Mawr needs her rest."

Elmira lumbered to her feet and shuffled behind me to the back door.

"Bye, now. You have a nice trip."

"Oh, I will. But I'm coming back."

Her merry blue eyes suddenly narrowed.

"What for?"

"Your daddy didn't just steal this land, Elmira. He stole my pappa's life. He stole my past. He took my father away from me before he got the chance to tell me who I was."

Elmira leaned heavily on one cane and used the other to push open the back door.

"My daddy never stole a thing in his life, especially from a nigger. You better get on out of here and forget you ever seen this place."

I stepped through the open door.

"How can I forget? I'm just beginning to remember."

Flossie reached past her and slammed the door shut. As I rounded the side of the house, I could see the same winding path that would bring Pappa home from the fields each evening. I stood there for a moment, half expecting to hear Shadrach yapping behind me. Or see Simon walking toward me, a beat-up straw hat crammed down on his bald head. Singing in his rumbling baritone about *a better day a-coming, by and by.*

I did hear footsteps, but they were not Pappa's. Flossie ran after me, waving the pocketbook I had left behind. She walked with me as far as the car.

"Miss, it wasn't no cause for that. She's a sixty-four-year-old woman with some of everything wrong with her. Bad heart. Arthur-itis. The Sugar."

I never remembered there being crows. They winged overhead in a noisy flock, cawing out lustily.

"Sixty-four. Seven years older than I am now."

"You're kidding." Flossie's eyes widened in amazement. "You sure don't look it. Hope I be looking that good when I'm pushing sixty."

"You know, when they took my father I wasn't but five or six years old. Scared as I don't know what and all by myself. Sent by unknown people to an unknown city to be raised by strangers. They were good people, my adoptive parents; Missionary Baptist church people. But still I was lost, disconnected from the source of my little river. Mrs. Bryn Mawr never lost the river of her blood. She knew who she was, her mother, her grandparents, and maybe their grandparents. She has her history. When her children and grandchildren ask her about the people they come from, she has pictures to show them and stories to tell."

"I don't know, honey." Flossie looked back toward the house. "She may got the history, but she ain't got no folks to speak of. They've all up and left her in her old age. In fact, all she got left is memories, and me."

"And she's paying you slave wages."

"Never mind what I said about that." Flossie was nearly fierce with loyalty. "You can't give what you ain't got. I been working for her near on fifteen years now and she ain't a bad old white woman. She just old and sick and lonely. It's terrible to get old and don't have nobody to do for you. All she got to hold on to is this house and this land. Your daddy's land, huh?"

"Simon Winfield." The name sounded like thunder in my mouth. I spoke it again. "Simon Winfield. He built a farm off the banks of the Illinois before this town had a name."

"So you're coming back. You going to take her to court, or what?"

"This is my father's land, Flossie. Simon's Acres. A Black man gave his name to this lily-white town. And everybody around here is going to know it, or my name ain't Earlene Winfield Josephs. I'll see you around."

I pulled out, headed west. The farms, the town, the cornfields all fell behind me. I crested the ramp onto the highway and immediately crossed the bridge over the Illinois. But I no longer wondered where it flowed. I knew now that not far away a little river had carved its own path to a big river, which flowed into a larger river, which flowed into the sea and on out into the world. I was connected to it, and through it to all waters.

One Mother of a Mountain

Going somewhere just to be going. That's all I was doing. Just going some-where to be going. Lord, but did it sound good though! Shirley called me on the phone, said:

"You want to go up to Montreal? I got to get out of this dead-ass town for a minute. Got some people I know up there and got me a brand new set of bags. Girl, you betta get ready come go with me."

Montreal. What did I know about Montreal? Not a thing. But just the name of it, child. The word sounded so elegant and sexy. Tall, dark, thin, serious-looking men with little mustaches and French accents must live in a city with that kinda name. A place where people sipped wine and served up crepes and caviar on crystal. A city where a woman was likely to fall in love. Did I want to go to Montreal?

"Hell, yes. Just tell me what time the plane leaves."

Wasn't until we were way up high in that cool, air-conditioned cabin in the sky did it occur to me.

"Shirley. Any Black people in Montreal?"

Shirley sucked her teeth crossly at my ignorance.

"Course yes, girl. What you think my friends is?"

So I settled on back in my seat to sip the complimentary wine the stewardess had handed around. Then I sat up again.

"Shirley. They speak French up there in Montreal, don't they? Well," I came back at her bored nod, "how we supposed to talk to the people? You know any French?"

Now don't you think that was a reasonable question? You go to a foreign country, you expect folks to speak a foreign language. But no, my slow-wittedness musta been too much for my girl Shirley to take. She shook her head and rolled her eyes on up to the airplane ceiling.

"Is you crazy, girl?" she snapped. "You don't need to know no *language*."

"Oh. Tell me something, then." I still wasn't what you would call convinced, but who was I to argue? I ain't never been to Montreal.

"Just relax, girl." All Shirley need to do is step on a plane and she turns into Miss Sophisticated. She smiled a superior little smile. "You gone enjoy Montreal."

Don't let Shirley Ann Moses fool you. She ain't had a way in the world of

knowing what I was going to enjoy. As far as I know she ain't never been no further than the corner drugstore, let alone some Montreal. And much as I like her, I
have to tell you that Shirley's the kinda woman pretend she know something
when she don't. Always been.

You know the type, you probably got a friend just like her. So scared to
look the fool that she winds up acting a fool. Me, I believe in doing like my
momma says:

"If you don't know, ask! Ain't nothing wrong with being ignorant, but you
don't have to stay that way."

I didn't aim to be ignorant. So by the time the plane landed I'd nearly worn
my eyes out peeping through the clouds trying to see Montreal from the air. I
mean, this here was some sure enough excitement. Me, Darlene Lou Josephs
Harris who ain't never been no further from Detroit than Toledo.

You see, up until that moment I was always just a stay-at-homebody. When
we were growing up other kids got a chance to go places, usually down South.
Since we didn't have no people that I knew of down there, I'd sit home and watch
my friends leave me every summer. My momma used to be an entertainer and she
traveled all over, even to Europe and places. Did Darlene ever get a chance to go?
Just once?

"Aw, Momma," I'd complain every time she got ready to go on the road. "I
want to taste some of that good Italian food you always be talking about. Can't I
go with you this one time?"

"Naw, baby. It's the middle of the school year." It always seemed to be the
middle of the school year. "You'll go with me next time."

But next time never came. I'm close to thirty years old and I'm still begging
the old girl to take me someplace. Old as Momma is, she still manages to
get around. Drove all by herself out to Davenport, Iowa, just a couple years
back, singing old slave songs for some young white folks. Then she got the
nerve to turn around and go back to some hick town in Illinois, talking about
transplanting roots in her little river. Me? I never got a chance to transplant
nothing. Got grown, got a job, got married, got divorced. Still ain't went
nowhere.

Momma be telling me how lucky I am to be a settled woman. To have a place
where I know I got roots. Momma claims these folks that's always running off
somewhere are just running away from the problems they got at home.

My brother Leroy sure did step in the wind just as soon as he could. He went
straight from the jungles of Detroit to the jungles of Korea. Left us crying blood
and sweating bullets for four solid years. I guess if you want to leave someplace bad
enough, you'll jump at the chance to spend some time in hell. Which is just what
Leroy did, and got the burns to show for it.

Still and all, Leroy got his taste of the world, as he calls it. Got him a little Ori-
ental wife out the bargain, too. Since then he ain't let no grass grow under his feet.
And whenever him and Lill went off for the weekend, guess who stayed at home
keeping they kids? Now those kids are grown and got kids of their own. And I'm
still home weekends, baby-sitting. Old stay-at-home Auntie Darlene, daughter of
the road-running motherless child Earlene.

I swear, child. Roots ain't all they're cracked up to be. Sometimes I feel like a great big old tree planted by the rivers of water, got all these cradles dangling in my branches. I got to stay put and watch the water run. Stuck in one place growing rings around my trunk, while everybody else is out there getting in the wind.

Well, honey, this weekend the wind blowed. The cradles fell. And the tree pulled up roots and walked, do you hear me? Hopped a plane and ran off to another country.

My first glimpse of the city was a little disappointing. I don't know what I was expecting, but it didn't look too much different than downtown Detroit. A lot cleaner, yes. A whole lot more tall, fancy skyscrapers rubbing shoulders with buildings of old stone. And those might have been the same Detroit women walking the twilight streets in winter coats and the occasional fur.

But no, come to think on it. It *was* different, once I started taking it in. Something fresh and foreign in the way the streetlight fell across the sidewalk. A different rhythm in the way pedestrians walked. Street signs at intersections written in English and French.

With my taxi window rolled halfway down, I could hear snatches of a language that wasn't mine. I was someplace else! Montreal. Quebec. *Canada.* I gobbled down the sights and sounds. I even sniffed the air to see if it smelled different. It did. Don't ask me how. One thing was worrying me, though.

"Shirley, where all the Black folks at?"

"Oh. They around," she blaséd back. "They around. And roll up that window, will you? You letting cold air in the cab."

The hotel wasn't the best. Wasn't really nasty or nothing, but you could tell it had seen better years. Wood kinda dusty and rubbed down. Rugs faded with a few bare spots. And a faint and musty odor hung in the lobby that reminded me of the smell of a nursing home. The scent of mothballs and old neglect.

A nice-looking little old brother carried up our bags for us. Course, I didn't see no reason for him to bother, it wasn't but one bag apiece. But Shirley wouldn't have it no other way.

"Let him carry that!" she hissed when I went to grab my grip. "That's what he here for."

Riding up to the eighth floor, the brother eyed me on the sly. You know those little mirrors that always be stuck, for some reason, in the corner of elevators? I glanced up there to check my hair and I caught his eye, steady on me.

He smiled. I gave him a little smile back, and a wink for good measure. Because I knew I was looking good. I may be a big woman, but I do try to keep myself up. And I know when I be looking good. That was one a them days. Had on a sharp little white sharkskin suit I bought special for the trip. And every piece of gold I owned.

"You don't need to be wearing all that white." On the way to Detroit International in the backseat of my nephew's Mustang, Shirley went narrowing her eyes at me. "White ain't practical to travel in and, well, you know . . ."

She let the words trail off, but I did know. She was cracking, trying to say I was too big to wear all this white. But hey, I ain't never been one to disguise my size with corsets and funeral clothes. I figure if the good Lord had wanted me to wear black every day, he wouldn't have created pink and purple.

And I don't care what Shirley Moses says, I *know* I be looking good in white. Besides which, this is all woman, every ounce. It ain't every man who likes a woman looking like a refugee from Hardtack, Mississippi. Plenty a brothers appreciate a lady with a little cushioning on her. They may not come right out and say it, but I know there's more than a few fellas out there who like what I got.

Like the brother who was carrying our bags into the room. I handed him a hefty tip, he flashed me a wink and went. Too bad he was so little. It's hard to get interested in a man you could crush in the clinches. Then again, some of these small men will surprise you.

"Why you flirting with that old nothing Negro?" Shirley wanted to know, all up in the full-length mirror, hit it first thing. Eyeing her spare little behind in dungarees.

"Flirting? All I was doing was being decent. I seen a Black face in a foreign country and I smiled at it. What's wrong with that? Course, he was kinda cute, wasn't he?"

"A bellhop. Nothing but a goddamn bellhop. I bet he don't make a dollar an hour." When a man's making anywhere near minimum wage, he's invisible as far as Shirley's concerned.

But just between you and me, I think the girl's face got cracked because the man ain't so much as stole a glance in her direction. Shirley's not the kinda woman take kindly to being ignored. Especially by a man, bellhop or no.

"Probably looking all in your chest trying to figure how to get his hands on all that gold."

What did I tell you?

"All that gold? It ain't but two of them, Shirley. And I've been told they're precious, but they ain't hardly made of gold."

See, I know how to shut Shirley up. Every since eighth grade she been burnt that I got the tits and she got the zits. But hell, you can't have your cake and pie both. She oughta just thank the good Lord for her size six, and leave me alone about my sixteen. But Shirley Ann Moses don't know how to leave somebody alone. That would be too much like right.

I hadn't hardly sat down good, getting ready to pull off the sling-backed pumps I was wearing, when Shirley jumped up ready to hit the streets.

"That white's too dressy. Slip on some slacks or something and let's get out of here."

"Out? Shirley, why don't we catch a little rest first?" I was tired and my feet were killing me. Good as they looked in those narrow spectator pumps, my toes didn't appreciate being overcrowded. And they were telling me so.

"You shoulda napped on the plane like I did. Busy staring out the window, wadn't nothing to see out there but clouds. You so country. Act like you ain't never been nowhere. Now we finally on the ground, you want to sit around. You coulda stayed in Detroit and sat. Come on, girl. We in Montreal."

So into the jeans (didn't do me half the justice of the sharkskin suit) and out the door I went, right behind Miss Busybody.

It had gotten good and dark by then, and a light rain was slicking the city streets. It was a nice night to be out. But child, Shirley be the walkingest woman! Up this street and down the next. Peeping up at dresses in this or that dark store window. My feet begging me for mercy all along the way. And you *know* it ain't no way you can enjoy window shopping when your feet be talking that way.

We finally stopped at a little French restaurant, had us a bite to eat. I shouldn't have been all that hungry, since I had ate something on the plane. But all that walking had worked up my appetite. And besides, it felt so good to be sitting. My feet eased out of them spectator pumps and whispered *thank you*.

"Where you want to go next?"

Can you believe this woman? We hadn't even got our food down good, just settling back to pick our teeth and Shirley was itching to get moving again, like somebody's hyperactive child. Some folks just can't set still. She whipped a guidebook out of her purse.

"You want to check out a nightclub? We got time. They say they don't close until three in the morning."

"Well, what about these here friends of yours? Don't you want to look them up?" Because I didn't look forward to no evening nightclubbing on my poor swollen feet. Maybe Shirley's friends had someplace quiet where we could set down.

For some reason Shirley looked real funny at that suggestion.

"Well." She twitched in her seat, sipping her *some kinda liqueur*. "I guess we could go by and see them. If they at home."

"Why don't you call over there and see?"

Whoever heard of a restaurant without a public phone? We had to get back out there in the streets, walking for what my feet would swear was another five hundred miles, before we finally hunted down a public phone.

"*Moses,*" Shirley was yelling into the receiver. "Shirley Ann Moses . . . yes, Moses . . . I met you all in Milwaukee, you and your husband . . . uh, yes. Madeline Brown's daughter's wedding. Y'all said to look you up if I ever came to Montreal . . ."

That Shirley. Got us traipsing off to Canada, coming to see *friends* don't even know who she is. That girl is a mess.

"Well, right now," she was saying. "Me and a friend of mine . . . umm-hmm. Just got in this evening . . . umm-hmm. Well, anytime. How about tonight . . . ? Really? Alright."

When she hung up she was looking like she just won the policy, didn't even know she had a ticket.

"They say come right over. They're having some friends by for drinks."

The Montreal night was one of shiny lights and deep, deep darks. Slick wet streets, white bright lights. A raw full moon shone like a white nickel against off-black velvet. I really ought to wear those eyeglasses I paid so much money for. What was that, a building? A tower? It seemed almost like something living, but as big and tall as that thing was, wadn't no way it could be alive. Could it?

I didn't study on it long. The tires of the taxi moving on the ground was making such a comfortable sound. Just the right kinda rhythm to lull you to sleep.

I had to fight it hard. Because tired as I was, once I gave in wouldn't nothing be able to wake me up.

"Just how well do you know these friends of yours, Shirley?"

"They're good friends of my friend Maddy." Her chin jutted out. "*Very* good friends. Came down for her daughter's wedding."

"Hmph." I wasn't going to say nothing more about it. But if these friends were anything like Shirley's hincty, social-climbing little girlfriend Maddy Brown, I didn't want no parts of them.

It was high-priced luxury we pulled up in front of. I could see that even without my eyeglasses. Had landscaped lawns and uniformed doorman, if you please. Shirley smirked proudly, like she owned the place and everything in it.

"Class," she whispered, nudging me in the side. I nodded. But couldn't help thinking that without the doorman and the potted plants, the place wouldn't look a whole lot different than the high-rise housing project Shirley grew up in.

Stepped into the people's apartment and I like to fell over, child. Shag carpeting so thick, you sunk in it up to your ankles.

A few friends over for drinks? Honey, this was a full-blown party going on here. It was so crammed with folks we had to elbow our way through. Me and my sore feet made for an empty seat at the dining table. Shirley, with a stiff smile stretched across her face (she was *impressed*, honey) went off looking for her friends.

People mighta thought I was a junkie or something that night. Because I set myself down to that table and commenced to nodding. I couldn't help it. The room was warm, my stomach was full, the hour was late, I had a little booze in my bloodstream, and I was tired. I propped my elbows up, put my head in my hands, and nodded back.

Don't know how long I sat there half-asleep, longing for my hotel bed. But some people sitting down to the table kinda shook me awake. They came carrying conversation with them.

Remember that fantasy I had about Montreal men? Between the two of them, they just about made up the picture. Wasn't neither one of them tall. He was a scraggly-headed little man, but he did have a mustache and a French accent. She was thin and dark. And they were both serious-looking. Him, gesturing and expostulating. Her, nodding and staring and asking questions. The stuff sounded serious to me.

"We are ze largest French-speaking city outside of Paree." The boy sounded just like them Frenchmens in the movies. "Over sixty percent of zis citee is Francophone. So why must everyone speak English in order to get ahead? Eh?"

The girl scooched closer, leaning over him intently.

"Umm-hmm." She nodded, staring at him with the blackest eyes and a little more interest than the conversation called for, if you ask me. "But don't you think people should learn both languages? We are a bilingual country."

Some of the scraggly brown hair fell across the fella's face. He reached out an impatient hand and flipped it back. If it was in his way, why didn't he just get a trim? If we were in Detroit I woulda told the boy about a good barber, Manfred Ellis. Does a real nice job on all heads, Black or White.

"But don't you see?" he was saying earnestly. "Ze English-speaking minority does not even find eet necessary to learn French. Eet is because zeh have ze power, no?"

"French- and English-speaking Canadians must learn to live together," the girl recited, sounding like something out of a schoolbook. "That is the only way we can prosper."

"No, no, no!" The fella was good and frustrated. He shook his head, sending those scraggly locks all over it again. Oh, Manfred come to Montreal and you'll make a mint. "We *do* live together. Zis ees not ze point. Eet is language, eet is culture which separates us. Not so?"

"We are all Canadians," the dark sister said stubbornly, leaning all up in his face. "No matter which language or culture."

"Ah, yes." He raised one finger in revelation. "But you must 'ave felt eet, ze racism. You, as a Black in a land of Whites."

By now I was interested. I felt like leaning over with a, *Tell it, brother!* But the man had continued on.

"So you must see zat we Francophones in Quebec feel eet. Ze English ees ze language of commerce, of politics. You cannot get a good position if you do not 'ave English. Eet is almost as in South Africa, yes? Ze majority is ruled by ze minority. Do you not agree?"

I nodded. It made perfect sense when he put it like that. But this child was having none of it.

"I don't know anything about Africa," she pout, like she proud of it or something. "I'm a Canadian, first and last."

"Yes, but you a Black Canadian," I busted out before I could stop myself. "Just like he's a French Canadian. Everybody here carrying something with them from somewhere else. 'Less they an Indian."

And black as you are, child, you need to be knowing something about Africa, I felt like saying. But didn't. It wasn't my place to point out the obvious.

Honey, the sister turned and looked me up and down, from the top of my head to the tip of my toe. The way she looked at me, you woulda thought one of them potted plants had got up and butt into their conversation. Then she whipped her head back without a word, ready to tune back into the discussion with the French fella. By then he wasn't looking at her, but at me. And asking me if I wanted to dance.

I was a head and a half taller than him, and had a few pounds on him to boot. But what the hell? I kicked off them tight shoes, got up off my seat, and gave him my hand.

See, this is why I don't like dancing with no short fellas, particularly when they white. They get a woman with a little weight, all of a sudden they forget how to lead. And this little man, child, he was a perfect mess. I tried to lean into the step, give him a little confidence to pick up the lead. Do you know he took two steps backwards and like to have fell over?

It was a miserable beginning to a dance that was beyond misery. In the first place, that plush carpet was made to swim in, not dance on. Number two, the man didn't know the meaning of the word *rhythm*. Number three, it was one of those long, long records. And he was determined to dance it to the bitter end.

Lucky thing the floor was crowded, couldn't nobody tell what was going down. I put up with the shuffling slow dance, my hand outstretched in his like we was doing the tango, the dude's head pressed earnestly against my bosom, and me looking down at a bald spot in the middle of it. All that scraggly hair and he had the nerve to have a bald spot smack dab in the center of his head. I guess that's why he kept that hair so long, trying to hide it. And Lord, he was trying so hard to keep the beat that a sweat popped out on his bare scalp.

The record finally ended, praise the Lord. He led me back to the table, hadn't said a word since he'd asked me to dance. Pulled out my chair, and if I'm lying I'm flying, said:

"You are a beautiful dancer, *mademoiselle*. I hope we can do eet again soon."

I'm glad he walked away, because I had to bust out laughing.

"Child," I said to the dark sister, still sitting hunched up at the table. "The man got two left feet."

Well, some people are just too saddity. You know. So stuck up they think their shit don't stink. She kinda half turned toward me, looking down that long nose over the tops of her glasses. Like she didn't know what the hell I was talking about. Miss Saddity's jaws musta got tight because her friend had asked me to dance instead of her.

Well she could have that old no-dancing dude. And I'd be damned if I was going to sit there and take somebody looking at me, as Momma would say, *in that tone of voice*. I got up and swished, bare feet and all, right into the next room. Which happened to be the kitchen. That's when I started having a good time.

I guess I'm used to putting in my party time in the kitchen. I love to cook and when I throw a party I want it so the food don't run out. I've spent many a party at the stove. Cooking, sipping, stirring, tasting. Chewing at the chicken backs so the guests can eat the nice meaty parts. Making sure there's plenty enough to go around, won't nobody leave away hungry. In fact, they don't even call my parties *parties*. They call them *Darlene's feasts*.

Well, Shirley's so-called friends had a little feast going just for themselves. Beverly was a pint-sized little something, with a round face and sleepy eyes. Couldn't have been a day over eighteen. She looked for all the world like a little Black China doll. Trevor was too fine for his own good. And he knew it, too; a big old handsome devil. Just the type of man to give a woman her weight in worry.

Beverly and Trevor were a lively West Indian couple, frying plantain in the kitchen and gossiping about their guests. I was surprised them and Maddy Brown had ever hooked up. Just some plain, down-home type of people who happened to live up in Boojie Heights and teach at the university. At least Trevor did. Bev said she works in some kind of shop selling Caribbean handicrafts.

"I tell you something bout these academic types, Sister Queen." Trevor was a charming rascal, flirting with me bold as daylight with his wife standing next to him, handing me a steaming plate of rice and peas. Beverly tried to play like she was too busy to notice. But she couldn't stop herself from cutting little anxious eyes at him from time to time. Poor thing.

"They wouldn't know good food," Trevor continued, chowing down, "if it hit them in the face."

"Well, I hope you know what you got going. Because this girl knows her way around the kitchen." I'd been known to have the same kind of anxiety attacks over the same kind of rascal. I wanted to make sure it came across loud and clear: *Uh-uh, baby. I ain't thinking about your no-good husband.*

"These university people don't know how to have a party, mahn. They want to come and sit on their backside, drink wine, and talk shop. Now when we party, we talking about some good rum, good folk, and good food, Sister Queen."

"I heard that," I had to testify, my mouth full of it. Three meals in a single evening was a lot, even for me. But hey, a party ain't a party unless you got a little something to snack on.

First time in as far as I can remember that I really got to sit down at a party and taste the food instead of snatching bites between frying and serving. And it was good. The red beans these West Indians called peas were plump and moist, the rice was fluffy and tasted a little like coconut. The fish had a spicy tang to it; I couldn't figure out how it had been fried so crisp without breading. Beverly said she had marinated it overnight with pepper and lime. She gave me the recipe for it. I'm going to try it as soon as I get home.

BEVERLY BARRETT'S FLYING FISH FOR FOUR
> Four small flying fish (if you can find them)
> Otherwise one big, firm-fleshed fish like snapper, cut into fillets
> 2 limes
> 1 bunch of chopped "ordinary seasonings": fresh scallion, parsley, thyme
> 2 Scotch bonnet peppers, minced
> 2 cloves of garlic, chopped
> 2 pinches of salt

Clean the fish, trim fins and tails, but keep it whole. Rub the fish with salt. Squeeze the limes over it and rub it in too. You can add the peels if you like. Put all your veg and seasonings on top of the fish, keep it in a covered dish in the fridge at least four hours. If overnight, that's even better. Turn the fish several times. Heat some oil in a frying pan. Dredge the fish in flour. Fry in hot oil on both sides. Pour off the liquid, but keep the marinade, all except the lime peels. Turn the fire low and add the marinade, veg, and seasonings. Simmer slowly for 8 to 10 minutes. Serve with rice and peas or coucou (turned cornmeal), fried plantain, and salad.

I really do think the kitchen is the best room for socializing. You can sit your guests at the table with their drinks and entertain them with stories while cooking smells tease their taste buds. You can serve your food right up hot from the fire, the juices still bubbling and the spices still sharp. A kitchen is a place you can be yourself, take your shoes off if your feet hurt. I always thought there was a lot more love in the kitchen than any room in the house. Honey, you ain't lived till you've done it on a squeaky clean kitchen floor.

I don't know how long we spent in there, the three of us. When I came out most of the company had gone home. There was one couple left on the dance floor. And talk about the clinches, honey, they slow-dragged to every tune, fast or slow. Tell the truth, you couldn't even call that dancing. It was foreplay on the floor.

Over at the dining-room table, there sat Shirley, that no-dancing French fella, and Miss Saddity looking just as stuck up as she did when I left her there.

"Shirley, I'm ready to go." I don't believe in hanging on to a party once the life's gone out. Besides, Beverly running the dishwasher and Trevor yawning was as good a hint as you could get.

"Not yet," Shirley whispered back. "The night's still young, girl. We in Montreal."

So I sat down, trying to keep from yawning myself. Trevor finished his drink and went on to bed. Beverly went around emptying ashtrays. And there Shirley sat, talking about some night still young. I told you that girl was a mess.

"So you work in a library?" Shirley was smirking up into the French fella's face. "How fascinating."

Looked like Shirley had latched onto something herself. No wonder she was in no hurry to leave. And there the man went, blushing and hitching himself up like a little banty rooster.

"Well, yes," he said important-like. "Ze university library has so many responsibilities . . ."

I do believe Shirley was trying to steal Miss Saddity's thunder. Miss S. just hung around the edge of the conversation, looking snooty and hopeful at the same time. The man shortage musta been even worse than in Detroit, if the sisters had to compete for little lopped-off fellas like this one here.

"And what do you do?"

Miss Saddity turned to me so sudden, the question so out of the blue that it threw me. I started to come back with a *What do I do when?* when it occurred to me that she meant for a living.

"I work in a hospital," I answered.

"Oh." She looked away with such distaste, you'da thought I just told her I worked in a whorehouse.

"Yes, assistant director of communications," I snapped back real crisp in my *company* voice. Now chew on that for a while, Miss Saddity.

Honey child, did somebody just tell the broad we were long-lost kin? She had the nerve to look astounded. Then for the first time since I'd seen her that evening, she smiled.

"That's very interesting. Is it something in the journalism field?" The girl looked so pathetic smiling. I tried to smile back.

"Not exactly," I answered. "But they're both kinda along the communications line."

Miss Saddity did a complete about-face, turned into Miss Eager Beaver. It kinda embarrassed me. Yes, she herself was in the communications field, a student of journalism. She studied at McGill University, where Trevor taught. And she was thinking of going on to graduate school in the States. Could I make any suggestions? She'd heard that Columbia was good, but was it the best? And how did I like working in the field? Was it challenging? And was I in Montreal in connection with my work? No, well there were so many opportunities for travel in journalism. And this, and that, and the other. Questions!

When the girl let me loose I was tired. Felt like I'd been through the fifth degree. Questions. I tried to tell her that paging doctors over the hospital P.A. was a long way from writing stories in the *Free Press*. But she wouldn't listen long enough for me to get a good word in.

Shirley, praise the Lord, broke into the conversation with some words of her own. Could she please see me in the kitchen? The girl was looking as smug as a housecat with a mouthful of canary and I soon found out why.

"Darlene." She leaned up against the refrigerator, looking dreamy. "I think I like that man."

"Who? Henry, the librarian?"

"*Henri*. He's taking me out to a jazz club tonight."

"Have a good time."

Shirley stopped talking and fiddled with her earring. She was either getting ready to lie or ask for something outrageous.

"I'm probably gonna take him back to the room with me. Do you mind?"

Mind? I didn't mind. I was flabbergasted. My hotel room? She couldn't possibly be talking about my hotel room. Not with my poor body crying, no, screaming for sleep. And Shirley Ann Moses wanted to roll around my bed with some old shaggy-headed white dude who probably wasn't any better in bed than he was on the dance floor. Impossible.

"He ain't white." Shirley shook her kitchen curls. "He is Jewish, I'll have you know."

See, I ain't never been one to judge. If that's the way you want to go, then fine. It's your business. But don't lie to yourself about it. I got eyes in my head. I know a white man when I see one.

"Girl, you too much." I meant it. Shirley and travel didn't seem to be agreeing with each other. It was bringing out the worst in her. Being phony and pretentious was just something Shirley played at in Detroit. Like a little girl in her mother's dress-up clothes. Here she was taking it all the way serious. Shirley don't generally be this bad, else I wouldn't have been friends with her for thirty years. I had to set her straight.

"Jewish is a religion, not a race. Being Jewish don't keep him from being white."

"So. Maybe he is. But he works, don't he? Got a good job and it sure ain't as no bellhop."

"Careful, Shirley," I warned. "The Lord don't like ugly and I'm not too crazy about it myself. Don't mess with me."

Shirley frowned and sucked her teeth.

"Darlene, you just too straitlaced. You ought to loosen up, girl. We here to enjoy ourselves. We in . . ."

"Montreal." I couldn't stand to hear her say it again, so I said it myself. "I know we in Montreal. Where, if you recall, I don't know a solitary soul. Where the hell I'm supposed to sleep tonight while you're entertaining? And how come the guy can't take you to his place? He must be married."

"No." But Shirley couldn't help from looking worried. "It's just that he lives so far out in the suburbs, the drive would take forever . . ."

"He's married." I was convinced. And also resigned. If Shirley wanted to have her little fun so she'd have something to talk about back home in Detroit, then let her. "The sooner you find a place for me to drop, the sooner you and *mistair* can get down to the good times."

Beverly was called in for a conference.

"So you and Henri got together." She gave our girl Shirl an appraising glance, a knowing smile. "He always did like his women on the dark side of brown."

Then she turned to me.

"We could have slept you on the sofa, you know, if it wasn't for that." She pointed through a counter cut into the kitchen wall. Past the dining area we could see into the living room, a heaving shadow of something snoring on the couch.

"Who's that?"

Beverly shrugged.

"Some drunk fool, me not even sure me know his name. Now, where we going to sleep you? I guess you could go to Cedella."

"Who's Cedella? Not that Black Canadian girl." Miss Saddity sure didn't look like no *Cedella* to me. *Penelope* and *Millicent* would be more her speed.

Beverly pooted with her lips.

"Canadian, m'backside. If that girl ain't West Indian, then I ain't. Tourist man find her in some Nassau hotel, bring her over here, and dump her down. She ain't going to be calling herself Canadian after Immigration them catch up."

So it was decided that that's where I'd go. All we had to do was let Cedella in on it. Beverly tugged me back when Shirley left the kitchen.

"What Cedella have to say about Henri and your friend?"

"She didn't say nothing. What should she have to say about it?"

Beverly shook her head.

"Let's just say, Cedella may think she got she claim staked. She might be a bit surprised."

A bit? Walking in there where the three of them stood, their coats already on, I was more than a little uneasy. Because Miss Cedella-Saddity was looking mighty blissful, like maybe she was expecting to take her stuff home with her. Poor thing. Just looking at her smiling up in Henri's face told me she didn't yet know the lay of the land.

"Cedella, you mind putting up Darlene for the night?"

"Oh, yes. I mean, no. Of course not." But Cedella looked around with puzzled eyes, an open mouth, and a look on her face that plainly said, *Darlene's definitely not the one I was planning on putting to bed.*

So out the door went Miss Shirley and Mr. Henry Hotshot, arm in arm. Cedella's eyes followed them, like a puppy left alone at home. Beverly looking on, shaking her head. Then sighing.

"Cedella don't live far. You want a ride?"

I opened my mouth to accept with a *Yes, Lordy!* but Cedella beat me to the punch. She shook her head like someone coming out of a trance.

"No, Bev. I think we'll walk it. I could use a walk."

I went and got my coat, and followed her out of the door, fuming. During the evening inside, snow had dusted the Montreal streets. It drifted in the air as we crunched our way across the street. These shoes definitely weren't made for walking, especially in the snow. My poor toes, cold and smashed together like frozen corn, protested loud and long. Just hope tomorrow they didn't go on strike.

The hell it wasn't far. Cedella walked me uphill, through a courtyard, across a low bridge over a slow, snow-covered river, around a couple of corners, and across a couple more streets.

We finally stopped in front of a building that looked just like the rest of the row it was joined to. *Rowhouses* we would have called them in Detroit. Except these looked odd. No stone steps or stoops, but long black iron staircases stretching up three stories, looking to me like fire escapes stuck to the front of the buildings.

Before I climbed down the stairs to Cedella's basement digs I got a peculiar feeling. Like someone was looking over my shoulder. I turned to look and of course there was no one there. Only the quiet street, and above it the once-clear sky, now misty with snow.

And against the soft black of that night sky was something softer and blacker still. Something solid and substantial looming immovable in the light of moon. Tomorrow I would find out what it was.

Cedella's apartment was nothing more than a couple of rooms wedged between a maze of pipes and fixtures. The only thing that looked inviting to me was the couch, so I made a beeline for it. Cedella disappeared into another room. I had pulled my shoes off, about to stretch out and get comfortable. When here she come, sailing in with a tray and two big cups of coffee on it.

Coffee. Now what did I want with coffee at this time of night? Sleep was so heavy on me that I felt drunk. My mind was so dull and tired that I had reached for the cup and was drinking from it before I even knew what I was doing.

"So." Cedella plopped down on the couch beside me, stretched her thin little face into a grin, and launched full speed ahead into verbal assault. "Tell me about your job as a journalist in the States."

Lord, where do they make these people? Please tell me, so I can call up and have them break the mold.

She went at me like a cat worrying a cold dead mouse. *When did I?* And *What did I think? Who shot John? How long did it take? How bad did it hurt?* Questions. Just like she did me at the party, only double time. Questions and more questions.

She prized answers out of my mouth and threw them away before they were even out good. Couldn't hardly wait until I'd answered one before she was pinning me to the mat with another one. Looking at me with bright big eyes and nodding, nodding, nodding. And wasn't listening to a word I said. If I had quizzed her on all this trivia she was collecting, she woulda flunked with flying colors.

"This is really my first time out of the country," I was answering to some inquiry or another.

The girl's head went to bobbing again, barely stopping to take a sip of coffee. Stirred in one or two *umm-hmms* to go with it.

"Go on." She bobbed. "Go on."

"I'm a little tired, Cedella." I had to try and put a stop to it. This kinda thing could go on all night. "Didn't sleep much last night and been on my feet since early this morning. Packing, traveling, unpacking. You know."

"Umm-hmm, umm-hmm." Bright eyes in a dark face, peering at me over the top of the cup. She looked like a dark little bird sipping coffee. "Did you have a nice flight?"

That was when I went from feeling sick and tired to feeling sorry. Poor Cedella. Sad soul that she was. Child-sized woman in a sweater too big, sleeves hanging past her wrists. Sitting, sipping coffee at three in the blessed morning with her legs tucked under her. Busy making manic conversation with a near stranger.

Cedella nodded her head again, though I had said nothing. I guess she was agreeing with the thoughts in my head. I couldn't help shaking it and sighing. Poor child.

"Watch it, woman," Hank Harris woulda said if he'd been there to see. "Your momma jones is coming down."

Now this ex-husband of mine had a theory that the reason we never had any of our own was because I was too busy mothering somebody else's. Course, I always maintained the reason was he was too busy *fathering* somebody else's. But that's another story.

Hank always said that I wasn't happy unless I was playing somebody's momma. He ought to know; he played the baby often enough during our marriage. But still, I had to admit the man had a point. Else, why was I sitting there fighting sleep in a basement apartment somewhere in Montreal? And the chattering little blackbird that was keeping me up, I suddenly had the urge to take in my arms and tell her *It's alright.*

Alright that she had to come home in want of a man, because my friend Shirley had walked off with what she wanted. That I understood how loneliness could come down in the dead of the night and you'd almost want to talk to walls. You'd take to shooting dice with the midnight mice just to have some company.

I didn't press the girl to my bosom. I did just as good. Gave her a smile and an ear. Forced back sleep, talked a little, listened a lot. Answered questions and drank coffee until near five in the morning.

When the girl was all talked out and I was listened out, I couldn't have told you what was said to save my soul. But it was over, praise the Lord. I finally got to curl up in a corner of that lumpy little couch and close my eyes. But not for long.

Seemed like hadn't but a minute passed when that crazy child wasn't shaking me awake, telling me I had a phone call. Shirley on the line, just as bright and chipper as if it wasn't nine o'clock in the A.M.

"Hey, girl. What it is?"

"Shirley Moses, what little mind you got, you've gone out of. Why you calling me up so early? Get on back to sleep, girl, and let me do the same."

"Wait a minute," Shirley called out before I could hang up on her. "I got to talk to you about something."

"Aw, hell." I struggled up into a sitting position. "You bout to worry me to death. Where'd you get this number from anyway?"

Shirley paused. Her normally shrill voice turned meek as a child's.

"Henri," she finally squeaked out. "He gave it to me."

"Oh, he did, did he? Lucky thing he happened to have it with him. Did he know it by heart, or was it written down in his little black book? And how *is* Henry this morning, all curled up in my bed?" Hank always did say I be an evil woman first thing in the morning. He always had sense enough to let me alone that time of day.

"He's just fine," Shirley snapped back. "And don't be sarcastic. Look, what time you planning on coming back here?"

"I don't know, girl. Whatever time I get there. Why?"

"Well." Shirley's voice went squeaky again. "We going out to brunch now . . . but we coming back here again. Try to make it late, okay? Not before one o'clock at least."

"Girl, you mean to tell me y'all been at it all night and still ain't finished? I didn't think that little man had it in him."

"Don't be so backwards, Darlene. This ain't Detroit, you know. This is . . ."

"If you tell me Montreal one more time, I'm coming over there right now and kick your ass."

That Moses woman ain't trouble, she's trouble's mammy! Maybe if she hadn't come waking me up, I woulda stayed in bed until one o'clock. Maybe. Wadn't no guarantee of that with Cedella on the case.

You ever heard of a night owl that likes to get up early? Honey, if Cedella was bee-busy that night, you shoulda seen her next morning.

"Oh, good. You're awake." She bustled in, gathering up the sheets and blankets I was about to tuck myself back into. "Come on in the kitchen."

Grumbling, I hied myself up from the lousy couch and followed her into the cubicle she called a kitchen. Thinking that since she didn't succeed in talking me to death last night, she aimed to finish me off this morning.

"Drink up." The little caffeine fiend pushed yet another cup of coffee on me. "We've got a big day ahead of us."

"We?" I sat at the kitchen table, my head as heavy as a bowling ball in my hands. Trying to peel my eyelids open. "I don't remember us making any plans for today."

"I thought I'd take you around, show you the city. There's so much to see in Montreal."

"I can't go nowhere looking like this," I protested, pointing to my slept-in jeans.

"You look fine." The little liar. She must want to see me out in her city looking tacky. "No, really you do. Just a little rumpled, but you can use my iron. I wish I had something to fit you, but . . ."

She inclined her head in my direction, and I hurried up and said it for her. These little chicks must get they kicks pointing out the size of other women's hips.

"I know you don't, honey. It'd take two a you to make one of me. Anybody can see that."

I went along with the plans Cedella had cooked up because I couldn't think of a way to get out of it. I sure wouldn't have been able to go back to sleep, between Shirley the Player and Little Miss Coffee. And didn't have nothing better to do between ten and one o'clock, anyway. So with hot coffee sloshing around inside and a bathtowel wrapped around my butt, I tried vainly to steam the bed wrinkles out of my jeans.

And then we were out in the city. The snow had melted, leaving little patches of wet on the ground. After that musty basement, the air smelled soft and cool and fresh. I breathed it in deeply and looked around.

And it jumped out at me. That dark center of a presence I'd only felt the night before. There it was, a proud brown lady sitting pretty. Right smack dab in the center of the city, no less.

"Jesus." I couldn't help but call the Lord's name. "If that ain't one mother of a mountain!"

"Oh, that." Cedella waved her hand carelessly at the majestic woman with trees in her skirt. I had stopped in the sidewalk to look, and she nudged me on. "You haven't seen the mountain? That's where the city's name comes from. *Mont Real.* The Royal Mountain."

"The Royal Mountain," I repeated, turning around for another look. "Well, how do you like that? And wouldn't I like to go up there. They let folks climb it?"

"Yes, but you don't want to go there at this time of year." Cedella was firmly guiding me down the street. "There's skiing when we have enough snow, and it's nice in the summertime. There's a park and a lookout point. But right now there's nothing up there but mud. Now come on. I want you to see Old Montreal."

I followed her down the street, but kept turning back for a peek at the Royal Mountain. A mountain in the middle of the city. What a notion!

"Old Montreal isn't far from here," Cedella was saying. "It's just a twenty-minute walk."

"No." My feet stopped me right in the sidewalk, obstinate as mules. They had decided for me. No twenty-minute walks this morning. "Don't they have buses or trains in this city? Why everybody got to walk where they're going?"

Cedella, like that Royal Mountain, looked different in the daylight. Her skin ashier, her face more pinched, her expression somewhere between a crotchety old woman and a pouty child.

"Alright." She shrugged. "We can take the Metro if you insist. But why you'd want to ride on a beautiful day like this . . ."

We rode. The Metro was heaven, honey. Wasn't nothing like I'd imagine a subway to be. Brand spanking new. The station was like a museum, hung with pictures and posters and works of art. Train rode just as smooth. And *clean*! I couldn't help thinking sadly how quick they'd mess this up back home in Detroit. Seemed like the nicer something was, the quicker it got destroyed.

The train ride was much too short. Less than ten minutes later we were out and walking. Walking around this here Old Montreal wasn't as bad as I'd thought. The sun was out and so were the folks.

Nothing like Sunday morning in Detroit. People walked the streets like they were on their way places, but not in a hurry. Vendors sold things from stands along the road, flowers and fruit and postcards. Children romped as children will, throwing things and calling out to each other in a fast language it seemed I knew, just couldn't understand. I knew I was in a foreign place, but not that foreign to me. I was beginning to enjoy myself.

But honey, would the child ever stop talking? Determined to play the tour guide, Cedella wouldn't so much as let me sit down to rest my feet and drink in the new sights. No, she just *had* to show me every old church and courtyard and cobblestone street. In the meantime, in between time, she chattered. This morning the subject was herself.

"I don't know whether to take French or Spanish," she fretted. "There's a language requirement at the university. I just can't decide."

"Folks here speak French, don't they?" I reasoned, not really caring. Those cobblestones were murdering my soles. "Take French."

"Ye-e-es." Her black eyes got wide, she cocked her head to the side like a bird. "But since I may be relocating to the States, maybe Spanish would help me more. Especially in a journalism career. What do you think?"

"I wouldn't know." I was getting good and tired of the girl and her nonstop chatter. "Do to suit yourself."

Cedella stopped in the street and narrowed her eyes at me.

"You don't seem at all like a journalist," she accused. "One would never know it from your conversation."

I came to a halt too, put my hands on my hips. We faced each other down in a silent duel, Dodge City on cobblestones. This little fool needed some serious talking to, and I was just the one to do the job.

"So what?" A hussy. "Your conversation ain't exactly sparkling either, if I may say so. And I told you, I don't know how many times I told you, that I work in hospital communications, not journalism. But you were too busy running your mouth. You just don't listen, that's your problem."

We stood squared off for half a minute. Staring each other down. I wasn't going to give an inch. I was ready to stand there all day if need be, cobblestones or no. But finally it was Cedella who turned away. You ever seen somebody punch the air out of a brown paper bag? That's how the girl's face just . . . collapsed. I felt a little sorry then, but hell. Hadn't she asked for it?

"I know I'm not being a good hostess. I'm sorry. I've been needing someone to talk to, and, well. You have such a kind face. Forgive me for talking too much." She grabbed my hand and pulled. "Come, we'll go to the Underground City for some shopping. You'll like it there."

I followed behind her, feeling a bit miffed. She'd gone and switched gears on me, turned from sassy to sorry and I'd made my point. Or had I? Because why was I running up behind her again, on my way to some Underground City (God only knew what that was, sounded like someplace moles did their shopping) when all I wanted to see was the view from the top of the Royal Mountain?

She stopped us at a bench in front of a little corner market just off the water. An old man in a plaid cap and dirty white apron came out to stand guard over his fruits and vegetables.

It's sad, isn't it? Soon as some folks see the color of your skin, they don't see a person. They see a pickpocket or a shoplifter. Cedella settled her thin butt on the bench and a little old woman (looking like a pile of old clothes) got up and moved to the other end. Cedella patted the space she'd left.

"Sit down," she invited. "We wait here for the bus."

"Bus? Can't we get where we're going on that Metro?" Cedella shook her head.

"You can see more of the city this way."

Sitting there between Cedella and the unsociable old woman, the suspicious shopkeeper hanging in the background, we waited. Waited and waited. Nobody passed, nobody came to buy anything, nobody said a word. Time might have been standing still.

It reminded me of that Otis Redding song. My momma can't stand it; she makes me turn it off anytime it comes on the radio. Then she waves her hand, like she's trying to whisk away any stray notes and melodies left lingering in the air.

"It don't make no sense for somebody to be that trifling and lazy. It's sinful, that's what it is. Downright sinful."

Momma never did like nothing that sounded too much like the blues. I just nod my *yes, ma'am* to make her happy, then walk around singing *Sitting on the Dock of the Bay* under my breath. I sat there in my wrinkled jeans, my butt sore against the hard bench. Wasting time. Smelling the scent of ripe tomatoes, freshly cut flowers, a breeze from the harbor, and the faint odor of cat piss. Which wasn't exactly what I had in mind when Shirley asked me to come go to Montreal.

"When is this bus coming?" I shifted on the bench, feeling splinters catch in my jeans. "It's taking forever."

The thin voice startled me. I'd almost forgotten that old lady sitting there at the other end.

"Sunday morning," she said in a voice that sounded like rust. "Always a wait on a Sunday morning."

"Indeed 'tis," the shopkeeper chimed in with a British accent. "A pity. Poor people always have to wait. No other way to get to church on a Sunday. You wait and you wait. What else can you do?"

Now me, I sure wasn't in the mood for no waiting. Turning into a statue, sitting on a bench with splinters in my ass. Shoot, for all I knew them old folks coulda been sitting there from time immemorial, waiting on the goddamned bus.

But Cedella's black eyes came to life. Head started to bobbing. Something told me the girl don't mind waiting. Liked to wait, in fact. She pounced into the old folks' conversation like a cat among pigeons.

"Umm-hmm, umm-hmm." She leaned across me, focusing in on the old lady. "It is a shame, isn't it? A real shame."

The more pointless the conversation became, the more intense was Cedella. Probing the old people with questions. From late buses to long lines at the butcher shop to the wholesale price of vegetables. Seemed like every word, every gesture was a jewel to that girl. She hung on to the people's words, hoarding them like nuggets of gold. They loved it, of course. They were what my momma called *professional old folks*. Life was what they used to have, the good old days were what used to be when the world was right.

Cedella musta been practicing to be professional old folks herself. Or maybe that career she loved to talk so much about. One in investigative journalism. The girl was an expert in meddling, rummaging around in the trash cans of other people's lives. Too busy pretending to be engrossed in other folks' stories, she wouldn't have to tell none of her own.

But even as I sat there, congratulating myself on my amazing insight, something hit me. Me and Cedella, maybe we were two of a kind.

See, my momma didn't believe in singing the blues. When she was low down depressed, she'd always sing *A Motherless Child*. She'd even make up a verse about being Jesus' child, just to contradict herself. Momma was good at that. Well, I guess my swan song should be *Sometimes I feel like a childless mother*.

If Cedella was trapped in the professional old folks bag, then my thing was being the professional mother. The big, comfortable woman with the kind face and ready ear. A woman forever in the kitchen cooking while the party's going on. Or at home baby-sitting while others are out tasting the world's flavors. Living other people's lives and putting my own on the back burner. Ready to be a pillow and a pillar to everybody but myself. I'd backed myself into the momma corner and was pretending to be happy there, while the world passed by.

Hank Harris was right. Self-sacrifice might save your soul, but it sure would ruin your life. Well, honey, I'm here to tell you. I was ready to take my life out of mothballs and put it on. Wadn't no sense of me playing momma to no more grown folks. Putting everybody's needs ahead of my own. I was tired of sitting in the kitchen nibbling the chicken backs of life.

And I'd be damned if I was going to sit on a bench like a pile of old clothes, squeezed between a manic chatterbox, two professional old folks, and pigeon shit. Shit. Not when I'd blown two whole weeks' worth of pay following Shirley Moses to Montreal. I decided to see to it right then and there that Darlene Lou Josephs Harris got out and got her own.

I was tasting the world and liking it. I was getting ready to come out moving like a mountain. What you mean a mountain don't move? Honey, have you ever seen a volcano? I was ready to rock like an earthquake and roll like a river of lava.

It started with me getting up from that splintery bench, waving good-bye to Cedella and company, and walking out into an unfamiliar street in an unfamiliar city.

The next thing would be to turn Shirley's overnighter out of the hotel room I was half paying for, so I could take a long bath and a short nap. Then get up, go put on some makeup, a white sharkskin suit, and all my gold. And get back out in the streets again.

I aimed to find a way to the top of the Royal Mountain. I was going to get up there and see what it looked like to have a city spread out at my feet. Don't care how muddy they got.

I hitched up my rumpled jeans and hailed a passing taxi.

Carry Beyond

MARITA

We go to market to buy a little flying fish for supper tonight. And I see this woman in market, she watch my Sara so. Miss Darlene is one of the Black ones come from States to teach we pickeni. Is good people, church people. Not Anglican, but is good church still.

I know she fancy m'child because of the fire in she. She come like a moth to Sara's light. I know right away the blackskin girl have hunger for some child of she own. And I can see with m'second sight there will be none growing in the belly. I know this kind of woman born with empty womb. People call them mules. Them without child is lonely women, pouring out love on other women pickeni. I know this feeling deep inside my soul.

I been loving Winston since I fifteen, soul. And I only get big with Sara after twenty-five years of it. I lose so many I stop counting. Some born too early, some too late, some born without breath. None of m'children decide to stay until Sara. That a real old child, take her twenty-five years to come to the world. And this other one in me, I don't know what to make of it.

Something strange in it. It don't seem proper to be getting big at such age. Fifty way past the mothering time. I rub the belly and feel trouble, see wind and rain in m'second sight. But this not the time to worry on that one. It's the one here in the land of the living that needs looking after.

Sara only ten, but she a clever ten. A ten about thirty-five years old. She have she own coal fire burning inside. She can be just like the blackskin girl from States if she have she chance. But she need firewood to keep she light burning, more kindling than I can gather.

But Schoolteacher, she a woman without pickeni to give sheself to. She can keep m'Sara's light from burning out. She can tend that fire and make it brighter. Sara must know all she know, have all she have. And more. That child is going somewhere, soul, or I know the reason for it.

Make I talk to Winston tonight and Schoolteacher tomorrow. Self, soul, I think it time for Sara to leave this island, go across the water. Just as well she not be here for the coming of the wind and rain.

SARA

Trapped in the spaces between hill and mountain. Between a rock and a hard place. That was her life in the land people at home called *Promised*.

It was a loneliness beyond separation from mother and land of birth, beyond language. It was a starkness there in that particular valley set between the foothills and ranges of the Blue Ridge in the late 1950s. North Carolina was markedly different from rural Barbados.

The sun shone down from farther heights. It was a sunny coldness that chilled her to the marrow of her bones. It took months for her to become warm again. It was also a land of silences. The people spoke seldom, a droning language it took months for her to assemble into words she could recognize.

They both felt like fish out of water: Sara Winston, a recent immigrant, and Darlene Harris, a refugee from inner-city Detroit.

Sara and her adopted mother made this valley home for six stark seasons. They called it the *War on Poverty*. Even at her young age Sara could tell it was a losing battle.

The Black families were truck farmers and sharecroppers living on the outskirts of Leeboro. Darlene taught their children in a ramshackle two-room building abutting tobacco fields. A school which regularly closed its doors for the planting and harvest seasons. When one year the schoolhouse was invaded by a plague of spiders, students took their lessons in the school yard. She and Sara shared a small house in the predominantly white town proper. Where few children were disposed toward befriending a tongue-tied dark-skinned girl.

And those Black children at school, the sons and daughters of farmers, were also not her friends. They would gather around in crowds to hear her island-accented English. They would repeat her words, laughing as they said them. *Marnin. Wah-tah. Vege-TAH-bles.* She stopped speaking to avoid such scenes. But they still found fun to make of the quiet girl with the starched dresses and wrapped sandwiches.

The roughened worldliness of these children alarmed her. They rode mules and carried cornbread, saltpork, and molasses to school in pails. They worked the fields with the adults and complained of aching backs from picking weeds and hoeing tobacco. Bolls and burrs clung to the hems of their overalls and hopsack dresses. They knew of things Sara did not, things that men and women did in the dark. Some of them had done those things themselves. Girls whose rounded bellies stretched the fabric of their hopsack dresses.

Sara learned to love silence. She played alone. Blacks were not allowed in the town's public library, so Sara reread the tattered storybooks her mother brought home from school, until she tired of them.

Out back of the house, a persimmon tree stood beside a quiet river. Her only friends in this foreign place. They reminded her of home, even though persimmons did not grow in the tropics and Barbados was a land without rivers.

The tree stretched up, high as a royal palm. Its branches ebony and aloof above the land. It seemed to look out beyond even the ranges of the Blue Ridge.

Out of season it rained down hard nuggets of fruit, like unripe pears. In season Sara feasted on the sweetsour berries whose taste reminded her of the guineps of her Caribbean childhood.

The river was slim as a blue ribbon and slow moving, more of a country branch some joker decided to call *Broad*. It gurgled like a baby as it meandered along, and Sara heard voices; invisible mermaids who whispered secrets to her.

She listened to voices under the shade of persimmon leaves and fantasized. One day the mermaids would help her build a boat, and she would sail away upon this river. She consulted a tattered atlas and plotted her escape route. She would go up to the Shenandoah, down the Potomac, across the Chesapeake Bay, out to the Atlantic Ocean, down to the Caribbean, and back to her island home.

But when she finally left Leeboro it was not by water. At the age of sixteen Sara and her adopted mother, Darlene, flew off to Washington, D.C. And again she became a stranger in a strange land. It seemed that every land would make a stranger of her. Her island accent was gone by then, locked away in a deep space within her.

The Southern dust she wore now became cause for scorn. Teenagers in the city's public schools were much more rough and worldly than those on the outskirts of Leeboro had ever been. Streetwise womanish and mannish children who teased her mercilessly about her shyness, her clothes, her speech, her country ways.

"Hey, country ga-a-al!" followed her down streets, echoed after her in school corridors.

In D.C. Sara learned to fight back, make friends, and live in a world beyond storybooks, persimmon trees, and talking rivers. She dated her womanhood to that first day in D.C. The dusty town in the Blue Ridge valley was something she dreamed in childhood, a long sleep between going to bed in Barbados and waking up in Washington, D.C.

Leeboro became yet another place to be tucked away in memory, a dried rose pressed between Bible leaves. Over time the two lands began to blur in the back of her mind, and Washington became yet another patina painted over the portrait of the girl she used to be.

Could it be that both places were shrouded in such blueness? Or was it the fine tissue of memory which wrapped the faded beauty, the shrouded hills? The shuttered stillness of childhood places.

The Spider's Web

I cannot be in two places at one time. After all, I am not a god, but a man. How can I properly be expected to weave your story cloth, when rivers run dry and also run rampant? Either they do not exist at all and there is no path to follow, or they overflow in all directions, even disappearing into underground channels. Not that I am complaining, mind you. It is only by way of explanation.

I have followed these three of your daughters into the backwaters where fate has led them. Your Gatekeeper might have found them too, if only she had the faith. They may be separated from the clan, but they are not lost.

You never miss your water till your well runs dry, so say your people on this side of the ocean. These three daughters may have lost the physical river of their descent; Lost River Clan members Earlene and her daughter Darlene, Sara Winston of the Sugar Island Clan. But they carry the memory inside of them.

It is their very intensity of longing for blood connections that has made it possible for me to find them. That has even made it possible, Queen Mother, for some of them to find each other.

Your daughters are moving about with increasing speed and frequency these days. How can they not, with the way the world is now? Movements of people and movements of minds are all around us: Antiwar and Antiapartheid, civil rights and Black power.

And of course, your rivers are always in motion. Sometimes they move in astonishing ways, crossing and intersecting, twisting and turning. Do remember the Priestess' prophesy of your Nine Daughters' fate:

> When a tree is bent from the beginning, it grows twisted. But if through fortune or fortitude its origins are upright, the tree grows straight. Your third-born child will be firm minded, though pampered and petted.
>
> One who breaks ranks may one day lead the herd. The seventh child will be born a leader.

It is one thing to lead, and another to be a guide. The eighth-born child will be helpful.

There are more daughters to become, Queen Mother; tributaries beyond this backwater. There are new courses I wish to explore. Without them your story cloth can never be complete.

PART IV

TRIBUTARIES

Beadwork

One must give the devil his due. Kwaku Ananse has located the bloodlines of our lost daughters, and for that we are grateful. But could this be more than just coincidence? It is not beyond a trickster to create the diversion for his own wild-goose chase. A spider has been known to deliberately lose a thing, only to call attention to the discovery when he finds it.

You may have noticed that Ananse has made more than a passing appearance in some of these stories. For a spider whose vanity prevents him from keeping earlier promises, who knows what hand he may have had in this convenient turn of events.

Whatever the causes, our daughters will never be lost to us again. Yet Ananse, in his infinite wisdom, reminds us that a related course of rivers remains unexplored. We are proud to say that we, their ancestor mothers, have never lost track of these tributaries. Though they have lived through great depressions and world wars, Jim Crow and northern migrations, they never stray far from river's edge.

Let us follow the Mississippi River to where it meets the Illinois, then veer northward along its course to where Illinois joins the Chicago. Somewhere along the course of time, a strange thing has happened. The Chicago has been taught to run backward! Modern technology can be a terrible thing.

So instead of flowing from the Illinois, it now flows into it, carrying along with it whatever debris it may have picked up on its voyage from Lake Michigan. And here along these waterways, a conscientious beadstringer may find the scattered lines of the Queen Mother's descent.

Ama Krah's blood would flow and flourish in a New World city with an Old Word name. Cairo can be found on a point of land between two rivers. From Zubena, that wild-spirited, short-lived, second-born daughter of Ama Krah Proud Mary, an entire family would be founded. Zubena bore but one child before her untimely death. That daughter, Ella Mae Beasley, would have a host *of children whose numbers include one Bohema, the tenth born. Accumulated time, wisdom, and three generations of descendants have given her a new name—Big Momma Bullocks.*

Farther north along this network of rivers, in the up-South city of Chicago, we find two families of Big Momma's bloodlines. From the loins of her daughter Truly come Lula Mae, and Lula's daughter Pat. And springing from one of Bohema's male descent lines is a granddaughter Callie Mae, and her daughter Allie Mae.

If any of the Queen Mother's Nine Daughters is destined to return to the River Where Blood Is Born, perhaps she will soon be found among this clan. But, before this can occur, that daughter must first find herself.

Sweet Jesus Club

'm writing it down. Every bit of it.

You ever write things down? I do it all the time when things get heavy on my mind. Not write it *up*, like you do with homework and stuff. I write it down so I can get it off my mind and on paper where I can take a good look at it.

Miss Tribbett, our Sunday school teacher, always makes us count our blessings. That's our homework every single Sunday. I never had enough blessings to make a decent list. So I been counting my curses, too.

Been making two lists. First one, all the things that are right with my life; a pretty short list. Second one, all the things wrong with it. I filled up both sides of a sheet of notebook paper and still haven't finished. Only reason I stopped is because it's time for me to get up and fix dinner for Mama and Benny.

Benny, my big brother, he retarded. He don't talk much. He been standing in front of the refrigerator for about five minutes now, just bouncing like he's got to go bathroom. The deeper his knee bends, the hungrier he getting.

Benny always be hungry. I wonder if they even feed him at that special education school he go to. When the bus drops him off here at four, first thing he do is run in here looking for something to cram in his mouth. That boy is always eating.

But don't get me wrong. I'm crazy about Benny. He's more like a little brother than a big one, what with him being retarded and all. I'll take up for him in a minute. Nobody better not mess with my brother or they ass is grass.

It's just that I don't see why Mama's always got to have him hanging around my neck. Benny Peeples Jr. ain't none of my baby. I ain't but twelve and a half, and these are the best years of my life. Alright, so Mama works two and three jobs and there ain't nobody else here to mind him. All that work, she still don't never have no money. So I don't see what the deal is.

Anyway, that's why Benny winds up on both my lists. He both a blessing and a curse. Right now Mama's only on one of them. The long one.

"Pancakes." Benny squeezes up under my arm, peeping into the refrigerator. "Eggs."

"No, boy. Pancakes and eggs ain't for dinner."

Benny goes to whining. In a minute he'll be crying, and the boy cries so loud you can hear him clear on up to the third floor. I know, because one day I was up there visiting my friend Laura Lee Flowers. And that was the day Mama was trying to give Benny a bath. He was hollering like nobody's business. I don't want to hear that kind of noise, so I go on ahead and make him the pancakes and eggs, which he wolfs right down.

"Girl, what kind of dinner is this here?"

I didn't hear Mama come in. I believe she does that on purpose, tips up on me trying to catch me in something.

"Mama! Mama! Mama!" Benny jumps up out of his chair and throws himself at her. It's embarrassing. He turns into a regular puppy dog the minute she gets home.

"Boy, get up off of me. I'm tired." She pushes him away, steady grumbling at me. "Hard as I work out there trying to keep a roof over your head and clothes on your back, I got to come home to pancakes and eggs for dinner."

You see there? No *Hello, how you doing, good to see you.* Just walk in the door and jump right on my case.

"I cooked it because Benny begged me and I didn't want to hear him crying. If you want me to, I'll fix you something else."

"Well, fry me a hot dog or something. And move your lessons off the kitchen table, do they get all nasty."

Mama calls everything I write *lessons.* She can't seem to see why somebody should be writing, unless a teacher was making them do it. I don't think I ever seen my mama write so much as a postcard.

She moves my blessings and curses lists to the top of the refrigerator, then sits down and takes her shoes off. She gives a low little moan, like a cat outside in winter, ain't got no place to go.

"You sure look tired, Mama." She wouldn't be such a bad old chick if she wasn't so evil.

"Lord knows I am." Talking about how bad she feels is one of Mama's favorite subjects. *She's the world's oldest young woman,* that's what Miss Flowers says. "Tired all in my bones. Don't know how I'm going to make it over to the Silversteins' tonight."

"You going over there again? That makes three nights in a row."

"I got to work, girl."

"Aw, *Mama.*"

"Aw, *Mama,*" Benny repeats, saying it just like I did.

"Why you always got to repeat what I say, you old simple-minded boy?"

Next thing you know, Benny is crying and Mama is reaching over to pop me upside the head.

"See? Now you got your brother to crying. Why you be such a evil little old gal?"

Because I'm my mama's daughter, I want to tell her. But I better not even fix my mouth to say those words, unless I'm ready to get smacked in it. It always be the same thing, every time Mama comes home. She makes me mad, I take it out on Benny, Mama gets mad at me. Next time I'm keeping my mouth shut so the whole thing won't get started.

Mama be the workingest poor woman I ever seen. The way she stays gone, we ought to be millionaires by now. Working all day in the hospital laundry. Working half her nights baby-sitting some senile old man for a white family in Rolling Meadows. Works all day Sunday at church and that don't pay a penny. Always working and don't never have no money. Always talking about how she puts food on the table and clothes on our back, when it don't be nothing but beans, hot dogs, and Good Will.

Look at Miss Flowers, Laura Lee's mother. She don't need to work. She got her welfare check and her boyfriends. Plus she sell a little reefer on the side. And she stays sharp. None of those Salvation Army rags Mama be wearing. This lady knows how to dress for real: high heels, bell-bottom blue jeans, earrings made out of 14-karat gold. She even got a fur coat one of her boyfriends gave her. You don't see her out work, work, working for nothing. She be at home with her kids, taking it easy and spending time with her boyfriends. Miss Flowers, she knows how to live.

After Mama leaves, I put Benny in front of the TV with a box of Ritz crackers, and I go on up the back stairs to see what Laura Lee and them doing. Their back door is wide open. They're all sitting around the kitchen table, talking and rolling reefers two to a plastic bag. Miss Flowers sells them a dollar a pack. Laura Lee and Miss Flowers' sister Chartrice are up there helping her.

"You sure this ain't oregano?" Chartrice sniffs a handful of the stuff. "This shit looking mighty green to be herb."

"Girl, quit talking and go get me some more sandwich bags."

"What do I look like, Steppin Fetchit?" Chartrice keeps poking around in the green stuff piled in the center of the table. "I ought to report you to the Better Business Bureau. These tea leaves ain't going to get nobody high."

"Don't worry. If the herb don't give them a buzz, then this will." Miss Flowers takes the reefer she just rolled up and gives it a long lick. Everybody laughs, including me standing outside the unlocked screen door. Chartrice jumps all nervous like.

"Mae, you need to keep that back door shut. Ain't no telling who might be creeping up those back stairs."

"That's just my girl, Little Miss Mae. Mae ain't no heat, is you, honey? Come on in. Take a load off."

Miss Flowers the only thing keep me from hating my name too much. Allie Mae is just about as country as it comes. People always bothering me about that name. *Forget you up your alley crack. Hope you die, don't never come back.* This real ignorant boy named Junebug Wilson used to follow up behind me singing that. That's why I didn't hardly associate with these low-life individuals around here. I don't care if they do call me *Allie with the attitude.* I don't deal with people unless they got some class. Like Miss Flowers, born Freddie Mae.

"And don't tell nobody, hear?" Miss Flowers had warned me. "Far as the world knows, I'm just Mae. Mae Flowers, like the ones April showers bring."

I sit down. Laura Lee tries to teach me how to roll, but I'm not catching on too good. She also tries to get me into some side chitchat about people at her school I don't even know. But I rather hear the woman talk.

Aretha Franklin is playing on a radio that's always teetering on the back of

the stove but never seems to fall off. Miss Flowers sings along, shivering like a
Sweetwater Missionary Baptist Church mother about to get the Holy Ghost.

A woman's only human,
this you must understand.
She's not just a plaything,
she's flesh and blood just like a man.

If you want a do-right
all day woman,
you got to be a do-right
all night man . . ."

"Sing it, 'Retha! Betty Flowers' baby daughter ain't never played with toys,
not since she found out how to play around with boys. I ain't nothing but a man's
woman, got to have me a do-right nigga, all night long. If I don't get it regular, I
gets evil."

"Girl, hush your filthy mouth." That's Chartrice, trying to play like she don't
talk just as dirty herself. "It's children sitting up here."

"They gone have to learn the facts of life one day. Girls, men is like penny
candy. Don't never settle for a *Now or Later*, when you can have some sho' nough
Good & Plenty. Get you an *All Day Sucker*, and make it last all night too."

"You so nasty." Chartrice went to giggling. "And for somebody supposed to be
a man's woman, why you ain't never managed to marry one?"

"Damned if I know. It sure would have been convenient."

"Convenient?"

"Hell, yes. Be getting it every night, right on the money." Miss Flowers snaps
her fingers.

"Girl, you a mess." Chartrice is laughing so hard all the herb falls out of
the reefer she's rolling. "You don't know a good thing when you got it. A husband don't give you nothing every night but a hard way to go, and a hard row
to hoe."

"If Johnny don't want to do you right, he ain't the only cock on the block.
Somebody else would be happy to have it. And would know what to do when he
get it."

Chartrice gives a little sneaky smile and a wave of the reefer stick.

"Honey, hush." Miss Flowers narrows her eyes at her sister. "Don't tell me
baby sister got her a backdoor man. Tell it, girl."

Chartrice rolls her buck eyes at me and Laura Lee, sitting there with our ears
wide open. Miss Flowers takes the cue.

"Get getting, girls. This is grown folks' talk."

I make my way to Laura Lee's bedroom, the conversation still on my mind.

"Laura Lee, what was your mama and them talking about?"

Laura Lee isn't too much interested. I guess she's heard it all before.

"Doing it."

"Doing what?"

"You know." Laura Lee makes an O with her thumb and forefinger, then sticks another finger through it. "The P-U-S-S-Y."

I've heard the word before. But I'm still not quite sure what it is.

"How they do it?"

"You mean you don't know about the P-U-S-S-Y?" She draws herself up like our old fourth-grade teacher, Miss Caruso, used to do before she gave a lecture on the digestive system. "That's when a boy takes his thing and puts it in your tee-tee hole. If he puts it all the way in, that's the P-U-S-S-Y. If he don't, it's just playing."

"Girl, you a lie. He puts that big old thing in you? That must really hurt."

Laura turns down the corners of her mouth and shakes her head.

"Naw, it don't hurt much."

"How do you know? Don't mean to tell me you did it before."

Laura shrugs like it ain't nothing.

"One time. With Junebug Wilson."

"You did? What was it like? Tell me, girl."

Laura shook her head.

"Ain't nothing to tell. I don't see why they make such a big deal out of it. It ain't much fun."

We weren't even in eighth grade good when Laura Lee dropped out, pregnant with her first baby. She said when her mother found out about it, she beat her butt so bad she couldn't sit down for a whole week. But what I want to know is this: if it wasn't no fun, how come Laura got interested enough to do it with Junebug again? I don't think she was telling me the whole story.

This pussy business. It seems to be a secret everyone knows about but me. Like once you do it, you're in a special club and can't tell nobody the password. Mama's a member.

"Don't be talking that filth at my kitchen table." When I ask her to explain the subject to me, she reaches over and slaps the shit out of me. "I don't know where you be getting this mess from. Yes, I do. It's Laura and that old whorish mama of her'n. That girl ain't even thirteen good and she already having a baby. You stay away from up there, hear me?"

Yep, she's in on it. Mama found herself somebody to do with in her bed the filth she don't want me talking about at the kitchen table.

Out of all the available men on the West Side of Chicago, you would think that Mama could do better for herself than Otis Clemmons. First, he's twenty years older than Mama if he's a day. Second, he's one of those high-yellow dudes with wavy hair, act like somebody supposed to bow down in front of him because of it. Third, he don't do nothing but sit up and drink beer, complain about his bad back, and try to boss somebody around like he their daddy. Which he ain't. Otis Clemmons is definitely going on my curses list.

He starts spending nights up in Mama's room. She brings him in late, when she thinks we're sleeping. Benny be snoring back. But I be hearing everything that goes on in this house. The first night it was such a scrambling and a rattling on the other side of our bedroom, I'm thinking we got rats in the wall. Until I hear my mama hollering.

"Lordy! Whoa, Lordy, sweet Jesus!"

Like it's the Lord doing it to her instead of that old slick-headed Otis. Before I know it, Sweet Jesus Otis is up here living with us. With his old stanky-feet, bad-breath self. Go up in the bathroom, stay in there a whole hour. Miss Flowers says that this is because he is full of shit.

"Full of shit and fake as a three-dollar bill. Always bragging about how his mama's a full-blooded Indian, when you and me both know his mama's as black as the ace of spades and his daddy was an old white man she picked up off Skid Row. Plus, I hear he's a minute man."

"What's a minute man?"

Miss Flowers laughs deep in her throat. That *I know a Sweet Jesus secret* laugh. "Never mind about that."

I figure it out for myself. But I don't know; that bed on the other side of the wall seems to rattle much more than a minute most nights.

Once Otis gets in here, he tries to boss us all around. Be telling my mother what to wear, how to fix her hair. Wouldn't be so bad if he got her to looking good. He just don't want Mama going outdoors with nothing showing, that's his thing. If he could wrap Mama up in one of those rags they wear overseas, the women don't have nothing showing but their eyes, old Otis Clemmons would do it in a minute.

"Girl, cover up your bust. And put a coat on. I can't stand these niggas looking all down my woman's dress."

He tries to control me and Benny, too. Well, Benny don't too much care, as long as he gets his TV and his something to eat. I told you he was retarded, right? But he's not illy-formed or nothing. He ain't got those bugged-out, slanty eyes like some of those kids go to his school. He don't be dribbling spit out his mouth or nothing like that. He's just like a big old baby. And he don't bother nobody, long as you leave him be. But Otis Clemmons wouldn't. That would be too much like right.

"Boy, you watches too much TV. Turn that thing off. And pick up all that popcorn off the floor." I guess Benny's not moving fast enough for him. He points a long yellow finger at him and hollers: "Do it!"

"Do it!" Benny looks up and points his brown finger back at him.

"Don't you mock me, fool. I'm a dangerous nigga."

He's dangerous alright. He ain't been here but six months when he has Mama sending Benny off to some home for the *profoundly retarded* in Waukegan. I'll never forget how Benny cries when we leave him there. And I'll never forgive Otis for making Mama do it.

With Benny out of the way, he starts in on me. First, he won't let me watch nothing I want to on TV.

"*Peyton Place?* What kind of trash is that for a young girl to be looking at?"

Then he starts trying to do me like he does Mama. Criticizing what I be wearing.

"You wearing that sleeveless blouse? To church? Go pull that thing off and put on you some *clothes*."

He really gets a shit fit when I start to sprouting titties. One weekend when Benny's out of his jail visiting home, I decide to give him a bath. He don't be too clean since he been up at Waukegan.

Seems like I've been washing Benny up all my life. It's not that hard to do, as long as you do it a certain way. Get lots of bubbles in there for him to play with. Soap him up everywhere but his face. He hates getting soap in his eyes. And let him splash all he wants. He loves to splash. By the time we finish, I'm just as wet as he is.

I go to Mama's room to get me a towel. As usual, Otis is sitting up there drinking. He looks at me real hard in my wet T-shirt.

"What the hell is the matter with you?" A red-eyed devil. "Parading around in front of me like that."

I just ignore him, searching for the towel. He keeps at me.

"Why ain't you got no bra on?"

"I ain't got one."

"Then get you one."

"With what? You got the money for me to buy it with?"

He clamps his red mouth shut then. With his cheap self. He ain't hardly got it to get Schlitz for his sorry gut, let alone buy me a bra.

He must have talked to Mama about it though. Next Saturday morning we rode the el downtown. I don't know where we're going until we get there: Junior Foundations at Montgomery Wards. She buys me two training bras, cost $12.50.

But after the bras, it's something else. It's going to always be something else. I'm wearing hot pants one day because it's hot. That's why they call them hot pants, you wear them when it's hot. It's ninety-eight degrees outside and I'm cooking biscuits inside. Sweat is running off me like rain.

Otis comes up in the kitchen, gets his Schlitz, and sits down. Hot as hell in that kitchen, he got to sit down where I'm at. Y'all *know* he wants to start something. I pass by him going to put the Crisco back in the pantry.

"Girl, if you don't get your black tail out of my face, you better."

See, you're not supposed to mess with people when it's ninety-eight degrees. Especially when they're baking biscuits in a hot kitchen.

"Leave me alone." That's all I say. That's all I want.

"Are you talking back to me, little evil gal?"

"What do it sound like to you?"

Otis halfway chokes on his beer.

"Is you lost your mind? Back talking me and swishing your little naked ass around this kitchen."

"Ain't none of your kitchen. Ain't none of your ass either."

Otis wipes the beer from his mustache.

"Bitch." He hisses the word between his teeth, like an old yellow snake. Ain't nobody never called me that word. "You better get your butt out of here before I beat it for you. Got your little ass hanging out like you think somebody want to look at it."

"You can look all you want." I'd give him his *bitch.* "Because you damn sure ain't getting none."

Miss Flowers had cussed a man out like that in a tavern one night. She said the man's mouth had dropped all the way down to the floor, he couldn't think of nothing to say back. Otis' red mouth does the exact same thing. And I walk right out the back door. Let the biscuits burn.

But Otis Clemmons is *a dangerous nigga*. I overhear them on the other side of the wall. The bed's not rattling tonight. They in there talking in hard whispers.

"Callie Mae, that girl is running too fast, too young."

"She ain't that bad, Otis."

"She is ruint. Won't be but a matter of time before she come up pregnant like her friend upstairs. Then what you going to say? *She ain't that bad?* That child is rotten. She needs more discipline than she's getting in this house."

"But, Otis. A place like that?"

"Would do her a world of good. She need to learn she can't run over everybody like she runs over you."

So that's what it is. Get rid of us so he can have Mama all to himself. All the little bit of love she can squeeze up, his love. All the little bit of time she has, his time. All her little bit of money, his money. But I ain't nobody's Benny to be sent off to jail crying. I'd sooner run away than let him send me somewhere like Waukegan. And I do.

First I go down to Phoenix, where I got some cousins who don't really want me there. Then to Chartrice, Miss Flowers' sister, who works me like a dog: cooking, baby-sitting, cleaning up after her and her nine nasty kids.

Mama catches up with me after about three weeks. One of Chartrice's kids lets her in the house. She comes tipping in like a guest not sure of her welcome. She sits on the far edge of the plastic-covered couch while I sweep up the front-room floor.

"How you doing, baby? You alright?"

Mama hasn't called me baby in so long, it makes me feel like crying. But it's not me, it's her that starts it up. The first time I can remember seeing tears on my mama's face. I can't blame nobody but Otis for putting them there.

"I'm sorry, Mama. But I just couldn't sit there and let Otis send me off to no home for bad girls. I ain't done nothing wrong."

"Baby, what I'm going to do with you? I tried my best to raise you up right. But I ain't done such a good job. I guess I ain't no kind of mother."

"You are so. You're a great mother. It's Otis who's the problem."

Mama acts like she don't even hear me talking.

"I stay gone so much, working. You having to stay home with Benny all them years. That's a lot to put on a young girl."

"I don't mind, Mama. Benny ain't been much trouble."

"You getting to be a young woman now. And I don't know how to protect you no more. It's all kinds of dogs and rats out there walking around on two legs. Some of them would just love to get ahold a young girl like you and use her for toilet paper."

"Mama, we never did have no problems in our family until a year ago. We were happy until Otis came along."

She hears me that time. And it don't do nothing but make her mad.

"Otis Clemmons is a good man! He treats you like a daughter. It ain't every man would take up with a woman with two kids and treat them like they was his own. And instead of praising the Lord for him, you act like *Ugly* was your middle name. Back talking. Chasing up behind boys. Stealing. Running away. Otis ain't doing nothing but trying to help you, baby. He don't want to see your fresh life wasted before you even start living it. He don't want to see you go wrong."

No, he don't want to see me go wrong. He just wants to see me go away. And he gets his wish.

I didn't tell you about the stealing, right? Okay, I stole some things. I stole some clothes. It wasn't my fault. First of all, Mama and them don't never buy me nothing. Especially since Otis been laying up there mooching off of her. I'll be starting high school this fall. What I'm going to look like walking up in high school in those mammy-made thrift store rags Mama makes me wear? They don't be fitting. They way out of style.

Occasionally Mama throws me something halfway nice.

"Here, girl. This blouse don't fit me no more. You might as well take it."

Problem is, something Mama's outgrown or got from the white folks' house would still be two sizes too big for me. And won't hardly be high fashion. I'm just tired of looking patched together, like somebody's little ragamuffin child. I want to wear things that come with the tags still attached. I want things picked out with me in mind. I want things that nobody else has worn before me. So I rip them off.

Only thing I can remember that was bought for me brand new is those two training bras. And even those didn't fit right. Mama bought them big, for me to grow into. But ain't no telling when I'm going to get titties that big. So I have to steal me some more.

The only problem with stealing is that I get caught. I'm not even in the store or nothing. I'm out on the street looking inside my windbreaker to see what all I got out with, when this cop comes up and asks me where are my receipts. Ain't nobody there but Otis when they call home, so he has to come down to the station and get me.

And then the Leslie thing. It's not fair. Mama and them swear up and down that I'm trying to do the Sweet Jesus with Laura Lee's older brother.

How Leslie Flowers got in that family, I'll never know. Otis says Miss Flowers went up to the north side and did it with a Puerto Rican. Old Otis got his nerve. At least Leslie don't look like he got yellow fever. He's nice and beige, like the inside part of a loaf of whole wheat bread. Of course, Laura Lee and Miss Flowers look more like the crust.

I'll admit that I do love me some Leslie Flowers. He is *too* cute, looks just like Smokey Robinson.

But Leslie ain't hardly thinking about me. Sometimes he'll call out, *Hey, Skinny Minnie* when he sees me over there visiting Laura, or alone out on the street. I think it's because he can't remember my name. Once he kisses me, but it's not a serious *in love* kind of kiss. It's more like he's kissing me off. Because Leslie Flowers is the kind of boy that girls go to him, not the other way around. He's got plenty of women, Miss Flowers says, who love to give it up.

Remember how Laura got her butt beat when she turned up pregnant? When she finds out one of Leslie's girlfriends is pregnant, Miss Flowers act like she proud of it.

"Well, at least the boy can make a baby." She flicks her cigarette ash into the cup of her hand. "Long as they don't be bringing it around here for me to raise."

See, Mama and Otis don't hardly have to worry about me turning up pregnant. As much as I love me some Leslie, I ain't hardly going to let something in me that (don't care what Laura Lee says) must hurt like a tooth getting pulled. And then to have a baby on top of it? Not me. I know from taking care of Benny all these years that a baby ain't no kind of fun.

But Mama and Otis, they don't believe me. They know the secret password of the Sweet Jesus Club and think I must know it, too.

So Otis gets his way. He has Mama take me down to the station. This train is taking me off to what kind of jail, I'm not really sure. I'm on my way, and out of his. Him and Mama free to make that bed talk as loud as it can while I'm gone.

Sitting here watching the West Side of Chicago disappear behind me, I can't think of a single thing to go on my blessings list. Everything is a curse. Don't nobody pay me no attention, don't nobody want to hear my side of it. But you know what? I'm going to make them listen.

I'm writing it down. I'm writing it all down, the whole story. And when I finish I'm sending it to Mama so she can see herself, and Otis Clemmons so he can see his ugly mug in it. She don't have to fret about somebody using me. She needs to worry more about herself. See, I ain't never going to get as turned around behind some no-account man as Mama is with Otis. I ain't about to make a man my religion, or be nobody's roll of toilet paper.

Yeah, I'm riding this train. I'm riding and I'm writing. But you think I'm going to sit back and let the bars close behind me? When I know how to get up and walk? Not hardly.

I may be sent away, but that don't mean I got to stay.

South for the Summer

MID-MAY

I told sweet Jesus it would be alright . . .

I t is not so much music as a moaning. A song some lonely old dog might howl at the moon. The song swells, filling the room. Pressing against walls. Settling into corners. Creeping under skin. Keeping meter with the movements of the old woman.

be alright
be alright . . .

A busy old woman. The young girl is not. As far as she knows, it is not alright and might never be. The room is too dim and the air is too thick. The smells around her are overpowering and unfamiliar. The moaning song is nagging to the ear. And there are noises in the twilight, vague sounds that she cannot decipher. They might well be spooks or rattlesnakes. There are certainly spiders. She spots a big one, dangling from a web in the dusty corner.

I told Jesus it would be alright
if he changed my name

The girl turns a sullen ear to the old woman's music. Stubborn in her traveling clothes, stock-still in a rocking chair. Arms crossed. Bottom lip poked out. Sent south to spend the summer with a woman older than time; a country-talking, church-song-nobody-ever-heard-of-singing, head-rag-wearing old woman she's never set eyes on before. To think she was missing her grammar school graduation behind some mess like this.

The woman works around her. Picking greens. Mixing cornbread. Humming spirituals. And carrying on a cheerful one-way conversation.

"Might as well to call me *Big Momma*. My kids called me that, my grands and great-grands, all the young folk around here. You just call me *Big Momma*, and I 'spect we'll get along fine. What you think of that, Little Daughter?"

That was one strike against her. Calling her out of her name. The girl does not respond, but turns to study something unseen in the far-off corner. Getting along is not in the plan. But the *Big Momma* person continues as if she were reading her mind.

"Don't worry, I call all my girls *Little Daughter* and all my boys *Little Man.* Else-wise, I'd be around here hollering *Come here, Lula Mae,* or *Supper time, Earlene,* or some other name you wasn't born with. I'm too old to keep up with names and it's too many young folks in Cairo."

That was another strike. Mispronunciation. If they had been on speaking terms, she would have told the old woman that Cairo is pronounced *KIE-ro,* not *KAY-ro,* like the syrup. But since she is not speaking, she bends to examine the dirt beneath her fingernails. She makes careful to sit forward so the chair won't rock. If caught rocking it might be thought she was enjoying herself here. Which she is not.

Big Momma casts a purposeful glance at the old gas stove with burners blazing and oven roaring. She walks deliberately to the stiff figure in the stilled chair.

"Now you, Little Daughter. Dinner going to be ready in 'zactly twenty min-utes. And them which works around here is the only ones which eats."

Strike three: starving a child. Even the worst witch in the fairy tales gave you a little something to eat, if it wasn't anything but a poison apple. And work? Whose little slave did she look like, anyway?

Yet smells waft tauntingly around the kitchen and her empty stomach betrays her. It carries on noisily, growling like a watchdog at the assailant cooking odors. She ventures forth a word.

"So." It comes as croak from her unused vocal chords, not so much a question as a statement.

"So?" the old woman repeats.

Not wanting to look at the face, she clears her throat and addresses the aproned waist inches before her. The apron smells good; like bacon grease and nutmeg and Ben-Gay.

"So, what kind of work?"

"Well, Little Daughter. If you going to eat you better get busy on that basket yonder by the machine."

Careful to maintain her citified cool, the girl strolls over. She peers into a battered basket crouching near the curved legs of an old-fashioned sewing machine.

"Ain't nothing in here but a bunch of rags," she protests.

"Scraps," Big Momma corrects. "Bits of some of everything. Overalls, some tafeety from an old petticoat. Hopsack, linen, lace. Now get to work, Little Daughter."

"Doing what . . . Big Momma?" She says the name with a side of her mouth turned down. Not knowing what else to call her.

"Sorting them, child. Match them up by color and piece them together with straight pins from that cozy up top the machine."

It seems deceptively easy. The girl is suspicious.

"That's all? Then I can eat?"

"That's all for today." Big Momma stirs the fragrant pot. "Come tomorrow you gone start learning to piecework."

Here I am in God knows where. Cairo. Don't seem like such a dinky old town should have such a fancy name. Don't seem like this backward place should even share the same state with Chicago. Won't be surprised if I die of boredom before this summer is through. And Otis Clemmons would get his wish. He probably sitting up somewhere with his Schlitz, patting himself on the back that his plans are turning out so good.

It's because of him that Mama carried me down to the station. Because of him I had to ride so long it was daylight when I got on and dark when I got off. Because of him I'm laying up here in some country shack next to a woman who snores and sleeps with her top teeth in a jelly jar. Wasting my summer in a place where people talk worser than the Beverly Hillbillies. And missing my grammar school graduation on top of it.

I'm out of his way now. I'm in Cairo, they in Chicago. They got that two-bedroom apartment to theyself, while I'm laying up in a three-room shack. They can hear car traffic and see streetlights from the window. Only light I'm writing by comes from a fingernail slice of moon. All I hear outside is the crickets buzzing and a dog barking someplace far-off. They all snuggled in the Sweet Jesus, while I'm mashed against the wall with my pen and paper. Trying not to touch this old lady who supposed to be my great-grandmother.

I can't think of a single thing to go on my blessings list. Everything is a curse.

LATE MAY

A faint breath of honeysuckle wafts in through an open window. Big Momma's needle glints like lightning, working in and out the quilt spread across her lap. She is singing as usual, a song about how she *just can't stop praising his name*. As she rocks, the old chair's joints chirp like crickets. The clickety clack of the sewing machine punctuates her pauses.

Allie Mae pumps out her last stitch on the old treadle machine. She lifts the foot, cuts the thread, removes the fabric, and holds it up to the light.

"You finished, Little Daughter." Big Momma adjusts her glasses, leans forward in the rocker. "Your first piece quilt. Tomorrow we going to dry goods, get you some muslin for the backing and some batting for the stuffing."

The girl wrinkles her brow. She is much dissatisfied.

"This ain't right, Big Momma." She points out the crooked stitches and uneven patterns.

"Child, I don't know what you talking. This is a work of art."

"Art?" Allie gently corrects her. "No, ma'am, this ain't artwork. Art is those paintings and stuff they hang in museums."

"Who says so? Look at these here colors, mixed up just as pretty. Look at the figures. See how nice that brightness look against the dark. It's better than pictures hanging just to look at. This quilt will keep you warm and pretty up your bed besides."

"But see yours." She points to the crazy quilt across Big Momma's lap. "It makes mine look so bad."

"Looka here, honey. Ain't nothing perfect under the sun, nothing 'cept the Almighty himself." She stretches out her own handiwork, squinting as if seeing it for the first time.

"Had the iron too hot on your mama's old calico dress. Couldn't get that scorch mark off to save my life. And these here velvet hearts. See, how one's brown and one's black? Did that on purpose. One's from Hosea's good Sunday suit. Couldn't take but a snatch before they buried him. I matched it with your great-granddaddy Joe Lee's old vest."

"That's a real pretty plaid." Allie points out a worn star in the center, its reds and oranges faded as autumn. "Where'd it come from?"

"Come from a little strip of hand-weaving my great-grandmama used to have. I do believe she brung it 'cross the water with her, all the way from Africy."

"Boy, that must be real old."

"Older than I am. And do you recollect this piece here?" She points out a piece of denim she is busy edging in bright red.

"Oh. Ain't that from my old pair of jeans?"

"Them britches was so tight your butt was bout to bust through. Here's some hair ribbon your cousin Pat had when she was a bitty baby. That child was born with a headful of hair."

"Looks like these pieces come from everybody in the family," the girl observes. "Like pictures in a family album."

"It's a lifetime's worth of work, honey. Been sewing at this old crazy quilt so long, I'm 'fraid to run it through the machine. *Don't never forget the bridges you crossed over on.*"

"What you mean by that, Big Momma?"

"Ain't none of us alone in this world, Little Daughter. Nana, my great-granny, used to keep a place in the corner with a little piece of something from all the kinfolk: buttons, baby teeth, locks of hair, scraps of cloth. I do the same thing with my quilt. These patches are our peoples; the born and the dead, the lost and left behind, the righteous and the wrongdoers. And what do you make of this red thread winding into each piece?"

Allie studies it. She traces a finger over the line of red, running through like a winding river.

"Maybe it's the blood that joins us all together. Hey, some of these patches got red running in, but none coming out. Did you forget to join them?"

"Everything pretty got some problem in it. That's what makes it interesting. You don't want nothing that's too perfect. Ain't no questions in it left to answer."

Still the girl is not satisfied.

"I don't know about all that." She squints and frowns, comparing the two pieces. "But I bet the first quilt you made wasn't as bad as this one here."

"Bet it was, too."

"No, it wasn't, Big Momma."

The woman eases back into her chair by the stove. She believes the heat helps her arthritis. The high bed has been moved into the kitchen for this particular purpose. Being the biggest room in Big Momma's house, it doubles as bedroom, living room, and sewing room. The parlor with its horsehair sofa is rarely used. The bedroom off the kitchen has become a pantry of sorts. It holds a deep freezer, the Frigidaire, and shelves of home-canned fruits and vegetables.

"You trying to call me a lie? Thing looked so bad, I ripped it up for rags. Yes, I did. Foolishest thing I ever did, too. Tearing up a piece I created. You ever do that with them stories you so busy writing?"

Allie is aghast.

"Rip up my stories. My *stories?* Big Momma, that would be like ... like murder!" She has acquired a taste for the melodramatic while watching Big Momma's *stories*, the television soap operas.

"Well, child honey, that's just what I did. Committed murder against my own soul. That was part of my life story I destroyed, a story writ with needle and thread. It ain't everyone been blessed with a story to tell. You got the gift, Little Daughter. Don't you be as silly and hardheaded with it as I was."

She smooths the quilt across her lap and contemplates it awhile.

"You think I'll ever get to quilt as good as you, Big Momma?"

"Tell you what, girl. Life kinda like learning to piece quilt. Ain't never going to get it perfect. But just keep on living, Little Daughter. The longer God spares you to practice, the better you gets to be."

I got a story to tell alright. A quilt crazier than anything Big Momma ever made. All problems, nothing pretty. Too many questions and not enough answers. I sure hope I don't be living like this for the rest of my life. Guess I just got to keep on living.

EARLY JUNE

Big Momma goes out there once a month. She replants flowers and digs up weeds around the family graves in Mound City.

Allie Mae can't imagine why dead folks underground would care about flowers growing up above. They are a collection of unknown bones with vaguely familiar names: *Ella Mae Beasley, Zubena Creek, Freedom Forest.* A very old headstone made of smooth rounded rock has a question mark for a birth date. The death date is May 12, 1899. *Proud Mary* seems to Little Daughter a strange kind of name. Maybe it should have been Mary Pride, and the gravestone carver misspelled the name and reversed the order.

Ray Bullocks, Joe Lee Bullocks, Berta Mae Bullocks. Allie recognizes her mother's maiden name. But her questions get caught in a tangle of names and dates and who gave birth to whom. It's like the red thread in Big Momma's story quilt, a thread that twists into Elijahs and Jakes, winds out of Hildys and Ruths. It all becomes a jumble of crazy quilt patches and she quickly loses the thread. These Sunday afternoons in the graveyard stretch on long and boring.

Deacon Frazier, Reverend Isley, or somebody else from church usually drops them off at three, and comes back before dark. But one Sunday their ride is late. The sun sets on them in Mound City.

Big Momma's gardening duties complete, she squats on the ground beside the strange *Proud Mary* headstone. She brushes it off, singing one of her familiar moaning songs. She carefully pours a teacup of water and props it upright against the rock. Now who did she think was going to drink that water?

Tree shadows lengthen. Lazy afternoon becomes spooky evening. A dog howls somewhere in the distance. The girl's heart lurches. She cowers down beside her great-grandmother.

"Big Momma," she whispers, worming under her arm. "I'm scared."

Big Momma hugs her absently.

"Now, Little Daughter. Ain't no use to be scared of the boneyard."

"Yes it is, too. Dead people buried here."

"Then you're going to be scared," Big Momma explains, "wherever you walk. Dead folks everywhere you go."

"What you talking about?"

"People been walking this earth a mighty long time. They fall down and die, get buried here and there. Grave markers get lost. People move on, or get moved off their lands. New ones don't know the old burial grounds. They build on them. Plant farms. Years go by. And here we come, walking on the graves of people long gone."

They sit side by side, watching the play of shadows. Reading the headstone before them. *Proud Mary, born in Africa?, died in Cairo May 12, 1899.*

"Big Momma, do you believe in ghosts?"

"I don't think nothing that was here ever leaves. The plants and animals, the dead folks in the ground get all stirred up, their bones and bodies helping trees to grow. Becoming a part of the water we drink, the dirt that grows the food, the greens and corn we cook. This air we breathing now may got somebody in it from long ago. In us, around us, little bits and pieces of them running in our blood.

"Maybe your uncle Ike, your granddaddy Joe Lee Jr. Maybe your great-grandmother's great-grandmother. I 'spect they're still around here somewhere. No need to be scared of the boneyard, Little Daughter. It's just a place you come to remember."

Big Momma said that Proud Mary was her great-grandmother.

If my great-grandmother's great-grandmother was born over in Africa, then I might be got some kin over there. It makes me wonder who they are and what they're doing. Do they live in houses or in trees? Do they still remember Proud Mary, the one who went away? Do they wonder what happened to her? Are they like those Africans in *Tarzan* who run away from fire and holler *bwana, bwana* all the time?

If I ever went there, I'd carry them some guns and cigarette lighters so people couldn't scare them so easy with bullets and fire. But I wouldn't know where to look for them, because I don't know them and they don't know me.

Blood is thicker than water, that's the way a family is supposed to be. Like the red thread in Big Momma's story quilt. Like the chart in Miss Caruso's science class, which shows the human circulatory system. The blood flows like red rivers through the veins and arteries. But all the blood in the body is connected, so it has to come back to the source. Which is the heart.

But it don't seem like our family is connected right. We ain't like other people with lots of uncles and cousins and family reunions every year. We don't halfway know each other. Mama's parents died when she was little; I don't even know their names. Some of the family's in Chicago, some in Cairo, some way out in California. Our bloodlines run every which way. I don't think none of it goes back to the source. It's a deep cut somewhere and all the blood just gushes out.

Much as I hated to come out here, I ain't that crazy about going back to Chicago when the summer ends. It just don't feel like home no more. It never really did. There ain't hardly no family there, besides us and the Browns, way out in Phoenix, Illinois. Which is almost as country as Cairo, even if it is close to Chicago. Live way out there in the sticks, got the nerve to be stuck up. Daddy up and left a long time ago, don't nobody know where he's at. Me and Mama and Benny seem to be blowing through the city like tumbleweeds. Not connected to no one but each other.

But now I'm in Cairo, Illinois. Cairo is named after a city in Africa. Africa is where the first woman in our family comes from, that's what Big Momma says. For the first time I feel like I'm connected to something. Like a tumbleweed putting down roots.

MID-JUNE

Big Momma works twice a week in Miss Elsie's kitchen. Elsie Wheeler is a retired schoolteacher, a widow with a sprawling old home on Millionaire's Row. She lives there all alone, but has another cook and what she calls her *cleaning girl* (who is probably the same age as Allie Mae's mother) to do all her housework. Big Momma does the biweekly baking. Miss Elsie says that nobody makes desserts and dinner rolls like *Miss Bohema*.

Miss Elsie always wanders in while Big Momma is working, dusty with nostalgia about the good old days when Cairo was a bustling river town. She claims the city's undeserved reputation goes back to the days when Dickens proclaimed this *dismal Cairo . . . a place without one single quality, in earth or air or water to commend it.* She laments that he never came back to see Cairo in its glory years.

She'll drift in clutching an old yellowed program book or a basket of Christmas tree ornaments, with a faraway look in her eyes. She'll sigh, *Wasn't it lovely when Christmas carolers sang along Washington Street,* or *Do you remember the year* La Boheme *came to the Opera House?*

Big Momma would answer *sho you right* and *yes, indeed* at the proper pauses.

But Allie knows she's thinking more about rolling crust out evenly or mixing biscuit dough properly than she is about Miss Elsie's chitchat.

She has been there three times already when Miss Elsie finally seems to notice her.

"And who might this little one be?"

"Allie Mae Peeples," she answers dutifully. Miss Elsie reminds her of Mrs. O'Neill, her grade-school principal.

"Allie?" Miss Elsie's eyebrow rises. "What an unusual name. It must be short for something. Allison, perhaps?"

Miss Elsie looks so hopeful, and Little Daughter has never liked her name to begin with. She grins and lifts one shoulder in a half shrug.

"Perhaps."

Miss Elsie finds *Allison* exceptionally well spoken. She has her read aloud from the *Cairo Register* as they fan flies on the front porch. Miss Elsie calls it a *verandah*.

"Lovely diction," she exclaims. "Simply lovely. The coloreds around here (and some of the whites, too, I daresay) could learn a thing or two from you about enunciation."

One afternoon Big Momma makes finger sandwiches and tea cakes. It is Miss Elsie's turn to host the women from the local book club and she is atwitter all morning with place settings and centerpieces, tea sets and floral arrangements. Allie wears a frilly white apron and comes out of the kitchen to hand around a tray of finger sandwiches. She is surprised to see that only one lady has shown up: Miss Eugenia Ammons, the birdlike, blue-haired next-door neighbor. The morning's heavy rain must have driven the rest of the book club indoors.

Miss Eugenia reads haltingly from *To Kill a Mockingbird*, squinting at the page and mispronouncing words. Miss Elsie, who fancies herself *a patron of les belles lettres*, apparently can't endure it. She winces and she sighs. She finally gets up and gently removes the book from her hands.

"Eugenia, I'm afraid you've forgotten your reading glasses again. Why don't we let Allison read it for us?"

"Well, I don't know." Miss Eugenia peers at her doubtfully.

"Nonsense. She is a very fine reader. Allison, dear. Page two thirty-three, second from the last paragraph, please."

Reading has always been one of the girl's favorite pastimes. She regrets that oral reading isn't done much past the primary grades in school. She used to read the dialogue in voices. None of the other kids ever thought to do that, and it was always very popular with the teachers. She takes the book and begins reading with gusto.

> "As you grow older, you'll see white men cheat black men every day of your life, but let me tell you something and don't you forget it—whenever a white man does that to a black man, no matter who he is, how rich he is, or how fine a family he comes from, that white man is trash."
>
> Atticus was speaking so quietly his last word crashed on our ears. I looked

up, and his face was vehement. "There's nothing more sickening to me than a low-grade white man who'll take advantage of a Negro's ignorance. Don't fool yourselves—it's all adding up and one of these days we're going to pay the bill for it. I hope it's not in your children's time."

"Bravo, bravo," Miss Elsie applauds when Little Daughter has finished the chapter. "Well done, my dear."

Miss Eugenia smiles at her kindly.

"Why, she's quite a clever little colored child, isn't she?" She sips her tea.

"Of course she is. She comes from Chicago, you know, and that does make a difference."

"Oh, yes." Miss Eugenia nods absentmindedly. "It certainly does."

"You know, I think it would be such a lovely idea to get a little reading club together for some of our colored people here in town. . . . Thank you, Allison." Miss Elsie takes back the book, hands her the tray, and nods her dismissal. "You may take it out to the kitchen. This only goes to show what I've always known. That given the proper guidance, these people actually can learn to appreciate *les belles lettres*. . . ."

The conversation trails off as Allie pushes through the swinging doors with the tray of untouched sandwiches. She is smiling, flushed with the recent success of her oral reading. Big Momma looks at her sharply, then quickly unties the apron that had to be double-wrapped around her thin body.

"Don't let those old white womens fill your head with foolishness, hear?"

On Big Momma's next work day, Miss Elsie takes *Little Allison* along on a trip to the public library.

"The next book club selection is *A Tale of Two Cities*. Now, don't tell me you're going to have to order that, too, Lydia. Because I know better."

"Oh, but Miss Wheeler." The librarian's cheeks flush pink. "I'm sorry, but you know . . . well, she can't stay."

The Cairo Public Library is for whites only.

"Nonsense," Miss Elsie snaps. "This child is a visitor to Cairo, all the way from Chicago. She has a long summer ahead of her with no reading materials to speak of except the local newspaper. And we both know the *Register* is hardly fit to wrap fish in. She will browse through our meager holdings here and select anything she likes. Carry on, Allison."

And she does. She chooses several Agatha Christie mysteries and a title by Dickens, thinking she'd like to see exactly what he had said about the town. There turns out to be nothing about Cairo in this book about a band of pickpocket boys in old-time London. But it's a good book anyway.

Whenever they leave Miss Elsie's on Tuesday and Friday evenings, she always places a waxed-paper-wrapped bundle in Big Momma's hands. It might wind up being two slices of pecan pie, a few biscuits, a half loaf of bread, or whatever is left over from the last time Big Momma baked.

"Now, then, Miss Bohema. Take this home for yourself and little Allison."

Allie thinks it strange that Miss Elsie should be making a gift from the leftovers of what Big Momma is hired to bake for her.

"And don't even dream of thanking me. Run along home and enjoy this with your grandchild."

Big Momma grumbles all the way to the bus stop.

"She coulda kept these stale biscuits and give us a ride home," she sighs as they wait for the streetcar.

But she carries the package home anyway. The next day it will be transformed into bread pudding, crumbled into cobbler topping, or simply brushed with warm water and reheated in the oven. She can always find a use for things. Nothing goes to waste in Big Momma's house.

Big Momma's been telling me that *life ain't nothing but a dressmaker's pattern. If it don't suit you, just take it apart and remake it.*

That's what I been doing with my life since I was little. Sometimes I'd look out my window back home in Chicago. I'd squinch my eyes just so. And instead of seeing dirty streets and slum buildings I'd see the broken glass glinting like diamonds. The sunshine turning dusty red brick into gold. Mama called it daydreaming. I liked the way my granddad said it better: *window shopping.*

We used to go to Silver City, a big vacant lot on the outskirts of K-town where a metal stamping factory used to dump their trash. There were piles of shiny scraps with fancy designs punched out. We'd get it and twist it into bracelets and necklaces and tiaras, then crown two kids as the King and Queen. They'd parade around the neighborhood, their silver crowns sparkling in the sunlight.

I was never picked to be crowned, but I would come home and think about it. My raggedy life as a poor girl in K-town would disappear, and I'd be living in the lap of luxury as the shining Queen of Silver City.

After the aluminum factory closed down, me and Laura Lee used to get old Sears catalogs and cut out pictures of all the clothes, jewelry, and furniture we'd buy, and the people we'd be when we were rich and famous. We'd make them into paper dolls, put them in paper houses, and fix them up with a life right out of the Sears catalog.

And that's what I do with books. It's like going into a paper world where I can make myself into any one of those characters—brave pioneers from long ago, people who are everything I ain't and have everything I don't—rich, famous, white, pretty. If a story didn't go the way I wanted, or end the way I liked, I would sit down and write it over.

Why should the miller's daughter have to marry that greedy king who was ready to kill her dead if she couldn't spin gold from straw? Let him fall into the bottomless hole, too, right alongside Rumpelstiltskin.

Sometimes Big Momma sews clothes by *pinching off* of patterns—the sleeves from a Butterick, the collar from Simplicity, the bodice from Vogue. Sometimes she even makes her own patterns from brown shopping-bag paper.

I do the same thing with stories. Pinching the princess from *Snow White*, the hero from *Sleeping Beauty*, the love story from *The Little Mermaid*, and the happy ending from *Cinderella*.

Big Momma says I've been blessed with a story to tell. More and more now, I'm starting to tell stories of my own.

LATE JUNE

They had been waiting patiently for fifteen minutes. The dry goods shop wasn't crowded. But as they stood a little ways back from the counter, several white women had come in, been served, and left out again. It wasn't until the store was empty that the clerk, a white man with glasses and a bald head, seemed to notice them standing there.

"Well, hello there, Bohema. What can we get for you today?"

Though it stews in her mind all day, Allie doesn't mention it until much later that evening. After the notions had been unpacked and put away, after the butter beans bubbling on the stovetop and the cornbread rising in the skillet. She mixes a pitcher of lemonade while Big Momma sits in the rocking chair with her spectacles on, reading her Bible.

"Big Momma, you scared of white people?" Having been forced down all day, it comes rushing out like steam from a pressure cooker.

The old woman closes her Bible, takes off her reading glasses, and tilts her head in consideration.

"No," she finally answers. "I reckon not."

"Then how come you let that man wait on all those white people before he took care of us?" Allie asks, trying to keep accusation out of her voice.

Big Momma's response, as always, is calm, thoughtful. She meets her question with one of her own.

"Is that why you think I was scared of that man?"

"He was rude to us." This time the accusation is unhidden. "He called you by your first name. And you didn't even say nothing to him about it."

"What would you have said, Little Daughter?"

"That our money was just as good as those white people's. If he don't treat us right, then we take our business someplace else."

"And where would we'd have gone? Future City? They ain't got no dry goods there. Cape Girardeau? White folks treat you the same way."

"I don't care what you say." Allie will not relent. "It still ain't right."

Dinner is eaten in silence. When the dishes are washed and the leftovers put away, Big Momma takes off her house shoes and puts on the oxfords she wore into town earlier that day. She ties a blue kerchief around her head.

"Where you fixing to go?" the girl asks. Big Momma always wraps her head before she goes out.

"Come on, Little Daughter. We taking us a walk."

Big Momma likes to stroll along the hump of land that forms the Mississippi River levee. Two rivers hug the town, each with its own levee system. As levees go, she prefers this one. As rivers go, she prefers the Ohio. She remembers when the Mississippi used to be wide and lazy, the color of weak tea. Then *mens got to messing around*, digging it out so big boats could pass through. Now the river churns like coffee bubbling in a pot. Its deepened waters and swift currents have been known to pick up a person *and carry them somewhere they don't want to go.*

"Before picking machines come into fashion we used to climb up in the back of some farmer's pickup and ride over to Missouri come cotton harvest. It was hot, hard work but the singing and joking would make the time pass easy. But while your mouth was busy singing, your mind had to be busy watching out for them cottonmouths. You couldn't be so 'fraid of snakes that it kept you from getting your work done. But you had to be careful enough to see you wasn't getting ready to pinch a mouthful of viper, 'stead of a ball of cotton.

"And that's just how I think about white folks. You ain't got to be scared, but you is got to be careful."

Allie swats mosquitoes. She sucks her teeth and sighs. She has picked up one of Big Momma's favorite expressions of exasperation.

"Hmph. Up in Chicago we don't take no mess off no white folks. They do me dirty, I slap them down. No questions asked."

"Is that so?" Big Momma seems genuinely interested. "Y'all must have lots of fights going on between the colored and the white."

"Not really," Allie brags. "White folks don't too much mess with us. They know we don't play that."

But even as she speaks, three ugly incidents spring to mind. When she was nine years old they had gone to Riverview. Mama had gotten tired of standing in the long lines, and didn't care much for roller-coaster rides. They were allowed to go off on their own as long as she promised to behave, and keep a close eye on her brother.

While waiting in line for the Loop-de-Loop, she noticed that Benny had dropped back, staring hungrily at the polish sausage sandwich another boy was eating.

"Benny, come on," she had called. He seemed not to hear. "Benny! Oh, shoot."

She realized she would have to get out of line. She squeezed to the side of the narrow barricade, allowing the people behind her to pass. They were a middle-aged white woman with teased blond hair, a big sunburned man who might have been her husband, and an elderly man in Bermuda shorts who could have been father to either one of them.

"Aw, look," the woman cooed. She had a soft Southern accent. "She's letting the white folks go first. Ain't that a good little nigger?"

Allie Mae froze in embarrassed silence. She hadn't said a word, but grabbed Benny's hand and rushed away to wait in line for another ride.

The second time, they'd been living in a terrible apartment on 16th Street. On the second floor, right above a tavern. Nobody could sleep on Friday and Saturday nights, the noise was so loud. You could hear the jukebox bass booming up through the walls.

It was overrun with mice. They set traps almost every night. As soon as the lights were out you heard traps going off. Bap! Bap! Bap! Mama had told her to make batter for cornbread once. She emptied the cornmeal into a bowl and a mouse fell into it, whitened with cornmeal and ghostly looking. It jumped out of the bowl and scurried off.

The front-door lock went bad, fell loose and dangled useless for over a month. She heard Mama on the phone every day, begging the landlord to come fix it. For security, they braced a dresser and couch against the door. Not that it would actually stop someone from coming in, but it would give the family time to escape out the back door. Mama finally picked up the phone and told the landlord she wasn't paying rent until he did something about that lock.

One day after school someone did come in. Pushed his way in, toppling the dresser over onto the couch. Mama was in the bathroom. Allie went banging on the door, yelling that somebody was breaking in. It was the landlord. He barged right in, climbing over the fallen furniture. Mama shooed the family out the back door, the landlord chasing behind them. He caught up and grabbed Mama's arm.

He was tall, freckled, and red-haired. He had come to collect rent money one time before and he had been friendly to nine-year-old Allie Mae.

"My, you sure do have a lot of books." He had smiled, pointing toward the bookcase full of paperback novels, a twelve-year-old set of *Childcraft*, and overdue library books. "I'll bet you've read them all."

He wasn't very nice now.

"You deadbeat," he hollered, shaking Mama by the arm. "Where's my money? Huh? Where's my money?"

Though Benny was slow in the head, he was big in size. At the age of twelve he was almost as tall as Mama. And he worshiped the ground she walked on. He launched himself at the man, kicking, screaming, and biting. The landlord shook him off and stomped away. They moved out the next day.

And then, two years ago, Mama got the bright idea to have her go across town to a school in a white neighborhood. *An experiment in integration,* the newspapers said. *Access to excellence.* She had been neatly dressed in a starched white blouse and cotton print skirt, white anklets, and last year's gym shoes, freshened with white shoe polish. She was not afraid. Her friend Clarisse sat by her side. They whiled away the time playing hand-clapping games in what they thought at the time was Africa talk.

Eena meena kipsajeena
ooka kamaleena
acha kacha booma racha
I love you

I love coffee, I love tea
I love the colored boy and he love me.
Step out you White boy, you don't shine,
'Cause I'll get a colored boy to beat your behind.

Throughout the hour-long ride down Western Avenue, they giggled at the older boys in the back of the bus. Who bragged about what they would do to the first *hunky muh-fucka* who even looked at them the wrong way. Black eyes, bloody noses, and broken bones were mentioned.

When they reached the school building it took ten full minutes for the bus to park, there were so many people. They saw a Channel 9 news camera in the crowd.

"Hey, Mama," a boy in the back yelled out the window. "I'm on tee-vee!"

The brown boys and girls tumbled out, eager to be the first one on the news. And across the street, a screaming mob of white housewives broke through a police barricade, coming straight at them. Hollering mean and nasty things; some of them had accents.

"Black trash! Get out of our community!"

"Go back to Africa, jungle bunnies!"

"Nee-gah! Nee-gah!"

She and Clarisse looked at the boys from the back of the bus. They didn't seem so big and bad now, their eyes bucked in fear. It was going to be every child for herself. They all turned and sprinted to the safety of the open school door. A squat White woman who turned out to be Mrs. O'Neill, the principal, ushered them in.

"Kiss my shiny black ass, hunky ho's," one boy paused to call before dashing inside. His remark made that night's news.

Clarisse never seemed sickly. But ever since she moved to Chicago from Mississippi she was always in and out of the hospital. And she always came out looking as strong and healthy as when she went in.

She was short for her age, but well developed. At eleven years old she already had big hips and meaty legs and wore a B-cup brassiere. She looked like a short, squat, fully grown woman. When she jumped double dutch the boys would crowd around to watch her breasts bouncing.

One Indian summer afternoon the geography teacher asked Clarisse and a white boy to open the windows. With the windows open you could hear the housewives out there hollering *Nigger, go home*, just like they did every day. Clarisse stood there on her chubby legs, watching helplessly. Then she just keeled over, falling away from the window.

She was rushed off to the hospital for the last time. They had slacked off reporting school desegregation, but her death made that night's news. One of the white wives came on too, claiming they had freedom of speech and Clarisse's death wasn't their fault.

But after that they stopped yelling. Instead they silently marched up and down the streets carrying signs, until they finally must have realized that yellow school bus from the West Side wouldn't stop coming. The groups got smaller and smaller until one day there wasn't a single housewife out there.

The mosquitoes drone. The sun sinks into the muddy Mississippi waters. Big Momma watches her intently, as if her forehead were a window she could read memories through.

"What you thinking about, Little Daughter?"

And she can only shake her head hard, as if to send that hateful history scattering off into the twilight.

Later on Big Momma watches the ten o'clock news while her great-granddaughter finishes up the dinner dishes.

"Come quick," Big Momma calls suddenly. "King's on TV."

Allie immediately thinks of her father, known by that name. She dashes over in just enough time to see a close-up of Martin Luther King's face, stricken with anguish and pain. Blood is streaming down his cheeks like tears.

"What happened to him?"

"Dr. King and his peoples was marching someplace in Chicago. They threw and hit him with a rock."

Tears spring to Allie's eyes. She doesn't know if she is crying for the stoning of Dr. King, for the father she hasn't seen in seven years, or for some other reason. Big Momma reaches out and captures her onto her lap, rocking her like the big baby that she is.

"Big Momma," she breathes between sobs. "Why white folks treat us so mean?"

"You ask hard questions, child. I don't know. I reckon they figure they can get away with it."

Later that week a Negro soldier is arrested in Cairo, AWOL. Nobody knows exactly what happens in that jailhouse. The next day the *Register* reports he was found in his cell, hanging by his own belt. An apparent suicide.

Allie and Big Momma go to a meeting at St. Bernard's Catholic Church. The place is crammed packed. People are angry. Some are crying. Some call for justice. Others for vengeance. The organist tunes up for the opening song. *We Shall Overcome Some Day.*

Martin Luther King's anguished, hurting face is magnified inside that sweltering church. Over and over and over again.

My father was King Benjamin Peeples. Benny was named after him. Him and Mama broke up when we was very young, so I don't remember much about him, except that he was real big and tall. I take after him in height, but my mother in size. My father comes from Baltimore and most of his people still live out there. I never met none of them but Dads. That's my grandfather. And he's dead now.

Seems like most of the family folks I hear about are the women. Me and Mama. Pat and Auntie Lola. Big Momma and her nana, Proud Mary. I wonder what happened to all the boys.

"Seem like all our menfolk die off," Big Momma told me, "or wander off, or never get born. We a family of womenfolks. Always have been as far as I know. That's just the way it's been."

I thought it over. Most of my male relatives did seem to be missing in action. It was like they'd all gone off to war and never returned. Daddy long gone, Benny hid away, uncles and male cousins far off. Grandfathers dead. Otis Clemmons, that sorry excuse for a man, seemed to be the only one in the picture right now. I guess Big Momma was right.

"Course now," Big Momma looked at me intently, "just because that's the way it's been, don't mean that's how it's always got to be."

"I don't see how I can change it."

"You sure about that?" Big Momma insisted.

Was she trying to say that one girl could turn a whole history around? When neither she nor the other women in the family had been able to keep menfolks around, how was I supposed to succeed where they all had failed?

Not that I hadn't tried. When I was little I was convinced that all I needed to bring my father back was to find him. I had found a Benjamin Peeples in the phone book, called him up, and asked him was he my daddy. He sounded like a nice man. He really seemed sorry to tell me, *Naw, baby. It ain't me.*

I remember when my daddy lived with us. He used to tell stories all the time, saying French words he learned overseas in the army, telling about different white men who had tried to fight him, cheat him out of his money, or do him some kind of wrong.

"But Mr. Charlie met this boy right here." He would grin and ball up his right fist, pounding it hard into his open palm. "Hit that cracker upside the head so hard, left a black streak on him."

Mama was always arguing with him about something. She would stand up on a stool or the couch to meet him at his own level.

"You can't keep a job to save your life," she would holler. "You stay in the street all hours of the day and night, leaving me alone with these childrens."

"I'm doing the best I can," he would answer. "What else do you want from me?"

"I want you to do right."

But she never said what that *doing right* was. Daddy didn't hit or holler. He talked low, pushing the words between his teeth so that his *s*'s made a little whistle.

"I got to take mouth from the white man all day long. Be damned if I'm ready to take sssshit from you, woman."

And he would leave, the keys jingling between his fingers or a coat slung over his arm. He'd close the door firmly behind him. Sometimes Mama would holler at that door long after he'd already passed through it.

I don't remember when he left for the last time, whether it was one of those days Mama talked to the door. Whether it was one night when me and Benny were sleeping. Whether he went to work one day and just didn't come back.

I be wondering about my daddy a whole lot. If he's living or if he's dead. Does he still remember me, does he wonder if I look like him. Sometimes I'll pass a tall, stocky man on the street and wonder if that might not be him. But I never say a mumbling word.

No baby. It ain't me. I don't ever want to hear that said to me again.

THE FOURTH OF JULY

Big Momma is barbecuing for the holidays. She and her great-granddaughter have been preparing for days. They've made mountains of spaghetti and potato salad, simmered homemade sauce, seasoned shortribs and chicken legs, baked biscuits and cornbread and sweet potato pies. The Frigidaire is crowded with gallon jars of strawberry Kool-Aid.

The Cairo relatives come; tiny Aunt Truly and her three red-headed, raw-boned sons. Big Momma calls them *The Boys*. They arrive with wives and carloads of kids; all girls, not a red-haired one among them. Hordes of aunties and cousins drive in from St. Louis, family members Allie has never met and whose names she immediately forgets.

Everybody eats too much. The grown-ups drink CC and 7 UP, and gossip about the ones who didn't come. The kids play *Captain, May I?* and *Miss Sue from Alabama* late in the day, and hide behind trees to pop firecrackers.

"Hey, Little Mama," one of *The Boys* calls across the porch to Aunt Truly. "Ain't that Lula Mae and them coming up the road?"

The Browns have driven down from Phoenix. They arrive just before twilight, after most of the food and many of the relatives are gone. Allie is so happy to see people she knows, she abandons a game of *Whichaway Your Billy Be* and goes running to the car as it pulls up. Auntie Lola gives perfumed kisses and tugs at her hair.

"Ain't you getting big to be wearing those braids?" she fusses. "You look like a big ole long-legged baby."

Uncle Clyde, as he always does, asks *How's your pocket, pipsqueak?* And without waiting for an answer, fishes around in his and brings out a fistful of coins.

Cousin Pat climbs from the backseat, wearing blinding white shorts and sandals. She looks disdainfully around her, and Allie suddenly sees it all through her eyes. The little house with peeling paint, the sagging wooden steps, the children running about with barbecue sauce–smeared faces, the trampled weeds and wildflowers.

"Girl." She seems to be speaking more to herself than her younger cousin. "Can you believe this mess?"

Allie suddenly remembers how much she admires, and at the same time dislikes, her stuck-up cousin. She is uncomfortable sharing a bed with her later that night. Pat is unhappy, too, resentful at having been left behind while her parents drive to a motel in Cape Girardeau. She complains about everything: the strange-smelling house, the scratchy bed linens, and *old lady witch* sleeping on the horse-hair sofa in the living room.

"How we supposed to sleep with all that snoring?" She frowns, propped against the pillow in a white nightgown with pretty pink flowers. "I can't wait until Lola and Pop come back for me. We supposed to be at Expo '67 right now."

"What's that?"

Pat gives her the withering look she had expected.

"Don't you know nothing? It's the World's Fair, girl. The World's Fair. We driving down to St. Louis and flying from there to Montreal."

Not wanting to reveal her ignorance of what World's Fairs were all about, she listens intently for some clue as Pat drones on about their upcoming trip. The cute boys she was likely to meet, the new clothes she'd be wearing, the restaurants she'd be eating at, the money she'd be spending.

Allie doesn't even remember having fallen asleep, when she awakens with a start. She feels a faint dampness on the sheet beneath her, and wonders with alarm if she has wet the bed, something she hasn't done in years. Careful not to disturb the girl sleeping beside her, she reaches a cautious finger between her legs and brings it back smeared with blood.

Before she can stop herself she gives a muffled shriek. Pat awakens, looking sleepily around her.

"What's the matter with you?" She frowns into her cousin's face.

"I'm bleeding," she can only whisper, as if whispering would wish it all away. "I'm bleeding down there."

Pat lifts the covers and looks, clicking her teeth together impatiently.

"It's just your period," she says shortly, hopping from the bed. "Look at this mess. How come you didn't wear your ministration pad?"

"What?" The younger girl shakes her head, confused.

"This your first time?" Pat is disbelieving. "Big as you are?"

She sighs like an old soul. She hops down from the high bed, walks from the room, and returns a few moments later with Big Momma at her side.

"You ain't having your first monthly, is you?" Big Momma asks anxiously, peering at the red stain spreading against white sheets. "Yes, I believe you is."

Her great-grandmother regards her with a mixture of worry and something else. Could it be pride? She smiles faintly.

"Well, honey. You a woman now. Pat, go get me some cool water and some white rags from the sewing basket."

Allie Mae waits. Her cousin brings a pile of rags and water in a beaten metal bowl. Her great-grandmother's hands strip the gown from her, washing her gently but thoroughly. She sees the thinness of her own naked body. The face Pat makes as she gingerly takes the spotted cloth and drops it into the bowl. The red stain that spreads through once-clear water.

She watches as her womankin oil her cleansed body, working together in the dark, silent room. A clean, folded white rag is positioned between her legs and carefully anchored there by a length of blue beads Big Momma flashes from a cloth sack. Pat peers at the beads coiled around her cousin's waist. She reaches to touch them, tentatively.

"The beads are so pretty, Big Momma. But why you got them strung on this ugly leather cord?"

Big Momma settles herself between them on the high bed, hugging a girl to her bosom on either side.

"That ain't just no ordinary string, girls. That's a sho' nuff lion's tail."

Allie bursts into a fit of giggles, while Pat rolls her eyes and sighs.

"Seems like ya'll don't believe me. But let me tell you something that will make you think again.

Back in the old days, it used to be a hunter lived way back off in the woods. He ain't had no kind of shotgun, so any kind of meat he needed, he would catch in one of his traps.

Come one winter, it was cold like I don't know what. So many critters died that winter, hunter couldn't hardly catch enough to keep a bird alive, less more a man. Every day he went out there to check them traps, every day they come up empty.

Now if y'all knew anything about trapping animals, y'all would know that there's times when a critter gets caught but not kilt. Trap built like a set of metal jaws, propped open and covered with some leaves. Thang clang shut when a critter step on it. Usually kill it on the spot. But sometimes it'll catch the critter by the foot or the tail. And he be trying so hard to get out, why sometimes he'll chew away that foot or tail, run off and leave it behind.

Old hunter thought he would starve to death until one day his trap caught something. He looked inside and saw it wasn't nothing but a tail. Long, skinny tail with a puff of hair at the end. Ain't had much meat on it, but the hunter was hungry. He took it home, fried it up, and ate it.

Round about midnight, here come a growling at the hunter's door.

"Tailey-po," something out there went to howling. "I want my tailey-po."

Old hunter sit up in bed real sudden, think he just hearing things. Here it come again.

"Tailey-po. Give me my tailey-po."

Hunter's eyes bug out just as big.

"I ain't got your tailey-po. Let me alone."

Hunter don't hear nothing again, so he go on back to sleep. Next night, same thing happen.

"Tailey-po," something howl outside the door. "I want my tailey-po."

"I ain't got your tailey-po. Let me alone."

Hunter go on back to sleep. But the next night, Lord help him.

"Tailey-po. I want my tailey-po."

This time the hunter come up right mad, because this thing been bothering him three nights in a row.

"Looka here," he hollers back. "I been done ate that tail. Ain't no way on God's earth you having it back, so let me alone."

Hunter man turn over, get ready to go back to sleep. Suddenlike, come a howl like you ain't never heard before, the door flies open. And here sits a big old mean she-lion in the hunter's doorway.

In two jumps she fly across the room, jump on poor hunter, and tear into him like he tore into that chicken-fried tail when he had it on his plate.

"Tailey-po," the lion finally say when she through. "I got my tailey-po."

"And this," Big Momma finishes, "is the very same lion tail Allie Mae got wrapped around the waist. What you think of that?"

Allie Mae reaches between the blue beads, fingering the withered cord, stiff and crackly with age.

"This a lion's tail for real?" she asks with wonder.

"No, that ain't no lion tail," Pat snaps. "It's a tall tale. How's a lion gonna be loose in Cairo, Illinois?"

"Who say it had to be Cairo?" Big Momma smiles mysteriously. "Our family goes back to other places, baby girl."

"Like where?" Allie wants to know.

"Africy. The old country. Guinea Land. And these beads been with us for a way long time."

Pat's sharp little face puckers, considering.

"Family heirlooms," she breathes. "I bet they're worth a fortune. Can I have them?"

Big Momma smiles, and pats her ponytailed head.

"Maybe one day, child. Just wait and we'll see."

With the bed sheets changed, in a fresh gown, her skin supple and glowing, the soft cloth nestled between her legs, and the blue beads hugging her waist, the girl is ready again for sleep.

Pat and Big Momma regard her, a knowingness in their eyes.

"You know what this means, don't you, Allie?" Pat lifts an eyebrow. "You can have a baby now. You better watch yourself."

Big Momma heaves a fulsome sigh and lowers herself to her knees.

"Yes, Lord. The first blood of her womanness. We gone have to pray for her."

Pat makes an impatient sound.

"Do we have to? I'm tired."

But something in Big Momma's firm manner stills her complaints. Sighing and reluctant, Pat sinks down beside her.

"God Jesus," Big Momma murmurs into clasped hands. "We want you to look after our Little Daughter here. Let her come into love in her own time. Allow her to know the gift of birth, but not before she's blessed to receive it. Don't let her be a mother 'fore she knows what it is to be a woman. We asks these blessings in Jesus' name."

"Amen," sighs Pat. "Now can we go to sleep?"

I can't sleep again for the rest of the night. I keep remembering the knowing look in their eyes. The cloth between my legs and the beads at my waist. The things I still don't understand. The new things I'm beginning to know.

I could have a baby now. But first I'd have to do the P-U-S-S-Y. Something tells me I don't have to worry about getting pregnant for a long time. A long, long time.

MID-JULY

Allie Mae had thought it might be fun having some company. But Pat makes a habit of being contrary. She never wants to do anything her cousin suggests, protesting that playing paper dolls and dress up, freeze tag and Hide and Go Seek are just *too childish*.

The only thing they have in common is their reading. And even then, they don't seem to share the same interests. Pat has a penchant for romance novels, the kind set among the English gentry, with the heroine handily situated as a governess on the hero's estate. Allie likes love stories too, but the ones where the hero and heroine have to ride the high seas, tame the flaming desert, and overcome great odds to be together. She also reads adventure stories and comic books.

"Why you like to read all those boy comics?" Pat asks one day as they lounge on the front porch swing. "You need to get you some *Archies*."

"I don't like *Archie*. That's just a silly red-headed white boy." The comic book character also uncomfortably reminds her of an old landlord, but she does not care to divulge that information.

"Oh, *The Incredible Hulk* and *The Amazing Spider-Man*. That's real serious, right?"

Allie Mae tries to explain her point.

"These are super heroes, Pat. They get to do things, go places. They have adventures. Let me tell you . . ."

"I don't want to hear it," Pat warns.

It is going to be one of their verbal tugs-of-war, and Allie is determined to be the winner this time.

"Just let me say this one thing. You see, this dude Peter Parker was a scientist bit by a radioactive spider and he got all these super powers, see . . ."

"I am not listening," Pat announces, fingers plugged firmly in her ears.

"No, let me tell you. It's exciting. He can make a web of super tensile strength and capture his enemies . . ."

"*La-la-la, la-la-la*," Pat hums loudly, trying to drown out her cousin's rising voice.

There is no telling how long the showdown would have lasted, the girls were capable of keeping it going all night. But just then Pat's grandmother shuffles onto the porch, a jelly jar of Big Momma's homemade muscadine wine clinking with ice cubes.

Allie always enjoys a visit from Great Aunt Truly. There is something delicious and vaguely scandalous about her. She remembers that Sunday at Mount Shiloh, Big Momma bustling about her ushering duties. Reverend Isley preached his sermon from John 4. Jesus asked the fallen woman at the well for a drink of water, but she said she had nothing to draw it with.

And just as the Reverend shouted:

"*And he whom thou now hast is not thy husband.*" She heard a hard whisper from the pew behind her. *Just like Truly, that hussy of Miss Bohema's.*

There is nothing much of the hussy in her appearance. Truly is short and bowlegged, round and brown. She has the kind of baby-fine curls folks like to call *good hair*, but she seldom bothers to get it done. Two unstraightened plaits are pinned across the top of her head, the tendrils around her temple plastered down with sweat. A faint mustache glows with perspiration above her upper lip. She settles heavily onto the swing between them, smelling of sweat and wine.

"What y'all girls know good?"

Allie thrusts the comic into her hands.

"I was just trying to tell Pat about the Amazing Spider-Man."

"*La-la-la, la-la-la!*"

Aunt Truly takes the comic from her, but instead of reading, she begins to fan herself with it.

"Lord, it's a hot one. Now, you girls think this boy in the funny book is something to write home about? I'm fixing to tell you about a real amazing spider man. Y'all ready?"

Pat sighs and moves her fingers from her ears. Allie slides from the crowded swing to the splintery porch floor. She snuggles between Aunt Truly's legs, counting the corns on her slippered feet. The sun slips behind the Mississippi River levee, like butter on a brown biscuit. A faint full moon emerges. Aunt Truly sips wine, fans sweat, and begins to speak.

You ever wonder why the spider runs around with that little bitty head on him? Wasn't always that way. Spider once had him a big old head, in more ways than one.

But you see, that spider just studied trouble. Seem like trouble was his middle name. Trouble took him some of everywhere, even to death and back.

One night just around twilight, full moon breaking through the sunset, just like it is now. Old big-headed Spider Man was looking for him some trouble. So he went a slipping across the bridge of life, off on into Dead Folks Town.

Soon as he got there he seen a colored woman, a white woman, and a Indian woman setting along the riverside. Now, these wasn't regular womens. They was old, poorly, hungry-looking ghost grannies.

"Hey, spider baby," they come calling. "What business you got in Dead Folks Town?"

Spider's big old head went right to work on his lie.

"Evening, grannies. I'm here to visit my old Aunt Sadie. Don't pay me no mind. Carry on with what y'all doing."

But the ghost grannies gathered round.

"And what you bring your Aunt Sadie to eat?"

No sooner had they said it, than Spider recollected that when you come to see your dead kinfolk, you had to bring along a little something for them to eat. He reached in his waistcoat pocket and pulled out a stale peanut, all soft and mushy. Held it out in his open hand.

But before he could say skit-skat, the grannies snatched that shriveled-up peanut, pinched it into three pieces, took one each, and gobbled it down.

"Y'all hadn't oughta did that. That peanut was for old Aunt Sadie." Spider was right mad, but not because his auntie would go hungry. He was meaning to chew that peanut hisself on the way back home.

The ghost grannies went to apologizing.

"Forgive us, son. We so hungry we done forgot our manners. Our peoples has just plain forgotten us. They ain't brought so much as a dry bone for us to chew on. Your auntie sure is blessed to have a boy like you."

"Well, least y'all could do," Spider grumbled, "is offer a man a cool drink of water."

Now the white ghost, y'all know white womens don't like to wait on nobody. She come a telling him: "We ain't got nothing to dip it up with."

But the red ghost, she said: "Hold on now, Sister. Spider is company, and the boy say he's thirsty."

Now, back in those days travelers used to carry around a cup cut from the end of a hollow squash. They called it a drinking gourd. They would use it to dip up sweetwater from any clean-flowing stream or river. Well, the ghost grannies ain't had no drinking gourds. So they took off their bony heads and dipped them in the water for Spider to drink from. Can you imagine that?

"You thirsty, baby? Here, take a little drink of water."

And after Spider had drunk his fill, the ghost grannies tucked those heads under their arms and went to dancing. Now dead folks, they don't dance like we do. They don't know nothing about Walking the Dog or the Funky Four Corners. Help me up, honey.

Allie takes the glass, Pat pulls her grandmother to a standing position. Aunt Truly puts a hand on one hip and begins a slow shuffle, her slippers slapping the wooden porch.

So they went to hamboning, shaking those knee joints and beating those thigh bones. Oh children, it was something to see. They took to beating the river with they heads, splashing up a storm and making a spooky kind of music.

Y'all girls know what is a shak-shak, one of them rattles folks used to make from a hollow gourd? Lord, them boneheads went to shaking like shak-shaks, the mouths in them justa singing.

> *The Black Dead beat the water with their drinking gourds;*
> >   *the Ghost Grannies Band!*
> *The Red Dead beat the water with their drinking gourds;*
> >   *the Ghost Grannies Band!*
> *The White Dead beat the water with their drinking gourds;*
> >   *the Ghost Grannies Band!*

Children, it was terrible. But Spider, he was really enjoying hisself. He shook his big head from side to side, dancing the jitterbug. And he commenced a-singing, too.

> *The Black Dead beat the water with their drinking gourds,*
> >   *the Ghost Grannies Band!*

But the ghost grannies hushed him up quick.

"No, baby. This a ghost song. When the living sing it, ain't no telling what might happen."

So Spider went on back across the bridge. Next day he told all his friends and kin-folk. But since Spider was known to stretch the truth from time to time, ain't nobody believed a word of it.

"Every child knows," said Take-It-To-Me, Spider's son, "that can't nobody go to Dead Folks Town and come back to tell about it."

"You little mannish so and so!" Spider smacked him upside the head. "I'm fixing to show you I been to Dead Folks Town."

And he commenced a-singing.

> *The Black Dead beat the water with their drinking gourds;*
> >   *the Ghost Grannies Band!*

The Red Dead beat the water with their drinking gourds;
   the Ghost Grannies Band!
The White Dead beat the water with their drinking gourds;
   the Ghost Grannies Band!

Then skit-skat! As quick as that, Spider's big head split open like a peanut shell. And there inside was a head no bigger than the shriveled peanut he had left behind on the other side.

"Oh, Lord, help me!" Spider went to screaming, running to and fro. "Ghost grannies of Dead Folks Town, give me back my big head!"

But all that crying couldn't help. It wasn't nothing they could do for him, way over yonder across the river.

"Well, Papa," Take-It-To-Me said, looking at his father's peanut head, "I guess you really have been to Dead Folks Town."

"And ever since then," Truly concludes, draining the last drop of wine from her jelly jar, "Spider Man been running the world with a peanut for a head."

"Hey, now. What you say! Can old Truly tell a story, or what?"

That night I dream I get bit by a radioactive spider and turn into the Amazing Spider Woman. Whirling like a dervish, I fire out a web of super tensile strength. The superweb stretches all the way across Cairo, from the Ohio River to the Mississippi. It shimmers with drops of water, shining like jewels. Caught in each drop is a woman's face: Aunt Truly, Big Momma, Mama, Aunt Lola, Pat.

And I am not afraid. Never have I felt such power.

EARLY AUGUST

They look just like a pair of pale brown breasts resting together on the plate. Big Momma lifts the cloth from the twin lumps of swollen dough.

"Is it ready to cook yet?" the girl asks anxiously.

"Be patient, child. This is just the first rising."

Big Momma gives one ball of dough to Allie Mae and takes one for herself. While they work the bread dough between their hands they work between their lips the news of the Ballards, a couple on one of the afternoon stories. Angela Ballard has plotted and successfully carried out the murder of her husband, Richard. Big Momma and her great-granddaughter carefully nibble at the crime, their regret seasoned with relish. As if dissecting the sordid tragedy of people they knew well.

"Well, honey, I'll tell you this. I hate to see somebody lose his life. And I know that killing's a crime before God. But Richard Ballard shoulda knowed he was coming to a bad end. That man wasn't right. He was a ill wind that blew no good."

"But he coulda been helped, Big Momma. If only Angie had gave him another chance, her love might have saved him."

"Can't one somebody be another one's salvation. Only one coulda helped that man was he himself."

"But she loved him," Allie insists. "She really loved him. And he loved her."

"Loving ain't everything."

"Big Momma!" The child is aghast. "Love conquers all!"

"Naw, honey. Sometimes all conquers love. I loved Simon Winfield. He left one day, took off upriver and I never seed him again. I loved Luther Patterson. He loved me, too. Plus all the other womens in Alexander County. I loved Joe Lee Bullocks, your great-grandaddy. He died. All my loving couldn't save nary a one of them."

The girl looks closely at her great-grandmother's loose arms and lined face. The idea of Big Momma loving all these men is cause for amazement.

"Big Momma, I didn't know you'd been married three times."

"Three times in the church. I'm not counting Hosea Ennols. We just lived together. Course we did have one child, your Great Aunt Truly."

"Big Momma! You mean to say people were shacking way back then?" The girl has forgotten to punch down her bread dough and it is slowly waning, like the passing of a full moon.

"Don't you be getting no ideas, Little Daughter. I was young, foolish, and I wasn't saved. I found the Lord after that and married all my husbands in the church. Now you get your mind off mens and back to work."

Beyond the kitchen window she can see a group of boys and girls romping in the overgrown weeds near the levee. It has rained off and on for four days and the Mississippi is beginning to flood. Her brown waters haven't broken through the levee, but are seeping up in puddles through the ground. Big Momma calls it *sipe water*. They can hear the children hollering and playing as they search the puddles for crawdads.

"Big Momma," the girl wonders. "What's it like being married?"

She sighs from somewhere deep within her. Somewhere past four husbands and happiness and heartbreak. Past one child lost, one dead at birth, and another three she's outlived. Past two children surviving, twelve grands, and nine greats. Somewhere past the four generations she's lived and the pain and pleasures that have seasoned her long life.

"I guess marriage kinda like making bread."

"Bread?" The girl watches Big Momma's hands deftly shape and reshape the dough.

"You got to tend it well. Mix it right, set it out, and give it time to rise. Work it, but don't worry it. Don't bake it before it's ready, do it falls right down." She punches down the dough flat with her fist.

"What about love?"

"That's the first ingredient. Like flour, you can't make bread without it. But you need more. The salt and the sugar, the leavening and the shortening. Yeah, I reckon making marriage is something like making a good loaf of bread."

Later on the brown loaves cool on the table, while Big Momma sharpens the bread knife. The baking has transformed the loaves and made their differences obvious. One loaf is as full and rounded as a well-endowed woman. The other is shrunken and flat.

Allie watches as Big Momma carefully cuts two slices off the full loaf and puts them on a plate.

"Want to try some of your'n?" The knife hovers above the dwarfed loaf. She thumps it with the knife and it makes a solid sound.

Allie Mae shakes her head.

"I wonder what went wrong."

"Musta forgot something. Not enough yeast. Or maybe you was so busy carrying on about love that you forgot to knead it right."

Big Momma wraps the rejected loaf in waxed paper. She will find some use for it. The girl is at the refrigerator door.

"You want butter or mayonnaise on your sandwich, Big Momma?"

"Neither one," she replies. "I like them but they don't like me. So I leaves them alone. Now what kind of lunch meat you get at the store?"

Allie unwraps the brown butcher paper to reveal four thin, pink slices.

"What's that supposed to be?"

"You mean you ain't never seen ham?" The girl carves off two thick slices of homemade bread, smears them both with a generous dollop of butter, and sandwiches two slices of meat in between. "Try it. It's good."

Big Momma snorts and eats her bread plain.

"Hmmph. They plump that stuff full of water and salt and sell it for a fortune. That's not what I call ham."

"I didn't know there was any other kind."

"You ain't tasted ham then. We used to home cure it ourself, back when we was keeping hogs. Every year at killing time we'd fix up about fifteen, twenty big ones. You pack your fresh meat in rock salt, then you smoke it for months, sometime near bout a year. And the last ham of the batch always tasted better than the first. Ham wasn't for everyday eating, like fatback and hock bones. Honey, we couldn't wait for holidays to roll around."

"Well, you'll never guess who I saw at the store when I went to get this ham." The girl's patience with ham has expired. She has juicier news to tell. "Mr. Holloway. You know Mr. Holloway, he's a deacon at church?"

"Been knowing him all my life. Fred Holloway bout lives on the front porch of that grocery store. Seeing him there ain't no news."

"Well, he asked after you. Said he'd love to come and call on you sometime." She darts a sly glance at her great-grandmother's impassive face. "He said you were a fine woman, to be your age."

Big Momma brushes bread crumbs from the table to her hand.

"Oh, he did? Did you tell him he was a no 'count stuff-talking somebody? To be his age."

"Aw, Big Momma. That's a nice-looking old man. Wouldn't you like to have somebody around to keep you company in your old age?"

"Not if that somebody's Fred Holloway. He don't do nothing with his days but hang out in front of the grocery store, and nothing with his nights but drink whiskey down to the Cavalier Club. I rather not to have nobody than to have me a lazy, trifling somebody."

"But don't you get lonely living here by yourself?"

Big Momma unwraps the corner of Allie's hard loaf and breaks off a piece. She chews on it thoughtfully.

"Hmmm. Taste kinda like a soda cracker."

"Big *Momma*," the girl insists. She wants her question answered.

"I'm coming, girl. I'm coming." Big Momma frowns. "Ain't nothing I hate worse than being rushed."

She pauses, breaks another corner. Allows silence to settle in the interval. Ignores the young one's nervous shifts and impatient shuffles.

"Little Daughter," she finally says. "The best way to have a man is not to need one. If God spares you to live as long as I have and see as much as I've seen, you'll soon find out that there's worser things than being lonely."

The girl picks up the invisible hat of another woman's style and puts it on.

"I don't know about that. I'm a man's woman, honey. A boy's girl, baby. Always got to have me a do-right, all night man."

Big Momma shoots her a quick look that cuts through her like a carving knife. The same look she aims at the mouse before bringing the broom down on him. A look that says *What kind of mess you bringing into my kitchen, creature?*

"You a man's woman, huh? How many mens you been a woman to?"

"Big Momma!" The invisible hat topples from her head. The sophisticated city woman is a girl again, protesting her innocence. "I ain't never did that before."

"Did what, Little Daughter?"

"You know," she squirms.

"I do?" Big Momma is going to make her say the word.

"I ain't never did sex with a man."

"Oh? Then what kind of man's woman are you?"

Her cheeks deepen, a blush on a brown D'Anjou pear.

"Big Momma, it's just a figure of speech."

"A figure of speech. What you mean by that?"

Big Momma could go on like that for hours. Turning her every stray remark into a question. Worming her way through the pear until she struck the core of truth.

"It's just something you say. Just . . . words."

"Oh, ain't no such thing as *just words*. When you say something, child, you got to be ready to own it. Sticks and stones will break your bones, but words will hurt you worser. Now you the one always be writing things down. You tell me what a man's woman is. Do that mean the man owns the woman?"

"No, no." She struggles to defend her crumbling position. "It's just that, you know. Men and women supposed to be together. Love makes the world go around."

"Thought you said love conquered all."

"Well, same thing. It's like, none of the books I read or the shows I watch or the dreams I dream, none of them don't mean much unless there's a love story in it."

"You didn't say *love story*." Big Momma wouldn't let it go. "You said *a man's woman*. I want to know what that means. The man wear the woman, like a suit of clothes? He find a new woman, he change his suit? She get a new man, she be the new man's woman? Or what if it ain't no man there, like it ain't none in my house? Then whose woman she is? Nobody's woman?"

The girl is frustrated, confused. Beaten down beneath the force of Big Momma's reason. Not knowing what to say, but unwilling to admit defeat, she resorts to one of her old tricks. Sullen disrespect.

"So I guess I'm supposed to never like boys or fall in love or get married or nothing. Just get old and dried up, sit around looking like death eating a soda cracker."

Big Momma is too wise for that trick. To respond to insolence with anger, and derail the lesson in chastisement. She surprises her with laughter.

"Lordy mercy, that's a new one. I been called *old*, but this the first time I been called *death*."

"I wasn't talking about you, Big Momma."

"If you going to say it, own it. Don't turn around and lie about it. And don't be putting words in my mouth, neither. I ain't never told you don't like menfolk. Love them. Love them with the fullness of your heart. But don't never make yourself into somebody else's woman. You ain't nobody's woman but your own. Even the Lord wants you to come to yourself before you give your soul to him."

Big Momma is quiet for a while, breaking off yet another piece of bread to crunch.

"You don't have to eat that, Big Momma. It can't taste too good."

The older woman shakes her head.

"You know, there's ways to make bread without leavening, Little Daughter. Hot water to cornbread will raise it up. And when Moses led the Hebrews out of Egypt they didn't have no time to take up yeast. They had to eat unleaven bread."

"How does it taste?"

"It don't taste bad. Kinda hard to get used to if you been eating risen bread all your life. But just because you ain't got yeast, don't mean you can't enjoy your bread. You just got to get used to a different way of living."

"Something tells me you're not talking about bread, Big Momma."

She continues on, seeming to speak more to herself than to the child.

"Get used to living without butter, when the butter don't do you good. Get used to doing without home-cured ham, if it ain't nothing but that pink meat in the butcher shop. Get used to living without the company of menfolk, when the good ones scarce and ain't nothing but trifling to choose from."

Big Momma gives her another one of those piercing looks. Like she can see through to the center of her soul.

"So you go ahead on and eat your ham sandwiches, Little Daughter. And let this old lady enjoy her unleaven bread."

MID-AUGUST

Allie Mae is shaken out of a deep sleep. She awakens expecting to see sunlight in the open space between the cafe curtains. Instead she is greeted by a full moon. It silhouettes Big Momma's kerchiefed head, topped off by a battered straw hat.

"Wake up and get dressed."

"What's going on, Big Momma?" Her voice is heavy with sleep.

"Don't you remember? We going fishing."

She sinks back into the comfort of the high bed.

"Aw, Big Momma. I don't want to."

"You going all the same. I told you to get yourself to bed early so you would be rested. But no, you had to set up and look at TV until all hours. Well, we ain't got time to waste now, Little Daughter. It'll soon be day. Rise and shine."

Before day, moonlight finds them tramping side by side. Heads bent slightly against the late summer chill. Each wears a pair of floppy galoshes, carries a pail and fishing pole. The girl is still grumbling, her drowsiness assaulted by the onslaught of fresh air.

"Why we got to get up so early?"

"Because the early bird catches the worm. And the fattest worm makes the best fishing."

They follow the railroad tracks along the edge of town for a time. When the tracks meet the levee and turn east, they bear west and cross Commercial to Washington. They pass through the center of town, past the library, the shops with darkened windows, the police station, and the Halliday Hotel. Right on the outskirts, before Washington Street gathers its breath to climb up and bridge the Mississippi, they turn off and walk down a dirt road.

They can hear water moving ahead, and after a short walk they can see it. In the failing moonlight, rivers converge from east and west, joining together at a point of land to make one way of water.

Moving down to meet the water at its own level, they settle on the narrow peninsula that juts out into the waters. Dawn is breaking. The water is so wide you can't see across it. If she hadn't noticed the Ohio and Mississippi coming together in the darkness, she would have thought this body of water a lake.

"Why we had to come so far?"

"The Point is the best fishing place in these parts. Fish get lost in some of these currents, they just swim in a circle, waiting to be caught."

"Why they call it *the Point?*"

Big Momma patiently skewers squirming nightcrawlers between chunks of cold salt pork, like shish kebabs on the curved hooks.

"If you see it from above, this little piece of land looks like a finger pointing out where the Mississippi meets the Ohio. Some folks call it Fort Defiance, 'count of the soldiers had this piece of land during the war."

"World War One or World War Two?"

"Civil War. This was a busy place then. Guns and all kinds of fighting goods came down here along the rivers and the railroad. General Grant and his boys camped out on this little piece of land, unloading supplies and watching out in case the rebels decided to come this way by water."

"You were around during the Civil War? But that was, let me see . . ." She busily calculates. "A hundred years ago!"

"I'm glad to see you know your history. But I ain't going to hit a hundred for at least another twenty years. When I was young I used to sit around and listen to the old folks talk when the war was still fresh on their minds. One old colored man, dirt farmer from out to Pulaski County. He had swore he'd never sharecrop for nobody. He joined up thinking he'd get to fight the rebels, wound up down here unloading barges. Never got over it."

The sun seems to stir, yawning in its bed of fluffy horizon. Then slowly it awakens, stretches itself out. And rises. It eases up the sky, lighting the water, waking the fish, and warming the bones of the child and woman sitting on an out-stretched rock, fishing rods dangling in changing waters.

Big Momma is right. The fish are plentiful this morning. Whenever she gets a bite, Big Momma wades out in her rubber boots and hauls it in. At every tug on the girl's string, Big Momma puts hers aside and shows her how to pull it in. Before long she has the hang of it.

Something about the morning doesn't call for much conversation. Woman and girl share a companionable silence sitting in the soothing warmth of sun, listening to the lapping of waters and the calling of birds.

By midmorning their pails are filled with glistening, flopping fish. Big Momma builds a small fire. With her great-granddaughter's inexpert help, she scales and cleans the fish, smokes them in groups of three over the fire, and wraps them in leaves.

"I guess it's time to be getting on back." Big Momma eases the battered straw hat back on her head. "The sun be overhead directly."

She stands up, stretches, then gazes along the water; first up the Ohio, then the Mississippi, narrowing her eyes as though she is searching for something unseen. The girl is curious.

"What you looking for, Big Momma?"

The older woman, as is often her way, answers the question with another question.

"What you see out there, Little Daughter?"

The young woman looks closely at the elements of the scene around them. And names them.

"Water. Sun. Sky. Land. Birds."

The old woman sighs, as if expecting a delivery that has not arrived.

"Then I reckon that's all there is."

Allie Mae waits. She feels a story coming on. She is not mistaken.

"Been coming here ever since I was small. Nigh on eighty years. Nana Proud Mary, my great-grandmama, used to bring me out here, just like I'm doing you. It was something about this place that was special to her. Almost holy. We'd come down here to fish and we would do us some fishing.

"Most folks will take their fish on home and fry it fresh. But Nana liked hers smoked. You salt it up good, smoke it slow, take it home, and dry it out. And when folks' fried fish is long gone, you still got some that will keep awhile outside the Frigidaire.

"Yeah, we'd come out here to fish, but Nana would be watching, too. Watching the water for I don't know what. Ain't had no way of knowing that one day I'd be down here watching.

"Folks say I'm old-timey for still using a pole when they got rods and reels at the hardware store. But Nana, she caught fish like I never seen nobody do then or since. In little reed baskets she made with her own hands. After Nana passed I still came out and fished by myself. Seemed like I always had me a taste for smoked fish. Seemed like this was the only one place I could remember her good. I could almost feel her, setting right here next to me. I reckon I was near about as old as you are right now. And it was here, right on this little flat rock that I first saw him."

"Saw who, Big Momma?"

"Him. Simon Winfield. I came out here before day and there was a oil barge anchored yonder. You see where them cattails coming up? The water is real clear and shallow there. Seen this bald head, just a bobbing. Simon Winfield was in there taking his morning bath."

Allie has heard the name before in Big Momma's stories. But it was always just another name in an endless procession of names and people and places she does not know.

"Who is Simon Winfield?"

Big Momma looks intently at the cattails waving in the breeze.

"Simon was my first real man. He was quite a bit older than me. About twenty-five years old, I reckon. He was a traveling man, a river man. Worked as a cook on that barge, docked here in Cairo taking on a load of cottonseed oil. When that barge headed up the river, Simon Winfield wasn't on it. He was courting.

"Mama and them didn't hold with me taking up with somebody like that. Said he had river water stead of blood running in his veins and wouldn't never be settled. Said he was too old for me, and I was too young to turn myself into a river man's widow. We had to run off and get married."

"What happened then?" Her curiosity is blazing.

Big Momma frowns suddenly.

"I ain't never been a traveling woman, Little Daughter. I always been one to stay put. White folks in Cairo didn't just get mean yesterday. They always been ornery. It was hard being colored in Cairo back in 1899.

"He said he wasn't stopping here but for a minute. He was always on me to pick up and leave with him. Especially after I had the baby."

The girl is shocked into momentary silence.

"You had a baby? When you were just fourteen?"

"Thirteen," she corrects. "Your age. I wasn't a strong healthy thirteen. I was weak and poorly, still playing with rag dolls. Had such a hard time with that baby, they didn't think I was going to make it. I had closed my eyes, ready to give up and meet my maker. I heard the sound of water running, seems like I felt my great-grandmama's hands on me. When I open up my eyes, my baby was in my arms. We named her Earlene, 'count of she was born early in the morning. Just before day."

"You mean I got a great-aunt Earlene. Where she at?"

Big Momma turns, gazing upriver in first one, then the other direction.

"Lord knows, child. I loved him but I didn't want to leave out of here with Simon. I thought my loving would settle him down. I was young and didn't want to leave my mama and daddy and all the peoples been knowing me all my life. Come on, child. Time to be getting back home. Noontime sun coming up."

They turn away from the confluence, their pails heavy with bundles of leaf-wrapped fish, still warm. They trudge back toward town, their footsteps weighted by their burdens.

"I knew that the Klan was riding the night. Colored folks losing their land and their lives. Simon Winfield just wanted better for his daughter. And I watched them boarding that barge. I waved them off. He said he was taking Early to see some of his people up in Cape Girardeau. She wasn't even two years old yet. Wasn't even talking good. But she talked that morning. Said *Bye-bye, Mama* just as clear. And they took off, upriver. Ain't never seen them again, neither one of them."

The story's ending hits the girl in the knees. She stops in the road and drops her pail, her pole and string.

"Big Momma, no." Fresh tears brim in her eyes. "That man stole your baby? Your first-born child? Just took her off and disappeared?"

Big Momma lowers her head, tilting the straw hat forward against the punishing sun.

"It was his baby, too, Little Daughter. Always said he wanted a life for her where she could come up on land of her own, not sharecropping for somebody else. Not knowing the fear of men in white sheets burning crosses in the night. I sure hope he found it."

They reach the rise where the dirt road meandered out onto Washington. They turn, looking back on the waters below them: the Ohio, lolling westward like a long blue tongue; the Mississippi churning eastward like a wide and brown arm. And at the confluence, becoming one way of water. They meet but do not mingle. The thin strip of blue, the wide swathe of brown flow side by side, southward toward Missouri. A barge moves down the middle, catching up the point where brown meets blue, trailing it out like a ribbon behind it.

Big Momma shades her eyes with one hand, surveying the scene below.

"As long as I live I'm going to remember little Earlene smiling and waving *Bye-bye, Mama*. Going to hear Simon calling out *We be back directly, woman.* And you know, Little Daughter, I believe my lost blood is out there somewhere calling me. I pray for my lost daughter, for all the lost childrens.

"If I had been a different kind of woman, I would have followed these rivers and looked for her. Took one of them, and if I didn't find her, then the other. But I wasn't a traveling woman. I was a waiting woman.

"I keep waiting, one year after the next. Waiting for Simon Winfield to bring my baby back. And it's been sixty-something years. I guess I'm just an old fool. I'm yet waiting, and yet praying. I still expects to see them back one morning, chugging down the river on that barge from Cape Girardeau."

I don't believe I'll ever get married.

Look what happened to Big Momma. Had a baby at thirteen, and the daddy comes and kidnaps the baby right in front of her face. Look at Mama, got a leech like Otis hanging on her. Look at Laura Lee Flowers, a mother at the age of thirteen. Look at me, walking around with a police record. All behind some no-account man.

I can see why Big Momma likes to live alone. I don't blame her. You love a man, he ain't going to do nothing but leave you anyway. Just like Daddy left Mama and me and Benny. Just like Dads disappeared, ain't never heard from him again. Just like Junebug turned his back on Laura Lee after she went and had a baby for him.

Big Momma is right. Love don't conquer all. All conquers love. I have decided right here and now. Menfolk are something I just ain't got no use for.

LATE AUGUST

The girl watches the hands of her great-grandmother. Brown and gnarled as old oak. The joints swollen with seamstress' arthritis. Strange how hands so old and stiff can move so nimbly. Like solid brown dancers, moving to the drumbeat of the treadle. Big Momma works the machine as if it were an extension of her hands. Smoothing out the fabric as it emerges, transformed by the needle.

"What you making, Big Momma?"

"Adding a patch to the family quilt. Snake Following the North Star."

Allie would have laughed if Big Momma's face hadn't been so grim.

"Where'd you get that idea?"

Big Momma pumps the peddle, pushes the fabric, and sighs.

"Look, child, I'm a God-fearing Christian woman. I don't hold with haints and hoodoo and suchlike."

Her hands push. The fabric flies. The old machine clicks and clatters like a rattlesnake giving warning.

"But God works in mysterious ways, his wonders to perform."

The girl heaves a sigh of impatience. But she knows better than to prod the story out. Big Momma's secrets are like the last drop in the syrup bottle. Slow to come, but worth the wait.

"Nana Proud Mary, my great-grandmother, she was a saltwater woman. Was brung over from Africy when she was young. Ain't much else we knew about her. She couldn't speak."

"Oh. Was she deaf?"

"No." Big Momma stops to examine some unseen flaw in the fabric. "Her tongue had been cut."

The clatter of the machine resumes. And so does the story.

"She couldn't speak a word, but I could usually get the gist of what she meant. They say she was well nigh over a hundred when she died. She used to take me out with her. Farming, fishing, gathering wild roots and weeds. She was what folks call a *conjure woman*. Knew grasses that cured fevers. Love spells. Potions for the pox. Poisons. She taught me what she know'd, that old woman."

"How could she teach you if she couldn't talk?" Allie wants to know.

"Oh, we had our way of understanding. She'd speak in grunts and motions.

Draw little pictures in the dirt. She even tried to get me to teach her how to read and write. But I guess she was too old. She couldn't catch on."

Big Momma pauses in her work. Her eyes get that faraway look the girl has come to know so well. The look that means she is contemplating things other people can't see. Her mouth works ever so slightly, as if she is reliving past conversations.

"Hmph," she says in a tone of finality. The only sound that follows is the clicking of the sewing machine.

Allie Mae has learned much more patience than she ever thought she had in her these three months with Big Momma. But she is bursting with curiosity at the untold story. She can no longer contain it.

"But what does that have to do with the snake following a star?"

Big Momma slices a glance at her, lips pursed. As if something has been said or done that she isn't pleased with.

"Nana came to me last night," she says sternly.

"Big Momma, quit it." The girl's eyes dart nervously to shadows in the darkened corners. "You're giving me the heebie-jeebies."

"Nana came to me last night," she repeats. "In a dream. I could see her just as clear. That white rag she always had tied around her head. That lemon grass chewstick she always had in her mouth. Them hands, all knotted and bony."

Big Momma glances down at her own knotted, bony hands as if they are strangers to her.

"Did your Nana say anything in the dream?"

Big Momma sighs, drops her head and shakes it slowly from side to side. A gesture that means she has seen or heard something she doesn't like to think about. The White Hats are still shooting colored folks down at Pyramid Courts. Belinda Lewis has left five babies at home alone, running off to East St. Louis behind some man. Orland McKenzie was struck by lightning working his dirt farm in a rainstorm. Black boys are going across the waters to fight in a war nobody understands. Some things are just beyond contemplation.

"That's the thing. Spirit and image of Nana. Only she had a voice in her that wasn't just mumbles and groans. She spoke to me."

They call me Proud Mary. Silence was the price I paid for my pride. But that's not the name I was born with. My babes no virgin births. They carried me across saltwater, seed in me. Snatched my firstborn from my breast at the slave breaking camp on the sugar island. They slit my tongue. Silenced my language. Shipped me to New Orleans. Sold me in the market. But they could not break me. I was born a daughter of the forest. Not meant for this life of cotton and chains.

I run. They beat me. I run again. A long walk from Mississippi. Look for Underground Railroad signs; Jacob's ladder quilted, hung on drying lines. Sleep on my own quilt on frostbitten fields. I've seen the insides of swamps. Grown friends with it. Been snake bitten. But I was born a daughter of the forest. I know the ways of water. Of healing and killing grasses.

Take refuge among the Apache warriors. I live and love and fight beside them. But the river calls and I must answer. I follow the North Star. Star of wonder. Did those wise men wonder on the faith that led them? Ever fear the light would be gone before they found Jesus?

I follow the way of water that should bring me back home. I know now that blood is seen before birth. I search for the Place Where Blood Is Born. But I come to a point where one way of water becomes two. Two rivers wander in opposite directions, one wide and brown. One thin and blue. Which one will take me to the source of blood? Which way will lead me home?

The way of water is split, like my broken tongue. It goes two ways now. Searching out its past, feeling for its future. Like a snake following the North Star, stilled at this passage.

My body is gone now but my blood still runs in the land of the living. The daughter of deepest memory will lead me home to the River Where Blood Is Born. And then I will be rested.

The rattle of the treadle fills the room, along with Big Momma's voice.

I told sweet Jesus would be alright
be alright
be alright

I told Jesus it would be alright
if he changed my name
Changed my name.

The girl is frozen in her seat. Afraid to move, but not fearful. Filled with a sense of something undefinable. As if suddenly connected to a long, winding lifeline.

"I do believe it's finished now." Big Momma lifts the foot, cuts the final thread. Little Daughter moves to the machine to look.

"Big Momma," she says finally. "You know what? She couldn't speak for herself. I bet she wanted you to tell her story."

Big Momma sighs. Drops her head and shakes it slowly. Puts away her pins and needles, her threads and scraps. Folds the finished quilt across her lap.

"And when I'm gone, Little Daughter . . . I want you to tell mine."

Changed My Name

You see a different side of things when you're coming at it from another direction. That's the same land I saw riding out from Chicago. The same hills and forests, prairies and farmland. The same small towns and railway stations.

But it looks different when you're riding back home, instead of coming away from it. I'm not the same person I was three and a half months ago. Even as I move into my future, it seems I can hear something calling me back. Something nudging me on.

I'm not a little girl anymore. I'm on my way to womanhood. I'll be in high school in a few days. I aim to learn everything they can teach me so I can graduate, go to college, and become a famous writer. Only one thing's got me worried. Whoever heard of a famous writer named Allie Mae? I'm going to have to do something about that.

"It ain't everyone that's blessed with a story to tell," Big Momma says. I been blessed. A pen is going to be my car and a piece of paper my road. A super tensile web of words is going to be my power. I'm fixing to write my way out of the ghetto. I know I got a way with words; I just need to get my grammar and spelling together.

I might even be the one to get all the Peeples back together. Maybe I'll find my father, and then I'll get in touch with all my different relatives in Chicago, California, Cairo, even Africa. We'll have a great big family reunion. And we'll all tell our stories of what happened when we were away from each other.

The city that works. Hog butcher to the world. Second city. That toddling town. City of broad shoulders. It's all a lie.

If the shoulders are that broad, then why does it always feel like I'm falling off? You got to know the place ain't got much going on for it, when truckloads of frightened farm animals headed for the stockyards is something that they brag about.

If nothing at all, these two years back in the city of onion grass have convinced me of one thing. My future is beyond these city limits. It's got to be. I got two Chicago lives going on, and neither one of them fits me right.

There's my K-town life, forty square blocks of blight from Roosevelt Road to

16th Street, from Kostner Avenue to Komensky Road. The neighborhood looks like somebody with a mouthful of rotten teeth trying to smile.

Crumbly old apartment buildings that used to be grand. Storefronts burnt out and boarded up from when they killed King and the West Side went up in flames. The smell of burnt wood still lingering, a full year after the fires.

Snaggle-tooth vacant lots where there used to be buildings, empty except for a few broken-down cars. Only one or two stores open on every block, and those are failing, all except the liquor stores. It's two o'clock on a Saturday afternoon and the corner bums are already out, drinking booze out of brown paper bags. Women struggling up the street with loads somebody should be helping them carry.

Then there's my Gage Park life. I got to get up at the crack of dawn and ride the CTA a full hour just to get to my first-period class. The daily bus trip to school, watching the riders slowly change from black to brown to pink. Watching yards grow from patches of dust to tufts of grass to neat flower gardens. Seeing the streets turn from filthy in the ghetto, to dirty in the Spanish territory, to sparkling clean in the white folks land. This part of Chicago has neat little bungalows, as picture-book pretty as that downstate town called Anna. Big Momma said the letters stood for *Ain't No Niggers Allowed*.

Mama says it's a good opportunity to be in this school. I should praise the Lord I was one of the few West Side girls that got to go. I don't know about all that.

I went to a white school in the seventh and eighth grades, but the few Black kids there got to stay together. Here in high school they split us up into three tracks; basic, standard, and honors. You can just guess where most of the Black students end up.

In a lot of my honors classes I'm the only Black person. The white kids look at you like you're an alien from outer space. I don't live but five miles away. Let them come out to K-town and see who the real alien is. I know I can make it in their lily white world; I been doing it since the beginning of my freshman year. But can they make it in mine? I doubt it.

Most of my white classmates are careful to ignore me, or they try to get in my business so they can ask a bunch of stupid questions. Like, *Do colored people get hickeys?* I don't do that kind of stuff with boys. But even the Black girls I know that lay all the way down, they don't get up with that boy's toothprints on their neck. Some of the girls around this school look like Dracula been biting on them. Mama always says, *Don't never let a man mark you like that.*

I keep my peace with Mama and them these days, by staying out of their way. They're married now and it looks like I'm stuck with Otis until I can get the hell out. Otis don't seem to be going nowhere, but in two more years I will. I don't know where I'm going, but I know I'm going somewhere. It seems I hear the world calling my name. And I'm getting ready to come answer it.

I feel like telling Mama there's more than one way of being marked. I watch her getting it every day. Everything she wears, every meal she makes, everything she says or does, got to pass by Otis first. It's pathetic. And every day she stoops a little lower, walks a little slower. Every day she gets older and Otis is the vampire sucking her youth.

Otis better leave me alone, I know that much. I believe he wants me to mess up, so he can have me sent off again. Fool me once, shame on you. Fool me twice, shame on me. I know better than letting myself get caught up in that trick bag. Anything he try to give me, I just throw it back at him. And Otis can't catch too good.

I'm on the school paper, so I be staying late a lot. That's fine with me, because the less I'm at home, the less I have to mix with Otis. If I'm there, he's subject to issuing orders like: *Empty this ashtray, girl*, or *Heat me up some chitlins*, or *Go get me the* TV Guide.

I'll empty the ashtray, alright. Then accidently empty out the tray along with the ash. *Heat you up the chitlins? Okay . . . oops. Sorry they got burnt.* Give him the TV Guide quick enough, but with today's page torn out. I read Dr. King in freshman social studies, you know. Learned a little bit about passive resistance.

He's taken to questioning me about my privacy.

"Who's that boy I saw you walking with?"

"What you doing in there with your bedroom door locked?"

"What business you got being up to school so late?"

I tried to explain that we had to stay late on Fridays so the school paper could come out Monday. And he went into this long, twisted story. About how teachers were keeping girls late at school so they could interfere with them when nobody was looking. Said he read where one teacher had been caught feeling on the breasts of an eight-year-old girl. And he looked at me close, to make sure I had heard it.

"Really?" I pretended to be shocked. "That's terrible."

When Mama got home I deliberately mentioned it.

"Did you hear about that teacher, Mama? Was squeezing on an eight-year-old's breasts?"

Mama's reaction was just what I expected. She closed her eyes and shook her head, shuddering like she'd just got an electric shock. It gave her the creeps to hear me talking that kind of sex stuff. Like having the words in my mouth might give me ideas about using them.

"Where'd you get that mess from, Allie Mae?"

"Otis," I replied promptly. "Otis, tell Mama about the teacher squeezing . . ."

"That's enough, now. I don't want to hear nothing more about it. And honey"—she turned to Otis—"what's an eight-year-old doing with breasts? Don't talk like that around my child."

See, I know how to get Otis off me. Just toss it back at him and let him fumble. You've got to watch yourself when you're a Black girl growing up in the ghetto.

Walking home from the bus stop one evening, the end of my daily trek from my lily white to dirty black life. I had been reading a book called *The Winds of March* on the bus, and had come to a very exciting part. The boy that Katie March was secretly in love with was making the moves on her little sister, Stacy. Ain't that just like a man? I couldn't wait to find out what happened. So I continued along with the open book in my hands, reading the pages by the streetlights on 16th.

I didn't realize they were behind me until one of the gangbangers walked up alongside and tried to veer me into the doorway of an abandoned building. I hollered for anyone's help. Leslie Flowers strolled over from the pool hall across the street, the cue stick still in his hand.

"Hey, Lucifer. Ant Man. What y'all doing with my lady?"

I was not his lady. I was his downstairs neighbor, his little sister's friend who had always had a crush on him. But the would-be rapists promptly turned me over to him, like illegitimate fathers of the bride. Releasing me over into the custody of the one who claimed my hand.

"Where you think you at, the library? Girl, this is the ghetto, not *Little House on the Prairie*. You better watch yourself."

Leslie walked me home, continuing his lecture about girls with heads so full of words they didn't watch where they walked. He took me right to my front door. Was this a kind of date? Did the occasion call for a good night kiss? He looked at me like a connoisseur.

"Allie Mae Peeples. Look like you're trying to get ripe, girl. Come here."

And he pulled me close and kissed me, his hands lightly skimming the curves of my body. I didn't try to stop him. But his kiss wasn't a lusty guzzling. It was a tentative sip, testing my mouth with his own. I guess he could taste the greenness of inexperience on my lips. He shook his head and put me away from him.

"You're not ready yet. Come back and see me when you're seventeen. Leslie Flowers will taste no wine before its time."

That was alright by me, although I had dreamed of kissing Leslie again, ever since that time two years ago when he pecked my cheek and patted my butt when he passed me by in the hallway. Because as cute as that boy was, I don't know if I could have kept him off me. Don't know if I would have wanted to.

Marsha Rivers used to ride the bus with me last year. She would spend the whole time talking about how much she hated white people. She didn't come back to Gage Park this fall; I'm sure it had something to do with that trouble.

I saw the whole thing happen in the first-floor girl's bathroom. They had just announced the assassination of Martin Luther King Jr. on the school intercom. School was letting out early that day. As I looked in the mirror to comb my hair, I noticed a commotion going on in one of the stalls behind me. Marsha Rivers had Katrina Kautsky by her blond ponytail, and was forcing her head down into the toilet.

"Allie," she called. "Help me!"

I went over to see what was going down. Marsha's eyes were wild and her mouth was set.

"You mutha fuckas killed our King," she growled into Katrina's scared, wet face. "Die, hunky bitch. Die."

And down went the head again, dunked into the toilet. Katrina Kautsky didn't die. But Marsha was suspended for a week. Katrina tried to drag me into the mess.

White folks were running scared then, nervous about sending their white ignorance to meet our Black anger. I sat in the principal's office with Mama and Otis, Katrina and her parents, watching the anxious pink stain on Dr. Prescott's face.

"What do you know about this matter, Miss Peeples?" He was twitching like anybody's little white rabbit.

"I saw it happen," I admitted. "But I didn't have a thing to do with it."

"But you didn't help," Katrina wailed. "You didn't do a thing to stop it."

"How you expect me to rescue you from the toilet water? Do I look like somebody's Wonder Woman? Wasn't none of my business what went on between you and Marsha Rivers. You fight your own fights."

I didn't feel the least bit guilty. This was the same Katrina Kautsky who had cornered me in freshman year, all pitying and self-righteous. *It must be very sad to be a Negro.* So now she had a little taste of sadness herself, had been baptized in it.

Aretha has a record out about a new generation of boys and girls coming up young, gifted, and Black. It's a hopeful song, but a sad one, too, when she admits feeling haunted by her own youth. Aretha Franklin, with all her money and talent and fame, looking back on her girlhood with regrets.

I don't know what her story was, but I can tell you mine. I ain't about to be haunted by nothing. If anything, I'll be the one doing the haunting. Otis Clemmons, Dr. Prescott, Katrina Kautsky; they can all kiss my royal Black ass. I am going places in this life, places they can't even pronounce.

I told Jesus it would be alright if he changed my name. I'm getting me a new name, finding me a new life that fits me right. Next year I'll be editor of our high school paper, the *Gage Park Alma Mater*. Just you watch. Year after that I'll be getting up out of here going to somebody's college. I might even be the first student from this school to become a multimillionaire.

Alma mater means *soul mother*. Well, I'm Alma Peeples, *soul sister*. The world's waiting for me. I'm young, gifted, and Black. And that's where it's at.

Coming Up Brown in Phoenix

May 2, 1967

Dear Diary:

You're the best birthday present a girl could get! Now I have someone to tell my business to, stuff I could never talk about with Lola or Pop, even Blondine. And it wasn't until just now when I sat down to write in you that I saw Pop had tucked a fifty-dollar bill inside. Fifty whole dollars. This is going to be a very exciting life, Diary. And Sweet Sixteen is just the beginning!

I'll never forget my party. Pop said he was going to make it the best *Sweet Sixteen* Phoenix, Illinois, has ever seen. Lola said she wasn't going to have no house full of rowdy girls trampling up her wall-to-wall. So Pop closed the barbershop for the whole day. Boy, were those men mad at him. Saturday is Pop's busiest day, when all the niggers come in to hang out and get their nappy heads cut. But Pop didn't care. He said his baby daughter was worth waving good-bye to a few dollars on a Saturday afternoon.

Pop sure knows how to do up a party. He had the shop strung with all kinds of streamers and ribbons. There had to be at least a hundred pink and white balloons floating around. You couldn't even see the ceiling. It was a happening party! Pop even let us sip a little champagne. It was all girls, the top girls at school.

Suzette and Anita and Tiara and Danielle and Blondine and Trici, they all were there. And they were looking sharp. Blondine had on a gold lame cocktail dress and a real fur stole that she borrowed from her grandmother. But none of them was looking better than me.

I was wearing pink and white to match the decorations in the barbershop. I had on white spike heels and a pink chiffon strapless. I had the longest hair there and the prettiest dress, too. But I sure wish I had a fur stole like Blondine. I'm asking Pop to get me one. Blondine has a lot of style. She really knows how to put outfits together. That girl is going places, just you watch.

It would have been a perfect party if it wasn't for Allie Mae. My piss-poor cousin from Chicago turned up, just as black and ugly as sin. She didn't call or anything, just showed up wearing those rags she tries to call clothes. And she didn't even have the decency to bring a gift, not even a pair of stockings. Allie Mae ain't going no place, you hear me? Doesn't even know how to dress and she live in Chicago and everything.

Suzette gave me a watch and Tiara gave me some *Jungle Orchid* perfume and dusting powder. Danielle gave me the latest Temptations album. Trici gave me a set of Nancy Drew mysteries. I'm not thinking about nobody's Nancy Drew. Trici thinks everybody likes the same thing she does. How much you want to bet she'll be over here tomorrow, wanting to borrow them? Anita gave me five dollars. She's just like Lola says, no imagination. But at least that was better than Allie Mae. She didn't give me nothing but the pleasure of her pitiful company.

But Blondine's present was the best. She's got plenty of imagination. She gave me a jewelry set, you could tell she had spent some time picking it out. A necklace, a bracelet, and earrings, all with Sweet Sixteen charms dangling. Fourteen-karat gold, Lola says. You know that had to be some money.

When I opened it up Blondine whispered, just like Marilyn Monroe:

"Sweet Sixteen and never been fucked?" Blondine is a mess. Everybody cracked up laughing. It's a good thing Pop had gone out to get some ice, because he would have had a shit fit behind that.

"Girl, you're crazy," I told Blondine, not knowing how to answer: to lie or tell the truth.

Blondine waved and jingled her bangles.

"Hey. Life ain't nothing but a party. You better get it and get off while the getting is good, girls." Who else but Blondine could say something like that and make it sound hip instead of nasty?

"Shoot." That was old black Allie, drinking pop like it was going out of style. "You ain't going to catch me doing none of that. You can get pregnant behind that."

Blondine got her told real good: "Stupid girls get pregnant. Don't nobody need to have a baby in this day and age unless they want to. Anybody with any sense knows how to get some pills before they lay down."

"Unless they're stupid," I reminded Allie Mae. And I wanted to add *And nobody invited you up in here, so you better shut up talking.*

But I didn't blow my cool and stoop down to her level. Blondine always says *Maintain your cool at all costs.* That girl is so smart. She got double-promoted in the fifth grade. Blondine's only sixteen now and she's a senior at Immaculate Heart of Mary. She'll be going away to college in just five months. I'm sure going to miss her.

Just then Pop brought in the cake. It was pink and white, of course, with sixteen red candles shaped like hearts.

"Sweet Sixteen and never been kissed!" Pop yelled. Blondine nudged me and winked. Everybody else saw it and they just about busted stitches. Pop thought he had told the funniest joke in the world.

By the time Lola got home everybody was long gone. Except Allie Mae, who came upstairs with me and fell asleep on the sofa. Call herself trying to come live with us. Pop had gone down the back stairs to the parlor, trying to get a stiff ready for a Sunday funeral.

Lola was loaded down with bags and boxes. She fell on the sofa, just about sitting on Allie Mae's feet. All tired out from a hard day's shopping.

"Lola, you missed the party. We saved you some cake."

"If I could have been here, I would have been here," Lola snapped. Hey, I wasn't trying to come down on her or anything. Like *Why did you miss my party?* I just wanted to tell her all what Blondine and them were wearing, because I know she's into that.

But she wouldn't hardly let me open my mouth, she was so busy yapping about how bad traffic was, stop and go all the way from Evergreen Plaza. Then she just sat back with all those packages spread around her feet, looking like a skinny yellow Christmas tree.

"I can't wait to see my birthday gifts. What did you get me?"

Now, Diary, there were at least seven or eight bags and boxes of different sizes. Three Sisters, Field's, Carson's. All the really nice stores at Evergreen. I just knew I had cleaned up. Like Pop said, *A girl don't turn Sweet Sixteen but once in a lifetime.* And do you know Lola handed me two bags? Two little bags! A real, real ugly sweater set and a green dress with a white Peter Pan collar. And the dress wasn't even my size! Can you imagine?

I'm almost a woman now, and Lola still wants to dress me up in bows and bobby socks and Peter Pan collars. I know what her problem is. She thinks she's the fox of Phoenix and she doesn't want any competition coming up behind her. She's trying to keep me down, that's why she does me like that.

All the stores at Evergreen Plaza, you can't tell me she couldn't find anything nice in a size five. She can't stand to see somebody looking good, or getting any love and attention, unless that somebody's Lola. My Sweet Sixteen and she couldn't even bother to come, too busy out there looking for something to put on her own back. And you know what else?

I've had my learner's permit for a year now and she won't even let me touch that car, let alone drive it. You would think that Cadillac was made of gold, instead of just painted that color. Don't tell anybody I said this, Diary, but sometimes I just hate her!

I wish the ground would open up and swallow Lola Brown right in it, so she can leave me and Pop alone. Let her go straight to hell and take Allie Mae with her.

Lola can try all she wants to keep me down, but she won't. I'm coming up brown as cinnamon and fine as wine. And one day I'm going to turn this little town on its ear. Just you watch me.

May 30, 1967

Dear Diary:

I hate them! I hate them! I hate them!

I could get a knife and stick it in them one hundred times. I could turn on the oven and gas them to death. I could get a gun and blow them away. Those evil creatures that call themselves my parents don't deserve to live in the same world with me.

Pop said that fifty dollars was mine, that it was mad money. He said I could do whatever I wanted with it. Well, I wanted an Afro wig. Blondine had one, a nice curly one even bigger than Angela Davis'. And some of the girls at school are wearing their hair in real Afros. Hey, this is 1967, not 1867. Afros are where it's at.

So me and Anita, we took the train downtown to Chicago and went to one of those wig shops in the Loop. I saw one in the window that was light brown, real curly. Even bigger than Blondine's. It looked so good when I tried it on that I paid for it and wore it right on home.

I had to go through the barbershop to get upstairs to the apartment because I forgot my key. One of those barbershop bums looked at me and yowled, just like a dirty old dog.

"Whoo-wee, Clyde! One of them wild Africans done made her way in here. You better set her down. She needs a trim real bad."

Pop nearly shit bricks.

"Girl, what is that on your head?"

"It's a 'fro, Pop. Everybody's wearing them."

"Afro, my ass. Take that mess off your head right now. And don't never let me see you looking like that again."

I wasn't taking anything off. It was mine. I paid my $19.95. I picked up the key and started upstairs.

"I said take it off!" Before I knew what was going on, Pop had reached over and snatched it right off my head.

I tried to grab it back. But Pop held it up over his head, pinching it between his thumb and finger like it was a smelly dead rat. He went out back and threw it in a pile of leaves he had burning out there.

I ran out after him, but it was too late. My wig was now a light brown lump melting on top of the pile.

"You got good hair!" Pop come hollering at me, raking the wig deep down in there. "Don't never let me catch you walking around here looking like no nappy-headed pickaninny."

I ran upstairs and called Blondine on the phone, crying. Blondine's heavy into Malcolm X and Black Power now. She said: "People like that handkerchief-headed daddy of yours are what's holding our people back. You ready to try a real 'fro?"

"But my hair's too soft," I told her. "It won't nap up, no matter how tight I roll it."

Blondine came over, cut about five inches off my hair, and gave me a home perm. It didn't take. My hair turned dark orange and frizzy. I looked like Little Orphan Annie. I came to dinner with a scarf on.

"Girl, if you don't get that rag off your head, you better," Lola said the minute she saw me. "You look just like somebody's old black mammy. Clyde, you remember Big Momma down in Cairo? That's just how she ties up her head."

Pop was dishing up mashed potatoes and smiling at Lola like she was the Queen of Sheba. I just don't know what he sees in that woman. She's not sweet and loving like a wife is supposed to be. All she cares about is money and clothes. I don't believe she ever gives Pop any trim. If she does, he probably has to beg for it. Or pay. But it seems like the worse Lola treats him, the better he likes it. He loves her funky drawers.

"Naw, girl. You still can't make me believe that old country woman is your grandmother. As fine as you are."

I eased down in my seat to eat while they were busy talking about how Lola was prettier than any number of white women on TV. I thought she had forgot all about my do-rag. But halfway through my fried chicken and peas, she frowned across the table at me.

"Pat Brown. Didn't I tell you to take that thing off at my dinner table?"

She reached over and snatched it right off my head. Pop took one look and moaned like he was hurting. While he was getting up from the table, Lola was busting stitches.

"Girl, what you dressed up for? Halloween been over."

"It's an Afro. It needs combing, that's all."

Lola got up and took a good look at my hair. She poked it and patted, ran her hands through it.

"It needs more than combing. It needs fixing. Don't look like no Afro to me, looks more like a Bozo. Got you looking like somebody's little colored clown."

"I do not look like Bozo. Mother!" I knew that word would make her mad. But I rather have her mad than laughing at me.

"The name's Lola," she snapped. "I told you that a million times. If you want somebody to call *Mama*, you got Clyde. What's he doing down there anyway?"

We soon found out. Pop came upstairs with one of those razor strops he uses in the barbershop.

"Clyde, are you crazy? Put that thing down and eat your dinner." That's just how Lola talks to him. The way she talks to me, and worse.

"I'm about to beat some sense into this little heifer." Pop raised the strop and snapped it. I just rolled my eyes and went on eating my food. Pop had never hit me in his life and he never would. It was all for show. Lola slapped down his hand.

"I said sit down and eat your dinner. Don't worry with that hardheaded child."

"But look what she did to herself. Hair all wild. She don't even look like she came from you."

Lola sat there pulling the meat off the breastbone. She always got the chicken breast, don't care who else wanted it.

"She don't have enough sense to know that long hair was all she had going for herself. She's short. She ain't that light. She's scrawny."

"I am pretty," I shouted at her. "Lots of people say I'm pretty!"

"You don't have nothing a hundred other girls don't have. Except that hair. And you don't even have that now."

"She had good hair, too," Pop mumbled. He had laid down the razor strop just like Lola told him, and was chewing on a drumstick. "I don't know why she wants to mess herself up like that. She was wearing one of those nappy-headed wigs when she came home. You should have seen it. I had to take the sucker out back and burn it up."

Lola sniffed the air.

"So that's what's been stinking up my yard. Clyde, you don't have no more sense than she does. How I'm going to get rid of that smell?"

"Don't worry about it, baby. I'll handle it. I just want to know what you're going to do about this child's hair?"

They sat there eating their chicken and talking about me like I wasn't even in the room. I might as well have been a picture on the wall, or a piece of furniture on the floor.

"I'm not doing a damn thing. She made her bed hard, let her lay in it for a while. It's just hair, it'll grow back. After walking around looking like that a few months she'll be glad enough when it does."

Have you ever seen such a hateful mother and father? I hate him. I hate her. I hate the way my hair looks. But what I hate the most, dear Diary, is that maybe Lola is right.

Maybe I'm not that pretty after all. Maybe all I did have going for me was my hair. Oh, God. I'll be so glad when it grows back again.

September 3, 1967

Bonjour, Dear Diary:

Did I have a summer! Did we have a time in Montreal!

They had all kinds of shows and exhibits there, but I wasn't thinking about that. But oh, the clothes! Those Frenchified folks really know how to make some clothes. I have a whole new wardrobe to start my junior year with. How much you bet I'll be the hippest chick at Immaculate Heart? My hair is growing out. It still has a little perm in it so it's reddish and curly at the ends. It looks real cute, if I say so myself.

Had to spend a week in Cairo this summer. Ugh! I hate that place. Nothing to do, nobody to talk to but Allie Mae. And I never done that much work in my life! I bet Big Momma saves up stuff all year long, so she can put me to work every summer. I'm asking Lola if I can stop going down there. I know she sends me south so she and Pop can get me out of the way when they take their honeymoon. Let them have their once a year screw, I don't even care. I just don't need baby-sitting anymore. I'm almost grown now, so what's the deal?

Tomorrow's the first day of school. I can't decide whether to wear my red walking suit or my new purple bell bottoms. What do you think?

February 12, 1968

I have decided to change my name, dear Diary.

The one I have is just too lifeless. Pat. Short for nothing. Not Patrice, not Patsy, not even a common Patricia.

Lola's always talking about how my friend Anita has no imagination. Well, what happened to hers? Seems like she could have thought up a better name for me than Pat. I know this had to be Lola's idea. If Pop had named me, he would have given me a pretty French name like some of my friends have.

Suzette. Blondine. Nicole. Charisse. Even as plain as Anita is, she has a pretty name. And what about that real ugly girl in my algebra class? She has a name so pretty it seems wasted on her. Why couldn't I have been called *Francesca*? If an ugly girl like that can have a pretty name, there's no reason on earth why I should be called Pat Brown for the rest of my life.

So I'm changing it. From now on I'm going by the name *Fondue. Fondue LaTrice.* It's fancy. It's classy. It's French. It's a name for someone who's not going to be sitting around Phoenix for the rest of her life. It's a name for a girl who's going places.

April 4, 1968

Dear Diary:

We got sent home early from school today. Martin Luther King got himself killed by some crazy cracker down South. I don't think those nuns feel bad about Dr. King dying, I think they're scared the Negroes are going to go wild and come after their white asses. And wearing those long habits like they do, they won't be able to run away.

I'm glad to have this time at home by myself, because I have some news I've been dying to tell you. These drops falling on your pages are tears of joy and sadness combined. I'm in love, I'm in love, I'm in love!

Love has come into my life and I'm so happy and blue I don't know what to do. Oh, Diary. The sad thing is, I know not his name.

I was working last Friday night at Lola's Place and there he was. Tall, dark, and handsome. His eyes like deep rivers. His arms strong and manly. His chest sexy in a University of Chicago sweatshirt. That's all I know about him.

But I believe that this is true love, love at first sight. I'm so happy, yet I'm so sad because I don't know if I'll ever see my loved one's face again. Fate may never bring us back together. So I have composed this poem that I will read and cherish for as long as I live.

POEM TO MY UNKNOWN PRINCE

Tall, dark, and handsome
My loving prince has come
But my heart breaks with cruel pain
Because I know not his name

Now I lay me down to sleep
And I lay me down to weep
Because I may much older grow
His loving kiss, never to know

Oh, my prince, hear me do
The weeping of your love so true
And come to me, my unknown prince
To share the passion of love's first kiss

The last line doesn't really rhyme. I couldn't think of anything to rhyme with *prince*, except *since* and *wince* and *mince*. None of those fit too well. Maybe I'll rewrite it later.

I think it's a pretty good poem, though. Maybe that's what I'll do when I grow up. I'll make a fortune one day writing about my experiences in the exciting life I'll be living. Oh, but Diary, the important thing is that I am in love. I may never see him again. But I love him. Oh, how I love him so.

Sister Mary Clementine says that the Virgin Mary carries our prayers to God. These BVM nuns are full of shit, selling the Madonna like she was a used car. Do you know that every single one of them has to take on *Mary* as a first name? BVM stands for *Blessed Virgin Mary*, but at Immaculate Heart we call them the *Black-Veiled Mafia*. Can't none of them get married or have sex, that's why they act so evil. If virginity was good enough for Mary, it's good enough for them.

See, there's a hole in that story a mile wide. They claim that Mary got the news off the Archangel Gabriel. Sounds to me like Mary and Gabriel must have got it on. Yeah, Mary had one hell of a heavenly screw, and then she married Joseph after she got knocked up, still claiming to be a virgin. Ain't no way in the world you can tell me Joseph kept it in his pants for nine whole months, pregnant or no. That so-called Holy Virgin might know a thing or two about this love business, after all.

Hail Mary, full of grace. The Lord is with thee. Blessed art thou amongst women, and blessed is the fruit of thy womb, Jesus. Holy Mary, mother of God, pray for us sinners. And while you're at it, please put a word in for me, so I might get a chance to see the man of my dreams again. *Now and at the hour of our death. Amen.*

May 25, 1968

Dear Diary:

I apologize for breaking our bonds of secrecy, but I didn't think you would mind this one time. I just had to let Blondine read you, just the last part about the Unknown Prince. Blondine's home from college for the summer. And I'm so excited about being in love, I wanted to share it with somebody.

She didn't have much to say, except that I need to work on my poetry, because poems don't have to rhyme nowadays. I guess she should know, she's in college and stuff. She's all so intellectual these days. Or maybe she's just jealous, because I'm still in high school and going for the college dudes. Don't you think Blondine's starting to get sort of fat?

Maybe I won't be a writer after all. I bet you I can make it as a movie star, or even a model as soon as I get a little bit taller. No sense letting this pretty skin and good hair go to waste. Blondine won't never be nobody's covergirl, a little blimpette.

She did give me some good advice, though. I confessed that my secret love has a little skanchy girlfriend. I caught her rolling her eyes at me that night I was watching her man. Blondine told me just how to handle it. I should march right up to the hussy and say:

"You don't want to mess with me, sister girl. Not only will I take your man, I'll break your man and send him back butt naked, not a nickel to his name."

That Blondine is something else.

May 19, 1969

Dear Diary:

I'm sorry to be away from you so long. But things have been so busy, with prom and graduation coming up. I'm trying to figure out what to do after that's all over, and it's pretty scary. I still don't know what I want to be when I grow up and I'm almost there. I can't decide whether to go to Chicago and get a job, go to college, or go out to Hollywood and try to be a movie star. I always thought I'd go to New York and be a model, but I'm too short and it looks like I'm not going to grow anymore.

I wish I had Blondine's talent of knowing what to do with yourself. What do you call that? Confidence? Determination? She's been downstate for two years now studying political science, whatever that is. And she's really serious about it. I've driven down to visit her twice. Pop got me a car for my eighteenth birthday this year, a brand new Corvair. Pop is such a baby doll. I love him to death.

And guess what? Me and Michael almost did it this time!

Michael's car was in the shop, so I had to drive all the way to Chicago by myself.

I cut class last Tuesday and while I was driving up there I was listening to WVON. I was wondering why Michael insisted I tune into that particular radio station. Then the DJ came on and said the next request was from Michael Jamerson, dedicated to Fondue LaTrice. That's the silly name I gave him when we first met. The song was about a virgin girl, fantasizing how this night her man would make a woman out of her.

I was so excited that our secret was being broadcast on the airwaves, if Michael had been with me I would have pulled over to the side and given him some, right then and there. But when I got into the city I got lost looking for his place. I finally had to call and have him come and meet me. By the time he got there I was mad, frustrated, and I wasn't in the mood anymore.

His place wasn't anything like I expected. It was little and raggedy, just two and a half run-down rooms he shared with another medical student. A very unromantic setting to be deflowered. We'd been laying on the sofa for about an hour and he was just begging me for it. I wanted to do it in a way, and in a way I didn't. He was trying to get me hot, kissing and feeling on me. I finally let him get my sweater and skirt off and decided, *What the hell? Let's do it.*

In flies this white dude, the Absent-Minded Egghead. He had on horn-rimmed glasses about an inch thick, and hair about an inch short. Diary, he looked like a creature that had just crawled out from under anybody's library. He stands up there squinting at us on the sofa in our underwear.

"Sorry, Michael," he says. "I didn't realize you were entertaining."

Entertaining! Can you imagine? Anyway, that put an end to everything. I got dressed and left. Michael followed me down to the car, begging me to come back, promising to get rid of Albert. But it was getting late anyway and I had to be back home before Pop and Lola got suspicious. Besides, it wouldn't hurt him to wait a little longer. Good things come to those who wait, isn't that what a wise man said?

It's funny how things turned out between Michael and me. It started out with me the one being head over heels, and him hardly knowing I was alive. Now it's just the opposite way around.

He used to come into Lola's Place with this little plain-Jane chick, probably from Robbins or somewhere else around here. She sure didn't look like she was worth driving no thirty miles to see, but you never know what turns men on. He was always with her, but I always had my eye on him. And one day I got up enough nerve to make my move.

See, the men's room has two doors in it, one of them the entrance, the other one opening to a storeroom. The only way you can get into the storeroom is either through a door in the back of the bar, or through the men's room. Somebody must have been high when they put that place together.

Anyway, I see him headed for the john one night, right? So I ran around the back of the bar, let myself into the storeroom, and waited back there in the dark with all those cases of liquor. I stood up against the men's room door, listening to make sure that he had locked the entrance door. And I took a big breath, opened the door on my side, and stepped into the room.

Girl, he was standing there peeing with his fine self. One fist on his hip, the other hand holding his thing. That was the first time I ever saw a man's thing.

Him: I think you missed a turn somewhere, sweetheart. This is the little boy's room.

Me: I know it is. (I tried to act bold, thinking how Blondine would handle the situation.) I just wanted to have a word with you, brother.

He grinned down at me like I was a little kid. Then he put himself back in his pants and flushed the john.

Him: Oh, yeah? Who do I have the pleasure of addressing?

Me: The name is Fondue. Fondue LaTrice.

He doubled over laughing.

Him: Fondue? I'm no gourmet, but isn't that a sauce you dip meat in?

You talk about embarrassed! I could have turned around and run right out that storeroom door. But I had to play it off. Maintain your cool at all costs.

Me: That's right, my man. I got the sauce if you got the meat. (Oh, I was so cool!)

That grin he was wearing went away, then came back real slow.

Him: You better believe it, baby. USDA prime, all day long.

Me: All night long, too?

Him: Oh, you wicked little woman.

(I like it when Michael talks street, then mixes it up with his little educated rap.) He leaned up against the wall, looking down at me and shaking his head.

Him: Baby, you look like jail bait to me. Just how old are you?

Me (lying): Eighteen and a half. Old enough to sleep in the bed without falling out.

Him: I would never let you fall out of my bed, Fondue.

I didn't know what to say back, so I just giggled.

Him: Well, Fondue. We've got to stop meeting like this. I'm otherwise engaged this evening . . .

Me: Yes, I saw what you walked in with. You can do better than that, can't you?

Him: Yes, I believe I can.

Then he reached out, pulled me to him, and kissed me. My first kiss! If he had tried to gobble me up, to get down to the nitty-gritty right there in the men's room, I think I would have run off or called Pop on him. I was kind of scared. But he was just so smooth! He kissed me slow, like he was licking a lollipop and had all the time in the world to finish it.

I was sweet sixteen and had never been kissed, let alone been fucked. But when he kissed me I suddenly wanted more. I remember standing up on tiptoe and leaning up toward his mouth, like I was thirsty and he was a tall drink of water. He didn't let me kiss him, he just drew back and kind of laughed.

Him: Eighteen years old and still don't know how to kiss? Fondue, your education has been sadly neglected.

This was almost a year ago, but I think that's pretty much how it happened. I remember going to bed that night feeling all excited because I had done something bold, like Blondine would have done.

But when I think back, I feel kind of funny about it now. It wasn't the real me in the men's room, doing and saying all that. I was just putting on an act to get his attention. And I guess it worked. If I hadn't done it, maybe we would never have got together. But I can't help feeling that this wasn't the right way to begin my first love. I used to dream that it would be flowers and candy and dates and dinner, not sneaking around with a man I can't introduce my parents to.

But it's like a game I started, and don't know how to stop. I went in acting wild and promising things I didn't know how to give. And I've been keeping it going for almost a year on the same promise.

Michael always tells me how much he wants me. *Like a bear wants honey, baby.* But he never says how much he loves me. Says he's tired of waiting. That I don't want to please him, I just want to tease him. But once he gets what he wants, will he still want to be bothered with me? He's twenty-five years old and in medical school. I'm just a high school senior. I don't even know how to talk to him about the things in his world. Blondine would. I wish she was here.

Plus, I'm scared it might hurt. Blondine said that when she lost her cherry she bled for two days straight.

What's going to happen after I give it up? I guess there's only one way to find out. Steak tartar is on the menu for Michael and me next time. Raw beef dipped in fondue. I'll tell you how it turns out.

June 30, 1969

I thought I was dead. I really did. It was only tonight that I know what I need to keep me alive.

Funerals never bothered me before. Death never bothered me before. I grew up around it. I used to play in Pop's parlor among the bodies. Old men with liver spots and old ladies with flat breasts and gold teeth. There were the crispy critters, people who had gotten burned up in fires. Suicides. Sometimes kids, they looked like stiff little Chatty Cathy dolls. I thought they were dummies, these bodies of people that used to be. I was never afraid of them.

Okay, let's start at the beginning. I just got home from Michael, when was it? Last week, I think. I wanted to surprise him. I went to his place and Albert the Absent-Minded Egghead was there. He told me where to find Michael. I told him to be gone when we got back.

You see, I had finally decided to give it up. I was tired of being a virgin. I told him so. No games, no teasing. What you see is what you get. So Michael turned into Speedy Gonzalez. He couldn't wait to get his pants off. I guess I had changed my mind on him so many times before, he wanted to make sure I wouldn't do it again.

But when we were all undressed and he started touching me, he jerked his hand back real quick. This look of shock and disgust came over his face. He told me: "Pat, I think you must enjoy tormenting me."

I was confused. I said: "I don't know what you mean."

He said: "Why didn't you tell me you were on your period?"

See, I had been playing a role all along. The Virgin Hussy. The Cocktease. The Scarlet Temptress. And I was really scarlet then, both with shame and menstrual blood. But up until then it had all been a game to me. How was I supposed to know the rules, the etiquette of the act?

He turned his back, pulled on his pants, went into the bathroom and ran the water. I hurried up and got dressed. I had to get out of there quick. I broke the speed limit driving back to Phoenix. I felt dirty, like I was flowing a river of blood.

I didn't know who I could talk to about it. My mother? When kids used to play the dozens, saying *yo mama is a man*, I couldn't call them a liar.

Pop had always been more of a mother to me than Lola ever was. I know he spoils me and lets me have my way too much. But he also tells me things, important things. He was the one who sat me down and told me about periods and procreation.

Lola is somebody you go to about practical matters. What earrings to wear with an outfit. How to tell 14-karat from 18-karat gold. But it was Pop who told me about the thing men and women did when they were in love. I'll never forget what he said when I was about thirteen years old: "Lovemaking is supposed to be like a little piece of heaven. It's a special thing, baby. You don't give up your heaven to just anybody out there."

So I don't know why I went to Lola. Maybe I thought her cool outlook would help me see things better. Maybe I figured she would know more about the etiquette of the thing. Pop would have just wanted to hang the man by his dick from the nearest tree.

She was in Lola's Place sitting at the bar. It was too early for customers to be in. I guess she was in there checking her stock or counting her change. The sun was setting and the light hit her straight on. With the sun in her face, you could really see the black in her. See, Lola has always been happy to tell anyone who wants to know that she comes from mixed blood. She calls herself a Creole and acts like she's all the way white.

Maybe that's why me and Lola never really got along. I always felt like a little colored child with a white stepmother. People say we look alike, but I don't see it.

Anyway, she wasn't looking like her old prim and proper self that day. Her lips weren't pinched like they usually are. Her hair looked like she had been running her hands through it. She always does that when she's worried about something. Seems like touching her own straight, white-folks hair is comforting to her.

It wasn't looking like white-folks hair that day. It was standing out around her head, like a chicken-wire Afro. The sun in her face made it look gold, instead of its usual washed-out yellow. She was leaning against the bar so tired-looking, almost like she needed its help to hold her up. She stared into the spider tattooed into her palm, as if it held the answer to some unspoken question.

I don't know what got into me. I hadn't even got in the door good before I blurted it out.

"Lola, I almost slept with a man."

She didn't even look surprised. Maybe just a little sad. She sighed and dropped her head. Shook it slowly from side to side.

"I guess it was bound to happen sooner or later. Did you use any protection?"

I answered no.

"Well, use some next time. Did you like it?"

I told her I didn't know. Lola narrowed her eyes at me and looked me up and down.

"You don't know? Either you liked it or you didn't. It's alright to like it, you know. Just make sure he likes it more."

I was trying to think about how to ask her what you were supposed to do when you were on your period. But she did something I never remember her doing. She took my hand and held it tight. This wasn't like her.

"I don't know how to tell you this, Pat. But one of your friends is there, in Clyde's parlor."

"Is it Blondine?"

That was just what I needed. A good heart-to-heart with Blondine. She knew how to make me laugh at embarrassing situations. To comfort me. To put things in order, tell me that *he ought to be glad to get it, bloody or not.*

"Yes, it is. But don't go, Pat. I'm not finished yet."

She was coming around the bar, trying to make me stay. But I was already on my way out the door.

"I'll be back, Lola. I just need to talk to Blondine."

Everybody knew Blondine was my oldest friend, probably my only friend. All the other girls I associated with, I never felt that close to. They were just someone to make gossip and small talk with. The same girls who grinned up in my face one day would hurry up and link arms with their boyfriends when they saw me the next. Like, *This is mine, hands off.*

That was back when Blue Island was still a boojie suburb, an island of white in a sea of poor Black towns like Robbins and Phoenix and East Chicago Heights. Blondine's was one of the only Negro families. We met in the sixth-grade band practice at Immaculate Heart of Mary, where Pop had sent me to get away from the public schools.

I was the first flute, Blondine was the second, although she had no business being in band at all. The only number she could play was *Three Blind Mice*, and even that she couldn't play well. I guess we became best friends because we didn't fit with any of the other two groups.

There were the white girls, little rich suburbanites who wanted no part of us. They were the cream. And there were the Negro girls, middle-class daughters of dark families trying to keep up with the Joneses. They were the coffee. We were both, we were neither. We were *half and half. Café au lait. Light, bright, and damned near white. Yellow fever.*

As kids Blondine and me would buy the movie magazines and get together on Saturday afternoons. We'd sit in front of the vanity and compare our features with the pictures of the stars. Angela Cartwright. Peggy Lipton. Mia Farrow. And we'd try to figure out which one of us had more movie star potential.

It usually came out to a draw. Blondine's skin and hair were lighter, but she had a wide nigger nose. My hair was straighter and my lips and nose keener. But my skin was at least two shades too brown.

Blondine had freckles and hazel eyes, a plus. But a big behind, a minus. I had hair down to the middle of my back, a plus. But bee-stung lips, a minus. Blondine had a white father and I had a white grandfather neither of us had ever met. So we spent many a Saturday afternoon in the mirror searching for something they may have left behind.

Did I tell you that Blondine had thrown away her Angela Davis wig and got herself a real natural? Cut her hair short, almost down to her scalp. I always knew she was going places. Blondine had been to Africa and come back changed.

"You've got to go, Pat. It's a spiritual thang. Never have I been so happy to be a Black woman."

She came back wearing tropical prints and tanned skin. She came back with a new name, *Imani*. She said it meant *faith*.

Faith had closed her eyes on me. She laid there naked, stretched out on Pop's embalming table. Her beige face was deathly pale, which made her freckles stand out like cinnamon bits in a bowl of oatmeal. Her natural was longer than the last time I'd seen it, smashed to one side of her head like she'd been sleeping on it. Her belly was as big and round as a watermelon. When had this happened?

A perfect round red hole was in her chest, right above her left breast. It wasn't much bigger than a cigarette burn on a sweater. But too far gone to be hidden by a scarf or covered with a brooch.

You know, when I was little I thought death was something you could outsmart. I saw people on TV who fell into a dead faint, but were quickly revived by water. All you needed was a bucket of water to bring you back. And those who were unlucky enough to wind up in Pop's parlor? Well, they didn't know the secret. They hadn't found water, or had found it too late.

"If I ever die," I used to tell Pop, "bring me water."

"I sure will, baby girl. I sure will."

Nobody had brought Blondine water. Whoever took her life away when life was growing inside her had done it so quickly, the smile didn't have time to leave her face. The bullet had caught her with her eyes wide open.

I looked into the clear hazel eyes I always wished were mine. Her fixed gaze stared back at me, looking into me. As if she had something important to say but couldn't find the right words.

"Blondine?" I asked, before I realized what I was saying. "What is it?"

A passing shadow broke the ray of sun shining on her face. Her clear eyes seemed to cloud over. She wasn't supposed to be dead. She should have stretched, turned over, and got up. She should have hollered *April fool!* She should have hugged me and asked *What's happening, ho?* But she didn't. And that's when I knew it was something stronger than water I needed to keep me alive.

The last time I saw Blondine alive was dancing. She had come up to Phoenix to get me and driven me back downstate to Normal. She opened the door of her dorm room, and there was a party going on. It was the kind of party where the music never ends. There was one slow, sweet song about an African violet.

Blondine danced a slow dance all by herself, balancing a wooden bowl of fruit on her head. She had taken off all her clothes and wrapped herself in this long African cloth. She went dancing around the party, passing out fruit from the bowl on her head.

"That's me," she said when she handed me my banana. "African violet. What the white man went to Africa looking for? Spice! Pepper for his pots, chocolate for his sweets. And look what they found. Me. Ginger, cinnamon, nutmeg, all rolled into one."

She was drunk on wine and high on reefer.

"Girl, you are a mess," I laughed.

"Spice is the variety of life." Blondine danced away as the record changed. "And you know what life is."

"Ain't nothing but a party!" I called out to her across the room.

She pulled out her rusty old school flute and played *Three Blind Mice* with her drunk self, until somebody snatched it away from her. After that she just danced.

Blondine was a beautiful dancer. I learned to pattern my style after hers. But she was reckless, too. She could get so wild in the magic of the movement that she wasn't watching the room around her. She would boogaloo into furniture, bop into walls. Maybe that's how she had blundered into death.

Or maybe it was the spice she seasoned her life with. Maybe she hadn't looked close enough and mistook poison for pepper. Shit for sugar. Maybe death was the ultimate cost to maintain her cool.

After Blondine's funeral I called Michael to come get me. He drove me back up to the Southside, and parked over at Rainbow Beach. Michael didn't try anything, for once in his life. He didn't touch me at all except for holding my hand and patting it every now and then. We parked and watched the waves wash up against the rocks. I felt like I was dying and the water wasn't saving me.

I raised the armrest that kept us apart. I scooted over to him and started unbuttoning his shirt. Can you believe it? Horny-ass Michael was pushing my hands away.

"You don't have to do this, baby. I know this is a bad time for you."

I didn't want his understanding. It was too late for that. I got his shirt off, but his pants were hard to remove in the sitting position. He was still protesting.

"Pat, honey. If you just want to be held . . ."

"I want to be fucked," I said. "And don't worry. I'm not bleeding."

Isn't life strange, Diary, my girl? Things do come back full circle. It had started with me begging him, then him begging me, and now it was back to the beginning. I was hungry for something; I felt empty inside. I was dying, and needed something to bring me back.

It hurt at first. But I didn't care. It was good to be feeling something, even if that something was pain. And then I started feeling something else. Let me see if I can describe it. It was like I was a empty balloon. And Michael was the air that filled me. I kept getting fuller and fuller and fuller until I knew I would pop. But for some reason I didn't. It was like all the air just came rushing back out again.

Michael said it was because this was my first time. He said most women don't come their first time. Maybe I will when it happens again.

But it was still good. Michael's touch, his arms around me, his body inside made me feel alive again. I could feel blood flowing in my veins. I had found the spice I needed to fight off death.

I wish I could tell you what I know now, Blondine. Spice is not just the variety of life. It is life itself.

October 20, 1972

Well, girlfriend, I guess this is it. Nine entries in five years. If somebody else were reading you from cover to cover like I just did tonight, I think they would be more curious about the things left out than the things written in. I've been like a bad friend, only coming to you in times of trouble.

It's a shame to have to end this with the pages half-full. But I guess I really didn't have the discipline to sit down and record the events of my life on a regular basis.

I'm leaving Phoenix tomorrow morning. I've been here way too long as it is. Anybody with good sense is long gone. I've already dropped out of Governor's State. I wasn't college material anyway.

Big Momma always used to say that *boys and books don't mix*. Maybe she was right. It was hard to sit and study in the library, when there was a party going on in the boy's dormitory. When people asked what my college major was, I always told them, *Men*. That seems to be the only thing I'm any good at.

Remember how I used to fantasize about growing up to be a writer or a model or a movie star? Well, I haven't become anything but a player. I chew men like gum, tasting them until the flavor wears off, then spit them out. And the killing thing is they let me do it to them time and again. And come crawling back for more.

Now, don't get me wrong. I love the pampering, the sex, the money spent. I don't set out meaning to break men's hearts. It's like I'm hungry all the time, but I can't seem to find the right food. So I taste a little bit of everything. It's like something's out there calling me, and I can't figure out who it is. So I go looking for the voice in every man I meet.

If only I could find someone who won't let me twist him around my finger like I've been doing Pop all my life. A man who will see something in me besides light skin and good hair. A man who will demand my respect. But I haven't found him yet. I haven't even found myself.

I guess I still don't know what I want to be when I grow up. But I do know where I don't want to be. And that's Phoenix. It's time for me to blow this ghost town. To get from underneath Pop's iron embrace and Lola's iron purse strings.

You remember my friend from high school, Anita Cantrell? She's living in Chicago now and she's been asking me to come stay with her. I spend more time in the city than in Phoenix anyway. And Pop has been giving me the blues about so many nights away from home. I might as well start spending my days there, too.

Pop's getting old and dropping heavy hints about marriage and grandkids. He wants somebody around to take over the family businesses when he's gone. But cutting heads and embalming stiffs in Phoenix couldn't be further from my mind.

Pretty soon that funeral parlor's going to be the only game in town. Phoenix is going down slow, full of dusty ghosts with empty pockets. Life here is becoming a life without spice. And life without spice isn't life at all, it's death. I'm not a ghost yet and I intend to stay that way for a while. So Pat Brown is moving up and out. I'll find me a job, find somebody or some bodies to keep me warm, and start living the spice of my own life.

You've been a faithful friend these five years. I almost hate to put you down. I know I never gave you the attention I should. I only came to you in times of need. But it was a comfort just knowing you were around in case I needed someone to talk to. I've always been a loner and sharing my feelings don't come easy.

But if I was too lazy before, I'll be too busy for you now. I'm getting kind of old to be talking to a bunch of bound papers like it was a real person. Keeping a diary is a teenage thing, and I'm free, brown, and twenty-one. I don't plan to be sitting around here writing life, Diary, my dear.

I'm going to be out there living it. I hear somebody out there calling my name, and I'm doing my damnedest to answer.

I Don't Know Nothin' 'Bout
Birthin' No Babies

October 20, 1973

Dear Allie Mae:

How is college treating my baby way up there in Providence?

Don't a day pass when I don't think about you, and miss you, and wonder how you're getting on. I'm counting the days until you home with us for Christmas. Wish we could afford to bring you home Thanksgiving, too. But you know how tight money is. This twenty dollars ain't much, but I hope it helps you some.

We all been doing fine. Benny fell off the toilet up at Waukegan and had to go in the hospital. He's doing better now, praise the Lord. Otis lost his little bit of disability money last month. Those peoples had the nerve to tell him he well enough to go to work, bad as his back is.

You remember Miss Nibbs out to Lombard, where I mind her mother Friday nights? She so happy to hear you in college. She give me these books and magazines she was fixing to throw away, thought you might could use them.

I see one here where they pay peoples to write about *My Most Unforgettable Character*. You know I don't have much education. I don't know much about story writing and what-all. But Lord knows I could use the money. And I have known me some Unforgettable Characters in my time. Maybe you could write it up for me.

I know I ain't never told you much about my childhood. I been spending my life trying to forget. It wasn't an easy thing coming up in Cairo. But if I learned one thing at the age of forty-five, it's the truth of that old church song. *I can't get above what made me.* I been thinking a lot about peoples I ain't seen in years.

Let me tell you about Lula Mae Jaspars. You know Cousin Lola, on my daddy's side? Her mama, my aunt Truly, was my daddy's half sister. I guess you could call us distant first cousins. They were the kin folk you never saw much of, come from living too close to the white folks' part of town.

Old Sheriff Jaspars was one of the ugliest mens you would want to see. Red face, red hair, big old red nose. Now you got to know he had a red neck. That didn't stop him from keeping his two houses. A big rambling one for his white wife and kids. A little white cottage for Aunt Truly and the kids they had.

I don't know how he done it. Maybe he would switch up days. Say, Mondays, Wednesdays, and Fridays with Aunt Truly. Tuesdays, Thursdays, and Saturdays for

Mrs. Jaspars, his white wife. Sunday to rest, you know he needed it. Between his two families, Sheriff Jaspars had twenty-something kids. Lula Mae was one of them.

They say Lula Mae was her daddy's favorite of the bunch. She didn't favor him, except for being kind of on the red side. How ugly Sheriff Jaspars made such a fine gal, I'll never know. Those light, funny-colored eyes of Lula Mae's. I swear they changed with the weather. Rainy days they was gray, sunny days they was green. She got that good hair too, used to wear it all down her back. Never did have the need of no straightening comb.

Lula Mae Jaspars grew up to be a traveling woman. Her daddy sent her all over. New York City. New Orleans. Texas. I wanted to be a traveling woman, too, but I was too chicken-shit to go off on my own. She was in San Francisco when I got it in my mind to go out and see her. I wasn't but about fourteen years old, but I went up there on the train all by myself. First time I ever set foot out of Cairo, I went halfway across country. Took me the better part of a week.

Lula Mae, who had been about the sharpest dresser in Alexander County, had took to wearing sandals, long skirts, headrags, and gold hoops in her ears. She had herself a Mexican boyfriend, and was passing herself off as a Gypsy fortune-teller, but she ain't used no crystal ball. She had a little black spider tatooed in the cup of her right hand, with all the lines in her palm stretched out around it like a web. For a price, she would tell them filthy-rich white womens up on Telegraph Hill what the spider saw in their future.

At first Lola, which is what Lula Mae had started calling herself, wasn't that happy to see her country cousin. But when it came to her that I could be of some help, Lola changed her mind and welcomed me with open arms. She got me on with the MacAvie family doing cleaning. It turned out I was doing her work and mines, too.

You know, thinking back on it, Dennis MacAvie might make a good story. That child was something else. I called him *Dennis the Menace*. I'd put him in his high chair while I cleaned up the house. He liked to be up high. And he'd be steady watching me with those big old blue eyes. He would wait for me all morning, just as quiet and patient. By lunchtime I would have that whole house spotless and the rest of the day left to play with Dennis.

The older he got, the more he swore I was his mama. But I wasn't soft like Mrs. Hightone MacAvie. I wasn't but fifteen years old, but Callie Mae Bullocks did not take no mess. I remember one day they give me some money to take Dennis to a picture show. Dennis wanted a cowboy picture. I wanted to see *Gone With the Wind*. Guess who won?

"Lordy, Miz Scarlet. I don't know nothin' 'bout birthin' no babies!"

Me and old buck-eyed Butterfly McQueen about the only black faces in the movie house. Dennis just would have to point at the screen and holler out: "Look! There you go, Callie Mae."

Child, I took him out of there and tanned his natural hide. If he had the nerve to show his behind, I had the nerve to whip it for him. Showing me out like that. I might be somebody's housemaid, but I wasn't hardly nobody's slave. If Dennis ain't learned nothing else, I made sure he learned that well.

"Are you my real mother?" he come asking me another time.

"Now, Dennis. How I'm going to be your mother? Look at you. I'm colored. You're white."

"No." Dennis shakes his blond head. "I'm colored, too."

I went and got his crayon box and a big sheet of white paper.

"Look at here." I drew a stick figure with the brown crayon. "This is me. What color is that?"

Dennis squinched up his eyes. He was just learning to name his colors.

"Brown."

"Alright." I picked out the white crayon. "Now this is you."

I rubbed and rubbed it on the paper.

"But Callie Mae. Nothing's coming out."

"That's right, child. You see, they call people like me colored, because we're colored brown or black. They call people like you white, because you don't have no color to you."

He frowned up his face and snatched the crayon away from me. He commenced to scratching it against the paper, trying to get a picture out of it. Finally it broke.

"Ain't nothing you can do to make white colored, Dennis MacAvie."

When it hit him that he couldn't make a colored picture with that white crayon, he bust out crying and wailed the whole afternoon.

Well, I've met colored people who wanted to be white so bad they would take a shotgun to their own shadow. And I've met many a colored person who don't have a thing in the world to hold on to but their color. I was one of them. But I ain't never met a white person who wanted to be colored so bad they would cry about it. Not until that day.

Lola said I was being cruel to the child. But you know as good as I do that Dennis would grow up and learn to love his whiteness. You know he did. But you better believe that he also grew up knowing that darkness can make a mighty mark. And Dennis MacAvie also ain't out there making a mammy out of every colored woman he comes across, do my name ain't Callie Mae Clemmons.

Of course I didn't have a way in the world of knowing how he grew up until near on thirty years later. Lola got in trouble with the family about bringing a man in the house to sleep in their bed when they was out of town. Dennis got an eyeful and couldn't wait to run and tell. And we were both sent packing back to Cairo.

But Lola wasn't a woman who would stay put for too long. Being run out of San Francisco on a rail ain't put a crook in her step. She hadn't sat down in Cairo good before she was off again to be with a man up in Phoenix. A black man this time. He had a little piece of change in his pocket, too. You know Lola had to have a man with some money.

Back then Clyde Brown owned the only barbershop and funeral parlor in town, right next door to each other. *Clyde's cuts will do you proud*, was one of his slogans. *Browns, for the Funeral of Distinction*, was the other.

Passing for Creole now (which I guess Creole is just about anything you want to make it), Lola went ahead on and married him. When she had the baby she come back down to Cairo and got me. I guess then she remembered how good I did her all those years in San Francisco when she was supposed to be baby-sitting

Dennis. Lola never been too good with kids, anyway. Her temper ain't as long as my toenail.

Anyway, I went on up to Phoenix to be Clyde and Lola's live-in. And here's where I met another one of My Most Unforgettable Characters. He was so unforgettable, I up and married him. But that's getting ahead of the story.

I thank Clyde Brown to this day. If it hadn't been for him wanting to stay home and play with his baby girl, I might not have never met your daddy. His name was Benjamin Peeples, but everybody who knew him called him *King*.

Clyde had set Lola up in a little business. She was queen of Lola's Place, a little juke joint that served watered-down drinks and live music. That night Clyde had come home from the barbershop or funeral parlor, one. He woke up Pat and started playing with her. She opened those big eyes and grinned all up in his face, nothing but curls and dimples. A little Daddy's Girl. If I had woke the hussy out of sleep she would have been screaming to beat the band.

"Go on out and have a good time, Callie Mae. I'm baby-sitting tonight."

"Where I'm going? I don't know nobody around here."

"Go on down to Lola's. If you want to meet you somebody, that's where they all at."

So down to Lola's I went. And I met me somebody. A big, black, burly somebody. Six and a half feet tall. King was there taking pictures of the colored folks dancing and drinking and flirting with each other's wives. He'd snap awhile, then duck back in that room behind the bar awhile. It was crowded that Saturday night, seemed like everybody wanted their picture took. King stuck his head out the door and hollered over where I was sitting drinking my soda pop, trying to make like it was something else.

"Come on in here and help me, girl."

Turned out to be, King had a darkroom set up in there where he was printing up the pictures as quick as he could shoot them. I got a quick lesson and was left to develop film and print pictures for the rest of the evening. We were a good team from day one. Just like a key and lock when they're well greased and not rusty. One works the other.

King, he was a natural-born salesman. Loud and friendly, could tell a Shine joke to a church mother and have her laughing at the filthiest lines. People just took a liking to him. He'd jolly them into having their pictures took; sweet-talk the womens, buddy up the mens. We'd sometimes pull in two hundred dollars on a good night. We'd work Chicago, Gary, Milwaukee, Peoria, and every place in between. Lord, wasn't that the good life?

See, me, I was the quiet type. I was happy to be in the back in the dark, with the noise and the music and the laughter floating back to me. I never missed a thing. Anything I ain't overheard, the pictures told the story the minute they start coming to life in the fix.

And if they didn't have nothing to say, King sure would. When the night was over we'd go on back home, count up our money, and King would tell me which woman got drunk and danced the hootchie-kootchie on the bar, who beat whose butt in what fight, what songs the band was singing that night.

King had him a good singing voice. He could croon just as good as that other man they called *King* who used to work the same juke joints we did before he went and got famous singing:

Unforgettable, that's what you are.

What went wrong with your daddy and me? The lock ran out of grease. The key wore down. Children started being born.

Maybe I should never have had kids. Lord knows I love you both. But when I had taken care of other people's babies it was so easy. When I had my own, it was hard as day-old biscuits. Hard as a pimp's heart. Hard as the sun-baked row you know you got to hoe. That's why I look after old folks now. Seems I'm better helping ease folks out of life than I am raising them up in it.

Your brother Benny wasn't right from the beginning. He wanted to go out of this life the minute he came in it. Maybe they should have let him. They worked on him a good twenty minutes to bring him back. But part of him stayed over on the other side. He always hung back. Slow to crawl, slow to walk, slow to talk. Took him ten years to get up to where most boys would be at two. And he ain't never went no further.

Big, lively King and his slow son, Benny. It broke his heart every time he looked at the boy. And it broke my heart when I saw him looking. He never laid blame, but I always felt to blame. Like I must have done something wrong to make a child that wasn't right. Maybe it was the smoke in the air of all them juke joints. Maybe it was the chemicals I always had my hands in.

When I got pregnant again King made me come off the road.

"You a mother now. Soon to be mother of two. These late nights and smoky taverns ain't the right life for a mother."

You was a normal child, even though you came six weeks early. Black as a raisin and smart as a whip. But Lord, I ain't never seen such a colicky baby. Always wanted somebody to be holding you. If not, you cried. Girl, you could lay up there for an hour, flailing those little legs and wailing those little lungs. Once you got started good, Benny would join in. Sometimes I'd have to go out on the porch just to get away from the noise and have a minute to myself.

King was away working nights, sometimes overnight. And my mind would be working overtime. I'd be seeing him with some woman in the corner of a tavern somewhere. I'd hear his deep laugh mixed in with her soft one, while I sat up and listened to babies screaming.

Motherhood turned me into somebody I didn't like. A prying, jealous, hateful somebody. The kind of woman who goes through wallets and listens in on phone calls. A woman who boils water and sharpens knives. King was a traveling man. I knew that when I met him. One day he went out on the road and didn't come back.

Well, they say what goes around, comes around. And I lived to have a man who would do me like I did King. You know who I'm talking about. A man so jealous-hearted he couldn't stand to hear another man's name on my lips. A man who burned up my clothes on the barbecue grill because he said they showed too much of me. A man who wants to own every step I take, every thought I think, every breath

I draw. I know you two never got along, but Otis ain't a bad man in his way. Sometimes I wish I had let him straight alone. It's too late to fret on that now.

And I don't hold hard feelings for King no more. He was a man who couldn't live with chains dragging at him. If I saw him today I would tell him that I lived to understand why he had to go.

Lola, Dennis, or King? Who do you think would make the best story? Or what would you say if I told you this? My most Unforgettable Character is me. Callie Mae Clemmons, forty-five years old. Born in Battle Creek, Michigan, raised up in Cairo, Illinois.

My daddy was a traveling man, too. He was an evangelist who went all up and down the country preaching revivals. He used to say that God got him up one morning and told him to spread the word far and wide. And he never stopped moving until a lightning bolt caught him while driving to a revival one night.

I never knew my mother. They say she used to go out on the road with him, singing gospel and passing the plate. I was born on the road, halfway between a church anniversary in Chicago and a revival in Detroit. My mother died giving birth to me.

Maybe that's why I come up wanting to be a traveling woman. Like that train named the *City of New Orleans* that would come whistling through Cairo in the night. I wanted to cock my hat to the side, jam my hands in my pockets, and jump aboard. Just move any which way the railroad would take me. I wanted to ride that train. I wanted to be that train.

But it took a while for the blood to take. Daddy stayed on the road, I stayed on the truck farm with Big Momma. Working the land, pulling at the roots of sweet potatoes, and feeling like I was growing roots that didn't belong in that place.

I just wanted to be out somewhere. Don't you remember being so little you couldn't even wipe your nose right, but always dreaming? Wanting to be out in the world with people who ain't known you since birth. People with things left to find out about them.

I ain't done too bad. I haven't traveled far, but I've been a lot of places. From Battle Creek to Cairo. Cairo to San Francisco and back again. Phoenix, Illinois. The night side of at least a dozen little cities in Illinois and Indiana. And Chicago, that's where it all ended up.

But don't a day pass when I don't wonder what I would have done and where I would have gone if I'd lived my whole life as a free woman. With no babies to keep me home, would I be laughing on King's arm right now in some other city? Ain't no telling.

Y'all kids are gone now. I'm as free as I'm ever going to be. I could go off tomorrow if I wanted to. But seems like once I got shed of one anchor, here come another one to weight me down. A piece of job to go to, a piece of house to pay on. A piece of man to keep me company as the years go by. Well, I guess my life wouldn't make no kind of story. I lived it long, but maybe not so well. But I tell you what.

I got me a daughter who is one Unforgettable Character. That's you, baby. Allie Mae Peeples. Still as black as a raisin and smart as a whip. I guess I give you a name something like mine because I thought you would be another one of me. But honey, ain't no such thing as making yourself over in somebody else. You don't belong to nobody but yourself. Allie Mae ain't hardly Callie Mae. I guess you calling yourself Alma now.

It tickled me to death when you went and done like Cousin Lola did. Changed your name to suit yourself. What you say Alma Peeples means? *Soul of a people?* It takes a writer to think up with something like that.

When I was coming up it wasn't no such thing as a colored girl making a living as no writer. But the only difference between *ain't yet* and *could be* is trying. You sure tried. Through no help of mine, Lord forgive me.

I tried to pass my ignorance on down to you. Tried as hard as I could to write *can't* on your soul. But I was writing with a white crayon that couldn't make a mark. So *can't* wasn't never a part of your makeup.

Remember when you started busing? You must have been about twelve years old. Livia was so happy when we got you and Clarisse in the white children's school. I wasn't sure about it at first, but Livia talked me into it. You girls was so smart, but that school you'd been going to wasn't for shit. To me and Livia, this was a chance to get our daughters a little piece of the future.

It wasn't nothing special we were dreaming of. You'd get to finish high school without having a baby. Go to college maybe. Get a job as a schoolteacher or nurse. Just the stingy little dreams of poor colored womens.

I knew it was going to be rough on you girls. But Livia said it like this; *at least there'd be two of you.* White folks was going to make it hard, but at least you would have each other to lean on. And be getting that good education, couldn't nobody take it away. Y'all got an education alright.

I seen what you went through every night on TV. It was just as bad as Little Rock ten years before. Bunch of grown-ass white womens, carrying signs and hollering at a busload of helpless children. Nothing I had ever taught could have got you ready to be called *nigger* by womens old enough to know better.

Livia didn't get nothing but grief for her dreaming. *What did Clarisse die from?* you used to always ask me. I didn't think that knowing would help, young as you was then. I guess I might as well tell you now. You remember that last time they carried her to the hospital? Clarisse had the sickle cell, she died in the County after having the fit that day in school.

What did I get for my dreaming? It's hard to say. You met the lynch mob at the age of twelve, lost your best friend to it. You know, I wanted to pull you out but Livia wouldn't hear of it. Said her baby's death wasn't going for nothing. Maybe you can tell me now. Was it worth it?

You stayed. Got that good education. And gone on to do much more in life than the raggedy little dreams I dreamed for you. You grew up strong, learning early on that to keep from being a beggar you had to be a fighter. But was it because of, or in spite of me? I guess I'll never know.

All I know is that I would come home from work so late most evenings, you was already done cooking dinner and putting Benny to bed. You'd be sitting up at the kitchen table, just writing. Sometimes so mad you couldn't even speak. But writing like the lessons on that paper would save your soul. And to tell you the truth, I don't begrudge you your anger. It helped you make a way for yourself in a world where most colored womens scared to walk.

I told you that I ran into Dennis the Menace again? I was on the ward one day, collecting my sheets for the laundry. And here comes this white man loping down the hall after me, hospital gown hanging all open in the back. Thirty years later and Dennis MacAvie still showing his behind.

The money his parents had and the gumption I gave him had made him a big shot in the business world. But he was still little snotty-nosed Dennis the Menace to me, just living high in filthy-rich Lake Forest instead of San Francisco. He couldn't believe that life hadn't taken me no further than the hospital laundry.

"If you'd just apply yourself, Callie Mae, you could conquer the world. Hell, you've got twice the balls of the average corporate CEO out there."

"Nigger," I said. Since the boy had been so interested in being colored, I felt free to call him by some of the worser names we're known by. "Don't be telling me to apply myself. I taught you the ropes when you didn't know your ass from a hole in the ground. You better be out there telling your corporate boys to apply themselves and get they feet off my peoples' necks."

I ain't asked Dennis for but one thing. I figure he owed it to me for raising him. It wasn't nothing for him to get you that college scholarship. And you acted like it was nothing for you to get it, too.

"Payback," I remember you saying when you was packing for the trip out east. "Just paying back a few pennies of the millions they've made off us for the past four hundred years."

I should have knowed that being a schoolteacher or nurse would never be my girl's speed. You been writing things up so long, I bet you still got ink stains on your fingers. I kept everything you wrote, too. Shoot, I still got shoeboxes in the closet, full of the lists and letters and stories you been writing since you was old enough to pick up a pen.

See, you're like your mama and your daddy and grandfolks before you; a traveling woman. You're going places in this life. You know how to go out, yet you know how to come home. You ain't a train, you a ship. Can pull those anchors up, and put them back down again.

Or being a woman of today, maybe I should say my Alma is a plane with wings spread wide. With the Lord beside you and the wind behind you, ain't no telling how far this life will take you.

Now I know what you going to say. *Mama, you lived the life. So you write the story.* But I just don't have the experience. So you take it and fix it up, make it so it reads right. I guess since you turned out to be My Most Unforgettable Character, it's only right that I split the money with you. So finish it up just as fast as you can, do we get that little piece of pocket change.

Be a good girl up there, now. Remember what Big Momma used to say. *Boys and books don't mix.* Keep your mind stayed on your lessons, don't fool around and get pregnant, and everything will come out alright.

Your mother,
Callie Mae Clemmons

Beadwork

Some of us have been around long enough to remember that wisdom once belonged to all men and women, until Ananse decided to hoard it all for himself. He gathered all the wisdom on earth and hid it in a pot, which he placed at the very top of a silk cotton tree. The trunk of this giant tree is studded with thorns, so no one could ever hope to climb it.

One day Ananse thought to check on his pot of hoarded wisdom. He spun a line that he flung to the top, then climbed it. But while in the treetops, he upset the pot, and down it fell. When the pot hit the ground, it burst into a thousand pieces. And wisdom was able to escape and return to the world.

But some of it was crushed in the fall. Wisdom is no longer in great abundance. It is difficult to find, and even harder to hold.

Those who seem to have acquired their fair share? Rest assured, it has never been visited upon anyone full blown. It is a lifetime task, a patient, painstaking harvesting. And while wisdom is a quality that can be shared, it is a prize no one will ever win in a sweepstakes or inherit from the family fortune.

Perhaps it is true that our daughters are destined to love unwisely. But who among us, living or dead, can say that they haven't? I, too, have been in search of spice, lovesick and desperate. Even in the afterlife I am weak for pleasures of the flesh, my phantom lover in the waterfall. And as a living woman I was known to stumble upon the road of love. It was only the offerings I made to my ancestors that saved me.

And we too have an obligation to help save our daughters. To help them learn to love well, and wisely. They also have obligations to themselves. They must shape a destiny where a man's love does not make, but enhances, a life well lived.

Every one of our daughters must find a way in life that moves her forward into the wisdom of her womanhood. Something she can master, like Proud

Mary's medicines here, Bohema's quilting in the living world. At the risk of immodesty, perhaps even my humble attempts at beadworking may be the way a poor Gatekeeper adds to the store of her collected treasure. For even in death a woman may become wise.

The Wisdom of Her Womanness

T he time would come when one of the Queen Mother's daughters in the land of the living was praying for the resources with which to travel.

"Travel." The Needleworker sniffs. "Is that not the province of men? Putting on their traveling shoes. Listening to train whistles in the night, hearing the road calling. Getting into the wind. It means nothing but leaving behind the ones they love. Running away from the problems every soul has to face. Now women want to do the same thing."

The Gatekeeper begs to differ.

"We've been doing it for quite some time. Market women and nomads, prostitutes and pilgrims. Why, your own mother was a wanderer. Seems to me, Sister Needleworker, that your heart must have been broken by a traveling man."

"The name is Emilene," she answers haughtily. "And if such was the case? I lived the story, so it's mine to tell. You show me one who roams, I'll show you a troubled soul. Someone who stirs up dirt to leave behind for someone else to clean. The mother gone off to the big city, leaving behind a houseful of children for some other woman to raise. The husband gone drinking and never heard from again, leaving behind his bills and bad debts. The spoiled child, running away from home. Running away never solves a thing."

Saltwater Ama, of course, would say her piece. If anyone can talk about being a traveling woman, here she is.

"But sometimes a new start can turn a troubled life around. Traveling isn't always a running away. It can be a running to. Farmers searching for fertile fields. Cattle keepers seeking out new grazing grounds. Slaves stealing away to freedom, sharecroppers striking out for independence. A river doesn't just ramble. It wants to connect with other rivers, to escape the boundaries of land. To taste the salt of sea. Show me a river that doesn't run, and I'll show you a lake. Landlocked."

It wasn't planned that way, but it seemed that a mother and daughter never able to know one another in life were destined to battle wits in the hereafter.

"What sense is there in wandering the world?" Needleworker Emilene insists. "Everywhere there are the same sunsets, the same full moons, the same stars in the sky. The same rascals and the same scoundrels. Tell me where they don't fall in love, make babies, get sick, worry over wealth, eat, sleep, and die? Why must one go away to find these things?"

"But don't forget, one of our offspring has a long trek ahead of her. The daughter of deepest memory must return us all to the River Where Blood Is Born."

"How many centuries have you all been saying that? Stirring up trouble and discontent in these women's lives? Calling to them across waters? Having them follow rivers that lead them nowhere? We've had our lives and lived them. We're dead folks here, old forgotten family. Jumbies and duppies. Haints and saints, spirits and unborn souls. I think we must forget this foolhardy quest. Let the dead bury the dead. Leave the living to get on with their lives."

"We are living, too, Needleworker Emilene. Our bloodlines run out into the village of flesh. Do we abandon our children just because we're no longer in a body? We stay alive because they need us there."

"And we need somebody's business to meddle in."

"My daughter, you surprise me. Where would the world be without our guidance?"

"The world doesn't seem to be in such a good way for it. People still hurting and dying. And womankind suffers the worst of it. Raped like dogs, beaten like drums, worked like mules. Look at us. Some in this village went traveling because we were made to move, not of our own accord. We went across water because we were carried. Some of us came to this Village of the Ancestors as sacrifices. We were the old women carrying wisdom. Why weren't any of you old ones meddling when they cut that one's tongue, stole that one's babies, stoned this one as a witch?"

"My child, my child. Even in death you are steeped in despair. Do you not realize how powerful you are?"

"Not powerful enough to have saved myself. Who are any of us to say that indulging in her idle whim to wander will save another?"

The Priestess, who had finally taken up permanent residence here, breaks into the standoff with her own dry brand of hilarity.

"Well, I move that we let her move, because if she can move, then we all can move. I've tarried here too long and I'm ready to go home."

"It also seems," the Gatekeeper ventured to suggest, "that one of our sisters here is discontented with the life she has led. She was born to be a bridge between two worlds, but time and a jealous ocean trapped her on an island without rivers. She never learned how to surge forth like sweetwater, never heard the call of blood. I believe she should be given another chance to become."

"If it is me to whom you refer," Needleworker Emilene responded stiffly, "then I want none of it. I don't care to go back to living all that pain, thank you kindly. I am tired. If I can't get some rest while I'm dead, then when will I?"

That was the first incident. Yet another afternoon, to pass the time at a riverside picnic, we begin to speculate on the outcome of our daughters' fortunes in the land of the living. Each of us has our favorites there, the team we root for on such occasions. Whether any among them will prove herself worthy in the end, even we cannot say. Just a harmless wager we engage in now and again, to wile away the time until we're called upon.

The women relax by the river in the setting sun, watching *As the Other World Turns*. Doing work with their hands as they sit—sewing, knitting, crocheting, whittling. They glance at the waters and the stories that flicker idly in them, like TV soap operas. Commenting on each as they appear.

"Ooh, look at that child rambling around that windy city. Just as fast as she want to be. She don't be careful she going to get in a world of trouble. Hope she ain't one of ours."

"Child, I'm glad I'm retired from all that. Heartbreak and unhappiness. Riots, weapons. War and rumors of war. It's a mess."

"Well, I'll put my money on Lola Brown. That's a get-up-and-go girl if ever there was one."

"Have you looked in on her lately? Her get-up-and-go has got up and gone. She's been sitting in the same place much too long. Of course, now she's got a daughter."

"That little womanish Pat Brown? Spoiled rotten and man-crazy to boot. Got a lot of growing up to do, that one."

"Well, they all do. But she has a lot of spirit, and that's a promising sign. If the plucky sparrow got nothing else from God, it got its dash. What say you, Needle-worker Emilene? Don't you have daughters out there among the living?"

"And I am sure that what my descendants do in their lives is not my concern. God alone is the end course of all things."

"Don't take that tone of voice with me, young lady. I've been watching since you were a mewling little newborn named Diaspora."

"Ooh, don't that girl got an attitude. Wonder what's eating her?"

"Don't mind her. Most of her team is trapped on some little fleck of sand in the ocean, a land without a single river to its name."

"I bet a nicely placed hurricane would blow some of them out into the world."

"I don't care how hard you make the wind blow. That gang of girls ain't about to budge. Move aside, sister. Let me see what's going on with these Peeples."

"What peoples?"

"Callie Mae and Allie Mae. The mother got out in the world a little bit, but now it looks like she's anchored down. Plus, she ain't got a penny to her name, and a woman needs a little money in her pocket to travel with. You think her young rookie's going to do any better?"

"Where that girl gone off to now? I ain't never seen such a wandering somebody."

"It was you who said let's give her some money to travel with. Why you complaining now that she's using it?"

"That girl don't know how to sit still. Makes me nervous to see somebody that restless. She's forever wandering. London, England. What a colored woman want over there, beside mixing it up with a married man? Washington, D.C. Where's she headed for now in the Carry Beyond?"

"The who?"

A jet plane circles above a green island. One of them leans forward, adjusts her glasses for a better look. Proud Mary, Saltwater Ama, stands up suddenly.

"The Caribbean. It's the sugar island, the place my tongue was taken. Where they tried their best to break me. We can't let her go there."

Emilene snorts over her needlework. "That was your life, old woman. They are no longer about the business of slave breaking on Barbados, I will have you know."

Proud Mary, Ama Krah, readjusts her glasses and stares at her first-born daughter. "If that be the case, perhaps it is because those that are there have already been broken."

The others hurry in with their opinions, before the argument can escalate.

"That traveling is a good sign, if you ask me. That's the one I'm putting my money on. What you call her name?"

"Born *Allie Mae*. Oops, look like she's about to change it. Oh, and here comes another one, just like the other one. From now on they'll be known as *Alma* and *Cinnamon*."

"How you supposed to follow the score when the names of the players keep changing? You think these children going anywhere in life, much less returning to the River Where Blood Is Born, when they don't even know what name to call themselves by? Don't seem like neither Allie Mae nor Pat got the natural-born wisdom of her womanness."

But wait, what is happening here? Perhaps they have exceptionally good ears, and hear their names being spoken in the Great Beyond. One begins to cry out without shedding tears. And such a cry it is, it clutches at the heart like the plaintive wailing of a child in pain. The other sheds tears without crying out. And such tears, they threaten to turn our river into a sea of salt. And the cause of all this misery? Ah, but that story is even sadder.

Just then the weather would change. Lightning would flash and thunder would rumble. A sure sign that a great ancestor is about to cross over.

She crosses a wooden bridge over a slow blue river and seems surprised to arrive at a picnic. Checked blankets and multicolored quilts are spread with mountains of fragrant food. All her favorite dishes are here, home-cured ham and candied yams, baking soda biscuits and cornbread. Smothered chicken and collard greens. Angel food cake and watermelon.

But before she can be properly welcomed, Saltwater Ama, Proud Mary, hobbles up. For a woman who couldn't speak for nearly one hundred years, she seems to be making up for lost time.

"It's about time you got here, girl. What took you so long? You've got to get ahold of your daughters. They got too much promise to let it go wasting."

No sooner does the new ancestor step foot on hallowed ground, than she is surrounded. It is clear that this gathering of fussy old ladies wasn't quite what she'd been expecting.

"Don't rush her," the Gatekeeper cautions. "Don't you see she just got here? Settle down and get your bearings, sister. Here, let me help you out of those heavy waist beads. Have a drink of water, a bite to eat."

"Listen," the woman speaks hesitantly. "I been a good Christian all my life. I want to know where I am and who you all are."

"Don't you know you're among family? Otherwise you wouldn't be here. Anybody here who knows . . . What's your name, honey?"

"Bohema Bullocks, thank you kindly."

Saltwater Ama seizes her, regarding her fondly in outstretched arms.

"Big Momma Quiltmaker. Child, it's me. Your nana."

"Nana Proud Mary? You sure? I ain't never heard you speak before."

"If the cow has never learned to speak, is it because she does not have a tongue? Don't tell me you don't recognize your great-grandmother. And," she reminds her as they embrace, "it's not quite true that you haven't heard my voice. I visited you at least once, as I recall. *Snake Following the North Star*. Does that ring a bell?"

"Lordy mercy," Big Momma breathes. "Seem like I've landed in the home of the haints. How could you know what happened in my dream?"

"We prefer to call it the Village of the Ancestors, dear one. This is your home now. And during your life, dream was the only way I could reach you. You wouldn't have had it any other way, a Mount Shiloh church mother like yourself. Ah, but you were a stubborn one."

"Now, wait one minute. Am I in heaven or in the other place? Cause if I'm in heaven, I expects to have my wings. I ain't missed a Sunday service in ninety-something years. If I don't deserve my wings, then nobody do."

A collective sigh is heaved. A conference is hastily called. Needleworker Emilene is pressed into service. It is not long before a pair of wings are stitched together from the white feathers of the great river heron. But before they can formally be presented, the picnic is marred by drops of rain. Women hurry to gather food as lightning flashes across the sky.

"Don't mean to say," the new one observes, "that it rains here in heaven."

"Big Momma Quiltmaker," the Gatekeeper whispers as they rush for shelter. "We are sorry to put you to work so quickly. But your help is needed. Your daughters, I regret to say, are in dire straits. So early on their road to womanhood, they've allowed themselves to become sidetracked."

"Sidetracked? By what?"

"What else?" Prissy little Needleworker Emilene thrusts forward the wings without ceremony. "Men. The downfall of every sensible woman."

"Now, I don't know about that," comes a mild reproach from Saltwater Ama. "Menfolks can be manageable. I think that Big Momma Quiltmaker can vouch for that."

"Well, it's been so long since I walked down that road."

They have arrived at the place sheltered beneath waterfall, where our Queen Mother lies abed, wan but luminous. Have you ever seen a goddess whom ailing becomes so well? She greets them from behind her canopy of flowing waters.

"Of the road and the river," she riddles, her voice a pleasant murmur, "which one is elder?"

"Well." Big Momma Quiltmaker stops to consider. "Don't we build a road to meet the river?"

"Well said!" The Queen Mother beams. "A wise one has come among us. We know you've taught your daughters well the lesson of owning their own souls."

"I reckon so."

"Those lessons seem to be forgotten," the Gatekeeper regrets to report. "One of them is dizzy in the desolation of loving one who is undeserving. Another is torn between our voice and the disembodied cries of a misdirected spirit. Your girls have lost their vision."

"Blinded?"

"To the hoodoo of their own power."

"Hoodoo." Big Momma is alarmed. "I don't carry on with hoodoo and such-like. I've been saved, praise the Lord."

"Then it is time for you," the Queen Mother gently instructs, "to help save your daughters. They need your medicine, your help, your hoodoo. Call it blessings if you wish. They need to be reminded."

Big Momma Quiltmaker is worried.

"But how I'm going to speak to them? I don't want to turn up like some haint in a dream, scaring my babies to death."

"You will find your way, just as you have found your wings. The good mother that you are, you will not see your child hungry and fail to feed her. See her hurting and not soothe her. See her drowning and not throw a lifeline. You will do what you must."

And so she goes, new spirit with white braids and wings to match. Determination in the set of her mouth, medicine bag slung across her breast. God's sunshine kisses her new wings. Causes them to stretch, to flex. Causes her to rise.

The Spider's Web

So it is the blame game our beadworker now plays? Accept the message, then slay the messenger? First, an innocent storyteller must shoulder the blame for last chapter's lost daughters. And after your spider goes to such pains to find them. That is gratitude for you!

Remember that proverb from the old country? *The ruin of a nation begins in the homes of its people.* Perhaps if the Gatekeeper, or any other of those present in the Great Beyond, had taken a more careful watch over their children, they would never have strayed.

Instead of expending her energies in competition with me, the Gatekeeper would do well to monitor her daughters more closely. Indeed they do seem destined to love unwisely. When Allie Mae Peeples carelessly proclaims herself a man's woman, baby, one should take that pronouncement as warning, if not a prophesy.

The Queen Mother's daughters reach a precarious point as they arrive at the threshold of womanhood, as did many an ancestor before them. Ama Krah's encounter with an unholy hunter was indeed a force in her downfall. Diaspora, Needleworker Emilene, was unable to choose the mate she favored. For Afro-Apache daughter Zubena Creek, careless loving would call her home to the ancestors long before her time. Callie Mae Clemmons allowed loneliness to cast her out of the frying pan and into the fire. And even Big Momma, Bohema Bullocks, made mistakes of love in her long lifetime.

In fact, the only one in the bunch who seems immune to men's wayward charms is that bold daughter with the spider tattoo—Lola Brown, née Lula Mae Jaspars.

Herein one is tempted to hold the sinful nature of menfolk into full account. But how does one weigh bad decisions made by delinquent daughters? It appears to me that, through no interference of my own, they are ripe to become sidetracked.

Will Alma, née Allie, indeed follow the song of her soul? Or will she let herself be led down love's dead-end lanes? Will Pat Brown, soon to become Cinnamon, live up to her own prophesy to go places in this life? Or will she stop in the road to sample every tomcat with a hairy dick?

One can only wait and see. And warn those who would cast blame that the messenger cannot be held responsible for the contents of the message.

PART V

CONFLUENCE

Beadwork

When did Kwaku Ananse become such an expert in the rearing of womankind? As far as I know, he has never raised a child of his own save Ntikuma, that sad excuse for a son.

Yes, it is true that adolescence is a delicate time in a woman's life. That is no news in our village, for the centuries of women who have lived these same growing pains. When the spider makes such pronouncements, perhaps in future he will contrive to tell us something we don't already know.

Yet again, another century soon draws to a close. Another generation of daughters emerges. We've roamed upriver from Cairo to Chicago. We have watched the evolution of an entire line of Big Momma's girls—from Lola Jaspars Brown to her daughter Pat, from Callie Mae Bullocks Peeples Clemmons to her daughter Alma, née Allie Mae.

And now two of those selfsame daughters have entered the age of their womanhood. We don't need Ananse's pointed reminders to realize that this is indeed a delicate turning in their lives. But they are not helpless, and neither are we. When a daughter makes a conscious effort to connect with our wisdom, that is when an ancestor mother must reach out a helping hand.

The Third Woman

TO THE FIRST WOMAN

I have never met you face-to-face.

But I find myself obsessed with the women who are loved by the man I love. I feel like the third point of an impossible love triangle. Or perhaps it might more properly be called a rectangle. I am, after all, only one of three women in his life.

Yet somehow I know it is you, the first woman, who has haunted me, taunted me, whispered to me from behind his shadow all these years. He has always hinted at your presence.

"Behind every great man is a great woman. And behind every great woman is a great behind."

It was one of those lapses I laughed about before I knew any better. Now I do. I know that great woman is you. It has always been his way, I suppose, to take our love for granted. Yet I can't help feeling that one day soon we will meet on our own terms. And I will finally know you for yourself, and not just as the first woman Trevor has loved.

Most women in our circumstances have this urge to let the "other women" know we exist. Let me tell you how it all started. I am nearly twenty-six years old now. That means I've been going to bed and dreaming about this man for seven years. That's longer than some marriages last. Of course, we have been more apart than together in these years. Railroad cars that couple for a journey and then move on, destined to join up again at some indeterminate point down the line.

He had no business doing it with me, you know. I was almost a child. And the man was my teacher. That's kind of like your doctor or your psychiatrist or your father. Some lines are not meant to be crossed.

I would have been content to fantasize. To watch him from my seat in the next-to-the-last row and whisper to my friend Nina, who made no bones about the hots she had for him. She busily speculated whether lecturing in economics turned him on, or if the bulge in his pants was there all the time.

"*Do me wrong, Dr. Do-right,*" Nina would murmur to the tune of a popular song. "*But don't let me be lonely tonight.*"

I would have been happy to worship him from afar in his fine, fiery splendor. I just knew he wasn't thinking about me. After all, I was green wine.

He'd called me to his office to discuss my first paper, *The Transatlantic Slave Trade & the Rise of Capitalism*. I'd spent long days in the library researching, and long hours at the typewriter composing it. He spent about five minutes shuffling through a pile in his briefcase to find it, and ten minutes reading it for what appeared to be the first time. He scribbled a B+ across the front page and thrust it at me.

I hesitated, casting down a surreptitious glance to see if the bulge was there. But he still had the briefcase in his lap and was rifling through it again. Nina would be disappointed there was nothing to report. He looked up to find me watching him, and seemed startled that I was still there.

"That'll be all for now, Miss Peeples."

And it was. I went on about my business and he his. His brusqueness didn't surprise or offend me. I didn't know how I was supposed to be treated. I was green and newborn, a freshman with no expectations. So when it all started it confused, but did not astound.

Back at school from break on Christmas Eve, a whole two weeks early. You wouldn't believe the mess going on at home with Mama and Otis. Marrying that man was the worst mistake she'd ever made. Now he thought he owned her body and soul. I couldn't take the drama and trauma of watching my mother, who never had to answer to any man, begging to be allowed to go Christmas shopping by herself. I couldn't wait to be gone, even if it meant returning to a deserted campus.

So you can understand why I was all attitude that night. Some men just love a mean woman. A slap upside the head or a dirty look turns them on like a hundred-watt lightbulb. Trevor was like that. It all went wrong when I traded in my evil attitude for naked admiration. But then I'm getting ahead of myself.

I was a taut, highstrung wire, nerves stretched to snapping. There was no rest. Mama and Otis' fights played over and over in my head on the flight east.

Out of the plane and into the terminal. I cussed myself out for being a weakling who couldn't carry her own baggage. I dragged it toward the exit. The bus was out of the question with this unwieldy load. I would have to take a taxi to campus, even though it meant I'd probably be celebrating with baloney sandwiches tomorrow night. Some Christmas.

And then this voice behind me, his voice. Nina always said that *Dr. Do-Right* could do no wrong with a voice like that; one-hundred-proof rum stirred into Blue Mountain coffee. If the ubiquitous bulge was there, it was hidden beneath his overcoat.

"That bag giving you a bit of trouble, young lady?"

I whirled, mad at Otis Clemmons and every man in the world at that particular moment.

"Any man with any manners would have offered to help."

Before I knew it he had scooped up the bag and was carrying it off to his car. Despite the extra weight, he loped rather than walked, covering great spaces in each step. I had to nearly run to keep up with his long-legged stride.

Family was on his mind, too. It was Christmas Eve, after all. He dominated the discussion during the drive to campus, speaking wistfully of the colleague just dropped off who was lucky enough to be going home for the holiday. He himself was aching with loneliness for an island one hundred miles wide. He told me I reminded him of someone on it. I know now who that someone was. She was the second woman.

He insisted on carrying the bag into my dormitory room. Helpless, I followed behind him. I was a woman without will. I was a tidal river, flowing first one way, then the other. He quickly became the current which gave me direction.

Nina had gone home to Brooklyn, leaving behind her bed unmade. He sat down on it uninvited, his long legs taking up half the room's length. He pulled me down to sit beside him. You see how I'm stretching out this part of the story? Like an alcoholic savoring the memory of that first taste.

He told me that I unnerved him. Watching me in class. In his office that day, so beside himself he could do nothing but shuffle papers, having completely forgotten what he'd meant to say to me. He, my fever, said this to me. And he rubbed my shoulders, reaching under my coat with his cold, hard hands. He pulled me close to him. The bulge was back with a vengeance.

It is strange to think that as thoroughly bad and bodacious as I had been in my early teens, I had made it to eighteen without doing it. Had never even been turned on kissing someone and wanted to go all the way. I was beginning to wonder if something wasn't wrong with me. It is therefore amazing that I was so instantly addicted. Or perhaps not so amazing, after all. Mama was once so rabidly afraid that someone would *take advantage of me*.

"No, you can't spend the night at Laura Lee's. That brother of hers might take advantage of you."

Maybe that is what I wanted after all, to be taken advantage of. It was a moment I'd been waiting for all my life, the sudden way his full lips met mine.

You know his love too. But have you ever felt his mustache moving across the surfaces of your skin? Have you noticed the smooth angles and sharp planes of his earth-black face when he closes his eyes? How he is transformed into a mask of anticipation, his features wreathed in desire?

If I could make you understand how wrong, and how completely wonderful this was. Then you would understand the makings of such addictions. How the first taste can leave you forever hooked.

He lowered me onto Nina's unmade bed. He undressed me slowly, one piece at a time. He tasted me in places I never knew could be so tender. Dewdrops of nectar bloomed between my thighs.

I wanted to unfold to him like a full-blown rose, but the bud remained tightly wrapped. He abandoned tenderness and tore into it. He uttered something between a sigh and a groan, and the searing space he'd opened was instantly flooded with a warmth and a wetness.

"Oh, Lord." He collapsed against me, murmuring into my collarbone. "Shit, woman."

"Dr. Barrett?" Alarmed, I began to cry. "What did I do?"

He reached into the pocket of his discarded jacket and removed a white handkerchief, a monogrammed B embroidered in red. Tenderly, he wiped the fresh tears, then the blood.

"God, girl," he whispered reverently. "It was your first time. I had forgotten what that needle-eye sweetness felt like."

It surprised me that the virginity I had come to regard as a nuisance was a thing he seemed to treasure. His fingers caressed the wounded space, and it began to tingle despite the soreness. If the world had ended that very moment, I would have died unutterably happy. I shivered with the sudden certainty of it.

"You're cold." He briskly rubbed my bare buttocks, as if the friction would bring a fire into being. "I believe the heat in here has gone off."

He took me away. Not to his own home, though I came to know it well. It was an old stone farmhouse that he had filled with precious pieces of art that had come to him from you. But first we went to an empty apartment in a nearby city that belonged to the friend who had traveled.

The situation defied all the stereotypes. I was the other woman, the third woman, and I had him to myself for the holidays. He tended the rose until it was full-blown and my cries no longer came from pain. I wept in his arms for two solid weeks until the semester started and we began our separate, entangled existences.

What do you know of wine tasting? I suspect that you prefer palm wine, kept fresh in calabashes in the sun, not dusty bottles in the cellar. But bear with me, if you will.

If I were wine, Trevor would have been the first man to have me, but not the first to taste me. I think of wine because of what the other man had said to me.

"Leslie Flowers will taste no wine before its time." A nineteen-year-old boy really, but seeming so manly and mature from my ant's eye view of the world at fourteen. Leslie was just past the age I would be when I became enmeshed in Trevor. Why did he seem so grown then, and I feel so green now?

Whether it was because Leslie knew when a child was not a woman, or simply preferred the flavor of riper vintages I will never know. I was only slightly crushed that he didn't want me. Crushed grapes.

By eighteen I had mellowed slightly into green wine. And now Trevor was the connoisseur. But he did not sniff the bouquet or test the aroma against his palate. He popped the cork and drank it down raw. Trevor was less discriminating than Leslie. Perhaps his appetite was greater, his tastes less refined. Or maybe his was not so much an appreciation for the nuances of new wine, as a yearning for the kick that comes with the mixing of the cocktail. My green wine, his Caribbean rum.

I was silent and alone on the island of our love. Trevor swore me to secrecy, though later I learned that our liaison was common gossip among students and faculty at large. Nor was it the only such one.

Trevor had a fleetingly jealous nature. Other men eying what he considered his private store of goodies brought it out. Once at an autograph party for a West African author visiting campus, I enjoyed a long, mildly flirtatious conversation with the guest of honor. I had been properly awed and he had been sufficiently flattered.

He talked about African literature. I questioned him avidly. He told me it was time for all African Americans to come home. From the come-hither sparkle in his eyes, he must have thought this particular African American could benefit by a get-acquainted course.

And Trevor, watching from the other side of the room, shot suspicious glances in our direction. Finally he stood and beckoned me away.

"Alma. Come over here."

I got up to leave, quick to answer the call of my master's voice. But the African author caught my hand.

"Will you come to the festivities tonight?"

And Trevor had bounded across the room in three long-legged strides, separating our entwined fingers.

"Comrade," he scolded. "This is my woman."

And he had taken me straight home. Undressed me summarily and laid me across his perfectly made bed. For a man Trevor was very neat. Made perfect hospital corners.

Standing fully clothed above my naked proneness, he addressed me. Sternly professorial.

"This is mine, woman." His hand wound into the briar patch between my legs. "My little honey pot. I'm the first one to taste it and I intend to be the last. Don't want no other man stirring around in here."

"Yes, Dr. Do-Right," I had deferred demurely. This was seven years ago, remember. My submissive stage. "But if you want to you can stir it up a little yourself."

From that day on, I couldn't hear Bob Marley's naughty invitation to *Stir It Up*, without remembering Trevor and the honey pot. And experiencing a twinge of shame to have been so flattered by his jealousy; I mistook it for a sign of love. To have been so possessed with, and willing to be possessed by, one man.

But bear in mind that I was young and impressionable and he was my first love. Bear in mind that he was a greedy grizzly, devouring the nectar of one clover pot until he tired of the taste. And moving on to sample the sweetness of other flavors. Jasmine. Sassafras. Sunflower.

Trevor was not a perfect man, as you well know. He was a flawed man. He had a weak spot in the fabric of his makeup. That weak spot was women; her, me, and you. And who knows how many others? But he also had a special core of wisdom in him. A wisdom so pure that the adulterated man which surrounded it would often be forgiven, forgotten. He would become a man who put his pants on two legs at a time.

Perhaps you understand the nature of such addictions. I think you do. You are beautiful, too, but not perfect. Have you any vices yourself? Perhaps you know that smoking is no good for you, but the nagging gnawing never stops until you've taken another pull. Perhaps you've had a white-powder monkey riding your back. Or maybe fulfillment beckons to you from the depths of liquor bottles. You don't want it but you need it.

All during the years of our sporadic union I kept guilt at bay. I knew he was a married man, although he and his wife did not live on the same land mass. I knew I was trespassing in another woman's space. Guilt gnawed at me just as steadily as my overwhelming need for Trevor. And that need always managed to shunt the guilt aside. Until one day. Actually, it was night.

Never having seen the second woman, never even knowing her name made it easy for me to pretend she didn't exist. Or to imagine her as some five-eyed monster with fangs. Who couldn't possibly appreciate, deserve, or need his love like I did. Anyway, she was thousands of miles away. I would never actually have to confront her, or so I told myself.

I went to hear one of Trevor's lectures. He was a dynamic speaker, excellent beyond eloquence. Charismatic. He brimmed with wisdom, with a deep and abiding sense of history. He knew so many things. And here in his glory all doubt was erased about why I loved him.

His talk was about the reconnection between the motherland and her scattered children of the African Diaspora. One day there would be no boundaries between her peoples, between her nations. He spoke of a new pan-African man and woman who would pave roads of freedom for our children to walk on. Oh, the exquisite intellect of him. The brilliance shining in history's eye. How could I not love this man?

The sterling wisdom and emotion in his speeches always stirred me up, turned me on. I would be ready to take up rifles and march off to revolution. To hurry back with him to the nearest dark room and make my body an offering. And our lovemaking would be luminous. I would take him inside myself and feel anointed.

His words were a blessed balm on that lily-white campus, where our blackness was made minor. *Speak but the word and my soul shall be healed.* But my Dr. Barrett was a man who could heal with his voice and wound with his heart.

On the particular occasion when I first saw you, it was May 25. I remember, because it was African Liberation Day. The half emptiness of the room rankled me. The whole Black student body should have been there. The whole campus . . . hell, all of Black America needed to have those words. Words like rain in the desert. Words like money to buy freedom with.

And I sat there drinking in his wisdom, glowing. And slowly growing hot and wet. Halfway through his speech a woman walked in. She was a beautiful woman, full figured and statuesque. Dark, bold features. A growth of dreadlocks sprouting from her head like forest. Clad in vibrant African print and high-heeled shoes. She carried a chubby child, perhaps one year old, just walking. A boy or girl, I couldn't tell which.

And do you know what she did? Of course you do. She did not sit down in one of the many empty seats in the huge hall. She squatted on her lovely high heels, right up front near the podium. Proprietarily. She attached a strap from her own wrist to that of her toddling child, to keep it from wandering. And then she turned full attention to the luminance of Trevor, mouth slightly parted to catch the fall of every ripe word.

I was able to see this because I had sat shamelessly (or so I thought before the dreadlocked woman arrived) in the first row facing him. And I watched the woman watching him. Not just listening, but drinking in every sparkling droplet. Once the baby tethered to her wrist began to fuss and she lifted her top without shame, and fed it from the fullness of her breast. Face still turned toward the beacon of Trevor. A fellow devotee worshiping at the shrine?

I knew it had to be the second woman. Trevor's wife. I just knew it. I got up and left, walking and crying the length of the campus. I thought of Trevor and the second woman naked and new as Creation. And me, the serpent in the garden. Slithering in not to tempt Eve's burning curiosity but to test Adam's appetite. Enticing his love away from his woman and child. I would have to give him up.

When I finally made it home Trevor was waiting on my front steps, tense and furious.

"Where the hell have you been, woman? I was ready to call the police."

"It's over. We have to end it, Trevor."

"End it? Why?" Trevor took me by the shoulders and shook me slightly, as if trying to snap me from a trance. "What has happened?"

"Until I saw your wife tonight it was easy to pretend she didn't exist. But now I know she's real and I can't live with the guilt of what I'm doing."

Trevor peered into my face.

"My wife? Are you out of your mind? My wife is on her own island, home with her mother."

"I saw her," I insisted. "Your wife nursing your child, right there in Kennedy Hall."

"You are mistaken, Alma. My wife has no child."

I tried to do the right thing. I tried to push him away, to send him back to Eden. I really did. But he took my keys and opened my door. Let himself in. Sat me down at my kitchen table. And insisted that there had been no wife in the place. That he couldn't even recall seeing such a dreadlocked woman dressed in African print. A woman squatting and nursing near the podium.

"Don't you think I would have noticed?"

He told me my storyteller's imagination was running on overdrive. That I must have just dreamed the image up. Making it real so I could write about it. I reached out and slapped him.

"That woman is a beautiful woman. That child is your child. How can you hurt them like that?"

He frowned, perplexed. And reached up to feel the place my hand had struck. Then he looked at me and smiled. He touched my cheek, as if there was a hurting there, too.

"It's you, isn't it, Alma? You are that woman."

"No, Trevor. Stop it. You're trying to confuse me."

I was hunched over my kitchen table, head in hands. I wore a roomy leather jacket Trevor had given me. It was a jacket with an appliqued map of Africa emblazoned in suede across the back. I hadn't taken it off all evening. Not just because it was dear to me, but because the night was chilly. I had on a thin sleeveless shell and had felt cold without it. He had smiled when he saw me with it on.

"I see you're wearing Africa tonight."

Trevor reached for me. Reached into Africa. Found my breasts and held one in each hand. He weighed them like ripe fruit.

"Is that what you want, Alma? A child, my child suckling these breasts?"

"No, Trevor." I was melting. "That's not what I want."

"I would want that, Sister Queen. For you to mother my child."

I was water, soft water held in the circumference of his hands. Held whole by a force more frightening than gravity. Unspilled water. *Sweet, sweet Jesus.* It almost seemed my nipples would swell open like eyes and run rivers under the tender insistence of his big hands. Under the quiet rumble of his deep voice. One-hundred-proof rum stirred into Blue Mountain coffee.

All things are possible. It can be easy, quite easy to make love upright in a kitchen chair. Especially when one is water and the other is vessel.

Our lovemaking took on a new frenzy for a time. We feasted on each other for nearly a year. I threw my pills out the open window and danced. Rushing to him between classes. Weekdays and weekends. Mornings and afternoons, twilight and dawn, I danced. Under, over, around, and beside him. And he danced inside of me. We moved to the rhythm of music telling us how beautiful the child we made would be.

Infant eyes you are my all.
Without your love the stars would fall
And the moon would lose its glow
And the rivers would cease to flow.

My own river ceased to flow for a time. My period stopped, breasts swelled, body became rounder. But it was a sham pregnancy. All that loving did not take. Creation was not made. No child was formed. I don't know if it was my egg that was defective, his seed, or that it just wasn't meant to be. The frenzy wore off, the fury died down. Gradually we talked less of babies. He began to complain. I began to cling. He became more absent. Was it, in the lyrics of the song I took on as an anthem, *our ages or our hearts?*

It was neither, as I was to learn. Clay in the hand of the master sculptor is what it was. I was content to be soft and formless, easily molded to a thing of his making. A river whose current had been turned to flow in another direction. Who had herself helped to engineer the diversion.

I'll never forget that line from one of Trevor's speeches:

"Consider, if you will, the ways in which we participate in our own oppression."

Let me count the ways. Making myself always and eagerly available at his merest whim. Changing my major to study in his department. Reading what he read, studying what he studied. Excelling at all, because I knew that he would want it that way.

Was it that the clay began taking on a form of its own, or was it that he tired of the task of working it? He started lecturing me about all the young men out there who would love me. He opened the door to our illicit entanglement and that is when the other women started coming in. Calling his name across campus. Knocking on his door in the small hours.

I did not have Trevor's finesse at steamrolling the opposition. I was impotent in my jealousy, my protests sounding shrill and whining even to my own ears.

I decided to go cold turkey. Kick the habit. Separate myself from the source of my supply. Before I left I asked him about the wife we had both made careful not to mention again.

He sat at my kitchen table in boxer shorts, reading midterm papers. I stood at the stove cooking.

"Do you really want to hear this?" he asked dubiously.

I didn't, but I knew I needed something to give me the final push away from him.

"I'm curious. You said yourself that it's been years since you've lived together. You're here in New England. She's in the Caribbean. What gives?"

"She doesn't like living in America. And this is my livelihood for now. I have to be here."

"Well if she won't be with you, why have you stayed married to her?"

He had set down the paper he was reading. And turned to stare out of the window, as if he could see beyond land and waters. Into another time and place.

"I've never told anyone else this before. I was a young man away from home for the first time, reading economics at the University of the West Indies campus at Cave Hill. Beverly was my first love, sixteen years old. It's hard to give up your first love. It stays in your blood forever, like malaria. Dormant sometimes, sometimes flaring up in fever. There's no cure for it."

Tell me about it, Trevor. I know the nature of such afflictions. The delirium of swamp fever. It distorts your sense and reason. But I've got to believe it can be treated.

The second woman had been given a name and identity. Beverly. Beverly Barrett. And this was enough to make me kick the habit. It gave me the strength to move on and out. Toward the time and place where I would be cured.

But I still haven't found my way, haven't come home for my healing.

I left in a huff, first semester into graduate school. First it was back home to my mother, then men of my own who were not Trevor. But we would find our paths crossing again, always by some coincidence. I would relapse into my old habit of him. And we would be together until the next time I left in a huff.

First encounter: one year later in Washington, D.C. He was with another woman who was not the wife who had been waiting for him all those years. I was with a member of the Mauretanian diplomatic corps, a man who liked to buy me things made of gold.

Somehow, somewhere between hello again and good-bye, we each ditched our respective dates. Trevor wound up draped across the sandalwood print of my Indian bedspread, taking the place of a man who had wanted to give me gold. And I woke up the next morning wearing Trevor's scent.

What is it I found in him? I have defined it; I long to find it in you. I thought I yearned for the thickness of his hair, when really I wanted forest. Perhaps I will find the whiteness of his teeth inside the heart of your yam, the richness of his voice in your drumbeat. His terrible, tender mercies in the dry wind they call *harmattan*. His wisdom must be tapped from the wine of your palm trees.

Why didn't someone tell me that it was not a man, but a mother that I needed? Why didn't I realize that Trevor had meant Africa to me, diamonds and ivory and drought? Why did I not know that I could find the quality of his kisses in the meat of mango and the spice of his sex in the taste of palm oil?

Perhaps I can have it all, and have it in a way that Trevor can never give me. A lover needy in ways that we both were, generous in ways he could not be. Because he knew Africa, but was not Africa. His touch could heal, but he was not the doctor you are.

You are one of the three women in my life. I always wondered who the first woman was whenever he said that to me.

I know now that you could not have been his wife because you are his mother. It was you who squatted by the stage that day, bearing witness to the wisdom of your son. Baring breasts to your daughter, and feeding her when she cried. Who had kept her attached to you, even though she wandered. Who will one day gently guide her home.

Trevor had been to Africa many times, as you well know. It is he who introduced me to the idea of you. Who purged the pollution of Tarzan and Jane from my mind and taught me to love you, too.

He spoke of you proprietarily, as if you were a favored lover. His rum voice caressed words like *Ashanti. Yoruba. Benin. Guinea.* He praised your colors and national character as if they were the hips and breasts of a woman he loved. He spoke of your droughts and famines as blemishes on the body of a perfect mistress.

I once felt a kind of rivalrous jealousy to hear him go on so. As if being compared to a woman with whom I could never compete. But I believe now that your harvests are too plentiful for hunger, even though we hunger. That your nature is too large for envy, though envy endures.

So now I know you are the first woman. What I question is this: Why has your love been so kind to this man? He still smiles at me with your smile, lures me with the scent of your perfume. Is it really fair that he reach forty-five with such grace, with such a gray-flecked beard? And with such a hold on me?

TO THE SECOND WOMAN

Second encounter: three years later. I have never met you, though I feel I have come to know you well over these past seven years. Do you know me, too? Have you ever suspected that I exist? What would you say and how would you feel if you knew this Yankee interloper were here sharing the same island with you? The same man?

I recognized his walk before I saw his face. My heart leaped to meet his long-legged stride. I was hooked again, firmly and helplessly.

He no longer seems so terribly much older than I. People move closer together as they age. Seven years had passed since I first sat in his economics class. By rights, twenty-six and forty-five should be a much more manageable combination than eighteen and thirty-seven had been. But the die was forever cast. I would always be the student, he the teacher.

He is a big man in the home he has brought you from exile to share with him. Minister of Tourism. I can honestly say that this I did not know when I accepted the invitation for the junket. I only knew that this sunny island had made Trevor, but how could I know I would find him there? Addressing the members of our press group on the natural beauties of beaches along the North Coast, with all the charisma of his lectures on political economics.

I wonder what happened in the intervening years. He had brought you out of your waiting to be by his side. Had his wild ways worn off? Was he now domesticated, content to purr in his own parlor?

There were ways, indeed, in which he had changed. But I hadn't. Perhaps you, a fellow sufferer, can understand my weakness for him. At least one of the other women in our group had set her cap for him. But it was me he took out for a drink after she and the rest were settled into the hotel. A nightcap, *for old times' sake*.

I went after your husband with a vengeance. He didn't take much persuading. We didn't even make it back to my hotel room, but consummated our reunion half-clothed in the front seat of his Mercedes.

I never got to flaunt the fact in my colleague's face. Perhaps Trevor managed to fit her into his schedule as well. I dropped from the press group at his insistence, conflict of interest and all. He was a philanderer with a sense of ethics.

I stayed on long after my seven days. And we were together for nearly a year, the three of us. You, me, and him. In the same city, the same island. But not in the same place. You were the one he took out into the world, the woman people meant when the question, *Where's your better half?* was asked. I was his secret, his mistress. The one kept hidden behind closed doors.

In his own land I was as helpless as a tortoise on dry sand, naked of its shell. I guess it was poetic irony. Now it was my turn to be the woman who waited. Trevor set me up in a small villa high in the mountains some miles above the city.

"The solitude here will be good for your writing. You can tell it in your memoirs. You had to come to the Caribbean to create the great American novel."

I locked myself in a cage fashioned from my own shell. Lost and alone in a land I was too strung out to explore. Gazing at blue mountains and blank pages and waiting to be fed. A ravenous baby bird trapped in its own love nest, all song and senses tuned to the moment of its mother's return. But how could he mother me, a fledgling who still needed to be mothered himself?

Solitary confinement did things to me. I went without underwear, took to wearing dresses he could easily dispense with. So that our borrowed minutes together could be a few seconds longer. The great American novel remained unwritten.

I wrote not a word and read plenty of trash in my idle hours. One story caught my fancy. It was the story of how a man had put a woman's name in hoodoo, locked it up, and thrown the lock to the bottom of a wide and very deep body of water. And until that lock was found and opened she would never be her own self. She was doomed to wander the world calling his name.

I questioned him avidly about you, the second woman. I don't know why I needed to know these things. Maybe knowledge would be my armor. Perhaps learning your secrets would immunize me to pain, unchain me from my prison.

Do you still sleep together? *Of course*. Did you do it on the same days he'd been with me? *Are you kidding? I'm not a young man anymore.* Which woman was better in bed? *You both have your moments, darling. But I must admit, you are a bit less inhibited. Caribbean women tend to be somewhat conservative in the bedroom.* Were there any other women besides the two of us? *Where would I find the time? I'm a busy man now.*

And a liar, too, I was sure. Still he answered each question, no matter how outrageous, with even-tempered equanimity. Even humor; he could afford it. He had the best of all worlds. He had the love of three women.

There were worse things, I told myself, than being a woman who waited. I wasn't being beaten, like less fortunate friends of mine. I was being kept in relative luxury, with no money worries to weigh on my mind. I didn't have a man owning my every hour, like Otis and my mother. Maybe I, like Big Momma, was meant to be a waiting woman. Maybe waiting was the price I had to pay to have the love I needed.

I settled into waiting as a way of life. I lived for the moments when Trevor walked through the door, and spent the long hours without him in suspended animation.

It didn't last, you will be relieved to know. What prompted the final separation? Trevor surely thought it was my paranoia about other women. But it wasn't. It was the same *you people* epithet that had eventually erupted from the mouth of every man I ever loved, all of them men from other places. And always eroded what had been between us.

Though both Caribbean citizens, you come from islands separated by miles of sea. Do those differences show their faces in obvious ways? Has *you people* ever come between you?

I nagged and wheedled to be taken out. On one of the rare occasions when we'd left the Blue Mountain hideaway and ventured out among people, Trevor had taken me to see dancers. I expected a concert of traditional Caribbean culture. What I got was an evening in a smoky bar with a crudely lettered sign out front. ALL-MULATTO DANCE REVUE. And inside, a collection of bewigged Black women of complexions varying from high yellow to midnight. All scantily clad. Bumping and grinding to beat the band.

A scratchy jukebox played a reggae version of Little Milton's blues:

Across the river a good woman cries
All because a foolish man lied.
She gave up all she had to show how
much she cared . . .

Trevor enjoyed it immensely. The last of the angry young men had become a dirty old one. He sat up close and threw currency on the stage. The women paused to collect the bills between bumps and grinds, stuffing it into their bras. And rewarded the giver with special attention. Cradling his head between their bosoms. Rotating their hips inches from his face. Turning around and tightening first one buttock, then the other in rapid succession. That was Trevor's favorite. He showered the stage with money, nearly breaking his neck trying to follow the movement of the bouncing buns.

I was incensed by the whole spectacle. It seemed that anger had become the by-product of all the waiting. He had uncorked the bottle in that dingy strip joint, and now the genie came hissing out.

"That's abuse, Trevor," I told him on the ride back up to the mountains. "Exploitation. Watching these women putting their bodies on display. Throwing cash at them like somebody's organ grinder monkey. You ought to know better."

Trevor veered close to the edge of the mountain road, making way for an oncoming country bus careening down its center. And between curses at the driver he flung accusations at me. Of being elitist, of looking down on the labor of proletarian women.

"Did you ever stop to think the sisters might actually enjoy their work? Like you enjoy yours?"

"More likely they have no skills, and no other way to feed themselves. And what about all those White tourists sitting up there ogling your country women? Don't you feel any shame?"

Trevor had shrugged. Tourists will be tourists and boys will be boys. The scene between Black women and White men was nothing new. He spoke of working down South during the civil rights movement, where one of the sisters in their organization was sleeping with the town's white sheriff. It was her contribution to the movement; keeping the heat off the rest of the workers' backs.

"Oh, righteous sister," I sneered. "Opening up her legs to save your Black behind."

I heard my voice sharp and shrill as Sapphire, the ubiquitous evil Black woman. I couldn't stop it.

"Is that what they mean by pussy power? The only position for a woman in the revolution is being prone? I bet you believe that, too."

"Alma." The very calm in his voice was infuriating. "When I was out in the red hills of *your* America getting my Black ass shot at, you weren't even old enough to wipe yours. Talk what you know, darling."

His condescension was the last straw. I exploded.

"Well, I know this. I'll never sit back and shut my eyes to this abuse of Black women's bodies. Whether it's them doing it to us or you doing it to us."

By this time we were high in the cool mountains with the lights of the city sparkling below us. I guess it was time to switch gears from rage to romance, from conflict to coitus. Trevor was taking off his shirt and smiling.

"Darling love," he cajoled. "Sister Queen. Don't get hysterical. You know that if anyone, Black or White, even thought of touching you I'd have his balls off with my bare hands."

And the conversation, like that out-of-control country bus, veered off course. He took my rage for fear and my need for understanding as pleas for comfort. As the understanding was not forthcoming, I settled for the comfort. Comforting became cuddling. Holding became fondling. And loving melted the ice of my anger. But still the *you people* lurked beneath the surface. And came out in the afterplay, exploding like a swollen seed.

"You needn't feel jealous that I enjoy watching the movement of other women's bodies." He cupped the fullness of my behind in the palms of his hands. "The way you move yours, you could be up there shaking it with the best of them. Why don't you dance a little for me?"

And I had leaped from his arms, the smoldering embers of anger flaring up again.

"You have the nerve to call yourself a revolutionary, you sexist bastard. Get out of here."

Trevor had gone about calmly collecting his clothing.

"Yankee prudishness has infected you people just as badly as the cultural imperialism you carry everywhere you go. I guess that comes from living so close to the White Man." He could have been lecturing me in one of his classes. Political Economy 101. "Don't try to impose your hang-ups on me, Sister. I'll be back in a few days, when you've had a chance to calm down."

"And I won't be here when you do," I had promised.

I made good on my threat. I was good at leaving in a huff. I had eight years experience in it by now. But maybe it wasn't so much the *you people* after all; the underlying assumption that we were not of the same people, and that mine was a less-than. That suggested that we weren't, after all, children of the same mother. The grown-up version of that *Naw, baby. It ain't me.*

Maybe it was my own realization. That I was probably no different from the shake dancers onstage, moving my body for my daily bread. Or worse still. I'd been one man's private dancer for eight years. A cocaine whore or courtesan, peddling my flesh for the substance I thought I needed to sustain me.

I left my Blue Mountain hideaway, more angry at the pitiful addict I'd become than I was with him. But by then a mission propelled my movements. I was ready to find a locksmith. It was high time for me to meet the third woman.

THE THIRD WOMAN

Whose woman am I now? Can I still be considered the third woman in these, the early stages of withdrawal? Or perhaps this habit is worse than the first. You would know that another addiction would come along to replace my eight-year flu.

I have become eccentric, superstitious. Carrying around this ancient, fraying strand of waist beads, I swing between moments of soaring faith and utter fatalism. I know I should be doing something with them, but I'm not sure what that something is.

Big Momma had given them to me on her deathbed. They were the same beads I had once been instructed to wear on the night of my first menses. I remember being embarrassed at the time at what I thought a silly bit of Southern superstition. But Big Momma had been so serious and her insistence so hard to buck.

The beads on this string are of two types. Small, round black ones like shiny stones connect the larger ones which are blue with swirls in them that look like running water. The feel and memory of them stayed with me throughout my girl-hood and into my adult years.

Finally, I got the courage to ask her why. And it wasn't always easy questioning Big Momma about her deep-seated beliefs. She was a woman who had been living those beliefs just short of a century. She carried them in her soul, and couldn't always articulate why she believed the way she did.

I do recollect what spurred the phone call. I was still in school then and passing acquaintances with a weird little West Indian woman who spoke with an affected British accent. Her name was Cedella, but she had suddenly announced she was changing her name to Cleopatra.

Cleopatra didn't live life, she played at it. One of her roles was professional student, for the past ten years a part-time Ph.D. candidate in theology. Another, I was later to learn, was as one of Trevor's occasional lovers. But that particular day she seemed to be going for a mishmash of Afrocentric earth goddess and mystical Indian madonna. She'd invited me to attend the puberty rites of her twelve-year-old daughter, Pocahontas.

It was a party celebrating the onset of menstruation. Cleopatra stood beaming in an unlikely combination of veil-draped head and velvet bustier. The young girl sat on an Ashanti stool looking bored, wrapped in African prints and decked in gold. And we, the women of the community, brought her gifts, welcoming her into womanhood. I had been reminded of the doubled rope of discolored beads which had been tied to my waist that night of my thirteenth summer.

"I don't rightly know why, child." Big Momma's voice crackled across midcontinent on the long-distance line. "You there, Little Daughter? Well, all I know is that I wore them when I had my first blood, and my mama did with hers, and as far as I can tell, so did Nana. She used to keep them hid away in this old croker sack and bring them out whenever one of us girls got her first monthly. I 'spect she had brung them over with her from Africy."

I still remember how my cousin Pat's eyes lit up.

"Family heirlooms. They must be worth a fortune!"

In the end I believe Big Momma clung to life by a hair's breadth, waiting until I got to her bedside so she could put them into my hands. Somehow among the slew of descendants which must have numbered into the hundreds, I had been chosen to carry the legacy. I felt completely uncertain and unworthy. Big Momma was not a woman who often made mistakes, but I was sure she had this time. Maybe she should have given them to my cousin Pat, who had valued them so much and wanted them so badly.

Never had I seen her so feeble. Her emaciated head seemed lost in the puffy white pillow. A pair of white pigtails curved around her ears, like wings. By then she was past speaking, almost past movement. But she found the strength to press the beads, encased in a blue felt Crown Royal bag, into my hands.

"Whiskey!" I had whispered, stroking the twisted, arthritic hand that looked so much like a bare tree limb. "So you've been fooling us all. Sneaking you a taste of whiskey all these years."

A smile had flickered across her hollow face and the tree limb lifted to lightly pat mine. And I swear to you, she winked at me. Even on the riverbank of death, Big Momma had paused for one last laugh before crossing over. That was the kind of woman she was.

Wasn't it she who taught me that death was a river you crossed when your time had come? And old age the bridge between birth and heaven? But in my grief I began to doubt. To think that maybe death was not a river, but a hungry crocodile that swallows you whole. And leaves your bones on the muddy bottom where no one knows, no one goes.

Because if Big Momma was just across the river, why wasn't I able to see a glimpse of her from time to time? To wave across to her? To hear her voice calling over to me? To see her smile from the distance?

Now that Big Momma was gone I scarcely knew what to do with that bag of beads. They gave me little comfort. I would have traded them and ten years of my own life just to have her back. To be able to ask the questions I forgot to ask. To demonstrate the love I rarely voiced.

For years the felt bag rested in the corner of my underwear drawer. I'd take them out now and then, but only because they reminded me of her. But there must be more to their secrets than memory.

In the long hours of Caribbean night I laid them across my bare, hungry body. They seemed to glisten like they had a light of their own. Endless, like a river that returns to itself.

I am alone in a cold place now, ashes in my fireplace and winter raging outside my window. Since I have taken up the story beads I am writing again, all the words stopped up back in those Blue Mountains now rushing forth like undammed waters.

My body encased in layers of clothing still longs for his missing touch. Like an instrument that vibrates long after it is strummed. But even in the deep bereavement I always lapse into upon these separations, I am hearing something else. A voice I hardly notice when enrapt in Trevor. I sense I am being called from somewhere far beyond myself. Am I going crazy here?

The last embers from a fire I thought extinguished flare up in the hearth. You can feel the cold pressing in, even through the walls. A wind from nowhere stirs the folds of Big Momma's story quilt, hanging above the mantelpiece. Am I seeing things?

Are those just flurries in the whirling snow, or did a small black bird with outstretched white wings bump against the pane? Could that have been a red thread dangling from its beak? Is it just the hawk I'm hearing, the infamous Chicago wind moaning outside my window? Or could it be the call of another winged creature? Could it be the first woman's voice?

Calling me, calling me, calling me home.

Ghost on a Bicycle

Going there was one of those spur-of-the-moment changes.
One day you wake up and realize that you want to be somewhere else. Somewhere unpredictable. You find that all your days, as far into the future as you can see, are dry as dust. The same names, same games. Same places, same faces. You are listening to your life and can hear no music. That is when you must do something different or desperate. Or resign yourself to a kind of death.

That is when the road calls and you must answer.

Alma had some sudden money. An unexpected sum from an unexpected source. She should have been practical. She should have tried to dent the towering mountain of debt that was threatening to topple and bury her in bills. She really should have.

But it was spring. Change was a brisk thing that charged the air. Frozen snow surging into flash floods. A keen green smell, potent as new dolls and pine. It wafted into rooms through open windows. She heard the faint stirrings of something like music. She shimmied to the tinny ice-cream tunes that played from white trucks. Good Humor plied the city streets, regular as the first robin.

The music played and Alma followed, a child in pursuit of the Pied Piper. She followed it into Pan American, where she bought a ticket on standby to London. She had really wanted Africa. She yearned for something even warmer than spring, a tropical sun whose sear she knew could heal.

The man she loved had given her a Benin bronze which she kept perched atop her desk. She placed it so that it watched over her while she worked. She called it *Déjà Vu*. Ancient memory seemed to tug at her soul whenever she watched it watching her. Its almond-eyed stare seemed pregnant with promises. Its full lips suggested sunshine and palm wine, rivers flowing through fertile forests.

But there hadn't been enough for Africa, only three figures in the sum. So she took a ticket to the place as far from home as she could afford. And then spring had also thawed out a deep frozen memory, but one not as ancient as Africa. Memory of a different year and a different spring. And a man of living Benin bronze, warm eyes and hands.

Five days before her flight she wrote a note.

Tony. It's been too long. Coming to town on May 17th. I'd love to see you then. Alma.

She hadn't given him time to reply. She didn't even know if the letter would reach London before she did. She was surprised when he showed up at the airport.

A contradiction of carelessness and an odd kind of style. Sky-colored faded jeans might have been the same pair he wore ten years before. His flat-to-the-ground moccasins made her taller by at least an inch. He shook her outstretched hand and smiled. Then pulled her to him in a brief embrace.

"Come over here, m'love. Long time gone."

Years of life in the British Isles had taught him to speak two languages. The clipped leaves of British tea, seasoned with the strong flavor of Caribbean rum. Suddenly shy, she could think of no word to say in return. She gave him her smile. He took the suitcase from her hand so that it would be free to hold his as they walked out into an English spring. Although the temperature was just a few degrees higher than Chicago's had been, Alma felt warm holding his hand.

She hadn't been sure she'd recognize him, but he was unmistakable. Though he had changed. And winding his car through the mazelike streets of a manicured suburb on the road to London, he told her the same thing.

"I wasn't sure I'd know you after ten years. But I recognized your walk right off. You walk proud, like a West Indian woman."

She looked at him carefully. The mustache was new, so were the gray flecks in his hair. The tiny laugh lines around his eyes somehow made him appear not older, but younger than before. Like premature gray on a child.

He'll still look like a teenager when he's sixty, she thought.

He felt her stare and returned it. Openly examining her face, both appraisal and appreciation in his eyes. A hand moved from the wheel and reached out for her. Perhaps he'd been meaning to touch her cheek, but his fingers found her open mouth. She nibbled them.

They laughed at the unspoken joke in the air. He leaned from the wheel and kissed her cheek. Winter was fading here in England.

Along the road she stole glances, trying to decipher the difference in him. It was something in the ease of his manner, the relaxed aspect of his movements. She seemed to remember him being a man more electric, more charged with nervous energy. Something must have calmed him in the intervening years. The thought descended like a thundercloud.

"You're married now." It was neither question nor accusation.

He didn't question the source of her sudden knowledge, but glanced at his left ring finger. She noticed for the first time a slim tan line there. Something of Tony's old manner suddenly charged his movements. He scooted forward at the wheel, increased his speed. Then looked at her longer, the corner of his eyebrow lifted.

He grinned, trying to make a joke of it.

"I couldn't wait for you forever."

She was dead serious.

"I didn't know you were waiting."

They moved along in silence for a while, passing a row of neat brick cottages.

"I live there." He pointed. "The one with the green shutters."

"Oh?" She looked, unable to distinguish one from the other. Trying to keep the pitch of her voice even, she asked him: "Is your wife at home?"

"No." A turned-down smile. "I hope we don't run into her, in fact. She's out here somewhere. Doing a bit of shopping on her bicycle."

There was a note of rueful affection in his voice. She tried to imagine Tony's wife, wheeling through these winding streets, a basket of bread and vegetables at the handlebars. For some reason the picture would not materialize.

"It's a nice, middle-class neighborhood," she observed. This time there was a hint of accusation buried in her studied indifference. Tony turned in surprise.

"It's not middle-class, you know. It's just England."

She looked straight ahead as the brick cottages passed by in her peripheral vision. Her mind worked feverishly, trying to reorganize her game plan for three weeks in England. Weeks without Tony's company at the blues dances and reggae bars she had made her reason for coming, that she told herself she would later write about. But her thoughts would not come into order. The unformed image of a woman on a bicycle kept intruding.

Though she had told him to take her to an inexpensive hotel, Tony pulled up in front of a spacious stone house which turned out to be the home of friends. An English couple who would be *happy to put you up*. He ignored her protestations.

"Nonsense, love. It's all been arranged."

Alma did not plan to sleep with him. She had quickly rewritten his role in the script. Former lover becomes deliverer of lodgings. She waited for him to leave her, duty done. But he sat close to her, talking and drinking with the couple. Afternoon stretched into evening and he had made no attempt to leave. The red wine, the slow conversation, the beginnings of jet lag were loosening her defenses.

And when Tony turned his warm eyes her way, touched his warm hand to hers, and suggested, *Let's go unpack now*, she went willingly. They did not unpack.

Tony was smoking now in a room devoid of light. Her luggage and the shapes of furniture huddled like frozen dwarves in the semidarkness. All illumination was caught in the contours of Tony's face, burnished bronze with cigarette glow.

Alma purred contentedly from her side of the bed and eased into his arms. He held the cigarette away, flicking ashes into something unseen at the side of the bed.

"You always did like to do it in the dark," she teased. "You would tear up the hotel room looking for something to shade that naked lightbulb."

"Really, now? I don't remember that."

"Just what do you remember?" The question was almost whispered. If he didn't hear, she would not repeat it. He brought cigarette to mouth again, as if there was memory in the smoke he inhaled.

"I remember that fleabag hotel in Bayswater. Not the perfect place for romance." A hesitation. "And you. Walking like a West Indian woman, loving like one, too. You were quite a sexy little craft. Still are."

"Oh. So that's the reason you came for me." She tried to withdraw, but he tossed away the burned-out butt and caught her in his arms.

"Come back here, Black woman. So I get a letter from America after all these years. I didn't know what you wanted. I just remembered you as a frail, delicate sort. I thought you needed looking after. Didn't want you to wind up in Bayswater again."

When she didn't answer he turned her body to face his.

"This wasn't the reason I came for you, love. But I'm glad it happened. Aren't you?"

She couldn't concentrate on his kisses. Her mind was rolling like a reel, casting back into the waters of memory. She couldn't remember having been called *frail* since childhood, when Mama used the excuse to push cod-liver oil down her throat daily.

"Don't play so rough with my daughter," the neighborhood kids were warned. "She's delicate."

Delicatessa had become her nickname.

But in retrospect, she could see how fragile she had been when time and London came together ten years back. She was not traveling then, but tumbling through Europe, trying to escape memory of the ubiquitous other man. She had been a satellite which had orbited the same planet so long, she felt weightless. Separated from her center of gravity without him.

Alma was doing Europe on the cheap along with Nina, her college roommate. They started out in Majorca on a leisurely itinerary, Eurail passes and student hostels along the way. They drifted along to Paris, where Nina took up with a man. A tall, fine Senegalese man. She spoke no French; he spoke no English.

Alma, who had two years of high school French, fell into the role of the interpreter. Until Nina decided she would spend the rest of the spring in his crowded flat, cooking the jollof rice she had learned to prepare so well that Ahmadu swore she was a Wolof woman in disguise. Alma was not invited to stay, translations no longer necessary.

Nina accompanied her to the station, carried her bag, and cried. She felt so guilty, abandoning Alma like this. She didn't offer to change her plans.

Before the parting their easy companionship had made traveling a mild adventure. A pleasant series of wanderings, of wondering which surprise waited beyond the next bend. Memory was kept comfortably at bay.

Now that she wandered alone she felt compelled, propelled toward the simple rewards she and Nina had found so easy to acquire. The leisurely strolls through Roman streets, laughing at the catcalls of the infamous Latin lovers. Soul food dinner at the home of a pair of Black American expatriates in Amsterdam. The people, fellow travelers and natives alike, whose lives intersected theirs for a time.

Now she was like a donkey with wisdom teeth removed, rushing headlong toward a carrot that just eluded her grasp. And running pell-mell from the apparition of a love that had ached itself into abscess. The pain was gone with the extracted teeth, but the space felt yawningly empty. Even if she reached the carrot, she wondered if she would be able to bite.

Once she made her way to London she stayed put, no longer feeling up to the task of deciphering different tongues. Tony remembered right. It was a crumbly old hotel, peopled by the great unwashed, unmoneyed student crowd. The toilets and baths were shared, the heating frozen in the *off* position. It had been a chilly spring. But beds were changed daily, and Alma was glad for that. Paris hadn't been so clean.

But it wasn't so much the cold, shabby room that bothered her. It was the memories which assaulted her when she was alone there. Days weren't so bad, with visits to the British Museum and Buckingham Palace. Matinees at Her Majesty's.

Such tourist traps she had never bothered with on the continent with Nina. They had been more interested in the human landscape than in sightseeing. But there was something pleasantly reassuring in losing herself among the anonymous crowds of tourists. It was the nights she found unbearable, alone in the musty little room in Bayswater.

It was not easy to move around as a lone woman in nighttime London. She wore vulnerability like a talisman some sought to avoid, others to prey upon. At night she felt like a loose moon, orbitless in an empty sky. Connected to nothing and no one.

But she couldn't allow herself the luxury of an early return home. Even though coming out here had been a running away of sorts, she couldn't bear the thought of running back. So she plodded on for the sake of experience. A solo voyager, intent on exploring an unknown planet.

She went off in search of Black Britain, hoping to connect with a community of kinship. Brixton was not picturesque. The people in it bumped about like captive tropical birds, searching the streets and markets for bits of home to carry back to their nest. A fog-bound sun shone down on grim streets. It rained almost every day. But behind closed doors she could decipher island-accented laughter. From half-opened windows she caught whiffs of plantain frying.

She roamed the streets, trying to develop the knack she never mastered. That of knowing people on her own. And into this fog of isolation a pair of almond eyes penetrated. A pair of warm hands reached in and pulled her out.

She sat at the bar of what Black Londoners called *a blues dance*. There was much dancing, but no blues to be heard. Patrons brought their beer bottles with them to the dance floor. Couples pressed against each other in *rub-a-dub style*. Women didn't wait for male partners, but took to the floor in groups. Single men somehow managed to dance alone, lounged against walls. And all swayed to the steady beat of a reggae band which played loud and long.

Alma had been there for a while when the music stopped. She nursed a rum and Coke and eavesdropped on the conversation of a group of Black men. Some of them seemed to be members of the band, on break.

There was a long, lean, light-skinned man with stooped shoulders. A bearded, dreadlocked, slightly squat, dark-skinned brother. And a slim bronze-colored man whose generous mouth and wide nose reminded her of *Déjà Vu*, the Benin statue which sat on her work desk, home on campus. She amused her bored fancy by assigning the men random names.

"I tell you, mahn. I tired of this reggae, reggae, reggae all the time," was the complaint of Banana Man as he sucked back a mug of beer.

"There you go again." The dreadlocked Chocolate Chip spoke in an unexpected English accent. "Get too much lager in you and you start talking rot."

"What did reggae ever do to you, mahn?" That was Déjà Vu. "You talk about it like a dog. And it feeds you, keeps you in all the lager you can drink and all the women you can eat."

Chocolate Chip gave a raucous laugh.

"Oh, so that horn ain't the only thing our boy's been blowing. My man's not just a saxophonist, he's a sexophonist."

Déjà Vu and Chocolate Chip hooted at the ribald joke. But the melancholy Banana Man neither joined the laughter nor tried to defend his besmirched honor. He drained his bottle and looked idly around for another one.

"I tired of all these limey women. Horny cows, the lot of them."

Déjà Vu seemed to be in charge of the drinks. He signaled the barkeep and obtained another beer for Banana Man. Scolding him all the while.

"Never bite the hand that feeds you. All you know is blowing that horn. What else can you do with your life, mahn?"

"I want to play jazz, mahn. Get outta England and go to America. Here you a Black musician, all they wanta hear is reggae, reggae, reggae. Dance and drink and smoke spliff. Jazz intelligent music, *to ras claat.* I go to America where a musician an artist."

The exchange broke off when Banana Man and Chocolate Chip were called onstage to play. Déjà Vu looked over at Alma and shook his head.

"Richard ain't never satisfied where he's at. He home in Kingston, he hungry to be in England. He's here now, he want to be in America."

"He's fooling himself if he thinks America's going to be his answer. He won't be there but a minute, and he'll be trying to think of someplace else to go."

The man looked intently at Alma, then moved in closer.

"Yankee, yes? Too bad Richard gone. He loves all things American."

"I'm not a Yankee and I'm not thinking about no Richard."

He lifted his eyebrow quizzically and motioned to the bartender.

"Give the sister another one of what she's drinking." He examined her face, as if the stamp of her citizenship could be found there. "Not American, eh? You walk like a West Indian woman."

"How do you know how I walk?"

"I noticed you the minute you came in, love." He handed her the fresh drink, even though her first was still half-full. "So is that what you are? An Americanized West Indian? Brooklyn Caribbean?"

"No, I'm not." The conversation was veering into deep waters. Alma braced herself for the bait, the line, the attempted snare. She turned slightly away. "Thank you for the drink."

He would not be so easily dismissed. He picked up his drink and came around to the other side, staring at her profile.

"African? No, I don't think so. Let me see your passport."

"It should be obvious what I am. I'm the same thing you are. America is my condition, not my identity. Maybe you don't identify with Africa yourself, but don't tell me not to. I know what I am." Alma paused to let the rebuff settle, then got up to leave.

Déjà Vu followed her. The band started playing again and they were caught on the dance floor. He took her hand and led her into dance. His arms went around her and his warm breath whispered into her ear.

"You dance like a West Indian woman, too."

His name was Tony. This she learned on the dance floor. He'd recently returned from road managing a reggae tour of West Africa. This she discovered over a plate of cook-up rice with Tony and the band at an after-hours shebeen. She told him how strong her urge was to travel *home*. This was said on the ride back to her hotel. He told her that Africa could no more be a panacea for her needs than America could be for Richard's.

"We've been away too long, love. Africa is no longer our home."

This he said beside her in bed, in her cold, shabby hotel room.

How can he say this, Alma wondered, his warm body entering hers, *when he is Benin bronze? How can he know Africa, and not know that he is Africa?*

Alma's week ran out and she extended her stay. Tony was her entree into a community she had not been able to penetrate on her own. His was the music world, and he took her into the shebeens and blues dances and music halls where the bands played. And the people would drink Red Stripe and rum, and dance and sing along to songs that reminded them who they were and where they came from.

After a month her period came. She spent the week confined to her hotel room, doubled over with cramps. Tony visited her, brought grapes, rubbed her back, and commiserated. But she was *frail and delicate*, and he apparently not interested in playing nursemaid. She saw him less. Back home in Chicago she wrote him and was not answered. Then came the years.

After a decade she knew she was now a different woman. Not exactly robust, but no longer fragile. Tony told her that her hair had grown longer, her breasts fuller. He told her she was the same, but different. She tasted smoke on his lips and wondered about the ways he had changed.

Despite the onslaught of jet lag, Alma had trouble finding sleep. She tried to relax against Tony, tried not to see the trolls her suitcases made hunched in the corners of the room. Her brain jangled with tiredness, with unsummoned images. The new easy languor about him. Déjà Vu smiling from her desktop, reaching out to hold her with warm eyes and hands. A brick cottage with green shutters. A Black woman on a bicycle tooling through English markets. *What's wrong with this picture?* She had to know, and nudged Tony into wakefulness.

"She's White, isn't she?"

"M'woman?" He woke quickly, his voice heavy with sleep, his island accent thick. He propped himself by the elbow and lit another cigarette. She didn't remember Tony as a smoker. Yet another change in him. He blew smoke circles toward the ceiling, then gave Alma a curious glance.

"Does it matter?"

"Yes."

"That I'm married, or that she's a White woman?"

"Both."

He turned to examine her in the dark.

"What are you looking for so far away from home, Black woman?" And when she didn't answer, "What do you want from me, Alma?"

How could she tell him she came following music? Beckoned by the warmth of his eyes and hands. The Benin bronze of him. The promise of palm wine and papaya. That she had heard music on the road and it led her across the waters to him. So her only answer was the whisper of bedsheets as they moved together one more time.

Sleep finally came. But it was an uneasy rest. She dreamed haunted dreams. And when the sun opened her eyes to another day, she watched Tony awaken in confusion.

He looked at her, jumped out of bed, then sat back down again. He said he didn't like being watched so closely so early in the morning. Cursed the absence of a hot cup of tea. Found his cigarettes and lit one. And began to sing praises of his absent wife.

"She'll be off to work by now. A hard-working woman, that one."

"What are you going to tell her about last night?" Alma settled back to watch him fret.

"What can I tell her? That I got into a fight and lost my trousers?"

"That you got into some wine and lost your mind. Then got into bed and lost your head. She'll understand." Alma was feeling strangely generous. She would give him the excuse he needed to escape scot-free. A bitchy Black woman. Sapphire on the rampage. This would send him running back to the arms of his little English lass.

"She's not a bad sort." Tony frowned and placed an arm around Alma's shoulder. "She's been sticking by me these years, putting up with my shit."

"Good." His arm grown heavy, Alma shrugged herself free. *Naw, baby. It ain't me* seemed to swirl in the flecks of his smoke-brown eyes, like grounds stirred up from the bottom of a coffee cup. "Black women been dealing in shit too long. Putting up with it, living with the smell of it, cleaning up behind it. About time somebody else took over in that department."

His eyes were no longer smoky, but brown and clear in the morning light. The Benin bronze of his skin took on a translucent tone.

"She's really a very nice girl, you know."

"Then what are you doing here with me? Why don't you go and tell that where it will be appreciated?"

Alma hustled from the bed and furiously dealt with the long-postponed unpacking.

As we grow older the seasons seem to crowd together. Spring becomes summer, becomes fall, becomes winter before you know what hit you. It was not a bad winter. It was warm inside. There was work in Alma's typewriter. Routine, noncreative work, yes. But the white pages would eventually transform themselves into crisp Yankee greenbacks.

Despite the snow she was dreaming of sun. Though she'd be leaving for work in Washington within the week, Africa was still on her mind. She was saving to buy a ticket home.

Alma would be celebrating Kwanzaa this year. *Déjà Vu* was dressed for the occasion. Gobs of wax coated his cheeks, like frozen teardrops. He sat in the semicircle of a kinara, where each night another red, black, or green candle would be lit.

Alma faced him, clattering away on the typewriter. Her fingers and brain were growing numb with facts and figures about whole life insurance. The ringing of the phone was a welcome relief.

"Alma?" A voice warm with pleasure. "Is that you, m'love?"

He could barely be heard above the noise of conversation and music in the background. His voice brought spring into her quiet room. Worked to loosen the brace of frost that stiffened her heart these days. She got up from the desk and sank into a nearby armchair.

"Tony. How are?" Her voice fumbled at careful conversation. "Where are you?"

"In your part of the world, love. Got one of my bands playing the Grist Mill in Montreal. Hold on, let me change the phone." He shouted something in patois to someone, then the line became quiet. "I miss you, African girl walking like a West Indian woman."

"You do?" Alma had the sudden urge to be up and walking. Walking not like a West Indian, but a Black Chicago woman. Walking quick and hard, scarved and coated, firmly booted feet annihilating snow. She couldn't think straight sunk in the soft of an easy chair. "Did you say that you miss me, Tony?"

"Missing you like crazy, m'love. Come up here to Montreal. It'll be like the old days, traveling with the band. You can fly here in about an hour."

"Just an hour? How do you know that?" Alma tried to hold back the softness that was threatening to spill over into her firm resolve. She had decided months ago to leave Tony alone. No more long-distance romance. No more married men. And most particularly, no more Black men whose hearts belonged to White women.

"I checked the schedule." He pronounced it the British way. *Shedule.* "Let me send you a ticket, love."

Alma hesitated, almost ready to move on the spur of the moment. She had moved that way before. She could see herself already, rapt in music, drowning in the smoke-brown waters of his eyes. Moving with him about Montreal, a city she hadn't yet explored.

"Hullo, love. Are you still there?"

His voice was low and husky in the receiver, as potent and intoxicating as rum. The memory of his hands and eyes sent a heartstring bridging their distances, stretched along the wires that connected them voice to voice. Alma wanted to reach out and twang it, to play it like a guitar. She thought of a green mirage opening up in the midst of a snowstorm. But then she saw something else in the midst of that mirage. A ghost on a bicycle.

"Where is your wife, Tony?"

"Back home in England, of course. Would I be inviting you up if she were here? She never comes out on the road with me, anyway . . . Alma, are you there?"

The long-distance line crackled a bit before she spoke.

"When I saw you last you had changed."

"How you mean? Ten years pass, everybody change, mahn." He spoke in teasing patois. He had discovered that patois disarmed her.

"I liked the change in you. You were calmer, more relaxed. You seemed happy. Marriage must be good for you, Tony."

There was a brief silence. Alma could hear his breathing at the other end. His voice came back crisper, more British than before.

"Well, actually things have gone a bit sour on that end. Maybe we can give you and me a chance. Wasn't that what you wanted, Alma? Isn't that what you came to London looking for?"

Was that what she had wanted? Was this the thing she'd been looking for and couldn't find, the search that had led her around the world? A man with warm eyes and hands to take her into his heart? If so, then why wasn't the news that things weren't going well with his white wife filling her with joy?

She could hardly believe the answer she gave. It was almost as if someone else were speaking with her voice.

"A lot of times people come together because they remind each other of someone else, something else. I think I reminded you of home . . . walking like a West Indian woman as you say I do."

"And who do I remind you of?"

Alma looked over at *Déjà Vu* atop her desk, the Benin bronze with wax-drop tears. And met his question with a question.

"You asked me what I was looking for the last time I was in London."

"And what is that, love?"

"I think I was looking for home. And I was looking on the wrong continent. Tony, I'm so tempted. But I know the properties of elastic. Things that come on the rebound have a way of snapping back. You can't hold them because they never were yours to begin with. Why don't you try to work out what's wrong between you and your wife? Meanwhile, I've got work to finish and a trip to get ready for."

She wished him happiness and good night, night such as it was an hour ahead in Montreal. And then she was seized by an overwhelming sense of regret. She put the phone back to her ear in time to hear the line disengage with a definite click. She held on and eventually heard the bleating of the busy signal. She hung up and felt as if a door had been slammed shut. She felt an immediate urge to call him back, but realized she hadn't gotten his number.

She looked over at *Déjà Vu*. She was flooded with the promise of sun, of palm wine and papaya. There would be no sun in Montreal; it was winter there, just as here.

And she returned to the work at her typewriter. Which was routine and non-creative, but would nonetheless become dollar bills. Which would join the growing pile of dollar bills. Money that would one day buy a ticket home.

Feeding the Dead

She doubted there would be any secrets here to discover. The island's very stillness promised no surprises, no stories to collect and string together like beads. At the very most she might manage to return home a shade or two darker.

Below the terraced hillside the calm Caribbean glittered like blue glass. The landscape was lovely, but somehow faded. Pale ocean against an even paler blue of sky. Bleached beige strips of beach hugging the shore. Gentle hills that faded in the mist to hues of mottled green. As if the merciless glare of sun had blanched the landscape into silence.

It all seemed remote, unreal. Of a picture postcard reality. From this height nothing moved, nothing changed. Perhaps it was fiction, a watercolor flat from some Hollywood back lot. Alma experienced a menacing urge to leap into the quiet picture spread below, to awaken the watercolors with a violent burst of life.

Instead she grasped her sweating tumbler of punch and quickly tipped it to the side. She paused to watch the droplets hit the ground, then took a sip.

"You keep feeding the dead, they won't stay buried," Sara warned. "Of course, they're probably right at home here on this graveyard of an island."

"But Barbados is beautiful," Alma protested, leaning into the view. "So quietly beautiful. How could you ever leave a place like this?"

Sara, across the table, looked as still and distant as the scenery itself. Her eyes hidden behind the mask of sunshades. A wide-brimmed hat shadowed the upper half of her face. Only her mouth could be seen, lipsticked red and bent into a slight smile. A watching stillness, Alma couldn't tell of what.

Her head was turned, not toward the view, but the business about the swimming pool. The terrace of the Oceanview Hotel had been quiet when they came out that morning. Now it buzzed with midmorning activity. Children screamed, men shouted, women splashed. All in a tangle of toys, towels, and suntan lotion.

The spilled droplet spread into a small circle on the concrete between her feet. A tiny black bird with white wings alighted and pecked at the damp spot before flying off.

Despite the frenzy around them, Sara sat calm and still in the shrill sunlight. A statue carved of cool brown wood. Her long fingers wrapped her drink and raised it to the red half smile.

"How could I leave Barbados? If you'd grown up on an island, child, you wouldn't need to ask that question."

In the three days they'd been there Sara's voice had taken on a different quality. Organically Caribbean but subdued, like the potent Bajan rum she drank at that moment, mellowed with Coca-Cola. Sara paused between sips, making musical clinks with her ice cubes.

"Most West Indians leave these islands looking for the *better life* and spend their whole lives looking. Not me, mahn. From when I was a child I knew that life don't get better unless you change, not the landscape. I never wasted my time chasing that illusion."

"Then why did you leave?" Alma insisted. "And why have you stayed away so long?"

"Twenty-three years?" Sara cocked her head, considering. "Is that such a long time?"

"Almost as long as I am old."

Sara stirred her drink with a finger.

"How can I explain? It's a funny thing about an island, you know. A limit on just how far you can go. Wherever you walk, no matter how far you walk, you going to always hit water. You're surrounded by the damned water, trapped by it. Anyone who's lived on an island knows exactly what I mean."

Alma struggled to understand.

"I lived in the Caribbean for a year, Sara. And honestly, I don't know what you're talking about."

But as Alma gazed into green hills, she suddenly thought of Blue Mountains. She remembered another, larger island whose mountains thrust aggressively skyward. An island of violent contrasts, whose deprivation seemed more abject, and plenty more abundant. An island whose people appeared more proud and less gentle than those here seemed to be.

She remembered a charming villa, whose distance from the city it overlooked blurred the poverty and decay apparent from close-up examination. She remembered wandering the well-furnished rooms, trying to avoid the accusatory glare of her neglected typewriter. And more than anything she remembered waiting. Waiting for the maid or gardener to show up and fill the empty silences of the day. Waiting for a man who was not hers to come and fill her empty arms at night.

On the evenings she ventured out alone, she worried that Trevor might show up in her absence. More often than not she kept at home nights, fretting until Trevor appeared, and despairing when he didn't.

Unbidden memories crowded her consciousness, as if to make a lie out of her earlier assertion. An overwhelming sense of depression and claustrophobia assaulted her senses. Alma was almost ready to cry *uncle*, to admit that her friend's point was well taken, after all. But Sara had not even seemed to notice her reverie.

"Small islands, small minds." Sara shrugged. "Some people are content to spend their lives planting the same little patch of ground. Me, I need more range than that. Besides, there's a certain mentality here. It can kill you."

"What kind of mentality is that?"

Sara shrugged again.

"When you meet the girls you'll see what I mean."

The sisters were coming. Some of Sara's siblings had heard it on the grapevine that Sara was on the island. Alma could never figure why Sara preferred to stay in a hotel when she had blood kin who would put her up. They lived, she claimed, on the edge of oblivion in a parish called St. Philip. They were due for a visit that morning; were rather late in fact.

"I can't wait to meet your sisters. I bet you've missed them after all these years."

"They don't give me a chance to miss them." Sara's thin shoulders lifted carelessly. "Every time I turn around one of them's up in D.C., suitcase in hand. There's Beverly, a schoolteacher with a husband living in the States. She married young, some rascal Jamaican. Who, as you know, are the worst men in the world."

"Yeah," Alma muttered. "Tell me about it."

"I've already told you about it. Find you a nice, manageable little white boy. Why you hurt your head trying to tame these tropical types, I will never know."

"Maybe your sister can explain their attraction."

Sara shook her head.

"I am sure that I don't want to know. I never met the man, but everything I hear convinces me he's a born-again bum. A very strange relationship they got going, Bev and whatever the boy's name is."

"What about your other sister?"

"Rita? Her only mission in life seems to be getting men and having their babies. I hear she got about six of them now, with almost as many different daddies between them. There's a whole heap of other brothers and sisters, but Rita and Bev are about the closest. Country girls, the two of them."

Alma smiled wryly.

"I think country folks tend to be pretty good people."

Sara sipped her rum and Coke, then made a face.

"They put too much ice, mahn. Make it watery. And don't tell me nothing else about your old granny down on the farm. Southern Illinois and rural Barbados are two different things."

"If you say so," Alma answered doubtfully, but decided not to argue the point. The drop had evaporated, the dead satisfied for the moment. She turned once again to watch the landscape and wonder what was going on behind the calm, impassive face of it.

THE SISTERS

They turned up late, well into Alma's second fruit punch, Sara's third rum and Coke. Alma sighted them, loaded down with packages and headed straight for their table. She knew them at once.

"Hey, mahn." One of them gave Sara's back a hearty slap. "We here nuh."

Sara jumped, spilling some of her drink.

"What de hell . . . ?" In that moment of surprise she sounded just like the Bajan she swore she no longer was. "Oh, you two. Is island time you walk with? Look here, Beverly, Rita. This is Alma, my American friend."

She waved vaguely at Alma, who was given a cursory glance, a nod, and seemingly dismissed. And the two women pulled up chairs on either side of Sara.

"So this we sister finally make it home." The one called Beverly spoke. "Life good up in States, yes?"

"Must be, she stay away so long. Twenty-three years she gone, seven since we ever see she again. Let me see what that she wearing." Rita reached across the table and pulled off Sara's hat. "Take this thing off, girl. Why you want hide that pretty face behind this big old country hat?"

Sara reached up to smooth her hair back into place.

"Ain't no country hat, soul. It's a sunhat. This Bajan sun too strong on my face. Turn me black as tar."

Rita slapped the table and hooted with laughter.

"Don't blame the sun for that, sister. Blame your mum and Old Man. That kind of black baked in from birth."

Alma decided she liked the sisters. No hugs, no kisses, no tears of emotion. They simply sat down and started up the banter where it may have left off seven years ago.

"And how you liking Barbados, m'dear?" Alma was so busy trying to follow the flow of patois, and accustomed to being invisible, that she didn't realize the question was for her. Beverly looked at her expectantly.

"Oh, you mean me? Yes, I love Barbados. It seems so peaceful."

Rita winked and patted her hand.

"Not a bit like Washington, D.C. That place fast and rough, yes?"

To which Sara laughed and waved at Rita.

"Hear the country girl talking? Anyplace but St. Philip must be fast and rough."

"No." Alma glanced at the bristling Rita and hurried on. "Not at all like D.C., or Chicago where I grew up. Of course I haven't had a chance to see much of the island yet."

The sisters swooped down on Sara like avenging brown birds. Alma was startled at their shrill scolding. Beverly reached over and gave Sara a sharp shove that almost sent her sprawling from her seat.

"Sara, why you never show the girl around? You shame we family name."

"Live so long up in States the girl come back with white man ways." Rita rolled her eyes. "Real high class up in Washington, this we sister. Must live in the White House itself, yes?"

"And if we didn't hear Sara come home, you think she would step first foot in St. Philip to see the family?"

For the first time she could recall, Alma saw her friend's polished poise ruffled. Sara sucked her teeth in something akin to embarrassment and moved to adjust a pin in her hairdo.

"Who in St. Philip want to see me, anyway? Same ones run me off twenty-five years ago?"

Rita began unpacking her tied-up bundles.

"How you mean? Your Uncle Herbie, and Marianna, and Junior? All the people knew you since you pickeni. And look all the food Muh Dear send you. Here. Mauby and pastel, black cake and coucou. Muh Dear say she know you don't get good to eat over in America. Say she don't know how you survive for twenty-five years, so."

Sara surveyed the mountain of packages.

"You say you get pastel? Lord, when have I last eat a pastel?" She unwrapped the leaf-covered packet. "So Muh Dear still around, then. How she keeping?"

"You know Muh Dear. Even when things bad, she go say things good. The old girl still work the fields, go to market every day. Cooking and caring for that Junior."

Sara bit into the thing she'd unwrapped.

"Junior still live off the old lady, then. The lazy bastard."

"And guess who else asking after you? The Old Man, sure."

"Girl, you lie." Sara stared disbelievingly. "The Old Man? What he ever want with me?"

Rita sucked her teeth.

"What he want with all of we this late in the day? Old Man say he ready to die off. Want all of him children come see him before he go."

"If that ain't something, then what else is?" Sara shook her head. "The Old Man want to see us. Imagine that."

The sisters settled back, sucking their teeth in tandem. In silence, Alma could see the family in their faces. The same smooth, earth-brown skin. The same rounded faces and sleepy eyes. But even in their sameness, different stories stirred behind their eyes.

Something in Rita's smile seemed bland and giving, a woman who asked little and was content with what she received. Beverly's slanted eyes darted with watchful tension, as though afraid she'd miss something vital. And just beneath Sara's carefully cultivated coolness was the hint of a smoldering fire. Alma thought she'd known her well these past two years, but now realized she didn't know her at all.

"Who is *the old man?*" she ventured in the interval.

Beverly too had the habit of shrugging.

"Is we father, girl. Just a tedious old man, eh?"

"But if he's dying?" Alma was confused at the lack of compassion. "What's wrong with . . ."

"With an old man wanting to see his children for the last time?" Sara finished for her. "Just a bit late in the day, is all. I can't imagine why, after all these years . . ."

She waved the questions away into the air.

Beverly turned to Alma with folded hands.

"You see, dear, we not really what you call the Old Man's proper family."

"Proper?" Alma frowned.

"Bev, stop trying to be delicate," Sara snorted. She cupped a hand to Alma's ear and whispered loudly into it. "What she mean is we born on the wrong side of the blanket. The outside children. Catch my point?"

"Yes, but you're still his children, even if he wasn't married to your mother. Aren't you?"

The three women looked at each other. The sisters. Something passed between them that bespoke the frustration, the weariness, the pained acceptance of a question often asked and often answered. Rita finally spoke.

"We're his blood, yes. But he never was a real father. He fathered us is all. And who knows how many more."

Sara barked out a short laugh and burst into song.

My papa was a rolling stone
Wherever he laid his hat was his home
And when he died
All he left us was alone

"Ain't that how they sing it? Because that just what Papa Winston was. A rolling stone. Rolling all over the West Indies scattering his seed. That's one reason it's good I get away from here fast. Got so many kin, I could wind up married to my own brother and never know the difference."

"Yes, mahn. They would have to make a calypso out a you." Rita's raucous singing voice was no better than her sister's.

Sara, Sara
Shame and scandal in the family.
That boy is your brother
But your Mommy don't know

"Enough, girl." Sara grinned. "You give up any ideas of making it as a singer, yes? And I think all this off-color humor is shocking Alma. But Old Man good for shocking people, the rogue. Wouldn't be surprised if he still giving girls the belly."

"Never again." Beverly shook her head solemnly. "Him too weak for it."

"Old Man too weak to get the pum-pum? Lord, he must be on his last leg, yes?"

"I tell you, sister." Again the shrug, this time from Rita. "Old Man know he got one foot on the other side. No other way he be wanting to see all a we black faces."

Sara looked down at her drink.

"Old Man still rich, is he?"

"Maybe," Beverly answered. "Maybe not. Nobody knows where the money go. Not on the house again; it falling apart. Plenty people think the Old Witch squander it long ago. Still, it worthwhile going up the hill, yes? Might get a little mention in the will."

Before Rita and Beverly left to catch their taxi back to the countryside, they made Sara promise to come down to St. Philip and pay the Old Man a visit.

If Alma was shocked, as Sara suggested, it was not by the ribald humor of the three sisters. It was their lack of emotion, the layer of casual contempt that filtered into their conversation about this Old Man. Their father.

Alma knew what it was to grow up without a father, with nothing but pictures to remember him by, and precious few of those. She knew what it was to not have him even in memory, and to have to fantasize a father into being.

She grew up without a father, but did have a Dads.

DADS

In the days before the girl Allie Mae became the woman Alma, he was paternal grandfather and secret best friend. He visited once a season, liberally dispensing coins, kisses, and tales of Baltimore.

Allie lived for his visits. He never made her do the things Mama instructed before she left for work. Pick up the front room, wash the dishes, make the beds. These would be saved for the last fifteen minutes before Mama was due to arrive home. Then they'd rush around in a whirlwind, tidying up the apartment.

But until that point in the day, Allie would be running the streets with Dads, taking a tour of the neighborhood haunts of men. Certain street corners he would find with uncanny ease. The pool halls, auto shops, taverns she otherwise would never have reason to step inside.

Along the way he'd tell jokes about how he outsmarted a certain white man or kicked a colored man's butt so bad he hightailed it back to Lilliput, Arkansas. He taught her to pitch pennies, play bid whist, and use profanity with style and grace.

Allie remembered him best eating barbecue. The Mississippi Disco Barbecue Palace was his favorite. He'd order a double of baby back ribs with mild sauce and fries. He'd hold the rib delicately between thumb and forefinger, draw back his lips, and nibble away at the meat with his small, white teeth. The naked bone would then join a pile by the side of his plate. And Dads would rub his round belly and sigh with satisfaction.

"Now that is what you call good."

Then would come his *after-dinner cocktail*. After he cracked the seal on each new pint of Canadian Club, he'd let a little dribble to the ground.

"For Cholly and Louey Bones, Big Barney, Tiny, and Steve," he'd count out the names, drop by drop, "and all those other dead partners. Gone, but not forgot."

"What you do that for?"

"You got to look out for your peoples, baby." He would measure the whiskey into the thimble-sized glass, and drink several shots down in neat succession. "Even dead folks need a little taste every now and then."

And Allie would screw up her brow, thinking. No dead folks came to mind except President Kennedy, and she really didn't know him. But just like Dads, she'd pour out a taste every now and then. For Bobby Kennedy. Marilyn Monroe. Malcolm X. Martin Luther King. It became a habit. And as Allie Mae grew into Alma, the Kool-Aid became chablis, the list gradually grew longer, and the dead closer to home. Junebug Wilson, MIA in Vietnam. Big Momma Bohema Bullocks, of natural causes. Her brother Benny, she believed of loneliness. Though the doctors said he'd been morbidly obese, and Down Syndrome victims rarely make it past thirty.

But back then Benny was alive, a ravenous shadow at her side. Always eating, rarely speaking, except for to name the foods he craved. *Duice,* for juice . . . or really, anything to drink. *Tatips,* potato chips. *Nanee,* candy.

One day, Dads promised, he would take his darling grandchildren away from their evil mama and bring them to live with him in Baltimore. He called Baltimore *God's country.*

Her fantasies were rich with pictures of a princess named *Allie,* a king named *Dads,* and the wonderful adventures they would have in the magical city of Baltimore. Maybe that was why, when she left Chicago two years ago, she had chosen to settle in nearby Washington. But by then the King of Baltimore had long gone.

Even when he was around, the presence of her grandfather never quite made up for the absence of his son. To be without a father in the house was not so unusual where Allie came from. But to have a father nobody knew how to find was a different story. Allie filled the void with Dads and fantasy. And hoped against hope for her father's return.

Which was why she couldn't understand the apparent hatred the sisters held for an old man who was at least a father that they knew was there, if nothing else.

THE OLD MAN'S EYES

They'd gone to bed, but not to sleep. The room was dark, smelling of the hibiscus that grew near the open window, and the sea. From the other side of the hotel room, Sara's voice continued, rich and fervent in the dark.

"Hatred? No, my dear. It's not hatred we feel for him. Anger, maybe. Resentment. But hate's too strong a thing for a person on the edges of your life. It's like love. You save it for those who mean something to you."

Sara said Old Man Winston came from a family of land-owning Bajan *browns.* Had always had a thing for the young girls. *Plenty young girls.* He was wealthy, educated, and once considered handsome. The women who'd been his were many, and so, too, the fruit. Women had welcomed the issue of a wealthy man.

"I remember Mum telling me she chose Old Man to be her lover. Said she wanted a man who could do something for the children he gave her."

"And what did he do for you?" Alma wondered.

"He did provide some. I never fault him that. I remember when I was young, Old Man would visit regular. Just before day turned into night, Mum would tell me, *Time to leave now,* and send me off to relatives. Plenty times I come home in time to see Old Man hitching up him trouser on the way out the back door. That night we'd have something special on the table."

A heaviness, a sweet closeness in the island air at night. Even in the hotel room, Alma could almost touch the swollen darkness. She sensed that so much more happened here at night than during the brilliant stillness of day.

"Old Man was there one day I come home from working in the cane fields. I hear him tell Mum: *Don't be sending that child out to work again. This is a clever one, she must go to school.* And soon he was bringing a few extra shillings for school fees and books."

Sara stopped. Her breathing grew measured. Alma thought she'd fallen asleep. But then again the rich voice, heavy as the same night.

"Wasn't him with Mum I minded. Young as I was, I knew that a woman had to have someone. Married or not, most women I knew had a man sometime. Least Mum had one could take care of us, give her a little money now and again. And wasn't around fighting most nights, like some of them that lived in regular. I suppose there's a certain amount of freedom in being the mistress of a wealthy married man."

Alma had never thought she'd live to hear Sara say such a thing. Sara was known around their professional circles by two nicknames. One was *Fudgsicle*. The other was *Sara Take No Shit Winston.* They had met when Alma started freelancing for the Office of Protocol, taking the wives and families of foreign dignitaries on shopping sprees and sightseeing tours of the capital city.

Sara was a high-level staff assistant known for her stern demeanor and no-nonsense attitude. Clad in carefully coordinated suits, her hair straightened slick and scraped away from her smooth brown face, her makeup always perfectly applied. She was a smooth, unruffled paragon of perfection, it seemed. Unapproachable and unassailable.

But Alma wasn't put off by her chilly aloofness. She had been attracted to the mystery of it. She suspected that behind the stillness of the mask she wore, secrets simmered. When she found out Sara was originally from Barbados, she pestered to be taken along for her next visit home. Alma had long looked forward to a return visit to the Caribbean. She yearned to reacquaint herself with a land and a people less disconnected from their past than she felt herself to be. Sara had stubbornly resisted the suggestion.

"I don't know why you added me to your collection," she had complained. "I'm not a real West Indian anymore. I've been living in America too long."

Sara accused her of collecting a butterfly assortment of Third World characters, a multinational menagerie of the students, diplomats, and ne'er-do-wells that Washington was full of. Alma plumbed their memories for stories many of them had long ago forgotten. She longed to know the tastes and textures of their lands, the secrets of the lives they left behind.

"*And here,*" Sara teased in a pinched, prissy little voice, "*you see the Reticulated Mauretanian Taleteller, while this is my prized Australian Fly-By-Nighter. And soon I will be jetting off in search of the rare Bimshire Backwater Wing. Don't forget to bring your butterfly net. You're going find yourself some specimens down there, I can guarantee you.*"

Sara had finally given in. Together they left for Barbados on a two-week vacation. Alma was finally seeing Sara at home. And tough little coconut though she was, the island seemed to be cracking her shell of self-containment. The music of the language was entering Sara's speech unawares. She was walking in a different rhythm, head erect as the market women who came into Bridgetown daily, wearing their burdens like crowns.

It seemed all the emotion Sara had drained from her beautiful, impassive face had entered her voice. Disembodied, it throbbed like blues in the darkness as she spoke of the man her father was.

"Never once, soul. Never once did he claim me as his child. Must have seen this man daily in and around St. Philip, coming out the back door of Mum's house. I don't remember him ever saying more than two words to me in life. I wasn't really a person to him. I was something he had produced.

"He lived in a fine house, high upon a hill. A big fine house, mahn. Yet even as we mothers warm his bed year upon year, I don't think none of Old Man's children ever enter. Till this day, I never know what my father's house look like inside. I guess we go find out tomorrow, eh? The bastards been summoned to Mount Olympus."

Alma thought of them as shepherds. Rita and Beverly came the next day to lead their Sara home. Returning the stray to the fold, as if after all these years she may have forgotten the path. Or perhaps afraid that left alone she might wander into the jaws of wolves.

The ride was long and bumpy, the landscape gently picturesque. As they drove east from the capital, country sprang up right outside city limits. The land gradually flattened into waving carpets of green. It seemed the entire country had turned into a giant cane field. Every here and there an oil rig loomed in the distance. Sara cursed every time they hit a bump.

"Tt-che-ew," she sucked air between her teeth. "These Bajan roads as bad as ever."

Rita had brought her youngest along. The baby slept soundly in her lap while she flirted with the taxi driver up front. Wedged between Sara and Beverly in the backseat, Alma caught snatches of scenery and conversation.

Over and around her the sisters tossed dialogue. When she listened only to the music of it, their patois was like a running duet; Beverly singing second soprano, Sara the rich vibrato of alto. Woven in and around, the man and woman's whispers and throaty laughter from the front seat created a chorus.

When Alma concentrated on lyrics, translating music into a language she could decipher, she learned interesting tidbits about people she would probably never know: Junior, Marianna, Muh Dear, Chita, Uncle Herbie. Amidst the medley of gossip she gleaned that the sisters all had different mothers. News was exchanged about an abundance of brothers and mothers and cousins, but word of Sara's mother was never mentioned.

The tenantry they pulled into looked to Alma like a Rip Van Winkle Village; as if it had gone to sleep for forty years and was just waking up.

The street was lined with trim chattel houses, propped on stone or cinder-block foundations. Few cars plied the narrow, rutted main road. Chickens and children strolled right down the middle of it. Women sat chatting on steps in front of low buildings, wherein calypso music played. Men in games of dominoes lounged under trees. A barber had set up shop on the sidewalk, working the head of one young man sprawled in a kitchen chair. The waiting customers clustered loosely about them. Even the clothes people wore looked Depression-era: threadbare shirtwaist dresses, battered hats tilted forward, shirts and trousers faded to indeterminate colors.

The taxi passed a modest two-story affair labeled simply *The Inn*, and turned off onto an even narrower dirt path. As the car jounced along, children materialized, running alongside and peering in.

"Ethel!" Rita called out. "Run tell Ma we home."

Rita's home couldn't have been more than four rooms, a modest wooden cottage in a clearing of bush. And here lived her mother, several younger brothers and sisters, and all six of her own. So many children. Alma couldn't tell who exactly was daughter or son, brother or sister. They danced about, excited at the arrival of visitors.

"Auntie! Auntie!" Sara was mobbed. Alma wondered how they even knew who she was. None of them could have been born when Sara left the island. "What you bring us from States?"

A house bursting at the seams, crammed full of children, bric-a-brac, and bustle. Alma was overwhelmed. A seat was found for her in the midst of it, while the three sisters disappeared out the back door on some unannounced mission.

Madara pressed food upon Alma, fragrant, unfamiliar dishes. Rita's mother was small-boned and delicate, not much larger than some of the children. Yet in this roost it was obvious who ruled. It was an ordered pandemonium. When Millie was told to bring *our visitor* a glass of mauby, or Michael sent to pluck a mango from the garden, they went scurrying to obey. No questions, no back talk.

Night had settled when the sisters returned. They ate dinner, washed dishes, and went out walking to see the Old Man. Alma, whom they insisted accompany them, followed blind in the liquid darkness. No lights lit the night, save those glittering in the distances. Sounds seemed magnified in the pitch black night: a woman singing somewhere nearby, the constant piping of tree frogs, an occasional punctuation of dog barks. They walked single file in the dirt road.

"Eh, eh. It dark, nuh!" Sara exclaimed. "I forget how black night get in the country."

But the sisters knew their way, moved with the rhythm of the Bajan night. They reached the main road and followed it through town, stopping to greet people every few paces. Cousins, uncles, and friends stepped forward to embrace Sara, the long-lost kin. To warmly welcome Alma, the visitor.

Then leaving town behind, they turned off onto another dirt road winding uphill. Panting behind the sisters, Alma climbed the rocky road and worried about rustlings in nearby bush and canebrake. Wispy tendrils of causerine leaves brushed their legs, like tentative ghosts trying to get their attention.

The road dead-ended at the top of a rise. A plaque above the double doors of a vine-entangled iron gate read THE RIVERS. And here they hesitated, obeying the unspoken rule that one does not enter her father's house.

A full moon shone now behind shredded clouds, casting a blue light over the house at the top of the hill. A house with secrets hidden away behind shuttered windows. A house in mourning. Alma shared the sisters' hesitancy. Even the lowing of cattle and braying of sheep from nearby stables seemed to echo with sad and sinister intent.

The silence was broken by footsteps on the path. Mingled male and female laughter sliced open the aura of grief. An elderly woman climbed the path, leaning heavily against a tall young man. The woman stopped suddenly, arms akimbo.

"Sara Winston. It ain't you." The mothering span of her arms opened wide. Sara went into them.

"Muh Dear." Her rich voice almost breaking. "How good to see you. Look at you, mahn. Young and pretty as ever."

Muh Dear waved a hand in dismissal.

"Liar. Get on with you." But she looked pleased nonetheless. "Why you keep gone so long, girl? We miss you past missing."

The young man spoke. Lazily, hands in pockets.

"Longer you stay away, harder it is to come back. Is so, Sara? Must have you a rich American husband tucked away in States, loving away all your time."

"Junior, you were too pretty for your own good when you were a toddling baby. And I see things don't change at all." Sara hugged him. "No, I haven't caught me no rich husband. And what of you? Breaking all the young girls' hearts?"

Junior didn't answer. Sara saw where his eyes were and smiled. They were fastened with interest upon Alma.

"I don't believe I meet you yet, darlin. Auntie, who be this lovely craft?"

"She's my friend Alma. And you leave she alone. Alma, watch out for this mahn, yes? He's a dangerous lady-killer."

Junior sucked his teeth lazily but did not disagree with that assessment.

Muh Dear ushered them all ahead, a bustling mother hen.

"Come, children, make we go forth. When Daniel ready to walk in with the lions, he never step back."

Junior linked arms with Alma and laughed.

"Only this time the lion, he have no teeth at all. Eh, Muh Dear?"

Tossing banter back and forth between them, they made their way up the drive to the house. But once they'd entered inside all laughter ceased.

So quiet it was from the outside, Alma hadn't expected to find the place filled with people. Men and women with Sara's eyes, tens and dozens of them came over to greet them. But none with the boisterous exuberance of earlier in town. Everyone here spoke in near whispers. Even the children were round eyed and silent. It may have been a funeral, in want of a body.

"Come, Alma, make we go and meet the master." Rita grasped her arm. "Might as well get this over and done with."

"Rita, are you sure? This is family business. Maybe I should wait out here."

"Oh come along, m'girl. Old Man will get a kick outta seeing you. Always did like a pretty face, that one."

"Might make him more kindly disposed toward disposing a bit my way," Junior added.

Sara slapped his hand and admonished him to hush. As a group they climbed the stairs. Rita, Junior, Beverly, and Sara. Alma brought up the rear. Muh Dear stayed behind with the relatives downstairs.

"Are all those people your relations?" Alma whispered to Sara as they rounded a bend in the staircase.

"Wouldn't be here if they weren't, I suppose. M'brothers and m'sisters, most of them. Their mothers, their children. Some of them though, I not sure I even know them. Old Man's bastards come from far and wide."

This room was even quieter than the one downstairs. It was dominated by a high iron bed. Empty. One wall was lined with chairs, where a row of people sat silent as schoolchildren.

In the adjacent corner, faintly illuminated by a tableside lamp, were two men. A gray-haired, gray-whiskered man in glasses, bent over writing in one chair. A bald man bundled in blankets, propped in the other. A frayed, faded strip of material folded across his lap looked like a piece of ancient *kente* cloth.

Their party made its way over to where the two figures sat. They stood before them.

"Good evening, sir," Rita began. "I am Rita Winston. Madara tell me to remind the Old . . . to remind him, sir. She get five children for him. And there's the grandchildren, too, twelve of them. My six, then Sally has three . . ."

Rita stopped. The man with the pen had motioned her away. She went to join the row of quiet people against the wall. And the ritual continued. One by one, they introduced themselves to their father. Told him their names and the name of their mother. The gray-haired man scratched away with his pen. The bald one bundled in blankets sat and watched. Alma thought of a medieval king and his scribe, holding court. Then it was Sara's turn. She stepped purposefully forward.

"The name is Sara. That's S-A-R-A."

The scribe looked up for the first time.

"Oh, yes. You're the one who went away."

Sara smiled her half smile.

"Not went away. Sent away. From this backward town by backward people. My mother is Marita Elders. Or should I say *was* Marita Elders?"

"She is deceased?" The scribe continued to scribble.

The voice seemed to come from far away. The other man had spoken, the man bundled in blankets. A thin, aged voice.

"Marita. Marita Elders."

Sara spun on him.

"Oh, you remember her, do you? One woman out of the multitudes, what an amazing memory. I guess you should remember, Old Man. You killed her. She died twenty-five years ago trying to bear you another bastard child. Do you remember that, old hypocrite?"

Beverly rushed to her side.

"Sara, no. He an old man, just a sick old man. He probably can't even hear you. Leave it, Sara. Leave it."

Sara let the sisters lead her away. But she turned back at the doorway. Her husky voice rumbled across the length of the room.

"You once told Mum I was a clever one. You were right. You sent me into the wilderness and I conquered it. And now I'm on your level, Old Man. Or better. I'm my own woman, got my own life, my own money. I don't care if you do disinherit me. You ain't got nothing I want."

Alma was frozen in place for a quiet moment, then made to hurry after her friends. But a voice called her back. A faraway voice from an aged body with ancient *kente* spread across its lap. A voice that seemed to have already journeyed on, and was calling to her from the other side of death. Alma approached timidly, looking back toward the doorway.

The Old Man's eyes were unnaturally bright. His bald skull and face the color of faded brown leather. Alma could just see a hint of Sara and her sisters in the face grown old. The same fullness, a similar bend of cheekbone. But the Old Man's eyes were his own. Bright and black as marbles. The Old Man wore a half smile. His head erect on a thin wrinkled neck, pivoted birdlike to the row of relatives lined against the wall. Alma thought of a king crow, gloating over his hoard of stolen corn.

"Who are you, young lady?" asked the scribe.

"I'm Alma Peeples. But I'm not from here."

The Old Man spoke again. His eyes bright on her.

"Who are you, my dear? Who is your mother?"

"You don't understand, sir. I'm not from here. I'm a visitor from America."

An old hand grasped Alma's. A strong grip in such an ancient, failing body. Alma drew back, startled. The bright eyes. The faraway voice.

"You are not American. Look." He spread her hand palm down against the faded *kente* cloth. "Your skin is black like mine. Your hair and your eyes, my hair. My eyes. Are you not a child of mine?"

The hand fell away. Alma opened her mouth to explain again, but the scribe interceded for her.

"She's a visitor, Mr. Winston. She says she's not your child."

Alma backed away. The stares of the silent relatives, the bright eyes of the king crow followed her out of the door.

Sara, Junior, and the sisters were nowhere to be seen. Disoriented, Alma walked the dark corridor looking for the stairway. She must have made a wrong turn. The corridor ended in an alcove. There sat a woman at a large bay window. Looking out into the still night.

"Excuse me," Alma whispered.

The woman turned. White hair against a whiter face. Blue eyes stabbed her with such an intensity of loathing that Alma recoiled.

"I'm sorry to trouble you, ma'am. Could you tell me where the stairs are?"

The woman didn't answer. She returned her blue gaze to the black night. And Alma returned to the hallway, where she eventually found her way downstairs.

Later there was laughter. Strolling downhill toward town lights. The quiet house was behind them now. Alma told them about the case of mistaken identity.

"So he thought you were his child?" Beverly laughed. "I tell you, the man believe he so prolific, every black face he see must be his offspring."

They parted with Junior and Muh Dear at a junction in town. But not before Junior had pressed his lips to Alma's ear and promised to come *check her* tomorrow. Muh Dear merrily waved her cane.

"So long, darlins. Come and visit me afore you're going, yes?"

They meandered on. Alma's next question was greeted by great laughter.

"Muh Dear. Is she your grandmother?"

The sisters looked quickly at each other as if checking the others' reaction. Then they stopped and stood, roaring in the road. Alma watched, bewildered.

"No, Alma," Sara gasped out between guffaws. "You won't believe this, but Muh Dear is we sister. Old Man's eldest child. I tell you, he been busy making babies in St. Philip for a long time now."

The laughter died away as the four women aimlessly wandered the quiet road. Sara did a quick dance step, suddenly boisterous.

"I wish there was someplace to go in St. Philip. Me, I want to get drunk, go dancing."

"Then it's the disco for you," cried Rita. "Make we go to the Inn."

"Disco?" Sara exclaimed. "You mean to say St. Philip get a disco? I can't believe. Progress come to the Bajan backwater."

The disco, however, was less than rousing. Almost empty this Sunday evening, a tinny calypso playing on an ancient jukebox. The women sat at the bar and nursed beers. The sudden gaiety gone out of the evening.

"Why he have to call us there?" Beverly asked bitterly. "The Old Man never care about us before. If he did, why he wait till he almost dead to see us?"

"Maybe," Alma began, then stopped. The sisters looked at her expectantly. "I think he draws comfort from you. It's as though he weren't really dying. Because . . . well, his blood lives on."

Sara snorted and returned to her beer.

"I think you giving the old fool more credit than he deserves. Me, I think all he want to do is take inventory. Counting us up, like chickens."

"Who was that old woman?" Alma remembered. "That white woman, in a room upstairs."

"You don't see the Old Witch, do you?" Rita was awed, almost reverent. "That old woman, she living here almost fifty years. Only one see her these days is the servants."

"I came on her accidentally after I lost my way upstairs." Alma shivered. "She gave me the most evil look you can imagine. Just pure hatred."

"Well, no wonder," Beverly explained. "That was old Mrs. Winston, Old Man's wife. She hate us, every last one. She probably like Old Man himself by now, half-crazy and senile. She mistaken you for one of us, Old Man's bastards."

"Why should she hate you?"

"Wouldn't you?" Beverly retorted, eyes lit with a sudden fury. "Old Man find her over Europe somewhere, marry her and bring her out here, then find she can't bear. Poor woman alone now, oceans away from home. And all she see in St. Philip is Old Man's children. Everywhere. She with none of her own."

Rita wrinkled her nose and sucked her teeth.

"That's what the old fool get for marrying a white woman. Mules, all a them. He shoulda known the white ones can't bear like Black woman can. Old Man wasted he seed planting in barren ground."

Beverly turned on her sister with fire.

"Rita, you a idiot woman, yes? What make you think white women can't bear? Where you think all a these white people in Europe and America come from, eh? I swear, girl, you vex me. You vex me bad."

Rita set her small mouth sullenly.

"You jealous, mahn. You think I don't know?" She turned to Alma. "She fear she just like old misses, sheself. Been married over twenty-five years and not the first child. And it ain't the man. He plenty busy fooling around. She should be vex with he for living high in States, loving every woman he find and leaving she alone in St. Philip. Not jealous of me and my children."

Sara, for once the mediator, raised her drink above her head.

"Truce, truce," she called, slightly drunk. "We don't show Alma enough dirty laundry for one day? And you know what make us fight like cats? It's men, yes? Old Man, Beverly's husband. Why it always have to be a man to make a woman lose her good sense? Hell, I guess I shouldn't even blame Old Man for Mum's death."

"Sara, Sara," Beverly soothed. "Don't do it. It's over, child."

But Sara wasn't to be comforted. Perhaps it was not over. Her eyes glittered as brightly as the Old Man's.

"I read about it in the papers. I hadn't been in America six months when Flora hit. *Killer storm ravages the Caribbean. Six hundred deaths.* I can imagine the calypsos sung about that one. And then I got Muh Dear's letter. All of St. Philip had to flee to Mount Pleasant, running away from Hurricane Flora. Everyone but Mum. I guess she tried to run but labor caught her in flight. They came down the mountain and found her in the cane fields. The baby inside stuck halfway between birth and life."

Alma saw Sara's eyes wild with unshed tears. The sisters moved to comfort her. Sara impatiently shrugged them away. The Fudgsicle was melting. And in her center was that store of secrets. Nuggets of pain as hard and bitter as unripened persimmons.

"How you like that one, Alma? There's something to add to your collection." She tilted her glass and let the liquid fall carelessly to the ground. "Here's a drink for the dead, the Wingless Wonder of St. Philip. Fifty-year-old woman, trying to give birth in a cane field in the middle of a hurricane. Loving an old man so hard she sent her only living child off into the wilderness. Loving herself to death. Where was her good sense, nuh? And you."

She turned to Beverly and Rita. The sisters looked back with stricken eyes.

"Sitting here fighting about which woman can make a baby and which can't. It's men got you doing this to each other. But not me, soul. I take no shit from no man. From no one. I'm like a Bajan palm, a Carolina persimmon. I stand alone, too tall to climb."

Sara downed her beer. The calypso song had ended and she shouted into the silence.

"Come on, sisters, let's drink. The prodigal daughter returns home. The king is dead, long live the queen. Hey, brother. Bring a bottle of that good Bajan rum. Tonight we go celebrate."

"DON'T I KNOW YOU?"

The celebration would become ritual, stretching on for days. They never bothered to check out of the hotel, but nonetheless wound up spending most of their days and nights in St. Philip.

Sara would disappear for hours, leaving Alma alone to dodge the clumsy courtship attempts of her nephew. When not trying to elude Junior, Alma spent long hours in the company of children, who told her Brother Nancy stories and frowned in disbelief when she assured them that the streets of Washington were not paved with gold. After a few days she grew bored and impatient, and decided to return to the city and wait for Sara there.

The colonial harvest holiday of Cropover had recently been revived, a century of pent-up expression exploding onto Bridgetown. It seemed that the entire city had taken to the streets. Alma wandered out alone, feeling safe and anonymous among the crowds of revelers, the costumed masqueraders, calypso music blaring from every open window.

The festivities went on for two days straight and Alma wandered in and out like a guest at some surrealist ball. She went out in the morning and joined the crowds, danced with strangers, fed the dead, and drank herself from the communal bottle of rum that always seemed to be passed around. She'd go back to the hotel to sleep it off, then come out again to find the same party going on.

On the second day of Cropover she spied a ragtag band of revelers playing wood and goatskin drums. They wound through the streets like Pied Pipers, leading a crowd in their wake. And she joined them, jumping to a hypnotic rhythm that seemed eons ancient and strangely familiar. Afternoon bled into evening. She didn't know how long she had been dancing when she heard someone calling her name.

"Over here!" a voice shouted from the sidelines. "It's me, Bev!"

Her body still pounding with the rhythm, her clothing damp with sweat, she danced over to the figure silhouetted in sunset, and embraced it.

"Lord help you, Alma." Beverly laughed, patting her sweaty brow. "Is not only we Bajans who does behave bad. Before I see it was you, I tell m'friend here, *There go one wild West Indian woman.*"

Beverly introduced the friend, a visitor who had just arrived that morning. Perhaps it was the failing light. Or could it have been the rum, the drums, the nonstop dancing? Alma looked into the strong brown face of the woman standing beside Beverly, and was seized with an overwhelming sense of déjà vu. She grasped the extended hand and peered into the vaguely familiar face.

"Don't I know you?"

The woman shook her dreadlocked head and smiled.

"If only I had a dollar for every time somebody asked that."

"You're American?" With her broad features and colorful tropical clothing, the accent came as a complete surprise.

"Not anymore. Somebody going to write a book, call it *Darlene Goes Native,*" Beverly joked. "Miss Josephs Harris Amagashie got more identities than she do names. When first we meet, she just a stick in the mud working girl from Detroit. Then she turn missionary, come way out here to Barbados and adopt my little sister Sara back in 1959. Next thing I know, the two of them living out in the sticks someplace in States don't even have a name."

"The town was Leeboro," Darlene reminded her. "Leeboro, North Carolina."

"Hmmph. Just a little bit of nowhere. And now that Darlene jump ship in Africa, she gone more native than the Queen of Sheba. She even knows the language now. Come, girl. Speak me some of that *booga-booga* talk."

Switching allegiance from the drum rhythms to girl talk, Alma followed the women back to St. Philip. They were sitting over dainty cups of English tea in Beverly's kitchen when it suddenly dawned upon Alma. *The dreadlocked hair. A full-figured woman dressed in tropical print, squatting and nursing near the podium.*

"I know where I've seen you. In or around Providence, some years back."

Darlene and Beverly exchanged quick glances.

"You lived in Providence?" Beverly asked with an uplifted eyebrow. "Rhode Island?"

Darlene reached over to pat her hand.

"A fair-sized city, sister love."

"True," Beverly shrugged. "Anyway, you must have already been in Africa by then."

"Yes, though maybe I did pass through New England around that time. It's been so long, it's hard to remember."

"You had a baby," Alma remembered. "A nursing toddler."

Darlene smiled ruefully.

"Musta been me then. It took the longest time for that child to give up the titty. Lord knows, I was the world's oldest living mother. Giving birth for the first time at the ripe old age of forty-five."

"And how is Zenzeli?" Beverly inquired. "She must be a big girl by now."

"Eight years old. I used to tell everybody that I went to Africa to become a professional mother. Never in my wildest dreams did I think I'd go and get knocked up in my old age."

Darlene seemed an unlikely type of Baptist missionary. Apparently Alma hadn't been the only person to think so.

"I went to Africa looking to convert souls, I wind up getting converted my ownself. Had to learn to speak the language in self-defense. Someone was always coming up to me saying *Don't I know you?* in Twi. And didn't want to hear no, *Mi no sabi.* I been accused of being a *been-to* on more than one occasion."

Alma had never heard of that ethnic group.

"A *Bintu?* You mean a *Bantu.*"

"I mean a *been-to.* The type of African who goes to New York on holiday, then comes back two weeks later claiming they can't remember their mother tongue."

In the bright light of Beverly's kitchen, Alma realized that Darlene was probably much older than she had first thought.

"It must have been really hard," she mused, "to uproot yourself like that."

"Tell me about it. I'd been on my job in a Detroit hospital since the age of twenty, and was looking forward to retirement. And suddenly I realized I had this misplaced mother complex I'd been struggling with all my life. Next thing you know, I was packing my bags and moving to Africa. Since I didn't have any kids at the time, I thought I might as well mother a whole continent. In fact, it was soon after I met Beverly. As I recall, y'all were living in Canada at the time, you and your Mr. America."

"That's right," Beverly remembered. "We were fresh, green newlyweds. Seems like a lifetime ago. Mahn, that place was cold. Took me years to thaw all the ice from my blood."

"And what about that man of yours? I thought he was finally back in this neck of the woods."

"It didn't last. If I don't know Mr. America, then nobody does. I can't stay in the States, he can't stay away. We get together until I can't stand him again, then we separate. I think that's how we stay married so long."

"It's funny," Alma mused. "I had me an island man, too, and taking a break from time to time was the only way I was able to deal with him."

"Some men ought to come with a warning," Darlene joked. *"Take only in small doses."*

"Use with caution," Alma added. *"This drug maybe habit forming."*

Beverly dished out the meal she had been preparing, a fragrant dish of spicy fish and rice seasoned with coconut.

"Hmmm, girl, this is good," Darlene remarked. "It reminds me of that first meal I had in your apartment, that winter in Montreal. You know, I believe I still have your recipe. I never have been able to make it taste quite this good, though. Fess up, now. What did you leave out?"

"It's never the same thing twice," Beverly admitted. "It's like making love. You always add a little extra something, just to make it nice and new."

Alma remarked how wonderful to be able to experiment so freely, both in the kitchen and in the bedroom.

"That's the thing about being married to a man you don't see every day." Beverly laughed. "Each time you get together, it's like the first time. But you know, I didn't really learn to cook until we went to live in Canada. I was cold all the time, lonely for my family. Tasting coucou and saltfish became my little piece of Bajan sun. It was the best way I knew of holding on to home."

"And holding on to that man with the hollow leg," Darlene reminded. "That's the kinda man you got to feed, honey."

The evening sprawled on, the women eating and drinking, sharing light-hearted recipes of aphrodisiacs and love tonics, talking long of love and loss, men and women, herstories of happiness and heartbreak. Finally Alma began to wilt, feeling the aftereffects of the long day's activities. Stray words, odd items she'd been telling herself were mere coincidences began to sound alarms in her tired brain—*Mr. America . . . Providence, Rhode Island . . . Montreal, Canada . . . Beverly . . . Beverly . . .*

"Go into my room and rest, child," Beverly instructed. "You look exhausted."

She led her into a darkened room and switched on the light. It was tiny, though lavishly frilly, obviously a woman's boudoir. Pushed against one wall was a single bed piled high with ruffled cushions. A man's portrait hung in a gilt frame above it, and Alma found her eye straying to it.

"But, isn't that . . ." she gasped, then found she couldn't continue.

"My Mr. America," Beverly responded, turning back the lacy coverlet. "In living color."

Staring from the picture frame was the unsmiling face of Alma's own dearest misery: one Trevor Reginald Barrett.

"Your husband?"

"My husband."

Everything fell sickeningly into place. Beverly Barrett came and stood with her, looking up at the picture with a faint smile. His eyes staring back seemed to size up the relative aspects of the two women, and Alma suddenly felt herself wanting. She could see herself towering, tall and gawky beside the petite Beverly.

Why would he ever want me, she found herself wondering, *when he had as his own this tiny brown flower standing beside me?*

Alma collapsed wordlessly onto the bed, a pulse pounding in her ears loud as carnival drums. She barely looked up as Beverly tiptoed to the doorway.

"She tired, poor thing. Come along, Darlene." Alma hadn't even realized the other woman had trailed them into the room. "Leave a soul to her rest."

"I'm right behind you," Darlene called after her.

But she continued watching Alma's stricken face, then gently closed the door without leaving.

"An island man in Providence, huh? I thought it was too close for comfort. Looks like we got ourselves a situation here."

Alma held hands open, helplessly to the air. As if in court, being asked to account for ten years of sin.

"I knew he was married. But how could I know it was someone this close?"

Darlene sighed. She sat on the bed beside her, placing an arm around her shoulder.

"I can see you're all shook up, so I'm only going to say this one thing. Beverly Barrett knows the kind of man she has and I suppose she's made her peace with it. Yet and still, this woman has let you into her home, her heart. Ain't no reason for her to know about this, is there?"

"There is nothing for her to know." Alma sighed, turning her face from the picture frame. "It's over."

When they were planning the vacation, Sara had changed her mind several times about coming back home to Barbados. Maybe this is what she feared. That once home she'd find herself unable to leave.

Alma returned alone, sated with stores of opened secrets that left her with more questions than answers. Dizzy and disoriented, almost drunk with sorrow. She'd gone looking to crack open secrets like coconuts, and had gotten more than she'd bargained for.

She'd cut the trip short, packed her bags, and come running back to

Washington. Exhausted and heartsick, she was certain she had lost her taste for foreign tales and untold stories.

Yet when nighttime came she couldn't stop herself from reliving images of tropical sun, Cropover drums, the Old Man, the three sisters, and the familiar face in the picture frame. She would awaken tremulous from troubled dreams, her face wet with tears. And then the package came.

She went to a diplomatic reception, found an old lover there, and brought him home. On the way inside she reached into her mailbox and discovered a small package. In the dim light of the vestibule she couldn't make out the return address. The crisp blue wrapping felt foreign. Perhaps it was a peace offering from the long-lost Sara.

She was curious at the contents, but too anxious to bring this man to her bed in an effort to replace despair with desire. She didn't look at the package until one bottle of white wine and twelve hours later. When the man was gone she ripped it open, uncovering a tissue-wrapped bundle and a single sheet of foolscap.

Dear Alma:

You remember my recipe for "manpower"? You mix up some dried sea moss, milk, a little rum, and if you can find it in America, some powder of an herb we call "bois bandee." If you ever decide you want to keep that island man of yours, just try it on him. I made it for my husband when he came down for my father's funeral, and he hasn't left yet.

Yes, Old Man Winston died in his sleep two weeks ago. Seems he took quite a fancy to you, Alma. I know you're wondering about this little piece of rag inside. It was some kind of security blanket Old Man took to carrying around in his dotage.

I don't know why he wanted you to have it. Everyone told him that nobody but him would value the threadbare old thing. But Old Man kept insisting: "I know she is a child of mine." I guess we're going to have to start calling you "sister." Take care of yourself, my dear.

Love, Beverly Barrett

She rubbed the scrap of *kente* between her fingers and the memories all came flooding back. The green island. The brown sisters. The face in the picture frame. The Rivers estate in St. Philip. The fold of cloth she now held in her hands. The thin, birdlike man propped in a chair; his strong hand on hers. His crow-bright eyes. It made her think of Dads.

Dads could hardly have been considered birdlike. Or at best a round, contented pigeon. Maybe it was something in the manner of the men. Like Mr. Winston, Dads enjoyed taking on the air of the refined gentleman. Both reveled in the company of women. And neither was quite like any man she had known.

Dads had been fond of saying: "Alma, don't tell your mama I said so. But one of these days I'm coming for you. I'll soon be taking my grandchildren back with me to God's country."

That's why she could never understand why he went away. Dads suddenly stopped coming to visit. Alma remembered asking her mother why. Mama sighed and said that Dads had *passed*. He'd gone to live with God. And her gruff, impatient tone also warned, *Don't ask me nothing else about it.*

Alma didn't. But she kept wondering. Why did Dads never call or send a birthday card from the place he passed on to? Maybe some day she'd be able to visit him there in God's country. And then they'd get a chance to do all the wonderful things he had promised they would in Baltimore.

Her memory cast over her life and the men who had inhabited it. Each distance and desertion, loss and unresolved longing, floated to the surface of consciousness, like dead fish in a tainted river. Her own biological father gone, the disappearance of the grandfather who had temporarily filled that space. The stepfather whose presence had complicated an already difficult adolescence. Such situations had been entirely beyond the control of a child.

Naw, baby. It ain't me. The childhood message that would echo into her womanhood. Even when her taste in men emerged, shaped by her long association with Trevor. The parade of intriguing, foreign-born men marching through her life would be just as elusive. She was learning now to throw them back almost as quickly as she reeled them in. *Sorry, Charlie. Only the best tuna get to be Starfish.* Learn how to use those words herself, to head off the eventual message in the back of every man's throat. *Naw, baby. It ain't me.*

Was this, indeed, the point of all her butterfly collecting and world wanderings: a running away from home? A desperate search, then desertion of love, before love could abandon her?

Alma refolded the letter, bundled up the scrap of cloth, and put them both away. She made herself a cup of tea and carried it to the windowsill. She watched butterflies flutter by and thought about birds. She looked out along the line of spindly city birches and thought of a woman who likened herself to a taller genus of tree. She tilted her teacup and let a droplet fall.

A tiny black bird with white wings alighted upon her windowsill, pecked at the spot of tea, and flew off again. A single white feather floated in its wake. She found herself wondering about secrets again.

The River Turns

How can you mend a broken heart?

Alma pitied the lovesick puppy on the radio. Didn't he realize it was simply a matter of willpower? Say *I do not need you* enough, and you will come to believe it. The inevitable *Naw, baby. It ain't me* would fall upon deaf ears.

She had willed herself into selective amnesia, diving headlong into work, the distractions of dating, even finding time to take an anthropology course at George Washington U. She rushed from man to class, work to play, too busy to let her mind stray into the abyss of memory.

And it wasn't just an academic exercise. She was tested early in the game; a case of sheer irony, too banal to be poetic. Sara Winston walked briskly into her office with a man in tow. He frowned as he followed, head hung like some recalcitrant schoolboy being dragged before the principal.

"My brother-in-law has been bugging me to show him the town," Sara announced unceremoniously, "and I have meetings all day. Then Eureka! I remembered a certain coworker who specializes in tropicals, so I'm dumping him on you. Can you take the boy off my hands for an afternoon, just to keep him out of trouble?"

She had turned on her stiletto heel and clicked off, just as quickly as she'd marched in. Alma had looked up from the typewriter, he had glanced up from his shoes, and their eyes locked in instant recognition.

I do not need you.

"Trevor." Shock had worked to her advantage; the calm, light tone of her voice surprised even herself. "We meet again. Can you give me a minute or two? I've got a memo to finish here."

Probing her will to see if any weakness remained, she found herself amazed at her own stores of steely resolve. She fulfilled the letter of Sara's request and nothing more; taking him out for lunch and a White House tour, begging off on his dinner invitation, and not returning his subsequent phone calls.

She was suitably nonplussed when he turned up at her apartment door a few nights later, interrupting the visit of a doe-eyed Ethiopian graduate student who hadn't yet become a beau. Who had, in fact, just been speaking of how lonely life was for a beautiful African boy trapped in the closet.

He was a challenge that intrigued her, the subject of an intended experiment. She had invited him over for drinks, and mixed up generous portions of an alleged aphrodisiac elixir whose ingredients included rum, milk, and sea moss. She had just settled back to observe the effect.

"This isn't a good time for me, Trevor," Alma murmured through the half-opened door. "I've got company."

"Oh?" His eyebrow shot up. "One of your men, I presume?"

And she'd been wondering exactly how to answer that question when he pushed his way in. He looked about to get his bearings, then marched right over to the young man on the sofa, innocently sipping his *manpower* and thumbing through the pages of a coffee table book.

"You may well have her body," he bellowed. "But I will always have her heart."

And Haile had spilled his drink, dropped his book, grabbed his keys, and scurried off with an anxious glance over his shoulder. He lived in the same building, so he didn't have far to run. Alma learned later that his flight was not motivated by fear for safety, but the rush of unexpected sexual attraction. Apparently the aphrodisiac had kicked in.

"What a powerful man," he whispered on the phone later that night. "Are you absolutely certain that he is not gay?"

And Alma had glanced over at Trevor, snoring comfortably in her queen-sized bed. He was sleeping off the aftereffects of the leftover *manpower*; a recipe which had been given to her by, of all people, his wife Beverly for just such a purpose.

"There are many unsolved mysteries to the man, Haile. But I don't think that is one of them."

The darkness of her bedroom was relieved by the intermittent glare of passing headlights, and the unaccustomed glitter of gold on her right ring finger. The stone itself reflected no light. It was lapis lazuli, a stone which did not refract light, but absorbed it into a glowing blueness crisscrossed with veins, like a network of rivers.

Trevor had explained, as he jammed the too-tight ring onto her finger, that he was supporting economic sanctions against South Africa and didn't believe in buying diamonds.

Seemingly satisfied that Alma's body had been saved from Haile's clutches, and her heart safely tucked in his back pocket, Trevor returned to New York.

Mr. America was back in the belly of the beast. Tourism was a failing proposition these days on his island home. He had resigned his ministerial post shortly after she'd fled their Blue Mountain hideaway, disillusioned over fallout from a war of words between his government and U.S. foreign policy interests, and political violence on the streets. Tourists were staying away in droves, and he had decided to cast his lot in international consulting work.

"New York City is as expensive as hell." He had shrugged cynically. "But then, UNICEF is paying thrice the wages I made back home."

Alma was relieved at his departure, and managed to squeeze the ring off with liberal applications of Vaseline. Engaged to be married to a married man; how did she get herself into these situations?

I really do not need him.

She reflected on it during the days after his departure, wondering how to extricate herself. But it turned out to be a moot point.

Governmental budget cutbacks brought her contract at the State Department to an abrupt end. Unable to find another position, and unwilling to squander her savings on living expenses, Alma held a house sale, abandoned what was left unsold, packed her bags, left Washington, D.C., and drove nonstop the seven hundred or so miles to her mother's house.

Two decades of marriage to a demanding, possessive hypochondriac had made Mama suspicious about men in general. Those few of Alma's boyfriends she met, she immediately suspected of having medical ailments. This one wore the wasted look of a TB patient, the other extended a handshake with seriously sweaty palms, while the prolonged bathroom visit of still another suggested hemorrhoids.

"And you sure don't want to spend your life looking after no ailing man."

When Trevor Barrett turned up at her doorstep, Callie Mae Clemmons called the Chicago law office where Alma was doing temporary work.

"There's a West Indian sitting up here in my living room," she whispered over the phone. "Got some big old flat feet. You know your daddy had them flat feet, always did give him trouble."

"Tell him to call back later. I won't be home until after six."

She actually didn't arrive until 7:30 P.M. She'd stopped downtown to have a drink with a coworker, then driven up north to pick up some produce from a specialty market. She suddenly had a taste for ripe mangoes, and good ones weren't that easy to find.

It seemed that Trevor had spent the entire day waiting, his fallen arches apparently forgotten. She walked into the back door with a sackful of tropical fruit, and encountered him in a grease-splattered apron frying chicken in her mother's kitchen.

Before she could say a word, Trevor had caught her up in his arms and covered her mouth with his. The paper bag split and mangoes bounced and rolled their way across the kitchen floor.

"Well, I do declare," Mama teased from the doorway. "Looka here, Otis. These lovebirds bout to burn up our dinner."

Trevor Barrett had won them over. Both mother and stepfather had fallen head over heels in love with him. Mama proudly produced a huge bottle of My Sin.

"Look what your fella brung all the way from New York. Ain't that thoughtful?" Alma had never known her mother to wear fragrance.

On the other hand, Alma was sure that Otis would get good use out of his gift. Enclosed in his ubiquitous back brace, he sat in an expensive recliner designed to raise him to standing with a touch of a button. He sipped Johnnie Walker Black from a beer mug.

"Good Scotch, son," he murmured, peering at the label. "Aged to perfection."

"You've really outdone yourself this time, Trevor." Alma was so irritated at his seamless insinuation into her family, she quickly hustled him off. Mama put up loud protestations.

"Now, Alma, honey. The boy ain't even tasted his dinner. What's your hurry?"

"Gotta catch up on those old times, Callie Mae." Otis winked broadly from his armchair. "You know what I mean?"

Once they were alone in the car, he reached for her hand. She dropped the lapis ring into his open palm.

"I'm afraid it's too late for us, Trevor."

And I do not need you.

It would have been a moment worthy of an Oscar. She fully intended to step out into the West Side Chicago street, turn away without a backward glance, and leave Trevor and his rented automobile behind forever. *Naw, baby. It ain't me,* never again to be heard.

But the river turned. Before she could make her exit, he had locked the car from the inside, started up, and screeched off into the sunset. He never stopped driving until he pulled into a rest stop just outside of Battle Creek.

"Kidnapping," Alma awoke from a three-hour nap, yawning into the Michigan midnight, "is a federal offense."

And Trevor Barrett deliberately reached for her, pulling her across the controls and onto his lap facing him.

"Don't you know by now," he took her face between his hands, "that you are mine?"

But I do not need you.

Alma continued protesting long past the point she actually wanted him to stop. There was something about her resistance, her failure to surrender that added to their excitement, urging them on to the ultimate conclusion. But at the end of it surrender would come. And despite that she was trapped between the steering wheel and his body, her legs cramped and clothing crumpled, it would be sweet.

"Alma Peeples," he murmured into her mouth, slipping a circle of gold back onto her right ring finger. She must have lost weight in the last month, because it fit perfectly now. "Please don't run out on me again."

"I can't make you any promises, Trevor." *And I do not need you.*

But the ring felt comfortable and she didn't remove it. Not during that night at a motel in Battle Creek, where they shared a twin bed and didn't sleep much. Not the next day, when Trevor drove into Detroit, turned in the rental car, and bought air tickets to New York.

Not even during the next weeks with him in New York, and the following in Geneva, Switzerland. Not even when the phone rang in their hotel room and she answered it to find Beverly Barrett on the line.

"Alma." She seemed genuinely pleased to hear her voice. "Girl, it's been a long time."

She told her that Trevor was unavailable, away at his conference.

"It's alright. Actually it was you I wanted to speak with."

She didn't want to face Beverly, and she told her so.

"Don't worry yourself, sister. You have nothing to fear from me. It had to be someone, my dear. I'm just relieved to know that it's you."

But I do not need him.

She felt herself on dangerous emotional ground. She found herself wavering, faltering. She tried to remember her mantra, but the words were fading. Could it be she needed him after all?

For one thing, she was on unfamiliar ground. She was in a place where no one knew her name. No one, that is, but Trevor. The mountains here were not blue, but white. Still, isolation seemed to breed devotion, as had happened before.

She was abjectly dependent upon him. All her belongings had been left behind in Chicago, so everything she owned was new. Her clothing, her bras and panties, her nightgown, her toothbrush. She had not so much as a sock, a lipstick, an eyebrow pencil that had not been bought for her by Trevor Barrett. She tried to summon the strength to resist being pulled into his undertow, then spat out again with the coming wave.

"Do you really want to love me, Trevor? Or own me?" The tentative tone in her voice might have been intimidation. They sat on the terrace of an embarrassingly expensive restaurant overlooking the River Rhone. Trevor looked handsome and masculine in his tan khaki *political suit*. They had just left a reception where several Third World diplomats had kissed her hand and expressed their delight at meeting *Mrs. Barrett*. Trevor had not corrected them.

"Not own, my darling." Trevor smiled across the dinner table. He expertly flicked open a linen napkin, bleached white as the snow-capped Alps that loomed in the distance. "Claim. I am old enough to know what I want. And what I want is you."

Apparently he knew what she wanted, too. In flawless German, Trevor ordered for both of them. Alma had never known that Trevor spoke German. She asked him what he had ordered, then decided not to object. He had chosen well, from the pâté appetizer to the Black Forest torte for dessert.

And the designer clothing they'd shopped for together did fit her well; the typewriter she worked on during her hours alone in the hotel was just the kind she used at home. Even when they slept at night, she seemed to fit perfectly against his chest, her head cradled in the crook of his arm.

Having Trevor all to herself should have been a dream come true. Yet somehow she strained at the cloistered intimacy, like a lap dog on a short leash. It all seemed too good to be true.

She wondered if it were the off-balance of being suddenly swept into his orbit again. Perhaps it was her natural inclination to run, to create discomfiting distances. Or could it be her guilt over the distress she was causing another woman?

"That should be the least of your worries," he scolded. "Beverly knows, and she accepts the situation. Why shouldn't you?"

"It feels wrong."

"It's been happening since the beginning of time. We are an African people. African men have always been polygamous."

"And polygamy has always been problematic. Somebody always gets hurt, gets the short end of the stick."

"I wouldn't hurt either one of you. And the stick is long enough to go around, if I may say so. I want to have you both, I can afford to have you both. She is the wife of my youth, you're the wife of my maturity. And besides, I'm ready now for a child."

"What if I'm like Beverly and can't produce one for you? Remember, we tried it before. Or what if the problem is yours?"

"Then we will adopt. Nothing can change the fact that I have claimed you as my woman, my third wife."

"Your *third* wife?" Alma repeated, though somehow she already knew.

"There is Beverly, and then there is Africa," Trevor admitted, "my first, and my forever love."

And Alma found herself looking wistfully out onto the Rhone, as if an image of Africa could be found in its muted waters.

"And I have never gotten to know her."

"Then you will." Trevor had what he wanted. He could afford to be magnanimous. "In African tradition, a new wife cannot be brought into the household unless the others agree. You have the approval of my second woman. You must now travel home to get the blessing of the first."

Alma realized that their loving had finally come full circle. Trevor's shadow had been a cloak she had learned to wrap herself in these years, a place to warm and shield herself. She had left its shelter like a runaway child from time to time, over the years. But the cloak had always been held open for her return.

She reached for it once again, and found it wanting. What had once seemed so voluminous, now barely had enough material to cover them. Something had shifted. She walked alongside him, feeling peculiarly naked and entirely unsure why she'd allowed herself to slip so easily into his aura once again.

What on earth am I doing? she often wondered, twisting the circle of gold and lapis settled on her right ring finger. She tried to imagine a future with Trevor, comfortably ensconced as the third woman in his life. Living with him in his New York apartment, raising his children. She found she couldn't make the image materialize.

Had she simply stopped loving him? Had she finally stepped from behind his shadow to bask in the glory of her own sun? Or was she shielding herself for the inevitable, the uttering of words this man had murmured more than once before? And neither the rum-smooth timbre of his voice nor the comfort of his arms could soften the coded message. *Naw, baby. It ain't me.*

For the first time since Trevor had come back into her life, a serenity of purpose settled upon her. She clung to him each night, listening to the rumble of his voice as he imagined spermatozoa on their way to rendezvous with ovum. She stroked his woolly head as he fantasized about children. A son named *Sekou*, twins they would call *Taiwo* and *Keyhinde*. But her thoughts were already several thousand miles away.

Somewhere in the back of her mind was the inevitable acceptance that it would all end. And when came the words *Naw baby. It ain't me*, Alma would have her answer already prepared.

So she accepted the ticket, took the money, warning him there could be no promises made, no strings attached. He sent her off happily, willingly. He took out his atlas, helping her plot her journey.

"Now where'd this critter come from? Alma, I believe you must have smuggled him in from Chicago."

A tiny spider scurried across the African map. She carried the page to the window and shook it free. She watched it catch the breeze, and be carried off into the European sunset.

Alma returned to Chicago wearing new clothes, the lapis ring still snug on her finger. She went deliberately about her travel preparations: inoculations against tropical diseases, applying for visas, buying summer clothing. She wasn't exactly sure what she was looking forward to.

She had surrendered herself to something, and it wasn't just being Trevor's third wife. Because, as she reminded herself, she no longer needed him. She felt for the first time she was not preparing herself for running away from life, but traveling toward it. She was ready to give up being a perpetual tourist, and become a permanent resident in her world wanderings.

The tide of time had reversed. The river had turned. Something was calling from the other side of the water.

In Search of Spice

Three women get out of a car and walk across the parking lot of a high-rise building. Two of them saunter, laughing at some pleasantry between them. Moving leisurely on toward their destination. But one of them walks slightly ahead, straining forward as she moves. Don't you see her prowling like a wildcat stalking prey? A small predator, hell-bent on the scent of something alive to feed her hunger.

Maybe this would be the time.

You may wonder at her name. Some men call her *sugar.* Others call her *honey.* Pop called her *baby.* Her mother gave her the name *Pat. Cinnamon* is what she has named herself. Cinnamon Brown.

Because she likes the way it sounds, the way it smells, the way it tastes. Something to sweeten your tea, season your toast, flavor your cocoa. She found out young that spice was the variety of life. And anyone who knows her will tell you her motto: *Life ain't nothing but a party.*

Parties promised pleasure, and pleasure was the primary of life's seasonings.

HOUSE PARTY

The living room was packed. Men and women claimed their spaces on the crowded dance floor and did their do. If you could call it dancing, that standing in one spot and shaking your body like it hurt, frowning all the while.

The room was steamy with the fumes of liquor and perfume and sweat. Cinnamon stood half-hidden near a potted palm in the corner. She sipped delicately from her wineglass, careful not to smudge her lipstick. This was a package presentation and everything had to be perfect.

She knew from working in the advertising business that a product had to be attractively packaged in order to sell. And strategically placed in order to be seen. She carefully plotted her next move. No one had asked her to dance for the past three records and Cinnamon knew she was being shuffled to the bottom shelf.

"What's the sense of sitting down at a party?" Cinnamon would often say. "I'm not here to sit down. I'm here to git down."

At which the friend would usually giggle and murmur *Girl, you crazy* and admire the cool, hard polish on the petite brown-skinned woman who knew what she wanted and how to get it.

Right now she wanted in. She wanted to get from behind the potted plant and out on the dance floor. She watched the scene, calculating. The cool-blue party lights gave a grayish cast to the writhing bodies. A smoky haze hung near the ceiling, shrouding the room in a kind of fog.

Cinnamon found the darkness a disadvantage, a film on the luster of her shine. If a man couldn't see you well, he damn sure wasn't going to ask you to dance. Especially if you hadn't been seen dancing already. Cinnamon always said that a man was like a dog with a bone. Didn't give a good goddamn about the bone unless another dog wanted it, then he'd fight over it to the death. Being out on the dance floor meant that you were the top bone; name brand and in demand.

She decided that what was happening was bargain shopping. These were low-class men who obviously wouldn't know quality if it hit them upside the head.

Shit, she said to herself. *Half those hussies wearing wigs, and them that don't, have chemical curls, the kind that wilt under this heat and sweat.*

Cinnamon's hand strayed to her own head, proudly patting her naturally wavy *Creole hair*. She knew she had a rare commodity; the kind of hair that didn't *go back*, didn't revert to naps under the threat of water.

Half-hidden though, behind a palm on the outskirts of the dance floor, no one was ever going to see it. At parties like this men went in for the obvious attractions, things they could easily make out in the near dark. Anything larger than life.

Cinnamon's practiced eye roamed the dance floor, sizing up her competition. Most of the women out there were Brand X or generic equivalent, using what little they had to sell their product. The fat broad there with the red halter top on, dancing with her chest stuck out. All bouncing boobs, nothing else. But men went for that. Stick a titty in a man's face and he'll follow you to hell and back.

And Willa. The Great Pretender. Cinnamon's lip curled as she regarded her friend decked out in ass-length braids. Out in the sunlight anybody with eyes could see that it was phony hair added on. But in this light either they couldn't tell or didn't care. Men went in for lots of hair, even when it was an illusion.

And that woman laughing in the center of the floor. Not all that pretty and just about bald with that mannish-looking Afro. But she was tall and skinny and ragged-out in a solid white jumpsuit. Men picked up on the clothes and the height.

Cinnamon knew that none of these broads could hold a candle to her in daylight. Her long, naturally wavy hair. Her small, shapely body. Her keen-featured brown-skinned face.

"My beauty's too subtle to be appreciated in a crowd." She pouted. Cinnamon was pissed.

The deejay had a trick of mixing the end of one record into the beginning of the next. There was no break in between. And the couples kept on dancing and sweating, from one song to the next. While Cinnamon sulked in the shadow of a potted palm.

Finally there came a break in the music. The couples drifted to the walls, waiting for the next dance record. And Cinnamon made her move.

Stepping out onto the empty floor just as the next song started, she slowly pranced her way to the doorway. A slight smile, head thrown back, her small behind swaying to the beat of the song. She couldn't have chosen it better:

Give me that fine brown frame.
Any other kind of woman
just ain't my thang.

As she moved she watched the men watching her. Their relative heights and body sizes. Their facial hair, the comparative leanness of their hips. The way they held their cigarettes, their drinks, and their women. And the satisfying slide of eyes in her direction as she danced past them. She imbued each movement with subtle sexual invitation. A good hunter doesn't just stalk her prey. She knows how to lure, to make them walk willingly into the trap.

And sure enough, just as she stepped into the doorway a man leaned out of nowhere and grabbed her hand.

"Dance?" he growled from way back in his throat. And she knew what kind of desire was masked behind that growl.

She smiled and looked away.

"Aw, I was just on my way to the little girl's room. Maybe next time."

She sauntered slowly toward the back of the apartment, aware that the man was watching the studied sway of her hips. She wouldn't dance with him though, except as a last resort. That man was hitting the bottom of the barrel. He was short and pimply, with bottle-bottom bifocals. She knew this type. Once he got up the nerve to ask for a dance, he'd hang around your neck all evening. And having a near-sighted albatross hanging on was almost as bad as not dancing at all. It scared off the serious prospects.

Cinnamon locked herself in the bathroom and critically examined her reflection. First she checked out her body from all angles in a full-length mirror attached to the door. The outfit was good, even if the color was a bit muted: a clinging bronze metallic top, skintight pants of brown leather. She unbuttoned the top, removed her bra and stuffed it into her matching bronze handbag. She rebuttoned her top halfway, leaving the top three open. She looked again and nodded in satisfaction. If it was titties they wanted to see, she'd show what she had. They weren't big, but they weren't bad.

She then concentrated on hair. She'd worn her long hair up in a topknot to give herself an illusion of height. But she saw now it was all wrong. No one could see how long it really was.

Deftly removing pins and placing them in her mouth, she let her wavy locks fall around her shoulders. The look was okay for the bedroom, but she couldn't let it flow loose like that at a party. It was so fine that it would just hang limp around her face. She pulled it all to one side and fashioned a flowing ponytail that just touched her shoulder.

She pulled out her cosmetics case and began to deepen her face color. Dark berry lips, bronze-lidded eyes, dusky rose blended into her cheeks.

Cinnamon's transformation had taken all of ten minutes and she was pleased with the results. She did look a bit on the whorish side, but that never hurt at a party.

Someone had been banging at the bathroom door for a minute or more. Cinnamon had simply ignored them. Whoever it was could wait. She'd had business to attend to. It was now done and she flung the door open.

"It's all yours, buddy."

"Damn," said the man. "What you been doing in there? Thought you weren't going to ever give up the john."

Then he took a hard look at her as she stepped through the door.

"Hey, hold up, baby. What's your hurry?"

Cinnamon smiled serenely, pausing to look up at him.

"Thought you had to pee so bad."

The man looked flustered and grabbed the front of his pants.

"Yeah, I do. But wait out here while I get rid of some of this beer. I got some talk for you."

"Better hurry up then. I'm getting ready to dance."

She didn't head back to the dance floor, but to the refreshment table set up just outside the kitchen. She refreshed her drink and looked over the tray of tired-looking snacks.

She wanted to give the man a chance to catch up, without making it obvious she was waiting for him. He looked promising. Not too bad-looking. A little on the other side of sixty, a little heavy around the middle. But well groomed, well dressed. Cinnamon knew money when she saw it and the man spelled M-O-N-E-Y.

He caught up with her just as she stepped through the doorway to the living room. The pimply dude was lurking there and made a feeble move in her direction. She dodged it deftly and spun around to smile up in the other man's face.

"Hello, stranger."

He wordlessly grabbed her hand and pulled her to the middle of the floor. And the music began.

Why must I feel like that,
Why must I chase the cat?
Nothing but the dog in me.

Cinnamon laughed to herself, dancing. The very idea. Men thought that calling themselves Atomic dogs made them dangerous, when it just made them predictable. Most of them were just puppies anyway. She thought of Twinkie, the flea-bitten mongrel who used to hang around Pop's barbershop.

Twinkie would do it with anything. Coats hanging on the racks. The barber pole outside. People's legs. He was pathetic. Twinkie was totally undiscriminating, and most men were just like him. Forgetting about the bone once it was buried. Chasing the cat but rarely catching it. Almost tame. Easily leashed and muzzled and carted off to the pound. Blissfully unaware that the feline is the real predator.

Cinnamon had hung a poster over her bed; a cat done up in high heels and pearls. Which read *Every dog has its day, but the night belongs to us pussy cats.*

The deejay went into a round of slow dance tunes. Cinnamon moved close to her partner, hooking her hands behind his neck and looking demurely off to the side. She held her upper body coyly away from him while they danced, but her hips twisted snugly into his crotch. She ducked her head and grinned at the results.

"Baby, I've got to know your name."

"They call me *Cinnamon.*"

"Well, they call me *Freddy* and you sure got me ready. You can put some of that spice in my dish anytime."

He swung her through the thinning crowd and over to the ubiquitous potted palm. And proceeded for the next three songs to (as she would later relate to her roommate Anita) *grind the hell out of me.*

By the fourth record she managed to pry herself away, pleading exhaustion. Grinding and groping was alright to begin with, but she didn't want to make it too easy for him. Hard to get was an essential part of the game. She strolled into the dining room, Freddy steady on her heels.

"Damn." Cinnamon surveyed the spread of drinks. "What happened to that white wine?"

"The bottle's empty, baby." His mouth came close to her ear, his hands gripped her shoulders. "Let's dance."

"Just a minute." Cinnamon twisted away. "I need something to wet my whistle."

She ducked away from his arms and went into the kitchen. She found a bottle of wine chilling in the refrigerator.

"Wouldn't you rather have something to tickle your nose?"

Cinnamon smiled. Cocaine was not her thing, but she didn't mind a man who indulged every once in a while. It sometimes had its benefits.

"You gonna do it here?"

"Right outside in my Benz, baby."

He stood back a little, examining her more fully in the bright light of the kitchen. He stroked his chin and looked her up and down, as if examining a car he contemplated buying. Cinnamon didn't mind the stare. A man who drove a Mercedes had the right to be choosy. And she was certain she measured up.

"Come on, let's get out of here."

But Cinnamon was in no great hurry. She didn't let just anybody in her bed. He had to have the right qualifications before he could pass *Go.* So she sipped her wine and did her best to find out all she could about Freddy Williams. Despite his street mouth and foul tongue, he bragged of owning a Pontiac dealership, a home in Pill Hill, a Mercedes-Benz. She had been right. M-O-N-E-Y.

Of course there was probably a wife and a couple of kids who went along with it all. But she didn't mind. Freddy looked like he had enough to spread around. She moistened her berry-red lips and looked up at him.

Maybe this would be the time.

"Where's your car parked?"

But Freddy didn't get to answer. A short, stocky woman close to his age suddenly appeared in the kitchen doorway. Her face, pinched with irritation and suspicion, had *wife* written all over it.

"Fred, what are you doing in here?" Her voice was as pinched as her face.

Hincty, Cinnamon thought. But ragging for days. Diamonds in her ears looked real. A fur coat was slung around her shoulders. She'd probably been afraid to put it down for fear of someone walking off with it. She was several shades lighter than Cinnamon herself. Almost white; the requisite color for a boojie wife. But her hair, though long, was nappy at the roots.

Old-fashioned press and curl, Cinnamon thought smugly, tossing her head so that the ponytail bounced off her shoulder.

Freddy was eyeing his wife uneasily, getting ready to grip. Wanting to have his cake and pudding, too.

"I'm just getting me a drink of wine, baby. Go on back there. I'll be out in a minute."

But the Mrs. was having none of it. She stared hard at Cinnamon, her mouth tight.

"Frederick, I am ready to go home. Now."

"Aw, baby," Freddy pleaded, eyes flicking nervously from cool Cinnamon to hot Mrs. Williams. "It's still early."

Cinnamon sipped wine and watched the woman plant herself resolutely in the doorway. Hands on hips, shoulders slumped, feet slightly apart, fur piece dragging the floor. She looked like a boxer ready to slug it out to the last round.

With a glance of regret Cinnamon's way, Freddy took the path of least resistance and obediently followed his wife.

Cinnamon shrugged, never one to worry over the one who got away. *Plenty more where that came from.* She made her way back to the living room and accepted a dance from the first man who asked, a stooped, light-skinned dude with green eyes and a trace of a foreign accent.

She danced the rest of the evening. The more the dance floor thinned, the more alive Cinnamon became. Twisting, smiling, styling, profiling. The night was getting late and the party was emptying out. Soon there'd be nothing left but the dregs. And no one had so much as asked for her phone number. Cinnamon worked it for all she was worth.

She left the dance floor reluctantly. Willa and Anita were frantically signaling her from the doorway. She sighed and made her way across the floor, hoping they weren't ready to leave. It would be a wasted evening if she had to go now.

Willa was the one driving and Willa was ready to go home.

"It's after three o'clock," she reported in an irritated tone. "Ain't nothing happening here, and I gotta get up and go to work in the morning."

Cinnamon examined her scornfully. Her braids were old and loose, a second hairline showing boldly above her own nappy roots. If a woman didn't keep up her hair, don't care how pretty she was, how expensive her clothes, she wound up looking like anybody's ragamuffin.

"Well, I'm not ready to go yet," Anita announced. She was looking pleased as punch. Cinnamon wondered why. She hadn't seen her dancing at all.

"I met a man," Anita reported, then blushed.

"You did?" Cinnamon demanded. "Where you been hiding out?"

"I was back in the bedroom." Anita blushed some more.

"Well, damn," Willa shrilled, hand on hip. "Talk about still waters run deep. You jumped into it mighty quick."

Cinnamon laughed and punched Willa with an elbow. "When I said get down, I didn't mean get all the way down," she teased. Though if the opportunity had worked out right, she certainly might have found herself in a more horizontal position.

"You all are crazy," Anita furiously rebutted. "There were a whole bunch of other people back there, didn't feel like dancing. We were just talking. That's all."

"Well, talk is cheap. If all you want to do is talk, talk to him on the telephone." Willa scratched aggressively underneath the nappy edges around her hairline.

Anita, usually so willing to go along with the program, jumped stubborn. She shook her head in quiet determination.

"I'm not leaving yet. You, Pat?"

As many times as she'd told her to stop calling her by that name, Anita never got it straight.

"I don't care." Cinnamon shrugged. "I can go or stay."

"Oh, please stay," Anita begged, grabbing her hand. "We can share a cab home. Or maybe Junior will drive us."

"You all suit yourselves." Willa's jaw jutted out. Her braids wagged belligerently at her back as she stalked out the front door. Meanwhile, Anita pulled Cinnamon toward the back of the apartment.

"Come on. I don't want nobody to grab up Junior while I'm gone."

Cinnamon glanced at her curiously.

"Who is this Junior, anyway?"

"He's so fine, girl. A West Indian steel drummer, the one putting on this party tonight." Anita smiled excitedly, her eyes alight.

"A musician, huh? I hope you know they're all dogs." This was pure speculation on her part; out of Cinnamon's many lovers she had never had a musician. A needle of envy jabbed her as she watched Anita pause at the bedroom door. Nervously fluffing her hair, preparing to reenter a private party that she herself had not been invited to.

The room was brightly lit, pungent with reefer smoke and body heat. People lounged on the bed and the floor, or leaned against the wall. Anita pointed out a tall dark man leaning back in a peacock chair, seeming to preside over the relaxed gathering. He smiled lazily, chatting with a woman she'd seen dancing earlier; the one in the Afro and white jumpsuit.

"I wonder who she is?" Anita fretted. "Junior didn't say he had a girlfriend."

"They never do."

"Maybe I should leave."

"Oh, no you don't." Cinnamon took her firmly by the elbow and propelled her into the room. "You better get over there and get what you want before someone else does."

Poor Anita. She was so anxious she actually twisted her hands. Cinnamon felt sorry for her. The girl had no self-confidence, no social graces. She had lucked up getting that man to notice her in the first place.

Cinnamon was therefore surprised when Junior glanced in their direction, smiled lazily, and made a beckoning motion. In fact, Cinnamon thought for a moment that it was she herself he'd gestured to join him. She smiled back at him and took a step in his direction. But Anita beat her to the punch, rushing eagerly across the room to the man in the peacock throne.

Cinnamon quickly recouped, glancing around her. Another man sat alone in a corner, smoking a joint and watching her with secret amusement. It was the same lean, hunch-shouldered man she had danced with earlier. She strolled over to his corner and sat down beside him on the floor.

"Are you sharing that joint?"

"Surprised you, didn't he?"

"What are you talking about?" Cinnamon knew exactly what he meant and didn't like it one bit.

"Junior wanted the other girl instead of you. You're not used to that." He looked at her speculatively, raising the weed to his lips. "Shocked the shit out of you, didn't it?"

"Hell, no," Cinnamon lied. "Why should it?"

He laughed, closing his eyes. His chest quaked but no sound escaped.

"Ain't you a woman?"

Cinnamon regarded him through slit eyes. Damn right, she was a woman. Just what did the fool find so funny about it?

"Junior always has that effect on women. Has their tongues hanging out from here to Lake Michigan."

"Does he, now?" Cinnamon did not find the conversation amusing. She glanced around the room, looking for another group to attach herself to.

Everyone seemed to have paired off. Junior still reclined in the peacock chair, Anita perched awkwardly on his lap. He murmured something to her, stroking her arm. Anita gazed down at his face, her mouth slightly open. Blushing all the while. Cinnamon didn't like what she was seeing. She snatched her eyes away to find the man at her side watching her again.

"Your girlfriend has it bad," he observed. "Real bad, mahn. I see it all the time. Junior has them in and out of here so fast, we ought to put in a revolving door."

"Oh?" She was careful to mask her sudden interest. "You live here, too?"

"Yes, mahn." He inhaled again, looked at Cinnamon, and laughed for no apparent reason that she could see. Damn, the dude was high. His eyes looked like they were melting into gobs of green wax.

"You a musician, too?"

"Yes. And you know what?"

"What?" Cinnamon breathed suggestion into the question. "Tell me."

"I'm the leader of the band. And I make twice as much as Junior boy. You're better off with me."

Cinnamon smiled and put her small hand on top of his, easing the joint away from him. She pinched it between her fingers and brought it to her berry-red lips, closed her eyes, and inhaled softly. She opened them again and smiled up at him. Ready for the kill.

Maybe this would be the time.

"What did you say your name was?"

The man with the melting eyes looked into Cinnamon's pert face. Glanced at her small body sitting beside him, feet tucked neatly underneath. He must have liked what he saw. He laughed again.

"I am Richard, the sexophonist. And you, my dear, look good enough to eat."

Sometime later she found out the reason for his title. He rolled from Cinnamon's warm body and spread his arms across the bed. They looked long and pale against the printed sheets.

"*Ras claat,*" he murmured. "You got some tasty pussy. Junior boy don't know what he's missing. Is your friend as good as you are?"

"I doubt it."

No, this had not been the time. She hadn't found what she had long been searching for. But still Cinnamon felt good, languid with electricity. As if she had been running on low and her battery was now recharged.

But thinking of Anita made her forehead wrinkle in the darkness. She sat up in Richard's bed, a mattress and boxspring on the floor. And began feeling around for her clothes.

"What you doing, woman? Lie back and go to sleep."

Cinnamon didn't feel the least bit sleepy. Her mind was racing to the other end of the apartment, the bedroom where she last saw Anita grinning stupidly into Junior's face. She was stabbed by sudden curiosity.

"I need to go and see about Anita. We're supposed to be sharing a cab home."

"Don't worry about that one. Junior probably has her between the sheets by now."

Which was exactly the thought that occurred to her. Carrying high-heeled boots in her hand, she padded to the back. Pressed her ear to the bedroom door. There was no sound to be heard.

"Anita," she called softly. She rapped lightly, then pushed her way in.

As expected, Junior and Anita were alone. Both were fully clothed, stretched out on the king-sized bed with every light in the room blazing. She was relieved to find nothing more than a lightweight petting session going on. Junior was busy trying to cop a feel. Anita was trying her best to avoid his hands.

"Come on, now, Junior. Stop that," she cried out, moaning just a little. Cinnamon never knew the girl had it in her. A full-fledged tease.

"Excuse me." She made her presence known, knowing full well the effect it would have.

"Pat!" Anita cried, jumping up as if cold water had been dashed down her back. She leaped from bed and began tucking in the loose ends of her blouse. Junior remained where he was, reclining in bed with his hands behind his head. Did he ever lose that lazy smile?

"Great timing your friend has." He examined Cinnamon from head to toe, seeming not to miss a single detail. "We thought you'd gone home."

"No. I was up front talking with Richard. And waiting for you." Cinnamon turned reproachful eyes to Anita, who predictably blushed.

"I'm so sorry," she apologized, fluffing her hair nervously. "I don't know what got into me."

"Nothing got into you, darlin'," Junior murmured. "That's just the problem."

"Junior, stop it," she exclaimed. "Oh, Pat. He's so bad. And so am I. We made you miss your ride and everything. That's okay, Junior will drop us home. Won't you, baby?"

"Junior will what?" A tinge of something deliciously tropical licked his words. His accent was different from Richard's, stronger and richer. He rose lazily from the bed, not bothering to hide the bulge in the front of his pants. Cinnamon was intrigued.

Ignoring her altogether, he moved up behind Anita, bent over putting on her shoes. He began nuzzling the back of her neck.

"Junior will do no such thing," he murmured. "Junior will not leave this room and neither will you."

If his boldness embarrassed Anita, Cinnamon admired it. She liked a man who went for what he wanted. Even if what he wanted wasn't her.

"Come on, Junior." Anita pulled away. "Pat is standing right there. And we've got to go home."

"We?"

"Pat does, and so do I. Come on, baby. You'll drop us?"

"Sure," Junior said unwillingly. "Whatever you say."

"Okay, let me find my purse. Now, where did I leave that thing?" Anita fluffed her hair again, rushing from the room and slamming the door behind her.

Cinnamon stood right where she was and regarded the brown giant before her. Fine was not the word for him. He was like brown confectioner's sugar, super fine. Medium tall, very dark, with eyes a lighter shade of brown than his skin. Lazy, dangerous eyes. The kind of eyes that hypnotized women, as Cinnamon was now.

"Thanks, darlin'." He inclined his head toward her.

"Thanks for what?"

He reached up to turn off a light shining just above the bed. Cinnamon felt her body quiver as it strained toward the magnetic pull of him.

"Thanks for your exquisite sense of timing. I'll think of you when I take my cold shower tonight."

He took a step toward her. All he needed to do was make the right move and Cinnamon knew she'd see to it he had no need for cold water. Anita and Richard be damned. But when he reached, it was not for her, but around her. He opened the door and gently shoved her toward it.

"Come on, you. Hit the road."

For once Cinnamon was speechless. Could not come up with a snappy comeback. Could only watch the man with the lazy smile and dangerous eyes. Could not even turn away from him, but stared transfixed as she backed out of the bed-room doorway.

"So you and Richard were up front talking," he teased as they moved out into the hallway. "That's all you were doing?"

"Just talking," Cinnamon lied smoothly. "That's all."

"Ah?" He reached down and chucked her under the chin. "You'll have to show me that trick sometime."

"What trick?" Cinnamon slowed as they neared the living room. They could hear voices, Anita's and Richard's.

"How you manage to speak with that part of your anatomy."

Cinnamon tossed her fine brown head. Her tousled ponytail bounced.

"That can be arranged," she murmured.

Junior's laugh matched his stride. Long, loose, and lazy.

"Junior?" Anita's anxious voice called out. "Are you coming?"

"No," he called back, striding forward. "But I wish I were."

Cinnamon watched him move toward the call of Anita's voice. The swing of his legs and arms, the narrowness of his buttocks, the tilt of his torso. His head turned back, but his body kept moving.

"Come along, m'dear. Party's over."

Cinnamon followed, helpless as a child in the wake of the Pied Piper.

OFFICE PARTY

"Help me, Pat. I can't decide."

"Girl, will you call me by my right name for once?"

"I'm sorry . . . Cinnamon. What should I get?"

A fellow secretary at the advertising agency had worked up to the zero hour, and was ready to drop the baby any day now. The surprise party had been planned by Anita, a *happy hour shower.*

The conference room tabletop was spread with champagne, canapes, pastries. Anita agonized over the desserts. Petits fours, gooey with gobs of butter cream. Puffy eclairs oozing custard. A cake shaped like a bassinet with a brown plastic baby inside. Anita's full figure ran toward pudgy. She was always dieting. But always begging for somebody's permission to break the diet.

"Go ahead and have it all," Cinnamon suggested. She wasn't interested in any of it. Too sweet and bland for her tastes. She preferred flavors more stimu-lating to the palate.

"I don't know," Anita fretted, teetering on indecision. "What do you think all that's going to be? At least a thousand calories. It'll just blow my diet. And this butt doesn't need to get any bigger."

"Well, then. Don't have any of it."

"Yeah?" Anita was still undecided. "Of course, Junior doesn't want me to lose a pound. You know what he says, girl?"

Anita ineptly mimicked his West Indian accent.

"I like de bum-bum big and round."

Cinnamon sighed with impatience and something else. She found the squeals of female laughter in the room suddenly irritating.

"Girl, you don't know what the hell you want. If you want the damn desserts, then have the damn desserts. Later for the consequences. And hurry up while you're at it. I don't want to hang around this hen party all night long."

THE PICNIC

"Horseback riding," Cinnamon snorted, stalking steps ahead of Junior and Richard. Anita rushed to keep up with her, skirting puddles of mud and piles of manure as they made their way toward the stables. "I thought this was supposed to be a picnic. Where'd you get it in your head to go horseback riding?"

"I don't know," Anita answered listlessly. "Junior's been promising to teach me. I just thought it would be fun to do. Something different."

"Different," Cinnamon muttered. "Damn right it's different."

She lifted her small, Gucci-booted foot and stepped over another pile of dung.

"Junior's supposed to be quite a horseman, you know." Anita turned around and gazed lovingly at him, walking beside Richard in their wake. He pranced boyishly, pretending to ride a phantom mount.

Cinnamon watched Anita watching him. She had fully expected Junior to dump Anita after he had gotten what he wanted from her. It was more than a little amazing that Anita and Junior actually seemed to have a thing going on. What a man like him could see in a woman like Anita, she couldn't fathom. Not with someone like Cinnamon herself standing there.

"Junior's a horseman, huh?"

Cinnamon found herself staring at him, too. Couldn't help herself. Out in the woods he looked like a Marlboro man. Tall, dark and lean in a pair of hug-me-tight jeans. A healthy head of steam escaping his mouth as he laughed. Next to him Richard looked as pale and uninteresting as boiled potatoes.

"Where's Junior from, anyway?"

"Barbados!" Anita breathed. She might as well have said heaven. "He has such a sexy accent. What about Richard?"

"Damned if I know." Cinnamon had never bothered to ask. She looked at Anita appraisingly. "What's Junior like? Is he good in bed?"

Predictably, Anita blushed.

"Girl, the questions you ask."

"And I'm waiting for the answer."

"He's a great lover," Anita whispered, darting a glance back at him. "I can't get enough of him."

"I bet you can't." Cinnamon surveyed the man's hard thighs and flat belly, his lazy smile and eyes. She could just imagine.

"Richard seems to like you a lot. I'll bet he's a good lover, too."

Cinnamon shrugged carelessly. Richard was certainly crazy about her. She'd gone out with him several times, just for the hell of it. She'd slept with him several times, also for the hell of it. But as always, she left his bed feeling less than satisfied.

"He's alright. I'll never go with a horn-player again, though. He's got these hard, muscled lips. Feels like kissing on a piece of wood. And he's a bit of a freak in bed, too."

Cinnamon could tell Anita was itching for the details, but too afraid to come out and ask for them.

"All he wants to do is suck pussy and come in my hair. Alright for appetizers, but what about the main course?"

Anita's blush was blended with a superior, pitying little smile. Obviously she wasn't missing out on any meals with Junior. It really wasn't fair. If only she had met him first. By rights, Cinnamon should be the one with Junior. They both had the same kind of style, the same concentration of spice. While color-less Anita and colorless Richard seemed so much better suited. Like white milk and oatmeal.

As the men moved into the stables to select their mounts, Cinnamon sighed over the injustice of it.

"Sometimes you got to tell a man what you like," Anita whispered confiden-tially. "Have you tried that with Richard?"

"Not really. But it ain't no big thing. I can take him or leave him."

Anita regarded her with worried admiration.

"You never do get that off into men. Me, I fall in love at the drop of a hat. How do you stay so cool, so uninvolved?"

Cinnamon shrugged.

"Life ain't nothing but a party, baby. And men ain't nothing but buses. You miss one, another's going to come along."

Richard emerged from the stable, gingerly holding the reins of a large dappled mare.

"Who wants this beauty? The man says she's the most patient, plodding thing they have. Never goes faster than a trot."

"Let Anita have her," Cinnamon retorted. "I want to pick out my own horse."

Cinnamon marched into the stables and encountered Junior. He looked natural there, like a Caribbean cowboy. Handling a stallion that looked a little like him. Lean, hard, and brown with just a hint of laziness about the eyes.

"Hey, there," Cinnamon called out softly, hoisting herself up against the stall's half door. "You look right at home."

Junior pushed the half door open so that she swung with it. He led the snorting brown beast from the stall.

"Do I?" he responded lazily. "I suppose I must. Used to do this sort of thing, you know. Worked horses at the racetrack home in Barbados."

"From stable boy to music man," Cinnamon murmured. "Rags to riches."

He cut his eyes sharply at her, as if to search out mockery. Apparently he found none, for he smiled and swatted her behind playfully. If his smile were sun, Cinnamon would have basked in it. Her rear end tingled pleasantly from the touch of his hand. She found herself singing naughtily.

*Though your girlfriend's
a friend of mine
here's my number and a dime,
Call me any time . . .*

Junior never stopped smiling. The lazy rays never dimmed, even when he shook his head and clicked his teeth scoldingly.

"I thought you and Anita were best friends."

Cinnamon walked over to where Junior stood, saddling his mount. She stroked the animal's firm flank.

"Were friends? Still are, as far as I know. Why?"

"Just asking, m'dear. Wouldn't want to come between friends." He led his horse toward the door, looking back over his shoulder. "Ask the boy to get you a horse. A nice, gentle one."

"I already know which one I want."

Cinnamon suddenly felt peevish and stubborn. She pointed to a small chestnut filly, tossing her head and prancing restlessly in her stall.

Junior shook his head.

"That one's a bit too frisky."

"I want that one," she insisted. "Get it out for me."

She could already see herself atop the prancing beast, her wavy Creole hair and the horse's chestnut mane whipping in the wind. She'd be looking good. And Junior would be sorry. He'd see just what he was missing.

"That one," she repeated.

Junior shrugged. He called the stable hand and had him saddle up the filly.

"You're riding Storm, huh?" the boy inquired. "Be firm with her. She's got a lot of spirit."

Cinnamon nodded absently. Storm. She even liked the name. It reminded her of herself. Sexy. A little wild, maybe even a little dangerous.

But she and Storm, for all their apparent likenesses, did not get along. Storm was wild and dangerous alright. Instead of trotting sedately beside the other horses, she broke into a canter and charged ahead. Cinnamon's backside slapped furiously against the leather saddle.

"Slow down, mutha fucka. Slow down!" she shouted. Her velvet beret blew from her head and was whipped away by the wind. She could hear the others behind her, shouting with laughter.

"Rein her in," Junior's voice rose above the others. "Rein her in easy."

Cinnamon tugged at the leather reins. Storm reared, causing her to slide sideways in the saddle.

"Quit it!" Cinnamon screamed in panic. "Cut it out, you ignorant beast. You hear me talking to you? Quit it!"

Junior galloped up beside her. From the corner of her eye she could see him sitting loose and easy in the saddle.

"I told you she was a frisky one."

"Shut the fuck up." Cinnamon's breathing came in gasps. "And get this horse to act right."

Junior edged his horse closer and reached for Storm's bridle. The animal let out a whinny and veered off the bridle path, heading straight for a river that ran parallel to it.

Too shaken for words, Cinnamon watched the blue ribbon of river jolt closer and closer. Felt the ground pound beneath her, the bite of the saddle. Storm waded right into the water. She stopped partially across.

The water lapped around Cinnamon's feet. She had let go of the reins and was holding on to the horse's mane. When Storm leaned forward to take a drink of river, Cinnamon pitched forward too, almost tumbling in. She screamed until she was hoarse.

"Grab the reins, girl. *The reins.*" She could hear Junior shouting behind her but she was too frightened to turn toward the sound of his voice. As Cinnamon clung to her mane for dear life, Storm raised her head a bit and shook it vigorously. River water and horse slobber flew into Cinnamon's face. She slid down further around Storm's slippery neck.

"Help! Somebody get me out of here."

"Just stay there, Pat," she could hear Anita calling from a distance. "Richard's gone to get the stable hand."

"A crazy horse!" Cinnamon hissed some long minutes later, back in the stable's musty darkness. She pulled off her river-sodden Guccis. "A crazy son of a bitch. Fucked up my two-hundred-dollar boots and tried to kill me, too. Damn diabolical beast need to be shot."

The group of them huddled about her broke out in laughter. Even Storm, being toweled off back in her stall, seemed to snort in derision. Cinnamon failed to see the humor in the situation. Quaking with rage, she stomped out to the car in her stockinged feet.

"A bunch of horseback-riding mutha fuckas!"

PRIVATE PARTY

Cry me a river,
cry me a river.
I cried a river over you.

She was awakened by the radio alarm set on the oldies station. It seemed the very sky was crying rivers that morning. The sun hiding behind thick clouds. Rain pelting the window. Cinnamon awakened stiff and saddlesore. Her throat rough and hoarse. She decided to call in sick.

While waiting in the kitchen for her morning pot of coffee to brew, she noticed that the spice rack needed dusting. While dusting it, she impulsively selected a jar of ground cinnamon, opened it up, and inhaled the scent. It wasn't satisfying. She sniffed the allspice, the ground cloves. Then the garlic, basil, coriander, sage. None of the spices smelled right. They were losing their potency. And Cinnamon was a woman who needed her food heavily spiced. She scooped up the whole lot and dumped it in the trash.

A feeling of numbness settled over her as she sat at the kitchen table, sipping her coffee. She carried her cup back into the bathroom and ran a bath as hot as she could stand, dumping in half a box of perfumed salts. And then, almost as an afterthought, she brought the telephone in from the bedroom. She made the toll call after settling into the steaming suds.

"Yay-low," he answered, like he always answered. "Clyde's cuts will do you proud. Who's on the line?"

"It's me, Pop."

"Pat, baby." If she could see him, she knew his brown face would be shiny with smiles. "Now what's wrong, little old girl?"

"Nothing's wrong, Pop."

"You can't fool me, angel. Don't forget I'm your father. I can hear it in your voice. Now what's that big bad city doing to my baby girl?"

"Chicago's treating me fine. Pop, I just wanted to ask you something."

"Go ahead and ask."

Cinnamon sat still and thoughtful in the hot water. Feeling five years old again and wanting her father to make everything alright. Trying to figure out just what she needed from him, but she wasn't quite sure.

"There's something I want so bad, Pop."

"What is it, baby? It's yours."

Cinnamon slowly shook her head, even though Pop couldn't see her.

"No, it's not something you can give me."

There was a pause at the other end of the line. Finally Pop spoke.

"Well, is it something you can get for yourself?"

Cinnamon paused, considering.

"I think so. If I really went after it."

"Then what's stopping you, baby?"

Cinnamon took another sip of coffee. Its familiar flavor seemed stunted today, dull.

"Because it would hurt somebody. Somebody I've known a long time."

"It's a man, ain't it? Old no-count, lying, tail-chasing man. Baby girl, half these men out there don't mean you a bit of good."

"They're not all that bad."

"Yes they is, too," Pop insisted. "I'm a man myself, that's how I know. Shoot, I hear these mens in here bragging every day about how many women's lives they done messed up. That used to be sport when I was a young man. Get a girl to give it up, then try to get next to her best friend."

"No, Pop," Cinnamon tried to explain. "It's not exactly like that."

"You tell that man you don't want no parts of him. Tell him to go jump in the lake and swallow a snake. Don't let nobody come between you and your friend, baby. You be done lost a friend and ain't neither one of you going to end up with the man."

"You're right, Pop. As usual, you're right. I'm glad I called you."

Cinnamon could hear a gentle metallic swish. She knew Pop must be clipping a customer's head, the telephone tucked between his shoulder and jaw. She could hear voices rumbling in the background, and could almost see the collection of old brown men. Lounging in chairs. Telling tall lies and short tales. Smoking cigars and chewing tobacco. She could almost smell the Murray's Hair Pomade and shaving cream and the gruff scent of manliness that permeated the air of Clyde's Barbershop.

"Why don't you come on down for the weekend, baby? We'll burn up a mess of barbecue. What you say about that?"

"It sounds great, Pop. I'm going to try to make it. I really am."

She heard the doorbell ringing and hurried off the line. She wrapped herself in a towel and went to answer it. Junior stood there smiling lazily, a beribboned cushion in his outstretched hand.

"I thought you'd be needing this today, darlin. Something soft to cushion the bum."

Cinnamon stood a long moment in the doorway before stepping aside to let him in. Her father's advice echoed in her ears.

"What you doing here?"

"I heard you weren't feeling well. I thought I'd come check you."

"Well, you're going to have to leave. I'm taking me a bath."

"Don't let me stop you."

"Alright," Cinnamon called over her shoulder. "You can let yourself out."

She opened the hot water tap, added more bubble, and stepped in. It's never the same coming back to something old. Old towns, old boots, old baths. You can never recapture the same comfort, the original sense of warmth. Cinnamon tried. She slid farther down, letting the sudsy water come up to her ears. It just wasn't the same.

"What you doing, girl? You want drown, or what?"

Cinnamon opened her eyes to see Junior's brown length bent over the tub. He switched off the tap.

"What the hell are you doing in here? I thought you were gone."

"Now, why you want to talk to me like that," he cajoled, "after I make you such a nice drink?"

Cinnamon sat up partially, careful to shield her nakedness with suds and water.

"What kind of drink? Liable to be some poison."

"No, mahn. I don't make it a practice to poison beautiful young women. Just taste it."

She reached out a soapy hand, took it, and tentatively tasted. The flavor was unexpectedly sharp. The fumes seemed to go right up into her head. It was warm. She thought she tasted rum, ginger, lemon, and something else she couldn't define.

"What's in here?"

"A magic elixir of love." He gave a devilish grin. "Man I meet tending bar at Sandy Lane give me the recipe, make me promise never to tell the secret. He use the thing on tourist women, make them all his love slaves. The man had more white women than he knew what to do with."

"A likely story." Cinnamon snorted, sipping the dark, warm liquid. "And when were you a bartender? I thought you used to be a stable boy."

"Just a poor man trying to earn his daily bread. Shovel horse shit, make mixed drinks. It's all the same."

Cinnamon finished the drink and placed the empty glass beside the half-full cup of coffee still sitting on the rim of the tub. She slid back down into the water.

"How did you wind up here, playing steel drums in Chicago?"

"Ah, now you get interested. And what if I don't tell you?"

Cinnamon reached out a slender foot to turn back on the hot-water tap.

"Won't make a bit of difference."

"Alright then," Junior agreed. "If you promise to sit back up, I tell you."

"Sit up?" Cinnamon narrowed her eyes at him. "Why?"

"Because it such a pleasing sight, mahn."

"Go to hell." Cinnamon slid down as far as she could. "Ain't no free shows in here."

"Something tell me the lady angry at me. What I do to make she vex so?"

"Like you don't know," Cinnamon grumbled. "You and Anita and Richard, you can all go to hell in a handbasket. Some cold, cold-hearted bastards. That crazy horse almost sent me to the bottom of the Fox River, and you couldn't think of nothing to do but laugh. I'll never forgive you."

Junior reached over to turn off the tap again.

"I wasn't laughing," he said softly.

"You're a lie."

"I swear I wasn't laughing at you. I was worried to death. Thought those tears would never stop, that river would overflow with your crying. You hadn't struck me as the sort of woman who made tears a habit."

"Well, I'm not. I can't remember the last time I cried. Not even at my best friend's funeral. Yes, I can. Fifteen years ago. I was sixteen years old and my father had burned up an Afro wig I bought."

"Your daddy did right," he observed, arms folded across his chest. "Your hair too nice to cover in some knotty wig."

"Nigger men and hair," Cinnamon hissed. "You all love straight hair better than a dog loves a bone. You probably just like that old bartending buddy of yours. I bet you like your women white as possible. That's what you love so much about Anita. Light, bright, and damn near white. Yeah, buddy. I got your number."

A heavy silence settled in the room, punctuated by the periodic drip of water into water. Cinnamon wondered if she'd gone too far, said too much in her anger. She stole a glance at Junior's thoughtful face.

"You calling me colorstuck?" he asked. "That seems a strange complaint coming from you. Anita couldn't care less about being a clear-skinned woman. You, on the other hand, seem to cherish that bit of white blood running through your veins."

The truth hit home like an arrow; it burned like boiling water. And Cinnamon reacted in rage. She tossed her coffee cup at him, but he had quick reflexes. He caught the cup, bottoms up. The lukewarm liquid dashed back into her face instead.

Before she knew it she was crying again. She, a woman who hadn't wept in fifteen years. As if the faucet, once rusted shut, had been loosened. The hot-water tap of tears overflowed.

Before she knew it she was being lifted by strong arms, lifted out of hot water and carried to the soft safety of her bed beneath the pussy cat poster. Cradled against a warm chest, like her father's would be when she'd come home bloody from fights or muddy from falls. When she'd seen death in her dreams and summoned him to chase it away.

"Was the coffee hot, m'dear?" A reassuring voice murmured into her hair. "Come, let me see."

And though she trembled, struggling to hide her tearstained face against his shoulder, she was overpowered by the tenderness she knew was stronger than her pain. He stroked her face gently, gently. Tucking blankets around her shivering body.

"I think it's alright. I never forgive myself if I mark that lovely face."

She collapsed against his chest again. The hiccupy tears began to subside. The river of tears dried in the warmth of his arms. She was feeling sleepy, feeling like Pop's little girl again. Newly bathed and ready for bed, tears kissed and hugged away. He continued to hold her, to rock her, to reassure her.

"No, Cinnamon. You're wrong. I never did like it white. That's your man Richard. You must know I'm a coffee man, that's why you toss me the cup, eh? I'm my old man's grandson, you know. I like my coffee all kinds of ways. Straight black. Café au lait. And I like it like this. Medium brown with a taste of cinnamon in it."

He kissed her. But it was not a kiss like her father's. It was a demanding kiss. A kiss that sucked away at the sweet warm sleepiness that enveloped her. And for once Cinnamon didn't yearn for a man's carnal touch to arm her against the approach of cold shadows. She simply wanted to be held the way her father would when he chased away death from her dreams.

She saw Junior's face moving toward her again, his eyes closed in anticipation of the next kiss. She veered away from his lips, scrambling out of bed.

"Junior, you're going to have to go. This ain't right."

Junior watched her struggle into her bathrobe. He frowned as he watched.

"What's the problem, now? You been begging me for it."

"I changed my mind. I don't think I want to sleep with you."

His frown creased into anger. He stood up and walked to her, took her by the shoulders.

"Girl, this a dangerous game you're playing. If I wanted to I could take it right now."

"Not if you don't want Anita to find out."

Cinnamon pulled away from him, escaping into the kitchen. She shakily poured another cup of coffee. He followed her there, watching her from the doorway.

"You would hurt her that way? Your best friend?"

Cinnamon looked into the well of stillness at the center of his brown eyes. And did not flinch.

"You would hurt her that way? Your lady?"

The only answer she heard was the sound of his footsteps walking away. And then the slamming of the front door.

She would break her promise to Pop. She would not come home to Phoenix that weekend. Nor the next one, nor the next. And by the time she did make it home she considered herself punished for having heeded the father wit in Pop's last words. His admonition that she deny herself spice for the sake of love.

BELLE OF THE BALL

Yes, she supposed she did love Anita. But it was a reserved kind of love. Rather like the love Anita's own mother professed when she wished her different. Cinnamon remembered Mrs. Cantrell, round and yellow as a butterball. A churchy, Southern kind of woman. And always pregnant.

"Yes, Lordy." Mrs. Cantrell would have some wriggling golden child pinned between fat thighs while she braided hair or wiped noses. "I sho' hope this next one be a nice brown-skinned baby, just the color of Patty there. We got too many yellow folks in our family."

And Anita, the oldest and lightest disappointment, stirring at the stove or taking cornbread from the oven, would blush in shame. Suffusing her pale cheeks with the color that her mother wished had been her birthright. Before Cinnamon met Anita she never knew that a person could be considered too light.

Anita had a thing about names. Cinnamon would always be Pat to her, no matter how hard she tried to remember. Back in the days when Blondine was her ace and Anita hung on the periphery of the friendship, Anita couldn't say Blondine to save her life. Or wouldn't. She always called her Goldie.

"Hey, Goldie!" Anita would come running up when Immaculate Heart of Mary disgorged them at the end of the school day. "Where you and Pat fixing to go?"

"Somewhere you ain't gonna be," Blondine would roar. "Until you learn how to say my name right!"

Anita had moved up in the hierarchy of friendship only after Blondine died. But still, Cinnamon loved her with the love reserved for second choice. Loved her and was disappointed that her soft lines could never be molded into the sharp silhouette Blondine had left as a template. That her brass shine could never equal Goldie's 24-karat luster.

Blondine had been more than a best friend. She was an original. A bold, brazen, fearless soul who didn't just live; she burned her way through the world. The fact that her candle blazed at both ends illuminated her short life all the brighter. Cinnamon had never had her daring. But she had studied her wit, her extravagant sense of style, her appetite for the spice of life, and made these things her own.

And now she wasn't sure where she left off and Blondine began. In the years since her death, Cinnamon sometimes felt she had become her. Had stepped into the aura left behind by a girl dead at eighteen. She felt it only natural that Anita regard her with the same sense of awe she once held for Blondine.

Blondine was never the sentimental sort. Her honesty and self-absorption sometimes caused her to be carelessly cruel. What would have happened had

Blondine been in her place? Would Blondine have had the man she fancied, dismissed him when she grew tired of him, and somehow managed to emerge with the friendship intact?

But just this once her father's wisdom had spoken louder than Blondine's ghost. And now that Junior was gone and Cinnamon had lost her chance to love him, she found herself wondering about the quality of their friendship. What would have happened if she had given in to the man, and Anita had found out? Would the friend tell her *Girl, you crazy* and forgive her her trespasses? Or would she never speak to her again?

She had taken Anita's friendship for granted these past twenty years. She thought of her more as a sidekick, a foil for her adventures. A Tonto to her Lone Ranger. And now she began to wonder just how her life would be without the faith of this neglected friend who persisted in calling her by her birth name.

Anita came home from work with a get-well card signed by all the other secretaries in the office. And Cinnamon, a woman who could always *maintain her cool*, suddenly felt hot. Emotions thundered in her chest like runaway horses; love, guilt, jealousy, regret. Attempting to re-create a sense of closeness she once had with Blondine, she found herself confessing. Her deepest, saddest secret.

"Do you ever feel lonely, Anita? I feel lonely all the time."

Anita patted her shoulder ineffectually.

"You just need some company, that's all. Why don't you have Richard come over?"

"That's the loneliest feeling of all," Cinnamon confided. "When I'm with a man. Out of all the men I've been with I still haven't found the one who could make me climb the walls. Every new man I have, I always think *Maybe this will be the time*. And it never is."

Anita was used to Cinnamon sharp and feisty. This vulnerable side seemed to make her uneasy.

"Do you mean to tell me," she asked tentatively, "that you've never had a man to make you come?"

"Never. One minute I'm all hot and bothered, my stuff clenching like a fist. Next minute I'm watching the man make love to a mannequin, not feeling a goddamn thing. Remember Michael, my first passion? He'd spend hours working on me, like I was a medical experiment in one of his textbooks. Touching this, touching that. *For every action there must be an equal and opposite reaction.* But I guess I defied the laws of physics. And he finally gave up on me."

"He quit you? For that?"

"You know that men's egos are tied up in their dicks." The Blondine voice erupted in her, cool and uncaring. "If they can't send you over the edge, then they start worrying about themselves. After a while I just stopped telling them about me. I let them think they're making the earth move."

Anita shook her head, perplexed.

"But if you don't really like it, why do you do it so much?"

"I do like it. I like making love for the comfort of it. I like being held by a man, being so close you can hear his heart beat. I like being worshiped by him, like I was some dainty, precious thing. I like the power of it, too. To feel some strong man trembling like a leaf. To know that I made it happen. And I always keep thinking maybe. Maybe this time."

Anita sat there blushing to beat the band.

"You just haven't found the right man yet."

"Damn right." Cinnamon shrugged. "That's why I aim to try out as many as I can, before I get too old and ugly to attract them."

"Did you ever think," Anita ventured hesitantly, "that all the fooling around might be keeping that Mr. Right from coming your way?"

"To hell with that. I can have any man I want to, any man out there."

"Any man?"

"Well," Cinnamon found herself admitting. "At least for a night. And one of these nights it'll be somebody worth working up a sweat over."

To which Anita shook her head like an old church mother.

"I ought to lend you Junior. He says lovemaking's not just an act, it's an art. That man could move a mountain to kingdom come."

That is when Cinnamon thought she'd discovered the ultimate test of love, of friendship. That a woman could consider offering a friend in need a man she loved. It convinced her that Pop was right. That giving up a man for a friend was the right thing to do. But that was then.

In the now, Junior, apparently trying to cover himself against blame, had blown the whistle. Exactly what he told Anita, Cinnamon wasn't sure. But it was something that had sharpened the round contours of Anita's face. Had suffused her pale cheeks with anger. Had made her move out in the middle of the night, spitting out epithets like *two-faced, back-stabbing whore*. And had left her solo to make the long train ride south from Chicago. Alone on to Phoenix for the occasion of her father's funeral.

Pop had always called her *Sweet P.* Once she thought that was her name. And she had called him *Popeye*. He could defeat any enemy, protect her from any harm. He was invincible. Would walk around the house lifting heavy objects to convince Sweet P. to eat her greens.

"See here, Sweet P. I'm the strongest man in the world. I done ate my spinach."

But by adolescence she had stopped calling him Popeye and started calling him *Pop*. And thought of him more as Wimpy. Mild, harmless, hungry Wimpy. By then she realized that Pop was not the strongest man in the world. That he lived under the will of Lola's golden thumb. Lola, her mother. The cold gold Creole. Sole proprietress of Lola's Place. And of Pop's heart.

Maybe it was deliberate. She missed her train and had to wait an hour for the next. Cinnamon reached Phoenix long past the time for visitation, long after the service had ended. The taxi dropped her off in front of the stone-faced storefront in which she had grown up. A building with three small shops squeezed together on the first floor, a spacious apartment on the second.

The living quarters above were dark, as was the window of the barbershop. She walked to the curtained plate glass of the funeral home. She was shocked to find the name *Brown's Mortuary* obliterated. When the only funeral director in town dies, who buries him?

She tried the door. Locked. The only light shining was in the space Clyde

Brown had long ago carved out for his queen. The place between funeral parlor and barbershop. A delicately etched spider's web stretched like lace, linking the words *Lola's* and *Place*.

Lola bustled around the lounge, arranging trays and platters of food. She wore a fitted black dress, a hat with a dotted Swiss veil, and house shoes. She sang along softly with an old Dinah Washington tune playing on the jukebox about how much a day could make a difference.

Lola looked different this day. Hardly the picture of a grieving widow. She wore her wavy reddish-brown hair in a short, sporty style. Her gilt face was heavily made up.

"Lola, you cut your hair," were the first words out of Cinnamon's mouth. "I never thought I'd live to see the day."

"Hey, Pat. About time you showed up. Take your coat off and come help me get this food together."

"Where's everybody at?" Cinnamon hung her coat.

"They should be coming back from the graveyard soon. I don't blame you for skipping the whole business. All that crying and carrying on. People trying to jump in when they lower the casket. I don't need that. I decided to come back here and get ready for the wake."

Cinnamon, mixing fruit punch at the wet sink, expressed surprise that the repast was being held in Lola's lounge rather than the apartment upstairs. Lola shook her head, bouncing her new curls and jangling her gold earrings.

"No, buddy. Not up there. I'm not going to have those Negroes tracking graveyard mud all over my carpet. I got an offer on the building yesterday, and I got to keep it looking good if I'm going to close."

"You're selling already? Pop's not even cold in the ground, Lola."

"You better watch your mouth, Pat. I'm still your mother. I brought you into this world and I'll take you out. Besides, how many times have you been down to see your father this past year since he's been sick? You ain't seemed to care much about him when he was warm. Why you all of a sudden so worried about him now that he's cold?"

"I *loved* my father," Cinnamon declared, righteously indignant. "He was much more of a mother to me than you ever were. I was just an inconvenience to you. And Pop was just someone to pay your bills and do your bidding. In fact, you're the reason I haven't been coming home like I should. You see? We can't be together more than five minutes without fighting."

Lola stood glaring at her daughter, her breath coming heated and heavy. Then she shook her curls and raised her right hand, as if to wave away the residue of her daughter's words. The spider tattooed into her palm seemed to be dancing.

"Pat, that really hurts me. You know I loved your father. Why else do you think I stayed in this dead-ass town so long? Shit, before I met Clyde I was a get-up gal, just like that old roadrunner they used to sing about. *Can't stay in one place too long.* If somebody had told me I would live in Phoenix, Illinois, for near on forty years, I would have said they're a liar and the truth ain't in them."

Mother and daughter worked in uneasy silence for a time. Lola was packing for the move, clearing away piles of papers and mementos that had collected for years in dusty boxes behind the bar. Monuments that marked her reign as queen of Lola's Place. She pulled out a large framed photograph and handed it to Cinnamon.

"Here, girl. You might as well take that home with you. That's you when you were about four years old."

Cinnamon examined it. A pensive-looking view of her earlier self. A chubby-cheeked, curly-haired child perched atop the bar. A young fifties-styled Lola stood behind her, smiling.

"Boy, was I a fat kid," Cinnamon noted. "Glad I lost some of that weight. And what were you looking so happy for?"

"Oh, I was so proud of you that day," Lola remembered. "It was Easter Sunday and we were having an afternoon set down here. Your Aunt Callie Mae dressed you up so pretty and fixed you those Shirley Temple curls. You must have collected at least fifty dollars from folks in here saying how cute you were."

Lola squinted, glancing from Cinnamon to the portrait.

"You really ought to cut about three inches off that hair and wear it curly again. Your face is so small, you need something soft around it."

Cinnamon was flabbergasted.

"You? Telling me to cut my hair? I did it when I was sixteen and you and Pop almost had a fit. I'll never forget you telling me that long hair was all I had. I still can't believe you cut yours."

"Honey, times change and so do I." Lola shrugged. "I been wanting to clip this mess for the longest, but Clyde wouldn't hear of it. I'm closer to sixty than I am to sixteen. When you young all that hair hanging down your back looks sexy. When you old, it looks witchy. It may sound cold-blooded to you, but the day Clyde passed I got shed of this hair. Left straight out of the hospital and went to the beauty salon. Told them to give me the same cut Lena Horne has, the exact same one."

Cinnamon gave her mother a critical stare.

"It suits you. In fact, you look a little like Lena herself with your hair that way. Very youthful looking."

Lola regarded her reflection in the smoked-glass mirror above the bar.

"I guess I have the black blood in me to thank for that. *Good black don't crack*, ain't that what they say?"

Wonders would never cease. To hear Lola refer to herself as Black was something Cinnamon never thought she'd live to witness.

"I guess my nigger side is coming out strong in my old age," Lola explained. "Some folks, the older they get, the darker they get. Lena used to be a shade lighter than I am. Now she's about your color."

"So now you're Black," Cinnamon teased. "What happened to Creole? That's what you always swore that you were. *I ain't colored, baby. I'm Creole.*"

Lola shrugged.

"Those were the times we lived in. To be a mixed white half-breed, that was nothing special. But to be a Negro Indian, a Gypsy, a Creole. Now, that was interesting. Exotic. People looked at you with a little bit more respect. I had a history that wasn't doing diddly for me, a bastard mulatto from Cairo named Lula Mae. So

I created my own name, my own history. Ain't nothing wrong with that, Miss Cinnamon Brown. But as you get older, child, you might find yourself slipping back into the person you used to be. Just like straightened hair going back to nappy, if you catch my drift."

Lola winked at her almost companionably. Cinnamon decided to ask a question that had been plaguing her all her life.

"Lola, why you never wanted me to call you *Mama?* I never understood that."

Lola regarded her reflection again. As if the answer was in the mirror.

"I know you think I haven't loved you enough. True, I never been a hugging, kissing kind of mother. It just ain't in me. But I love you, in my way."

She turned from reflection in the mirror to daughter at the bar.

"But, Pat, I never wanted to be nobody's mama. Never did. Some women just ain't made to mother, and I always knew I was one of them. I told Clyde that when I met him. Told the man I would give him a love affair that would keep him happy till the end of his days. But I wasn't about to give him no babies. And he said okay. Said I would always be his Baby. In fact, before you were born he used to call me that."

Lola's forehead creased in sudden memory.

"But after a few years he started in on me. Talking about how pretty a baby I would make. How bad he wanted to be a father. But still I wasn't about to change my mind. So he changed it for me."

"Pop changed your mind?" Cinnamon interjected. "That's hard to believe."

Lola clicked her tongue and glared.

"As much as you've been screwing, I know you would have you a houseful of babies if you wasn't on that pill. See, we didn't have that back then. We had rubbers. Had to rely on Clyde to use them. And the man went and doctored the things. Probably sat up and poked holes in them."

Cinnamon felt a whole new kind of love for her father well up in her. That he had wanted so badly for her to come into being, he would risk the wrath of the woman he worshiped. Tears brimmed in her eyes. She turned her face to hide them. Lola hated to see anybody crying.

"When I found out I was pregnant I almost hit the roof. I even thought about getting rid of it."

Lola looked at *it* sitting at the bar before her. Smiled and shook her head.

"But I didn't."

"Thank you, Jesus," Cinnamon murmured.

"And then you were born. I was scared to death. What the hell did I know about babies? Clyde was so proud you'd have thought he'd birthed you himself. That's when he slipped and told me what he did. *I knew you were going to change your mind when the baby came.* Girl, you talk about mad! I was furious. The man had gone and made me have a baby. Now you know that ain't right. What if your boyfriend went and *made* you have a baby?"

Cinnamon shook her head. The very idea was unthinkable.

"That same day I got out of that hospital bed and left. Went down to my granny's in Cairo and stayed there a month. Clyde caught up with me, brought you down wrapped in blankets. Begging me to come back home. *This baby needs a mama, Lola.* I told him I never bargained on being no mama, that he had forced this on me. It was his baby. So if he wanted you to have a mother, he was going to have to be it."

"That explains it." Cinnamon understood now. "You never really wanted me in the first place."

"No," Lola admitted. "And it wasn't love at first sight. But just like it was with Clyde, I learned to care for you over the years. I just wish I had had more mother love in me to give. But you can't give what you ain't got."

"Well, Pop had more than enough," Cinnamon assured her. "He made a pretty good mother. But he's gone now. It's just you and me. I think you're going to have to get used to me calling you *Mama.*"

Lola made a face and patted her brand new curls.

"I guess I could learn to tolerate that. Since I'm near about the age for some-body to be calling me *Grandmama.*"

"Don't hold your breath," Cinnamon warned her. "After all, I am my mother's daughter."

"And the fruit don't fall far from the tree, huh? Child, I don't hardly expect you to produce no grandkids on my account. If you have them, you damn sure gonna have to raise them."

She stuck out her hand for Cinnamon to slap five. They both fell across the bar, convulsed in laughter. And at that moment the door of the bar burst open.

Lola's Place began to fill with mourners fresh from grief. Dozens of aunts and uncles and cousins, most of them from the Brown side of the family. They rushed over to Lola and Cinnamon, pressing them against perfumed bosoms and rough-whiskered faces. Kissing their cheeks with lips chilled by winter. Telling them how like himself Clyde had looked. Testifying how good a man Clyde had been.

Lola was not well suited for the role of grieving widow. She was more used to being bar hostess, making sure her customers were well watered and comfortably settled. Her charming hospitality seemed to alarm the mourners with tears yet wet on their cheeks.

"Well, look what the cat drug in," Lola called out cheerily. "Callie Mae Clemmons! Cousin, I haven't seen you in a month of Sundays. Is that your girl we been hearing so much about? Honey, the child has gone and got good-looking on us. And who's this handsome gentleman by her side?"

The handsome gentleman hanging on the arm of her cousin Allie Mae Peeples turned out to be none other than Junior Winston. Startled, Cinnamon fell back into the shadows of the bar, watching him glide forward to take her mother's hand.

Allie Mae moved off to greet other family members, leaving Junior there with Lola. Cinnamon watched his extravagant flirtation with dismay. *She must have been a child bride, so young looking she was. How tragic it was that such a beautiful woman should be left alone in the arms of mourning.* And he kissed her hand! Lola lapped it up like a cat in the cream. Cinnamon was sure she heard purring.

She felt outrage mounting. Not so much at Junior, who was a victim of his own charm. Who didn't seem to know how to do anything with a woman but flirt.

SANDRA JACKSON-OPOKU • 309

But Lola! At her age, with her own husband fresh in the grave. Cinnamon found it nauseating.

Junior had once called attention to Cinnamon's poor sense of timing. Who knows how things might have turned out if this tentative new friendship between her and the widow she was learning to call *Mama* had had time to blossom. She remembered her father's last words to her.

Don't let nobody come between you and your friend, baby. You be done lost a friend and ain't neither one of you going to end up with the man.

Cinnamon backed away, ducked into the storeroom Lola had converted into a card parlor. She pried open a case of Crown Royal, opened a bottle, and drank from it straight. She sank down onto an old sofa and sulked.

The door cracked open, pouring in light and noise. Her long-gone second cousin stood, silhouetted in light from the open doorway.

"Pat Brown? I know you're in there."

"Close that door, Allie Mae. And don't call me Pat. I go by the name Cinnamon now."

"So don't you call me Allie. This is Alma you're looking at, new and improved."

Cinnamon laughed in spite of herself. She held out the open bottle in invitation.

"Ah. So this is where your mother hides the good stuff." Alma reached for the bottle with graceful, manicured hands. The gritty West Side accent Cinnamon remembered was completely gone. Words fell from her mouth as smooth as cultured pearls.

Cinnamon had heard about the cousin who had gone away. She had never expected Allie Mae to amount to much. Now look at her, sleek and sophisticated. Dressed to the nines in a slinky black dress, a rakish hat with a huge white feather curving under her chin. News of fascinating jobs and travel to exotic places were filtered back to her through Lola, who made no secret of her comparative disappointment.

"Callie Mae raised that girl all by herself. Dirt poor on the West Side of Chicago. You had all the advantages. Look how far she's gone, and look at you. Allie's going to be your madam and you're going to be her maid one day. You mark my words."

Alma collapsed on the sofa beside her, accepting the proffered bottle.

"I'm so sorry about your father. Clyde was my favorite uncle. If it hadn't been for that man, I probably wouldn't have even been born."

"Oh, yeah? Don't mean to tell me Pop made your mother get pregnant, too."

"Are you calling my uncle Clyde a lady's man? Smile when you say that, pardner." She turned her finger into an imaginary pistol and aimed it at her cousin. "Girl, where you been? I'm surprised you haven't heard the story, your father used to tell it so much. How he sent Cousin Callie Mae Bullocks down to Lola's one night, and that's where she met her future husband. My father."

Her voice suddenly broke, and Cinnamon examined her cousin's face in the dim light.

"Are you crying?"

Alma shook her head, contradicting the evidence running in rivulets down her cheeks.

"He was a good man, Cinnamon. He was gentle, and kind, and he cared about people. You don't know how lucky you were to have a father like Clyde."

By now she was convulsed in sobs, and Cinnamon hugged her absently. But she couldn't still the niggling, peevish suspicion she was being cheated out of her grief. She herself was the one who should be breaking down in tears, she was the one who should be comforted.

Her tears hiccuped out, Alma settled her head against Cinnamon's shoulder and sighed, fiddling with something shiny in her hands.

"Girl, where did you get that?" Cinnamon was shocked to see her father's favorite stickpin, the one shaped like a pair of open barber shears. It had been her Father's Day gift a few years back.

"He was wearing it in the casket. I managed to get it off before they closed the lid."

She straightened suddenly, dislodging Alma's head from her shoulder.

"Why, you little grave robber." Cinnamon didn't know whether to laugh or cry. Maybe Miss Sophisticated did have a chink in her armor; a kleptomaniac. Wait until she told Lola.

"Oh, this isn't for me," Alma protested. "I'm going to Africa within the month, God willing and the creek don't rise. Uncle Clyde used to always talk about how much he wanted to see the motherland. Don't you remember?"

"That's right." Until Alma mentioned it, she'd quite forgotten Pop's African fantasy. "*Ghana, my motherland, is free forever.* He saw Kwame Nkrumah come on TV in 1957 and never did forget it."

Alma dangled the stickpin between thumb and forefinger.

"Well, Cinnamon. When I go across those waters, Uncle Clyde is coming with me. The flesh may be weak, but I know his spirit is still willing. You ought to come, too."

"Africa? What I look like chasing behind some jungle bunnies?"

The laughter left Alma's smooth brown face and her eyebrow shot up. Lola was right, Cinnamon thought. Alma was dark, but she was pretty. Time had turned her from a skinny little ghetto girl to a graceful, willowy woman.

"You could learn a thing or two from some jungle bunnies."

"Really? Like what?"

She took a long swig of Crown Royal and settled back in contemplation.

"You know," she mused, seeming to speak more to herself than her cousin. "African people believe that the spirits of the dead ancestors live on after they're gone. That they're an invisible world, guiding us along our life journeys."

"Sounds like the same mumbo jumbo those BVM nuns used to brainwash us with."

"African juju sounding like Catholic doctrine?" Alma hooted. "That'll be the day."

"Well, it's true. They used to claim we each had a guardian angel watching over us. We were supposed to leave a space on our seats for them to sit next to us.

That shit used to give me the creeps, thinking some Peeping Tom with wings was there watching me get dressed, take a crap."

"Helping you across the street, keeping you out of trouble," Alma pointed out. "You know, sometimes I feel the spirit of Big Momma around me."

"Girl, that sounds like something out of those ghost stories Grandma Truly and Big Momma used to tell us. Tailey-po. Spider Man in Dead Folks Town. That's some spooky shit."

"Not really. It's comforting. You know you can trust Big Momma to do the right thing, even if she is a ghost."

"Well," Cinnamon thought about it, "to tell you the truth, I sometimes think somebody else is there. It's a feeling I get, like someone's trying to reach me, to tell me something. Maybe it's Blondine; you remember my best girlfriend in high school?"

"She's dead?"

"As a doornail. Shot to death. Damn, it's been almost twenty years. It seems like yesterday. Seems I can still hear her flute playing *Three Blind Mice*. That girl was a fearless soul. *Spice is the variety of life, and life ain't nothing but a party,* that was her motto. *And men ain't nothing but buses . . .*"

". . . *You miss one,*" Alma finished for her, "*another's going to come right behind him.* I've heard that one long enough, you'd think I'd learn my lesson by now. It takes a man to make a good woman do right, then turn around and do wrong."

"*Make you come home ear-lay,*" Cinnamon sang drunkenly. "*Make you stay out all night lo-o-ong.*"

Together they caterwauled the remaining verses of *Love and Happiness*, making up the forgotten parts as they went along.

"Move over, Al Green," Alma drawled as Cinnamon soloed, approaching the bar where, overwhelmed with emotion and lost for words, the singer *moans for love*. "Sit your narrow butts down, Supremes. We got the cousins, coming at you. Take it to the bridge, Cinnamon. And don't forget to give the drummer some."

Alma handed her an imaginary microphone, then commenced to beating a tattoo against the whiskey bottle with the purloined stickpin. Cinnamon threw back her head, wailing to the ceiling.

"*Eee-heee-eee!*" she began, then stopped suddenly. "Speaking of drummers, where'd you get that no-good Junior Winston? I almost had a heart attack, seeing that man coming up here in my father's wake."

"Oh, you know Junior?" Alma smiled. "This world is too small for coincidence. Seems like certain people are entangled somehow. Something invisible connects us. Everywhere I go I run into someone I know, or should have known. I had to travel all the way to Barbados to stumble upon the wife of the man I loved. And Junior? Well, he's her nephew. After we met over there he kept writing me, bugging me to sponsor his immigration to the U.S. I brought him over here two years ago. Put him in touch with this crazy horn player I met over in London."

"That's downright kinky. You sleeping with the man and his wife's nephew, too?"

"No, no, no," Alma held up a hand. "I don't go that way. Not with Junior. That's too close. My friend's nephew, my lover's in-law. I'd feel like I was sleeping with my own kin. It's bad enough I've been fooling with the same old married man nearly half my life."

Cinnamon felt the Blondine voice bubble up, bold and brash.

"Honey, if you want the man then have the man, married or no. You don't help yourself, somebody else will."

"It's not like that." Alma shook her head. "I've tried to leave him so many times I can't count them. Seems like we're connected to each other by rubber bands. No matter how many times I leave him, eventually he comes snapping back into my life. Now he wants me to be his third wife."

"Oh, so he's getting a divorce?"

"No such luck. He wants to have us all. Girl, I wish I'd never gotten myself mixed up with these tropical types. I should have found me a nice, chitlin'-eating brother from the West Side somewhere. Do you know that all the men in my life have been from another place? I don't even know what it's like to have a regular Black American boyfriend."

"Really? That would be like going through life without greens and cornbread. How come?"

"I don't know." Alma laid the bottle gently against her chest, like she was burping a baby. "Probably a flaw in my makeup. Like the brother who can't interest himself in anything but a white woman. I've always been attracted to Black men from other places. The Caribbean, Europe, Africa. Seems like I'm wearing a sign that says *All aliens, please apply here*. I've even had an Australian aborigine."

"Really? What kind of man was that?"

"Like all the others," Alma answered. "A Black man trying to get next to the America in me, while I'm busy trying to touch what's not America in him. Anyway, I've decided that the best way to have a man is not to need one."

"Girl, I cannot imagine living my life without a man in it," Cinnamon admitted. "I wouldn't know what to do with myself."

"A man ain't necessarily the answer, though. Remember what Big Momma used to say? *You got to be your own woman before you give yourself over to anybody, even God.* I think we wind up looking for something in these men that might not even be there."

"Yeah," Cinnamon sighed. "Is this going to be the one to make my loneliness go away?"

"Who won't wind up telling me *Naw, baby. It ain't me?*"

"Who'll finally satisfy me in bed?"

Alma's eyebrow arched like a blackbird's wing.

"Really, now? That's one thing they're generally good for. You mean to tell me Junior, the lover, hasn't shaken your tree? That must be a bitter pill for him to swallow."

"I haven't slept with Junior. I wanted him like crazy at first, then he wanted me. But I never let it happen."

"Why?" Alma wanted to know.

And this was the only thing Cinnamon could think to answer: "Because Pop told me not to."

Alma took the half-full bottle and set it on the floor.

"Look, girl. Uncle Clyde is gone, rest his sweet soul. Do you have to obey your daddy from beyond the grave?"

Cinnamon thought about it. She slowly shook her head.

"No, I guess not. Pop said forget the man and keep the friend. But the friend is gone and I still haven't had the man."

"Then enjoy Junior Winston if you want to. But don't love him. Men like that aren't made for loving. I'm a living witness, cuz."

Alma's dark eyes sparkled with sudden, drunken mischief. She raised a slender finger to her mouth.

"Imagine that! Cousin Cinnamon, you're what the romance novels call *an unawakened woman*. Wait right here. Don't leave."

Alma left the dark room and Cinnamon alone in it. The drone of voices and music in the main room and the undiluted liquor in her bloodstream lulled her into an uneasy sleep.

She dreamed of Pop. Pop pushing her in a swing he'd hung from the crab apple tree out back. He was pushing her high and hard. It was fun at first. But then the ground got too far away. She was sailing up into the sky, feet almost touching clouds. And she was afraid. She called out to him.

"Too high. Too high."

But he didn't hear. And she fell, as she knew she would. Plummeted down to earth like a broken-winged bird. Falling toward the yawning emptiness of an open grave. But she was caught by something other than death. Gathered up in arms that held her warm and safe. Pop's? How could they be?

"Cinnamon, m'love. Fancy meeting you here."

A voice intruded into her troubled dream. It wasn't Pop's voice. It belonged to a man from another place. Cinnamon's eyes fluttered open.

"Junior." She saw him kneeling over her, grasping one of her shoulders in each of his hands. "Junior, what are you doing here?"

"Someone said you needed me." He rearranged her limbs on the sofa, made a space for himself to lie beside her. "Is that so?"

"No." But she settled herself against his warmth. And when she felt him moving to leave her, blurted out: "Yes, I do. Do you know I've never had a climax?"

"Haven't you, now?" His hands roamed the contours of her body. "We must see what we can do about that."

Before he lowered his lips to meet hers, she thought she saw a spider descend, dangling on a line from the ceiling. But she fell instead into the web of his clear brown eyes. His shadow blocked out what light there was in the room, all but a faint halo about his head.

He cupped her chin in his hand, and teased her lips open. The taste of his mouth was, inexplicably, like raspberries. And she told herself, *This may be it, this time.*

His kisses were medicine to drive away cold shadows. An artist summoning colors from a blank canvas, he painted pictures on her pliant body, tracing designs up and down her back, across her buttocks. His hands roamed her breasts, gathering each aureole between the ball of his forefinger and thumb. And he never stopped kissing her.

He pulled open her blouse. She could hear the buttons hit the floor. He stopped kissing her then, and made his lips busy elsewhere. He lifted her bra with his teeth. He applied his tongue and her nipples strained like baby birds, stretching toward their source of nourishment. Beneath his ministrations her body began to stir. She told herself, *This is it.*

He lifted her skirt and lowered her panties. He stroked her like a harpist, tuning the tender cleft between her legs. His hands were pulling her from the dank dark of an open grave.

He came in for a closer look, and exclaimed over what he found. He kissed her gently, again and again. With the tip of his tongue, he teased a comma out of hiding and turned it into an exclamation point. He spoke the language of passion: nuzzling, and nibbling, and nudging.

Yes, this was it.

He had not even entered her when she felt herself beginning the freefall. With only his mouth and his hands, he had sent her floating like a skydiver miles above earth. Rolling downhill like an overripe berry that must burst before it reaches bottom.

But the berry remained unbroken, the parachute unopened. The storeroom door did instead. They felt the sudden breeze, the rush of sound. Junior instinctively shielded Cinnamon's body with his own. As one they turned to look. Lola, an outraged queen, stood watching from the doorway, her face red as blood.

"Pat." Her voice was hushed and harsh. "You doing this here? At your father's wake? What kind of woman are you? What kind of daughter?"

And the red queen rushed upon them. *Off with their heads,* thought Cinnamon drunkenly. Lola snatched up discarded pieces of clothing and hurled them at the fully clothed man, the completely naked woman, reclining on the sofa. She sent the bottle of Crown Royal crashing into the wall above their heads.

"Get out!" she screamed. "This is my place, not some whorehouse. My husband's wake, not some drunken sex party."

Cinnamon placed both feet on the floor, suddenly sober.

"I'm sorry . . . Mama. I didn't mean no disrespect."

"Don't you call me that! Don't ever call me that. You are a spoiled, selfish brat who don't think about nothing and nobody but yourself. Going after your own pleasure, even if it means somebody else's pain. Always got to be belle of the ball, even when it's your own father's wake. Get on out of my place with your nastiness. I don't have no daughter."

No, Cinnamon wanted to say. *It was not she, but Lola herself, who always insisted on being belle of the ball. Who made sure all attention was riveted to her. Who had to have the lion's share of Pop's love. Who had to be star of her very own solar system. Wasn't it?* Or was she more of her mother's daughter than she knew?

Cinnamon searched around for something to cover her shame. Though only his belt buckle had been opened, Junior hurriedly refastened it.

"Come on, love." He pulled her to her feet half-dressed, out of the room, through the crowd of bereaved ones; drinking, eating, and remembering Clyde Brown. Pulled her past the curious eyes.

"You're just jealous, Lola," Cinnamon shouted before stepping out into night. "You wish you had been the one he was fucking."

She wore the imprint of Lola's slap for many days to come, a curious shape like a spider bruised into her cheek. And realized she had finally fulfilled a childhood self-prophesy. *To turn this town on its ear.*

Junior tore up the road driving the thirty miles back to the city. Whether he was rushing from disgrace, or toward the climax of their unfinished business, she couldn't tell. A numbness had crept over her. Cinnamon felt weightless, separated from her body. As if hovering in the night above the highway, watching the silent man and woman, the car hurtling toward its destination.

He took her to his place in the concrete high-rise. Where she had first seen him beckoning lazily to the woman who had been her second best friend. He laid her across his king-sized bed and began to touch her. Unhurriedly at first. Then with increasing urgency. But Cinnamon still couldn't find her way back into her body.

And she told herself, *This is nothing.*

And when it was over she was unmoved. Still detached, watching the dark figures sprawled nakedly against pale sheets. Witnessing the opening of the door. And Richard's head stuck inside.

"Junior, mahn. Don't tell me you forget rehearsal again . . ." And the dropping open of the other man's mouth, the stopping of his speech. And then his slow, sly smile. "What is this, now? M'girl and m'best buddy, *in flagrante delicto.* Horror of horrors."

She floated above herself, watching Junior's body roll away from the woman on the bed. And Richard's moving into the room, closing the door.

"So who gets to keep the woman, you or me? Or what of this? You think she have enough for us both?"

There the three of them watched. Junior looking at her with naked speculation in his eyes. Richard standing at the foot of the bed, unbuckling his belt. And she saw it, too, the woman lying crumpled like a rag doll, beside herself with emptiness. And death had danced in the room's cold shadows. And Cinnamon Brown had hovered high above the frozen tableau, watching it all. And wondering.

Maybe this would be the time.

The Spider's Web

I realize that this may be an unusual request, Queen Mother. But a deserving ancestor has just crossed over. And I respectfully request that this one be accepted into your village.

As blood parent, the departed ancestor has mothered one of your daughters with as much devotion as any woman. The only problem being, he is not a woman.

I can personally vouch for his credentials. Clyde Brown has lived his life as a fine, upstanding, hard-working family man. Of all the people in this life or the hereafter, no one loved Cinnamon Brown better. Nor, with the possible exception of one person, has had as much influence upon her.

I suppose that your Gatekeeper may want to stand on ceremony and refuse entrance to a male ancestor. But keep in mind that Cinnamon has become something of a wayward daughter these past years. You saw where the last story ended. Shocking!

And if her father is not empowered to reach through life and intervene, who knows what fate might befall Cinnamon Brown. She has been receiving messages from the great beyond, but not from any mother spirit.

A pregnant teenaged ghost has been seen hanging around the bridge into eternity. For years she has used her proximity to the Village of the Ancestors to plant chaos and confusion in the life of her former best friend.

The choice is simple. Between Clyde and Blondine, which one would you prefer as Cinnamon Brown's guardian angel?

Homecoming

Sometimes I feel like a motherless child
A long way from home.

A song signals her arrival long before the new ancestor crosses the bridge of life into the Village of the Ancestors. Though with all the confusion here, it isn't much of a homecoming. We thank God that the serenity she found in life has accompanied her over to the other side. I suspect she will need it.

It is but a ragged little welcoming committee we can muster; myself and Big Momma Quiltmaker, her long-lost mother. But in times of crisis one does not stand on ceremony.

"You are motherless no more, Earlene Winfield Josephs, henceforth known as Singer. Welcome, sister. Life well lived."

She floats into our open arms.

"I'm mighty glad to be here. I knew I'd get the chance to meet my mother one of these days."

"And I knew you'd be coming on home directly." Big Momma Quiltmaker beams. "Who say it don't pay to be a waiting woman?"

"I have felt your presence for all my life," Earlene confesses. "I always knew that I was not alone. And I thank you for sending this angel to guide me home."

What angel? Not this wild-haired, whiskey-eyed young thing with bulging belly and a bullet hole upon her breast, stepping boldly through the mist and humming *Three Blind Mice* beneath her breath.

"Young lady," I demand. "Whose mother are you?"

"Mother?" Blondine clutches her petrified belly. "Been carrying this load almost twenty years. If that don't qualify me as a mother, then nothing does. Where's the party?"

"Singer Earlene," Big Momma Quiltmaker inquires intently. "My first-born child. What kind of little gate-crashing haint you done hitched up with?"

"She was waiting at the bridge and followed me here. I assumed she was sent."

"That's straight, old girl." The wild one laughs. "Cinnamon Brown's been calling my name for the longest. Can't call me a gate-crasher when I got an invitation. Seems this function could use a little livening up. Don't y'all know that death ain't nothing but a party?"

As if things were not already at the point of collapse in this village, we should be invaded by such a visitor?

"You're a troublemaker, young lady. And trouble is not something we need at this moment. Get thee behind me."

"Alright, I'm outta here." She tosses her tousled head, stepping back onto the bridge. "I been kicked out of better parties than this one here. Of course you know this means war."

And she is gone.

If that Blondine doesn't remind one of that troublesome little Zubena we used to have in our midst. Of course, calm can be distilled from the muddy waters of calamity. For Zubena has grown up nicely in the personage of our new Singer, Earlene. Who has been watching quietly through all the confusion.

"Welcome home, Singer Earlene. It will be good to have music in this place again." I guide her to her place in the village. "Now let me show you the best vantage point to watch over your daughters."

As Gatekeeper of the Great Beyond, the Queen Mother's right hand, one learns to dole out information on a need-to-know basis. And of this latest development, I choose to say nothing. There is no way the widespread knowledge can possibly help the situation, only harm it. Even more chaos could descend upon the queendom, if such a thing is possible.

Though our leader lies near death, it is best that her followers know nothing of the matter. Though she hasn't been herself since we left the old country, her quiet leadership has been the force that keeps us going. What would become of us here without her direction?

And so this sunset vigil at waterfall is not a typical tryst with my phantom lover, but an occasion to send up the most urgent of prayers.

Oh, Great God in the Sky.

I am but a gatekeeper, an intermediary who delivers messages from our daughters in the land of the living. But sometimes we must appeal to you with prayers of our own. Our River Mother Goddess has grown so gaunt, I fear for her survival.

And hers is not the only soul in decline. Chaos and confusion reign like falling waters. We are meant to be mothers united by a common cause: to watch over our daughters in the land of the living. To guide one of them home, here to the River Where Blood Is Born. But it seems we have lost our purpose.

Our village is being invaded by strangers from all quarters. Liars and losers of all sorts. White women, brown women, women of all races claiming to be mothers to our daughters. Errant spirits, male line ascendants.

Why, yesterday a man arrived calling himself Barber Clyde, the Undertaker. Can you imagine that? With a bald head and barber strop and silver stickpin, swearing he had mothered a child. Kwaku Ananse himself couldn't have planned a more bizarre encounter.

Though in truth, few of us even seem to care. Though we cannot see her among us through the dust of trampling feet. It was irony indeed to predict that the homecoming of

Singer Earlene would bring music to this place. Blondine is back with a vengeance. Her flute bewitches our ears with bizarre riffs of Three Blind Mice *and we churn about like dammed-up waters, boiling ourselves dry. See how they run? Of all the times for festivity, when there is so little here to celebrate!*

Death indeed ain't nothing but a party *now; an empty ritual of idlement. We laugh without mirth, sing and dance without merriment. Those of us still watching the waters are merely checking for their own reflection. We have grown as selfish as that witch queen whose reassurance of her own worth came from the shallow depths of a looking glass.*

Our progeny is all but forgotten, abandoned to the wilds of the world. They wander about motherless, surviving only at the mercy of the executioner's ax, the fickle whims of strangers.

The riverbed is running dry, our bloodlink to the land of the living slows to a trickle. We are becoming disremembered among our descendants. Some of us fallen from the lack of tribute are further trampled by careless celebrants. And we, locked in our desperate dance of despair, merely step over the bodies and move on, like rats in the wake of the Pied Piper.

I sit by our Queen Mother's sickbed, stringing the story beads she may not survive to wear. I hover over her as helpless and blundering as a cow elephant whose matriarch has fallen. Who hangs about the carcass even as vultures and hyenas gather. Futilely fondling the ivory, attempting to nudge some movement from the fallen giant.

I humbly beg that action be taken and quickly, lest in time we shall cease to be. I beseech you to look down on us in your infinite wisdom, in your abundant compassion, and hear our prayer.

"Hear it here! Gather round everybody, don't miss the news."

When you dance to the music, you must pay the piper. We have paid the price and those of us left stumble through the debris, dazed in the aftermath. The macabre festival over, the last lingering notes of *Three Blind Mice* wafting away into the mist. Can it be my prayers have been answered?

The party is over, but a commotion still brews. It's like an old country marketplace with women milling about and conversation buzzing. We blink into the sudden sunlight, shaking the haze from our eyes. Ancestors who haven't stirred for centuries have hobbled out to hear the news.

It seems only fitting that it be delivered by the one who first crossed over. The gathering becomes hushed as the voice of Proud Mary, Saltwater Ama, the self-appointed conductor, cries out again in the voice once lost on her original journey.

"Sister spirits, looks like we're ready to make that journey. God has finally seen fit to grant our prayers.

"Those of you who aim to go better get ready quick. Put on your traveling clothes, but pack light. We've been here nearly two hundred years and we don't want to come back hauling excess baggage. Don't tell me you want to keep hanging around this ghost town you call a village. We're pulling up stakes and going back home. Let's get a move on.

"Those that are strong, stand up on your hind legs and walk. Those that are weak, lean on somebody strong. Those that are ailing, climb on somebody's broad back. And I don't want to hear your complaints. They used to be your bridges, it's only right that now you carry them when comes time to cross the water."

And they come. An assemblage of spirits gather around her clad in faded *kente*, linen, hopsack, buckskin, flowered Sunday dresses.

"Who all are coming? Can I hear a roll call?"

And they come . . .

"The First Wife here."

"I am her daughter, Abena Anim, mother of Ama Krah."

The Saltwater woman reminds them of her original name: "Proud Mary, the one who crossed over. Born Ama Krah, daughter of Abena Anim. Mother to Diaspora, Zubena, and Freedom. Grandmother of Ella Mae Beasley. Great-grandmother of Bohema Bullocks."

"Ella Mae Beasley, born to Zubena, mother of Bohema."

And they come . . .

"One Bohema Bullocks, the Quiltmaker. Born to Ella Mae, mother of Earlene, Joe Lee Jr., and Truly. Grandmother of Callie Mae Clemmons and Lula Mae Brown. Great-grandmother of Allie Mae Peeples and Pat Brown.

"Singer Earlene Winfield, lost daughter of Bohema Bullocks, mother of Darlene Josephs Amagashie. Seems like I can't get away from wandering. I just got here and I'm traveling again!"

And still they come . . .

"I have decided to be bound by ocean no more; I, Needleworker Emilene Winston (née Diaspora), lost daughter of Ama Krah, great-grandmother of Sara Winston, Rita Winston, and Beverly Barrett."

"Always did want to see Africa. Sure hope Nkrumah's around to meet Barber Clyde, the Undertaker, father and mother to Cinnamon Brown."

And they come . . .

"We are all together, those who study songs and daughters. Spirit mothers, guardians of rivers and other waters, saints and *loas*, *orishas* and ancestors. And you are not forgotten, the one who is mother to us all . . . the soul of our people, Queen Mother of the River Where Blood Is Born. We can no longer see you, but we feel you stirring within us."

There is a hesitation two hundred years ancient; none seems willing to take the first step. Big Momma Bullocks appears at her great-grandmother's side, her angel's wings spread wide.

"Don't know about y'all, but I believe I'm ready to take that ride. Let's get to the airport quick before we get left behind. That's right, the airport. We came over here steerage, but we're going back first class. Let's climb onboard that silver bird.

"Come on now, take your time. No need to push, there's room for everyone. Y'all some sho' nough country haints, can't take you nowhere. Settle right in there on that wing.

"Yes, I know you're anxious to get settled somewhere warm to soothe that arthritis in your bones. Just take your time, honey. Take your time. And you. I realize you ain't had a decent meal in something like sixty years. But you've been waiting six decades, just hold out for another six hours. Yes, you too. You haven't had palm wine so long, you've almost forgotten the taste. It'll be there for you. And I realize you've always walked into the east to renew yourself, Changing Woman. But what's wrong with flying? What do you mean, if you don't like it over there can you come back home? Honey, you are going home. Now everybody get settled. We got a long ride ahead of us, but it's nothing compared to the years we've been waiting.

"Anybody got a traveling song to make the journey light? What's that? *Swing Low, Sweet Chariot?* No, that's too mournful. This ain't a funeral, it's a celebration. How about that jazzy version, New Orleans style? Yes, Singer Earlene, that's a good choice. Everybody ready?"

Swing down chariot
stop and let me ride
I've got a home on the other side . . .

PART VI

WATERSHED

The Spider's Web

Does it strike you as ironic, Queen Mother, that most disasters occur when the traveler is within one mile of his or her destination? Do not take this as a prophesy of doom, but merely a warning. One of your daughters is pulling into the last stretch of a long journey. But the hardest part still lies ahead.

What has sustained her in the wilderness? Perhaps it was traveler's palm. When there is no river to drink from, no oasis to slake their thirst, wanderers have come to know a desert tree which harbors a source of sweetwater at the heart. A thirsty nomad need only to know its secret, to part the fronds and find the well. And they will be quenched with living waters.

But having been so long in the desert, having subsisted upon so little, will they now know the river when they find it? Will they recognize their own reflection in the face of your waters?

Some may come back changed, winter pallor bred into their souls and strange syllables falling from their lips. Some come dragging rusty chains, but still they come. And they have not lost their taste for okra and black-eyed peas. And they have not lost the admirable fullness of their African buttocks.

They come with syncopated drum rhythms translated into jazz and reggae and samba. They come with gods renamed Mary and Santa Barbara, though some may still remember Asase Yaa.

They teeter like tightrope walkers on a spider's web stretched from one shore to the other. We pray that balance does not fail them now. They come riding the wings of great silver birds. We pray they do not fall.

They, who came here weeping tears of such weight that the Atlantic was made saltier by their passage. And weeping they return, arms held open to embrace their long-lost kin. We hope that their tears are not wasted, that arms may be open in return.

We pray that they find welcome upon these shores.

Bedrock

I don't know why I felt the need to take them out. Big Momma's story beads were wrapped like a rosary around my right hand. I held them throughout the flight, fingering each bead as we sliced through air, hurtling in the direction of the rising sun.

It was barely twilight pulling out of JFK. Puffy white clouds carpeted the sky, first above, then below us. And as we glided out above the Atlantic I could see a patch of black storm clouds whirling above the white, galloping above the clouds. They seemed to dog the plane, chasing it like late travelers running for a train that has left them behind. And they caught it. They appeared to wrap themselves like shreds of diaphanous rag around the tip of the plane's left wing which I was positioned over. I decided you had sent guardian angels to guide my journey home.

You gave me a good night kiss; the heat of setting sun pressed briefly against my face with the promise of more to come. I was on my way home to you.

There was turbulence all the way across the water but I didn't find it alarming. It wasn't a wild rumbling, but a constant, steady creaking. Like ours was a huge iron cradle and wind was the hand that rocked it.

Soothed and contented, I slept. My head crooked at an unnatural angle, smashed against the cold window. And every time I awoke I could see night cleaved by the long silver airplane wing. And beyond it the black shreds of my guardian spirits. And beyond that a deep and endless blue.

When I awoke for the last time during this abbreviated night, the landing announcement was sounding and the sun was rising. Out of the window night was drifting away like smoke. I hurriedly fished into my flight bag and brought out my camera. I snapped away furiously, so busy taking pictures that I didn't really see my first glimpse of you until I had the roll developed some weeks later in Monrovia. And this is what you looked like.

The knife blade cleaved the newborn dawn. And at the tip of its point the sun balanced on it like a swollen, blood-red orange. And beyond that the blue of sky and the blue-green of water. And beyond that the brown of earth and mountains.

I was home at last, in my mother's house. But this only began my journey. I still desperately seek the way back to myself, to my source. I run like the Niger, that river that bends back toward the place where it is born. I know now why I have been sent here. It is not to seek permission. It is to embark upon a mission.

From one African nation to another, I carry these story beads. And I tell the story, what I know of it, of Big Momma and the African great-grandmother who gave them to her. Somewhere in them lies the secret of her life, and so of mine. Somehow they are the lock fished from salt water, for which I must find the key. And somewhere here in your house, someone must know where it can be found.

I wonder at times whether I've embarked upon a pilgrimage or a wild-goose chase. I have gotten such widely varying reactions to my sojourns. From Darlene Amagashie, a Black woman from Detroit teaching English in Ivory Coast, applause.

"Go ahead on, girl. *Roots* revisited. Put Alex Haley to shame!"

From Boumi Akande, a Nigerian woman lawyer, scorn: "Oh, please, Alma. This sounds too much like the kind of primitive hocus-pocus we're trying to put behind us."

From Kwesi Omobowale, a dreadlocked journalist from Los Angeles I have taken up with, amused skepticism: "Well, it's an interesting and charming story, but these kind of trade beads are as common as tsetse flies in West Africa. What can you possibly hope to find from them?"

"The first woman," I would always answer.

I pressed an easterly route, along the bosom of your western coast. Senegal, Sierra Leone, Liberia. Stepping onto a boat on the River Gambia, the Crown Royal pouch had fallen out of my flight bag and floated down to the river's muddy bottom. Unthinking and fully clothed, I had plunged in after it. I took to wearing them around my waist as I had done that night some twenty years ago.

Perhaps it is poetic justice. Just as I am beginning to know you, the first woman, I have become entangled with the third man.

My mind had cleared from the confusion of who you really were; not my lover's wife, but both our mothers. In my journey home to you, there have so far been two key men in my life. The long sojourn with Trevor, punctuated by periods with Tony, all seeming to lead me to the road I am now walking. The road that leads me home to you. Then came Kwesi, who would be so entirely different from any man I've known.

I needed another man like I need a hole in the head, right? I was on a mission, a holy crusade. I would venture forth celibate and unencumbered, like a nun or a saint. I came across the water to meet my mother, to connect with memory, not to fool around with no man.

Am I being honest with you? No, I guess not. It actually had more to do with men than I was willing to admit. After all, it was a man who sent me running this way.

I wish I could claim that it was Big Momma whispering in my ear that brought me home. I came to you like that two-faced Roman god. Are you on speaking terms with European spirits? Do you know the one with an extra pair of eyes in the back of his head? Ever looking back as he moves forward. That was me.

And it was all over that man. His influence was harder to shake than I realized. A miasma that floated across the Atlantic after me. A ten-year flu. A virus in my blood. And I turned to you for a healing.

But even as I roamed, brave and adventurous, I would see myself showing off for Trevor's eyes. *See there. You aren't the only one who can squat around a common bowl and eat fufu and meat with your fingers.* Or, *This man is looking at me. Is that longing in his eyes? I imagine him kissing my shoulder. And oh. First one breast, then the other. I may not be able to live without a man's touch, but I can certainly live without yours. After all, I do not need you.*

I am sorry to have used your love like that. As revenge, a medicine to lance the wound and draw the poison out. Until one infection replaced another and I was in love again. But you are a lover yourself. Maybe you can understand.

The best way to have a man is not to need one, I can remember Big Momma saying just as plain as yesterday. And from the moment that I met Kwesi I was resolved not to need him, though we quickly became constant companions. What had made us fall so easily together? Roam so freely with one another? What had formed the basis of our collective being? It was my role as damsel in distress, and his as Jim Dandy to the rescue.

I first saw him at the airport in Abidjan where I was being detained for entering the country without the proper visa. And I stood there miserably at the customs desk, listening to the two officials arguing in French around me. About me. Occasionally directing an English insult to me.

"You come here alone on holiday? To do what? We don't want your kind here-o!"

I stood there stewing, trying hard to hold my temper. And I noticed the walk before I noticed the man. Off in the distance. Though I never studied on it before, I realized that there was a certain way that African American men move that sets them apart. A syncopated swagger, with a dip of bravado in it. As if offering the world an unspoken challenge: *I dare you to mess with me. Cool as I am.*

Then I noticed the mane of locks that were more manicured than wild. African garb that draped his body in a manner that told me he had not grown up wearing it. A tarnished pocket watch, on a golden fob dangling from his waistband, bounced against his right thigh.

When I found out his name it was a dead giveaway. Kwesi Omobowale, meaning *male born on Sunday*, and *the child returns home*. Nobody but us Diaspora Africans had the gall to mix up such a linguistic cocktail: equal parts Ghanaian *akpetshie* and Nigerian *ogogoro*. But it was his walk that first let me know he was a brother from the other side.

And Kwesi Omobowale noticed me. Perhaps he, too, caught a glimpse of something familiar in my demeanor. He sauntered over and began chatting with the officials in East Los Angeles–accented French. Soon they were laughing and shaking hands. And just like that I was released. Perplexed, I turned to him for some explanation.

"They said they didn't want my kind in this country. What kind might that be?"

And he had explained. Abidjan was the unofficial prostitution capital of West Africa. Women flocked here in droves from near and far, smuggling themselves across the borders. Lone women pouring in to sell their wares in the lucrative flesh market.

Kwesi appointed himself my protector. My dreadlocked dreadnought in shining armor. I had not come to Africa to become dependent upon another man. I had come here fleeing from it. But it had been so easy falling into the syncopated rhythm of Kwesi's footsteps.

We watched each other warily for a while, neither of us willing to make a move. After a full day haggling for masks at the local market, we wound up exhausted back at his hotel.

He recommended the modest two-story inn with the grandiose name of *Le Palais Ivorien*, both for its food and reasonable rates. I had treated him to dinner in the restaurant before we discovered that the hotel was fully booked. He offered to share his room for the night, no strings attached. I was suspicious enough to look a gift horse closely in the mouth.

"Don't even think," I warned, climbing fully clothed into the spare bed, "about trying anything. I don't play that payment-in-kind-for-services-rendered business, contrary to the opinion of your boys at the airport. Understand?"

He laughed heartily, as if such an idea had never occurred to him.

"Don't worry," he assured me with an face-splitting grin. "Your precious body is safe with me."

And he was as good as his word. Without having discussed the matter, we found ourselves platonic roommates and traveling companions. We roamed our way through Ivory Coast, and across the border into Ghana.

He was a better listener than any girlfriend. I would pour my heart out to him, and he listened patiently to my woes about Trevor in particular, and men in general. He was old-fashioned in many ways; holding doors open, walking on the outer sidewalk, escorting me anywhere I wanted to go. One night before bed he asked if I had anything for the laundry. I stuffed my lingerie into the requisite plastic bag, the laundry ticket filled out.

"This is flimsy stuff," I cautioned. "Make sure they understand about the gentle cycle."

"No problem."

The next morning I found each one of my bras and panties carefully washed on plastic hangers in the bathroom. Amazed, touched, and slightly embarrassed, I told him I wished he hadn't. He merely grinned.

"Oh, you can never trust hotel laundries with fine washables."

He never touched me, unless taking me by the hand to help me out of a car or guide me through a crowd. He never looked at me with anything remotely resembling desire, even that night when the air-conditioning failed.

At this particular point we were sharing a double bed in a campus guest house; all quite celibate and chaste. The room was sweltering and we both slept above the sheets, completely in the nude. I woke up once and watched him sleeping there like an overgrown boy, one hand unconsciously shielding the flaccid nakedness between his legs. I was overcome with tenderness. Maybe I'd let him have a little sugar, after all. I leaned over and kissed his cheek. He sprang instantly awake, looking around the room in confusion.

"What?" he asked, disoriented.

"I just gave you a good night kiss. Go on back to sleep."

"Oh." He gave me a sidelong glance, then put on his glasses and consulted the ubiquitous gold pocket watch propped open on the bedstand. "What good night? It is three o'clock in the blessed morning."

At which he removed his glasses, plumped his pillow, placed a protective hand over his crotch, and was soon snoring again.

I decided that he must have been gay; all this attentiveness and restraint was all well and good. But even in an undersexed heterosexual male, it would have been too good to be true. And so we relaxed into our relationship as a reluctant pair of running buddies. Any reluctance was admittedly on my part; he seemed to be perfectly happy with the arrangement. Until the incident with the African author.

I ran into a paragraph from my past. Not a chapter, not even a page. Just a sentence or two in the overall story. Kwesi knew that a particular man had been my dearest misery for nearly all my adult life. And he knew that I was still getting over him. So when we met the African author, he just assumed.

Remember the African author? Visiting professor on campus during the college chapter of my life, when I enjoyed a brief, harmless flirtation with him. This was not the first time he would be the object of another man's jealousy. That first man was Trevor, long gone and left behind. But jealousy still looms in all its poetic irony.

I ran into the African author again, this time at a faculty party at the University of Legon. He did not remember me and I would not have remembered him had he not a public name outside of himself. And still he was smooth as oil, as flirtatious as ever.

I entertained the party with my tales of Big Momma and Nana, embellishing the story for my appreciative audience. Avoiding the skeptical roll of Kwesi's eyes, I announced that I was in Africa trying to trace my origins.

The African author became very interested. Insisted that I show him the two-hundred-year-old beads which were an integral part of this herstory. I lifted my top a bit to reveal them coiled like a blue snake around my waist.

The African author reached out and touched them. He told me that beads identical to these were used in his village to this very day. Not, so far as he knew, to mark adolescent girls' onset of puberty, but to hold up the diapers of babies.

"Of course you haven't connected with your ancestors. You have been looking in the wrong places. Gambia, Cote d'Ivoire, Senegal. Everyone knows that *Nana* is an Akan word. It means elder, old woman, grandmother. You are home now."

You know I was beside myself with excitement. A lead! A clue! I fell upon the African author, turning him every which way but loose. Questioning him about beads and rivers and anything I could think of that might give me something to go on.

He smiled disarmingly, taking my face between his hands and tilting it to the side.

"Do you know, you look so much like an Ashanti woman. Your skin is very dark, and we Ashantis believe that the blacker a person's skin, the closer the person is to the earth, to the ancestors, to the gods. You could almost be my cousin."

Kwesi snorted into his jollof rice. It was quite common for both of us to be assured that we were descended from this or that particular people. Africans know I am not from their place, but something in me makes them think I am from somewhere nearby. I'd been told on innumerable occasions by dozens of people that I was certainly Wolof, Hausa, Fulani, Yoruba, Mandinka, or from any number of different nations.

But even Kwesi would have to admit it. When I took a good look at the African author, I realized that we did look something alike. Tall bodies, slim builds, dark skins, rounded faces.

He said that he must know how to contact me. All in the pursuit of cultural inquiry, of course. I must go to Kumasi and consult with the historians at the palace of the Asantehene, king of the Ashanti people. He himself could assist with a contact, a letter of introduction.

When the evening was over I realized I'd spent it all in the company of the African author. Kwesi was uncharacteristically quiet on the ride back. We stopped at Labadi Beach and were surprised to have it all to ourselves. In the full moonlight its deserted sands shone not like the gold these coasts had once been called, but rather like silver.

We stripped down to our underwear like kids, and waded out into the midnight waters. The ambience called for indolence, and we lolled about rather than swam. Even the ocean was tame tonight, rolling in lazily and lapping against our skins.

I playfully splashed him, scooping a handful of sand into his boxer shorts. Kwesi sighed and turned over, doing the dead man's float. If I hadn't known better, I'd have thought he was acting like a jealous male.

"Maybe you should have picked a native-born African as a traveling companion." He lifted his head, murmuring into the surf.

"Who said I picked you? It seems more like you picked me. And what makes you think I need a continental African?" I dipped beneath the surface and floated underneath him, trying to see his face in the dark waters. He flipped over, sighing again.

"You seem to require so much more than I have to give."

The revelation was astounding.

"Like what?" I wanted to know.

"A sense of belonging, of finding the African in yourself. It seems that's what you need from a man."

If Trevor acted out his jealousy in possessiveness, Kwesi's was played out in misery and martyrdom. I was having none of it.

"I'm not looking for myself in somebody else. I don't need no man to tell me who I am. I know who I am."

"Do you, Alma?" This was a new side of Kwesi. Depressed, morose. "Then why are you here in Africa?"

"But Africa isn't outside of me," I insisted. "It is in me. And I am in it. It is my genealogy."

We argued on into the night, into the gentle waters. Kwesi telling me that I was romanticizing the motherland, glorifying a past I did not understand and could never fully know. Asked me if I realized that this very type of trade bead I wore around my waist had been used as currency in the precolonial era. Had helped turn one African people against another, used for trade in whiskey and guns and slaves. Told me to contemplate the possibility that one woman's bondage might have been used to finance the decoration of another woman's body.

"How can you glorify your Africanity when you don't even appreciate your humanity?"

"I'm sure I don't know what you're talking about."

"Don't you know that I see you, Alma?" he said gently, rising from the water. "I've been where you're at right now. Running away from who I am, trying to catch up with my past. Isn't that why you've always been attracted to foreign-born men?"

"But Kwesi," I whispered. "What on earth is wrong with that? With loving someone who has a sense of wholeness, of belonging, that I have never had? What's wrong with men who own themselves, own their souls? At least that way one of us will."

He said I was placing the same impossible burden on the back of Mother Africa. Oh, he was so discouraging. Told me I was looking for a needle in a haystack, a grain of sand at the beach.

"Well," I dipped beneath the waters and filled both hands, "I'm in the right place for it."

He was not amused. Told me that even a tumbleweed had roots. Asked me when I was going to stop chasing the wind. I tossed his question back at him.

"When are you?"

He smiled. And I realized that he had not been arguing with me all night, but himself. Because it was he who chased the wind. I was the one who followed rivers. Which could be unpredictable, too. Full of surprises and unexpected twists.

"That's different, Alma. Me, I'm a professional wanderer. I've been at it so long I've forgotten what I set out looking for."

"So why are you trying to discourage me? Maybe I'm a nomad, too. Maybe we were meant to wander together."

Kwesi shook his head ruefully, releasing himself from the seductive pull of the ocean waters. We collapsed upon the beach, stretched out my *lappa* like a blanket, and lay upon it, side by side. The antique pocket watch Kwesi said had been handed down to him from his father's side of the family ticked faintly in our ears.

"Maybe I care too much about you to feed your fantasies. Or maybe I envy you the energy which gives purpose to your wandering. Which makes it less aimless than mine. Maybe I don't want you to find what you're looking for because then you won't need me anymore."

Can you believe it? A man afraid to hear the very same words that have haunted me all my life? *Naw, baby. It ain't me.*

"Kwesi." The time was past for talking. It would be morning soon and something was about to change between us. The possibility hung in the air, like a dewdrop suspended from the petal of a rose. "I've been looking for you all my life. What do you mean *I won't need you?* I'll need you then. And I need you now. Right now."

And he turned toward me, cupping my face in the palms of his hands.

"Do you think you're ready for this, Alma?"

"I think so."

That is when he took my hand and pressed it to himself. He was like a rock beneath his wet boxers. It startled me so that I automatically snatched my hand away. And then let it timidly wander that way again. How long, I wondered, easing into his arms, had he been waiting for me? The dangling dewdrop gathered itself slowly. And fell.

We didn't sleep that night. Though the gentle alluvion of ocean gurgled a lullaby to us. We rocked ourselves deep into sand still warm from yesterday's sun. We cooled off our heated bodies in the water, and found ourselves rocking again. If I'd only known how this loving would be, I wouldn't have let so much time go by.

In the intervals I rested in his arms and listened to the sea breeze stirring in the shoreline palms. And thought, for some reason, of forests. Of deep green trees reaching out their arms to hold us. I listened to the roar of ocean and seemed to hear beneath it the quiet song of sweeter waters. As if cast for centuries upon shifting sands, my feet had finally found the firm rest of bedrock.

He continued to court me long after. A mango to meet me in the morning, perfectly sliced upon the plate. A plucked petal of hibiscus, its pinpoint of nectar pressed against my tongue. A metal object folded into my hands; a naughty goldweight figure of a tiny man with enormous genitalia.

"Open your mouth and close your eyes," he'd tease, "and you will get a big surprise."

His open mouth would meet mine, and in it a cool mouthful of palm wine. A gravelly morsel of guava. Or simply the melon sweetness of his tongue.

We continued to wander along the coast. Across Togo and into Benin. We made a moonlight visit to a French-speaking Yoruba priestess in a dusty, roadside village. She chewed on the plump cloves of kola and read my fortune in the toss of palm nuts. She told me I must make a pilgrimage to the mother goddess. I must go to her shrine on the banks of a river. I must take her an offering: a crayfish, eight pigeons, eight bags of cowries. Only then, I was assured, would I find the answer to the question I was seeking.

I paid her a thousand CFA francs cash for the amulet she placed around my neck, and another thousand francs for permission to take her picture.

Kwesi laughed and called her a con artist. In the taxi, sang teasingly in my ear:

*I got my Yemoja working
and I'm going try it out on you . . .*

But still he promised to take me to her shrine at Ile-Ife. Yemoja, the mother of all waters. He said it was one of Africa's *must-sees*, even for the nonbeliever. I don't know what I believe anymore. But I do know an old song or two, myself. And one of them says that *freedom's just another word for nothing left to lose*.

I have lost weight since I've come home to you. The constant walking. The spare diet of rice, fufu, and tropical fruit. Big Momma's story beads hang loosely around my waist now. As I walk they click against each other, echoing the soft percussion of Kwesi's heirloom pocket watch. *Tsk, tsk, tsk*. Like a mother scolding and at once reassuring her child.

Sheltered in the house of the first woman, in the arms of the third man, the voice I seem to have heard all my life becomes clearer. The rattling of Big Momma's story beads, the ticking of Kwesi's watch punctuate the constant calling. When the night falls in some inn or resthouse along the coastline, and when we move together in the ancient fertility dance of loose limbs and sweet fire, I can hear them, too.

These story beads speak to me in a language I had long forgotten. They come alive in loving, rattling like a snake giving warning. Like the rumble of far-off drums, or the call of nearby waters.

Sweet River

A heated breeze rushes in through the open window. Roadside palms rustle like whispering ghosts. Save the ribbon of asphalt unfurling before us, this stretch of coast seems curiously untouched.

"Like slipping back two hundred years in time," I murmur into Kwesi's ear as we crest a bridge over the Sweet River.

. . . like the scent of offal that remains, even when the act has been buried. Memory seizes the mind like a monkey which mistakes a hunter's head for its mother's back.

Jojo drives up front, we ride in back. I watch the coast unfold and recline in Kwesi's arms. There is something vaguely familiar in the landscape, something undefinable in the air. I think Kwesi senses it, too.

They bathe in the waters of the Sweet River, singing to each other and washing away the soil of their latest mating.

For some reason he is very affectionate this afternoon. Every other moment he is touching my hair, holding my hand, or gathering me to him in an embrace so tight it almost hurts.

"Kwesi, poor man," Jojo laughs, watching him from the rearview mirror. "You love this woman too much."

Who does he think he is, this forest dweller who has never seen the inside of any city? This one to whom she habitually opens her legs?

The winding road stretches westward and disappears into the distance. On our left is ocean, fringed by beige rises of beach. The sand is littered with the drying husks of coconut fruit fallen from shoreline palms. The slender trunks lean toward the sea, as houseplants do toward sun. They could almost be beaus, vying for the hand of the same lover. Ocean is the woman they woo.

I had had but one taste, one tantalizing bite and that tasty dish was snatched from my open mouth. If only he had waited until I ate my fill, perhaps I might have allowed him my leavings. Everyone knows you do not take from a man that which he has prepared for his own palate.

They have given a name to these waters. Abena, born on Tuesday, a woman to be both revered and feared. A tempestuous goddess to whom fishermen pray for a share in her harvests, and who they hope will not one day claim their lives in exchange.

Ah! But these women will betray you. And other men, they will take what is yours.

I learned my lesson early. You must become a predator, or forever scurry in the bush as prey.

Abena is at ease this midmorning. Perhaps because today is Tuesday, when it is taboo to disturb her waters. Swelling softly in her blue-green garments, she waves as if in welcome. Her pungent perfume wafts in the air, a blend of sea salt and fresh fish. Time and again, Abena rolls up to embrace the bosom of a coast once called *Gold*. As if comforting a sister robbed of her riches.

My mother had no daughter to assist in her woman's work. So she tried to make a woman of me. I went about with younger siblings tied to my back, worked the farm with the women, cooked groundnut stew on the coal pot. The other boys jeered, called me a woman's boy when they saw me bent over the cooking fire. But that did not prevent them from coming to taste my meat at mealtimes.

Along the blue curve of Abena's hip, we move toward the widening horizon. Up ahead a town emerges, a collection of buildings huddled together in a self-embrace. It seems a guileless sort of place, as calm and charming as any in a number of West African villages. Elmina is her name. A virginal young girl of a town, flowers in her hair one would suppose.

But such is not the case.

There are moments when release of the arrow, when the spurt of blood or the thrill of the kill does not satisfy. When a man lays down his traps and spears for other weapons. When he yearns to plunge into the valley of fresh, charmed flesh.

Though she still smiles, her innocence has long been pierced. In her center stands a monument to a people's amputated past. An edifice still anchored firm in the rocky peninsula on which it stands. This is our destination.

Sao Jorge da Mina, St. George of the Mines, the five-hundred-year-old fort built by a Portuguese expedition. We are amused to learn one Christopher Columbus found himself accidentally onboard, a full ten years before he blundered upon the New World.

One day when I had a taste for it, I pounded fufu, crushed fresh palm kernels in the mortar, and made a meal for myself. Steam rose from my calabash, hot and spicy. I tore off a ball of fufu, dipped it into the stew, and tasted. Ah! Could the second taste ever match the first? I would never know.

But we haven't yet arrived. We can see Elmina up ahead of us. For some reason we hesitate on her outskirts. As if gathering the sustenance we need to journey on.

My mother stepped from her room and sent me to the river for water, a task everyone knows is reserved for girls. When I returned, a boy from a neighboring village was sitting before my calabash, wiping up the last bit of stew with the last ball of fufu.

Jojo pulls the car to the side of the road. We get out, the three of us. We cross over to the beach side of the road. Which is deserted. Africans do not love sun just for its own sake. Feel no need to toast their well-browned bodies. When they swim it is generally a matter of necessity, not leisure. So beaches tend, as likely as not, to be deserted save for the company of fishermen and wandering children. And the occasional traveler, like ourselves.

Ah! If these bush people only knew what lies at the mouth of this river.

Cramped from the drive from Cape Coast, we wander toward the ocean.

Warm sand brushes the sides of our sandaled feet, inviting our toes to mingle. We move to take off our shoes, but Jojo advises against it. He points to scatters of prickly plant life, half-buried in the sands.

"Those things go chuke your leg," he warns in pointed pidgin.

We follow his advice and remain shod.

Further on, the sea beckons, a taunting temptress calling thirsty travelers to her. She holds no cooling liquid to slake our thirst, this we know. It is a water heavier and saltier than tears. We approach Abena, we dip our feet in her waters. They will dry streaked white with salt.

The girl would come to weep and curse and, yes, even strike me, when she saw what I had done for her. For us. She, who did nothing but complain about the old woman. "My mother hoards me like salt. She refuses to let me climb down from her back." You would think she'd be grateful to me for removing that witch from our path.

On our return to the car, a grinning boy with cutlass tied to his waist comes running up to us. A fine-looking child, face bronzed ebony with sun. A boy with broad, bare feet. Obviously unafraid of sharp things blooming in sand that will *chuke* the feet of strangers.

He bargains with Jojo, most businesslike. Still darting us smiles between negotiations. We think he has come over as much to examine the strangers at close quarters as to make a sale. And then the boy, barely ten, runs to the nearest coconut palm. He deftly scales the bare trunk and tosses down two football-sized green pods. He returns to earth and halves them with his cutlass. We take a half each and taste. It gives up a cool, sweet water to quench our thirsts.

This is not the coconut we are used to, the one hardened over time. This is the soft, vulnerable stage. And the fruit surrenders easily, sweetly. A milky jelly for our hunger; we scrape this away and eat it with our fingers.

After all, it was I who first crushed this palm kernel, who cracked this coconut, who opened up the passage he now plunders.

It is both sweet and somehow sad, this succulent. Young and defenseless. Yielding. Having not yet developed the fierce and hairy outer shell, it is tender and easily taken. We wonder if Elmina was once this way, at a time before her name was changed. Before the eyes of a nation turned outward, toward the invaders crawling her coastlines.

Any hunter will tell you this is true. To kill a beast, you must first become that beast. You must come to know the ways of antelope, know the heart of elephant. You must learn to live as the lion, think as the lion, be as the lion. Only then can you capture the lion.

Up close she is a sleepy town, eyes half-closed in the sun. Driving through her scant business section, we are reminded of the kind of frontier settlement one sees in American westerns.

Everything is bleached deadwood white in the salty sun. The sandy streets are framed by parched wooden buildings, supported in front by splintering posts. We almost want to peer behind them to make sure they're not really jerry-built sets. But then, it would have to be a West African western shot in this town. There is no Deadwood Dick, no Annie Oakley roaming these streets, six-shooters slung low at hips.

Avoiding sun-bleached wooden sidewalks raised slightly above the ground, people, chickens, and one or two goats saunter in the road. They walk with confidence, as if they own these streets. Which they do. We are the visitors who must drive carefully around them.

Up ahead another obstruction. At a rise in the road we come upon a procession. They are about thirty some souls in number, dressed in identical African print. And marching directly up the center of the street. They carry a carnival spirit with them as they march through the quiet town. Singing, carrying baskets of plantain and yam upon their heads.

As we breast the marchers, some lean over to sing into the car. They smile for the camera. Jojo tells us this is a wedding procession. The people here are family to the groom, marching as one to meet the bride's family with gifts of food for the wedding feast.

And this one dares to trifle with the likes of me? I am no longer a woman's boy, you know. In my manhood I am the husband of three wives. I drink European liquor. I have tasted the meat, cured the hide, and worn the skins of many animals. I have seen leopards tremble in death throes. My mates and I have captured whole villages. Grown men prostrate themselves before me, begging me to spare their lives.

We cross the low bridge over the Benya, now a dried-up riverbed made over into a marketplace. Beneath us and beyond, fishermen sell their catch, market women hawk their wares.

Then a wide shadow shades the road. Elmina Castle springs sharply into focus. It is balanced on a promontory that juts above the sea, guarding the harbor of the town. The great stone walls cast a cold gray shadow.

Opposite the castle on a hilltop across the road stands a cathedral. The place where resident slave merchants once went to worship. It seems that these traders of women and men took churches with them wherever they went. Did they suppose that prayer would save their slaving souls?

And it is me they call the unholy. See them rutting like beasts on the bare ground, desecrating Asase Yaa, our Mother Earth. Even hunters like myself know that one does not sleep with a woman in his mother's bed.

The pair of medieval Portuguese fortresses loom strange and stony, out of place above the quiet town.

We get down to take the tour. It is nearing noon when we climb from the little car and into the white-hot sun. Sensible people usually siesta away this sweltering time of day. Who was it that wrote only mad dogs and Englishmen venture out in the noonday sun? Add to that Black American travelers. And Japanese tourists.

Entering through the iron gates we run smack into an exiting group of them. All men, wearing Bermuda shorts and Nikons around their necks.

We find that we've missed the morning tour. The afternoon session won't start until 2:30 P.M. Since Jojo must return to Accra that afternoon, the two of us decide to do some exploring on our own. Jojo remains behind, finding a shady place to nap. He is blasé about this atrocity, having lived at close quarters with it all his life.

But at times it is not enough to snare an antelope, to fell a buffalo. There are times when a hunter hungers for greater prey.

We roam the courtyard looking at plaques and inscriptions etched in bronze and stone. Elmina seems to have had a long line of *gentleman callers* over the centuries. Each one has left his calling card. Yet the spirit of this great rock remains imprisoned in a vaulted shrine, powerless to halt the centuries of predation.

We wander past a second set of iron gates. Here is an inner courtyard, surrounded by a labyrinth of cells and dungeons, stairwells and balconies that stretch up several stories. For fear of getting lost in the maze, we limit our explorings to the ground floor.

We retrieve from a pocket the Elmina Castle guidebook obtained from the National Museum just yesterday. In it we find a floor plan of sorts, which we study.

We look into one of the many small iron-barred cells that ring the courtyard. According to our guidebook, female captives were kept in these cubicles conveniently situated beneath the governor's quarters, prior to being loaded onto ships.

"Aye, in you go." Kwesi grabs my arm, drawls a pirate's brogue into my ear. "Me comely Coramantee wench."

"No, Kwesi *Obruni*, sir. I beg-o."

I obligingly play along, whimpering and struggling, beating his chest in mock resistance. He tugs wide one of the iron doors and swings me inside.

"Har, that's a willing lass." He stretches his face into a comical leer. "Cool yar heels for a bit, me lovely."

It is dark and cool here, away from the sun. Try to imagine this cell crowded with women. Try to conjure up the stench of fear, of beings packed and panicked in such a tiny space. Perhaps among them the great-grandmother of your great-grandmother.

After I killed the mother, the girl would no longer have me. Though I called, she would not come. She hid from me. She went to lie with another in the shelter I built to spare Mother Earth the insult of our mating.

But I have trouble making the image materialize. Is it the welcoming coolness here after such punishing sun? The almost soothing sense of silence?

Kwesi clangs shut the door and jangles an imaginary bunch of keys. I clutch the cold, unyielding iron. My field of vision is suddenly limited. All I can see is the cell directly across the yard.

"I'll come for ye again, me bonny lass." Kwesi flips open the battered pocket watch dangling from his belt loop. "Midnight sharp."

Is she dazzled by the trinket this bush boy wears at his waist? I would wager he's never known the red rawness of the European's skin. The feeble click of his white man medicine is nothing compared to the might of a white man's musket, spitting fire from the hands.

It grows yet quieter. All the noise and laughter in the world might have been called to a halt. What if you were trapped here inside this stone tomb? If this were not just an afternoon sightseeing excursion? If a comfortable bed were not just an hour's drive away? If you must trade Kwesi's sweet embrace for nighttime visits from the governor and his boys? What if you were to be taken away at this very moment, leaving all you knew behind?

As for her, she must also pay. She will answer to me, or by the Great God in the Sky, I will know the reason why.

A cloud passes over the sun. A shadow hangs over the gray stone courtyard. A chill deeper than freezing enters my blood.

I would sooner have the white men ride her, see her sold across ocean waves, than let a bush boy feast on a meal prepared for my own palate.

"I don't like this game, Kwesi. Let me out of here."

He quickly twists the iron handle, but the rusty latch does not budge. I push against the iron bars in sudden panic. But it does not give. *It does not give.*

I have tracked them for many days now.

I throw full weight against cold iron. A handle creaks and I tumble out into the courtyard, into Kwesi's arms. He grabs my hand and for some sudden reason we are running.

This one believes himself to be a hunter because he may trap a bird or fell an antelope. He is but a bush rat, a small rabbit waiting to wander into my snares.

Running, running. Running toward noise and heat and healing sun. We run.

Soon their sweetwater songs will drown in saltwater blues.

Jojo has abandoned his cat nap. He is in the outer courtyard, standing atop a rusty cannon like a conquering warrior. We clamber up to join him, panting and out of breath. But the clanging of the cell door has brought our presence to the attention of the day watchman. Disturbed from his midday rest, he irritably issues us away.

"The castle is closed," he shouts. "Come again at half-two."

We leave the premises. We will not come again.

For the greatest of all hunters is the warrior; he who tracks the human animal.

On the ride eastward past Cape Coast toward Accra, Abena is blue-black and churning in the dying sun. I do not join in the cheerful conversation of the men in the front seat. A part of me remains behind in the cold stone castle . . .

This small boy hunter will soon know what it is to become the game. Perhaps I will watch him beg for his life, then let him meet the metal of my musket. Perhaps I will sell him downriver to the obruni traders at Elmina.

. . . reliving the time when Time no longer existed. The moment of fierce uncertainty and absence of sun. Before the ship and after the gun. The moment our memory became anonymous and the language left our tongue.

No man devours a dish I prepare for my own palate.

We drive toward Accra in the dying evening sun.

Lady in the Slip

People moved about catlike in the near darkness. A smear of dying sun lit a purple oil-painted sky. Sounds of African night swirled dizzily around us. The bleating of a goat, the blare of car horns, one hundred voices almost singing in a foreign, familiar tongue.

Kwesi clutched my hand and we plunged into the hazy crowd. He found ours with uncanny ease; a nondescript Volkswagen minivan with *God is Driver, Holy Ghost is Wheel* carefully lettered across the back. Though all of the vehicles in Agege Motor Park made such metaphysical promises, not a single one gave a clue as to its destination.

Yet everyone seemed to know without asking which one would take them where they wanted to go. As Kwesi did now. Loaded down with bags and suitcases, mostly mine, we struggled aboard and settled into a wide seat at the back of our *danfo*. These share-taxis had earned the title because men who drove them reputedly did so like *damn fools*, despite the enigmatic inscriptions which suggested otherwise.

The vehicle was only half-full and our driver seemed in no particular hurry to leave. Leaning against the side of the minivan, he chewed groundnuts and called out at periodic intervals.

"Ife, 'fe, 'fe, Ife-o."

Two young men in blue jeans, one with mirrored sunglasses hiding his eyes, twisted around in their seats to get a good look at Kwesi's mane. They pointed and commented loudly in unself-conscious Yoruba.

"*Se alafia ni?*" Kwesi smiled and greeted them.

Kwesi was like that. His dreadlocks drew a great deal of attention wherever we wandered. I couldn't believe his ubiquitous good humor. He acknowledged every curious glance with a smile and a greeting. Often it would evolve into a conversation, sometimes a friendship. Kwesi was a master of what I called *the walking blues*. Taking the lemon and making lemonade. Turning a potential confrontation into the possibility of camaraderie.

But this time his overture was not acknowledged. One of the two shifted his gaze to me. Long, jean-clad legs, tropical print top, sandals, close-cropped natural.

"*Akata*," he commented to his fellow.

"African," I corrected.

341

I didn't have Kwesi's unself-conscious friendliness. I bristled at the nickname which when roughly translated meant *wild animal*. Unable to summon Kwesi's good humor, I crossed my arms and stared them down until one pair of eyes and one pair of mirrors returned their focus forward.

"Don't take it so hard, Alma," Kwesi whispered in my ear. "*Akata* ain't so bad. He could have called you a Negress."

"Not if he wanted to live to tell about it."

Our wait was interminable. I shifted nervously, anxious for us to be on our way. But no one else appeared to mind, Kwesi included. After five years in West Africa he had adjusted his internal clock to African time. A patient, unhurried pace of living. The serenity that came with the acknowledgment that schedules were not worth the paper they were printed on, if in fact they were printed at all. The patient acceptance that comes with learning how to wait. The *danfo* would not budge until every single seat was occupied. And neither would we.

We leaned back and watched the night. Agege Motor Park surrounded us, no more than a busy patch of red mud where enterprising men with motorable vehicles picked up fares to Cotonou, Ife, Benin City, Ibadan, and other points in and around western Nigeria.

Nearby Ikorodu Road, the world's deadliest according to the latest *Guinness Book of World Records*, was a noisy blur of moving cars. Traffic zoomed in and out of Lagos with pointed disregard for stoplights and speed limits.

Challenging the threat of Ikorodu death, hawkers scampered across the road to Agege balancing on their heads a veritable supermarket of items. Trays of cigarettes, groundnuts, packets of biscuits dipped and swayed, but did not fall. Vendors of bananas, transistor radios, and suitcases milled about beneath our windows, advertising in musical Yoruba or shrill pidgin English.

"Peel' orange. Peel' orange. Sweet peel' orange."

"*Ikpa, ikpa, ikpa-o!*"

"Boil' egg here, madam. Na fine boil' egg."

Buying on the market was an art. If you didn't know how to bargain you were a lamb in lion's country. Sure to be fleeced. Kwesi had become an expert.

"*E ku oja-o?*" He beckoned a woman wearing a pyramid stack of oranges like a crown. He grabbed three oranges from the point of the pyramid. "*E lo ni orange?*"

He had asked how much they were. And the woman quickly looked him up and down, assessing how much money was likely to be in his pocket.

"*Shile meji-meji,*" she said firmly. Her hands reached back to adjust a child tied to her back.

"Ah, ah!" He gave a wounded gasp. He'd been charged thrice the going rate. "Make you carry your orange commout. You think say I get Central Bank for my pocket?"

She narrowed her eyes and hesitated. Her hands were engaged in unwrapping the crying child on her back. She held him under the arms to urinate in the dust.

"Twenty *kobo* last price," she insisted, retying the baby with a length of folded cloth. All the while, mind you, the tray of oranges never teetered. African women are masters of balance.

Kwesi hissed loudly, sucking his teeth in feigned exasperation.

"You think say orange na gold. Bye bye-o!" He waved her away, but I noticed he still held on to the oranges.

I started laughing. I couldn't help it. Kwesi, wearing that pained, injured expression. The woman, one hand on belligerent hip, oranges on head. The round-eyed baby watching from the perch on his mother's back apparently found Kwesi's playacting amusing, too. He burst into a fit of delighted giggles.

How can you be a shrewd businesswoman with a laughing brown elf peering over your shoulder? The woman sighed and surrendered.

"Okay. You want me give orange for gift? For you, only ten *kobo*. Bring de money." And she cupped her hand to receive it.

Kwesi grinned. He paid her and handed her the oranges to peel. With a thin knife that was tucked within the pyramid, she deftly separated peel from oranges in long, unbroken strips. A fine spray of scent wafted into the Nigerian night.

We sucked our oranges in companionable silence. The vehicle was slowly filling up. A short, balding man with a portable boom box climbed aboard. All the other seats had been taken and he squeezed into the backseat with Kwesi and me. The driver and his companion finally boarded and made ready to pull off. The engine gunned, the door creaked shut.

Then suddenly a shrill female voice pierced the night, almost a scream above the noise.

"Wait now, please. I beg-o!"

The door was pried open from the outside. A woman's tousled head poked through and she struggled in. Our friend in sunglasses hissed irritably.

"Ah, ah! Hurry now, enter. Make you no waste we time." His sudden impatience amused me, since we'd all been sitting idle for nearly an hour.

Clambering over baskets and bundles crowding the narrow aisle, the woman searched for a seat.

"Eh. Which kind woman be dis?" someone whispered.

All eyes turned on cue to where the woman stood. One mud-splattered foot poised in the motion of climbing over a pile of ripe plantain. Her longish hair stood out on end, a bristling helmet of porcupine quills. One eye looked bruised and swollen. Both were tired and reddened.

The faint scent of old sweat and cheap perfume wafted in with her. She wore a dingy black nylon slip. Nothing else. No shoes. Not the requisite bag or bundle African women always seem to have in hand or on head. Like a sleepwalker she stumbled, staring around her as the *danfo* started. Clasping one hand in the other palm upward, the African gesture of supplication, she appealed to a woman with a child sleeping beside her.

"Please, madam, I beg. Take the child in lap. I want sit."

Madam gave her one sharp look and turned her eyes to the window.

"We no get seat for here."

"Wey t'ing, woman? You no get eyes for head?" Sunglasses demanded. "We done full-up finish. Seat no dey. Make you go down." His companion grunted in agreement.

Shoulders sagged in resignation, she turned tiredly toward the door.

"My sister, come. We will make room for you here."

Who was the Good Samaritan around here? The words coming forth from my mouth surprised even me. Three of us occupied a seat that could have comfortably accommodated two. I could have kicked myself remembering how I insisted we take the backseat, which was slightly wider than the rest. Thinking foolishly that we'd have it to ourselves. I shrugged in answer to Kwesi's lifted eyebrow.

"She's got a story," I whispered back. "And I've got to hear it."

Kwesi sighed and squeezed in closer to our seatmate, the grumbling round man with juju music blaring on his radio. In turn, I moved closer to Kwesi, one hip perched upon his lap. Amid much belabored shifting we just managed to fit her in. She sandwiched sort of sideways between me and the open window.

"Chmph!" our seat mate hissed, wiggling uncomfortably and looking disapprovingly in the direction of the newcomer.

The *danfo* started abruptly, then stopped. We piled into each other. A whispered conference up front. The driver's mate, a stooped skinny man, buttonless shirt hanging open, scurried to the back. He held his hand out to the lady in the slip.

"Make you pay de money."

She reached into the bosom of her skimpy garment and extracted a greasy paper tied with string. Before she could unwrap it, however, Kwesi had intervened.

"Wey t'ing dey happen here?"

The man shifted from one foot to the other.

"*Oga* say make he pay now."

"I don't care what *oga* says." Kwesi's jaw hardened. "Person usually pay de money when he reach destination. Na bi so?"

"Yes, *oga*." So now Kwesi had been elevated to the status of boss man. The man glanced uncertainly up to the front. "Na so he bi."

"Fine. Madam go pay you when she reaches Ife." Kwesi nodded in dismissal, and the man lurched back to his place on the floor next to the driver. The minivan started up again.

"Thank you, sir." The lady in the slip tucked the bundle back where it came from and smiled tiredly, trying to pull the skimpy garment above her half-exposed breasts.

The van swung recklessly into Ikorodu, creeping along through miles of *go slow* until we left the noise and traffic of Lagos proper. Once outside the city the air cleared of auto fumes. We zoomed along past long stretches of bush, dotted here and there by clumps of thatch-roofed huts. Night air rushed in through the window along with the inevitable mosquito. I tossed out the sucked-in shell of my peeled orange and watched it disappear into the bush.

Up ahead beyond a curve in the road I saw a dark, low-slung shape separate itself from the shadow of trees and scurry right in the path of our vehicle. The animal huddled in the road, eyes glinting green in our oncoming headlights.

"Watch out!" I shouted too late, as the creature bumped and tangled noisily against our wheels. The van did not stop, but a dozen pairs of eyes turned to stare at me, curious at my alarm.

"What was that?" I was somewhat shaken, slightly embarrassed.

"Bush rat," replied the man on the other side of Kwesi, smacking his lips with gusto. "Uhmmm. That na de real chop meat."

"Bush rat? You eat it?"

I couldn't help shuddering, hand over heart. Kwesi whispered into my ear in teasing pidgin.

"No worry sista, na delicacy. When we reach Ife we go chop fine-fine bush rat stew."

The man with the taste for bush rat meat had been watching Kwesi with growing interest.

"Which kind person you be self, juju priest?"

Dreadlocks were not exactly high West African fashion in those days. They were usually reserved for those on the outside of society. People who lived in service of certain spirits, and those who suffered afflictions of insanity. Because of this Kwesi was usually assumed to be either a juju priest or a madman.

I remembered the man I saw in Jankara Market. I don't know if Shango, the Yoruba god of lightning, had shot his eyes with blood and twisted his hair into ropes. Or perhaps the demons of insanity had captured his mind. Where he walked people scattered. I was fascinated and stopped to watch him. There might be a story in it.

Then he focused bloodshot eyes on me and started to move in my direction. I thought of the spectacle I had run from. The fierce, vacant eyes, the shabby clothes, the Medusa locks. And then looked over at the gentle man sitting beside me.

Kwesi glanced back at me and sighed. He was all too used to such questions.

"No, my brother. I no be Shango priest. Just a lazy man with the luck to have lived among the Rastas in Jamaica." He raked a hand through his shoulder-length locks. "Thought it was a good idea at the time. All the time I'd save not having to comb it. The money I'd save on haircuts."

This was Kwesi's standard reply. But I always wondered what really committed him to maintaining what was certainly a difficult choice, especially here in Africa. I knew myself that Rastas, maybe the juju people, too, felt that the hair was a living extension of the body, capable of receiving vibrations from the air around it. Like a cat's whiskers or an insect's antennae. Was this it for Kwesi? Or was he simply attracted to the idea of marching to a different drummer? I would question him on it one of these days.

But not now. The man with the radio, wearing the traditional pajamalike garb of Yoruba men, was gesturing in excitement.

"Ah! Do you know Jamaica? Me, I am Jamaican."

We listened to him as he told his curious tale. A man, he told us, calling himself *Mansfield Duncan* left his island for a place he knew of as his lost homeland. Duncan worked for years on the building of the Nigerian railroad and when his work ended, he decided not to return to Jamaica. He settled in the old Brazilian quarter of Lagos, married a Yoruba woman named *Comfort*, and raised seven children. Our current Mr. Duncan, grandson of the old Jamaican, seemed exceedingly proud of his hybrid heritage.

"And how is Kingston now?" he inquired fondly, carefully pronouncing the name of a city he probably only knew from his grandfather's stories.

I muddled over the paradox of it. Here I was in Africa, on an eager search to recover a lost heritage. And here a Nigerian man, proud to call himself *Duncan*, looked back with pride and nostalgia to a land and identity far outside his homeland.

As the men chatted I studied the faces around me, partially obscured by darkness. What kind of stories were locked away behind their eyes? The young woman with child who'd declined to share her seat with the lady in the slip. She sat staring out of the window with the child now sleeping in her lap. Her face was as round and innocent as an infant herself. A teenaged bride, I wondered? And where was her husband, her family?

An old woman with strong muscled arms, surrounded by bundles of yam, sat calmly chewing kola nut. A market woman returning home with wares unsold? A grandmother bringing gifts of food to a wedding feast?

The two young blue-jeaned men sitting ahead of us were collapsed against one another, snoring. Best friends traveling to a nearby city in search of adventure? Brothers from a broken home, on their annual trek to visit the father they seldom saw?

The woman in the slip, wedged between me and the window, sat hunched forward. Her eyes were reddened and weary, her brow crumpled in thought. What could possibly have happened this night to make her board a share-taxi to Ife in a black nylon slip? If only I had a key to unlock her secret story, her personal history. I had always wondered about the hidden secrets of people from other places. And here in the Africa I had come home to, I was ever the outsider. Still wandering and wondering.

I sighed and turned to watch the night outside. It was deep black velvet. A thick, impenetrable darkness, broken every now and then by the sight of a man walking along the road. A roadside village of thatch-roofed huts. The moon shining through a grove of trees. A river, twisting off into the distance.

And I wondered if I would ever really know the full fabric of African life, a fabric in which my own life was so intimately interwoven. Or would it always be night to me here, a night lit by tantalizing glimpses through windows that would always be closed to me? The thought was wearying. I leaned back upon the headrest.

"Tired, sister?" Kwesi put his arm around me. "Here, rest."

My head nested on Kwesi's shoulder, bumping along the road between Lagos and Ife in the darkness of night, I drifted into sleep.

I was jolted into wakefulness, mildly surprised to find myself on the floor of the halted *danfo*, someone's sandaled foot planted inches from my face. The vehicle and everything in it was tipped ominously to the right. I was not the only one who had fallen in the pitch darkness; other bodies littered the aisle. Someone's arm was flung across my back. There was a pregnant moment of silence, then a scream. All pandemonium broke loose. Kwesi leaned over and hoisted me up into his lap.

"Are you alright, Alma?"

"Yes, darling. I think so."

"Are you sure?"

I felt about my body. Nothing, save a mildly throbbing elbow, seemed out of the ordinary. But perhaps I was merely numb with shock. I listened uncomprehendingly to the voices shouting in shrill Yoruba around me.

"What happened?"

"I think an accident. We seem to have run off the road." It was the lady in the slip, whose presence I'd almost forgotten. Hers was the only calm voice among us. All the rest were shouting and scrambling, trying to pry open the jammed door.

Perhaps it was our ignorance which shielded us from panic. I wondered how the lady in the slip was able to exhibit such self-control. Something told me it might just be despair; the nonconcern of the uncaring.

We finally climbed from the vehicle. The other passengers had piled to the front, struggling to be the first ones off. We pried open the back door and climbed out, into the cricket-shrilled darkness. We stood along the roadside, barely able to decipher the movements of our fellows up front. The night's quiet shell was shattered with the aftereffects of the accident: shouts, tears, people running aimlessly to and fro.

"I think no one is hurt," the lady in the slip assured us. She seemed to have taken on the role of hostess, of simultaneous interpreter. "But they are quite upset. Our people can be emotional."

"So what happens now?" Kwesi asked, automatically accepting her new role.

"We wait."

I looked at the scene around us, my own panic starting to rise.

"Wait for what?"

The lady in the slip beckoned us to a fallen log.

"Please sit," she instructed, doing the same herself. "Either the accident will be repaired or help will come."

Kwesi seemed uncharacteristically impatient. He stood near our seating place, shifting nervously from one foot to the other. He began pacing.

"Let me see if I can't be of some use," he finally blurted out, and began striding toward a group of men who were flitting around, trying to upright the tilted van. Then he turned back. "Will you ladies be okay here by yourselves?"

Unconsciously, I turned toward the lady in the slip for the answer. She patted my hand.

"Yes. We will be fine."

Silence followed as we sat there, side by side. My handbag had somehow exited the van with me. I opened it and rummaged around, more for something to do with my hands than looking for anything inside it.

The shock of the situation must have affected my judgment. Grateful for her concern, it suddenly occurred to me that I might have something I could offer the lady in the slip. A long-handled Afro pick was tucked into a side pocket, and I had reached for it and handed it to her before I realized what I was doing.

The lady in the slip looked at the comb in my outstretched hand. She touched a hand quickly to her bristling hair. For the first time since I saw her, she smiled. A loud, harsh, heartbreaking laugh burst from her chest. A laugh that seemed dangerously close to a cry, seasons of sadness buried within it.

"I must look a madwoman," she rasped, taking the comb from my hand. "Thank you."

Her hair was long and thick, resistant to her efforts to tame it.

"Here, let me help," I offered.

The lady in the slip lowered herself to the ground, her head resting against my knee.

There is something magic about the touch of hand on head. I'd seen it time and again as a little girl in beauty shops. Hairdressers would lather shampoo through tangled locks, massage tired scalps. And with these ministrations secrets would be loosened. And flow forth free with the rinse of hot water. Disappointments at the way children have turned out, hurt at the hands of men, the blues of empty pockets and gray hairs growing.

I combed through the tangles, fashioning an awkward line of cornrowed plaits.

"Oh, my sister." The lady in the slip sighed. "No one has done this for me since I was a very small girl."

She leaned back her head, eyes closed in memory. My hands wove designs in her thick black hair. I twisted three strands in two hands, my free knuckles rubbing her scalp as I worked. Secrets loosened, and slowly, memories began to flow. The first thing I learned about the lady in the slip was her name: Olabisi Laoye Okeke.

Olabisi was a quiet child, for a time her father's favorite.

In the early days when her mother was young and her father had but one wife, Bisi would climb onto his lap in early evenings.

His room was placed directly in the center of their small compound. She came there after dinner had been served and eaten, and the sun was fading. The chickens cackled as they settled in for the night, like old women sharing a joke between them. And here, in the dying of day, her father told stories of people, both seen and unseen.

He told tales of the ancestors who rested on the roof, protecting them from the evil of errant, unhonored spirits who wandered the world in search of a home. He explained why weekly sacrifices were offered to those mothers and fathers who had moved on, but not away. He told her of the world of the gods . . .

Of Shango, the capricious ruler of lightning and thunder. His laughter licked the sky on rainy evenings. Of Ogun, god of iron. Who governed war and was patron of travelers who roamed the land, sea, and skies in vehicles made of metals. And of Osun, the goddess who lived in a nearby river. Who, when she was happy, would bless them with rain and children.

It became apparent after many rainy seasons came and went that her father's wife was not one so blessed. Bisi would be her mother's only child. For it was said that her mother was haunted by Obanje, a wicked spirit who loved birth but did not love life. Obanje entered pregnant women's bodies and came into the world as an infant. Only to die young and be born again. Obanje had claimed the lives of seven of Bisi's brothers and sisters.

And when her father took another wife no one was surprised. More wives meant more children, and a man's children were a blessing to his name. More than anything Bisi's father wanted a son. But Jumoke wouldn't give him one, anymore than Bisi's mother. Daughters followed, one, two, three. And those quiet times at sunset with her father ended.

The rains came again and again. Her father moved his two wives and four daughters to Ife. Bisi, who had gone to the Oshogbo mission school, was now enrolled in an all-girls' middle school. Her quiet village life retreated to memory. After living awhile in what her teachers told her was the birthplace of the Yoruba people, Bisi couldn't imagine why she'd ever been happy in that primitive village with mud huts and outdoor toilets. And where there was no Clara.

Bisi loved Clara with all of the loyalty of first friendship. But even Bisi had to admit that Clara Olufemi was an odd sort of child. She was thin, thin with legs like reeds. Her skin the color of peeled yam. She resembled more her mother, a tiny yellow-haired woman from a land called *England*, than her father. Mr. Olufemi spent most of his time in Lagos, working at his big job with the colonial government.

Mrs. Olufemi preferred to live in Ife where her husband would join them most weekends. She found the capital dirty and depressing. She loved the leisurely life of comfort and genteel society among the small European community in Ife. Where she and Clara could live like queen and princess.

But for some reason, perhaps at Mr. Olufemi's insistence, Clara was sent to study in the African middle school. Most of her classmates here avoided her company, scornfully referring to her as *oyimbo*, a black white girl.

But Bisi was not repelled. She was intrigued by the smooth texture of Clara's hair, the pale surfaces of her skin. She asked Clara how she had become that interesting shade of yellow. And Clara told her she was regularly polished, not unlike the hide of leather shoes. Bisi went home and told her mother that she too wished to be polished.

After classes Bisi would come home with Clara and become part of a strange world. A large pink colonial home at the end of the road, shaded by palm trees. A house with few family members and many servants. The housegirl gave them sweet and elegant things to eat. Sugar biscuits, tiny sandwiches, tea with milk and sugar. Clara would show Bisi her possessions sent by a grandmother from abroad. Dozens of dolls with soft bodies and porcelain heads. Dainty beribboned frocks. And more than anything else, books.

There were more books in the Olufemi house than Bisi had ever seen. Much more than in the library at school. High stacks of them lined the walls of Mr. Olufemi's study. Clara had her own library. Crisp pages with titles like *Oliver Twist* and *Wuthering Heights*. Lying across Clara's canopied bed, Bisi would dive into books. Devouring words like they were meat in her mother's *egusi* soup.

Bisi would only be able to read in snatches. Clara's mother did not allow her to lend her books out. And Clara herself would always become bored with Bisi's silences when books had her full attention. Clara was not overly fond of reading. She preferred to play pretend.

"What do you wish to be," Clara asked one day, combing long hair before her mirrored vanity, "when you are a big lady?"

Bisi thought about it. She had been reading from an exciting book, the biography of the great Dr. Livingston who had braved wild animals and unfriendly natives to bring the word of God to darkest Africa. She told Clara that she'd probably grow up to be a missionary. Or study at the medical school in Lagos and become a physician. Maybe both.

Clara turned her sharp little face to the side, considering.

"Hmmph!" She finally wrinkled her pointed nose in distaste. "You can have your stuffy old university. I want to become a mannequin and wear all those lovely, lovely frocks." The mother-of-pearl-handled brush hovered above her head. "Or an airline hostess."

Bisi went home that day and asked her father if girls could become doctors. He smiled indulgently as he'd done before.

"Why, of course they can. And you will be the best of them all."

Actually, Bisi's father had been rather preoccupied of late. He'd just taken a third wife and she was expecting a baby. Bisi rather liked Dayo, who was not that much older than herself. Her mother complained and disapproved of the friendship.

"This is my only child. Why must she do me as her father does? Why does she spend more time in that woman's room than she does with me? Does she make a better soup or sew a straighter seam?"

Dayo did neither. She was more like a playmate or an older sister. But Bisi had learned to sew from her mother, and also to prepare the palm nut soup and *eba* that her father loved. She taught Dayo all she knew.

After thirteen years of daughters, when a son was born to the household there was much rejoicing. Bisi's father named him *Babatunde*, for the dead father whose spirit he believed had climbed down from the rooftop and returned to reside in the house. Dayo's status as the favored wife was thus guaranteed. To the extreme resentment of her co-wives, she delivered twin sons three years later. Her husband presented her with a brand new sewing machine.

In her final year of middle school the eldest daughter of the household brought home her own bit of good news. She had passed her A levels with flying colors and won admission to Queen's College in Lagos. She rushed home, shining with luck. Her father was proud, but not exuberant.

"Bisi," he said gently, "I cannot afford to send you to Lagos. School fees for your younger sisters are high. I am still in debt for the naming ceremonies of your brothers. You are becoming a woman now. It is time you gave thought to marriage."

But Bisi resisted the stream of suitors her mother began to welcome into the household. She was much more interested in books than in boys. And she stubbornly set her vision on Queen's College. Throughout the rainy season she thought of nothing else.

Despite her dreams of becoming a high fashion model, Clara was bitterly complaining that her father was packing her straight off to the London School of Economics.

Bisi's father had plans for her as well. One day he told her to dress herself well and come to his room. When she arrived, head and body wrapped in her mother's best wax print, he said to her: "Olabisi, please greet your husband."

Sitting beside her father, his hand dipped in her mother's bowl of groundnut soup, was the rotund Moses Ologboni. A friend of her father's already with one wife and two children, one of them the same age as Bisi herself. His right hand was greasy with soup, so he pointed his elbow at her. Bisi shook it obediently and left the room as soon as she reasonably could.

Bisi had always been an industrious and frugal girl. The bit of sewing money she made helping her mother was never spent. One day in September of her sixteenth year, Bisi took the money from its hiding place, packed a small bag, and secretly boarded a share-taxi for Lagos.

Wedged between two very large women in the backseat, she saw very little of the scenery on this, her longest trip away from home. Clara had often spoken of the Jenkins family, American friends of her mother who lived in Lagos. Bisi found the Jenkins home in Ikoyi and managed to get on as a housegirl. Still determined to eventually make a way for herself to attend Queen's College one day.

Hope dwindled quickly. The hours of washing dishes, sweeping floors, and caring for the fat, pink Jenkins baby translated into pennies. She realized she could work a lifetime and still not have enough for school fees and books for even one year. Then the Jenkinses were suddenly transferred and Bisi was left with neither home nor job nor dreams.

And she was swallowed into the bowels of the city. Lagos was not a village community, like Ife had been, despite its size. Lagos was a place where people did not know you, and did not wish to know. And Bisi was just one of a thousand girls like herself who had come to the coast following dreams. Finding dust.

She had finally acquired the polish she long admired in the luster of Clara's skin. She obtained it from numerous jars of Venus de Milo bleaching cream. She had also found a job of sorts. Working nights as a desk girl at the Bellerest Hotel, a dark hole frequented by the numerous prostitutes of the Yaba area. Night after empty night Bisi collected two *naira* notes and handed out keys for an hour of bliss. Retrieved the keys and called the maidservant to turn sheets on rumpled beds. And handed out keys again.

At eighteen the fire had gone out of her eyes, but her body had belatedly blossomed, despite her meager daily rations of starchy *eba* and often as not blank, meatless soup to go with it. Venus de Milo had not polished all the pigment from her skin. Like flecks of brown on a ripe banana, stubborn dots of freckles still lingered across the bridge of her nose. And the freckles on her nose and the roundness of her cheeks and the fullness of her breasts would belie the emptiness of her eyes. Some men took them even as invitations.

And they would receive curses from the impatient girls they had picked up in the bar. Because it was Bisi they wanted, gleaming arms and lips dark like bruised peppers. Bisi of the brown freckles on polished gold.

Bisi resisted the tension that pulled at her. That would have her accept a few pennies more and walk the street with the disillusioned. But it was a tension that ever stretched and would have snapped. Had it not been for Chike.

Chike was a hardworking, poverty-stricken Ibo boy. He, too, had come to Lagos chasing dreams. Like Bisi, he had been more hungry than satisfied. Had been bruised and battered by the unending storm of urban life. But unlike Bisi, he had held up and held on. He was possessed of a thicker skin. He was of another people and accustomed to bucking the odds of being a stranger in a strange land. And he was a man.

Chike, after ten years, had begged and bribed enough influence to land a job as a bank clerk. And had finally been able to buy himself a motorbike. On late afternoons when his diploma course at the university was over he would ride past Yaba and notice a beautiful Yoruba girl waiting at Yaba bus stop. And offer her a ride.

Bisi was indifferent. Chike persistent. And one day she finally, grudgingly accepted a ride to her evening's work. One month later she allowed him to take her to an Indian film at the Metro. And some of the old glimmer returned to Bisi's eyes. And sometimes she laughed. She cooked bush rat and yam potage in her one room for Chike. And they ate from the same dish.

She wrote home to her father. Her mother answered. A dutiful Yoruba daughter does not keep company with an Ibo boy. She associates with none other than a boy of her own people, who has been selected with her mother's approval. And was this what Bisi had been doing *for two good years when we do not know if you are living or dead?* Moses Ologboni, her betrothed husband, was still willing to accept her. She should break all contact with *this stranger* and return home immediately.

Bisi cried for an hour, crumpled the angry letter, then determinedly sat down to sew up yards of yellow lace on a borrowed machine.

The wedding was a motorcycle ride in yellow lace to the registry in Ikoyi. And afterwards, Star beer and kebab for a handful of friends at the bar of the Bellerest. And marriage became cooking and keeping house in a two-room compound in the mud flats of Surulere.

It is always muddy here. I do not think this is a place where people were meant to walk. The ground holds on to rain much too long. It seems the very earth sucks at the feet, pulling you to it. I do not think it is a place people were meant to live. But it has been our home for fifteen years.

Fifteen years and my breasts, once firm, have fallen with childbirth and nursing. I am a seamstress of ladies' garments in *adire* cloth and native wax prints. And for those who have the money to pay, the delicate Brussels lace.

I take my bath this morning as every morning, a splash of cold water in the stone-floored ablution hut behind our compound. I scrub my skin with a sponge of dried fruit. I dry myself and wrap last night's sleeping cloth about me. And make ready to prepare the day for my family.

The beauty I once had has gone to seed. When I was young it ran wild like bush flowers. I had not the inclination to tend it. Now I have not the time. My life is not my own. It is for my family.

Four children so far the gods have given me. Four fine children with bright eyes and quick minds. The eldest is Funmilayo. Indeed *God has given me wealth* with this, my fourteen-year-old daughter. She is almost like a junior mother to the younger ones. And there are Taiwo and Keyhinde, the treasures. The twins. Had they been born in old Iboland would they have been smothered by the midwife at birth? Or taken to the bush to die alone?

I know among Chike's people that twins were once taken to be evil spirits. I know that when they were born Chike called in a medicine man for purification rites. But among my people it is not so. Yorubas believe twins are a cause for joy, a blessing of magic. Taiwo comes out first and calls behind for Keyhinde to follow. *Yes, my brother. The world is a sweet place and we must stay to chop.* The gods have smiled upon a man whose wife bears him twins. Women such as I are rewarded with the title *Iyabeji, mother of twins.*

And then there is Omalara, the third born. My jewel of two seasons has awakened early and waddles to me crying. She has been a difficult one to wean and still asks for the breast. Though she is getting heavy to be carried, I give her an orange to suck and tie her to my back. It is hard to concentrate when Lara is following one about, crying. And there is work to be done.

Before the father of my children rushes off in his motorcar to the white man's bank at Lagos Island, I serve him his morning meal of *dodo*, plantain which has been allowed to ripen, fried crisp in palm oil. And his porridge of ground cassava, sugar, and tinned milk.

I do not leave the room to eat with my children as I usually do. But hang back like a housegirl at the door. He eats and rustles the pages of the *Nigerian Tribune*. The sound of the talking drum signals that a voice on the radio will shortly read the news in nine Nigerian languages.

"May I have your ear, *Father of Funmi?*" I address him so. To speak his raw name to him is considered a sign of disrespect.

"Yes, woman. Speak."

My husband is impatient with the years that have made him fat and important, and with me; a simple housewoman. I fear that I am no longer good enough for the man. It is not that I do not understand how people grow apart. I do. We were apart from the beginning.

He has been a stranger here for twenty-five years. He will always be a stranger. He is of a people who have been made to feel less than. And so in turn, I am made to feel less than. I know this man better than he knows himself. I do understand. And weep for us both.

He has not lain with me for many months, since long before the birth of my youngest. My children squat in the kitchen. He sits alone at the table. With his newspapers and his glasses. Lines are carved deeply, like tears, around his eyes. And I can hardly summon the words to speak to this man frowning, father of Keyhinde and Taiwo. He who once ached to taste my lips. He who once begged to simply hold my hand.

My hands are hard now from work and water. They twist and wring like wash hung out in the wind. And I tell him what I've told him before. I beg him as he once begged me. Our eldest daughter will soon come to the end of middle school. Since the day she was nearly as small as Lara and learned to read even before her primary school, I knew this child would be the special one.

And did he remember, in those days when laughter was easy in the air, that he used to call her *Little Professor*? I wanted Funmi to go to higher school at Queens College, the school I had yearned to enter a lifetime ago. I wanted for her books stacked high, like those in Clara's library. And motorcars and money not only in her husband's name, but that she might claim.

I wanted for her fancy frocks from overseas. I wanted for my daughter a life of never having to look over her shoulder at lost dreams. I wanted these things for Funmi and for all my children. And the taste of it was like kola nut in my mouth.

And Chike tells me that which he has told me before. That the cost of living is high and money is dear. That higher education is wasted on a girl who will simply marry and become a mother. That Funmi should learn well her woman's work. To cook and keep house and sew, like her mother before her. To ready herself for marriage. He says this and rustles his pages in dismissal. He whose girl-friends, I've been told, ride to chop bar and nightclub in his motorcar, wearing fine dresses from abroad.

I leave the room choking on this bitter leaf. And go to my children in the kitchen. The twins have already eaten, and ready for school wear their khaki-green uniforms. They look like bright-eyed soldiers. I pick up my youngest to feed her, while my eldest stirs the pot. She looks at me with questions in her eyes.

"Do not worry, child," I tell her, though I worry for her. "We will find the money. Hurry now. Do not be late to school."

She is happy now, my childwoman slender as a young palm. She runs with her brothers, her school bags slapping against her side. Her laughter is like music. And I will not break my promise to her.

Chike is gone now. The sun crawls up the sky. With the other children at school, my youngest has joined her age mates nearby for play. And the sounds of morning settle like a familiar song.

I hurry through my woman's work. Sifting the *gari* for tonight's meal. Washing the clothes. Bending to sweep each grain of dust from the concrete floors.

When it is over I bring bundles of pink lace to my black iron machine. My shop is a shed near the road. And before I have finished my work, Flora Bankole has arrived for her fitting. Flora is my friend, a large lady who sells fortunes of decorated calabash and gaudy seed necklaces outside the Mainland Hotel. Flora is a widow woman and has grown so rich on the tourists of Lagos that she is paying for her son in university.

She takes off her shapeless top and *lappa* to try on the lace *boubou*. Pulling it around her body, I kneel with a mouthful of pins.

"Do not move so, Flora. These pins go chuke you."

Flora is impatient. She squirms, full of news.

"Make you finish quick, quick. I get big news for Mainland Hotel." And her eyes dart to me, like those of a lizard.

"Flora." I am weary with such stories. "I no want hear nothing at all about Chike, him women."

"Ah, ah. Make you hear-o!" And if I do not know Flora, no one does. Gossip bursts her cheeks like a mouse with a mouthful of okro seeds. It must come out.

"This time, Bisi, my eyes go drop for head. I tell you, I see 'am for Mainland Hotel in de broad daylight. Na yellow girl, like so." And she snaps her fingers for emphasis. "First time I think he be *oyimbo*, na white woman. Then I see 'am well, well. Small pickin like Funmi, na so he bi."

I dropped hands to my hips in disbelief.

"So now for Chike it is children. Are there not enough whores in Lagos?"

Flora is satisfied with my reaction. She goes on.

"Eh heh. Is de two of 'am, Chike and yellow girl. Come walka in de broad daylight. And dis yellow girl, eh! Wey kind dress he put on?"

Flora makes a motion across her overflowing bust to indicate a plunging neckline. The other hand pulls back her new *boubou* to demonstrate a skin-tight skirt. Closing her eyes and pursing her lips for effect, she prances delicately about the sewing shed. Swaying her huge hips.

"Na so he dey walka. In de broad daylight!" Suddenly she yelps and snatches her hand from the unfinished garment.

"Ai-ai-ay," she whimpers, shaking her hand. "Pin, he dey chuke me-o."

And when the pain is past she continues. Wags her finger in my face and lectures me like a mother.

"Bisi, this Ibo man dey make housegirl for you. Make you leave this bush boy, *ojare*. Make you leave 'am."

"Flora, no make *shakara*, now. Take off the dress." Flora's news is not new, nor is her admonition. I have heard it all before. "Me, I no care if Chike, him women be yellow, no black, no *oyimbo*. I give this man fifteen good years and I want something in return. I only care self for my children, them go get education. Na so. The dress be ready for tomorrow."

I ask Flora to take Omalara for a few hours. And they leave, small Lara waving to me from her perch on Flora's back. Then a shadow passes over the sun, swiftly turning the day gray. And I suddenly know my life will never be the same again.

I run to the kitchen. The secret is still there, a fat envelope buried under the charcoal pile. I count the worn notes, knowing full well that it is not enough. I return the money to its hiding place.

A garment is hidden in the small room stacked with sleeping mats where I and my children take our rest each night. It is a black nylon slip bought many months before Lara was conceived. But never worn. I wear it now. Over this I tie the soft wrapper of yellow lace, the one I married Chike in.

I remove the frayed cloth from my hair and undo the plaits. On the coal pot I heat a seldom-used stretching comb. I use it. My hair falls new, soft and straight against my face.

Beneath the threads and bobbins in an overflowing basket in my sewing shed I find three items. Over the years my skin has deepened to blend into the freckles that dusted my nose when I first met Chike. Before the mirror near the bed where Chike sleeps alone, I carefully smooth cream from the jar of Venus de Milo. I apply bright red color to my dark lips. Cheap English perfume to my wrists. I step back and look. I am ready now.

A strange woman with polished face, with lips wet and red like new blood, looks back at me from the mirror.

After the beginning it became a bit easier.

Bisi did not go to the Lagos Island and Ikoyi hotels frequented by foreign tourists and businessmen. No, it was the Yaba she once knew as home. The noisy palm-wine bars that rocked drunkenly from morning till morning. And the Bellerest Hotel was still the same. Dim and quiet. Ceiling fans creaking noisily over dingy beds. A sleepy, sullen girl would hand her the key.

It was not hard after the beginning, though sometimes she washed for an hour on returning home to muddy Surulere. Again and again she rubbed rough soap into her skin and watched the soft gray water settle into the drain. Her body was often tight and drawn before she was ready to slice the okro and pound the yam and soak the bitter leaf for her family's evening meal.

The sewing machine gathered dust, rats scurried in the corners of her shed.

Days crumbled by. Another *harmattan* season came. Dry choking winds blew down from the north. And Bisi walked the windblown streets. The Yaba dirt dried into a powder that was stirred up by wind and cars. The stench of things rotted and tossed into the gutter with the sweetness sucked out had an actual color that was flat and rust.

Bisi walked in the invisible code. African woman with no bag or load on head. And her occupation was obvious. They had to travel lightly. Prostitutes were favorite prey for thieves and pickpockets. Sweaty *naira* notes rested in the valley between her breasts or were tucked into the folds of her *lappa*.

Today business was not good. Bisi had haunted the Bellerest bar for hours and there were no takers. And that is when she began to walk. She walked, though she knew it would soon be time for her husband to be home.

She walked in the time between day and evening when things hang suspended in twilight air. A curious time when most of those with day business have made their way home and those who work the night have not yet surfaced. The market women at Yaba bus stop have gathered their dusty fruits, their oranges and cigarettes into baskets. Bottles full of the strong *ogogoro* gin people called *Kill Me Quick* were corked and added to the basket. And balanced on the women's heads. The end of day's work, the long journey home.

Dust blew like powdered blood in the narrow streets. It settled into the clothing of passersby, turning them a sweaty rust. Dry winds stiffened their lips. This land did not love water, did not hold rain into itself like swampy Surulere. When the rains came, waters ran off and into the overflowing gutters to be gone. But this was not the rainy season and there was no water to run. It was *harmattan*.

Bumping into, almost overturning Bisi, a young man darted by, adjusting his clothing. Behind him chased a screaming girl bare of foot and breast, *lappa* trailing like a banner in the wind. And all the laughing prostitutes and idle passersby joined in the chase.

"Come back, *ojare*! Make you pay-o!"

Bisi did not follow the procession. No money had been made this night and Funmi would soon complete her A levels. There was work to be done. Bisi stumbled on. She had heard there was much money to be made among the

Europeans and Americans who frequented the Shrine. But she had never gone there. A prostitute with a few principles left, she had not liked the idea of selling her body to the whites. This night it seemed not to matter. She walked in that direction.

A huge concrete flyway loomed overhead in the distance, designed to whisk motorists above the clogged Yaba streets. And the flyway had itself become clogged with *go-slow*. The concrete contraption like a huge honeycomb that people swarmed over and under.

Enterprising boys took advantage of the logjam of cars to hawk miscellaneous toys and plastic items, appliances that may or may not work. Motorists who bought took their chances, the buyer beware.

Graceful girls sold roasted groundnuts and cashews packed in whiskey bottles. And swayed in and out of traffic, dancing with death and calling for customers.

While beneath the shadow of the flyway was a shelter of sorts. Men with haggard faces settled into the dust of evening. Men with lines of the Sahel etched deep into their faces, *harmattan* in their spirits. The drought whistling like death's rattle, the starvation of cattle, the long trek to the cities of the south. They shooed away the occasional dog or rat which dared venture into this space they had made home. Shielded by concrete from stars and rain.

Wisps of rags that had once been turbans tattered about their heads. The men held on to babies that did not know how to cry. The women and children littered the flyway above and the streets beyond. Clinging to moving cars, hanging on to the arms of passersby.

"Dash me money," they begged, the only English they knew. And would point to their open mouths in the universal gesture of hunger.

They hung on until some soul a few pennies better off might toss a coin or two their way. Or entwined in their own troubles, might shake them off.

"Yellow beggars! Go away."

The girls and women were wrapped in black, silver bangles carelessly lining their arms. Some had become artful in the style of the wink and smile. They were learning a new nomadic culture, a living to be made in the hotels and palm-wine bars.

While the women and children begged and bartered, the men did not. Settled into the hollow hush of evening under the concrete sky, they gnawed withered meat or perhaps a bone. Five times a day prayers would pierce the air.

"Allah, most merciful. Bless this money given by the nonbelievers."

Bisi drifted past the concrete honeycomb, on toward her destination.

In the streets almost empty of people a purple sunset lit the western sky. The last dull gleam of sun shortening around the corner. She was moved by some invisible companion that whispered her on toward the Shrine. That playfully lifted the corners of her *lappa* as if to see what could be found underneath it. If you asked her what brought her to this place, Bisi would say it was *harmattan*.

And suddenly there was music in the air. Three kinds of African drums, European horns, and guitars which had been taught to sing another song. Bisi's sore soul was soothed by the far-off sounds. She followed the aural balm into the Shrine.

A settling darkness hugged a low ragged building with no roof. Music seeped languidly through the top to mingle with the stars.

> *If you call a woman African woman*
> *no go 'gree*
> *She go say,*
> *she go say I be lady-o . . .*

Bisi entered the Shrine and found it rich with night smells. Roasted chicken, spilt beer, the pungent burning of Indian hemp. A circle of moonlight poured through the roof and formed a makeshift dance space on the floor.

On the stage the man who called himself *high priest* was singing. A smooth brown man bending a horn like it was a bottle from which to pour libation. He stopped again to sing. Bisi took his words as invitation.

> *Call 'am for dance,*
> *she go dance lady dance . . .*
> *African woman go dance,*
> *she go dance the fire dance . . .*

Bisi entered the moonlit dance space. She danced the fire dance. She needed no partner because she danced with *harmattan*. Fire danced with wind, rapt in the music. She felt she was becoming the music. That her body was tuned and taut, rounded as the talking drum. That she was the horn the high priest played, bent like a curve of gold in his mouth.

> *She go say 'im equal to man.*
> *She go say 'im get power like man.*
> *She go say anything man do*
> *himself fit do.*

Those who watched her swore she was drunk, or drugged from the fumes of Indian hemp that wafted about the place. The women who leaned at the bar hissed at the antics of the intoxicated interloper who would *spoil we business*. But they could not know that the high priest's exorcism had metamorphosed her into music. Had filled her emptiness like a vessel. And when he sang:

> *She know 'im man na master.*
> *She go cook for 'im,*
> *She go do anything he say.*
> *But lady no be so . . .*
> *Lady na master.*

It only confirmed what Bisi had known long ago. She was not destined to be a lady, like Clara and her kind. She would always be an African woman. One who worked onto death, who carted heavy loads, and continuously went to the river to draw water. Who put shame aside and begged the family's bread when the man was too proud. Who lay back on the bed with opened legs. Who collected the payment only after the thing was done and the man was so inclined. Who would never be master, even of her own soul.

She had come to the Shrine aware of the possibility of free-spending white men. And so it did not surprise her when the pale man, husky in dusty *agbada*, stumbled onto the floor like one bewitched. She accepted the *naira* notes he sprayed her with as her due. As she did the thick arms went around her waist, leading her from the dance, up the stairs to a darkened room. But the music was still with her, playing around and through her. And she was the music. Until it stopped and the bubble burst above her head.

Bisi was snapped from the trance, sober and sound. Stretched out on a bare mattress. Her black slip damp with mingled sweat, clinging to her body. A ceiling fan creaked overhead, stirring the heat. She could hear the high priest start up another song. She could feel the vibrations of his band music through the floor and walls. The room's window looked out over the Shrine. And through it she could see tiny figures jumping like juju on the stage.

"*E lo ni-o?*"

Bisi hadn't expected a white man to ask her price in Yoruba. For the first time she really looked at him. And she could only stare in disbelief at the stocky man standing at the foot of the bed, fingering his fistful of money.

He calmly looked back with deep red eyes, his free hand rubbing himself with a threadbare towel. But this was no American or European white. He was a man completely without color. And Bisi was frightened both of the apparition, and the realization of what she had done.

A scream opened up as if it came from somewhere else, outside of herself. The albino pulled on his pants, tossed a few bills her way, and fled. Bisi could not stop screaming even as the ghost disappeared out of the door and a sea of people poured in. Irritated women with pinched faces in various stages of undress peered in and snapped their fingers in disgust. The men with them looked in, laughed, and left.

"Make you shut up-o!" someone yelled in.

But the scream echoed on an endless note, a treble C on the high priest's saxophone. She sat in the bed in her black slip and heard it issuing forth from her throat.

"Eh, eh. Why dis woman dey cry so?" A fair-skinned girl with hair like Clara's walked right in, examining Bisi in bold curiosity. "De thing, he no be good-o?"

Still another head poked in, a neatly trimmed male head with glasses on. And a hand caught the hand of the laughing girl, as if to pull her out. He glanced at the woman in the slip, screaming like a sacrificial goat upon the bed.

In three bounds Chike leaped across the room. Bisi stood up and the scream stopped, caught like a fishbone in her throat. His fingers fastened like a noose around her neck. He bounced her back onto the bed, striking her about the face and pouring out every epithet in the Ibo language. Bisi's hands flailed and struggled futilely. Men entered, trying to pull him off.

"Na madman. He go kill-o!"

His enraged, swollen face was finally lifted away. His fingers pried from her throat. Bisi gasped for strength and ran. The room, the stairs, the dance floor, the stage flashed by in fast motion. Out on the street, a *cabo-cabo* picked her up and the driver surely wondered at the woman in the slip, face bruised and anguished.

She ran into her compound. Hearing in her head the sound of Chike and his male relations storming down the street to beat her, to kill her. The unfaithful wife. She dug through the charcoal pile until her fingers ran blood. She found the envelope and crammed it into the bosom of her garment.

When she looked up her Funmi was standing in the doorway, horror driving sleep from her eyes. But Bisi knew that one day her daughter would understand. And she told her this before she fled.

The driver waited outside her sewing shed. She told him to take her to Agege. And she arrived just as a *danfo* for Ife was pulling off. She called for it to stop. She climbed inside.

She didn't know what awaited her at home in Ife. Was there still love for her in the heart of her father? A meal of *eba* and *egusi* soup at her mother's cooking fire? Or would she be a stranger there now, a bringer of disgrace to the household?

And as she drifted off into sleep she made a decision. This would be her last night as an African woman, hewer of wood and bearer of water. Somehow, home in Ife she would find a way to become a lady. Living her life to please herself. A lady who, as the high priest accused, would *take piece of meat before anybody*. And if she couldn't find this for herself, she knew that she would see to it that her daughters would have it. Whatever she had to do, Funmi and Lara would never know what it was to be another's housegirl.

I had finished. My skill surprised me. Concentric lines of cornrows circled Bisi's head, like the rings around whorls of wood.

We had all returned to rest in the uprighted van. Rains had come in the night. It was not a tropical downpour, but a fine spray that misted the windows of the quiet *danfo*. *Harmattan* was over. The rainy season had begun.

The lady in the slip rested on the floor of the van, her head pressed against my knees. Kwesi was sleeping too, his arm around me. I leaned my head against his chest and listened to the reassuring drumbeat of his heart.

It seemed that all the passengers were sharing this fellowship of slumber. The sound of snores and deep breathing echoed comfortingly through the vehicle. We could all have been a large family of brothers and sisters sharing the same bed.

Besides the driver and his companion smoking and talking low up front, I seemed to be the only one awake. No one else seemed to notice the tentative turn of the key, the whine of the starter. The engine coughed spasmodically, then caught. The van pulled out into the road, and we were off and running again.

I glanced down at the lady in the slip. She was sleeping, too. Sleeping and weeping. But despite the tears which slipped from her closed eyes, a transformation had taken place upon her face. Her face beneath the crown of cornrows had somehow changed. The strain was gone. I noticed an incongruous sprinkle of freckles scattered across her nose. And a small, faint smile upturned the corners of her lips. I couldn't put my finger on it, but she reminded me of someone.

My mother, maybe. A hard-working woman who had labored away most of her life. Being both mother and father to her children. Whose tightly drawn face dared to relax only in slumber. Or numerous other women I knew who had been given more burden than they could bear, but bore it still. Or perhaps myself. Fleeing a troubled past, rushing toward an uncertain future.

And finally I knew what made the lady in the slip smile through the tears. It was the faint, faded remnants of hope. It clung to her as tenacious as the dried dust, as tentative as the black nylon slip she wore.

I prayed that hope would not betray her. Because if an African woman could not go back home after two decades, what hope was there for one who had been away for two centuries?

To Those Who Come Behind Me

ILE-IFE, NIGERIA

ALMA

I've figured it out. If she were as long-lived as Big Momma, then my great-grandmother's great-grandmother would have left these shores some two hundred years ago. Would have been between fifteen and twenty years old when she was captured away across the ocean.

And I am still searching. I haven't yet found the way back to the river of her genealogy. But still I do my Langston Hughes against the landscape of Africa. *I wonder as I wander.* And now there is a faith which fuels it all.

There is a poetry in motion. I know that's a cliché, but please allow me just this one. The continually changing faces of the land and waters. The grasses that bend with the wind on the African savannah. The flickering candlelight along city roadsides at dusk.

The way men walk with men, and women with women. Unashamedly holding hands in fast friendship. The slow flow, or rapid surge of various rivers. *Niger. Volta. Gambia. Oshogbo.* The shine of moon upon water at the shrine of the river goddess in this holy place.

Kwesi seems to know someone nearly everywhere. He was able to engineer our entry into the shrine long after it had been closed to the public. It was past midnight when his friend let us in. We were warned to take neither pictures nor anything else away with us.

It's probably a personality disorder. I've been like this since birth. No sooner would someone tell me not to do something without giving me what I considered adequate explanation, than I would feel immediately compelled to go off and do the thing.

Oh, that's what happens when you shake up a bottle of seltzer? Well, why didn't they just say so? Do not use chlorine bleach. *Well, why not? . . . Oh, that's why not. They could have at least explained it.*

Hardheaded is what my mother called it. So consequently most of my lessons were bought ones, paid for dearly with hard knocks.

Of course I went and took a picture. It came out beautifully, by the way. Even in the dark without a flash, you could see the outline of a tranquil river in the moonlight, my offering a shadow upon its bank. I'm still waiting to see how I'll be punished for that particular sin. I think I've already received my comeuppance for the other transgression.

I picked something up during our quiet walk in the surrounding forest. A flattened, hairy pod I saw lying on the forest floor. I scooped it up and dropped it into my purse as a souvenir. I still have it now, afraid to touch it. Because soon after I first held the thing, the palm of my hand burned and stung so that it was painful to take a pen in hand and write these words.

Just call me Pandora. What spirits of evil did my willfulness let loose? Perhaps my punishment is simply silence. A failure of the displeased goddess to give answer to the question I came to her with.

And I began to fret.

"Kwesi, do you think it's the picture I took? Or the thing I picked up? I must have offended her spirit. I should go back and beg her forgiveness."

Kwesi shook his head in amused disbelief.

"Alma Peeples, you are certifiable. Come on, let's get back to Lagos. I've got the possibility of some work there. And you need a dose of reality. A nice, dirty, overcrowded city. A sane, rational university environment. You're taking this stuff altogether too seriously."

You do know that I was sent here? I came to the Mother of All Waters with offering in hand and question in heart. I haven't gotten my answer yet. I haven't found the river of my descent, the Place Where Blood Is Born. But the experience has compounded my faith.

My great-grandmother's great-grandmother was a saltwater woman. And somewhere within the lands and waters of West Africa, I know I will find the river of her genealogy. I just know it.

KWESI

Of course we were all kings and queens before we got ourselves kidnapped, never mind the fact that the kings and queens were the ones organizing the slave raids. And the ignorance cuts both ways. Some Ugandan chap in grad school wrote a long, convoluted paper trying to convince himself that Africans signed up for slavery on a voluntary basis. Guest workers, so to speak. Oh, the things we believe trying to make ourselves whole again.

Alma Peeples is no exception, bless her superstitious little soul. Now, the withered old thing looks just like a bullwhip to me. Probably a piece some enterprising slave snipped from the driver's cat-o'-nine, just to lessen the sting. But she swears up and down that great-grandma's trade beads are strung on a lion's tail. A lion's tail! How does she prove it? Some family fairy tale she refuses to challenge.

It may just as well be a tiger's tail, let alone the fact that tigers are not native to Africa. You see, I've met the tiger and her name is Alma. I've got a feisty little she-cat by the ninth tail, and she's dragging me along on a wild-goose chase. Wandering all over West Africa, hot on the trail of myth and superstition.

We made it into Ile-Ife after a particularly hellacious journey. I'll never ride another *danfo* again, if I can help it. It was a stroke of good luck finding Femi teaching here at the university, and getting him to let us into the shrine.

Of course, we had to endure his rambling lecture *cum* prayer immediately afterwards.

He's a peculiar kind of brother, always has been since our days at Cambridge. A complex blend of African superstition and western pragmatism. He thinks nothing about bending tradition, but has to turn around and ask the ancestors' forgiveness when he does so.

I don't go in for all this supernatural mumbo jumbo myself. But there's a strange kind of déjà vu being with Alma here in Africa. She's a woman no less wild and adventurous than myself, always happy to follow me on my wanderings, and to lead me on some of her own.

And there's something about her that reminds me of someone or something I just can't place. Is it the smoothness of her, her skin like a ripe papaya? Her eyes as black and gleaming as papaya seeds? The smile that turns up the corners of her full, dark lips? The sweetness of her pussy? Lord knows, that's some powerful poontang.

It is amazing how easily I let myself become derailed by this woman. Even before we'd slept together, I found myself caught up in the aura of her. One moment I am footloose and fancy-free, roaming through Africa on a wing and a prayer. The next moment I'm firmly attached.

She's the type Africans call a *mammy water*. The Greeks had them too, though they knew them as sirens, those water nymphs who set sailors off course with their otherworldly song. It gets in your mind, under your skin, into your blood, and you just can't shake it loose.

Sometimes I think I'm just as daft as she is, traipsing around West Africa searching for some mysterious ancestor who may never have existed. Oh, well. Who was it that said it's not the destination, but the journey? Somebody else said it even better: *He who rides the tigress fears to dismount.*

LAGOS, NIGERIA

ALMA

"Water, water everywhere," so said the ancient mariner.

And I can understand how a body could be overwhelmed by the sight of so much water. I am by no means ancient, nor a mariner myself. But I have seen the Atlantic, albeit from the air. I have traversed the Niger several times. Visited the holy sanctuary of a sacred river said to be the temple of Yemanja, the Mother of All Waters. And now it is lakes.

I am told that *Lagos* is Portuguese for lakes. And this city is full of them, not lakes actually but lagoons. Some of them are saltwater inlets of ocean. Others are freshwater haunts of fishermen, like the one Kwesi and I have discovered. The narrow beach is tucked away within the campus of the university and completely deserted, save the transparent jellyfish which wash ashore from time to time.

We have not had each other in two weeks. I had not realized how keenly I would miss the closeness of Kwesi's body next to mine. Not just the act, you know.

There is something even more intimate than sex which comes from sleeping together. The ways in which two bodies meet in slumber, cupped or curled around each other. The way two heartbeats find the same rhythm. The clicking of his pocket watch echoing the rattle of my story beads. And I do swear that in sleeping head to head, you dream each other's dreams.

Kwesi has hunted up some kind of hustle here at the University of Lagos. He's teaching part-time, and assisting in the editing of a new journal of African arts. A very exciting project, from what I have been able to ascertain. But our living arrangements are not.

We have been staying in spartan student quarters at the university, strictly segregated by sex. It feels strange being back on campus after more than a decade, sharing rooms and showers with other women. Exchanging deodorant and nail polish and late-night camaraderie. Not altogether unpleasant. But I do miss the closeness of nights with Kwesi.

So we have been prowling the campus, searching for a quiet spot where we can be alone. And have stumbled upon this little strip of beach upon a lagoon. May I be blunt with you for a moment? When the surroundings are right there is little need for foreplay.

Find this spot for yourself, somewhere in a far corner of the compound of the campus of the University of Lagos. Come upon it just at the time of twilight when the sun and moon share the same sky.

And let there be the sound of drums in the far-off distance. And arrange it so that just before loving, you catch sight of a fisherman riding his craft. He flings out his nets, they hover briefly above water like a low-flung constellation before settling into the element. And the wind will be a bit balmy, puffing the remnants of day into night. And see if you aren't both as ready as we were for each other.

Making offerings by rivers. Crossing over oceans. Loving by lagoons. So much water and so much confusion. Because Big Momma had been told in dream to follow a certain river to the Place Where Blood Is Born.

How will I ever know which way of water is the one to follow?

KWESI

I hadn't planned on coming back to Lagos so soon. It's not exactly my favorite city in West Africa, but how does a man say no when his pockets are empty and there's a little money to be made? Taking over Ahmadu's African lit class at Unilag while he's honeymooning in London with his British bride, means there'll be a little something in the kitty to send us on along to our next destination.

What is this thing we've got about getting it on down by the waterside? Maybe it's because of that first time down at Labadi Beach.

It started out innocently enough. She was showing me some kind of acrobatic move at the lagoon, bent over backwards on her hands and feet, her body arched in the air. The wind blew up her skirts to reveal those *beads of water* on the alleged lion's tail, coiled like a blue river around her waist. And before I knew it, without so much as a hug or a kiss, I was entering her.

When it was over, I wanted to beg forgiveness for taking her that way, but when she looked up and smiled that luminous smile of hers, I knew it wasn't necessary.

Watch out, Kwesi, my man. Not only do you have a tiger by the tail. Looks like you got a mammy water in your blood.

YAOUNDÉ, CAMEROON

ALMA

Did you know there are tidal rivers which change their nature from fresh water in the flow, to salt water in the ebb? Did you know that some Africans here believe that drinking small amounts of ocean is medicinal? Did you know that when newborn babies cry, it is often without tears?

Here in Cameroon I have seen my first African mountains.

I have been to the top of one and gazed upon a tranquil valley below, set between this range and the next. The lush greenness surrounding a volcanic lake in the nearly hidden valley below is so beautiful that the truth is hard to believe.

That the devastation of death and breathtaking beauty are sometimes brothers. That beneath this lake's tranquil surface the volcano's spirit still rumbles. And periodically emerges to spew the countryside with a poison more powerful than napalm. A sulfuric gas that only five years before killed nearly every man, woman, child, and animal in the village. All save an infant whose very crying expelled the poison from its lungs and saved its life.

The horror story haunts me for days. Maybe this is what has gotten me so jittery. My nerves seem oddly on edge these days. I've become a walking accident waiting to happen. Incompetent with clumsiness.

We are here in the French-speaking capital, where Kwesi is doing odd work for, can you believe this? The International Girl Scouts Organization. The man is a nomad and he takes his harvest wherever he finds it.

But I was telling you about this sudden, disconcerting attack of butterfingers. Elisa, the Anglophone Cameroonian woman with whom we are boarding, has taken to calling me *Dropping Things*. It usually happens at mealtimes. I have destroyed so many of her dishes and glasses it is shameful. At this rate we'll leave Yaoundé next week deeply in debt.

The open-armed, full-hearted hospitality of Africa sometimes embarrasses me. I feel uncomfortable being waited upon hand and foot as a guest in another woman's home. Elisa is going to the office to work every day, as is Kwesi. And I sit around idle, carefully instructed to lift my finger in no household task. I feel like Minnie the Moocher. And I tell Elisa so.

"Fine," she answers, retiring to her room to read. "You will prepare the evening meal."

Now I have never been the best of cooks. I think it's an act of rebellion from childhood. I cooked for the whole family from the age of eight onward. The task was always an intrusion when I wanted to be off in a library reading, or at the kitchen table writing something down. In fact, almost anything was preferable to tending hot pots. And as soon as I went away to college and didn't have to do it anymore I deliberately lost the knack of cooking.

And now a slave to western labor-saving devices, I have burned my meals with the best of them. Aided by gas stoves, food processors, and microwave ovens. What can I possibly do in Elisa's kitchen with a strange one-burner stove hooked up to a bottle of propane?

I decided to keep it simple. Fried plantain and eggs. I peel the plantain, careful to scrape away the tough inner fiber I have heard can be toxic. I slice it into uniform circles. And wonder of wonders! I am able to figure out how to operate the stove without asking for instructions. I heat up a pan of palm oil and fry the plantain perfectly. Perfectly! Crisp and lightly brown around the edges, without burning.

I crack open ten or twelve guinea fowl eggs, just the right number for three people. They are tiny, brown-flecked things I can never get used to after the almost obscene ovalescence of the American supermarket variety. I whip them up frothy and add to them hot peppers which sting my fingers as I mince them. The chopped bits of tomato stain the mixture with curious bloody streaks.

I reheat the oil in which the plantain was fried. The eggs are scrambled adequately, thick and yellow, still with those bloody streaks. But looking delicious and smelling like heaven. I turn off the burner and turn to slice a loaf of the French bread on the table. French bread, mind you, baked by a real Frenchman. There are plenty of Europeans living in Yaoundé, almost as many as in Abidjan. And they seem to have brought along all the comforts of home.

As I stretch for the bread I hear an ominous crashing behind me. And I turn to see my carefully prepared pan of eggs, steaming up-ended on the floor. Elisa had appeared in the door, book in hand. Almost gloating. *I knew I could never trust an American woman alone in my kitchen,* her smug smile seems to say.

"What now, *Dropping Things?*"

And I can only shrug my helplessness.

"I don't know what happened. The pan just slid off the burner. At least nothing seems to be broken."

Except a near-dozen guinea fowl eggs. You make an omelet, you break some eggs, right?

Elisa helps me to salvage the top layer of eggs, untouched by floor. We stoop over the spill with spoons and plates.

"You know," Elisa tells me. "If I were from the villages and superstitious I'd tell you why you are always dropping food."

"Why?" I throw my hands open to the air. "Tell me, so I can figure how to stop doing it."

"That your ancestors were hungry and wanted to be fed. That's what I'd believe if I were a superstitious woman from the villages."

Elisa was of a new breed of African woman. College-educated, urban-dwelling, living on her own in a city without family. I didn't know if she was superstitious or not. But I had enough of it for both of us. And as I threw the discarded eggs to the cannibal chickens who clucked at the back, I thought of one particular ancestor squatting by strangers' doors, gaunt with famine.

Here in the vastness of West Africa, of mountains and deserts and rivers and savannah, how would I ever find my way to her. So that her hungry spirit might be fed?

AMA KRAH

It is not clumsiness which has unsettled you, my dear. It is something more, much more. A mixed blessing which will reveal itself in due course.

No longer do we wait by strangers' doors. On the contrary, we are nourished by your faith and devotion. By the food you prepare and the liquids you pour. We are remembered ones, the blood in your veins and the memories in your soul. We are stirring inside you, blooming into the birth of something new.

You are moving home toward us, sweet daughter. Winding toward the source of sweetwater.

And soon we will hunger no more.

IN AIR, EN ROUTE FROM YAOUNDÉ, CAMEROON, TO ACCRA, GHANA

KWESI

You know the thing that makes me so impatient with Alma Peeples? It's her acquired superstitions.

This isn't a woman who grew up steeped in voodoo and ancestor worship. She ain't no New Orleans Creole or Caribbean animist. She's a missionary Baptist from the West Side of Chicago, for Christ's sake. A sensible, sane, educated woman who has been out and about in the world.

So why does she come to Africa and suddenly begin to embrace the possibility of some nebulous other reality? What is this desperate need to trace her African roots? What will she do with the information when, and if, she finds it? We were just discussing it here on the plane.

"You know that you are of Africa. Why this desperate determination to connect to a particular place, when you can claim the whole continent? What difference does it make what village one of your ancestors hailed from?"

"But these story beads, Kwesi. They are my connection to something particular. They were brought to America by my great-grandmother's great-grandmother. Probably worn on the slave ship that brought her over. I know that she came from somewhere here in West Africa. And I need to know her story."

"But what about your other ancestors? Those of Africa, and those of other places? Don't you want to know their stories, too?"

"I can't go chasing every star in the sky. I've got to follow this one."

I guess I'm just as bad as she, in the end analysis. I try to reason her out of this wild-goose chase, yet I'm all too willing to lead her on it.

She says it's an unspoken promise she made her great-grandmother on her deathbed. I guess it is the kind of faith that cannot be measured by reason, this determination to find the River Where Blood Is Born, or to die trying.

ACCRA, GHANA

ALMA

I think Trevor is out of my system now. I'm going to say this one last thing about him and hope I won't have to mention his name again.

Having been the first man I loved, and having loved him for such a very long time, he had become the standard against which all subsequent lovers were judged. His height, his size, his eyes, his intellect. His style in bed. I unconsciously measured all my men against him and usually found them wanting. Until Kwesi. Because Kwesi is so entirely opposite, and so much his own man.

Do you remember Aretha's infamous lovesick love song? The one where her voice sounds like a celestial flute? I clasped each lyric to my heart, went around the apartment crooning so much my mother would have to hush me up.

"I never heard of such silliness. The man ain't never gonna come back with all that moaning and crying."

Mama was married to Otis. What did she know? This was how true love was supposed to be. Loving past the heartbreak, past the ignored phone calls and attempted flight. Swallowing your pride and begging. Waiting and wailing in a plaintive soprano, tapping on his windowpane like a prowler or a poltergeist.

I've always liked me a good love song. But music can sometimes be a dangerous thing. Most of those songs are all wrong. Teaching us to feel the wrong ways about each other. To be cool when we should be hot. Foolish when we should be wise. They will have you thinking that loving is supposed to hurt. That men are to be worshiped and women to be mastered.

Loving doesn't hurt with Kwesi. It is easy to know him, easy to love him. He is not like Trevor at all. He's not stylish, nor terribly tall. In fact he's exactly my height, maybe even an inch shorter. Forever fiddling with a pocket watch so ancient I'm surprised it still keeps time. He wears horn-rimmed glasses and carries that pocket watch, like somebody's absentminded professor.

He is a man who asks more questions than he gives answers. Who has not Trevor's studied style in bed, but who comes to me eager, sometimes clumsy, with tenderness. And whose vulnerability lies just beneath the surface of his skin.

I sense in him a person who has been hurt, perhaps badly. But who still is not afraid to love. And that is what I love so much about him.

KWESI

One of the first things I noticed when I came to Africa was the night-soil man. A funky wretch with his face covered by a dirty rag, walking through the streets with a bucket of human waste balanced on his head. Too low to even speak to his fellow man or woman, he'd beat the bucket like a gong, warning people out of his way. I always wondered where the night-soil man went to dispose of his burden. Never did find that out.

In one of his songs, Fela Anikulapo Kuti claims this is not a traditional custom. According to him, Africa's systematic downfall can be traced to the acquired habit of carrying shit. A practice introduced by . . . who else? The White Man. Sometimes I wonder if the boy deserves all the credit we give him. Just because he brought us the bucket, does that mean we had to shit in it?

Quiet as it's kept, I feel like I'm going through Africa carrying my own bucket of shame. The shit is not just on my head, it's in it. My own private shit pile sent me running all the way to Africa. That's the thing about shit, though. You can run, but you can't hide. It always catches up with you.

Actually, it goes back much further than that. It started with chicken shit. Grew up wild as a weed in the streets of Watts. Father gone, left nothing but a beat-up old pocket watch to remember him by. Mom working around the clock to keep the wolf from the door, doing the best she knew how. The TV set and comic books got me through childhood. Then I hit my teens, the streets called, and I answered. Gangs became the family I never had, the father I never knew.

One day I went to stick up a rich-looking Black lady. She moved like a movie star in her fur coat and high heels, climbing into a ruby-red Jaguar convertible that matched her lipstick. She took one look at me, shook her head, wagged a finger in my face, and said:

"You're better than this, boy. You know that, don't you?"

She sat me down in her front seat and gave me a lecture I never forgot. Spoke of possibilities that a little thug like me might actually have a future. Mentioned higher learning, gainful employment, things I'd never considered in my limited existence. She wrote down her name and number, pressed it into my hand.

"When you're ready to give up the streets, give me a call."

And she kissed me, that fancy Black lady. Kissed me, a dirty little street urchin who had meant her nothing but harm. Leaned over, kissed my cheek, and shooed me out of her Jaguar.

The telephone call led to a job, a diddly do-nothing gig, but at least it wasn't mugging people. Odd-jobbing and running errands at the Metropolitan Opera House, where Grace occasionally sang bit roles in a trilling, three-octave mezzo-soprano to standing ovations.

But Grace wasn't happy there. She complained that all the plums went to less deserving white singers. She was constantly threatening to jump ship in Europe, where her dusky countenance and musical genius would be appreciated.

The Opera House gig led me to junior college, a brief stint in the military, more college, some travel, during which time I lost touch with Grace. We crossed paths again in England where I was in grad school, and she was living with an Italian tenor who publicly referred to her as *negrita mia*.

I promptly fell back in love with Luigi's *little negress*. I was so flattered when she left him, I quit Cambridge to follow her around Europe like a lap dog. And she treated me like one, too. Kept me on a short leash, occasionally patting my head, tossing me a bone, a few francs or lira or deutsche marks. A little scrap of pussy when she felt like it. Grace had me hypnotized with my daddy's own pocket watch, I'm convinced of that. Dangled the thing in front of my eyes and whispered.

"You are in my power. Your eyelids are heavy. You are getting sleepy . . . sleepy . . ."

I sleepwalked for years while she cavorted openly with other men and the occasional woman. In those rare moments of backbone when I attempted to shake off the spell and confront her faithlessness, she never failed to remind me she *had picked me up out of the gutter*. When I finally got the balls to leave, that is where she predicted I'd end up again.

Off I went to Africa pussy-whipped, tail between my legs, shit balanced on my head. A sinner saved by Grace, dogged by disgrace. And here I find myself playing the tour guide on somebody else's desperate search for identity. A sheer case of the blind leading the blind.

Still, you never know what you'll find when you're looking for something else. It's ironic what the shadowy search for Alma's ancestor accidentally turned up. My lost dick! Been wandering through Africa a dickless wonder, figuring I'd left my johnson behind when I went scurrying out of Europe. That it was missing in action, added to Grace's collection of broken hearts and other body parts.

But then I looked at my mammy water that night in Accra, glowing in the moonlight of Labadi Beach. Eureka! Suddenly my missing manhood jumped back in my pants. Thanks to you, Alma Peeples,

I got my mojo working now
and I'm going to try it out on you

And maybe even one day, with your help, I'll get up the nerve to:

. . . lay my burden down
down by the riverside
and carry shit no more.

LEGON, GHANA

ALMA

The river spirit has finally seen fit to answer me. Not the answer to the question I've been seeking, but an answer all the same. When I was first sent to the Mother of All Waters I didn't realize this same spirit was a goddess of fertility.

You know they say that one member of every family will turn out to be barren? I always figured I was one of them. I've been sexually active for something like sixteen years now. And for much of that time, I never bothered to use anything. And never got pregnant.

Not until now. I come to Africa looking for my roots and wind up growing branches. Don't you just love the poetic irony? It is entirely unexpected and a bit of a problem.

Telling Kwesi won't be the problem. The problem will be knowing whom to tell. I did say I wouldn't mention Trevor's name again, but this changes things, doesn't it?

But then, that is not for you to worry about. You have much bigger and harder questions in your time, I am sure. You have an earth to save and worldwide wounds to heal. The fractured legacy we have left you to mend. Let me not add to that burden more than you can bear.

Surely you will want to know why I am here. In a suburb of a modern city on the West African coast. Wearing a worn cotton blouse and *lappa* that feel good against my skin. Sitting beneath the generous shade of a mango tree. Holding this pen and page, pausing only to swat flies or simply think about what it is I want to say to you.

Do you know that in this home of Kwesi's friends, who are musicians and batik artists, one of the women knew of you before I did? She smiled at me and patted my flat belly.

"You de get picken."

I asked her what made her think I was with child. I showed no signs of it, save missed periods in a cycle that was never very regular. I was in fact thinner than I had ever been. And I wanted to know how she knew.

"Some of us," she said, smiling. "We can smell it."

What is the scent of fecundity? Is it something you could smell yourself, curled there within the waiting place? Is it rich like ripening fruit? Or loamy, like the delta soil which rises out of rivers?

I feel myself balanced at the apex of a pyramid whose base is buried in centuries of sand. And a wind has just come to blow the years away. Or perhaps I am in the midleaf of a thick book. The years unfolding both behind and before me. And I in the middle of a story I know neither the beginning nor ending to.

Did she, the one I seek, ever wonder as I do? About her future. Who and what her generations would be. Would her descendants live to shame or glorify her name? And who exactly was this first mother? How far do you go back before all humankind is linked? And how did Eve, if you believe in her, learn to mother when she was not mothered?

What would it have been had the seed never left these shores? What would I have been had my branches grown and spread out only on this side of the Atlantic? Would I have been the same person? Had the same urge to write and roam, to collect stories and string them into beads? Would I have had the wherewithal to do so?

But it is useless speculating this way. Because I am who I am and you will be who you are. You, the ones who come behind me. The one within me waiting and the ones waiting within her. Or him. My generations spread out beyond me. The base of the pyramid which holds me up.

The time will come when you will hunger as I have hungered, for a sign that reassures you there is some link between you and your past. And I will be your past. So what I wish to say to you is this.

Listen to the click of your story beads. Know that there is drumbeat in your blood, and know too the source of this drumbeat. Know that blood comes before birth and also after death. Blood is the living lifeline, the river that connects us.

Your heartbeat is river music, dear ones of my blood. Keep your ear tuned to the pulse of it.

Beadwork

I know delaying tactics when I see them. Just when the end is in sight, the spider would stir up sediment to cloud the waters.

As spiritual mothers of the clan, we are always pleased to welcome a new child into our midst. But honestly, the timing here could not be worse. How will our daughter find her way back to the River Where Blood Is Born with pregnancy slowing her steps and romance clouding her mind?

Of course, we all know why Kwaku Ananse weaves his web in the path of progress. It is fear, plain and simple. He is reluctant to see this project end, in apprehension that his work will not hold up in the cold light of day. That flaws and mistakes may be found in the cloth he's been weaving for the past two hundred years.

Ananse suggests that their long sojourn in the New World ill prepares our daughters to face the challenges of the Old. Perhaps there is truth in this observation. Perhaps.

But consider this. They are not the only ones who've been transformed by their journey. Could Ananse be more worried about his own readjustment?

This trickster of a spider has grown quite accustomed to the fast life, bright lights, and relative plenty of the Western world. Does he really feel at home in modern Africa, with all its turmoils and travails? Can it be he hopes to entice them back?

We shall see. We indeed shall see.

In US

I look quite the odd duck waddling about Kumasi. That is precisely why I try to do as little as possible. But I can't stay indoors all the time, as much as I would like to.

So I shuffle along with both arms cradling my belly like an inflated beachball. The streets are crowded and I'm often filled with the irrational fear that some passerby will accidentally elbow me in the stomach.

The market smells I used to find so intriguing have suddenly become nauseating. I have been back in Ghana now for nearly one month; I have been with child somewhere around seven. And I cannot wait for this baby to be born.

I often find myself peevishly wondering why I should be going through this alone. I need someone to lean on, someone to run out and buy the odd items I crave in the middle of the night.

But then I must remember that being on my own was a choice I made. However much I hobble alone, I am hobbling with my pride intact. It was destined to end, after all. Isn't it always better to leave than to be the one who is left?

Still, it's hard not to feel sorry for myself. Not that it's really me shambling around in the too-small dress. Somewhere inside is my old self; the slim, independent, unpregnant Alma. She shakes her head sadly at this imposter who's replaced her; the rotund and bloated, slow-moving creature she's become. *Here's another fine mess you've gotten us in.*

I could have known that being in Africa on my own would be difficult. But in Africa alone, and pregnant, too. It's more than a notion. My funds are running short, my clothes are straining at the seams, and I find myself walking everywhere in an effort to save a few *cedis*. The heat is hard to take, as are the long waits at the maternal health center. I am beginning to see how difficult life is for an African woman.

Just walking through the marketplace is a major undertaking, let alone bargaining to buy something. That's why I decided to go to one of the shops. The price for a length of cloth would be higher, but the experience less stressful than negotiating the jumble of Central Market. And I must have some new clothing made before I burst out of these.

The place was empty and the shop girl rushed over to assist me.

"Yes, madam. What do you need?"

I leaned tiredly against the case displaying African prints and imported fabrics.

"I need about ten yards of fabric for maternity dresses. Plain white cotton, the cheapest you have."

The girl, a young woman of about eighteen, suddenly smiled and ducked her knee in a curtsy.

"Oh, madam. You are from US. I am happy to know you."

I waited patiently for the request that usually came with such a greeting. A letter to be carried out and delivered to a loved one living abroad. My help in obtaining a visitor's visa. An offer to buy my American dollars on the illegal currency market. The young woman whipped out a pad and paper, wrote something down, and gave it to me.

Miss Elizabeth Osei Esubonteng
c/o Kwabena Akosa, Esquire
Chief Purchasing Officer
Cocoa Marketing Board
P.O. Box 327
Ashanti, Kumasi
Ghana

"I want to be your pen pal," Elizabeth said eagerly. "I want to write to you when you are in US."

I scribbled my Chicago address on the pad she handed me.

"I'm visiting Ghana now," I warned. "I don't know when I'll be back in the States to answer your letters. Why don't I give you my Accra address, too?"

Miss Elizabeth smiled and shook her head firmly.

"Oh, no. I prefer to write to you in US, please."

I shrugged, irritated at the girl's obvious infatuation with the land of my birth. Maybe it was a projection of my own guilt. Now and again I found myself surreptitiously longing for the conveniences, the creature comforts, the relative ease of life in a place I once called home. Twinges of secret nostalgia for TV and Häagen Dazs. Twitches of impatience with the idiosyncrasies of African life.

Though I had sworn not to leave until I had traced the river of my descent, I'd lately been toying with the thought of returning to Chicago just long enough to have the baby and make some money to finance an extended return. Some reorganization was in order. Especially since I was now alone, without Kwesi.

This is not the first time I've been out on my own in the world. And it's still the same. The knowledge of it slaps me in the face. It is not easy for a woman to move alone. There are doors which slam shut the minute I approach. Not just because I am alone, and I am a woman. But because I am both, and a stranger here.

At Kwesi's side I could go practically anywhere, anytime. To the hotel bar if I had a taste for a beer at two o'clock in the morning. For a walk along the beach at midnight. We could wander as a couple into a nightclub anytime to hear live high life, no questions asked. Or Kwesi could easily enter alone. But just let me come walking in there by myself.

Now that I was alone in Africa my movements were circumscribed. I was suddenly conscious of the curious stares whenever I ventured out. The occasional warnings from other women. Who had accommodated their own lives to the stricture that the only women free to wander openly were prostitutes and market women.

"For a woman in your way, it doesn't look too okay to be alone out here." They'd stare at my belly and frown disapprovingly.

And that was the thing about Africa. The longer I knew her, the more I loved her. And could also begin to see her faults. She was a loving mother, but at times an intolerant one. And there was a troublesome tendency in her to let some of her children stray into the reaches of the outcast; those whose peculiarities did not fit the norm.

Kwesi, who often found himself on the perimeter of the outcast circles, explained that Africa did not worship rugged individualism, but embraced the collective. And was willing to sacrifice the stray leper for the overall good.

But it seemed to me that the leper colonies were growing. Africa's people were in a state of change, her children becoming dispossessed in greater numbers. And haggardly drifting to other lands in an attempt to satisfy their hungering spirits. It was not because they did not love Africa. It was because they felt themselves exiles in the land of their birth.

The honeymoon was over for me here in Africa. I had given up any romantic illusions I may once have had about *The Motherland*. But I was still in love. And determined to make the marriage work. I was in a different condition of life now. It was a state of being, like pregnancy. I would never be the same again.

Even if I returned, I could never be completely in US again. I was in the *us* of Africa now, an Africa I claimed as my natural mother even though I had been adopted out at birth. I might well return to an uneasy truce with the orphanage America. But I would always be with Africa in spirit. I was a changing woman.

Even as I chafed against the strictures, I found a certain serenity settling upon me. I missed Kwesi badly. But I made peace with my loneliness. I was no longer afraid to be alone, and the knowledge was liberating. I realized that however difficult, this was something I could manage. Kwesi had made it easier for me here in Africa, but his absence didn't make it impossible for me to function.

I was becoming stronger. Learning how to negotiate my own way in the African world. I did not yet feel completely at home. But I was becoming less of a stranger. During the months we were together I had become overly dependent on Kwesi's companionship. Like an infant whose only view of the world is from the safety of the mother's back. It is a warped perspective. Only when the child climbs down and walks on two feet can she say she knows the world.

Yet an odd kind of camaraderie linked us; like brother and sister, or an old married couple. Sometimes we'd find ourselves completing each other's sentences. Sometimes I'd be hit by an overwhelming sense of déjà vu, as if we'd been through this journey before.

Our individual lives seemed to have run on a parallel course long before we'd met. Humble origins, big-city upbringing. We'd both studied in New England universities around the same time; I in Providence and he in New Haven. We'd traveled through Europe around the same time. We'd lived within miles of each other in Jamaica during the exact same year, if different circumstances; I in an uptown lap of luxury, he in a downtown Rasta colony in Back o' Wall.

I never thought I'd take up with another writer. Too much introspection there. Sometimes I sensed us watching each other for a story, like two scavengers waiting to pick the same bone. Though we wrote in different disciplines; he a journalist and jack-of-all-trades, me essentially a poet and storyteller. But we had a way of picking up on the same things. Sometimes we'd even laughingly argue over it.

"Hey, that's my story. I saw it first."

Ghana at that time was not your typical tourist destination. It was a poor country, and there were no playgrounds to draw in vacationers who expected the land to cater to their carnival appetites, who discarded inhibitions like winter clothing. But every now and then you would run into an aberrant adventurer holidaying off the beaten track.

Early to meet friends one evening in the lobby of the Continental Hotel, we both noticed the same incident at once. Kwesi's mind undoubtedly raced to explore the journalistic angle, mine probed the poetic irony.

A lean, leathery, sunburned white woman smoked at the bar. Kwesi said he could tell she was European by the way she held her cigarette. We watched her from the moment she determinedly walked in and took up her perch. She ordered her drink and sipped it, eyes wandering the premises like a practiced bird of prey. Her cool gray gaze lit on Kwesi for a moment, slid over to me, then drifted on.

Three young Africans were drawn into the orbit of her eyes. They surrounded her, laughing and competing for her favors. She bought drinks for the whole group, chatted with them for a while, then made her pick of the bunch. She downed her drink, picked up her bag, tossed down a few bills, and disappeared with him into the elevator. We timed it. The whole thing had taken twenty minutes.

"Can you believe it?" I turned to Kwesi. "That old hawk preying on these young chickens. I've seen them in the Caribbean, turning innocent men into beachboys."

Kwesi chuckled.

"Reminds me of an old buddy, a dread from up Trelawny way. Ras' Mau Mau would come down the mountain whenever he needed some cash. He'd let down his locks and hang out at the beach, looking picturesque and whittling these little wooden lions he sold to the tourists. When a willing white woman stopped to watch, he'd offer to let her *sit in de face of de lion.*"

"What on earth does that mean?"

"He was willing to eat a little pussy . . . for a price. Brother man was going to make his sale, one way or the other."

"Interesting marketing technique," I observed dryly. "No wonder African nations are in no hurry to develop their tourist industries. Look what goes along with it. The girls can look forward to rewarding work as call girls, the boys as gigolos."

Kwesi was visibly amused at my indignation.

"I'm sure the man doesn't consider himself a victim. Being used for a night or two, but having the drinks, the sex, maybe a little bit of money to show for it. Who's the culprit?"

"The one with the power. The buyer, not the seller."

"Ah." Kwesi held one finger up in revelation; that was one of his favorite gestures. "But victim is not always blameless. Sometimes you give the master permission to oppress you. I know whereof I speak. I was once in similar straits."

Now it was my turn to laugh. My gentle, bespectacled Kwesi. A beachboy? A paid prostitute? A gigolo?

"How much do you really know about me, Alma? Do you know just why I've been wandering the past five years of my life? I am hounded, trying to stay one step ahead of disgrace."

And Kwesi told me a story I could barely believe. He had fallen into the orbit of a beautiful opera singer who'd made her home and fortune in Europe. Who thrived on the adulation of her European audiences, but yearned for the attention of Black men. Young, struggling Black men she could play *sugar momma* to. Kwesi was one in a string of them. She dragged him across Europe by her purse strings. Her name was Grace. Kwesi called her Disgrace.

According to Kwesi, the Diva was beautiful, charming, and entirely faithless. Played cruel games of pain, love, and manipulation. And staring into the foam at the bottom of his beer mug, Kwesi told me of pillow talk he had overheard. He had come upon Disgrace snuggled in the sheets with another woman, boasting to her of his sexual prowess. The other woman had been disbelieving. The Diva had, as proof positive, offered her the opportunity to sample his services.

Though I have always been curious to the point of prying, I had never probed too deeply for Kwesi's secrets. I sensed anguish churning beneath his easygoing charm. I was afraid of puncturing the surface calm of him, of the pain that would seep out. I might see something I didn't want to know about.

Kwesi reminded me of Daniel Aguirre, a little brown boy in the fifth grade. Everyone ignored the slight accent with which he pronounced his own name: Dan-YEL ah-GEARR-ray. They called him Danny A-gwire, to rhyme with fire.

Danny had the requisite qualities of a 1950s cute boy: bronze skin, curly hair, curious hazel eyes. He was the only one in the whole school who had eyes like that, and they made him much sought after. All the girls in the fifth grade had crushes on Danny, all except me. I feigned adoration along with the rest, but there was a morose quality, a melancholia about him I found unsettling.

One day I had stood behind him at the water fountain, watching his curly black head dip into the stream of water. Danny turned around and saw me watching. He looked at me speculatively.

"Hey, girl. You want to see something?"

And before I could answer he had lifted his shirt, displaying a skinny chest mottled with huge, angry burn marks. His sad hazel eyes fixed on my face all the while, like a wounded cocker spaniel. Pleading eyes, I couldn't imagine what they asked of me. I had backed away from his pain, then turned and ran off.

Kwesi looked at me that way across the table, beer mug clasped between his palms. Eyes sad and questioning, challenging me to recoil. But this was the woman Alma, not the little girl Allie Mae. His open pain only endeared him to me. The comfort I offered was only a small portion of what he had given me.

And he spoke of her often after that, as if saying her name could suck out the poison of snakebite. Sometimes he cried in my arms at night. Of course I understood the nature of such suffering. I hd been through the fire myself.

But wise men and wise women caution against speaking too often of the demons which haunt one. For to speak their name might summon them up, might call them into being.

Money was running low and we were both budgeting. That is the only reason we decided to attend that fancy function at the American Embassy. We planned to take full advantage of the abundant spread of food and drinks, then cut out before the speechifying started. We had never even bothered to inquire into the occasion of celebration. We never knew until much too late that the Diva was the guest of honor.

I could see why Kwesi was so obsessed with her. She was much too beautiful. Middle age had added patina to her finely chiseled features, had molded them like a piece of sculpture. Her skin was smooth as silk against high cheekbones, around slanted eyes. Hair swept into a cornrowed topknot adorned her head like a tiara. I knew who she was without asking. Kwesi stiffened at the sight of her. I caught his hand.

Grace uttered a cry of welcome and rushed to Kwesi's side. Embracing him, then kissing him full on the mouth. Noting my raised eyebrow, my hand still holding his, she tossed me a careless laugh.

"Forgive us, dear. Old friends greeting one another in the European manner. You will excuse us."

It hadn't been posed as a question, but a command. I hesitated, unwilling to step aside. She stepped into that hesitation and whisked him away. I watched him move beside her, his face drawn. Grace on his arm, whispering into his ear.

I don't know where they disappeared to. I lost track of the time; was it one hour or three? Had they found someplace quiet to have a quickie? Or were they merely sitting head to head, holding hands and reminiscing? And which was more alarming?

I found a seat off to the side and lowered myself into it carefully. Nobody but me seemed to notice that the room was shaking. The ground I had thought so solid was shifting beneath my feet. Why was I thrown off center by it, when I had never really had a man of my own before? They had all been borrowed, like past-due library books. I should have been accustomed to the notion of man-sharing by then. Why should this one have been any different?

It was bound to happen, the voice of experience seemed to reproach. *When you balance your life on the promise of a man, the bottom drops out beneath you. Sooner or later you're going to hear those words: "Naw, baby. It ain't me."*

Eventually Kwesi returned to my side. I avoided looking at him, afraid of the scars I might see in his eyes. He caught up my hand, grabbing it as if it were a life preserver. He nervously fondled his pocket watch with his free hand, popping it open and clicking it closed. *Pop, click. Pop, click.* Over and over again.

I struggled to hold on to understanding. Knowing that I too was capable of relapsing into fever. That I might have done the same had my nemesis walked into the room.

The Americans were escorting Grace to her evening of rest. She must retire early and make ready for her command performance tomorrow. The celebration of the nation's twenty-fifth year of independence, at which festivities she was the star performer. Grace paused before us on her way out. An artful glance over her shoulder.

"Ka-WAY-see," she breathed his name in three theatrical syllables. "Come to the villa for a nightcap. Your friend, too, of course."

I bristled at the afterthought I'd become. Kwesi shook his head and glanced away from the magnetic pull of her. As if distrusting his own voice. His grip on my hand became tighter.

"Very well. Enjoy." Grace darted me a look that I couldn't quite fathom. Scorn? Appraisal?

She took two steps away and turned back to toss a disarming smile.

"Expecting, are we?"

I could only nod, off balance. I hadn't yet found the way to tell Kwesi. I was stunned to hear my secret falling from the Diva's bee-stung lips.

"How . . . how did you know?"

She laughed a laugh of tinkling silver, eyeing Kwesi all the while.

"I can always tell, darling. Something in the body language. Ka-WAY-see?"

He looked helplessly at her. *Pop, click. Pop, click.* She smiled and blew him a kiss. And then she was gone. But my relief was short-lived. Before we left a waiter pressed paper into Kwesi's hand. He unfolded the note, read it wordlessly, and handed it to me.

Darling:

How poetic and prophetic that we should find ourselves together in the Motherland. Come to me, Kwesi. We still have something burning between us. And I can ease you out of this sticky dilemma. You are a free spirit. You don't need to be weighed down. Loving you madly after all these years.

Grace

And the Diva's kiss was imprinted on the bottom of the page, a perfect fire-engine red set of lip prints. Audacious and unsmeared. I returned the note to Kwesi, who absently shoved it into a pocket and did not offer further comment. Until morning.

Kwesi was a morning person. No matter how late we'd gone to bed, he always got up before me. So even if I tried, it would have been impossible to hide it. Morning sickness visited me for the first time. I woke up and ran retching to the bush, passing the mango tree under which Kwesi sat reading.

When my stomach had ceased its heaving, I looked up and saw him there. Watching me. His expression unreadable.

"So it's true."

"Yes," I answered, any escape in lies or half truths impossible now. "It's true."

"How far along?"

"I don't know. Maybe three, four months."

"Am I the culprit?"

"I . . . I can't be sure."

He stared at me for a moment. Then he spoke. His voice was soft, his eyes pleading, like a wounded cocker spaniel.

"*Akwaaba*," the gentle word of welcome. There was no bitterness, only pained resignation in his words. "Disgrace has come calling and found me home."

When he turned back toward our room, Grace's kiss fluttered from his pocket and fell to the ground. I stood alone in the garden, shivering despite the warmth of the morning. His retreating back told me all I needed to know. *Naw, baby. It ain't me.*

I had been putting off telling him for weeks. I knew that I eventually would, but I thought I would be able to choose the right moment, the right method. I had thought I'd be able to cultivate the comfort of his acceptance, to lull his uncertainties. I thought I could make him feel that same apprehension edged with gentle anticipation that I'd come to feel.

But the news had fallen from the fire engine of Grace's smile. And now I and the small thing fluttering in my belly were a dilemma which weighed him down, the disgrace that Kwesi had spent half a decade running from. Disgrace was the chain that shackled him to me. That weighed him down with baggage too heavy for him to roam with in the true freeness of his spirit.

"When you travel light, you travel right," Kwesi was always admonishing, as he struggled to handle my overweight luggage. I decided I had to carry my own weight. I opened the shackles and set him free.

With sandals on my feet, braids in my hair, a return ticket in my bag, and a baby in my belly, I walked out to the road and waited for a taxi.

I left Ghana for an extended visit with Darlene Amagashie and her family in Ivory Coast. We had happened upon each other during my first week in Abidjan when I accompanied Kwesi to a dinner party, only to discover that the hostess was someone I had bumped into before.

"First Providence, then Bridgetown, now this," Darlene joked. "We must be related."

Darlene's Ghanaian expatriate husband was also called Kwesi, though most people knew him by his Christian name, Peter. Darlene jokingly tagged the two men as Pete and Repeat. An even more drastic coincidence cropped up on my second visit. The Darlene who met me at the airport was heavily pregnant with her second child, what she wearily referred to as a *menopause miracle*.

"See what a bad influence I am? First you hook up with a repeat offender, then you get yourself knocked up. What you going to do when I decide to jump off a bridge?"

But I was a pampered houseguest and my visit stretched on for several months. I wallowed in the comfort of an Africa adapted to Western tastes; the air-conditioned quarters, the swimming pool, the sumptuous French dishes prepared by Prospère, their Ivorian cook. I even squeezed into party clothes on the occasional evening out, and circulated among the cosmopolitan cloister of the cocktail circuit. I didn't bother to contradict Darlene when she introduced me as her *Chicago cousin*.

But I knew my mission in Ghana was not complete. I had not gone to Kumasi to beg audience with the King of the Ashantis. I had not yet found the river of my descent. And so I returned.

But I have found precious little to encourage me in my interviews with elders and historians, my visits to the Asantehene's Palace. The growing weight of my pregnancy has slowed my movements and sapped my energy. I was beginning to wonder if I was in the wrong place after all.

And most troubling of all, I was running out of money. It was hard to part with the notion that money spelled freedom. Money had long been a preoccupation with me. I'd never been a gold digger, but always wanted a man who had a little money of his own. It meant he was able to make his own way in the world. That he was not helpless in the hold of a nine-to-five. That he was not owned.

I knew poverty from intimate experience. And poverty meant being helpless and afraid. At the mercy of landlords and bosses who control your labor and dole the fruits back to you in crumb-sized increments.

But even more than a man with money, I always wanted to have some of my own. And spent years chasing it, trying to catch it and keep it from flying in the front door and out the back. And now five years of my hard-earned savings were melting like ice in the African sun.

Nor did I have Kwesi's faith that money would always come. Didn't have his knack of discovering untapped wells of opportunity. I felt like Old Mother Africa's foundling dog, rooting about for a bone in bare cupboards.

The only sizable resource I had left was my return ticket. I toyed with the idea of returning to that place across the ocean that I had learned to stop calling *home*.

But the need to connect with my African past was almost as strong as my fear of the demon Poverty. I dreamed of voices clearer and closer than they had ever been, women's voices calling out to me. I still didn't know where to go, or how to answer. And if I never discovered the place my great-grandmother's great-grandmother was from, if I never reached the River Where Blood Is Born, would the unanswered voices continue to haunt me? Or worse still, would they one day fade away?

I teetered on the brink of indecision. It was perhaps a sign that G. S. Akbar's fabric shop was situated directly across from the Pan Am ticket office in downtown Kumasi. I made a sudden decision.

Anxious to follow through before I changed my mind, I hurried through transactions with the chatty shop girl who seemed more interested in questioning me about life *in US* than in selling fabric. The material bought and bundled beneath my arm, I walked out to find it raining. The Pan Am ticket office seemed to beckon from across the boulevard.

I stepped out to cross over, the driving rain turning the street almost into a river of red mud. But a car pulled up and blocked my way. A man I am sure I did not know beckoned to me from the driver's seat. I walked on, ignoring him. The car followed, the driver gesticulating wildly, honking his horn. I walked faster.

The car quickened, driving through a huge potholed puddle, splashing my outgrown dress with muddy rain. The red Kumasi mud ran down my legs like blood. I halted in my footsteps, trembling, shaking my fist at the vehicle dogging my heels. The troublesome stranger in it.

"Look at what you did, you careless creep! Can't you find anything better to do than harass pregnant women?"

I dashed out into the street, shouting all the while. My epithets were disregarded. The car swung a U-turn in the center of the street, pulling up directly in front of the Pan Am office.

"I'll get the law after your sorry ass," I threatened, my face running rain. And in case my point was missed, I added the very insult a market woman had spat at me the day before when I suggested that her plantains might be overpriced: "Go way you! Bloody fool!"

The Nissan's back door opened. An umbrella emerged first, then a familiar dreadlocked head.

"For God's sake, Alma," Kwesi called calmly. "Will you quit running your mouth and get in here?"

Confused and hesitant, I stood in the driving rain. Shifting from one foot to another. Kwesi got out of the car and maneuvered me inside. I'd never seen him so formally attired before; he was wearing a three-piece suit, European cut. His dreadlocks licked the sharply tailored lapels.

"Where's the funeral?" I asked wanly.

"Hope it isn't ours. It's going to be a downpour, you know." He clicked his ubiquitous pocket watch as he spoke. As if resuming a conversation interrupted minutes before. "I hope it doesn't mean more mudslides in the hills. The roads will be impassable."

I sat silent while he spoke, a body's space of seat separating us. I was too jarred to join in the one-sided conversation. To even ask where he was taking me. He discussed the unseasonably heavy rains, the possibility of flooding in one of the region's rivers. We left the streets of Kumasi proper and wound into the forested hills above it.

The car paused before crossing a bridge. The river below it churned in the rain. The driver blew his horn, although I could see no one in the road to be warned.

"What did he do that for?" I asked, curiosity penetrating my catatonia. Maybe there was a story in it.

Kwesi laughed as we pulled across the bridge.

"Ain't nothing but superstition," he snorted. "Right, Ansere?"

"Right, sah," the elderly driver grinned in agreement. And tooted his horn for emphasis.

"You'd love this one, Alma. Superstitious soul that you are. Ansere believes that the river's children might be playing in the road. He always slows down and blows his horn to warn them of his approach. If he ran over the river children, their mother might get mad and turn his car off the road."

"Oh. We wouldn't want that to happen," was all I could think to say. I believed in many things I didn't understand. Maybe that was why I suffered.

We finally pulled up to a crumbling colonial bungalow, its white walls spattered rust with muddy rain.

"Whose place is this?"

"Mine," Kwesi answered. "At least for now. I've been doing a contract with UNESCO at the Technical Institute. I heard you were here in Kumasi but I've had the devil finding you."

This one-way conversation went on while Kwesi deliberately led me to an upstairs bedroom.

"Where are your things?" he asked.

"At City Hotel."

"Good. I'll send Ansere to settle the bill."

"No, Kwesi. You don't have to do this . . ." But my pleas fell upon silence. Kwesi had already left the room and I could hear his voice outside, brisk with instructions.

He bustled back in, sat me down in a chair, and pulled off my sodden shoes. He took off his jacket, loosened his tie, squatted before me in his British tweeds, and began methodically to strip me of my clothes. Shocked and disconcerted, I slapped his hands away.

"Just what do you think you're doing?"

Kwesi looked up at me, frowning. As if I were the one behaving irrationally. As if I were peremptorily undressing him after not having seen him in three months. And he resumed his task.

"Come on, Alma. We've got to get you out of these wet clothes. You'll catch double pneumonia in your condition."

When I was completely naked he took me into the shower. Ignored the soapy water that splattered his tweeds. Washed me up, washed me down in a steam of hot water. Around my neck and under my arms. Between my breasts and thighs. Over the hump of my protruding belly. Washed away the residue of red Kumasi mud from my legs. Carefully, deliberately.

And when I was cleansed he dried me. Wrapped me in a *kente* cloth that felt new. And brought me to the bed. Rubbed the areas of my skin that were still exposed with shea butter.

I was lying flat on my back. In this position the baby loved to kick. I wondered if Kwesi noticed the rippling of my belly beneath the cloth. Or if he were too busy talking to see it.

"I'm glad I caught you before you went into that place." Rub, rub. Readjust the cloth. Rub again.

"It was an airline ticket office, not a house of ill repute. And I have business to take care of there. You're going to have to take me back."

"Bullshit," Kwesi replied calmly. "You're going back to United States of America over my dead body. You'll be having this kid right here. Why do you think I took this assignment, got this house?"

"I wasn't planning on going back. I was going to cash my ticket in. I need the money. And just where do you get off planning my life for me? Telling me what I will and won't do?"

The movement of Kwesi's capable hands slowed. He suddenly rested his head against my swollen stomach and whispered into it. The little one inside of me fluttered in response.

"I've been looking for you a long time. A long, long time. I've been lost, wandering that deep bush without you. You are my soul mate, Alma Peeples. I need you. And you need me, too. Just look at you."

"But you don't have to rescue me," I insisted, capturing his moving hands into my own. "You don't have to shackle yourself to my disgrace. You're a free spirit."

And Kwesi looked at me. His hands escaped my restraint and were once again rubbing oil into me. Up my arms, my shoulders, my neck, my cheeks. With a hand on either side of my face, he brought it to his own.

Kwesi was not a classic kisser. He did not press his lips to mine. He licked them carefully, first the upper, then the lower. As if testing their flavors. He coaxed my mouth open and gently explored it with his tongue. And then pulled back, his wounded eyes looking into mine.

"Yeah, baby," he breathed, almost wordlessly. "It is me."

And he unwrapped the cloth covering my body, as if opening a present. He continued his ministrations of oil against flesh. Rubbing shea butter into the tautening skin of my back, my breasts. He rolled my bulging nipples between his fingers until drops of clear liquid trickled forth, like tears. He pushed the beads aside to massage my quaking belly. He let a hand rest there gently, as if testing for seismic activity. Did he know there was quaking in other places, too?

"Now lay on back, woman, so I can love you."

Who would have thought that Kwesi, the pragmatic agnostic, the dialectical materialist, could have a superstitious streak all his own? He stopped short on the doorstep of passion and said he couldn't go on. Fear shot through me and I almost found myself glancing around the darkening room, searching out the presence of ghosts. Maybe Grace at the window, or Trevor under the bed. But no, that was not it.

He said that entering me now would be like walking into a temple with muddy boots on. Would be defiling the new life inside the sanctuary. I said I couldn't bring myself to see the tender instrument that must have planted the life within me as muddy boots. But he was insistent. And he did not enter the temple. But worshiped on the steps of it, polishing the door.

Eventually I was able to make him change his mind. During one of my research sessions at the university library, I found an obscure anthropological text explaining that Ashantis believe regular lovemaking, up through the eighth month, to be essential for the healthy development of the fetus.

"We've got a good three months to catch up on," I whispered in his ear as he finally entered inside me, "if we want this kid to develop right."

As the pregnancy advanced, the string of waist beads began to bind. I had to take them off. I slipped them back into the Crown Royal bag I had brought them over in. And wondered if this signaled a giving up. A settling in. A resisting of the urge to wander, to seek out my source. Of nesting in a place where I could spread out my belongings. Read my books and write my stories. Give birth to my baby. And one day perhaps call *home*.

I wondered how having a child would change our lives. Even if we got the urge to roam again, how would I wander with a baby on my back? Would Kwesi, the professional nomad, adapt to a settled life with me? Would our mating endure past the nesting period?

Kwesi said that giving in was not necessarily giving up.

"The African identity you've been searching out so long, Alma. This child of yours will have it."

"Ours," I corrected. I saw speculation appear in his eyes.

"What do you suppose the chances are that I am the father?" he asked.

"I don't know," I admitted. "But the law of averages is in your favor. I was with the other man over ten years and never got knocked up, even though I tried. Had known you only one month when I discovered I was pregnant."

He seemed to do some quick arithmetic in his head.

"You're eight months pregnant now and we came together only eight months ago. That means you would have had to conceive almost the first time, that night at Labadi Beach. Is that likely? I've never gotten a woman pregnant before, never even been accused of it."

"First time for everything," I assured him. "And it only takes one shot to hit the bull's eye."

But shot through the tentative jest was anxiety in both our hearts. And hope. That no matter who sired it, he might find it in his heart to love this unborn one. Who may have been carried over the Atlantic, or may have been planted here in Africa. But who would be born in the *us* of Africa, and Africa in it.

The hills above Kumasi climbed up toward the sky like stair steps. And beyond the hills were mountains. Every now and then a stone would come tumbling down from the heights and land at my feet. Almost as if there was someone up there throwing, trying to get my attention. Or merely skipping stones across the hills.

I never skipped stones as a child. There was nowhere in the crowded city for me to do so. Unless you counted the polluted city river that ran like bad blood several miles from my home. A river not made for skipping stones. It was a water whose flow had been reversed. A tame beast, made to run contrary to its course.

The banks of the Chicago were too steep to access by foot. And the bridge was several stories higher than land. I grew up frightened of both the towering stretch of bridge and the waters below it. As if the mineral-heavy water sought some magnet in me and worked to pull me toward it. I was drawn to the tame city river, like a child with the urge to pet a weak and rabid dog. Attracted to the beauty that was still there, repelled by the sad, sick, dangerous thing it had become.

Just a glance over the railing was dizzying. I would have nightmares about riding my bike across, only to have the drawbridge open up below me. And I would drop through the yawning opening, like a coin into a wishing well.

The dream haunted me into my waking hours, into my adult years. Once I traveled east from Charleston to Isle of Palms, South Carolina, at dawn. I drove alone the mile-long stretch of suspension that bridged peninsula to island. Sunrise along this bridge was said to be a spectacular sight. I saw not a ray of it.

Inching along ever so slowly, cars blaring behind me, a sweat seeped out of every pore. I felt like an ant crawling a shining knife blade some sadistic soul had set across a bucket of salt water. Frightened and diminished by the water surging in all directions. By the time I reached the island I was a prime candidate for the funny farm.

But now I believed my phobia was cured. A river ran not too far from our home in the hills. It was not a large river. But it had a lot of force in its narrow flow. It rushed down from the mountains and ran through these hills, taking on the red tinge of its soil. Ansere, who has adopted us into his extended family, told me this was once a much larger river.

The river had diminished in size over the generations since the Europeans had come and captured the soul of the people. It was said that the river mourned the loss of the golden stool of Ashanti, the exile of the Asantehene. Even when negotiations were made with the British and the Asantehene returned to his stool, the river never regained its former dimensions.

A medicine man had been called in. He told the people that a sacrifice must be made to appease the river's stunted spirit. A full bottle of lice, the body of a fair-skinned person. Those insects which burrowed under the skin and fed on the blood of their host were easy enough to find. And there were a handful of whites governing their parcel of Gold Coast from the regional capital in Kumasi. But human sacrifice had been outlawed generations ago. And so the river remained unfed, gaunt and hungry.

But somehow I don't mourn the diminished properties of this river. Though she is transformed, she never flows against her nature. She clings tenaciously to the lifeline of her course.

And despite her hunger she still runs. I know one day she will be fat and fabulous, returned to her former glory. Sometimes I can hear her singing. One day soon I will follow that song to the place it begins.

She didn't know which was more compelling at that particular moment, her urge to visit the toilet for the umpteenth time that afternoon, or her idle fascination with a spider spinning its web on the underside of an Ashanti stool that sat before her.

I will get up and go to the bathroom, she told herself, *as soon as this spider has finished its business.*

Alma was seized with the irrational thought it might be a mother spider, preparing a place to lay her eggs. She made a promise to guard her, protecting her handiwork from any hazard that might come along.

Either that, she figured, *or I'm too lazy to haul my overgrown ass up out of this rocking chair.*

She had spent hours alternately watching the spider, and arranging an assortment of objects. In the burst of energy that often comes in the last stages of pregnancy, she'd decided to create an ancestors' shrine.

Big Momma's family quilt was spread on the seat of the Ashanti stool, an appliqued patch depicting a *Snake Following the North Star* prominently displayed at its center. Atop that sat a small bottle of *akpeteshie* native gin. The story beads rested inside their customary Crown Royal sack. The scrap of *kente* cloth bequeathed to her by a dying old man in Barbados sat beside it. And with the two pieces lying side by side, Alma suddenly noticed that the snake applique handed down from Big Momma and the worn scrap of *kente* seemed to be from the same cloth. And on top, a crumpled twenty-dollar bill her mother had sent when she first went away to college, never spent. There was also Kwesi's ancient pocket watch, which had suffered a *fatal injury* and suddenly stopped keeping time. A guidebook from Elmina Castle. An amulet she'd obtained from a Yoruba priestess. A luxuriant white feather found on her windowsill one spring morning in Washington, D.C. A list begun just that day, of her blessings. At the moment she couldn't think of any curses to go on the other side.

An odd legacy to bequeath to an unborn son or daughter. But she was nonetheless happy with the assemblage. The spider had finally begun to converge toward the center of its web of concentric circles, and Alma had started uncorking the bottle of *akpeteshie* when Kwesi came out onto the verandah with an envelope in his hands.

"I hope that's not what it looks like," he observed, planting a kiss on her forehead, then leaning over to sniff the open bottle. "So you've waited until you're nine months pregnant to try out African moonshine? Bad idea."

"Oh, it's not just for me." Alma tilted the bottle and dribbled its contents onto the flower bed bordering the verandah. "This is for Big Momma, Uncle Clyde, Dads, my great-aunt Truly, Grandmama Ella Mae, Nana—and any other ancestors who might happen to be hanging around."

"Hmmph," Kwesi snorted. "Don't see why the ancestors can't buy their own booze. Here's a letter for you; New York, by way of the American Embassy in Accra."

"From whom?" she asked lazily, tipping the bottle so that the last drop of gin touched the tip of her tongue. The liquid burned like fire, freezing the taste from her tongue.

"Just initials. TRB."

The bottle froze in Alma's hand.

"Trevor Reginald Barrett. Shit."

Kwesi held the unopened envelope up to the sun, pretending to read it.

"H'Alma Peeples," he boomed in his best attempt at a Caribbean accent. "I don't send you to H'africa to wind up barefoot and pregnant, shacking up with no natty dreadlocks boy, y'know. Bring your backside 'ere to New York, mi no want have to come out dere h'after you."

All she could muster in response was a deep, heartfelt sigh.

"Now I can think of something to go on that curses list."

Kwesi regarded her with an inscrutable squint, thrusting the letter toward her. "You'll want a minute alone with this, I expect."

"Hell, no," Alma responded. "Throw it away."

"It could be important."

"Nothing Trevor has to say could be that important. Just get rid of it." She stopped rocking and froze suddenly in her seat. "Oh, Lord. Shit, I don't believe I sat up here and did this."

"What is it?" Kwesi quickly dropped the letter onto the stool, and knelt before her. "Are you okay?"

"Sitting up here watching a goddamn spider make a web, listening to some mess about Trevor Barrett. And . . . and . . . and . . ." Without warning she began to cry.

"And what, Alma?" Kwesi asked, holding her hands. "What's the matter?"

"I peed on myself!" she wailed, burying her face in his shoulder.

He patted her head, stifling the laugh that bubbled to his lips.

"Aw, baby. You're permitted to pee on yourself. You're pregnant. Come on, let's get you off to the bathroom."

He hauled her awkwardly to her feet, then happened to glance down at where she'd been sitting.

"Since when did you start peeing in Technicolor?"

She looked down at the seat. The brilliant red spot was like a flag waving. The bull lying still in her midsection lurched to life and began its charge.

"Blood is seen before birth," she whispered, patting her belly and smiling wanly through tears still wet on her face. "I think it's my time, Kwesi Omobowale."

As he helped her through the open door, the spider finished its work. It had no eggs to lay, though. It scurried to the top of the Ashanti stool, waving its eight legs and blessing each of the objects there, finally coming to rest upon the envelope with the New York postmark.

Dear Alma:

Your mother tells me that you're pregnant. Could this possibly be true? Do I finally have reason to celebrate?

Your mother also forwarded this letter to me. She said it arrived a few weeks ago from Ghana. She isn't quite sure of your whereabouts at this point, so I promised I'd use some of my diplomatic contacts to track you down.

When I suggested that you travel to Africa to meet my first wife, I merely wanted you to understand the dynamics of polygamous marriage before you chose this as a lifestyle. Don't you think it's about time for you to come home now?

I'm overjoyed at the prospect of becoming a father. I always felt you would give me a son. I'm anxious to see you again. Please write and let us know what's going on.

You'll find the letter from Ghana enclosed within.

With love,
Trevor

My Dear Madam:

How are you there in US? By God's grace, my family and I are well. And if the Saviour continues to bless me, I will soon be journeying to your country.

A man who is here from US wants to marry me. He is a Ghana man and many years older than I. He is very kind. He says he loves me well and wants to bring me back to US with him. I think that I will go.

I want to be in US very much. To see the wonderful things you have there. To one day become rich as the other Americans like yourself. Here the poverty is too much. Every day we struggle to find food to feed our bellies. I am tired of struggle. I would like to enjoy an easy life like you and your people in US.

When we met at Akbar's you asked me about the place I am from. I was ashamed and told you I was a Kumasi girl. But I shall be punished by the Great God Jehovah unless I own up to the lie and replace it with the truth.

My surname Esubonteng means deep water. I come from a mountain village some thirty miles from Kumasi, high up in the Maase Mountains. It is a beautiful place, deeply forested in the hills and fertile farmland in the valleys. Its name means the Place Where Blood Is Born, because it is the source of a river which is called the Blood River. A very peaceful village where there is plenty yam and bush meat.

But it is also very primitive. There is not an indoor lavatory in the whole village. And many of the people are pagans who have not surrendered their souls to Our Lord and Saviour, Jesus Christ. They still believe in witches and spirits, and worship at a shrine where the river begins. This place the pagans believe to be sacred.

It is a very backward and Godless place. When girls are ready to be women, they can shave your head, rub you in shea butter, wrap you in beads, and display you nearly naked before the village. You may not believe this, but it is true. When I found that my grandmother was planning to do this to me, I ran away. I am thankful that I was able to come to my uncle in Kumasi.

Kumasi is a fine city, but I think my spirit will never be satisfied here. Prices are too much, money is too small. And some people have a need to go out beyond our borders. I will not be feeling fine until I am there with you in US.

I am so happy to be your pen pal. I will look forward to receiving my first letter from you. And I will be even more happy when my husband takes me to join you there in US.

Pray for me please, that my wish might be granted. May the Almighty God, in his infinite wisdom and mercy, bless you and keep you always.

Your friend and sister,
Elizabeth Osei Esubonteng

EPILOGUE

Renaissance

The peal of water trickling down the mountainside rings like champagne pouring into crystal. The music lightens our hearts as we wile away the idle hours, working and waiting. I wrap beadwork around my busy hands. The sun sets, yet each bead of water passing between my fingers seems to catch a fading ray, holding the spark deep within its heart.

Our village has moved to new quarters, a more likely sort of limbo than the last. We've set up rocking chairs on the verandah of a stained white bungalow in the foothills of the Maase Mountains. The portico curves from the front to the side to display a panoramic view of the sprawling city of Kumasi below, and the verdant foothills above. A perfect perch for ancestors to watch the comings and goings of those within.

We wear new clothes for the occasion, vibrant prints of red and orange. Even the more conservative ones have wrapped their heads or white cottoned waists in colorful strips of *kente*.

Some have picked up the old traditions again. One has remembered the craft of arranging black *adinkra* symbols onto pure white cloth. Others fashion pottery and basketry. Yet another has begun experimenting with the weaving of *kente* strips, although her seniors sigh and shake their heads.

"If only you had the experience," one Abena, Mistress of the Adowa, patiently explains, "you would know that weaving *kente* has never been women's work."

"It is now," Needleworker Emilene insists, brow furrowed and lips bitten, fingers fumbling at the loom. "There's no telling how long we'll be waiting for that child to make up her heart. Better to keep busy, learn something new. Idle hands are the devil's workshop."

A halfhearted argument erupts among the others.

"You know good and well there's no such thing as no devil," Singer Earlene scolds. "You ought to know better."

"Child, what you talking, it ain't no devil?" Big Momma Quiltmaker interjects. "Begging your pardon, I done met the man. Just study evil, that old Satan."

"Naw, Mama, that weren't Lucifer. That was your second husband."

But as they sit waiting, passing around the *akpeteshie* and palm wine that they've begun to acquire a taste for, an old priestess is morose. She sits silent, face turned toward the mountains. Head tilted slightly, ear strained to the sound of running water.

"So near," the Priestess moans. "And yet so far. How much longer must we wait?"

"That child is pregnant." Big Momma Quiltmaker, the mother who knows her best, rushes to her defense. "You been waiting two centuries, you can give my baby two more minutes. We can't have her running through these hills in her condition, do she catch her death of pneumonia. Then she be sitting up here with us, and we all back where we started."

"How on earth did we let that happen?" Needleworker Emilene wants to know. "It seems I remember a long ago plea from someone sitting here: *Look after our daughter. Allow her to know the gift of birth, but not before she's blessed to receive it.*"

"I remember my own prayer." Big Momma Quiltmaker bristles. "I ain't senile. I didn't want my great-grandchild to make the same mistake I did, becoming a mother before she had a chance to be a girl. That child is good and grown now. 'Sides, she went down to that water just like a good daughter, asked for blessings well and proper."

"That doesn't count so far as I am concerned," the Priestess interrupts. "The Ile-Ife is not our river. Yemoja belongs to the Yorubas, not to the people of the River Where Blood Is Born."

Big Momma disagrees. "How you know the child ain't got some Yoruba in her? And it's the thought that counts, anyway. She did the right thing."

"Nine months pregnant and not even sure who the father is," Emilene sniffs from her loom. "You call that the right thing? I call it downright foolish."

But there is a sympathizer among them.

"Don't be so quick to judge," Proud Mary Ama, the Saltwater Woman, interjects. "Have you walked the world in her sandals?"

"I know who my child's father was," the Needleworker insists. "You can be sure of that."

"And you are my daughter," Ama reminds her. "My first-born child. When I crossed over with you inside, gave birth to you in mid-Atlantic waters, I never knew for certain whether the seed had been planted by the boy I loved, or the unholy hunter who sold me hence. You may know your child's father, but do you know your own?"

And so her mother continues into the stunned silence.

"Though I may not have known which one fathered my child, I at least was the one who made those choices. Can you say the same for yourself?"

The scolded one is silent.

"Well, you know what they say." I hurry to make the peace. Those two are always at it. My role seems to be more of a Mediator than Gatekeeper these days. "You may not know the father, but you can always be sure of the mother."

The Needleworker mutters the last word: "Hmmp. Mama's baby, Papa's maybe. How many times have we heard that old sorry song?"

"Let us not quarrel," I interrupt. "I do believe that we have a baby about to be born."

And our ears listen for the unmistakable moans of labor, the deep breathing, the grunting of the push. Each one of us braces her body in memory, and when the pain becomes too much for a mortal woman to endure, we hold hands and absorb the excess onto ourselves.

No event in a woman's life brings her closer to the ancestors than childbirth. Swells of pain wash the shore of life in mounting succession, each wave breaking higher than the last.

Some of us have been known to drown, dragged into the riptide. Some reach out for the ancestors' hands and never let go. At the precise point when new life thrusts forth from the Place Where Blood Is Born, some of us have been known to surrender to death.

The breathing techniques begin to abandon the woman abed with the bulging belly. Her focal point also fails her; the fluttering curtain at the open window more disquieting than calming. Shuttering her sights against the crescendos of pain, she concentrates instead upon the bloodbursts behind her own eyelids.

And inexplicably, the pain leaves her. Her eyes flutter open in surprise, but still she sees red. And against that red a glowing blueness, like a tongue of flame dancing across smoldering embers. She watches it in curious detachment, wondering if her attempt at natural childbirth might be sending her into a pain-induced delirium.

The flame lengthens, softens, settles into the form of a river. And it runs as rivers do, bubbling blue against a landscape of red earth. From its headwaters rises the figure of a woman . . . a woman at once newborn, ancient, and ageless. A luminous waterfall draped about her shoulders, shimmering *beads of water* wrapped around her waist. And she smiles from the center of her heart, the same smile seen in a mother's eyes as she urges the child to take the first step into her waiting arms.

Other figures break the surface of the water, one by one. There are faces seen before; grandmother, great-grandmother, great aunt. There are other images, too: unknown but faintly familiar. Each smile brimming with love, with gentle expectation. Each one reaching out with open arms.

And that is when both the mother to be, and others gathered about the birthing bed, would swear they heard the sound of running water. And a heartbeat afterward, the plaintive cry of a newborn soul.

Cupped in the shelter of its mothers' palms, stirred by the warmth of the women's breath, a silkmoth cocoon unfolds, stretches its delicate wings, and takes flight. The ancestors and elders, mothers and priestesses, sigh with satisfaction as they watch the new one make its uncertain way toward life.

"Perhaps," one of them ventures, "this will be the one. For what is said of the ninth-born child . . ."

"The ninth child always brings fortune and luck to the mother who bears her," comes the long-quiet voice of the Queen Mother of the River Where Blood

Is Born, murmuring like smooth running waters. Like a mother humming lullabies to her loved one.

In a blooming of blue mist, she materializes among us, she whom we feared would never be seen again. She is the same Queen Mother we have always known; it is as if she has never been away. And we rush to her side.

She smiles her welcome and draws us to her, a mother bird thought lost in the storm, now returned to rest. Counting each egg, noting each newly hatched chick. Blessing each upturned face.

Kwaku Ananse is nowhere to be seen, but it is obvious he has been about. A luminous new *kente* cloth is draped about the Queen Mother's shoulders, cascading in waterfalls about her body.

And what a miracle it is to behold, its blueness shimmering like waves upon the water. And when one examines the design, Eureka! There is story woven into every fiber. With each movement she makes, images, actions, faces, figures, shift like the pictures on a TV screen. Indeed the weaver has outdone himself.

But do not fail to notice the sheen of finished beadwork I fasten about the Queen Mother's waist. They seem subtle enough at first glance; *beads of water* strung on a lion's tail.

But observe their graduated pattern: Birth. First blood. Adolescence. Love. The sacrament of sex. Childbirth. Old age. Death. Each bead a bridge bending back toward the original passage; the River Where Blood Is Born.

Discern the hues of blue within them; the long and short of each life, each happiness and heartbreak. See the waters which swirl within them: Afterbirth and mothers' milk . . . the fluids of sex . . . sweat, tears, and menstrual flow. Note the delicate, ovumlike curves of their contours. And the spark of blood each one carries within its heart

Our Queen Mother rises wrapped in new magnificence, rapt in restored magic.

"You have studied long and well the lessons of songs and daughters," she sings. Story cloth wafting in the breeze. Story beads tinkling like birdsong. River waters flowing like music. "I believe we have met our moment."

The Spider's Web

    "Heh, heh, heh. When spiders' webs unite, they can capture up a whole pride of lionesses."

    Hidden overhead in the foliage of a nearby tree, I spin out a line, toss it down, and slowly descend. Floating earthward, I am privy to a bird's-eye view of the entire scene. I watch them, a swarm of insects caught firmly in the weave of my spider's web.

    The women mill about the riverbed, agog with admiration at the Queen Mother's raiment. As well they should, for a finer length of fabric cannot be found in this world or the next. Yes, there may be minute imperfections. I am an artist, not a technician. Nor am I some court artist hired to favor the queen's vanity by rendering perfect portraits of her imperfect children.

    So there are rough spots in the material. Each mishap causes one to appreciate the marvels. In fact, these flaws were placed there by design. It is a simple matter of metaphysics. The fault within otherwise perfection allows an exit point for any evil spirits abiding within it; this trick I learned from my Native American counterparts. I trust my skills will never again be called into question.

    As for the Gatekeeper's baubles glowing dimly about the goddess' waist, their simplicity rather adequately complements my design. Beginner's luck, perhaps. Or maybe the competitive challenge spurred her on to accomplishments far beyond her normal talents.

    For sheer artistic merit, her primitive beadwork can never hold a candle to the spider's web. After all, any toddling child can thread a bead onto a string. Weaving is a skill, nay, an art form which requires a practiced eye and years of mastery. Considering, however, this Gatekeeper's limited imagination and restricted mobility, she has not done badly for herself.

    Still I pity those whose meager accomplishments send them into orgies of self-congratulation. See that Gatekeeper off in the distance, beaming with pride at her homemade handiwork. As smug as any five-year-old whose parent humors her by donning the misshapen product of her kindergarten craft.

Notice them all, these avowed ancestor mothers. They twitter and chitter, jostling each other like hens vying for a peek at the peacock's plumage. See how the old Queen preens and poses like a girl one-hundredth her age. But then, isn't vanity the way of women, young or old, living or dead?

But whether the Gatekeeper has ultimately strung a superior set of story beads or I designed a finer length of cloth, is entirely beside the point. Any fool knows that it is not the ending point which matters, but the road which leads one there. It is the process, rather than the product. As a wise man once uttered: "It is not the destination, but the journey."

Predictably, the Gatekeeper has once again become negligent. You do recall that it was obsessive lust which originally flung her into my web. I suspect that this time undue pride may be her undoing.

The gate to the Great Beyond has been left unguarded. The Place Where Blood Is Born, a bubbling pool that shelters unborn souls for life to come, is once again ripe for plunder. And I, Kwaku Ananse, the man who is a spider, the spider who is a man, have a secret mission to fulfill.

I have become exceedingly bored banished here to the bush. Fufu and palm wine are no longer enough for my enlarged appetites. The scent of the New World, the taste of the road, the flavor of moonlight on urban streets; these I have become accustomed to during my two-hundred-year sojourn. Africa can no longer satisfy my big-city tastes.

Nor should it surprise anyone, that stifled within this big village the Ashantis call a capital, yet another deepwater daughter of the Queen Mother's clan is ready to escape. Even now she makes ready for an uncertain journey across saltwater. And young girls should not travel alone.

It is for the child's own good, the Queen Mother's posterity. It is only fair that I undertake the weaving of story cloth from a new selection of silkmoth cocoons. It is only prudent that I fasten a line onto this prodigal daughter and ride her; nay, guide her on her New World journey. It may be her life, but the story belongs to him who tells it. After all, my original agreement with the Queen Mother of the River Where Blood Is Born was that:

"This is my story I have told. If it be sweet, or it not be sweet, take some for yourself, and let some come back to me."

A woman with a bowlful of rice will not begrudge one fallen grain, an old priestess once said. The Queen Mother finally found the daughter who has been dedicated to her. The other one belongs to me.

Beadwork

L ust may well have been my undoing. Pride indeed may be my penance. But fool me once, shame on you; fool me twice, shame on me.

Kwaku Ananse does not bother to hide his laughter as he scrabbles back across the bridge with his ill-gotten booty. Well, I ask you this, my people.

Is it likely that his latest antics were observed by us all? Could it be that sham cocoons were planted in the River Where Blood Is Born? Might one big-city slickster soon discover he has nothing but spun sugar with which to work his new magic? Do you suppose the master weaver will turn chef in self-defense, creating edible works of art? Shoofly pies and marzipan lies?

Could it be that the master trickster has finally been outdone?

Ananse thinks he has the last laugh. But as one old lioness who had faced her share of hunters pointed out, "It is the lion who moves the tail, not the tale which moves the lion."

Some may pronounce her defeated, this one wounded without manner to swat the occasional fly or shoo away the pesky spider. Yet she preens in her pride, triumphant as anyone who has eluded the hunter's snare. She sharpens her claws, waves her stump, and calls out clearly in the language of lions.

"Victory or defeat resides not in the doer of the deed but in the song sung by the teller of the tale."

Acknowledgments

Though the baby may not have been born in Africa, that is certainly where she was conceived.

The first germ of what would become *The River Where Blood Is Born* stirred its way to consciousness following my first trip to Africa in 1975. If I had known then how challenging this work would be, how thoroughly it would take over my life, perhaps I would have attempted something very different for a first novel. As it happens, I did not so much pick this story to tell, as the story picked me as an unwitting mouthpiece.

A work which has gone through countless lives and incarnations, it was painstakingly assembled over the course of some two or more decades and could not have happened without the support of so many people.

I thank Sherifat Akorede, Hilary Beckles, Barry Gaspar, Cheryl Johson-Odim, Leslie Palmer, Edward Reynolds, Hamlet Theodore, and various members of OBAC Writers Workshop for their helpful readings and comments. Judy Ingram and Shirley Smith of North Carolina; Helen Bishoff, Preston Ewing, and the resources of the public library of Cairo, Illinois, contributed wonderful layers of memory and hometown texture.

In addition to other research sources, *A Slaver's Logbook of 20 Years Residence in Africa* by Captain Theophilus Conneau and *The Journal of a Slave Trader* by John Newton proved most useful in my attempts to re-create a culture and language of the Middle Passage. *Adowa Songs* and other works of Ghanaian scholar Dr. Nana Nketsia, as well as the works of Caribbeanist historian Dr. Hilary Beckles, provided invaluable cultural and historic perspective.

Karen Bovard and Shelley Putnam provided important technical advice on quilting and the textile arts. *Afrique Newsmagazine*, the Barbados and North Carolina Tourist Boards, the CCLM/General Electric Award for Younger Writers, the Cummington Community of the Arts, the Illinois Arts Council, the National Endowment for the Arts, the Ragdale Foundation, and also Ragdale's US / Africa Writers Project all provided much appreciated financial and material support for the development of this work.

I am most grateful to the friends and family who have seen me through: the emotional support of the Jackson girls: blood siblings Sheryl and Wendy, spirit sister Angela; the patience, pride, and understanding of my own Kimathi and

Adjoa, who've had to share their mother with this mammoth task their entire lives; as well as the encouragement of the Deckart Family, Tanya Edmonds, Lisa Gillard, Akua Lezli Hope, Kareen Karim, Bisola Marignay, Susan Ackoff Ortega, Naurice Roberts, Rose Tompkins, Hamlet Theodore, and others who held my hand, kept my kids, and commiserated when I needed a shoulder to cry on, or time to get away and write.

I acknowledge the griot voices of Richard Thelwell, Michael Thelwell, and Jimo Omo Fadaka, who first introduced Africa to me, both in idea and act; my parents, Doris Jackson and the late Roscoe Jackson Sr.; Kofi A. Opoku, Kandi Bourne, Seli Boni, Abena Joan Brown, and others whose patches of history and life experience have greatly added to the grand design.

A thousand heartfelt thanks to my agent, Susan Bergholz, for the eleven years of faith and patience that have brought me this far, and for not allowing me to "settle" for less than what could be; to my editor, Cheryl D. Woodruff, for her spiritual guidance, artistic vision, and pushing me past my own limitations. And to "Historyman" Michael West for blessings too numerous to count, among them a place at his dinner table, a pillow to lay my weary head, a space to work, the river at his window, and five years of encouragement, special kindnesses, and caring.

And finally, I honor the ancestors who whispered this story to me in patches of dream, vision, and lived experiences. I thank them for guiding my hand and Cheryl's eye in the final stages of editing; threading the beads, weaving the cloth, and nudging the story from its twenty-year cocoon and out into the world.